AMERICAN DECAMERON

MARK DUNN

First published in 2012 by M P Publishing Limited
6 Petaluma Blvd. North, Suite B6, Petaluma, CA 94952
12 Strathallan Crescent, Douglas, Isle of Man IM2 4NR

1 3 5 7 9 10 8 6 4 2

Jacket by Iain Morris
Typeset by Maria Clare Smith

Dunn, Mark, 1956-
American decameron / Mark Dunn.
   p. cm.
   ISBN 978-1849821636 (Hardcover)
   ISBN 978-1-84982-253-4 (e-book)

1. Short stories, American. 3. Short stories. 3. United States --Social life and customs
--Fiction. 4. United States --History --20th century --Fiction. I. Title.

PS3604.U56 A44 2012
813/.54 --dc23

A CPI Catalogue for this title is also available from the British Library

For my nephews (who remain little boys in my heart):
Daris, Ryan, Bren, and Zach,
and to the memory of Chris, the little boy who left us too soon

CONTENTS

INTRODUCTION

As its title suggests, *American Decameron* is comprised of one hundred short stories, each either set in the United States or featuring Americans in far-flung places, and each assigned to a different year of the twentieth century, which historians often refer to as "the American Century." Although the stories here are presented chronologically, it isn't necessary for them to be read sequentially, with the exceptions of "1901: Arboreal in Texas," and "2000: Convergent in Connecticut," which serve as prologue and epilogue for the book and should be read first and last, respectively.

The stories, though discrete in terms of time and place, tone and subject matter, are complementary components of a singular journey through the century now past. Together, the one hundred different narratives create a patchwork of American life in an era that seems at times familiar, at other times wholly archaic compared to the way we live our lives today.

While it was never my intention to write a different story on *every* aspect of life in the United States during the twentieth century (although I have achieved my personal goal of setting at least one story in each of the fifty states of our union and Washington, D.C.), I have tried very hard not to tell the same story twice. Some of my stories are subversive, and with a tip of the auctorial hat to Mr. Boccaccio, who penned the original *Decameron* in the fourteenth century, I have even dropped a handful of purposefully naughty tales into the mix. (Parents and teachers are advised to preview a story before sharing it with a young reader.)

Obviously, these stories are greatly informed by my own interests. On the other hand, I've made a deliberate effort to expand those interests so as to be as catholic as possible. My goal has always been to create a work of fiction that my readers will enjoy both for its uniqueness (Günter Grass's

My Century, published in 1999, is constructed upon a similar concept, but is laid out with intentional economy; few of Grass's one hundred historic and social portraits of Germany through the past century are longer than three pages), as well as for the worth of its individual constituent stories.

Although fantasy, the occult, and science fiction have always interested me, these are literary genres you'll have to seek elsewhere. *American Decameron* is about people who either really existed in that bygone century, or *could* have existed. All of my characters' feet are planted firmly (if sometimes a bit unsteadily) on terra firma. (The two literal exceptions would be *1915* and *1945*, which take place in the Atlantic and Pacific oceans, respectively.) If you have any doubt as to which category a character in a particular story belongs—real or not real—do the twenty-first century thing: Google him. I have not been at all shy about appropriating flesh-and-blood historical personages to use as characters in my stories.

A good rule of thumb here: If something sounds too incredible to be believed, it probably really happened.

And if you end up enjoying this book half as much as I enjoyed writing it, then I'll be a happy man indeed. You might even encourage me to try my hand at the nineteenth century. (Did I actually say that?)

Mark Dunn

1901

ARBOREAL IN TEXAS

Gail Hoyt came into this world on March 1, 1900. There being no Galveston County Records Office at the time, scrawled mention of her birth appears only in the baptismal ledger of the church where her father and mother worshipped, Tremont Ecumenical Chapel. The minister, stubbornly insistent that 1900 was a leap year just as was every other year divisible by four, inked next to her name the date February 29, 1900.

The minister was wrong. There was no leap day in 1900.

Gail Hoyt nearly left this world that same year on the occasion of the Great Galveston Hurricane, which blew in with historic fury and killed thousands of Gail's fellow Galvestonians—including both of her parents. The swaddled child was deposited high within the brachial embrace of a storm-denuded live oak tree. Perhaps it was not the storm itself that placed her there; hurricanes have personalities far less mercurial than tornadoes, which have been known in their more erratic moments to transport babies—unscathed—to all manner of remarkable resting places. More than likely it was someone who did it—someone who perhaps had escaped the rising floodwaters with the little girl tucked under arm, only to be whisked by wind or wave into oblivion.

Much has been written about the Great Galveston Hurricane. And no small measure of ink and typewriter ribbon carbon has also been devoted to the "Rock-a-bye Girl," as she would soon and ever thereafter be called—a girl who from that point forward was to spend her life ascending things, and gazing down at the world from great heights. Like the sailor who rejected solid ground for the constant pitch and roll of the restless sea, Gail Hoyt sought the vault of the sky and the bird's-eye view, some special, lofty aerie to call her own.

The Rock-a-bye Girl would grow up to turn her love of the towering and the altitudinous into both vocation and avocation. There would be very few men in her life capable of climbing to such heights as she, but those who *did* make the brave ascent found favor in Gail's embracing arms. Two in particular won Gail's heart for a time: a circus tightrope walker and a celebrated aviator. There was another man whom she coaxed to the top of flagpoles in the madcap twenties, but he plummeted with the stock market, the loss of his family nest egg sending him into a swan dive over the pavement of Upper West Side Manhattan.

High upon cliffs and hilltops and towers Gail exalted herself, for the young woman had no fear of falling—none whatsoever. She was human avatar for a nation that was also on the ascension—a country that sought to climb and clamber its way up through this new century to sublime heights of its own.

"Born with the century," said Mrs. Pell, administrator of the Seaside Home for Storm-orphaned Girls, an institution of that woman's recent founding. "And she will grow old with that very same century—the *American* Century. Don't you agree, my little Rock-a-bye Girl?" Mrs. Pell nuzzled the baby, nose to nose like a Maori, and then lifted her from the crib she shared with two other orphaned girls of nearly the same age and unfortunate circumstances. As Mrs. Pell raised Gail high above her head, the child—who had been sluggish and largely unresponsive—curled her little lips into a simper of infant delight, and before Mrs. Pell could put her down, was giggling in bubbly bursts of baby glee. Perhaps Gail was imagining in her tiny inchoate brain that she was a bird taking wing (for there was a recurring pattern of birds in flight upon the wallpaper in the room). Overhead was a gasolier and Gail reached for it, as if she might swing monkey-like from its brass hardware.

"What an extraordinary child!" marveled Miss Falcongentle, assistant to Mrs. Pell, as she took the baby from her middle-aged employeress and held her aloft as well. And all was fine and gay on that day in early 1901 when Gail was just ten months old. That day would shine in sharp contrast to the one that came later in the year—a day that would send Gail upon a very different path than Mrs. Pell had first sought for her.

But let us tarry for a few moments longer on that day upon which Gail made infant claim upon the supernal: January 2, 1901, which—depending upon which side of the table in the Seaside Home for Storm-orphaned Girls' dining room one sat—was either the second day of the new century or the three-hundred and sixty-seventh.

The case for the former was made by Mrs. Pell's suitor, Mr. Aloysius Mannheim, who had successfully survived the storm by being conveniently situated in an Austin hotel sitting room some two hundred miles away while it was about its deadly business. Mr. Mannheim had been meeting with representatives of the National Biscuit Company, who were considering the prospect of engaging him, a factory designer by trade, in the construction of a Texas UNEEDA biscuit factory—a factory expressly required for the dual purpose of baking the UNEEDA crackers and then sealing them hermetically and hygienically within the company's unique "In-Er Seal" packaging. Mr. Mannheim was a roving man of commerce; this is one of the two reasons that Mrs. Pell demurred at becoming his wife. The other reason was that her former husband, Mr. Pell, had been dead less than four months, washed out to sea in the terrible storm. And though the marriage had never been strong (for Mr. Pell had a weakness for juniper berry wine—known more commonly by its more economical denomination, "gin"), Mrs. Pell could not bring herself to remarry so soon. Other widows and widowers had done it and had been condemned by this city of mourners for their disregard for the dead.

The case for the latter (with regard to the aforementioned calendrical debate) was made by Mr. Hayes, a boarder at the orphanage, whose former rooming house had blown away like so many toothpicks.

"When did the Year 1 A.D. begin?" queried Mr. Mannheim, gesticulating with a UNEEDA biscuit pinched between his thumb and forefinger.

"What are you getting at, Mannheim?"

"That there was no Year Zero, A.D. *That* year was called Year 1, which means that the first century in the Christian era and every century thereafter must include for its 100th constituent year the year that you so ignorantly ascribe to the *next* century."

"Stop confusing Mr. Hayes, Aloysius," castigated Mrs. Pell. "And give me a cracker."

As Mr. Mannheim pulled a cracker from its unique In-Er-Seal wax paper packaging, he continued: "There shouldn't even *be* an argument here. The year 1900 belongs to the century past. Ergo, our new century began two days ago. Case closed."

"Perhaps, my dear Aloysius," said Mrs. Pell, calmly munching upon her cracker, "the first century of the Christian era was an anomaly. It had only ninety-nine years. Did you ever think about that? Stranger things have been recorded. Why, my little Rock-a-bye Girl was found wedged high within the branches of an ocean-lashed live oak tree, as if placed there by the gentle, salvational hand of God Himself. She's a special child. She hardly cries. I want you to meet her, because I'm considering adopting her."

Mr. Mannheim cleared his throat and adjusted himself in his chair. "You told me, my dear woman, that you had no plans to adopt *any* of these girls. In fact, you said that once you had found good homes for them all, you'd leave the orphan-rearing profession altogether and move with me to Austin."

"I've had a change of mind. All of my little motherless lambs are dear in their own way, but little Gail has staked the strongest claim in my heart."

"Let's shelve this conversation for some other time." Mr. Mannheim pushed himself from the table and away from the picked-clean chicken carcass that represented the first truly satisfying meal taken in this house since before the hurricane, food being hard to come by throughout that dismal preceding autumn, especially food that once ran about on two legs and cackled. "It's late. I must rise early to assist in repairs to the hospital that bears my family's name—a name that you will one day bear yourself, my love, once we can come to a meeting of the minds on this matter of adopting other people's children. It isn't enough that you have spared these little ones from circumstantial abandonment; must we also make them our legal wards?"

"Aloysius Mannheim! You have now shown a cruel and selfish side to yourself that gives me troubling pause!"

Cross words between the two lovers continued back and forth until each participant could little bear another moment and fled the field of battle in different directions. Mr. Hayes was left to empty the box of crackers in solitary silence, and then to poke at the fire and wonder what had become of the flaxen-haired girl who resided that previous summer in his rooming house (just down the hall from his own room) and who, no doubt, survived now only in heavyhearted memory and doleful, recurrent dream.

That later life-altering day of previous reference arrived in the warmer season, when Galveston was clearly on the mend, its citizens once again drinking deep from the waters of hope and high expectancy for a century that promised progress and prosperity and permanent recovery.

However, such was not the fate destined for Mrs. Pell, who woke early in the morning to the tocsin of her assistant Miss Falcongentle's frantic, frightened calls. There was a child upon the roof of the orphanage, and that child was none other than Gail Hoyt.

"How in the name of the blessed virgin did Baby get up there?" cried a hand-wringing Mrs. Pell, as Mr. Hayes held the ladder so that Barnacle, the orphanage's liveryman and general do-all, could scramble to the girl's rescue.

"I have no idea, Mrs. Pell," answered Miss Falcongentle, her face a worrisome disc within the circular frame of her flannel sleeping bonnet. "Her little bed was empty and I looked all about the rooms and was ready to scour the grounds when I heard her mischievous chortle coming from this most unlikely location."

The chortling had, in fact, hardly suspended, for Gail was continuing to take a toddler's delight in her present predicament, sitting negligently upon the pitch of the wood-shingled roof as if she had been comfortably lodged there since birth.

And then it happened: just as Barnacle reached out for her, the Rock-a-bye Girl lost her balance. It was not the only time that such an accident was destined to befall Gail.

Down came baby in a roll and a tumble, bouncing off the eaves as if there were springs attached to her diminutive bottom, and then landing with perfect convenience in the outstretched arms of Mrs. Pell. The child was unharmed, but Mrs. Pell's right arm was wrenched in its socket, a place in her neck pinched, and her left hip would never be the same again.

Miss Falcongentle took Gail from the woman who had, in fact, saved the little high-flying girl's life through involuntary maternalistic outreach. Yet it was the last time that Mrs. Pell would ever touch the child.

There would be no more nuzzling, no more cuddling of Gail Hoyt. "I can no longer abide her," confessed Mrs. Pell to a grateful Mr. Mannheim, who now saw no further impediments to the marriage. "There are signs of willfulness even at this young age which give ample evidence of the potential for a lifetime of conflict between the two of us. It saddens me to be bringing to such swift end my hopes for adopting the child, but it simply cannot be otherwise."

There was nothing else that could be done for the toddler except to secure her a good home. Five and a half years would pass before this outcome could be effected.

The husband and wife who adopted Gail were loving and kind, but well into their middle years. They had not been able to have a child of their own, but now decided to make a go of it with one of the many needy orphans of Galveston. But there was another reason for why the Harrisons took her in. Burt and Reva Harrison were trapeze artists. Perhaps you know the song:

They'd fly through the air with the greatest of ease,
That daring middle-aged couple on the flying trapeze.

And Gail Hoyt had already demonstrated her suitability for the profession.

There is more to this story of how Gail Hoyt came to be upon that roof. If you guessed that the perpetrator was Mrs. Pell's jealous, black-hearted suitor Mannheim, you would be all but technically correct—it was a man that Mannheim hired who did the dirty deed.

When the wind blows, the baby shall fall
And Lana and I shall marry after the bawl.

But in fairness to the veritable multitude of characters who are waiting to march, strut, stroll, stride, tramp, tiptoe, goose-step, mosey, limp, stumble, sashay, ramble and/or promenade in the cavalcade that is this book, we must leave Gail to the care of her leotarded, high-flying adoptive parents. However, it should be noted that our protagonist's life was destined to take no small number of interesting twists and turns before her candle finally sputtered out in 2001. Should you wish to spend a few moments with her in the year before her death, by all means skip to the final pages of this book and have done with it. But if you will be patient, you'll be rewarded by a visit with Gail long before then in a story that puts her back upon a roof and once again in harm's way.

Because Gail Hoyt Hopper Rabbitt, human analogue to this century now past, could not keep herself content and quiet and still. It simply was not in her nature. Nor was it in the nature of that which has been called the American Century to go quietly into the annals of history.

It is a fact from which, this author hopes, we will all derive profit.

1902

VEHICULAR IN NEW YORK

"I should think that he would have better sense. He looks like an absolute fool."

"Who looks like an absolute fool, dear?"

"Haven't you been listening to me, Mother?"

Rosalinda Eames turned from the window to face her mother, who sat knitting across the room, the older woman's spectacles resting halfway down her aquiline nose, so that she should better see her daughter just over the rim. The picture was one of maternal scrutiny writ casual, almost transitory.

"Of course I've been listening to you. But you have yet to say his name—the object of your studied observation. Am I to guess it? It's much too early in the morning for games, my dear."

"It's Cadwalader, Mother." Rosalinda returned herself to the serious business of descrying. With the sleeve of her green-checkered muslin blouse, she wiped away a little of the condensation from her breath that had clouded her view through the pane

"*Cadwalader*? I had heard that the poor man had taken to his bed. What's he doing standing at the end of our lane looking like a fool, and so very, very sick in the bargain?"

Rosalinda heaved a theatrical suspiration of impatience. "It isn't the father to whom I'm referring, Mother, and you know it. It's Wilberforce. *The son.*" Rosalinda was set to punctuate her superfluous clarification with another labored sigh, when suddenly her exasperation demanded expression of a different sort: a gasp of overwhelming indignation. "Just look at him—shaking his fist like a character in some wretched melodrama."

"At whom is he shaking his fist, dear? God?" Mrs. Eames set her knitting down upon her lap, taking care not to surrender her skein of yarn to the calico that lay at her feet, the creature, no doubt, cogitating upon the skein's many playtime possibilities.

"Not God, Mother. The tree. *Our* tree. Our cherry tree. He's run his machine into it and then to add insult to injury, he has stepped out of that awful crumpled contraption to indict the tree."

"Why has he hit our tree with his motor, dear?"

"Because he doesn't know how to steer it, apparently. Had he a carriage, the horse would certainly have avoided collision. As a rule, horses do not run themselves into trees. Oh, for the love of God, Mother, he's coming this way. He's heading directly for our door. He'll want to use our telephone, I'll wager." Rosalinda stepped away from the window and quickly drew the curtains. "Be very quiet. Perhaps he'll think we're out."

"It's quite early, dear. He must know that people like us don't leave their homes at such an early hour. It's only the servants who have business in town betimes."

In a strained whisper: "Yet *he's* out. Out and about at the crack of dawn like the insufferable fool that he is."

"You judge people much too harshly, dear. It isn't becoming."

Rosalinda sat herself upon the divan and tried to compose herself. The door chime sounded and within a moment, Mary Grace, the housemaid, appeared in the adjoining foyer.

"Mary Grace!" summoned Rosalinda in a raised whisper. "We are not at home."

"But of course you're at home, miss. I can see you sitting right there."

Rosalinda turned to her mother. "She's a dolt, Mary Grace is—a perfect dolt. Sack her, mother. Sack her this very morning."

Mary Grace, who now stood halfway in the foyer and halfway in the drawing room, frowned. "I heard what you said, miss. I may be a perfect dolt but I have perfect hearing as well."

"What I *mean*, Mary Grace, is that you should tell him—Mr. Cadwalader— you should *tell* him that we are not in. In short, you are to lie. We pay your wages, Mother and I, and so you must do what we ask without question."

Mary Grace nodded and went to the door. It was not possible for Mrs. Eames and her twenty-two-year-old daughter to see the door from where they sat in the drawing room, but it was quite easy for them to hear the exchange that took place over its threshold.

"Good morning, Mary Grace," said Cadwalader in a voice that seemed almost too sonorous and refined for his youthful twenty-three years. "I've had a mishap with my machine. It has hit a tree and is no longer operable. I must have it removed to my garage for repairs."

"Begging your pardon, sir—what's a garage?"

"It's like a stable but for automobiles. May I use your telephone?"

Mary Grace hesitated. "Are you not going to ask if my mistress and the baby mistress are here?"

"Well, it isn't necessary for me to speak to Mrs. or Miss Eames. I simply require access to a telephone."

"Because they aren't here. They have both gone into town."

Mary Grace, having failed to place herself sufficiently in the way of Cadwalader, was unable to successfully prevent his incursion into the foyer and, subsequently, his sighting of both Mrs. and Miss Eames, neither of whom appeared to be out. In point of fact, both women were sitting in close proximity, their heads identically cocked in an eavesdropping posture.

Cadwalader removed his cap and brushed the shoulders of his duster with opposite hands. "I believe that you are mistaken, Mary Grace," he said, with an arch grin. "They are returned already. Here they are. Good morning, Mrs. Eames. Good morning, Miss Eames. I seek use of your telephone, if you will permit me. I have had a vehicular mishap."

"You have rammed our prized cherry tree is what you have done!" gnarred Rosalinda, bounding up from her chair. "Planted by my grandfather with great care and devotion. It came all the way from the Orient and will be most difficult to replace."

"I have every intention of indemnifying you fully for your loss, Miss Eames. Remind me: where is the instrument so that I may place my call?"

"Please take Mr. Cadwalader to the telephone, Mary Grace," said Mrs. Eames in a composed manner. "Mr. Cadwalader, you are welcome to remove your horseless carriage from our front lawn by whatever means best suits your purpose."

"Thank you, Mrs. Eames. I'm most grateful." With this, Cadwalader disappeared along with the house servant. The sound of retreating footsteps was quickly replaced by the removed voice of Mr. Cadwalader speaking into the telephone in the library.

"The absolute nerve!" raged Rosalinda under her breath. "To come barging in here as if he were master of this house. The arrant presumptuousness!"

"Calm yourself, dear. It was not a burdensome request. Indeed, had we actually *been* in town, I have no doubt that Mary Grace would have done the proper thing and permitted use of the instrument without a moment's hesitation."

"That is beside the point." Rosalinda sat back down and drew her hands together in her lap so that the fingers should interlace one another and twiddle and fidget with a sort of nervous energy commonly found among the constitutionally overstrung.

Not another word was exchanged between mother and daughter before Cadwalader reappeared in the doorway that led from the foyer into the drawing room. "Thank you again. My man Millard is on his way. Irony has won this day: I am to be towed by horses. May I sit here while I wait?"

"You may…with *impertinence!*" muttered Rosalinda.

"Sit as long as you wish, Mr. Cadwalader," said Mrs. Eames in a louder, more accommodating voice.

Cadwalader nodded his gratitude and settled himself upon a cushioned settle across the room from the two women. After a silent moment, he said, "So, Miss Eames. Have you given any further thought to the question I put to you last night?"

"I beg your pardon. Are you addressing *me*?"

"I am. The question I asked you yesterday evening within this very room—have you an answer for me?"

"I have."

"And do you intend to give me that answer today, or does my request require another day's delay?"

"I'll give you my answer right here and now if that is your preference, Mr. Cadwalader."

The "Baby Mistress" collected herself.

"I will marry you, Mr. Cadwalader. I don't know why but you shall have me."

The young man beamed. He rose and crossed to Rosalinda. Bowing to her, he took her hand with mock chivalry and kissed it upon the knuckles. "I have no doubt that I shall be the happiest husband on Earth."

"And I shall be the most miserable wife upon that selfsame planet. Don't look at me that way."

"What way?"

"As if I am some prized heifer you've won at the Dutchess County Fair."

"But Miss Eames, you have it all wrong; I regard you—as I have always regarded you—with only the most heartfelt devotion." A look of concern now betrayed the disparate thought that now crossed the young man's mind. "I must check on the machine. There were some boys nearby who seemed the sort to engage in a bit of mischief in my absence. I'll return shortly."

Wilberforce Cadwalader departed the room with a gladdened spring to his step. The front door opened and then closed.

"The audacity of the man!" growled Rosalinda. "Thinking that I would so easily accede to his proposal of marriage."

"And yet you have, my daughter."

"And did you notice the way he took his leave? That look of smug entitlement—how it adulterated that most ruggedly handsome countenance. And the insolence in his words and in his bearing—at such odds with so fine a figure and such an appealing muscular form. I'll live to rue this decision, Mother, you may be sure of it."

"And I am equally certain that you will not, my dear," said Mrs. Eames to her fretful daughter, as the elder of the two once again took up her knitting. "For you are looking for contradictions between complexion and character where none actually exist."

"Piffle!" declared Rosalinda. She had returned to the window and opened the curtains to gaze out at her fiancé, her eyes clinched, her brow constricted. "Oh, just look at him—chasing after those boys like a clown at the circus."

Then a sigh. The melodic sigh of a woman in love.

"The man absolutely appalls me!"

1903

DEDUCTIVE IN MICHIGAN

Elizabeth Ellsworth handed the revelatory letter to her husband, Thomas. She had found it on her daughter's made bed, propped up against the bolster. It was addressed to *My dear mother and father*. Elizabeth had opened the letter then and there, and read it three times. Keeping her emotions in check, she had gone into the sitting room to share it with her husband.

There was another family member present in the room: Tad. Tad was twelve, a studious, spectacled boy who thought himself brilliant and therefore rejected the general rule that children should be seen and not heard.

"She must have left in the night," said Thomas, looking up from the letter.

Tad shook his head. "It was at daybreak. I heard her go. He was with her. I could hear their whispers."

Elizabeth frowned at her son. "And you didn't wake us?"

"How was I to know that she was *eloping*! You know that Longnecker comes by early some mornings to visit with her before he goes off to work. Sometimes she'll walk him all the way to the sanitarium. May I read the letter?"

Thomas surrendered the letter to his son with a sigh. "She's twenty-one. She has the right to run away and marry whomever she pleases— even lowly hospital bedpan emptiers who have scarcely held their job for two months. It's the twentieth century. Young women have rights now."

"They don't have the right to break their mothers' hearts," said Elizabeth, blotting her moist eyes.

"Sit, Elizabeth." Thomas led his wife to the sofa. "Ethel knows that we don't approve of the young man. We know hardly anything about him, but apparently she wants to marry him anyway. Elopement was the only course available to her. Where's Tad?"

Tad had left the room.

"Tad! What are you doing? Bring that letter back!"

Tad returned to the family sitting room. He was wearing his Sherlock Holmes deerstalker hat of plaid wool. Tad now had a magnifying glass in his possession.

"What's this?" asked Thomas, irritation creeping into his voice. "Your sister has run away and you've decided to spend your morning play-acting?"

Elizabeth blew her nose. "He isn't play-acting, dear. He's going to solve the crime. But there is no crime, Tad, dear. It isn't against the law to turn your back on the love of your family and run away with a man who will probably bring your life to ruin." Elizabeth sighed. She looked out the window upon a beautiful spring morning that defied her dark spirits.

Tad sat down at the walnut escritoire where his mother kept track of the household accounts. He laid the letter down and began to scrutinize it closely with the magnifying glass. "Yes, yes," he said to himself. Then he turned to address his parents. "The letter appears to be in Ethel's hand."

Thomas rolled his eyes. "That's a relief, son. For a brief moment, I thought that it might be a forgery and your poor sister had been kidnapped."

"I wouldn't, as of yet, rule out the possibility that the young woman has been abducted, my dear Watson," said Tad.

"I am your father, Tad. I'm not Dr. Watson."

"Indubitably," said Tad, lapsing into deep thought.

"Tad," said Elizabeth, with deliberate patience, "perhaps you might want to see what Albertha's preparing for breakfast. Are you hungry?"

"I can't eat," said Tad, his focus returning to his investigative work. "Not until I solve the 'Case of the Disappeared Daughter.'"

Tad's retort now elicited from his father a loud, inarticulate response seated largely in the throat.

"Granted, she has written the letter," continued Tad, "but one must not discount the possibility that it may have been penned under duress."

"You believe there could be that possibility?" asked Elizabeth, whose general wearying indulgence of her son had suddenly become supplanted by a genuine interest in his theory.

Tad nodded eagerly. "Because I have deduced the following: Ethel wasn't happy with Longnecker. And Clara has confirmed it."

Thomas sat down next to his wife. "Which Clara?"

Tad swung around in his chair. The deerstalker hat, which was two sizes too big for his small head, flew off and onto the rug. "Ethel's friend

Clara Puckett, of course. Clara said that Ethel knew Longnecker was a ne'er-do-well but she didn't know how to get away from him."

"Oh dear," said Elizabeth.

Tad went on: "That's why I think he might have *forced* her to leave with him."

Elizabeth stretched out her arms for her son to come to her. Reluctantly he got up and allowed his worried mother to embrace him. "You're too young to have such mature theories about things. You should run and play with children your own age and leave such complicated matters to your elders."

Tad shook his head. "The time for childhood games is behind me. There are more important things for me to be doing with my life."

"Like solving crimes?" asked Thomas.

Tad nodded. "Now, if you would be so good as to excuse me," he said, retrieving the letter and magnifying glass from the writing desk and snatching up his hat from the floor, "I will be in my room trying to make some sense out of my sister's alleged elopement, which flies in the face of all reason. Have Albertha bring my breakfast to my room on a tray."

Not waiting for a response from his parents, Tad departed the room, the seriousness in his carriage evincing a sense of grand purpose.

After a silent moment, Thomas turned to his wife and said, "It does seem strange, if indeed it be true, that Ethel should run away to marry a man she no longer loves."

"*Or* trusts," added Elizabeth. "Oh, that seems frightening even to contemplate—that he may have gotten her to leave against her will. And yet the letter offers no clues as to possible coercion. I refuse to believe it. I choose to believe, instead, that she took careful stock of her feelings for the young man and decided that the good clearly outweighed the bad. If you recall, Tommy, I did the very same thing prior to *our* wedding."

"What do you mean, 'if you recall'? What did you do, Lizzie—put it all down in a ledger?"

"As a matter of fact, I did. Happily, the good did win out, my love. Else I wouldn't be sitting here today." Elizabeth's nascent smile suddenly evaporated. "Oh, Tommy. Where do you think the two of them could have gone?"

Thomas looked upon his wife with compassionate eyes. "We can't go after her, Lizzie. Marrying Longnecker and moving away with him is her decision to make. Perhaps she'll write to us shortly."

*

Seated at the desk in his room, Tad read and reread the letter his sister had left behind. It was most assuredly in her hand, but there wasn't the ease of expression that he was used to. Ethel's trip to Europe with their aunt the previous summer had generated a number of letters to him, and these he now drew from a drawer in his desk to compare to this far more consequential missive.

Ethel was a good writer, and though her letters usually had a frothy, whimsical feel to them, they were remarkably well-crafted. This farewell letter was well-crafted, to be sure, but the voice was without variance in tone, and the meringue was entirely absent. This aberration of character was the first clue that Tad took from it.

After twenty minutes or so there came a knock at the door. Albertha, the cook, entered with a breakfast tray. "Set it there upon the bed, Mrs. Hudson."

"My name ain't Hudson, and you know it." Then in susurrant appendix: "You snot-nosed little mischieviant."

"'Mischieviant' isn't a word, Mrs. Hudson. And don't think that I don't appreciate you. Your cuisine may be a little limited but you have as good an idea of breakfast as a Scotchwoman."

Albertha set the tray upon the bed. "You've said that before, Master Tad. Is it be something your Mr. Holmes says?"

"Perhaps it is. Come over here. I want to show you something."

Albertha went to Tad. She peered over his shoulder. "Is that the letter—the one from poor Miss Ethel?"

Tad nodded. "Why do you call her '*poor* Miss Ethel'?"

"Because I don't reckon she wanted to go with that young man."

Tad turned around. "Why do you say this?"

"One night I overheard them two fussing on the back porch—fussing like cats in a bag, but with their mouths half-closed-like, so as to keep their voices low, I suppose."

"What was it that my sister and Mr. Longnecker were quarreling about?"

"Why, that very thing, Mr. Tad! He wanted her to marry him and she didn't want no part of it. But he lays the law down on her—says she's his and no other man gonna have her."

"Did you tell this to my parents?"

Albertha shook her head. "Young people in love—they get all het up sometimes. They say things that no person in his right mind gonna say. What was it you wanted to show me?"

"It's quite curious, Mrs. Hudson. Look closely. What is the first thing to strike you about this letter?" Albertha took her reading glasses from her apron pocket and hooked the end pieces behind her ears.

"The stationery's got a nice, pretty look to it. And it smells like roses, don't it?"

Tad got up from his chair. "Sit here, Mrs. Hudson. Examine the letter as closely as you wish."

Albertha sat down.

"With what instrument do you think my sister has penned this letter?"

"It don't seem to have been penned by a pen at all, but by a pencil."

"Precisely. Now why do you think that she chose to write the letter in pencil?"

"Well, can't rightly say."

"*I* have a theory. Would you like to hear it?"

"Please. And hurry yourself up, child. I have to fix your father's sack lunch before he leaves for work."

"Look at the words, Mrs. Hudson. See how some seem to have been made darker than the others?"

"Yes, I do."

"And what could be the reason?"

Albertha shook her head and gave a little shrug.

"Oh, but certainly you *must* see, Mrs. Hudson!" Tad exclaimed, rocking upon his heels with a kind of boyish exuberance not at all replicative of the severe and intellectually gelid Mr. Holmes. "She's written the letter in code. It is absolute brilliance! And it is our job now to decipher it."

"And just how is it we do that?"

"By taking each of those words she has made slightly darker than the others through pressing the pencil harder upon the page—by taking those words and assembling them into a form of sentence anagram to give us the true, hidden meaning of her letter."

"That sounds rather farfetched to me, sport," said Mr. Ellsworth, who was now standing in the doorway of his son's bedroom. "Albertha, do I pay you to cook our meals or to duck off and play Watson to my son's Sherlock?"

"To cook the meals, Mr. Ellsworth." Albertha rose quickly, her head bowed in humble subservience. But even in the midst of her haste to return to her duties in the kitchen, the Ellsworth cook allowed a little sauce to bubble from her pot: "Excuse me, Mr. Ellsworth, but I ain't

Watson when I'm in this here room. I'm Mrs. Hudson, and you best be remembering that."

During Albertha's withdrawal, Tad let slip a smile that was quickly transmuted back into the stone face of the impassive detective.

"Your mother is handling this quite badly, Tad," said Thomas to his son. "I don't think either of us approves of your making sport of it. Please give me the letter, and let's have an end to all this nonsense."

"It isn't nonsense, Pop. Sis has written the letter in code. You can help me if you like, and Mom, too, but I won't relinquish the letter until I've finished deciphering it."

Thomas scratched his head. "I don't think I've ever seen this kind of impudence from you. You may have always been Peck's Bad Boy, but now you've become Peck's Hopelessly Incorrigible Boy, and I'll not have it."

"And *I* refuse to give up this letter until I've tested my theory. I love my sister far too much to do that to her."

All the wind had suddenly deserted Thomas's sails. He dropped down upon Tad's bed like a lead weight. "Why would she write to us in code?"

"Because she couldn't do anything else."

"Why did she not come to us and simply say that she didn't want to go with Longnecker? If he is the dangerous man that you now purport, we could all have stood against him."

"Maybe he's more dangerous than we could even imagine, Pop, and she didn't want to see her family harmed."

Thomas thought about this. Then he said, "Let's decipher the code and see what it is that your sister's trying to tell us."

Dear Mom and Pop,

My **husband has** won **my** heart at last. **I'm** sorry to **hurry** off like this as you **nap** so peacefully, and I **will pine** away for **you** like a little **kid** without his **marbles** in the **street**. But it will not **kill** me to try to be a good wife to Adam who loves me so much. It will **help** me immeasurably if you try to understand. **I'm** not a little **lost** lamb. I am a grown woman now, and it **fits** me. I **get** pleasure from making Adam happy. And he has **come** into my life only to make me happy. He has great plans for us away from Battle Creek. **Soon** he is going to buy **me** evening gowns of lavender and tulle, and diamond solitaires and a bright red **Cadillac** Model A. Please **don't come** looking for me. **If** you do, it will mean that you don't trust **me** to make this important decision about my life.

You will always be **in** my thoughts and in my heart. Adam **has his** own parents, but they aren't half as wonderful as you are.

Love,
Your Ethel

husband has my I'm hurry nap will pine you kid marbles street kill help I'm lost fits get come Soon me Cadillac don't come If me in has his

Through employment of the anagrammatical talents of Tad, his mother and father, Albertha the cook, and the chief inspector of the Battle Creek Police Department, the message was, within a matter of three hours, successfully and decisively decoded:

Help. I'm kid nap. Come get me. I'm in Cadillac, Pine Street. Hurry. My husband has lost his marbles, has fits, will kill me if you don't come soon.

Ethel was rescued with all speed. Adam was returned to the lunatic asylum from whence he had escaped. And Thomas and Elizabeth Ellsworth's oldest child vowed never again to fall in love with a good-looking newcomer to Battle Creek who wanted something more from her than simple directions to the Battle Creek Sanitarium. She vowed something else as well: to value every moment her younger brother spent in the thrall of his fictional detective idol, for she had laid her hopes for rescue at the feet of Tad's inquisitive nature, inspired by Mr. Holmes.

Love and trust between siblings can be powerful forces for good. But then, everyone knows this. It is, to borrow from the famed sleuth, elementary.

1904

IN MEMORIAM IN PENNSYLVANIA

The man writing my husband's obituary asked where he went to college. "Haverford College," I replied. Then I smiled. Just that morning I had asked my grandson Tommy to go out and buy me a Haverford College sweater. I wanted to bury Lindsay in it, you see. My late husband had always said he wanted to be buried in his old college sweater. Because the moths, as I had earlier discovered, had had other ideas, I was forced to improvise.

I'm a resourceful widow.

I may be mistaken, but I think my Lindsay was the last surviving member of Haverford's Class of 1904. He was almost ninety when he died this week. He had been in touch with several of his classmates—the "Nineteen Fours" they called themselves—throughout their entire lives. Deep friendships were forged in those days, the kinds of friendships I don't think the college kids of today could ever understand.

The saddest thing about my husband's senility was the loss of all those memories. We've had a good marriage, and a long one, but there was something special about Lindsay's college days that no love of wife or child could take the place of.

In the last year of his life Lindsay would often forget who I was, or he'd fail to recognize his children and grandchildren. I would also have trouble making sense out of the things he'd say—things sometimes mumbled, sometimes spoken with volume and authority but still totally incomprehensible. The doctor said that Lindsay's gibbering was nothing more than the expression of thoughts—fractured, disjointed thoughts— that his brain could no longer assemble and process in a rational manner. I tended to agree with his opinion. For this reason, I never prodded

Lindsay to explain any of the random statements he made. I'd nod and smile and comb his hair because it was always mussed. The attendants at the nursing home could have done a better job of keeping him looking nice. Lindsay was a beautiful man. He was kind and funny and good to the children and me. It seemed in those last few months that he was dead already—that some stranger had come to take his place, or worse, some living entity incapable of speaking beyond senseless prattle, unable to love in the deep way that my husband once loved, powerless to remember even a single detail of a life well worth remembering. To be robbed of memory seems to me the most insidious assault of all.

On one of my visits last summer I thought that I would write down some of the things he said. It was a silly thing to do, I know it. But the words were delivered by a familiar voice that still resonated for me, because this was all that I had left: the shell that resembled my husband in appearance and the voice that used to come to me from across the dinner table, from behind the steering wheel of our car, over the telephone from his office, in the intimacy of our nocturnal bed.

"Gods and hook fish!"

I scribbled it down. "Gods and hook fish." What did it mean? Well, it can't possibly mean anything, can it?

"Ye gods and little fishhooks, Baldy!"

Baldy's getting sentimental. Somebody muzzle him. He sits by the fire and sucks his pipe and reminds us that it will all be over soon. Our final quarter. One quarter more and then it's out the door—or doors: those stately doors of Roberts' Hall. Funeral-marching. Diplomas in hand. Must we, Baldy? Must we think about it?

Who knew that 1904 would be the year that our bully lives came to a crashing halt?

Bonny seems poised to speak. Bonny has a tendency to get philosophical. He's got those big ears and he looks about twelve but he's the class sage by reputation and he won't let us down. He'll say something that will take the lumps out of all of our throats. Say something, Bonny. Say something soothing and sagacious.

"Remember Lester? Down in the dumps because nobody would dump him?"

I nod. I remember. Poor ol' Lester—the only freshman who didn't get his turn at being dumped out of bed from a sound sleep. I think it hurt his feelings something awful, to think that nobody liked him enough to want to toss him to the floor and throw his mattress on top of him.

"Good things finally come to he who waits for his dumping," Lester says through a guffaw. "I got mine soon enough. And a little more to spare. You chuckleheads broke the ventilator over my door with all your roughhousing and you knocked down my bookcase like it was the wall of Jericho!"

Everybody's laughing now. We're sitting around the fireplace in Lloyd Hall and all the memories are flooding back. The lump is still there. It's late. The night and the quiet (save for the crackling of the logs on the fire) have sent our thoughts to dark places where good things are destined to come to an end—all the things that will be so sorely missed—new chances to beat Swarthmore on the gridiron, or to beat whoever has the guts to face us on the cricket field—Cornell, Harvard, the New Jersey Athletic Club!

"Baldy, Thorny, Marmy, Had."

Baldy remembers forming a bucket brigade the night Denbeigh Hall burned down, and Thorny describes with his customary sailor's seasoning how we used to fumble with our academic gowns in the blustering winds of our senior year. Damn those gowns and the antediluvian chucklehead who first decided that seniors should wear them! Marmy waxes gastronomical over four delectable years of steak a la Bordelaise, asparagus on toast, iced tea and strawberries and fudge and ice cream. And "Had" puts us all into hysterics by recalling the day the electrical lab short-circuited.

We should—all eight of us—have suspended our group reminiscences and gone back to our rooms to start penning the opening paragraphs of our respective graduation theses.

"A History of Isthmian Canal Failures."

A History of Isthmian Canal Failures by Jack Thomas. Wireless Telegraphy by Benny Lester. The Philadelphia Filtration System by "Battery" Clark. The Negro Problem by Edgar "Psyche" Snipes. There probably wouldn't have been such a Negro problem if classes like Nineteen-Four hadn't put up as their contribution to Junior Play Night a black-face minstrel show of such pasquinading offense as to make even the racially accommodating Mr. Booker T. Washington apoplectic.

"Ethel and beloved Maudie."

Thoughts of the end of our college careers moving with astonishing illogic (as all thoughts eventually do) to the fairer sex. The nearness of the rosy-cheeked maidens of Bryn Mawr and the utterly unattainable theatrical Misses Ethel Barrymore and our own beloved Maudie—that is to say Miss Maude Adams, who was ours not in reality but only within our heartfelt fancy.

And now into this late hour of throbbing longing suddenly step the conjured wraiths of every girl we have ever loved and those to whom some of us are presently engaged. And suddenly we are facing our own futures as we have never faced them before, accompanied by the women—both real and imagined—whom we will woo and wed and with whom we will make our families. And into that void steps my dear...

"Flora."
"Yes? What is it, Lindsay? Do you want something?"

She is there standing before me, among the corporeal companions of my collegiate youth. There in that room before the fire, late in the third quarter of my last year at Haverford. And all has come together on this night of mystical invocation—the boys who grew to manhood before my very eyes. And my beloved...

"Flora."
"Yes, I'm here, Lindsay. I'm sitting right beside you, darling. I have your hand. Are you thinking of me? Am I *there*, my precious darling? Somewhere within your broken thoughts?"

I take Flora by the hand and we walk together in the midnight moonlight, breathing deeply the bracing wintry air. We walk through the Conklin gate and catch sight of Barclay Hall in all its Victorian Gothic glory, with its abbey-like spire rising up from walls of dark ivy. We stroll along the granolithic walk under chestnut trees bare of leaves, yearning for spring. I show Flora the place where once I was so very happy. A time when life held every promise and there was so much that still lay ahead. It is meet and proper that you should be here, I say to her. It is meet and proper that you should be with me at the beginning, for I do not know if you are with me now at the end. Are you there, Flora? In all those other places? In those places that took the place of Haverford? Where should I seek thee?

"For I do so miss thee."

"I miss thee, too," I said.

Did I tell you that my husband Lindsay attended school among Quakers? Even before the senility set in, he would sometimes lapse into the language of his Haverford elders to make a poetic point.

> *So when life's long years are almost o'er*
> *When thinking of those times with Nineteen-Four*
> *Amid the myriad memories which rise,*
> *That college ideal stands before our eyes.*
> *The brightest recollection of those days*
> *Seeing it grow real before our gaze*
> *Find we ourselves to be that youthful vision.*

Words penned by our class poet Howard Haines Brinton, who sits next to me before the fire, smoking his pipe like all the others, a cup of cocoa at his side. Quiet. The night so quiet. And then the silence broken by a wet snowball splatting the windowpane. We look out to find the fresh and the sophs engaged in mortal brumal combat. And there was a time when without hesitation we would have joined this battle royal wearing only our nightshirts and worsted slippers, eagerly defying the winter cold for pride of class. But not now. Now we are preparing with somber sobriety to troop, instead, into the valley of the shadow of adulthood…

…Or would have, had Helbert (more intimately known as Hellbird) not cried, "Ye gods and little fishhooks! Are we going to let those insolent underclassmen bastards get away with this?"

No, my dear sir, we are not. Avenge this assault upon the honor of Nineteen-Four! We're still here for three months more!

And out we all went into the embattled night.

"Yes, out I go into that dark night."

"Don't go just yet, my love," I said to my husband, my eyes brimming with tears. "Stay with me, just a little bit longer."

1905

GENEALOGICAL IN RHODE ISLAND

Here is my draft of the Official Record of the 17th Reunion of the Livergood Family Association of Warwick, Rhode Island, September 27, 1905. Nota bene: I will entertain suggestions for changes to this document in the event that the notes taken by our treasurer and my secretarial assistant Mrs. Medora Livergood Markham (which I have liberally appropriated for this record due to the fact that my withered hand prevents note-taking of my own) are found in error or discovered to be in any other way deficient.

I observed at the September 27 gathering that Mrs. Markham was often inattentive, either in a sort of woolgathering state or engaged in animated conversations with other female Livergoods, whom she perhaps had not seen since last year's reunion, and thus was not as scrupulous in her transcribing as she might otherwise have been.

THE LIVERGOOD FAMILY ASSOCIATION held its seventeenth annual reunion at Warwick, Rhode Island, September Twenty-seventh, Nineteen Hundred and Five, Mr. Fred R. Livergood of Warwick, President, presiding. The morning session was called to order at 9:33 o'clock after repeated raps of the gavel, due to an unwillingness on the part of several Livergoods by marriage to suspend their conversations, having never before attended a Livergood Family Association Reunion and being largely ignorant of its serious purpose and solemn nature. One must also indict Professor Elisha Livergood for his disruptive absence. Professor Livergood was tarrying in the corridor and could be heard, along with two attendees from the female branches, Messrs. Gleason and Looney, singing "In Zanzibar, My Little Chimpanzee" (although my husband contends that the song was

"Won't You Fondle Me?"—the two songs sounding to my ear not a bit similar and my husband being deliberately perverse).

REV. ABNER HOADLEY, DD, Pastor of the West Warwick Congregational Church, offered the Invocation.

MRS. MARY BLUNT LIVERGOOD of Kingston, Rhode Island, sang a song that she and her husband Chester had written about the Livergood family, entitled "O Joy! O Bliss! O Livergood!", which included a brief musical interlude on the harp played by Miss Annie Capwell, whose claim to Livergood family affiliation is still under advisement by the Committee of Ancestry Eligibility. For this reason she was asked not to play too overtly.

PROFESSOR ELISHA LIVERGOOD, chairman of the Committee of Publication of the Revised Genealogy, informed attendees of the near completion of the latest edition of the published genealogy and explained the particulars of subscription and purchase. Professor Livergood's remarks were interrupted by Mr. George Pardee, who argued that those, like himself, in the female lines descending from our common ancestor, the venerable and much esteemed Cockchase Livergood, should be eligible for a discounted price, given their second-class status in the family. There ensued a lively debate among the various members of the male and female branches over the disparity of privileges and appurtenances redounding to both, e.g. the fact that female branch descendants and their spouses are relegated to sitting in the back of the hall and required to drink their coffee in demitasses and eat their luncheon on dessert plates. The latter half of this statement was said in jest and there were some who derived pleasure from it; but the first half was spoken in earnest, as those in the back of the hall were quick to attest. There was no resolution to the debate, and though a vote was suggested under "Roberta's Rules of Order" (Roberta being Mrs. Roberta Livergood Fuller, who frequently lampoons Parliamentary Procedure in her monthly squibs for *Pshaw!* magazine), there was no consensus as to whether a vote in actuality would be taken, since descendants of the female lines are allotted only one half of one vote and must attend our annual meetings in a veritable swarm if they are to ever hold sway.

Professor Elisha Livergood completed his appeals and sat down, but missed his chair and landed on the floor, this gluteal mishap being accompanied by shrieks and caws of uncharitable laughter. There followed a motion that the assembly adjourn for lunch, the motion being offered by the perpetually famished Mr. Stewart Livergood of Usquepaug, Rhode Island. It being only 9:59 o'clock, the motion went unseconded and Mr. Stewart Livergood proceeded to chank a corned beef sandwich on rye bread in lip-smacking defiance of prandial propriety.

HON. DUDLEY LIVERGOOD of Pawcatuck, Connecticut, PROFESSOR ELISHA LIVERGOOD of Providence, Rhode Island, and MR. DELBERT LIVERGOOD of Fall River, Massachusetts, were appointed a nominating committee over the objections of members of the female branches and three newly arrived young men who stood in the doorway with folded arms for a quarter of an hour and eventually demanded a say at the meeting by virtue of their bastard lineage to Cockchase Livergood by John Livergood, Cockchase's great grandson, and a fecund whore named Beriah Scrants. The Sergeant-at-Arms was promptly awakened and encouraged to remove the three toughs from the premises, though an arrangement was ultimately effected in which the three would be permitted adjunct membership to the body and afforded one quarter of a vote (upon payment of one quarter of the required annual membership dues) but were exiled to one of the children's tables at the luncheon, whereupon President Fred R. Livergood adjourned the formal meeting for lunch.

I observed in that interim that Mrs. Markham was not very observant, assuming—correctly as it were—that partaking of victuals did not necessitate the taking of notes, but I should like to make the brief interpolative comment that Miss Clementina Denslow and Mr. Edgar Livergood should think twice before pursuing a romantic attachment to one another until it can be fully established that Cockchase Livergood is their only mutual ancestor, so as to spare themselves the heartache of bearing imbecilic children.

THE AFTERNOON SESSION OF THE LIVERGOOD FAMILY REUNION was called to order by President Fred R. Livergood at 1:15 o'clock, whereupon the nominating committee presented its slate of officer candidates for unanimous approval, this list including MRS. FANNIE FLOWERS of Warwick, Rhode Island, descended from one of the female branches, for the office of vice president, the nomination being viewed as "highly commendable" and "a long time coming" by celebratory members of those branches, and "odious" and "anarchic" and "a splat of pig dung upon our fine Livergood family escutcheon" by members of the male lines, who immediately offered up the name of HOWARD LOOMIS LIVERGOOD of Westerly, Rhode Island, to contend for that selfsame office. A vote was held, and a tally made, with all parties voting along branch lines and the three intrusive bastards who were descended from that whelping whore voting on the side of Mrs. Flowers. The final totals for the office of vice president stood as follows:

Mrs. Fannie Flowers: 28 ¾ votes
Mr. Howard Loomis Livergood: 53 votes
Abstaining: 4 votes

When the results were announced, supporters of Mrs. Flowers proceeded to rip apart a chair. Order was restored when Mr. Loomis Livergood, in an act of familial reconciliation, withdrew his name, and Mrs. Flowers was elected by acclamation. In the spirit of family unity and togetherness, Mrs. Mary Blunt Livergood led the assembly in a verse of "O Joy! O Bliss! O Livergood!" although several disrespectful youths were clearly heard singing, "Oh Joy! Oh Piss! O Liverwurst!"

THERE FOLLOWED SEVERAL SHORT ADDRESSES to the body as noted below:

MR. WINTHROP LIVERGOOD of New York City, New York, delivered an address entitled, "Mr. Cockchase Livergood and his early home in England."

MR. DOANE WALLACE of Hartford, Connecticut, spoke on "Mr. Cockchase Livergood and his early home in Scotland."

Near fisticuffs ensued over the competing claims, but amity between Messrs. Livergood and Wallace was quickly restored when the two gentlemen were reminded by Miss Madeleine Livergood that Jesus was watching them and passing judgment upon their behavior from His celestial throne.

MRS. JETTIE LIVERGOOD RABBITT of Barrington, Rhode Island, began to speak on "Mr. Cockchase Livergood and his invention of the potato masher," but was silenced by a chorus of hoots and catcalls from the floor by those who annually reject the claim. There followed unkind charges that Mrs. Livergood Rabbitt was mentally unsound. She was compelled to flee the room in tears, and when she returned an hour later she stumbled and flannelled her words with obvious inebriety, and vowed "retaliation on those who would so malign and maltreat me."

MR. HAYDEN LIVERGOOD of Cranston, Rhode Island, offered "A tribute to the name of Livergood," the speaker itemizing moments of historic achievement in which Livergoods were active participants, notably the burning at the stake in Canterbury, England, in 1566 of Henry Livergood for being both a Protestant and keeping a miniature family of doll people. Also mentioned by Mr. Livergood in this fascinating study of famous Livergoods throughout history was Charles Livergood, witness to Burgoyne's surrender. By all accounts, Charles was dispatched to take the news to General Washington but got turned around and ended up in Spanish Florida, where he took up the ways of the Seminole. More recently, the publisher John Crocker Livergood was famously set last year to publish Mark Twain's collection of essays, *Things I Have Said for which God Should Punish Me upon My Death if There Were, in Fact, a God*, the publication of which was halted by judicial injunction sought by the Women's League of Christian Decency.

Interspersed among the addresses were the following musical selections performed by MRS. GLADYS LIVERGOOD ROUSE of Norwich, Connecticut, with accompaniment by MISS ADA POGUE on the piano-forte: "Please, Mother, Buy Me a Baby," "I'm on the Water Wagon Now" (for the abstainers), and "On the Banks of the Rhine with a Stein" (for the imbibers).

MRS. MEDORA LIVERGOOD MARKHAM delivered the treasurer's report.

MRS. BEDELIA MCQUIRK LIVERGOOD read greetings from association members who were unable to attend this year's reunion. Some were comical, others poignant, one was posthumously delivered, and one was written in Chinese characters and left everyone wondering if it was, in fact, a greeting at all.

THE FINAL ADDRESS OF THE AFTERNOON was delivered by PROFESSOR ELISHA LIVERGOOD, who charged us all to perpetuate the name Livergood with pride, and to honor our fine heritage and the memory of our common ancestor Cockchase Livergood. Professor Livergood also reminded us all to purchase our subscriptions for the third edition of the Livergood Family Genealogy, and then quieted the room to speak from his heart about his long but ultimately successful battle to end his addiction to opium cough syrup.

Before the valedictory prayer was offered by REV. ABNER HOADLEY, DD, all those present joined hands and together recited the motto of the LIVERGOOD FAMILY ASSOCIATION OF WARWICK, RHODE ISLAND: "Head good. Heart good. Livergood. All good. Peace of God be with you until we meet again."

A booklet is being printed as a keepsake of the event. It will include photographs of those of you in the male lines who posed for Mr. Cleary from Providence Plantations Photography. We regret that there was neither time nor room within the publication for the inclusion of photographic likenesses of those in the female branches.

Signed this day, September 30, 1905,
Mrs. Bedelia McQuirk Livergood, Cincinnati, Ohio
Secretary, The Livergood Family Association of Warwick, Rhode Island

1906

PUNCH(ING) DRUNK IN PENNSYLVANIA

The older brother, Randall, lived in Philadelphia. He installed skylight glass for the Benjamin H. Shoemaker Glass Company. The younger brother, Elijah, lived in New York City. He was a sculptor. The brothers hadn't seen each other for over two and a half years. Randall didn't approve of Elijah's bohemian lifestyle. Randall imagined opium-clouded assignations with Rubenesque models.

And Elijah drank.

The brothers' father had had an unquenchable thirst for spirits. A piano-forte instructor at the Philadelphia Music Academy, Randall Broddick Sr. had ended his employ at the school when his two sons were in their teens, and had ended it with a theatrical flourish. He arrived to perform at a faculty recital, highball in hand, dressed in the livery of a chauffeur: frock coat, striped trousers, patent leathers, rolled-brim derby, and butterfly bow, having traded clothes with the cab driver who had brought him that night to the academy. He had paid the driver well for the waggish exchange, but Randall was the only one who found it funny.

It appeared to Randall Jr. that his brother Elijah was following in their father's staggering footsteps. It was good that the two brothers kept to themselves and cities apart, though Randall's wife Elise wondered if the two would ever be close again and tutted over the tragedy of fraternal estrangement.

Randall and Elise had just bought a row house on Pine Street from one of Randall's coworkers at Benjamin H. Shoemaker. Although the windows were new and snuggly fitted, everything else about the house seemed in need of repair. The pipes leaked. The baseboards were rotted. The roof was falling apart and the furnace in the basement rattled and groaned through the night. Men would need to come and fix these things.

Elise had been sick. The three children needed attention. All was at sixes and sevens. It simply was not a good time for Randall to see his younger brother.

And yet the brother was coming down. That evening, in fact. The reason for the visit was an appointment set up by a sculptor whom Elijah had befriended in New York by the name of Samuel Murray. Mr. Murray had seen one of Elijah's pieces in bronze in a Bowery shop and had been quite impressed. After meeting its creator, Murray expressed his wish that the talented sculptor should come to Philadelphia and meet his friend, Thomas Eakins. "Eakins is a very good man for a young man of your talent to know," Murray had said.

This made Elijah laugh. "You flatter me, sir," he had said, "to think that I am *that* good *and* to think me so young. I'm certain that I'm almost as old as *you*."

"I'm thirty-seven," Murray had replied, snapping his finger for the waiter. The two men were dining on oyster cocktails and potato salad at a table d'hote establishment where Elijah took most of his meals (avoiding whenever possible the bland boardinghouse fare that came with his lodgings). "You *are* good, whatever your age, and I have every confidence that Tom will appreciate your talent."

"I'm laughing for another reason as well, Mr. Murray. I am no stranger to Philadelphia. I was born there, you see, and my brother lives there still."

"Is that a fact? You'll see your brother when you come?"

"There is a rent between us, but perhaps it can be mended. Especially if I'm finally to make something of my talent, which heretofore has only marginally sustained me."

Elijah had sent a wire informing Randall that he was coming. After discussing the impending visit, Randall and Elise agreed that it was only right that the two brothers should see one another. Accordingly, there was orchestrated an embrace upon the doorstep and an exchange of warm fraternal smiles that betokened reconciliation.

After seeing his sister-in-law and his two nieces and one nephew, and after marveling aloud at how the little ones had grown and how the wife had aged not a single day since his last visit, Elijah accepted his brother's invitation to take a leisurely stroll to talk frankly of the separate courses of their lives.

"I'm happy to hear that Eakins could help you win commissions here," said Randall. "If things go as you wish, will you be moving back to Philadelphia?"

Elijah shrugged. He stopped at the street corner to pull a couple of pepsin tablets from a roll he kept in his pocket. The meal he had taken on the train trip from New York that morning was giving him dyspepsia, although Randall wondered privately if their meeting again after so long an absence had contributed to Elijah's gastric discomfort. "I haven't thought of just what I'll do."

"Just like our sainted father. Never thinking more than a day or even an hour ahead. Life lived in the recklessness of the moment."

"The *spontaneity* of the moment, brother," replied Elijah, parrying his brother's jab with a smile.

"Elise would like you to have dinner with us tonight, and I'd like you to stay with us while you're in the city. There are workmen and repairmen coming and going throughout the day, which may be of some inconvenience to you, but at least you'll sleep well before your meeting with Mr. Eakins on Friday. Elise convinced me of the need for a good bed in our new guest room, so you'll be the first to lie upon this downy cloud and tell us how it feels."

It was late November. A crisp wind brushed past the two men. It carried with it the sounds and smells of a city at the zenith of its workday: the odor of hot asphalt from a street paving nearby, the clicking keys of typewriters within a second-story business school, the pungent smell of boiling turnips, the incongruity of "In the Good Old Summertime" cranked by an organ-grinder on a busy street corner. There was everything to take the two brothers' minds from the central conflict between them that had yet to be remarked.

"I've booked a room at the Windsor, Randy. I didn't want to be a burden."

"You wouldn't be a burden."

"I like the Windsor. And I also like not having to join the temperance league for the next three days."

Zing!

"You will at least try to keep yourself sober before your meeting with Mr. Eakins?"

"I have no intention of climbing upon the water wagon while I'm here, Randall. But perhaps it will comfort you to know that I intend, while in this city, to limit myself to only a couple of beers and a single pony of brandy a night. Will that help you to sleep better?"

"I sleep quite soundly as it is, Elijah, because I know that your life is your own. It's your choice whether to pursue the path of dissolution blazed by our father, or follow the more constructive and far more sober course that engenders success. You're very talented, Elijah. I've always known this. I've been quite proud of you, though I've never really had the chance to say it until now. Here's a golden opportunity to better your situation. Embrace it, I beseech you, with an unmuddled head."

"I'm not the man you knew three years ago, Randall. And I'm not our father."

Randall slapped his brother upon the back. "I'll give you what I've rarely given you before: the benefit of the doubt. Now let's select something sweet and cream-filled at the bakery around the corner, a contribution to the feast Elise is busily preparing for our return."

Three days later Elijah was introduced by his new friend Samuel Murray to the sculptor's lifelong friend and teacher, Thomas Eakins. Elijah produced his portfolio, containing photographs of several of his most exemplary pieces. Eakins nodded and clicked his teeth ruminatively as he gave lambent consideration to the pictures in the book. And though he was momentarily taken with an art school sculpture that Elijah had created of a muscular Roman Centurion, Eakins being much more drawn to the male form than to the female, the celebrated Philadelphia artist was only moderately impressed overall and pronounced Elijah, a man who would soon be turning thirty-six, a "young artist of some promise."

"That would mean—mean what?" asked Elijah, who had been drinking and jumbled his words a little as he spoke.

"It means that in time—"

"In *time*?"

"I do not wish to offend, but my assessment, Mr. Broddick, is that you have yet to reach the pinnacle of your talent. This is my opinion. My friend Sam here may think differently, but I am not inclined to recommend you or your work at the present time. And there it is."

Elijah allowed the anger that had been kept in the bud to blossom to full furious flower. "You arrogant son of a bitch!"

"Sam, get him out of here."

"If you had talent yourself, sir," railed Elijah, whiskey-scented droplets of saliva atomizing from his mouth, "you'd be working in Paris or in New

York. You are here in Philadelphia, sir, because you are nothing more than a journeyman portraitist, a hack sculptor, a Muybridge pretender in the field of photographic experimentation."

Murray, his face an amalgam of shock and painful disappointment—not over the fact that Eakins had not agreed with his own more positive evaluation of Elijah's work but at Elijah's mortifyingly obstreperous behavior in the presence of a man whose reputation as one of America's foremost artists was universally unassailable—took Elijah by the arm to lead him from Eakins' atelier. But Elijah would not go easily, roughly disjoining himself from his escort and nearly striking him with wildly swinging fists—fists emboldened by the liquid courage that Elijah had found necessary for this encounter with artistic greatness. In short, the courage that Elijah had acquired in a South Philly groggery prior to his interview betrayed and disserved him, just as his brother had predicted.

All in all, there was ample mortification to go around—mortification that was relayed in abject detail by the younger brother to the older later that day.

"What difference did it make whether I'd been drinking or not? Eakins thought my work was shit!"

The parlor door was quickly latched shut by Randall's wife Elise to keep the three children from hearing words she did not wish them to hear coming from their spiritually vanquished, profligately profane uncle.

"The difference, Elijah," said Randall, who was pacing now, "is that had you been sober and of a composed disposition, you would have accepted Mr. Eakins' comments with good grace, remembering that your friend Murray would gladly have remained your advocate and is not without his own influence in the art world. You have now slammed your door to both Mr. Eakins and Mr. Murray, and it is largely your love of demon rum—to put it in temperance terms—that has done you in. Change your ways, Elijah, I'm begging you. Or else you'll end up in a premature coffin just like our ossified father."

"And *you*, my sainted brother, may go directly to hell!"

With this final imprecation, Elijah fled from the house, nearly upending the man at the door who had come after a lengthy delay to repair the faulty furnace.

That night Randall spoke with his commiserating wife beneath the sheets into the early hours. Both had headaches. Even their two daughters and their son had headaches. The harsh words, the paint and varnish fumes, the sound of perpetual hammering—it all seemed to be too much for the greatly beleaguered family. Yet Randall blamed his own headache and restlessness on his brother, who had shown up after a deliberate absence of two and a half years with the express purpose, Randall now sincerely believed, of depositing the shards of his own shattered life upon the doorstep of his brother, thence to stomp them in a paroxysm of alcohol-fueled failure into much smaller and more inconvenient pieces—not so easy now to be carted away, to allow for the sound sleep of the just and meritorious sibling.

Randall took a sleeping powder.

Elijah, however, did *not* sleep. He was more angry this night than ever he remembered in his life. He continued to drink. In a saloon, he punched the face of a man whom he had never before met but who had cast a disdainful look in his direction. Elijah was punched back. He was ejected from the saloon, still thoroughly intoxicated, his lower lip bleeding, his mind reeling with thoughts of every grievous injustice that had ever been done to him. Why was his life such a struggle? Why was strong drink—the only thing that uplifted him, raised his spirits when the artist's life left him so often professionally, personally, emotionally unmoored—why was this one thing, so efficacious, so invaluable in the short term, his worst enemy in the long run? He slipped into the icy bath of jealousy over all the good fortune that fate had bestowed upon his brother: a beautiful and devoted wife; three healthy, happy children; a job with a solid weekly paycheck; a new house, which, after the chinks had been filled and the pipes soldered and leaky roof patched, would be a home that any man should cherish with pride. There was nothing in Elijah's life for which *he* could be proud. Even Eakins had pronounced him merely a man of some promise. And what if that promise was never to come to fruition?

Here in this City of Brotherly Love, Elijah was now determined to go to his brother's house and to pound upon the door until he woke Randall from his happy, carefree repose. He would spew hatred into the face of this greedy recipient of every ounce of fortune which by all rights should have been split evenly between the two siblings.

And go he did.

There was a bell and he rang it. He rang it over and over again. He hammered the door with his fist and kicked it. He stepped back and looked to see if a light had come on.

No light.

Were his brother and his brother's wife waiting him out in the dark, hoping that his drunken rage would subside, that he would simply wander off and let them (and all of their neighbors) slip back into contented slumber?

No, Elijah would not release his brother so easily. He would ring and pound and kick until Randall was forced to come to the door, even if the effort exhausted him.

Like a madman let out upon the street, Elijah did this and more. He took a stone from the gutter and shattered the fanlight above the door into a shower of glass. The rudely awakened neighbors poked their heads out of their own windows and yelled for him to quiet himself.

An officer quickly appeared. Seeing the hysterical man at the door and the broken glass for which the hysterical man was, no doubt, responsible, the officer stepped forward, squaring his shoulders to make his arrest.

Elijah stopped. As he was about to turn, wholly prepared to defend the indefensible, the front door of his brother's house opened. Randall appeared, pale, groggy, coughing heavily. "Gas. Leaking from the furnace," he said, his voice rasping, desperate. "All through the house. Help me get Elise and the children out of the—" Randall's eyes suddenly rolled back. Elijah caught his pajama-clad brother as he collapsed into Elijah's arms.

Elijah set Randall down away from the glass. He and the police officer dashed into the house and pulled the mother and her children from their beds. They put them out of the house as neighbors telephoned for an ambulance. The rescue was effected in a matter of two or three minutes. Had Elijah not persisted, bent upon waking the metaphorical dead in the house above, those who slept inside would have perished in actuality. The house had been filled with gas from the ill-repaired furnace in the basement. The windows were airtight; an expert glazier—a colleague of Randall's—had installed them.

The family was rushed to the hospital and all were eventually revived.

Elijah was standing by his brother's bed when the latter regained consciousness. Randall took Elijah's hand and squeezed it in silent gratitude. When later the two were able to speak, Randall shook his head in wonder. "You saved our lives. To think that everything that was wrong and bad—your hard drinking, the anger and belligerence that grew from it—were at the root of our deliverance. Who would ever think that it should be your ulcerated jealousy of me which would, in the end, rouse me from my death slumber and restore me to my family and my family to me?"

Elijah didn't know what to say, except this: that love and hate can be partners in a random, nonsensical universe. And hate—not the everlasting variety but that which rises up in temporal fitfulness, only to recede in reparative repentance—can, on a rare occasion, do good as well.

As for his enraged frenzy upon his brother's doorstep, Elijah was never asked to apologize. He was, paradoxically, thanked ten-fold.

1907

PROBLEMATICALLY BETROTHED
IN MASSACHUSETTS

Ada and her husband Roland Wilmer had been up all night discussing what must be done. The private detective had made his report earlier that day. Now there was confirmation: their daughter Carrie had chosen badly. Their daughter had, in fact, chosen disastrously. Carrie's fiancé, Scott Goodhue, had a secret, and now Mr. and Mrs. Wilmer knew what it was, though Carrie, they assured themselves, did not. Had it been otherwise, would she ever have agreed to the match?

Granted, Scott came from Brahmin stock. The Goodhues were doing business on the bay before America was even a twinkle in the eyes of her patriotic patriarchs. The Goodhues were first whaling men, then exporters and importers. Their wealth agglomerated with each subsequent generation. Scott Goodhue himself was a successful businessman, the owner of a lucrative fish warehouse. But Scott Goodhue was something else as well. According to the report delivered to Mr. and Mrs. Wilmer, Goodhue was the father of a bastard daughter, born of an Irish maid. The Goodhue family had kept it quiet. Yet the fact of it got out through an anonymous letter addressed to Mr. and Mrs. Wilmer which began, "There is something of dire importance that you must know pertaining to your daughter's betrothed, Mr. Goodhue."

Now that the detective had confirmed it, there was no question that Mr. and Mrs. Wilmer should tell Carrie what they had learned and ask her to break the engagement, even with the wedding set for Saturday—only four days away. Even though the scandal of canceling the wedding at the last minute would cast a cloud over the Wilmer family that would not evaporate for many years, far more grievous consequences were bound to result should Carrie be permitted to proceed with the wedding unawares, including but not limited to a humiliating, very public rotogravure divorce.

In the bedroom the Wilmers shared in their large house outside the village of Newton Lower Falls, Ada Wilmer, her face bathed in milky lunar luminosity, agreed with her husband that their daughter should be told the very next day, and that Ada should be the one to do it. The opportunity would come during the two hours that mother and daughter had set aside to take an inventory of the wedding gifts.

It was the first chance the two would have to spend some time together since Carrie's gown-fitting. In the ensuing days, Carrie's life as prospective bride had become a whirl of parties and teas and other congratulatory prenuptial soirees lavished upon her by the Newtonian social set.

Ada watched the dining room clock as the minute hand crept past two. She folded and refolded a stack of embroidered napkins and a crisp linen tablecloth and a cambric washstand covering whose poor stitching could not be believed (although there was no mystery to it; it was bestowed by the foreman of her husband's factory—a man whose wife was notoriously cheap).

At a quarter past Carrie fluttered in, her head in a cumulus, her heart captured and held hostage by the man she believed she would soon marry. "Forgive the delay, Mother, dearest. Shall I dictate and you write, or will you have it the other way around?"

"Sit, dear. There's something I must discuss with you. It's very important."

Ada indicated with a nod the empty chair beside hers. The dining room had become repository for the hundreds of wedding gifts that had been descending upon the Wilmer manse over the last several weeks: silver boxes and cloisonné, crystal vases, apostle spoons and cut glass cake dishes, andirons, a new, self-threading sewing machine, a china tea service, porcelain knick-knacks, a Maytag Pastime Washer, and a large sterling silver punch bowl that Ada wished she could use for the reception because the one the Wilmers owned was old and chipped.

"You seem upset, Mother. Is the rector ill? Has Aunt Violet suffered a relapse?"

Ada shook her head. "I'm simply going to say it, darling. And I want you to be brave." Ada took her daughter's hand and held it. "Scott has fathered a child. It goes without saying that it was born out of wedlock, since your fiancé has always been a bachelor."

"Oh," said Carrie calmly. She removed her hand from her mother's clasp and straightened herself in her chair. "I have no idea how you've come to know of this, but Scott's told me already."

"He has?"

"Moreover, Mother, I've forgiven him. He's made amends. He has promised me that his profligate days are behind him."

Ada stood abruptly. She gripped the back of her own chair to steady herself. "I don't mean to cast aspersions on the character of your fiancé, darling, but I can't possibly think it an easy thing for a man who has exhibited such debauched behavior in the past to transform his character by simple proclamation."

"And that is where we are different, Mother. I take him at his word. He loves me and will not disappoint me."

Mrs. Wilmer put her hands upon her daughter's head. Slowly she began to smooth the tresses with a gentle application of the fingertips. "Oh darling, darling daughter. We've done too good a job of sheltering you from the world. I should have been more honest with you about the ease with which some men fall victim to temptation."

"Scott is sorry for what he did, Mother. Very, very sorry. Do you not believe in forgiveness? In redemption? Or is it the idea of trust that you find so equivocal?"

"Your father and I want only for you to be happy, darling. Both now and forever."

"My happiness—the only thing? Do be honest, Mother. Is it not also terribly important that no shame should come to our good family name?"

"Do we not owe that to your father for everything he has done for us, my darling?"

Roland Wilmer had started his career as a teacher of the deaf. He had worked alongside the famed teacher Sarah Fuller, who had taught Helen Keller, among many others. Mr. Wilmer had used his familiarity with the needs of the deaf and his scientific background to start a business that specialized in ear trumpets, ear tubes, acoustic table urns, and other devices that assisted the hard-of-hearing. Most recently he had filed for patents and begun developing hearing aids that employed electrical amplification. The business was destined to grow and thrive, especially under the shrewd stewardship of Wilmer's son, Darius. But for the present, Carrie's older brother, a hydraulic engineer, was helping to build the Panama Canal. "I appreciate very much what Father has done for us," said Carrie, thoroughly chastened.

"I know you do," replied Mrs. Wilmer, before placing a delicate kiss upon her daughter's forehead.

Not another word was exchanged between mother and daughter, and Mr. Wilmer did not raise the matter with Carrie.

Saturday came—the day of Carrie's much-anticipated wedding. The February sky, typically cinerous and dreary, was powder blue with hardly a cloud in sight. Even without the foliage that served as natural adornment to St. Mary's Episcopal Church in Newton, the Federal Style meeting house was the chromo-perfect picture of New England simplicity and charm. Inside, the high box pews and square columns of the colonial sanctuary were festooned with smilax berries, the altar graced with white Easter lilies and white and pink rhododendrons. Pots of hothouse azaleas were distributed generously.

In one of the bedrooms of the rectory, Carrie's toilette was being prepared by her mother and her bridesmaids in a giddy, fussy pinwheel of activity. Roland Wilmer stood in the doorway not quite believing that the little girl he had once bounced upon his knee was now the beautiful young woman who stood radiant before him. Roland had spared no expense in giving his daughter all she desired, including the dress both she and her mother had sought from the finest couturière in Boston: a princess-style gown of white satin, trimmed with point lace. Atop Carrie's head was a pompadour large enough to hold a lengthy tulle veil and orange blossoms that replicated the blooms in the lace upon her shoulders and her silver brocade shoes.

Carrie caught her father's eye and the two smiled at one another. But a different look passed between her parents—a look of only slightly disguised apprehension. Mr. Wilmer shut the door and proceeded to another room, assigned to the groom and his attendant groomsmen. He opened the door to find his potential son-in-law arrayed in a species of sartorial splendor that perfectly complimented the look of his bride. Standing before him in Prince Albert frock coat over a gleaming white Marseilles waistcoat, his pearl gray cravat tied with perfection in the puff style, Scott demonstrated that it wasn't merely a prodigious knowledge of salted and frozen fish that defined him; he also knew how to dress well, especially when it counted.

"I'm wondering if I might have a word in private," said Roland.

"Skidoo, fellas. The old man wants to give his soon-to-be-son-in-law 'the talk.'" The four young men, two of whom had been playing mumblety-peg with a pocketknife upon the rectory's wooden floorboards, took their hasty leave.

"I'll save you the breath, Mr. Wilmer," said Scott, slapping a hand on Wilmer's shoulder. "I promise to love, honor, and yes, even to obey your remarkable daughter."

"Goodhue, I don't want you to marry her."

A stunned silence. Then,

"You're joking. But you aren't, are you?"

Wilmer shook his head. "I won't beat around the bush, young man. I know what you've done."

"What have I done?"

"Don't sport with me. You have a bastard child."

Scott looked about for a place to sit down. There were hymnals stacked upon a chair. He removed them. "You may wish to sit down, as well, Mr. Wilmer. This may take a moment."

Roland cleared a chair for himself and pulled it over to Scott.

"The maid was in the employ of my father. Did your private dick tell you this? Did he tell you that the woman died in childbirth?"

"He did not, but that makes your crime all the more reprehensible. Where is your child now?"

"An orphanage. But she isn't my child."

"You expect me to believe this?"

"I do. I expect you to believe it—though you are never to let this fact escape your lips—when I tell you that the bastard child's father was my own father. When the maid became pregnant, a rumor began to be circulated among the servants that it was I who was responsible, because I used to give the maid a bit of flirting attention from time to time. We—my father and mother and my two sisters—we let the rumors stand. We decided that should word ever get out, I would take the fall for my father. I would take the fall, Mr. Wilmer, because the damage to my reputation would be far less onerous than that which would come to him, especially as he planned to put himself before the Massachusetts General Court as a candidate for the U.S. Senate in 1906. I had never intended to marry, Mr. Wilmer. It was the bachelor's life for me, sir, though I must emphasize that I would never, could never live the sexually degenerate life which you ascribe to me by your accusation.

Of course, I didn't foresee that someone as wonderful as your daughter would come along and steal my heart as she did."

Roland Wilmer shook his head. He could not contain his skeptical and cynical nature. He was forever fearful that his laboratory might become infiltrated by industrial spies working for Mr. Alexander Graham Bell, whom he believed had a larcenous nature, since there was widespread contention that Bell had appropriated from Mr. Elisha Gray crucial details of sound transmission which facilitated his invention of the telephone.

"You will have to do better than that, Goodhue."

"I'm prepared to give you the proof you require. That is, should you wish to see it. Latch the door behind you, sir, and I'll show you the reproductive wound I sustained with the Rough Riders in Cuba. It impedes my ability to sire any children, bastard or otherwise."

Roland cleared his throat with a nervous cough. "You're being serious."

"Dead serious. Give me just a moment to unbutton this fly."

"No, no, no. That won't be necessary. Does Carrie—does my daughter know this?"

Scott nodded. "Her love for me far exceeds her desire to bear her own children. We have already taken the first steps toward adopting the child my father sired. We intend to love her as if she were our very own daughter."

"I regret, Goodhue, that I grossly misjudged you."

"It is water under the bridge, sir. Shall we shake hands on a pledge to put all of it behind us?"

The men shook hands with a hardy pump and Mr. Wilmer opened the door. His wife was standing on the other side. Taking Ada into his arms, he said, "All is well, and I will explain everything to you after the ceremony."

"But all isn't well with Carrie. She's decided that she doesn't want her father to give her away."

"Though I have only been looking after her best interests?"

"She sees only antipathy to the man she loves. Will you talk to her?"

It was fifteen minutes past the time that the ceremony had been scheduled to begin. The wedding guests, comprised of members of both the Goodhue and Wilmer families, along with friends, business colleagues, and employees of the various businesses owned by those families, were growing restless in their boxes. The groomsmen were playing mumblety-peg again despite flustered interdictions by the rector, and Miss Sarah Fuller, famed teacher of the deaf, was allowing her own impatience to reinvigorate her defense of her friend Alexander Graham Bell, her peroration being ill-received by those associates of Wilmer's who sided with Mr. Gray in the historic controversy regarding the invention of the telephone. "And for the record," Miss Fuller held forth, "Mr. Bell did not famously say, 'Mr. Watson, come here. I want you.' What he said, in point of fact, was, 'Mr. Watson, come here. And bring Miss Fuller with you!'"

Roland Wilmer sat with his daughter in the little bedroom in the rectory. Carrie was weeping upon his shoulder. "I have asked for your forgiveness, my darling daughter. Will you give it to me?"

"You are quick to find imperfection in others, Father. I agree that no man or woman who has ever walked this planet is without some blemish—"

"Save our blessed Lord Jesus," interjected the rector, who had stepped into the room to offer religious counsel as needed, but more pertinently to remind the bride and her father of the time.

"But my dear Scotty's blemish is in his nether region and it was a bullet put there by a Spaniard in the heat of battle."

Mr. Wilmer nodded as the rector tapped upon his pocket watch.

"You will then accept the fact that your own father is also merely human. Your mother as well."

"I will."

As the bride and her father were waiting in the vestibule, Roland Wilmer leaned over to whisper a question into Carrie's ear: "Have you any idea who sent the anonymous letter aspersing the character of your fiancé?"

"We may never know it, Father," replied Carrie, "but Scott wonders if it may not be one of his Harvard Porcellian Club brothers to whom he owes a great sum of money. Scott is indebted to a large number of gentlemen and to some men who could not be characterized as gentlemen at all."

"Whatever is the reason for the debt, my darling girl?"

"My fiancé gambles, Father. Poker, baccarat, faro, fan-tan, hazard. It is a mania with him. When he wins, all is happiness and joy between us, but when he loses—especially when he loses quite dramatically—I must soothe his troubles with loving kindness and tender mercies, the poor, poor dear."

The bride came down the aisle, followed by a six-foot train, her expression incandescent, rapturous. The man who accompanied her looked deathly pale, and the smile upon his lips seemed hardly sincere at all.

1908

VOLANT IN NORTH CAROLINA

"I'm too damned old for this," said the first man.

"Quit your belly-aching, Jimmy," said the second.

"Belly-aching is the very thing," said the third. "Are we belly-crawling all the rest of the way, Salley? If I'd known this would be a possibility, I'd have packed my truss." The third man then took out a handkerchief and blotted his sweating forehead.

"It isn't much farther," said the young man named Salley. "Look up and you'll see the tree I climbed to make my first observation."

Salley's four male companions, three of them newspaper and magazine correspondents, the fourth a fifty-one-year-old news photographer from Great Britain named Jimmy Hare, looked up.

Although it was a tree of average height, the imposing sand dunes that surrounded it seemed to dwarf it by proximity. Upon this isolated, narrow strip of seashore the sand hills swallowed up the entire landscape—both figuratively and literally. The men chanced upon large clusters of pines that all but disappeared under the glistening white mounds. Reaching this spot had been an adventure for the group, four of whose members had come all the way from New York City. Only Bruce Salley could claim a local connection and that was putting it broadly, this "string-man's" beat stretching all the way up and down the Virginia and North Carolina coastlines.

Upon assignment by their respective editors—each of them skeptical men who refused to take Salley's word on what he had seen with even the smallest grain of Atlantic Ocean salt —the newsmen had made their way over from Elizabeth City, and then by one-lung motorboat had chugged across the Pamlico, Albemarle, and Roanoke sounds, finally reaching the quiet village of Manteo on the island of Roanoke—an island which, for over three hundred years, had been haunted by the tragically unresolved fate of Sir Walter Raleigh's lost colony. These intrepid reporters set out from the village the next morning to discover for themselves if what Salley said he had seen was true and verifiable.

At the break of dawn they had climbed into the open launch that would take them to the Outer Banks. There they hiked ten miles over sand dunes that exacted an enervating toll with each sunken step. They established their day camp about a half mile from that which they had each come to see on behalf of their respective employers.

"I don't get the reason for all the cloak-and-dagger, Salley," said a reporter named Hoster, who wrote for the New York *American*. "You said yourself that you didn't stay hidden. You said that it wasn't any time at all before you were chin-chinning with them just like old friends."

Salley nodded from behind his field glasses.

"Then they had to have known that others would come after you. Men with more impressive credentials. Men with cameras that don't lie."

"Unless, of course, you're taking pictures for Hearst," interjected a reporter named Ruhl, with *Collier's Weekly*.

All the men laughed except for Hoster, who had a habit of never disparaging his employer, even when that employer was six hundred miles away.

Salley handed the binoculars to Hare, who was happy to take up something lighter than his bulky press camera. The thickly mustached Brit enjoyed a private laugh. As a young man, he'd walked away from an apprenticeship with his father, a successful camera manufacturer, because of a frustrating reluctance on his father's part to make smaller, handier cameras. This one was small—but it wasn't small *enough*. He also worried that his fragile lenses were becoming scratched from all the blowing sand. When it came time to take the photograph that would make history, he wanted a perfect print.

If that time ever came.

"They don't want the press around," explained Salley. "They haven't removed all the bugs from the new model. You remember what happened to Langley's aerodrome back in '03."

Ruhl nodded and snickered. "As I recall, the *Washington Post* said the craft slid into the Potomac like a handful of mortar. Oh, was that harsh!"

Ruhl laughed until he lapsed into a noisy smoker's cough that threatened to betray the secret press encampment.

"I'm only saying," resumed Salley, whose youthful earnestness betrayed his appreciation for being treated as an equal to these more established and seasoned men of the American press, "that Langley's well-attended aeronautical debacle is probably the reason that nobody paid much attention to the reports coming out of this little patch of sandy wilderness. After all, the brothers' first flight took place hardly a week after Langley's flying machine received its well-financed bath."

"*If*, that is, you are among those who believe that such a flight ever took place here," qualified Ruhl through his muffled hacks.

Unfortunately for the newsmen, each hoping for the scoop of the century, that first day was a bust. All the sand and the stealth and the *New York Herald* correspondent Byron Newton's near-death encounter with a slithering, dauntless copperhead had been for naught. At the other camp—the one under surveillance—there had been activity of a sort. The machine was brought out of its shed and there followed hours of tinkering, and then the twin propellers were made to turn, each glistening tauntingly in the bright sunshine, and as the five men of the press waited eagerly in their minimally concealing blind, the machine sat decidedly immobile upon its wooden skids and its specially built monorail and nothing else of note occurred. Before the onset of dusk and the hampering darkness, the quintet gathered up their supplies and made their long, laborious, grumble-inflected trek to the boat that would return them to their inn at Manteo.

The next day: a virtual reenactment of the day before.

The third day seemed equally unpromising. By midmorning, with the prospect of continued aeronautical stasis, Salley was lambasted by his colleagues for what surely must have been faulty eyesight and then excoriated over what surely must have been faulty memory and finally condemned for having been catalytically responsible for all of their present tribulations by virtue of his very birth. Each of the newsmen wondered to himself if the brothers who had invented the fantastical machine had been made well aware of the newsmen's interloping presence and were therefore waiting until their permanent departure before perpetrating anything historical upon these windy dunes. Or was all of this exactly as the world press had snidely surmised? Was it not the Paris edition of the American paper, the *Herald* (to which Bruce Salley had earlier sent his fervent eyewitness dispatches), that said in early 1906, "They are in fact either flyers or liars. It is difficult to fly. It's easy to say, 'We have flown.'"

The answer to all of these questions came in the form of a sound—that of spinning propellers. Rather than the clanking clatter redolent of a grain reaper, being the sound that had earlier broadcast itself from the vicinity of the rotating blades, there now came a crisp rat-a-tat-tat—the rataplan becoming sharper in tone as the blades spun faster and with greater assurance. Now, as Salley's companions looked on, first with spiritless half-curiosity, and then, suddenly, with full, unbridled anticipation, the men witnessed exactly what the youngest and least experienced among them had already seen with his own eyes several days earlier and had tried to convey, had tried to put forth with the same convincing detail that characterized the accounts of that select handful of privileged men and women who had seen it, too—had seen that which Orville and Wilbur had done and done repeatedly ever since that first blustery day in December of 1903, when history was made and then promptly and roundly ignored. This newly privileged crop of correspondents watched as the Wright Brothers' flying machine glided smoothly and quickly down its monorail track. They heard shouts of encouragement as it lifted itself up into the air, as its white wings caught the angled light of the morning sun and shimmered, as Wright Flyer III defied the gusting wind and rose thirty, forty, then fifty feet into the air. And then Jimmy Hare, in his thickest, most theatrical cockney brogue, cried "My Gawd!" and snapped a picture that all the world would later see and take as proof.

It was the kind of proof necessary to convince a doubting world. For man was never meant to fly. That was axiomatic. It was an impossibility that ranked with equal weight alongside the concept of terrestrial immortality and the absurdity of amity between the Russians and the Japanese.

It had taken only five years, and numerous flights both from the lofty dunes of Kill Devil Hills and the flat, grassy fields of Huffman Prairie in the brothers' home state of Ohio for the world to come to a settled acknowledgement of their accomplishment. In the first decade of the twentieth century, faith and belief were largely reserved for the ethereal, and not for those who would puncture the ether with their corporeal flying machines.

Late that night at the inn in Manteo, after the men had virtually commandeered the telegraph office of the United States Weather Bureau to wire their own breathless-cum-deathless accounts back to New York, the newsmen reiterated their apologies to their string-man colleague over a second round of beers. The evening adjourned with

Mr. Hoster's pronouncement that "history was made today, and we are its witnesses."

Bruce Salley shook his head in rebuttal. "History was made in all actuality on December 17, 1903. The Wright Brothers flew through the air while we were all looking in the opposite direction. Let us not congratulate ourselves too effusively for having simply and belatedly turned our heads."

1909

MORBIFIC IN NEW YORK

The cottage looks less like a cottage and more like a railroad depot. This was the first thought that entered Ruth's head.

The structure's situation upon the small island wasn't quite as Ruth had presumed either. She had imagined the small bungalow to be nestled in a sylvan grove, perhaps adjoined by a motley cutting garden. Instead, the house sat exposed and unadorned next to a church, only a few hundred yards from the East River. Its previous occupant, the superintendent of nurses, may have enjoyed the view from its riverside windows, but was perhaps otherwise ambivalent about giving it up to its notorious current resident.

The bungalow's present occupant had lived there for over two years. She lived alone, as was required, but was permitted to keep a small mongrel dog for compensatory companionship.

Ruth had wondered at first if the woman would even permit an interview. Ruth's letter seeking permission to write about her for one of the magazines for which Ruth worked had been answered, but not in the way that she expected. The request had provoked a long and vituperative attack upon all those who had conspired to imprison this woman on the island, and an equally impassioned defense against all the charges that had been hurled at her.

Ruth smoothed down a rumpled pleat in her skirt and patted a rimple in her salmon-colored shirtwaist. She straightened her modestly trimmed hat, knowing that the riot of flowers and feathers that characterized the millinery of most of her contemporaries would certainly have elicited contempt from the object of Ruth's visit—a poor Irish immigrant given to simple tastes in accordance with her diminished means.

Ruth St. Croix knocked and then waited. She waited for so long, in fact, that she began to wonder if the woman she had come to see—the woman whom she had taken extraordinary measures to interview—had, with the arrival of that mutually appointed hour, changed her mind. Had Ruth come all the way over from Manhattan Island this breezy summer day, the East River nearly claiming her hat when a gust pinched it (hat pins and all), simply to be mischievously jilted?

No further dark thoughts were allowed to enter Ruth's head, for the door to the cottage finally opened and the woman sought by Ruth St. Croix, intrepid female reporter of the stouthearted Nellie Bly stripe, stood before her, engaging Ruth with weary blue eyes that looked her visitor up and down in naked assessment.

"Welcome to North Brother Island," said the woman, the bounce and lilt of her native brogue having been modified by years of service to non-Gaelic American families. "How do you like me wee cottage prison? Will you add bars to the windows in your description of it? Will you tell your readers that I eat watery gruel to tug at their heartstrings? I give you permission to color me circumstances here as miserably as you may wish. Do come in. Mind the stair."

The woman stepped back and held the door open as if daring Ruth to enter. Ruth accepted the invitation and stepped inside. The front room was dark, curtains drawn over most of its windows. Yet even in shadow, the woman appeared to be comfortably dressed in accordance with her situation, simply but tastefully and crisply arrayed, and smelling to Ruth as if her frock had been freshly laundered.

"Please sit down," said Ruth's circumstantial hostess. "I do get the pleasure of a guest now and again, but they generally don't enter me cell." With a conspiratorial whisper: "They like to come and peer and gawk at me through the windows—like I'm some monkey in a cage. Do you see me the same way, Miss St. Croix? Do you find me to be akin to some animal in a zoo?"

"Well, of course not," said Ruth, glancing about the little sitting room. Though sparsely furnished, the space had a warmth and snugness to it that put Ruth at some ease.

After offering her visitor a seat upon the room's small sofa, the woman sat down in an armchair with a large and elaborately stitched lace antimacassar draped over the top and a profusion of doilies imbricating the arms. She had not put her blond hair up, and so it cascaded negligently over her shoulders, framing a youthful face, though Ruth knew the woman to be past forty. Perhaps her plumpness enhanced the semblance of youth. "So what do you want to know? I suppose you already know the reason they've put me on this island of ghosts."

Ruth produced her stenographer's pad and pencil from her bag. "Why do you call North Brother's Island an 'island of ghosts'?"

"Because of all of them what died here not five years ago. Do you not remember the *General Slocum* fire?"

Ruth nodded. "Yet I had forgotten that it was near here that the steamship went down."

"Abide upon this wretched island for more than a few hours and you'll hear the voices, too. Them shrill, panicked cries of the littlest babbies—you'll find these the hardest to bear. They laid most of the bodies right upon the bank not so very far from this cottage. 'Tis the worst sort of cruelty to put a person like me upon a ghost island like this. I do not deserve to be haunted so."

"There are those who say that you are fully deserving of such a fate."

The woman glared at her guest.

Ruth had been forewarned of her interviewee's famous temper. Lighter observations than Ruth's had been known to throw her into a raving frenzy; still, Ruth had chosen words that were deliberately, daringly provocative. "Did you come to hear my own side of things and the very good reasons for my release," said the woman, with obvious restraint, "or are you no better than all them others—the ones what bollocks and abuses me for sport?"

Ruth clasped her hands together and leaned forward upon her chair. "No, Miss Mallon, that certainly isn't the purpose of my visit. But there are questions that I feel I must ask. Your lawsuit against the city which demands your immediate release under habeas corpus proceedings—is there to be a ruling soon?"

"Very soon says Mr. O'Neill."

"Mr. O'Neill is your lawyer?"

Nodding: "But even if I lose, I intend to throw myself upon the mercy of me captors. I'll agree to everything they ask of me, I will."

"Meaning that, to begin with, you will no longer seek employment as a cook. That you will no longer infect others with the typhoid bacillus."

The woman known the world over by the unkind moniker Typhoid Mary lowered her eyes in contemplative silence. Then she raised them to impale Ruth with a contemptuous glower. "I have never been sick with typhoid—not a single day in me entire life."

"But you have been tested and, still and all, the typhoid germ does live inside you. It resides within your gall bladder, does it not? Was it not the case that you could remain free forever if you would but submit to an operation that would have removed the diseased organ?"

"An operation that most assuredly would have killed me. And I am not ready to die. Miss St. Croix, have you come here to plead for my release through your magazine? For this was what I understood you to mean from your letter. Or were you letting on for personal benefit—that you should meet me and then go and write about me just as all them others have written? If this be the case, then I must ask you to leave my home immediately, but I should like to strike you first for having wasted me time." Mary grinned. "On second thought: join me for lunch. A cold salad, I think. For it is me cold collations, they say, which appear to be the deadliest."

Checking her desire to rise and flee, Ruth collected herself and then calmly replied, "May I know why it is, Miss Mallon, that even though you don't believe yourself to be a silent carrier of typhoid fever, you've never engaged in those sanitary practices that could only have absolved you from all suspicion?"

"You mean why did I never wash me hands after attending to my business in the w.c.?"

"Frankly, madam, yes."

Mary thought for a moment while chewing upon her bottom lip. Then she shrugged and said, "Because it is not in my nature, I suppose. And for that reason I never took up the habit."

"I see."

"Of course, I suppose that it shouldn't have been such a terrible inconvenience for me to have done it."

"No, I should think not."

The two women regarded one another for a brief, silent moment. Then Mary said, "Miss St. Croix, I have no friends."

Ruth nodded. "Yes, I have heard this."

"I am a pariah."

"With only a dog for company."

Mary nodded. "I have a dog who doesn't care if I wash me hands or not."

"Yes."

Then suddenly, in spite of Ruth St. Croix's assiduous efforts to meet with Typhoid Mary and in spite of that previous desire on Ruth's part, given her humanitarian heart, to do good by this poor, lonely, hygienically uneducated woman, there remained nothing else to be asked or said. And so Ruth St. Croix stood, preparatory to taking her leave.

"Well," said Ruth in a vocal haw.

"*Quite* well," responded Typhoid Mary with an ironic smile.

As Ruth placed her hand upon the doorknob, regretful that she had not worn gloves that morning, a chill came over the formerly intrepid reporter and she felt herself in that moment surrounded by all the ghosts who resided on North Brother Island in the middle of the East River. But these were not the ghosts of the *General Slocum* tragedy. They were specters born of an Irish immigrant's ignorance of germs. And Ruth knew that once the woman was eventually released, she would in no time give sufficient cause for re-incarceration, hand-washing not being a component in her squalid nature.

The winds were even stronger during Ruth's return trip to Manhattan Island. Despite being affixed to her hair with multiple hatpins, Ruth's hat—an understatement of peacock plumage—was rudely seized from her head and sent flying in a gust that nearly pushed the rest of her over the gunwales and into the roiling brown river.

Chastened by her experience, Ruth St. Croix did not that year attempt another story that discomfited her (and for which she had a good chance of losing another hat—even though it be expendably under-trimmed). Nor did she set out to write another story whose subject so easily earned her disfavor. Ruth, who quickly abandoned any thought of writing about Miss Mallon, fought hard against feelings that depreciated the ignorant Irish, while making the customary boasts to her editor (and to the editors of the other enterprising progressive journals which employed her) of her general liberal nature.

And like a twentieth-century Lady Macbeth, Ruth St. Croix began to wash her hands several times a day to the point of crazed obsession. The soap she used was made of lye and the laving with such was quite punishing to her hands. By the end of the year, great patches of Ruth's epidermis had been abraded away. She was forced to wear large, paw-like protective mitts and to be laughed at, especially by the Irish, who, by their general nature, had a healthy sense of humor.

1910

PORCINE IN NORTH CAROLINA

The boy had never known a permanent home. At the death of his father when he was only seven, he was taken away from his impoverished mother, separated from his six brothers and sisters, and delivered to his mother's younger sister and her husband, a dry goods dealer in Wilmington. When the sister wandered off late one night in her bed robe seeking Jesus and was found the next morning floating face-down in a lake, the boy was removed to the custody of a spinster great aunt in Raleigh, who ultimately could not abide his energy and rambunctious nature and so was regretfully obliged to give him up to a paternal uncle who was a cooper, and his wife. Here in Winston the boy was to be made an apprentice when he reached the age of twelve, but due to the incapacitation of the husband, the victim of concussion by the injurious aim of a sprung stave, the boy stayed only long enough to learn the difference between a rundlet and a tierce, a hogshead and a firkin, and then he was off again to live in Durham with a different uncle, who was a phenomenon of sorts—a college-educated blacksmith—and his wife—a transplanted New England Bluestocking dressmaker—and their son, who was close to the boy's age and would have been a boon companion had he not been sickly and nearly always bedridden and eventually dead.

With the death of the son, Master Eugene Ramp, as the boy had come properly to be called, prepared himself to be sent off yet again, shuffled away to some other reluctant North Carolinian relative or village man wanting an apprentice. Yet, to Eugene's surprise, the decision was made by the grieving uncle and his grieving wife that it was not Eugene's fault that his first cousin was of a sickly constitution and could not do a better job of surviving childhood, so Eugene was kept. And though he wasn't at first any sort of replacement for the dead boy, young Eugene, now eleven years of age, was treated as *somewhat* of a son and loved as best as his uncle and aunt were able, except that the aunt was intolerant of energetic and high-spirited boys, and frequently punished him for his unbridled youthful ebullience.

"You will come in and sit down to dinner when I call you!" commanded Aunt Helen at the back door. "Send all of your colored playmates home. They know they aren't allowed in our backyard after sundown."

As Eugene was nodding goodbye to his dusky playfellows, his aunt cautioned him against coming inside without having first washed his face and hands at the well pump. This he promptly did, though his blouse was equally drenched and the aunt put to even greater ill humor. Then nephew and aunt sat and waited until the uncle came in from the adjoining blacksmith's shop and made his apologies for his tardiness and washed up, and then the three said grace with a mumbled amen from the areligious blacksmith and something even less than that on the part of Eugene, for he at the young age of eleven had concluded that God had long abandoned him and that he would return the favor.

There was a roast chicken on the table, and potatoes and freshly baked bread and some of the peas that had been put up last year in surfeit. Eugene was ravenous from having run and played after coming home from school and from having given away his lunch to the poor, hungry boy who was his desk companion at the schoolhouse, and from the fact that his Aunt Helen didn't believe in afternoon snacks. And so Eugene ate quickly and voraciously with both hands, reaching and grasping and shoveling food into a willing, gobbling mouth. At first the scene didn't register with the aunt, who was caught up in her private concerns over the fact that her blacksmith husband was seeing fewer and fewer customers. Was it because the carriage horses were being fast replaced by automobiles? What did the future hold for men like her artisan husband in this increasingly mechanized world? And what of Eugene when it came time for him to become a striker and work alongside his uncle?

With the thought of Eugene, the aunt turned to see her nephew stuffing a large wad of buttered bread into his mouth and was revolted.

"Young man, I have asked you repeatedly to respect this table and eat as an adult and not as a pig in a sty. Yet you refuse to listen."

"I'm sorry," said a cowed Eugene, his mouth still filled with bread, the butter basting his lips with an oily sheen. Could his aunt not see that his unruly attack upon his supper was testament to his appreciation of her fine cooking?

"And I do not intend to ask you again to display manners that my own dead son showed even in his sleep. You will suspend eating and you will go to your room."

The uncle, who nearly always took the side of his nephew (at least privately), for he knew that it was hard being an orphan (for Eugene's mother had died while he was being sent along from one relative to the next) and felt that some degree of latitude should be given, petitioned his wife with a look that bespoke a need for compassion and leniency. But the look and the implied request did not move her.

Eugene sat upon his bed, surrounded by residual evidence of the other boy who had once occupied this room. Gregory's books were still there and his hand-drawn pictures remained tacked to the walls (for Eugene's cousin Gregory was a gifted artist), and there were rocks and pinecones and other trophies of an exploratory boyhood. Eugene, who was frisky and exuberant by nature, now sat very still and tried to hear what his aunt was saying to his uncle. But he could glean only two words for certain: "pig nose."

This made no sense to Eugene whatsoever, although an hour later the words made quite a bit of sense, for Uncle Oswald came into the room carrying an artificial pig snout that he had fashioned in his shop, made of papier mâché and fixed to a string that allowed the nose to be put on top of a human nose as if for a masquerade. "Eugene, I've made this pig nose, which your aunt wishes you to wear for a week. I made it a month ago when you attacked the Sunday meal with reckless abandon in the presence of Reverend Gardner and his wife, and I was successful then in talking your aunt out of your having to wear it. Alas, I have lost the battle this time around and you must now put it on. While I would not portray your behavior at the table, my boy, as that of a greedy, snorting pig, it is your aunt who governs within these walls and she who has final say in all manners of domestic discipline. Put on the nose. She'll want to see it on you before you lay yourself down to sleep."

Eugene put on the nose. He did indeed look like a pig—or rather a creature that was half pig and half human in physiognomy.

The aunt now appeared in the doorway with folded arms. "You will remove the nose when you sleep so that it won't hinder your breathing, and then again when you take your meals. But at all other times you will wear the nose as a necessary reminder that boys who act like pigs will be regarded thusly."

"But must I wear it to school, Aunt?" Eugene's voice sounded different. It sounded as if he were holding his nose. And why should it not? The papier-mâché nose was tight and it pinched the nostrils nearly shut.

Aunt Helen nodded. "You may take it off when you eat your lunch. Only then."

Eugene was not a boy for whom tears came easily and this night would prove no exception. He reconciled himself to the ignominy of his fate, though he dreaded what his schoolmates would say and do when they saw him looking like a pig.

And they did not disappoint. There was no small number of snickers and guffaws and puns directed at Eugene that involved pigs and piglets and hogs and shoats and pork and ham and, naturally, all things nasal. Eventually, Eugene's teacher, Miss London, declared a moratorium on all future raillery, if for no other reason than the simple fact that she was tired of hearing it.

"You wear me out," she said to her class with a sigh of exasperation. "And there isn't an ounce of originality in anything you've thrown at poor Eugene today. This classroom is an absolute graveyard for cleverness. It batters my heart."

While the children were taking their lunch outside upon the sunny playground (the arrival of emancipative summer being just around the corner), Miss London detained Eugene to ask for the true story of the nose, since he had earlier attributed it to an affinity for oinkers.

Eugene, who had always been fond of his comely young blond-haired teacher, who was both gentle and wry—a fascinating cross between a nineteenth-century no-nonsense school marm and a twentieth-century pedagogical subversive—told the truth about how he came to receive the nose and related the sad fact of the length of his punitive sentence.

Miss London shook her head sympathetically, a few strands of her long, carefully gathered blond tresses escaping their confinement upon her head and hanging in free filament. "It's a small matter to make a boy wear a pig snout around his own home, but it's something far different to force a child to wear it where others will see it and taunt him over it."

"I don't mind the jests, Miss London. I myself would point and laugh if one of the other boys was made to wear it."

"Well, take it off. In my schoolhouse you're to be a boy and not a pig."

Eugene shook his head. "I cannot. I am under strict orders from my aunt to wear it at all times except when I eat and sleep."

"How will she know if you're wearing it here or not?"

"She said that she'll send Caleb, our hired man, to come and look in the window from time to time to make sure that I'm in compliance."

"What a predicament!" marveled Miss London, leaning back in her chair and drumming her fingers upon her lips. "Perhaps I should have a talk with your aunt tonight."

Miss London came that night but Aunt Helen wasn't home. Aunt Helen was at her missionary society meeting discussing heathen brown babies throughout the world and how best to bring them to Christ. Miss London went instead to talk to Uncle Oswald, who had been working late in the forge, scouring his tools and anvil. Eugene had been assisting his uncle prior to Miss London's arrival, though at present the two were munching potted meat sandwiches like hungry bachelors. "Eugene, if you will excuse your uncle and me," said Miss London, "there's a private matter that I wish to discuss with him."

Eugene picked up the remains of his sandwich and the pig nose, which lay next to him, and obediently left the forge. (He had been ingesting his sandwich very slowly to postpone the return of the false snout to his face.)

"Mr. Ramp, I cannot say that I'm a big fan of humiliation as a means of correcting misbehavior."

"Nor I, Miss London," said Uncle Oswald. "And yet my tacit compact with my wife—the compact which opened the door to Eugene's coming to live with us—is that within the sphere of discipline, all will be left to her and her alone. She isn't a heartless woman, Miss London, nor even, may I add, misguided. She simply sees things differently than do you and I."

Miss London paced a moment with her fingers interlaced behind her back. "Then Eugene is doomed to be a pig for six days more."

Uncle Oswald nodded and wiped a trickle of sweat from his brow. The forge remained forever warm regardless of the season.

"And what a pity it is," said Miss London. "He's a good boy in the main. And not a pig."

"No more a pig than you or I," agreed Uncle Oswald, who was, nonetheless, remembering how Miss London had attacked with hedonistic glee a particularly tasty blueberry pie at the county fair when a more contained and cultivated judge would have simply placed the fork daintily to her lips and withheld her full assessment until the distribution of the prize ribbons.

The next morning there was more fun to be had by several boys who had thought of new things to say, and there was even a comment on the part of the visiting nurse who came each month to check for head lice and suspicious coughs, and who, in seeking a tally by Miss London of all the children in attendance that day, couldn't resist appending her request with, "including the pig."

The following day, which was a Friday, was quite different from the two days that had preceded it. In the first place, when Eugene came down for breakfast, his uncle was missing. Before Eugene could inquire of his aunt, who stood frying eggs at the stove, as to his whereabouts, Eugene's uncle made his appearance in quite a dramatic fashion. He dashed into the room, and, snatching up the plate of sausage and bacon from the table, addressed it in the voice of melodramatic tragedian, "Oh, Mother! What has happened to my poor, dear porcine mother?"

The fretful wail had a logical explanation. Uncle Oswald was wearing a pig nose—a nose with the same look and construction as Eugene's.

Nor was this the end of things. When Eugene got to school he was greeted by a pig-snouted teacher and twenty-two pig-nosed classmates. Eugene's Uncle Oswald, by all evidence, had been up all night in his blacksmith's shop making pig noses to match the one worn by his nephew. He had taken them quite early to the school, and Miss London had asked her other pupils in confidence to come early to put them on. And all had agreed and had delighted in the frivolity of it, and Eugene's aunt's choice of punishment for her nephew became undermined in a way that did not in the least put him at odds with her, for even the aunt had at last come to see the folly of it all.

Yet ever thereafter Eugene sat up straight in his chair and displayed his very best manners when taking meals with his uncle and aunt. And over the ensuing years Eugene came to be loved by both of his surrogate parents just as deeply as they had loved their own infirm son.

When as a young man Eugene Ramp left to join the American Expeditionary Force to help deliver the world from German barbarism, he took his papier-mâché nose with him and wore it to coax a laugh from his fellow doughboys and to keep up their spirits when hopes would ebb. When he fell at the bloody Battle of Château-Thierry in France, Eugene was still wearing the nose. At the request of his fellow Yanks, he was laid to his eternal rest with the fabricated pig snout firmly emplaced.

Back in North Carolina there was a memorial. Punch was served, along with cheese and crackers and a tar-heel honey ham. Most in attendance thought the ham an appropriate touch.

1911

EFFLORESCENT IN MAINE

Penny Rutland was an only child. She was also an only grandchild on her father's side. The uniqueness of this status placed a heavy burden upon the twelve-year-old. For the last six years, she had been sent to her paternal grandparents' landed estate on the Western Promenade in Portland to spend the summer in the constant company of her sixty-year-old forebear who, though under-demonstrative in her affection for the girl, did love her in her own way and sought to instruct her in all those things that a young lady of good breeding and cultivated refinement should know. Penny would have liked to romp and play with the servants' children, but she couldn't risk soiling her pinafore. She would have liked to sit upon the vespertine verandah and listen to war stories told by Mrs. Rutland's butler Jenkins, who had served as a spy for the Union Army during the Civil War, but there were, according to Penny's grandmother, far more ladylike and much more productive things for the young girl to be doing in her postprandial hours.

There were teas—these attended by her grandmother's West End friends—and there were gatherings of the distaff members of St. Luke's Cathedral for the purpose of discussing matters of both a spiritual and morally inculcating nature. Penny was expected to sit politely in white muslin with her hands folded neatly in her lap and to be the perfect little girl. Penny was expected to knit when her grandmother desired a knitting companion and to read to her grandmother when she sought a mellifluous rendering of one of Mrs. Rutland's favorite books, and each day Penny was required to accompany her grandmother in her daily matutinal promenade through her English rose garden, which was the woman's pride and joy and one of the finest private rose gardens in the state.

While Penny didn't dread her rosaceous catechism at her grandmother's side, there were fifteen or twenty things she would rather have been doing on these cool, dewy summer mornings. But Penny was a good girl and properly indulgent of her grandmother's efforts to instill in her a love of the floral, and more specifically to share with her all the many mysteries and particulars of rose horticulture, including the salient aspects of both the hybrid perpetuals and the tea roses (which do quite well in light soil if manure is added and plenty of water is given in the dry season).

"And what have we here?" asked Mrs. Rutland, suspending her stroll alongside her granddaughter to linger before a peculiar-hued tea rose climbing upon the old stone wall that encompassed the garden. The rose was yellow with streaks of red and gold—a distinct coloration that upon some earlier tutorial session Mrs. Rutland had compared to a J.M.W. Turner sunset.

"Is that the L'Ideal?" asked Penny.

Mrs. Rutland nodded and smiled approvingly.

"And this variety here, sitting low against the wall?"

Penny thought for a moment and said, "The Gustave Regan?"

"Not *Regan*, my dear. *Regis*."

"Regis," repeated Penny.

"And those lovely creamy yellow buds—what did I tell you they were often used for?"

"For button holes?"

"Precisely, dear girl. They make the most *exquisite* button holes."

"May I sniff them?"

"Oh, my darling girl, you may sniff any rose in your grandmother's garden. That is the twofold reward bestowed upon us by the most beneficent family Rosaceae. Its constituents are ravishing to behold with the eye and they are delicious in fragrance—except for the Baroness Rothschild over there, a nearly faultless rose both in its color and aesthetic composition but without any scent whatsoever. A rose without a scent. It's absolute apostasy! Yet I grow the Baroness for her beauty and overlook her deficiency as best as I am able, for the lovely pale pink of her petals delights and enchants. Look all about you, child. Have you ever seen in one singular spot so many delectable variations of color? All the different whites and yellows and salmons and pinks and reds? Oh, such reds! A near riot! It's my favorite color, I must confess. Is it *your* favorite color, Penny?"

"I like red. I like blue, as well."

"And who could *not* like blue? How blue the sky is this morning! How beautiful the world on a day like this. Now, shall we visit the pillar roses or spend a few minutes with the dwarf teas?"

"I'd be happy spending time with either one," said Penny. She took a parting sniff of the Gustave Regis. The sweet scent was strong; all around her the air was infused with its pungent redolence.

"Grandmother, may I ask you a question?"

"Of course you may, Penny. There is so much to learn about the World Rosaceae. There is much still for me to know. Should we find the gardener and put our questions to *him*?"

Penny shook her head. Then she swallowed and said, "Grandmother, when I woke this morning there was blood on the inside of my panties. It was…" Penny looked about, her eyes settling upon a cluster of blackish-maroon blossoms. "…*this* color."

"That is the Prince Camille de Rohan, my dear. It's one of the finest dark roses to be had and extremely difficult to grow. Hardman and I, we have been quite astonished by the extent to which it has flourished here. And once the plant is established in full, we shall be amply blessed by a prodigious number of blossoms."

"I have blood in my panties, Grandmother. Should I see a doctor?"

Mrs. Rutland shook her head.

"What am I to do?"

"Has your mother not spoken with you about this?"

"I've never bled before."

"She will speak with you, I'm certain, when you return home in the fall. Let's go and see how Madame Plantier and the Marquis of Salisbury are doing."

Mrs. Rutland walked in silence to another section of the rose garden and examined the forenamed pillar and her companion tea rose, as well as their floral friends Grace Darling and Marie van Houtte, the latter festooned in soft blossoms of striking pale lemon yellow, each petal tinged with delicate pink along the edges. Mrs. Rutland sighed contentedly. "This could very well be my favorite among all my tea roses. Shall we make a bouquet of these beauties for the front hall?"

"What if I bleed again?"

"It is nothing with which to concern yourself. It will all be explained to you in due time."

"Will *you* explain it to me?"

"I think it best that you discuss this with your mother."

"Mother doesn't discuss things with me. She treats me as if I'm still seven."

"That will change, I assure you. This hedge here. Directly behind you. Do you recall the name of this variety?"

"Something to do with New Orleans," sighed Penny.

"You very nearly have it. This is Léopoldine d'Orléans. And there is the Dundee Rambler. Note how *luxuriantly* it rambles!"

"Why won't you tell me the things that really matter to me!" Penny suddenly exclaimed. "What is wrong with me? Am I going to bleed to death?"

"Your mother has been derelict. It is not my place to discuss such things with you. I am the grandmother. And, Penny, you will refrain from ever raising your voice to me again. My gracious word!"

With that, Penny's unwontedly flustered grandmother gathered her skirts in one hand and fled the garden. The gardener, Hardman, who was nearby upon his hands and knees weeding and therefore wasn't noticed by Mrs. Rutland, now stood up to make himself known to Penny.

"The garden is nearly perfect," he said. "I can't imagine what she saw that has put her in such an agitated state."

"She hasn't a problem with the garden," was all that Penny said in response.

There was a tea that afternoon attended by several of Penny's grandmother's friends. Penny said that she didn't feel well so that she would be excused to go up to her room and read a book and write letters to her friends back in Boston, but mostly to sit upon the window seat and look out her bay window at her grandmother's rampant English rose garden and wonder if she was dying.

Her dismal reverie was interrupted by a knock upon her door. The visitor was Mrs. Rutland's downstairs maid Hildy. "Begging your pardon, miss, but I have a question for you, if you could but spare me a moment."

"What is it, Hildy?" Penny, who had been sitting with her knees pressed against her chest and her arms wrapped tightly around her knees, now granted freedom to all of her limbs and stretched herself cat-like upon the window seat.

"I noticed the spot in your panties. Will you be needing a rag or two?"

"A rag or two?"

"Now that you're blossoming into a young lady."

"I don't know what you mean."

Hildy stared at Penny for a moment without speaking. Then she said, "You haven't been told a thing about it?"

"About what?"

"Your mother and grandmother—one of them hasn't…?"

Penny shook her head slowly, uncomprehendingly.

Hildy tutted. She shut the door behind her. She crossed to Penny and took her by the hand and led her to the bed, where the two sat down next to one another. "It's nothing to be afeared. I'll tell you everything you need to know. Your grandmother knows her roses but she apparently don't know a thing about the rose that blooms in every young woman."

"I'm not dying?"

Hildy smiled and nearly laughed, but held herself back, for it would have come at Penny's expense. "No, my dear little girl. You're just beginning to *live*."

Then Hildy told Penny everything there was to tell, even those things that Penny could scarcely believe.

At table that evening there was more talk of roses between Penny and her grandmother as her grandfather read his newspaper and nearly nodded off in his soup. After a subdued evening spent reading and listening to Caruso on the gramophone, Penny was sent up to bed with a kiss upon the cheek from her grandmother and a mumbled goodnight from her preoccupied grandfather. After Penny had left the room, Hildy was rung for and a sum of money changed hands and Hildy was made slightly richer, though Mrs. Rutland had asked nothing from her.

The day came near summer's end when Penny was packed up and put on a train back to Boston. There had been not a word spoken on that brief exchange in the garden. It was as if it had never happened. On the train Penny wept for her grandmother whose world she felt was too narrowly circumscribed, but she knew the woman wasn't unique in this respect. It was the way of things with the upper class, for whom the natural and elemental were made floral and fragrant and gay, and any discussion of pruning and budding and disbudding was forever limited to the literal and never to the analogous, though rose gardens do blaze with all sorts of sanguineous possibilities.

1912

TRISKAPHOBIC IN WISCONSIN

Dr. Remley paced. It was one o'clock in the morning and it wasn't like him to lose sleep over any one particular patient in his care. But John Schrank was a special case. Since being committed to the Central State Mental Hospital in Waupun (after first having spent time in the Northern Hospital for the Insane in Oshkosh), Schrank, called "Uncle John" by the younger of his fellow inmates, had been a model ward of the state—pleasant and scrupulously well-behaved. During his twenty-eight years of internment he had rarely exhibited any of the symptoms by which he had earlier been assigned the diagnosis of "dementia praecox, paranoid type."

Schrank was a quiet, solitary man, obsessed with politics, but interested in little else.

During all the years of his institutionalization he'd never had a single visitor. The sole love of his life, a young woman named Elsie Ziegler, had died in the *General Slocum* steamer disaster in 1904. It was through Schrank's references to Elsie and the tragedy that surrounded her death that Dr. Remley got his most revealing look into the soul of a man whose psychopathic criminality should have suggested nothing but violent depravity without compunction.

Uncle John was truly an enigma.

"I remember the day of all the funerals, Doc," Shrank had once confided to Remley. "June 18, a Saturday. There were over 150 of them, most in Kleindeutschland—that's the neighborhood in New York where most of us lived in those days. The bells tolled without stopping. Nearly every door and window in our neighborhood was draped in black. I remember wandering the streets with all the other men—weeping men, tortured men, their faces pallid and drawn. Since most of those who died were women and children—the innocent of innocents—it was the husbands, the fathers, the fiancés and boyfriends who were left behind. The church outing took place in the middle of the week, you see. Those of us who hadn't taken that fateful trip—it was our duty now to carry that heavy burden of grief upon our shoulders to the end of our days.

"In the midst of all those ambling, listless men, I spied a young girl walking with an older man. She was eleven or twelve years old. She reminded me of Elsie. The girl had Elsie's hair, Elsie's eyes, the turn of my Elsie's cheek. I asked her name. Catherine Gallagher, she said. She told me that she'd been on the boat but had survived—one of only about three hundred who did. She'd lost her mother, her nine-year-old brother, a baby sister. I hugged her in the street before letting her go on with her grandfather to the funeral of the family members she'd watched die.

"It was hard for me to understand how life could be ripped away so easily. That those who most deserved to live often did not, and those who did *not* deserve the precious gift of life—such as the man I fired upon in 1912—survived in spite of heavy odds.

"I don't know what happened to little Catherine Gallagher. I have always nurtured the wish that she should have a very long and happy life to make up for what happened to all those who were not as lucky as she."

That night in 1940, the doctor had tried to get Schrank to talk about what was troubling him. Why was he sitting at the window, unable to speak, or even to eat or sleep? Why was Uncle John, in his mid-sixties now, and usually quite genial in his dealings with the other inmates and the staff—why was he now so refractorily uncommunicative, so completely unreachable? Was he reliving the loss of his beloved Elsie with more intensity than usual? Or was it memory of that other day—the one in 1912—that drew him so deeply inside himself?

The night after President William McKinley died from an assassin's bullet, Schrank had had a vivid dream. The deceased president spoke to him. In a room filled with crepe and flowers, McKinley's lifeless body suddenly became vivified, the murdered president waking from his death slumber to sit straight up and point to a spot in the darkness. "Avenge my death!" he commanded of Schrank. The one in the darkness who was being fingered for the crime wasn't the man who had actually pulled the trigger, an anarchist named Czolgosz. It was the man whom Schrank would later stalk from city to city until destiny finally brought them together in Milwaukee.

Luck had been against Schrank when the time came to exact revenge. On one occasion he had stood waiting by a particular door only to have his quarry unknowingly give him the slip and go out another. In a different city there had been far too many people standing between Schrank and his target for him to get off a good shot. In Chattanooga, the potential assassin had a good opportunity to make his kill but he lost his nerve. In Chicago, Schrank had hesitated again. Standing at convenient proximity to his victim outside the Hotel La Salle, Schrank's desire had been arrested by qualms about bringing notoriety to the city of Chicago—a city he loved.

Yet he had no such qualms in Milwaukee.

First he steeled himself with several bottles of beer in a saloon near the Hotel Gilpatrick, where the former U.S. president was having dinner. Then, after the candidate had finished his meal and was waiting to be driven over to the city's auditorium to deliver a campaign speech, Shrank would make his move.

John Schrank had always been at home in saloons. He'd been a saloon-keeper himself back in New York City. He presented himself to his fellow bar patrons not as an assassin-in-waiting, but as a newspaper reporter. He became friendly with the bartender, with the bar musicians. He asked them to play something patriotic. They obliged by striking up "The Star-Spangled Banner," and he bought them all a round. At a few minutes past eight o'clock, Schrank walked over to the hotel to wait with all the others who wanted to cheer the man who was running for president again, who was asking for a third term in the White House beneath the standard of a brand new political party: the Progressives.

John Schrank wasn't drunk. He was clear-headed. He was primed and loaded for—not bear—but bull moose. He positioned himself close to the parked car, among those who now surged forward, having gotten word that Colonel Roosevelt was on his way out.

Schrank watched as TR first sat down in the tonneau of the open vehicle, and then impulsively bounced back up to acknowledge the cheering crowd. He flashed his famous toothy grin, lifted his hat in salute, and then…

Bang!

One shot was all that Schrank was permitted to get off before being tackled and pushed down to the ground. The gun was wrenched from his hand. A moment later he was dragged to the ex-president, who enjoined the crowd, now rising up as its own overzealous lynching party, not to harm him. Schrank was to be brought forward so that Theodore Roosevelt could look into the face of the man who had sought to kill him. After studying his assailant for a moment, TR turned to the police officers who had subdued him. "Take charge of him," TR said. "See that no violence is done to him."

Perhaps, thought Schrank, Roosevelt remembered that McKinley had prevented his own assassin from being beaten to death through similar pacifying words. Or perhaps it was simply in Teddy's nature to be concerned for his attacker's safety. Schrank didn't hate Roosevelt. In fact, when TR died six years later and reporters sought a word or two from the hospitalized madman who had previously tried to kill him, Schrank was quoted as saying with absolute sincerity and quite unexpectedly, "A good man is gone. I did personally admire his greatness."

What Schrank despised wasn't TR the man. It was TR the "third termer." The fact of the former president's lust for another four years in the White House, which had motivated the creation of a new party to accommodate him, was the sole reason that this sufferer of "dementia praecox, paranoid type" wanted to have him removed permanently from the political stage.

George Washington had set a precedent that all other presidents had respected. Ulysses S. Grant would have preferred a third term, but delegates at the 1880 Republican convention had other ideas. TR hungered for the chance to step out upon that stage for a rousing third act, and it was up to John Schrank, a nondescript saloon-keeper, originally from Bavaria, to stop him.

By killing him.

And he almost did. Were it not for the fact that the bullet had to pass through both a metal eyeglasses case and a fifty-page speech (folded over), the missile would have gone straight into Roosevelt's lungs rather than into the taut muscle of the ex-president's barrel chest, where it remained, only a moderate inconvenience, for the rest of his life. Schrank had, to his misfortune, directed his bullet at the most armored spot on TR's body.

When examined by Chief of Police Janssen at the Central Police Station of Milwaukee, Schrank answered quite a few questions, a good many going to motive. And yet it couldn't be any simpler: America had the Declaration of Independence and the Constitution to guide her. But she also had her traditions, and Schrank felt that the most sacred of them all was the unspoken two-term limit for occupants of the White House. It was so sacred to him, in fact, that he would kill to keep it upheld. Was there any other reason Schrank had pulled that trigger? Well, yes. It was because William McKinley had told him to.

It wasn't only that one night after McKinley's passing—this dictate of revenge from beyond the grave. A second spectral injunction was delivered to Schrank over a decade later: on September 15, 1912, to be exact. It manifested itself in the early hours of the morning in the form of a disembodied (though familiar) voice. Speaking to Schrank in a low and melancholy tone, the voice had said, "Let no murderer occupy the presidential chair for a third term. Avenge my death!" This second decree, ambiguous in its earlier incarnation, now had explicit clarity: Theodore Roosevelt deserved to die because he was trying to achieve what no man throughout the course of American history had done before. The monk-habited, famously mustached figure in the dark (was there a doffed Rough Riders' cavalry hat resting in its lap?), complicit in the death of the man he'd served as vice president, was now culpable of a most grievous additional offense in the sick mind of John Schrank. A week later Schrank was off on a single-minded mission to deliver the White House on November 5 to either President Taft (whose rupture with his friend and mentor TR had contributed to the creation of the Progressive or "Bull Moose" party) or the priggish Presbyterian academic Woodrow Wilson.

To the shock and consternation of those who formed the ex-president's entourage in Milwaukee, the Bull Moose chose, in characteristically operatic fashion, to deliver every word of the prepared speech—all eighty minutes of it—to those who had assembled to hear him—this in spite of having just been shot in the chest. Only after completing the address did he consent to be taken to a hospital.

In the end, the former president made a full recovery. Unfortunately, the delivery of that speech (deemed inspiringly heroic by some and suicidally reckless by others) failed to sway the masses by numbers sufficient to win him the election. The prize went to the priggish Presbyterian academic.

On November 15, a court-ordered sanity commission was convened to determine if Schrank was sufficiently *compos mentis* to stand trial for his crime. The committee's unanimous finding: the lonely, politics-obsessed saloon-keeper wasn't sane by even the most generous definition of the word, and was therefore not accountable for his actions.

Which brings us back to 1940, whence this story began. Dr. Remley had lain awake, had walked the halls, had fretted without respite over a patient who had up to that date, July 18, seldom troubled him before. It was all quite mystifying to the doctor, especially since Schrank, generally a rapt observer of events of national political import, had stopped listening to the gavel-to-gavel radio coverage of the Democrats' National Political Convention—had simply switched off the radio and not switched it back on, retreating silently inside himself.

Failing to glean the cause of this change in Schrank was the good doctor's own fault. Had he cudgeled his brains just a little harder, he might have come to realize that the reason for his patient's debilitating despondence lay in the very day itself. Because July 18, 1940, was a red-letter day in the annals of presidential politics. It was the day that Franklin Delano Roosevelt (fifth cousin to Teddy) formally accepted his party's nomination for a third term as president of the United States.

And there wasn't a thing in the world that Uncle John could do about it.

1913

CLAIRVOYANT IN NEW YORK

It was clear to all three of the siblings that their mother had been swindled. Several important aspects of the confidence game being perpetrated upon her became painfully apparent to Carlotta Cramford's two sons and one daughter through the course of that revelatory evening in February when Dodge and Porter Cramford and their baby sister, Violet Cramford Gooch, pinned their mother down on the matter of a certain disappeared inheritance. Where had all of the money gone? They knew that Mrs. Cramford wasn't investing in the stock market or in real estate. They also knew that she wasn't dropping fat, dimpled bags of coin into the collection plate on Sunday mornings, or sneaking munificent donations to the city's many settlement houses.

"I'll tell you where it's gone," said Mrs. Cramford, with a defiant glare that was betrayed by the tears which moistened her lace handkerchief, "if you tell *me*, Violet, why you remain married to a man you do not love."

Violet, finding the question irrelevant to the matter at hand, would not offer tit for her mother's tat. Additional prodding and lachrymose cajoling were required before Widow Cramford was finally forced to admit that she had given most of the money left to her by her deceased husband, a successful bridge designer, to the psychics whom she saw sometimes several times a week: local seers and Cassandras, mediums, card readers, crystal ball caressers of both genders—every one professedly clairvoyant, clairaudient, telepathic, and second-sighted, and every one located in the city of New York. Mrs. Carlotta Cramford had been for the past several months, hands down, the easiest mark in town. Everyone had her number (which, by the way, was seven), and each took every opportunity to filch from her bountiful pocketbook until there was nothing left within it to be passed down to her children when she eventually joined her husband in the Hereafter.

"There oughta be a law," railed Porter, the second oldest. "Taking advantage of a poor old lady like Ma."

"She was a willing party to it," countered Dodge, who had been to college for almost a year, and though he was a men's clothier had a head for other things besides haberdashery.

"I'd like to get them all into a room," said Porter, who kept his voice low. The two brothers stood smoking on the front porch of their mother's Forest Hills Tudor, but the windows were open and Porter was afraid that his distraught parent, presently being comforted by her commiserating yet equally appalled daughter, might overhear.

Porter had made his money in ways that he'd never shared with his family. He had twice been imprisoned in distant states for crimes he chose not to disclose. Porter Cramford had never played by other men's rules… or *laws*, for that matter.

"And what would you do, brother, were you to get them all into that room? Put a knife to their throats and demand the return of all that money? Because I have no doubt that every penny's been spent. These lowlife charlatans live from pillar to post. They dined well while they had our family fortune to diddle with, but those days are over."

"I'd show them up for the humbugs they are. I'd use their chicanery against them."

"How?" Cigarette smoke swirled about the brothers' heads as each pondered the enticing prospect of revenge.

Porter sat down upon the old porch swing where as a boy he had plotted his future in the promising field of criminal mischief (the porch swing having been moved from former family lodgings in the city of Brooklyn). He draped both arms over the top of the slatted swing-back and grinned. "We gather together several of the most egregious offenders under the pretext of finding a certain lost article, with a substantial reward awaiting the one who succeeds. Divination, as we both know, being nothing more than robe-swagged flimflammery, all will fail and the price will be a choice at the point of a *gun*—so much more efficient than a knife, don't you think?—and *this* gun, in particular…" The gun was now conveniently produced; it lived strapped to Porter's right calf. "…a bullet to the head for having stolen our family's fortune through cunning lies and deception. *Or…*"

Porter inhaled deeply from the stub of his cigarette.

"Or what?"

"Or they sign a document that will then be promptly delivered to the *New York World* for next-day publication admitting to one and all—including all potential future clients—that they are arrant frauds."

"I subscribe to every aspect of your scheme, dear brother, except for the part having to do with pointing firearms at people and threatening to use them."

"But it will only be just that, brother dear: a threat. Who will agree to have his or her brain matter splattered across a wall, when we are permitting him—or her—to simply sign a piece of paper, pack a suitcase, and move to the safety of some other burgh? All of Gotham will thank us for ridding this city of the worse kind of predator—one who takes full advantage of the most gullible among us."

"You mean gullible like Mother Dear?"

"Sad to say, 'tis true." This from the baby sister Violet, who had just stepped outside to join her brothers for a smoke. Only a moment before, she had succeeded in getting their mother to stop disparaging her husband of eight years, a huckster in his own right—a trafficker in electrical warming and vibrating devices with dubious therapeutic value.

"Let it be known to each of them what bilked our poor mother, let alone her three innocent children," Dodge went on in a comical voice, "that we have come to town with a vast fortune to spend in hopes of recovering our long lost—our long lost *what*, my brother and sister?"

"I saw the loveliest vase in the window of the flower shop where I bought Ma that bouquet of roses," squealed Violet.

"A vase? A simple vase?" Porter rolled his eyes. It was the most tempered among his arsenal of contemptuous looks for those less clever than himself. "There isn't a counterfeit psychic in the world who couldn't by dumb luck direct us to a vase, there being only, perhaps, five million in this city. What makes *this* particular vase unique?"

"It had the most beautiful poppies in it."

"So our challenge then, if I am to understand you, sister," said Dodge with exasperated indulgence, "is to have our psychics, upon pain of death or career disfigurement, tell us the location in the city of a vase containing poppies. I must agree with Porter, Sis, that your obsession with the floral has produced a challenge that doesn't seem to be very challenging at all."

Violet's look turned suddenly murderous. *"Poppies do not grow in February as a rule. You know nothing of poppies!"* With that, the severely offended Violet retreated back into the house to sniff her mother's fresh bouquet of hothouse roses and to mutter foul blasphemies against her two brothers.

"Sister has a short fuse," chuckled Dodge.

Porter nodded as he scratched his nose musingly. "Of course, if it is truly an oddity to find poppies for sale out of season, then perhaps it isn't such a bad test for our snared charlatans. Poppies in a vase—I cast *my* vote for it. Do you vote likewise?"

"Vase of poppies it is. Let's make Sis happy."

Sis was indeed made happy. She could hardly contain her joy at seeing the four mediums gathered in the hotel room the three siblings had secured for the purpose of exposing their frequent shams against the trio's overly trusting mother. Each seer seemed completely unsuspecting of Dodge and Porter and Violet's true motive (sufficient reason in and of itself to impugn their psychic bona fides).

There were two men and two women who had avariciously answered the call. Each had been visited on numerous occasions by Mrs. Cramford, to whom advice was proffered, matters of concern instantaneously resolved, conversations held with the dead (the late Mr. Cramford often conversing with his extant wife through a variety of unseen human "controls," who wailed and swayed and brought all the trappings of the afterlife into Mrs. Cramford's present life). And even when the various results were incompatible, the old woman agreed with the psychics (who could only have had her very best interests at heart!) that in the spiritual world all was fluid and transitory and so it was necessary to confer even more often with those human Baedekers of that land of mystery to get its fullest lay. Porter and his brother and sister had no doubt that the network of fortune tellers in New York City often spoke insultingly of their mother in their private conclaves and shared information with one another of communal value, expressing all the while the great joy they felt at having at their disposal such a dependable and lucrative pigeon to dupe and cash cow to milk.

The older man's name was the Great Belcazzadar. He wore a loose-fitting and slightly tattered black frock coat mantling an excessive amount of avoirdupois. The younger of the two women went by the moniker

Madame Cassandriana. Her face was overly rouged, her costume a simple but sprawling red cloak. Her female companion was Countess Nadia, Mystic of the East. She was turbaned on top and draped and looped with strings of clinquant paste beads.

The last of the four looked nothing at all like a medium. His name was Edward Reese. He was young and handsome and came dressed as if he had just stepped from Dodge's own men's clothing shop, his rig crisp and exquisitely tailored. There was even a carnation under his lapel.

"That one's slick," observed Porter in an underbreath.

"And smug. The worse kind," replied Dodge, who still could not get over the young man's lack of circus theatrics, both in the manner of his dress and in his demeanor, which was disarmingly casual, almost indifferent.

Porter quickly got down to business: "We have a proposition for you all. There is a vase of poppies somewhere in this great polis. Our poor, memory-deficient sister saw it yesterday in the window of one of our city's many flower shops. Alas, she has forgotten the name of the shop as well as its location. And yet she wishes now to go there to purchase the vase and flowers, to bring some morsel of joy to her sad, prematurely senile life. It's a beautiful vase and the poppies are quite dramatic in their claret petals. Are they not, sister?"

"If that's what you say. But my memory is so deficient I can scarcely remember my own name. Is it Rose?"

"No, it's Violet."

"Is this a joke?" wheezed the pursy Great Belcazzadar, who apparently found little humor in the presentation. "Because we are far too busy to endure it."

The two female mediums nodded in vociferous agreement.

"It is no joke," said Dodge with sudden clarion authority. "You are, no doubt, on close terms with our mother, Mrs. Cramford?"

There were shrugs and half-nods. It wasn't clear to the quartet at this early point in the interview if events set presently to transpire were to redound positively or negatively on them. But all became clear in the next moment as Porter produced his gun and the terms of the challenge were laid out. There was shock and some fear on the part of the two women and the Great Belcazzadar, though Mr. Reese remained calm and collected. It was almost as if he were pleased with the sudden turn of events.

It was the garishly beaded Countess Nadia of the East (or, rather, Lower East Side) who surrendered first. Her patrician accent fell quickly away, leaving Delancey Street in its wake. "I'll sign d'Goddamned paper. Just take the gun outta my face, yoose—yoose hooligans!"

And she was gone.

At least Madame Cassandriana gave it the ol' college try: "I'm getting an image. Yes, yes, it's coming to me now." The madame's eyes were squeezed tight, her lips pursed in intense concentration. "I'm seeing the window of Amorelli's Florist Shop on Mulberry. The vase is *there*, is it not?"

Dodge shook his head and handed her the pen. Madame Cassandriana scribbled her signature at the bottom of the document that was to end her prognosticating career in the city of New York, while regretting aloud everything she would miss about the city—a berg in which she'd made herself quite a nice living predicting things that on rare occasions actually did come true (because even a stopped clock gives the correct time twice a day).

As for the Great Belcazzadar, he bristled and blustered and held to his contention that he was a legitimate seer, but there were times when the spiritual world was inconveniently opaque and it couldn't be helped, and then he swept a tear from his cheek, signed the document, and left in a Patchouli-scented pique.

"Well?" said Porter, looking now at the chisel-jawed and sartorially spruce Mr. Edward Reese. Porter glanced knowingly at his brother and sister and then bore down upon Reese with deep ocular penetration. "What will it be?"

"Neither the gun nor professional disgrace for me, sir," answered Reese, smiling sedately. "Because I happen to know exactly where your vase is."

"Do you really?" asked Violet, her voice suddenly devoid of all skepticism.

Edward Reese nodded.

"Bull's balls," croaked Porter.

"I second the sentiment," added Dodge, and then, because he could not help himself: "Say, where did you get those swell threads?"

"I'll take you there," replied Reese, his grin remaining fixed.

"To the place where you buy your clothes?" asked Dodge.

Shaking his head: "To the place where you'll find the vase with the poppies. It isn't, *ahem*, a flower shop."

The three siblings traded looks of intrigued interest. "Lead on," said Porter. He put the gun away. Perhaps the young man might take it to mind to flee. But then again, where would he go? He certainly couldn't ply his trade in secret. They would eventually track him down; it went without saying.

Edward Reese was right; it wasn't a flower shop. It was the 69th Regiment Armory on Lexington Avenue, site of the popular International Exhibition of Modern Art. "It turns out," said Reese to his companions as he led them into the large Beaux-Arts building, "that your sister didn't see the vase of poppies in the window of a flower shop at all. But perhaps van Gogh did. My friends, I give you 'Vase with Poppies.' It's quite lovely, isn't it?" The four now found themselves standing before that very oil painting, one of the artist's later works.

"You've always known it was here?" asked Dodge through a grimace of defeat.

The young man shook his head. "I was *told* that I would find it here."

"By whom?" asked Violet, not taking her eyes off the rubrical painting, though she was constantly being jostled by other attendees to the exhibition, "Vase with Poppies" apparently a favorite.

"By one who converses with me from the spirit world: by the painter himself." Suddenly, the self-confident young man's tone changed from brazen cocksureness to gentle, even charming solicitude. "My dear woman." Taking Violet's hand: "Did you on your last visit here have the chance to see van Gogh's 'Mademoiselle Ravoux'? It's just around the corner. I ask because she happens to bear a striking resemblance to *you*."

"Is that your studied opinion or just a glancing impression?" asked Violet with accompanying erubescence.

"I'll let *you* be the judge."

After the two had glided away arm in arm, brother turned to brother and acknowledged the disappointing reversal without exchanging a word. A moment passed. Porter released a sigh, and then wondered aloud if young Mr. Edward Reese *had*, in fact, known that the painting was there all along.

"Well, of course he did," said Dodge huffily. "And wasn't *he* lucky?"

"Some psychics are *very* lucky, my brother. It's almost as if someone's watching over him."

Porter nodded as he ground his teeth.

"Say," said Dodge, brightening. "Duchamp's 'Nude Descending a Staircase' is around here somewhere. Let's see if Comstock has swooped in and covered the poor woman up, although I would challenge him to point out the naughty parts from among all those shanks and planks."

The two brothers laughed.

Perhaps the brothers would have taken things less in stride had they known the truth of what had actually occurred: that Mrs. Cramford, having overheard her children's plan and the item with beautiful claret petals that was to be the principal part of it, had promptly telephoned her favorite psychic to let him know what to expect when he arrived at the hotel the next day. As it so happened, Mrs. Cramford had attended the exhibition only a week before and was quite taken with the van Gogh floral still life. It was she who had told Mr. Reese exactly where it was to be found. The ulterior motive at play here had everything to do with her daughter, who was a perfect match for the young bachelor-mystic. Reese had impressed the old woman with his fine looks, his innate charisma and charm, and his financial success in a profession that rarely brought great wealth. There was only one thing left for Carlotta to do to secure the deal: encourage Violet to divorce that lout of a husband of hers. It should prove very easy. One of the psychics she had been secretly seeing in Hoboken, New Jersey, had told her so.

1914

DEVOTIONAL IN ILLINOIS

Saturday, June 27

I used to enjoy what Papa calls our "Chautauqua summers." It's all so old fashioned, I know, and half the folks who come here walk around the place with their Methodist noses stuck up in the air like they're trying to sniff God, but I did used to have fun. I learned to swim and dive and to play croquet and tennis. We went on hikes through the woods on the bluff, and picked wildflowers along the Jerseyville Road, and Miss Dawson, who conducted the girls' classes, was warm and kind and funny, and I'll miss her now that I've outgrown her.

I've outgrown everything I used to do here. I don't even think I should like to take a swim in the pool because it's either filled with the little ones splashing around like otters or those older than me who, truth be told, also splash around like otters. I just turned eighteen last month. I am between worlds. I am dreading my nearly summer-long stay here with Mother and my Aunt Carolyn, and glimpses of Father as he motors in from St. Louis on occasional weekends.

I am going to die of boredom here. I absolutely know I am.

Monday, June 29

Today I climbed the bluff unattended (to Mother's consternation) and watched the sun go down in all of its violent color and still wished that I were anyplace else on Earth. All the girls I knew from summers gone by have stayed in the city where it is hot, but where they are not minding the heat in the least because they're seeing boys and going to dances. They have dances here but there are few boys around my age who aren't in the employ of the New Piasa Chautauqua or who don't go to Lover's Bridge and drink corn liquor or smoke behind the Pavilion, and I absolutely hate them. I hate all boys, to tell you the truth. Why did I look forward to growing up?

I am adrift.

Saturday, July 4

It is Independence Day and my boredom is made almost bearable by the celebratory events of the day. There was a concert band performance and a bicycle race and the funny Fat Man races. (Papa was here and I begged him to enter, but he found my request to be an affront to his efforts to reduce.) After supper we all gathered at the riverfront for a fine display of fireworks. The sound—like small cannons going off—frightened Aunt Carolyn (who frightens easily, I must say), but the shapes and colors were beautiful. And there was no one who enjoyed the show more than I— except, perhaps, the young woman who stood next to me. She said her name was M.K. (which stands for Mary Katherine) and she told me she works as a chambermaid at the Inn. Mother and Aunt Carolyn and I have lodgings in the Piasa Springs Hotel, for which I must consider myself lucky as Aunt Carolyn tried to secure a room for the three of us at the Women's Christian Temperance Union Cottage, which would have been simply unbearable, as the women who stay there are far too prim and proper, and they pray far more than is customary here at this Methodist outpost on the river, where people already pray too much in my heathen, hell-worthy opinion. But Mother—thank God!—would not have it, for where would Papa stay when he came for his visits?

Anyway, M.K. was funny and very gay. I am hoping that I have another opportunity to see her.

Saturday, July 11

A very good day, I must say. I watched the girls playing basket ball in the afternoon and there was a diving contest at the swimming pool. Mother wanted me to enter, but I couldn't remember all that I'd been taught and feared I would make a fool of myself. At supper tonight, Mother took me aside and said that she would have no more of my maundering about in a non-participatory manner and that I would have to start attending some of the lectures with Aunt Carolyn and her, especially those having to do with the cooking arts, since every girl my age needs to know her way around a kitchen.

Ugh!

But the day ended on a very good note because Mother and Aunt Carolyn and Papa, who was visiting this weekend (two weekends in a row, callooh callay!), and I all went to hear the world-famous Miss Maude Willis read from various works of fiction and drama. And I thought that she was very good, especially when she read a couple of passages from *A Girl of the Limberlost* (which I had read myself when I was sixteen) pertaining to Elnora's tristful rambles through the swamp, collecting moths and wishing that her mother would not hate her for trying to be born while her father was busy dying in the swamp. As I was being moved nearly to tears, who should suddenly appear but M.K., who opined in a rough whisper that Miss Maude Willis was a fraud and a theatrical poseur and New Piasa Chautauqua would have been better served by having the "Divine" Sarah Bernhardt sitting on stage and belching for an hour instead. I burst out laughing and earned a glare of displeasure from my aunt, who was sitting nearby.

Before we parted, M.K. whispered that I was downright "adorable" and that she would like to spend some more time with me. She said she had tomorrow afternoon off, and asked would I meet her at the Pagoda and perhaps we could go rowing together?

She gave me a little kiss on the cheek in parting and I kissed her back. I was giddy to have made a new friend, though Aunt Carolyn looked at me oddly.

Sunday, July 12

I did not meet M.K. at the appointed hour (2:00) because Papa had decided to stay until tomorrow morning and Mother and Papa and Aunt Carolyn and I were to have a picnic. I stole away after the service to try to find M.K. and tell her that I would have to break our engagement, but I could find her nowhere about, and I regret not asking the name of the boardinghouse where she was staying.

I felt miserable, but I didn't tell Mother the reason. Papa thought it was because I was not seeing enough of him and I pretended he was correct in this assumption and hugged him tight while holding back tears, which seemed quite incongruous since M.K. was nothing more to me than just a friend.

Thursday, July 16

I finally caught a glimpse of M.K. this afternoon upon the verandah of the Inn, sweeping among the rocking chairs. I know she saw me, but she pretended that she didn't. I don't blame her. I wondered how long she must have waited for me at the Pagoda before concluding I'd changed my mind. I would have gone to her and explained everything, but Aunt Carolyn and Mother and I were on our way to hear a lecture by Mrs. E. F. Ford on beautiful houses—their location, arrangement, furnishings, and sanitation.

Early this evening I noticed M.K. again. She was sitting on the other side of the auditorium attending, as was I, a performance of "fantastical legerdemain" by Mr. Dana Walden, "Magician Extraordinaire." Again, M.K. pretended not to see me, and my chagrin was hardly dispelled by the droll occurrence of a small white rabbit hopping over my shoe.

Saturday, July 18

Oh miracle of miracles! While Aunt Carolyn, Mother, and I were leaving the School of Household Science late this morning after attending a demonstration on bread-making, I spied M.K. carrying a basket of laundry across the footbridge that goes to the Inn. I excused myself and went directly to her. I apologized for missing our appointment and she accepted my explanation with jolly grace. I vowed that I would see her at the Pagoda the very next day at 2:00.

It is after one o'clock in the morning as I write this. I can scarcely sleep. It has now been three weeks since I got here and M.K. is the first real friend I can claim for myself. I don't care that she works here. It is not her fault that diminished circumstances have required she support herself in this way. I just know that she is funny and wise, and I absolutely cannot wait to spend the afternoon with her.

Sunday, July 19

I reached the Pagoda at the appointed time and M.K. wasn't there. My heart sank. I wondered for a moment if she was playing a trick on me for what I did to her, but then at five minutes past the hour she arrived, breathless, her face red with cheer. She picked me up and spun me around and set me down and said how happy she was to see me.

We took a hike deep into the woods beyond the bluff and I knew that the farther we went the more trouble I was going to be in when I returned, especially since I was destined to miss the late afternoon vesper service and set Mother to worrying over what had become of me. I knew Aunt Carolyn would be particularly unhappy (which she was), for she alone has come to the conclusion that I am an apostate child, a deserter of my faith.

M.K. taught me how to smoke a cigarette, as sophisticated women in the big cities do and working women do throughout the land. I coughed and choked and felt woozy in my stomach, but I wanted so much to please her. I cannot say this with certainty but I'm feeling a fondness for her that I've never felt for anyone before. It frightens me and makes me joyously happy at the same time.

Before we hiked back down to the Chautauqua grounds, M.K. kissed me again, this time upon the lips, and I could hardly demur at such a concerted and affectionate overture. I kissed her back with wanton abandon and felt dizzy in her embrace.

M.K. said the word. She said it boldly and without a moment's hesitation.

Love.

Monday, July 20

This is the week that the Epworth League Institute descends upon New Piasa Chautauqua and there are hundreds of people coming and going who were not coming and going only a couple of days before. There are to be lectures throughout the week about temperance reform and Christian citizenship and Methodist missions, and there will be prayer meetings and sermons and addresses and Bible study. And M.K. cannot see me until Sunday. She doesn't even get her usual Tuesday afternoon off because of all the new lodgers at the inn, all of them expecting their rooms to be just as clean, says M.K., as their whiter-than-snow Christian souls. M.K. is a Roman Catholic and she laughs when she contemplates hanging a picture of Pope Pius X in each of these rooms to see how the Epworthians will react.

This morning Mrs. Ford talked about "Milk as a Food." I could scarcely concentrate.

Tuesday, July 21

Mrs. Ford talked about "Meat as a Food" this morning and demonstrated receipts that naturally included meat. Mother said that I seemed inattentive. I said I wasn't feeling well and then stole away to the Inn in hopes of seeing M.K. Alas, I couldn't find her. M.K. said that sometimes she is kept in the laundry room for long hours. I think I will call her Cinderella the next time I see her. I wonder if the original Cinderella was also a Roman Catholic.

Wednesday, July 22

This morning Mrs. Ford gave a demonstration having to do with "Cornmeal as Food." Afterwards when I was walking back to the hotel, who should stop me upon the lawn, but M.K.! She said she missed me desperately and that it was a tragedy we should only be able to see one another on Sunday afternoons. She asked if I might be able to steal away this evening and come to the boardinghouse where she lived with some of the other housemaids. She said she would be waiting for me on the porch in the rear no matter what time I should come.

I missed her so terribly and said that I would try, but I didn't know how in the world I was going to make it happen, for I am sharing a bedchamber with my aunt. Aunt Carolyn has already asked where I spent the previous Sunday afternoon. (I wouldn't tell her.) I absolutely deplore my aunt, whom I have begun to call behind her back "Miss Nosy Parker," and several other things that I cannot put down here.

The day crept by so slowly. When night finally came I had to endure "An Evening of Dramatic Entertainment by the Morse School of Expression" with my mother. I returned afterwards to discover that Aunt Carolyn was already fast asleep in our room. Shortly thereafter my mother retired for the night and an hour later I felt that it was safe enough for me to creep out, traverse the hotel lobby—dodging the eyes of the night desk clerk—and make my way to the rooming house beyond the cottages. As promised, M.K. was there with open arms. We waited until the coast was clear and then stole up to her tiny room. There was a little crucifix on the wall and a framed photograph of an old woman on the bed stand. M.K. said that the picture was of her grandmother, who had raised her but who had died two years ago and left M.K to her own devices.

M.K. rolled cigarettes for the both of us, and we sat and smoked and talked about how different our life-journeys had been so far. Then M.K. put out her cigarette and took mine and put it out as well, and came to me and began to unbutton and unfasten me with tender, loving hands. A chill came over me, not only because nights at New Piasa Chautauqua are cool, but because there was a frisson of something absolutely wonderful that goosed my flesh—happiness made palpable in the presence of one who cared so deeply for me and whom I loved with equal ardor.

As we lay together in the dark, quiet room, things were whispered between us that seemed to meld our hearts from that moment forward. I fought the caress of sleep's sweet entreaty, wanting so much to surrender to it in M.K.'s arms. In Mary Katherine's arms. In Mary Katherine Healy's protective embrace.

But I had to go. It was time.

"Don't go," she said. "Run away with me."

"When? Now?"

"Tomorrow morning. You and me. We'll go anywhere you like. I'm a vagabond, Jennie. Let's be vagabonds together."

"But what of my family? I'm my mother and father's only child."

M.K. pulled a strand of hair from my eyes. "You'll write them. You'll see them. But on your terms. You aren't their little girl anymore. You're a beautiful woman. And now you are mine."

M.K. was robbed of my answer by a hard knock upon the door. "Who is it?" she called, pulling the covers up around us to shield us from potential interlopers.

"It's Mrs. Barnes. Unlock the door or I shall unlock it myself."

"Just a moment, please!" called M.K. There was trepidation in her voice. I had never seen her afraid before. "I must dress."

M.K. pointed to the window with urgency. But how was I to dress and escape in so short a span of time? How was I to negotiate the fire escape from the third floor of this large house? It was an impossibility. M.K. saw that the broth was made. We would have no choice but to eat what we had set upon our table.

After she had drawn on her frayed dressing gown, she said, "Will you? Will you come with me?"

I didn't answer. I couldn't answer. I simply could not make such an important decision in the blink of an eye. In the blink of her eyes. Eyes that spoke so sweetly yet so urgently to me.

The door flung upon. Mrs. Barnes, the lady of the house, had company: my mother and my Aunt Carolyn. Mother appeared distraught. Aunt Carolyn seemed cool and self-possessed. This was, no doubt, the moment that confirmed whatever it was she had speculated about me—whatever she had finally said about me to my mother.

"Gather yourself up, Jennie," said Mother in a voice that sounded broken and dispirited.

"You are never to see this girl again," crowed my aunt, who appeared to be taking special delight in saying that which my mother in her present distressed state could not bring herself to say.

"That shouldn't be a problem," said Mrs. Barnes. "I will speak to Mr. Gillen this very night. Miss Healy will wake tomorrow morning to find that she is no longer in the employ of the New Piasa Chautauqua."

"Come, Jennie," said my aunt, her lips unpursing to utter her edict, then pursing themselves again in comical rectitude.

"Stay," countered M.K.

"Upon my word!" ejaculated my horrified aunt.

"Come," said my mother calmly, putting her hand out to me.

"Stay," M.K. repeated through plump, Irish lips that only an hour before had blissfully explored every inch of my hungry, yielding body.

Time stood still.

The room grew silent.

I could not speak.

And then.

And then my heart cried out its need. It trumpeted its desire. I listened in ecstacy.

I attended.

And I obeyed.

"I am a grown woman now," I said to my mother, taking care not to dignify my odious aunt with even an acknowledgement of her presence. "And I choose to be with M.K."

Mother swooned, not nearly so melodramatically as did Miss Maude Willis when reading the part of the young mother who received news of her husband's death upon the battlefield, but frightfully and painfully so. Yet in the end this display of maternal injury was insufficient to wring from me a change of heart.

I belonged to M.K. now.

And so I stayed.

Thursday, July 23

This morning Miss Dawson led the girls' clubs in "rhythmic work." The boys enjoyed "freak races." My Aunt Carolyn listened to Mrs. Ford of the School of Household Science speak on the "value of fruit in the diet." I understand there was a canning demonstration, as well. Mother didn't attend. She spent that time saying goodbye to me. Papa, who had gotten word in the night, was there to bid me adieu as well. They didn't need to tell me how strongly they opposed my decision to follow my heart. I commend them for registering their objection only through tears and plaintive expressions.

I don't know if I'll ever come back here. I suspect that the time of my "Chautauqua summers" has come to an end. There is so much I've learned in this place. Though I think, in the end, the heart is the best teacher of all. M.K. agrees. (That last sentence was penned by her own hand.)

1915

HAVING A SINKING FEELING
IN THE NORTH ATLANTIC

And so they all sat down. And so the conversation began.

Elaine opened the gates to her memories of the trip and the dastardly act that abruptly ended it. Rich choked back tears and cursed the headache that underscored the pain of his own recollections, but held back not a single detail of his own part of the story. Will and Olive Donnell added their own harrowing account of the eighteen minutes that passed from the moment the torpedo hit to the last gasp of the great liner before she sank beneath the humanity-clogged waters off Old Head of Kinsale.

There was fresh corn soup and deviled clams. But the soup grew cold and the clams went untouched.

It was a chance meeting that brought the two couples together four years after the trip that nearly claimed their lives. One hundred and twenty-eight other American men, women, and children had not been so lucky. In all, the deliberate wartime sinking of *RMS Lusitania* took the lives of 1,198 of her passengers and crew.

Over the intervening years, none of the four had found the right time or place to share with family or friends the particulars of that tragic day, and so they—Elaine and Rich, and Olive and Will—had kept it largely to themselves.

The memories were the most oppressive for Elaine. The sinking was a ghost, haunting her and keeping her anxious, and frequently tearful. It sabotaged social gatherings. It stole all the joy from her heart.

At first Rich didn't think that his wife would remain in the Donnells' hotel room once the two couples had gathered for drinks. He worried that once conversation steered itself to the ill-fated voyage, Elaine would excuse herself to go and drink alone in the saloon downstairs and wait. She would wait until her husband had completed his visit. She would hide there in the saloon so that the couple couldn't see the residual pain in her eyes or the look of practiced impassivity that so often characterized her public face.

But Elaine surprised her husband. She stayed. In fact, she remained for the entire evening, which was long and cathartic and, in the end, just the emollient her long broken spirit had required. Some of the things remembered and shared within that hotel room were these:

As the *Lusitania* backed herself into the Hudson River just after 12:20 p.m. on the afternoon of her departure, the ship's band played "Tipperary" at one end, while a Welsh male chorus entertained passengers on the opposite end with "The Star-Spangled Banner." The vessel's final voyage began in brilliant sunshine.

One always approached Captain Will Turner with caution. As a rule, the crusty captain disliked most passengers, whom he called "bloody monkeys." (The recounting of this fact constituted one of the evening's few moments of levity.)

Elaine made the observation that there was an unusually large number of children on board for this particular crossing.

Elaine and Rich accepted an invitation to dine onboard with Alfred Vanderbilt. The multimillionaire was on his way to attend a board meeting of the International Horse Show Association for which he served as director. He was also planning to offer a fleet of vehicles for use by the British Red Cross. Vanderbilt had, coincidentally, booked passage on the *Titanic* in 1912 but changed his mind before it sailed. The dinner was a delight.

Just as they hadn't bothered to heed the notice published in New York newspapers by the German Embassy warning American passengers against traveling on British vessels while a state of war existed between Great Britain and Germany, few bothered, as well, to read posted instructions on how to put on their life jackets. When the time came, many passengers tied them on backward or upside down, with fatal consequences.

As the *Lusitania* entered waters off the coast of Ireland and the dreaded danger zone, passengers were puzzled by the fact that there was no discernible increase in speed. They were told that the enveloping fog made such an increase a hazardous prospect. Additionally, the ship was conserving its coal in this way and keeping reserve steam up so that if a submarine were spotted she would have ample power at the ready to remove herself from harm's way.

The Irish coast was the most beautiful shade of green Olive Donnell had ever seen. Its nickname "the Emerald Isle" was well deserved, she asserted.

In spite of London's promise, there was no British escort.

Rich was among those who witnessed the approach of the U-boat's torpedo. It cut through the water with moderate speed, followed by a spumy wake, akin to the trail of an outboard motor. At the time of impact, Elaine was lunching with friends she had made during the voyage. The explosion threw several of the women to the floor.

Will watched a plume of coal and debris rise high above the ship's Marconi wires. This was followed by a wall of water that knocked him violently to the deck. A few moments later came a second explosion from somewhere within the ship.

The list to starboard made for great difficulty in launching lifeboats from the port side. Will and Olive watched in horror as the boats slammed into the side of the ship, spilling passengers—mostly women and children—into the waters below. Ropes snapped or slipped from the hands of those guiding the boats down. The lifeboats smacked the water like heavy stones.

Rich, on his way to meet up with Elaine in the dining room, chanced upon the ship's doctor and its chief purser strolling up the Promenade Deck calmly chatting and smoking cigarettes. Rich asked the men if they had taken leave of their senses, only to be told that the captain had assured them the ship wasn't going down. It would right itself soon and the worst would be over. Rich said that even if this were true there were still injured people both on deck and in the water in need of medical assistance. Rich, who was also a doctor, had, for his part, just finished attending to two such passengers only a moment before. The ship's doctor took a breezy drag on his cigarette, announced his lack of desire to go anywhere, and indicated with a dismissive flick of the wrist that the colloquy was over. Rich, an amateur pugilist in college, responded by punching the doctor in the nose. The purser received a cuff to the jaw.

Having witnessed one deadly launch after another, both the Tattersalls and the Donnells realized that the lifeboats offered little guarantee of survival.

"And yet this is where they kept putting all those poor women and children," said Olive. "I began to beg people to stay out of the boats—to wait until the right moment to jump, and then swim quickly away from the ship."

Will nodded. "I watched a boat on the starboard side laden with passengers smash itself against the superstructure and splinter to pieces. I saw another fall stern-first directly on top of those poor souls who had just spilled out of the boat right next to it."

"I remember the sounds of the day with the most clarity of all," said Rich, the pages of his own catalogue of memories turning quickly before him. "The deafening scrape of wood against metal, the banging and clanging as the crew members tried to release the boats from the listing ship. The cries and shouts of frantic fathers and mothers; the bawling of lost children; the anguished moans of those suddenly crushed and mangled."

Elaine took a sip of her Old Fashioned to moisten her dry mouth. "The little girl said her name was Harriet. She couldn't find her mother. I instructed her to stay with Rich and me. She had no life jacket. Rich went off to find her one. The boat began to tilt at such a sharp angle that Harriet and I had to cling tightly to the rail to keep from being knocked off our feet. She said she was eight. I waited for Rich and he didn't return."

Rich took Elaine's hand as if to remind himself of their ultimate reunion. "I pushed my way through a mob of people ascending one of the interior stairways and rushed down a corridor in which I had remembered seeing a wooden locker marked 'life jackets.' I retrieved one from inside and made my way back to the stairs. Now water had begun to cascade down the stairwell and directly into the corridor. I turned to find another means of egress and slogged my way toward a set of stairs that proved more promising. By this time, however, I had forfeited easy passage to the deck where I had left Elaine and the little girl. For the next several minutes I engaged in an ultimately fruitless attempt to make my way back to them. I was thwarted at every turn by debris. It was as if the ship were in the process of dismantling itself right before my eyes. Every passage I found was blocked by thick knots of desperate, panic-stricken passengers and impotent crew members. Men and women were pushing, shoving, clawing their way through the pack, while still others stood or sat immobilized by shock. I passed one of the ship's saloons. An old woman sat alone in a wicker chair, awaiting the inevitable. Water lapped at her ankles. She was staring vacantly at the wall—staring at the ornately paneled wall of that once stately room."

Will continued his own family's story: "I felt that our best chance was on the starboard side, so I took the hands of my two little girls and Olive took the hand of our little boy, and we headed in that direction. Our path was strewn with crushed and bleeding bodies. Few of the still ambulatory were able to stand now without holding onto the railing. As the angle of the deck became more pitched, I felt my youngest daughter's hand slip from my own, but I was able to catch her in time to pull her up and into my arms. She wrapped her arms and legs around my chest like a tree monkey while we moved in fits and starts to the other side of the ship. On the starboard side we encountered even more pandemonium, even greater panic. It was at this moment that we realized that the ship was sinking too fast for everyone to get away. I lost my footing, as did Olive, who also lost her hold on the railing. Frankie slipped away and tumbled down the deck. Lucy slipped away and did likewise. I held on to the little one, Dorothy, as tightly as I could. The water rose to meet the three of us. I witnessed the horrible sight of my wife being pulled under by the strong suction."

"I remember blackness," said Olive. "Things were slamming into me, first from one side and then from the other. I remember a hand in the water—a ghostly hand already stilled. I remember losing any sense of what was up and what was down. And then I recall popping to the surface in an area so choked with bobbing, flailing bodies that I imagined I had arrived in Hell—a numbingly frigid cesspool in Hell."

"I swam with Dorothy clutched to my side," said Will. "I paddled like a sloppy-pawed dog in the water, the life jacket making every stroke a trial. I called for Olive but my voice was drowned out by the cries of hundreds of others."

"I feared that the worst had happened to Rich," said Elaine softly, "so I vowed to try to save myself and the child. With luck I chanced upon a crew member who had been distributing life jackets. He had one left. I put it on little Harriet. I then sought out a place for us to jump. I waited until the water had risen high enough that the drop wouldn't prove injurious."

Rich leaned forward in his chair, resting his elbows on his knees. He massaged the back of his head. Staring down at the floor he said, as if in fresh disbelief, "I couldn't get back. Every path was blocked."

He looked up. "From the listing of the ship I now concluded that I wasn't going to be able to make it to Elaine and the little girl. I knew that the odds were against their even still being where I had left them. Within only a few minutes the *Lusitania* would go under. I prayed that Elaine had somehow gotten the girl a life jacket and found a safe way off the vessel. Seeing the liner's screw propellers and rudders fully exposed above the water line, I knew that the time for my departure had come. All around me people were jumping or sliding down wires and ropes, burning and flaying skin in their desperate descents. I wanted no part of this. Babies were being thrown overboard, to be caught by men standing in lifeboats, or never to be seen again.

"I turned and to my surprise saw Vanderbilt and his valet Ronald surrounded by a circle of women and small children, frantically securing life jackets around first one and then the other. 'Give me a hand, will you, Doc,' he said, and I stepped over to assist in getting the jackets put on the group even as the sea rose to meet our feet. One by one the young women—who were they, I wondered: mothers? Governesses? Total strangers?—took a child or two by hand and floated off and away from the ship.

"'Lousy luck, huh, Rich?' Vanderbilt asked. I nodded. 'God save you and me and King's Navee.'

"'God be with you too, Alfred,' I said. Then Alfred Vanderbilt plunged into the water. His body was never found.

"Through all the chaos and confusion I could faintly discern the sound of young women singing in delicate, Irish-brogued voices, 'There is a Green Hill Not Far Away.' I could make out the green hills, too, tantalizingly near, yet far too removed for anyone to think of swimming for them. I slid into the water and began to kick away from the ship. The *Lusitania* was entering the final stage of her submersion now, the strong suction pulling me back, forcing me to swim as hard as I could away from her. Finally free of her, I watched men dragged under by the funnel stays, others entangled by falling wireless aerials, still others drowning in tangles of ropes. A man dangling from a rope over the ship's stern was sliced in two by a still-revolving propeller."

Rich's three companions nodded. They had seen such things themselves.

Rich continued, locked inside his memories: "A moment later there was a violent explosion from below. A thick cloud of steam burst up from the surface. A tidal wave surged outward from the place where the ship had gone down. In its center, giant bubbles of foaming, churning water brought deck chairs and oars and unidentifiable wooden and metallic flotsam to the surface, along with the bodies of those already dead and those nearly so. The centrifugal wave engulfed everyone in its path."

Rich grew silent. Elaine picked up the story. "Then the sea calmed itself. All movement upon the now gently rippling water—all movement now belonged to the survivors."

The sea, in Elaine's painful memory, had been transformed into a mass of waving, flapping arms. She and young Harriet had jumped into a thickly clotted mattress of animal, vegetable, and mineral that bobbed upon the undulating water's surface. Too many had met its icy waters without life jackets and now clung with slippery fingers to pieces of floating wreckage. Screams of terror had given way to a long, lingering choral-like keen— one great collective moan from the bereft and the bereaved, from those for whom life held fast and others for whom life would drain away through exposure to the cruel, cold water. Unlike those passengers of the *Titanic*, floating in the icy North Atlantic southeast of Newfoundland, for whom death from hypothermia came quickly and in some ways mercifully, the survivors of the *Lusitania* had longer to await resolution to their predicament. The lucky ones were pulled into lifeboats during the long hours between the sinking and the arrival of the first rescue ships. (Many of the larger vessels enlisted for rescue were reluctant to venture out into U-boat-treacherous waters until they could be assured of their own safety.) The unlucky ones, who either found themselves outside the vicinity of the lifeboats or were refused a spot in boats that were already dangerously overloaded, were forced to float and shiver, to fight to stay conscious, to keep their air passages clear of the oily water, to keep shock and derangement at bay. Some succeeded. Many did not.

Olive found the words to continue her own account. "I could see Will and Dorothy perhaps two hundred yards away. I wasn't sure if they could see me. I swam toward them, nonetheless, passing men and women clinging to buoyant corpses, people without life jackets supporting themselves by hanging onto those for whom life jackets did not, in the end, assure life. Through a thick film of oil and ash, I swam to the side of my husband and my youngest daughter. I wept in gratitude for having found them, and they wept as well. If we were to die, at least we would now die together."

Elaine took her turn: "Harriet and I floated for what seemed like over an hour. I despaired of ever finding Rich, just as I despaired of being spotted by one of the few lifeboats still gathering up survivors from the water. Finally, I caught sight of a half-filled boat that seemed more than willing to take the girl and me aboard. As it rowed toward us, I assured little Harriet that she'd get dry and warm now. Things would be better for her once we were taken into the boat. I received no response. I turned to look at her. Her eyes were closed tight, her head tilted back, her beautiful long brown hair trailing in the dirty water. Her skin had turned a dark, bruised color, and there was froth upon her lips. The little girl I had sought to save was dead.

"I let her go, gently releasing her to the arms of the sea. A moment later someone pulled me into the lifeboat and wrapped a blanket around me."

With the passage of time, the floating island began to break apart, and people began to drift off with the current. Rich found a lifeboat bobbing upside down. He and several others held on to it as best they could, but as muscular paralysis from the cold began to set in, they would one by one lose their grip and drift away. In time he found himself alone.

"I lost track of time," said Rich. "I became delusional. I saw Elaine behind every floating crate, or perched upon every hencoop or jagged flat of planking. I knew that my time was short, yet fear had begun to subside to be replaced by a kind of peace—the peace of acceptance. Some of us would survive this man-made catastrophe. Others would not. It was so ordained: I was to be among the unlucky ones.

"Then, as these stories sometimes turn at the most hopeless moment, I saw a miraculous thing—a lifeboat. An empty upright lifeboat—not one of the twenty-two wooden vessels, only a few of which were successfully launched—but one of the collapsibles, each of which had been designed to float free of the ship should it sink, but very few of which actually did so. I learned later that the bloodiest of all bloody monkeys, Captain Turner, had decided not to loosen them when the ship reached the war zone because he was concerned that they would slide across the deck. This one, to my good fortune, not only slid across the deck but slid itself right into the water to be discovered by me a full two hours later.

"I climbed inside and spent the next several minutes trying to raise the boat's canvas sides and get them lashed into place. It had taken on much water and I spent a good deal of time bailing. I had recovered my wits in this newly minted desire to survive, and in very short order had succeeded in picking up several other passengers nearing their own ends and effusively appreciative of receiving this last-minute reprieve from death by exposure to the icy waters. They were additionally pleased to learn that the boat's newly commissioned captain was also a doctor of medicine, and I set myself to rendering medical assistance as best I could."

"'Do you have room for three more?' I believe that was the first thing I said to Dr. Tattersall here." Will turned to his wife. "Isn't that right, dear?"

Olive nodded.

"Yes, it comes back to me now," said Rich. "The very polite man with his wife and young daughter. I was happy to see that a family had survived intact. I wasn't aware—" Rich stopped himself.

"No, you weren't aware," said Olive stoically. "How could you have known about our loss?" A sad, sepulchral silence descended upon the room.

Olive took a moment to compose herself. "I've totally neglected to ask: have you any children, Elaine? I recall that you and Rich took that trip as newlyweds."

Elaine nodded. "Yes, we'd just gotten married a month before sailing. Rich and I—we were on our way to work in a military hospital in Great Britain. I'm a nurse, you see. Yes, we have a little girl. She's two."

"What's her name?" asked Olive, taking Elaine's hand.

"Harriet. We decided to name her Harriet."

The Tattersalls stood and the Donnells stood with them. The evening had come to an end.

"Please ring us up the next time you're in town," said the doctor, placing a hand warmly on Will's shoulder.

"Of course," said Will. "And we'll speak of *other* things. I'm a saltwater taffy man, by the way. Olive and I run a couple of concessions down in Atlantic City."

Later that night, after the Tattersalls had returned to their apartment in Gramercy Park, Elaine entered her daughter's dark room and kissed her little girl as she slept. She wept for the first Harriet and for the two children whom the Donnells were unable to bring home. Elaine knew that, even though she'd finally brought herself to speak of it, she'd never be whole again. Not really. Yet that shared moment, standing sadly transfixed before a poster for the Cunard steamship line outside a Manhattan travel agency's window—that moment that had brought Elaine and Olive together in silent, grieving kinship—had led to the chance to at least give a name to what they had communally endured: survival.

For those who can find within themselves the will to go on, there is no better consolation to tragedy.

1916

INCARCERATED IN OKLAHOMA

The younger of the two men, Ames, slept in the less-convenient upper bunk, and the older, Tyson, slept in the lower. This was as it should be; there were still twelve years left to Tyson's sentence, while Ames, serving time for manslaughter, would be up for parole in four.

Tyson had big shoulders and beefy arms. He had a prognathous jaw and an overhanging forehead that gave him a slightly simian look. He was a smart man, though you couldn't tell it just from looking at him. Ames, on the other hand, was tall and wiry, and the horn-rimmed eyeglasses and the arresting symmetry of his face gave him an owlish appearance.

It was a barroom brawl that put Ames into McAlester. He had delivered a fatal brain injury to a fellow roughneck by shoving him into a mirror. Ames's father, a Bible salesman without a sense of humor, noted humorlessly the appropriateness of his son's sentence of seven years, the crime having involved a broken mirror and all.

Tyson had never told his cellmate the details of the felony that had landed him in the Oklahoma State Penitentiary. He'd only said that he'd taken the life of a man without malice aforethought, but clearly not by accident—the textbook definition of second-degree murder.

Both men were prepared to do their time, take their licks, and then, once released from McAlester, try to get on with their lives.

In the meantime, though, there were the stories.

Early in his sentence, Tyson, a storyteller of the first order, began to regale his cellblock neighbors with tales of his family and all the colorful, comical characters who populated the small western Oklahoma farming and ranching community where he'd grown up. Tyson saved his more personal tales, though, for Ames alone.

These tales got told just before sleep in that drowsy hour after lights-out. They were delivered in soft whispers from Tyson's bed to the vicinity of the chair that Ames pulled up alongside it, so that not a word should get missed.

One muggy night in the summer of 1916, Tyson told the story of his youngest brother among a brood of eleven. Tyson had spoken often of his many siblings and how his tenant farmer father and mother struggled to keep all their young 'uns fed. He had spoken often of the lengths to which his parents and their older sons and daughters had gone to earn a few extra pennies to keep starvation away.

And how relentless and unmerciful was that struggle.

And even to this day, after the passage of over twenty years since Tyson was taken as a teenager and stood before a judge and sentenced to spend a good half of the rest of his life behind bars, he could still feel the gnaw of hunger in his gut and knew that this was what had motivated his father to do the unthinkable: seek to end the life of Tyson's two-year-old brother.

This is the story that at long last got told in the thick, quiet air of the midnight prison cell, when, having offered up every other narrative from his childhood, Tyson finally decided to relate the one that until that night lived only within his darkest memories. Its telling had come about this way:

Ames had made a comment about the newest resident on their cellblock. The man—half Choctaw, it was said—appeared slow, of limited mental capability. Ames wondered if he would be treated cruelly by the other inmates—especially the hardened ones—or would he, instead, be shown compassion for his intellectual frailty?

Talk of Grinning Pete brought Tyson's two-year-old brother to mind, and what became of him.

The boy's name was Wink. There had been a fever going around, and the Tyson family had weathered it and kept themselves intact by either luck or God's good grace, even as other families in the county had lost one, two, or even three beloved sons and daughters to the epidemic.

Seventeen-year-old Broderain Tyson, who at an early age had taken from his surname the nickname Tie, and his older brother and two older sisters were assembled by their parents upon the rickety wooden porch that fronted the family's sharecropper shack to discuss a family matter to which the sleeping younger children would not be privy. Ma sat upon her rocker but did not rock. Pa sat uneasily upon his whittling chair with empty hands. The four oldest children, having found places for themselves upon the steps and floorboards, wore expressions that anticipated nothing good from this exclusive family conference.

"Now, children," began the father in a serious, preacher-like tone, "times is hard for the poor man and they's gettin' harder. Crops are good this year as we all know, but Mr. Jimson, he don't give us any more for 'em than the usual. He's a Christian man, I figger, but it seems he ain't looked in the Good Book in a long while. Else'n he'd see some verse or two about how a land-man's miserly ways can put his croppers in a sorely bad place, and how that ain't the sort of thing that Jesus would abide."

"Amen," said Tyson's mother, who seemed naked to her son without a pan of shelling peas or a half-mended work shirt in her lap.

"Now your ma and me, we been talkin' things over—talkin' 'bout hard things we gotta do to get us all through this bad time. And there was a thing that got decided, and I gotta say that your ma ain't for it, even though she's agreein' not to throw herself agin' it."

Tyson's pa looked over at Tyson's ma, as if expecting a nod of concurrence, but there wasn't one—only an almost imperceptible movement of the head from side to side as if she had suddenly been seized by pangs of private, profound grief.

"Have any of you children told anybody of your younger brother Wink's recovery from the high fever?"

Tyson and his brother and oldest sister shook their heads, while his next oldest sister said, "No, we ain't, Pa. Warn't more than two day since the fever broke and he got his little self back on the mend."

"I wisht that he ha'n't," said Tyson's father, his eyes searching for something that could not be found. "Would've been an easier thing if he'd a been taken by the Lord right there upon that sickbed."

Tyson understood why his father had said this. Wink was an idiot boy who could hardly do a thing for himself. Most children with a mind like Wink's would have died early on—would have died in the womb, for that matter—but Wink did not. He showed a remarkable resilience in spite of his deficiencies, and now extended his special facility for survival to beating back an illness that by all rights should have claimed him.

Tyson knew what his father planned to say next.

"Now it's a good thing that you ain't told nobody how your little brother pulled through. 'Cause we got to say now that he died. We got ourselves a lot of mouths to feed on this sorry little farm, and his is one mouth too many, 'specially considerin' that Wink ain't gonna do nothin' from here to the end of his days that'll be of help to this family. Why, you take Tie here. He was collectin' them chicken eggs ever morning when he was scarce older than Wink!"

"And droppin' a goodly number of 'em," responded Tyson in an underbreath.

Ignoring the commentary, Tyson's father pressed on. "It's a hard thing we gotta do, but it's what's done in nature when a runt comes along without a fighting chance. And our little Wink is worse than a runt. He's a runt with the mind of a frog or a turtle, and ever bite of food what goes into his little turtle mouth is a bite that don't go to fillin' the empty bellies of all you other young 'uns. Now I ain't lookin' for your say-so; I brung you all together this evenin' just to let you know what's what. And to tell you that tomorry mornin', my brother Henry, he's a-comin' to take Wink down to Dead Indian Lake and drown the boy and then bring his little body back here and we gonna put him on the sickbed and tell the doctor he was taken with the fever.

"I tell it to you, children, because you got to keep the little ones away, both when Henry, he comes, and then when the deed is done and Henry bring him back. Do you hear what your pa is a-tellin' you?"

There were nods in the midst of all the tears now flowing from the eyes of the three females upon the porch, while the eyes of the paterfamilias and his eighteen- and seventeen-year-old sons were similarly glistening.

The word of Tyson's pa was law and there was no arguing against the course he'd chosen. And Tyson's bachelor uncle was the man for the job. He had an empty place inside him that allowed him to come to his brother's farm and do all the killing without compunction. Henry Tyson was a valuable asset at hog slaughter time.

The next morning, after a sleepless night for all those who had gathered upon that porch, a night spent by Tyson's mother whispering sad valedictions to her baby boy, the oldest four of the Tyson brood rose early to take all but the youngest of their siblings on a turkey hunt in the grassland.

It wasn't long into the turkey hunt—a hunt that at best would offer only a distant sighting or the sound of faraway gobbles for all their efforts with slingshot and rude bow and arrow—that Tyson made known to his older brother and two older sisters that there was a sickness in his stomach and an urgent need within him to return to the house. And no, he would not be talked out of it, even under the hard looks of disbelief, and all the dread and fear that came from thoughts of their father's wrath when Tyson came home sooner than expected.

But, as it turned out, Tyson had no intention of returning to the house. Once out of sight of his brothers and sisters, he ran all the way to Dead Indian Lake, praying that he wouldn't arrive too late to stop his uncle from the murderous act that his own conscience, regardless of the consequences, simply could not abide. Yet, as Tyson put it to his friend Ames, "the hand of fate had swooped down too soon. The boy was dead, his tiny body being carried limply in the arms of my uncle—a man who felt no pity for the boy a'tall. It was like he was carryin' the carcass of some animal he'd slain for the table that night."

At this point, Tyson could no longer continue with his story.

Ames didn't ask for the end of the story through any of the days and nights that followed. In fact, he wondered if this was a memory that should have been kept locked away forever. Perhaps Tyson had only shared it to cement the bond of close friendship that existed between the two inmates. For that, Ames thanked Tyson in his heart, and the two quiet men never went to such a dark place again.

Four years later Ames was released from prison. Upon the day on which he was to become a free man, the two friends shook hands and the sadness of their parting wrung each of their hearts.

"Still goin' up to Tulsa?" asked Tyson, once he had regained his voice.

Ames nodded. "My brother-in-law has a good job working in the oil field. He thinks he can get me on there. Now you take care of yourself, Tyson. And I aim to write to you, and you sure as hell better find somebody to read them damn letters to you, 'cause I ain't gonna waste my time writin' 'em otherwise."

Tyson nodded.

"And I'll see you on the outside when you get out."

Ames didn't get a job with his brother-in-law. But he did get a job—a lot of jobs, in fact. All those years of incarceration had delivered unto Gordie Ames a wanderlust even stronger than that which enspirited all the other young men of Ames's age, many of them veterans of the Great War. Ames hitchhiked all over Oklahoma and Kansas and northern Texas and took most of the jobs that were offered to him before finally settling down in Alva, Oklahoma, and marrying one of the daughters of a cook at the

Northwestern Oklahoma Teachers' College and getting himself hired on as building custodian for the school's ornately Moorish "Castle on the Hill."

Ames continued to write to his quondam cellmate for the next several years, just as he had promised, though only once did he get a letter in return. It was a letter that told a thing or two more about the story that Tyson had been unable to finish—the one about Wink. It had been dictated to the warden's comely secretary, who'd taken a decided liking to Broderain Tyson.

The reason for the original letter was this: Ames had met a young man in Elk City whom Tyson had every reason to know. The man worked as a busboy in a diner there—Crutchen's Diner. Though diminished in his intellectual capacity, he performed his job well, was marginally communicative, always in good spirits, and beloved by both his fellow workers and by the diner's regular customers. Ames had overheard the man being called by the name "Wink." Racked with curiosity, Ames had asked a waitress if there was more to the man's name than that simple nickname.

"Always known him just as Wink," she said, "but I'll try to find out." The waitress returned to Ames's table shortly thereafter. "Nobody knows. When Mr. Crutchen brought him here all them years ago, Wink was just a toddler."

"Where'd Mr. Crutchen find him?"

"Ain't you one with all the questions?" asked the waitress with a grin. "His brother, a sheriff up in Dewey County, brung him down. He was a foundling—left by the roadside, as it was told. They called him Moses for a while. Like Moses and the bulrushes. Mr. and Mrs. Crutchen, they sort of adopted him—didn't have no trouble with the fact that he was slow. Why do you wanna know so much about Wink?"

Ames had no answer for the waitress, but Tyson had one for Ames. The answer was this: that he had lied about what happened that day at Dead Indian Lake. That he had lied because of the shame of that day. Tyson had gone to save his little brother Wink even if it meant tucking him under his arm and hopping a freight train with him. His father and mother hadn't looked for a special place for the boy when he was born; the looking would have been hard in western Oklahoma at any rate, there being no orphanages or asylums around for children like Wink. But Tyson was determined to find a home for the little boy, no matter how long it took—once he had rescued him from their homicidal uncle.

Of course Tyson didn't have the chance. He reached the lake, thankfully, before his uncle had done the deadly deed: before he had forced the boy below the surface of the water, had held him down until all the oxygen had fled his tiny lungs. Tyson reached the lake at a time that worked to his baby brother's benefit. Yet the uncle would have none of Tyson's appeal on behalf of Wink. He was there to do the job assigned to him. According to the incensed uncle, Tyson was a kid who was listening to his heart at the expense of his whole family.

There was a scuffle as Tyson reached down to pick up the boy, who sat upon the grass, playing with a twig. There was a hand that took up a rock. There was a rock that was smashed into the side of a man's head. And there was sudden stillness from that man. Then there was a sheriff who came and took the baby boy into his own custody and delivered him into the arms of his wife, and then delivered Tyson to a Dewey County jailhouse cell.

There was a trial. The father and mother, abetted by the compassion of a jury of hungry, impoverished fellow sharecroppers—"there but for the grace of God" hardscrabble folk—were acquitted, but were forced to give up custody of their little boy Wink.

There was another trial. This one sent Wink's seventeen-year-old brother not to reformatory school, but to jail—specifically to the Oklahoma State Penitentiary, from which he would not be released until the year 1928.

1928 would be a very good year for Broderain Tyson, known as Tyson to his friends and fellow prisoners, Tie to his family, Honeybunches to his newlywed wife, and Brother to his youngest brother Wink, with whom he would be happily reunited. This year saw another reunion as well, between two former prison cellmates, who over time had become the best of friends. Wink would never be told how his life had been saved. Even if it had been carefully explained to him, he wouldn't have fully understood. And yet there was something in his regard for his brother—a look of intense esteem and affection—that gave Gordie to wonder if perhaps there was a *sense* there—a feeling that Wink somehow knew that Tyson had once done a very good thing for him, a thing for which he should be forever grateful.

Or perhaps it was merely the affection that one brother will feel for another when all impediments to allegiance and devotion have been removed—something that Gordie Ames fully understood. For it worked the same way with friendship.

Yes, it worked the very same way.

1917

PRINCIPLED IN MASSACHUSETTS

When the magazine was first published in 1831 it was called *A Boy's Companion*. It offered articles and stories of interest to young male readers. In 1857, the magazine began to cater to a readership of both boys and girls. Its name changed to *The Young People's Companion*. In 1892, the magazine reinvented itself yet again and became *The Family Companion*, with pages devoted to every member of the family. There was even a section, titled "Remember When," that revisited the halcyon days of America's innocent youth (while deliberately avoiding mention of slavery, child labor, female indentureship by marital contract, and institutional discrimination against immigrants).

Dennis Bailey had written for *The Family Companion* for the last ten years. His office was on the fifth floor—the editorial floor—of the Family Companion Building, perhaps the most striking sandstone structure in all of Boston. The building was a commanding Romanesque edifice of arched doorways and windows, and elaborate oak woodwork that made Dennis, himself nearing the venerable age of forty, feel as if he were some titan of Boston finance rather than a mere scribbler of short stories.

Because it was a family magazine, the incredibly popular periodical had an editorial policy encouraging its writers to avoid pieces of an overtly political nature. Its editor-in-chief, Douglas McCalley, had agreed with his friend, former president Theodore Roosevelt, that there was far too much muckraking going on among the nation's periodicals. "Best to leave political commentary to other, far less family-friendly magazines."

However, this policy changed in dramatic fashion on April 6, when President Woodrow Wilson, scarcely a month into his second term in the White House—swept into office in large part through application of the chest-thumping isolationist slogan, "He kept us out of war"—asked Congress to declare war against Germany. On that day, America—and *The Family Companion*—committed itself hook, line, and sinker to the Franco-Anglo cause.

Dennis Bailey wasn't happy. Several weeks later, after having read the Memorial Day editorial that McCalley planned to run in Thursday's pre-Memorial Day issue of the magazine, Dennis called down to McCalley's office and asked for five minutes of his employer's time.

"For you, Bailey," came McCalley's jaunty response, "I'd be willing to give up nine, maybe even ten minutes of that precious commodity."

McCalley was a jovial man who tried to see the humor in things. America's sober involvement in the Great War—"The war to end all wars," as President Wilson, a man given to meaty aphorisms, had called it—required that McCalley be a bit more sober himself. It was a behavioral change the sixty-one-year-old editor struggled daily to achieve.

The two men shook hands with the strong grip that bespoke their ten years of manful friendship. McCalley slapped his most popular writer of muscular fiction upon his sinewy back. "Been a while since our paths have crossed in this brick beehive of ours. Let me see your nose—not whittled down *too* much from application to that literary grindstone." McCalley laughed and tried to coax a smile from his favorite staffer.

There was a glimmer of something agreeable in Dennis's solemn countenance. But it quickly faded.

"Have a seat, Bailey. I enjoyed very much your story about the rescue of that lad from the ore conveyer. It was a ripping yarn—terribly good. You have a knack for writing just what our male readers, young and old, wish to read."

"Thank you, sir."

"And I'm sure that you have something even more exciting in store for next week's issue." Dennis wrote for alternate issues of the weekly magazine. Some of his stories, like "Ore Bucket of Death," were relatively short. Others, like the nautical tale "Shipwreck of the Sophronia Bordeen," which had been published in the March 1 issue, ran over five thousand words and was greedily snatched up by the Famous Players-Lasky film company for immediate motion-picture adaptation.

"I just finished a first draft of a story about a young man compelled to enlist in the American Expeditionary Force."

"Excellent. And will we see him upon the field of battle? Put some years and a thick moustache on him and we'll call him Teddy Roosevelt. TR wants in this fight, you know. He's going to petition the president to reassemble the Rough Riders."

"Not a lot of room for cavalry horses in those trenches, sir."

"True, true. I'm not quite sure just what it is that the colonel has in mind, but you can be certain it will be heroic. So the young man in your story, he goes off to war and what happens? Are you sending him over with the first infantry regiment?"

Dennis shook his head. "In actuality, Mr. McCalley, I'm not sending him over at all. His wife pleads for him to stay home with her and their newborn baby, and in the end he accedes to her wishes and exercises his exemption."

"Oh. Well, we certainly can't have *that.*"

"Why?"

"It sends the wrong message to our readers. *The Family Companion* is going to be behind this war one hundred percent. That means the stories we publish must also come out in support of the thousands of men who will be fighting under the American flag."

Dennis cleared his throat. "My young man will be very supportive. He'll buy Liberty Bonds and whatnot, but he won't go off and run the risk of leaving his wife a widow and his new son without a father."

"Hundreds of thousands of our French and British brothers have made that ultimate sacrifice with commendable dignity, Bailey."

"Dignity, Mr. McCalley? Most of them died gruesome deaths far from the loving embrace of their wives and children."

McCalley, who had been sitting behind his desk, now got quickly to his feet, knocking a framed photograph of his own family to the floor. "Bailey, dear boy, you astonish me. I had no idea that you possessed anti-American tendencies. Nothing you've ever written for this magazine has led me to believe you to be anything but a true-blue, red-blooded American patriot."

"This war is folly."

"Perhaps, then, you should be writing for *The Masses.*" McCalley, having rescued his family's portrait from the floor, wiped the dusty glass with the elbow of his suit jacket. He returned it to his desk.

"Why? I'm not a socialist. Although I do find much to agree with in what Mr. Eastman and his colleagues have said about our involvement in this war. Like Eastman, I don't wear patriotic blinders. Where some see only the flag, I perceive opportunities for imperialistic land-grabs and financial aggrandizement on an unprecedented scale. Industrialists in Europe are growing fat and rich as a consequence of this war. The same will happen over here. The French troops have had their fill of it. They're deserting their battalions in droves. I don't, by the way, see you publishing that fact in our magazine."

"Of course not. Our job is to get this war over with and all of our young men sent back home."

"With or without their limbs and faces."

"That sentiment, Bailey, is loathsome. I can't possibly understand why you've taken such a stance. Do you not realize that once anti-sedition legislation gets signed by the president talk of that kind could put you behind bars?"

"If I'm not mistaken, sir, the First Amendment guarantees me freedom of speech."

McCalley shook his head. "In times of war we are required to surrender a few of our freedoms for the good of the cause. That's the way it's always been. Otherwise, national morale is undermined and the war lost. Do you wish to live beneath the yoke of German tyranny for all the rest of your days?"

"That's what I wanted to see you about, Mr. McCalley, and thank you for reminding me."

"Remind you of what?"

"The particulars of your Memorial Day editorial."

"What's wrong with it? I thought it rather good. I wrote every word of it myself."

Dennis drew a folded piece of paper from his pocket and read from it: "On this Memorial Day we do more than commemorate those who died more than half a century ago in the cause of preserving this Union. We honor as well those American men who will soon be sacrificing their young lives upon French soil to preserve the union of *all* the civilized people of the Earth. The problem of Negro slavery which pitted Blue against Gray in our homeland could never, even in its worst instances, be compared with that savage inhumanity represented by the slavery presently imposed upon the people of Belgium and Serbia and Armenia."

"You own to this, Mr. McCalley? Really? Every word of it?"

"Dear boy, we are fighting for the cause of liberty—not just for our own people, but for all the peoples of the world!"

"Most of whom live under oppressive monarchies. Sir, I cannot in any stronger words tell you how objectionable I find this editorial. Not only what it says—downplaying, for example, the inhuman subjugation of the American Negro in antebellum times—but the very fact that you felt impelled by the present jingoist, militarist climate to actually write it."

"You're skating on very thin ice, Mr. Bailey."

Dennis stood. He combed his hand through his mussed hair. The look on his face was that of a man upon the horns of an all-too-familiar dilemma: to stand proudly on principle with all manner of negative consequences in attendance, or to abandon principle for purpose of self-preservation. "I take it you mean thin ice with regard to my employment here."

"That in the short run, yes—but far more cautious men than you will find themselves ostracized for saying quite a bit less than what you've said to me this morning. I don't believe you to be a traitor to this country, Dennis, but others will. It would be the end to your writing career as well. Do you seek it? You have a wife, three children."

"That's right."

"And Juliet, always in such poor health, and all of those doctors' bills."

Slowly, Dennis Bailey returned himself to the chair he had previously vacated.

"This is not a good time to be a socialist, Bailey. Or even a Progressive, for that matter. In times of national crisis, we are called upon to kiss the flag even though it may have stopped representing in totality all those things we have been taught that it stands for."

Much of the fire was now gone from Dennis's delivery. "I don't see the war the way you do, Mr. McCalley. I don't believe German troops have the wherewithal to invade this country, or that the Kaiser is any more of a monster than those men who will manufacture our own murderous armaments for enormous profit. And I well know why you included that reference to American slavery. I've worked with you long enough and have seen you often reward your 100,000 Southern white readers for their allegiance to the *Companion*—those Sammie and Rastus cartoons, this illusion you put forth on our editorial pages that all is harmony and bliss between the races in the South. I believe I'm reaching the end of my allotted ten minutes. I will think about what you've said and talk it over with my wife."

"And you'll rework your story so that the young man goes off and fights valiantly for his country?"

Dennis stood. "And comes home without his legs and blinded by the mustard gas?"

"If that was said in jest, Bailey, you'll notice that I'm not laughing."

Dennis didn't answer. He stared out the window at busy Columbus Avenue. It was nearing lunchtime. The street was thick with cars and vans and the occasional horse-drawn delivery wagon. The sidewalks were filled with people bustling here and there—businessmen in suits, working men in overalls, shop girls and female typists wearing monochrome and serge—all seemingly unmindful of the fact that the country they loved, the country which they had always felt had only their best interests at heart, was about to engage in a war which would leave nearly 117,000 of its citizens dead and another 205,000 wounded. In Great Britain, in France, in Germany and Russia they would count their dead and wounded in the millions. The age of modern warfare had arrived. McCalley's friend Teddy Roosevelt would be left on the sidelines, holding the reins to his obsolete mount.

"This war will be a terrible thing for us all," Dennis finally said, "while upon the pages of this magazine which has employed me for the last ten years will be found only stories of battlefield heroism, of young boys marking off the days on their calendars until they are old enough to take up arms themselves. You've already said in so many words to me that there will be no place within this magazine for exposing the degenerate side of war—the side which sanctions the killing and maiming of others and creates without apology widows and orphans on the home front.

"But I will not be a part of it. I don't need to talk this over with Juliet. I've made my decision already: I am not for this war. I am not for any foreign war. I see no glory in needless bloodshed and no honor in fighting for a nebulous or even specious cause. You are right, sir: no one will hire me. At least not until this country returns to its collective senses. Until then, I will have no choice but to set down my pen, for I have no desire to write for Mr. Eastman's *Masses*. I wish to write for the *true* American masses—those I see below—those whose allegiance to this country has become nothing more to you than a commodity to be traded upon the open market."

"You don't have to set down your pen, Bailey, if you will but bend a little."

"I can't write things that I don't believe, Douglas."

And with that, Dennis Bailey turned and walked out of the office of the man who only a moment earlier had been his employer. The departure

ended a decade of stories from the imaginative pen of Dennis Bailey—
adventure tales, tales of the sea, stories of the breaking of the plains and
the taming of the American West, narratives of muscle and valor, of
knights of old who fought for vaulted ideals, of American patriots who
took up muskets to win their freedom from colonial servitude.

Of those stories about America's war for independence from England,
one in particular, "A Riotous Little Tea Party," had been adapted for the
stage and was set for production in New York City in the fall. Unknown to
Dennis on this day was the fact that investors were being quietly asked to
withdraw their financial backing. Such a play, said the war propagandists,
would send the wrong message about the relationship between the United
States and its present ally, Great Britain. Particularly injurious to the cause
of an Allied victory was the fact brought out in both the story and its
theatrical adaptation that America, in its infancy, had come only one vote
shy of making its official language…

German.

Sometimes the past must be ignored to achieve the goals of the present.
Everything now was about the war message.

And *The Family Companion* would do its part, with or without Dennis
Bailey.

1918

TREPID IN FRANCE

Oh God, did I hate that infernal gas mask. The straps itched and burned. The rubber tube made my jaw ache, and after a while I began to drool like a baby. Running while wearing the blasted thing winded me to the point of near suffocation. I cursed the Goddamned Boche for introducing these deadly gases into this war, along with everything else to which my fellow doughboys and I found ourselves rudely subjected. War is hell, as they say, but this diabolical twentieth-century war was especially hellish in ways you cannot imagine: lousy food and tepid coffee, always being cold and always being wet, sharing bedding with rats and lice, and the possibility of permanent hearing loss from all the shelling.

Did I leave out death and bodily dismemberment?

I was a nobody—a lowly private in Uncle Sam's army. We were there to finish the job that the British and the French could not, the Tommys and the Poilu who loved us for showing up and hated us for taking so long to get there *and* for our Yankee arrogance. But who was I to make an opinion? All I wanted was just to get the thing over with and hightail it back to Mom and Pop and Sis—to put myself back behind the counter at the family candy store and back into the arms of my girl Suzie, with whom I'd cuddle and coo on the front porch, serenaded all the while by the cicadas and the nightingales. Nothing chirred or sang in this part of France. Everything that didn't carry a bayonet or skitter and crawl with parasitical designs through the trenches had left this place in one way or another auld lang syne, as the skirt-wearers say.

At thirty-one, I felt like an old man. A few steps closer to death among all those pups.

For several days our artillery units had been intermittently bombarding the German lines. It wasn't the first time I'd been exposed to the sound of modern heavy artillery, but this was the loudest by far. With each thunderous blast, everything in the trench clattered and shook, the attendant vibrations traveling up my feet and through my entire body. Along the several-mile front held by Allied troops in this region of northern France great guns were speaking, and the German army was being forced to listen. I resigned myself to listen, too, and to spending the rest of my life—should I be so lucky as to survive—half-deaf with a brass ear trumpet stuck in one ear like my ancient Aunt Ernestine.

Over the last couple of days, the skies in the east had turned gray and overcast, made darker still by the brume of war. Great clouds of airborne dirt marked where each new shell was being detonated. Billows of black and white smoke competed for prominence in the middle distance. It was deadly to poke one's head over the top of the firing trench, but even from my vantage point tucked below in the support trench I could see lace-like shrapnel wreaths hanging low above No Man's Land, blossoms of artillery clouds dissipating for fleeting moments to reveal the contorted skeletons of once-proud trees, the tops of bullet-perforated posts marking the location of our defensive wire entanglements, distant chalk bluffs riddled and riven by trench mortars and French-made 75 mms.

On the third day of the bombardment, near the end of a three-hour shelling, I had an interesting encounter with a young man from our companion platoon—a fellow private.

The blasts had become more powerful as the shelling went on. With each explosion the ground shook, clods from the revetment falling around me as I sat upon a muddy wooden crate and leaned uneasily against the dirt wall.

War, to me, can best be described as waiting and waiting, and then something unspeakably horrific happens, and then if you're still alive you go back to waiting again.

There was little that one could do during this period but count off the minutes until the tumult was scheduled to end. Earlier, some of the other boys and I had passed around our letters from back home. Some were scented. It was odd smelling something so fragrant and appealing in such a putrid place. Suzie never perfumed her letters. They always smelled of whatever her mother had been cooking as she scribbled away at the kitchen table.

I had ventured from the relative safety of the dugout, where I was being bivouacked here on the front lines. I had tired of my earthen cave—a dank and stifling place, odoriferous in a variety of ways, including most offensively the overriding stench of stale feet. I preferred the slightly less noxious air of the open trench. Adjustments had been made to the usual rotation of troops from the front trenches to stations offering temporary relief and recuperation behind the lines. Fewer of the men were being removed to relative safety in the rear, our commanders fearing a German counter-assault upon our defensive positions that could be compromised by a depleted troop presence. Like everyone else, I wondered if at some point the Huns would have their fill of our deadly artillery assault and climb from their trenches to retaliate *en masse*.

The young private I met this day, whose name I later learned was Cantwell, didn't even try to speak—not that I could have heard him if he did. He looked ill; a bit deranged, upon closer inspection. As he approached me, I wondered what he was up to. I had heard about the very young ones, new to the fighting. The ones who gave in to their fears, who reverted to frightened children. Even the more seasoned soldier could be alert and fully functioning one moment, and the next—as if someone had flipped a switch—suddenly be shut down to all thought and feeling, removed, as it were, from all engagement with his surroundings. Still others would remain active witnesses but spend their time screaming hysterically until they, too, succumbed to merciful catatonia.

I wondered what it was that this young man wanted from me. Surely, he wasn't in his tortured mind mistaking me for a Boche raider and making ready to plunge his bayonet into my side. Yet I readied my hand upon my pistol and held still to my position, lest movement on my part be cause for some frenzy-fed attack upon me. The young man—he didn't seem much older than twenty-one—moved slowly, almost hypnotically, toward me. With each new blast his whole body jerked like a clumsily manipulated marionette, his head turning first this way, then that, but his eyes always returning their penetrating gaze on me alone.

After reaching a spot about three or four feet away, the boy let his rifle slip from his grasp and fall to the ground, almost as if he'd forgotten it was in hand. Then in one sudden, fluid move, he drew up beside me. He curled himself next to me upon the oversized crate, burying his face in my tunic.

He began to cry, gushing sobs rocking his entire body.

I didn't know what to say to him.

There were men in my company who would have denigrated him for such a "show of obvious cowardice"—who would have used this display to, by convenient contrast, build up their own reputations for battlefield bravery (or bravado). I could have told him that for this reason alone he needed to fight the fear that had reduced him to sniveling and quivering. It betrayed the honor of his manhood before his fellow soldiers. But I said nothing. Even if he had been able to hear me, I couldn't bring myself to attempt to restore manhood to a man whom fear had already defeated. And so I let him sit next to me and draw strength from me—such as he was able. Perhaps he saw in me someone he had always trusted—an older brother, perhaps, or an uncle. (I was, obviously, much too young to be the age of the soldier's father.)

Eventually, the guns retired for the day and relative quiet returned. The boy stopped shaking, his sobs subsiding as well. Yet I did not seek to extricate myself from his presence. Nor did I stop patting him gently upon the shoulder.

In time he fell asleep. I soon grew groggy as well and retreated to the dugout. As I was walking away I saw something of my younger self in that boy. No one is without fear, I thought. It is what we do with fear in the course of overcoming the obstacles that have been placed in our way that defines who we are and tell of what we're made.

Two days later, the Germans had had enough. They decided to give back as good as they got. That morning, hell visited the AEF's front lines. Fatigue parties had spent most of the night repairing and fortifying the firing trench with additional sandbags. Still, we all wondered if we could withstand the kind of shelling that we had been dishing out to the Huns all week. We were at stand-to when the first mortars came over. All along the opposing lines, German artillery of every description headed in our direction. The German command had figured out our game and was set on preempting our anticipated attack with all the firepower in their arsenal.

The waterproof sheets that had been protecting our machine guns from night dew were pulled away. Our Maxim guns answered the German assault. We stood at the parapet and strained our eyes to see through the early morning shadows, to find and nail our targets. Shrapnel burst above us, around us. Exploding shells flared intensely white, dull orange. Here and there explosions of other colors—no beauty in this fountain of detonated shells and signal bursts, the coloration of the deadliest kind of war known to man. Through the general cacophony one could distinguish the singing of machine gun bullets, the whiz of the whiz-bangs. High explosives cratered our front trenches. I saw men go down to the left of me and to the right, limbs blown off, heads opened like smashed cantaloupe, brains and blood splattering us all. The worse was yet to come: a barrage of German cannon fire that shook the ground with earthquake intensity. Hundreds of shells landed in straight rows, short of the trench, behind the trench, squarely within the trench.

The captain signaled retreat into the communication trenches. If this deadly counter-barrage kept up, there would be no men left to mount the troop assault. A potentially catastrophic error in planning had now become evident. The multiple-days' bombardment hadn't hurt the Germans to nearly the degree that we had hoped. There was fire and fight left in them.

We prepared for our inevitable attack. Thousands of other men crushed toward us, the communication trenches filled with soldiers—shoulder to shoulder, checking the luminous dials of their radium wristwatches, steadying their rifles, stuffing more wads of cotton into ears already stuffed, passing assault ladders overhead.

I found Cantwell hunkered down in the shadows, tears streaming down his boyish face.

I looked up. Against the hazy blue of the morning sky tufts of smoke hung here and there. A black, acrid-smelling blanket of gloom settled upon us.

We shook it off. Some of the boys made jokes. I took a moment to look at faces that, when the order to don gas masks came around, I wondered if I would ever see again.

Cantwell put on his gas mask with difficulty, his hands fumbling, his fingers tremulous. I fought the urge to go to him and help him. There were things that soldiers in the Great War did for one another: heroic things, acts of fraternal self-sacrifice. Helping a shell-shocked kid put on his gas mask was not one of them.

It started with a whistle singing shrilly above the din: the "follow me" signal. The moment had arrived. The captain waved the men of our company forward, and we climbed in slightly disordered fashion up the assault ladders to the top of the sandbag parapet, a place in which every fear found justification and in which death was a permanent companion.

No Man's Land.

Yet it was not a place that I would see on this foray, because a German bomb—delivered right to our doorstep—sent me, along with those men who climbed next to me, back into the arms of those behind us. These men shook us off and clambered up and out as I felt myself falling in slow motion to the bottom of the trench. I was still conscious, though dazed, the clouded eye-glass of my mask making it difficult to see anything—not that there should be anything in that moment to see but a blur of legs and arms and swinging bayonets: men on the move, men following the orders of other men as I lay helpless and suffocating.

After the trench was emptied of all able-bodied men—only the dead and wounded remaining (and I wasn't sure for those first few moments exactly which group presently claimed me as member), I tore off the mask with my blood-spattered hand so that I might breathe. Even mustard gas, I thought in that crazed, head-clouded moment, had to be better than dying in this face vise. I saw a soldier that I knew lying next to me, still and lifeless. The muddy duck boards of the trench were carpeted with the bodies of others whom fate had kept from going over the top.

Among them was Cantwell. He wasn't moving. I crawled over to him, wondering if taking a fatal concussive blow *before* facing his ongoing living nightmare was a better thing than that which awaited him over the bags. Had circumstances—in cruel irony—been merciful to the frightened young man? I removed his gas mask to discover a place in his temple where a bullet had entered—a small spot, really, almost surgically produced.

There was a wounded man lying next to him, the khaki of his uniform darkened at the shoulder by fresh blood. He was fumbling for a cigarette.

"Was he a friend of yours?" the soldier asked between grimaces.

I shook my head. "I didn't know him. Not really." I touched my left arm and winced from a sudden stab of pain. Something—shrapnel perhaps—had imbedded itself in the crook of my arm. I wondered where else I had been hit.

"I've been watching him. We've *all* been watching him," the young man said in a voice raised to be heard over the roar of battle, "wondering what would happen when the time came. He didn't disappoint."

"How do you mean?"

"I mean, when we all moved forward, he just sat down, fixing himself to that spot. Lieutenant Lyster had apparently been watching him, too.

When he refused to advance any further, the lieutenant took out his pistol and drumheaded him."

I swallowed, didn't speak.

"Hell, I probably would've done the same. A soldier who doesn't fight is a risk to every man who *does*. Say, is somebody gonna come get us, or do we have to get ourselves to that fucking field station under our own steam?"

I shrugged, shook my head. The sounds of war made it difficult for me to speak below a yell. My bloodied companion was having no difficulty, but I didn't have the strength. I looked at Cantwell. The fear that had lived upon his face was now gone. It had been replaced by an expression of eerie contentment. Even peace.

Wherever the young man was now—the pavid young man who had curled up beside me—it had to be a better place than where he had been in those moments that preceded his summary execution.

In a war so nonsensically cruel, there were special cruelties meted out that made this conflict even harder to understand. And one was this: that a young soldier had been killed for the crime of not wanting to die.

It's pretty funny when you stop to think about it. But you'd never catch me laughing.

1919

VESTAL IN NORTH DAKOTA

The war was over, but where one might have expected celebration in the streets, there rose up, instead, a chorus of acrimony and dissent. The thoroughfares of America were crowded with strikers of every stripe and hue. Inflation was running rampant and wages weren't keeping up. In Gary, Indiana, steelworkers picketed; in Boston, policemen ripped off their badges. Even actors in New York City refused to go on the boards.

1919 was the year America got dyspeptic.

It was also the year that life lost even more of its intrinsic value. This trend toward human depreciation had started in the death-trenches of France and continued even after the killing machines had been decommissioned. 1919 was a year in which contempt for one's fellow man became especially fashionable. There were race riots in twenty-six different American cities. Anarchists protested recent laws against sedition and deportation by being violently seditious and subsequently getting themselves deported. The industrial and political power brokers found package bombs in their mailboxes. Arsonists set fire to factories.

Archie Hawke had seen what fire could do. Shortly before moving with his wife and young daughter from northeastern Minnesota to his new job in Jamestown, North Dakota, he and residents of several Minnesota counties had watched with collective horror as over one quarter of a million acres outside of Duluth burned to ash in a massive fire—the worst natural disaster in the history of the state. Thirty-eight communities had been destroyed, 453 lives lost, 52,000 Minnesotans injured or displaced by the conflagration.

Archie and his wife Cathy and their little girl Janie lived with Archie's mother in the Duluth rooming house Mrs. Hawke ran. For several weeks the three were crowded into a small bedroom to make room for all those soot-covered refugees who had come into town from the charred countryside with nowhere else to go.

Archie was pleased when the company for which he worked, Bridgeman-Russell, transferred him to the new creamery it had opened in Jamestown the summer before.

Jamestown was a picture-postcard sort of town, comfortably situated upon the arcadian James River. The town's many elms and elders did a fine job of shading the bucolic cinder-and-gravel drives meandering through its lovely green parks in late spring, summer, and early fall (the remainder of the year—unspeakably cold—being seldom evoked in service to Jamestown boosterism).

The new creamery was the pride of the town. All of its equipment— the large capacity churns, the capacious refrigerators, the coiling steam pipes and warming vats, the modern Pasteurizer—reminded Archie that, in spite of his good head for business and his can-do entrepreneurial spirit, there was a lot he had yet to learn about the nuts and bolts of American industry, and working for a company that had its eye on the future wasn't such a bad way to crank-start his own professional life. Archie was thirty. He had a wife, and he had a daughter who would soon be turning four; for now, a dependable weekly paycheck was what mattered most.

Archie liked everything about his new job as director of payroll and personnel. A special aspect to his job very much appealed to him: taking groups on tours through the factory's top-notch facilities. He especially enjoyed spending time with all the schoolchildren. Machinery fascinated the little ones—the whirring, booming, chugging sounds of a large, fully operational food plant thrilled and delighted his young visitors. Sometimes the operations manager, Waldo Spraig, came along on tours to answer the questions that Archie could not.

Archie didn't like Waldo. He was a textbook know-it-all. Waldo sometimes made Archie feel unprepared or under-informed. Archie was well-versed in company operations; it was the new creamery and its modern hardware that tripped him up. Waldo knew this and he seemed eager to help Archie out. This came with a price.

Waldo had a daughter of his own. Her name was Angeline and she was six. Angeline, aptly named, was Daddy and Mama's little angel. Archie had never met the girl. She wasn't among any of the grammar school children who tramped in strepitous tandem through the factory during those first weeks after Archie's arrival.

"Does she go to school?" he'd asked Waldo. "My little Janie is champing at the bit to start school and she isn't even four."

"Your daughter's very pretty."

"You've seen Janie?"

"Last week when your wife met you here after work—didn't she have Janie with her?"

"That's right."

"She has beautiful curls. My little Angeline has natural curls of almost the same color."

"What school does Angeline attend?"

"She doesn't go to school. She doesn't belong with other children."

"Why is that, Waldo?" The two men were walking through the vat room to meet a group of third graders waiting with their teacher in the front office. Surrounding them were great holding vats and warming vats with tortuous coils of steam pipe and a vat in which the Pasteurized cream sat undisturbed, sufficiently heated to kill the last errant bacterium that might be lurking there.

"I don't think that the other children would treat her very well. She's a very special little girl. Children can be injurious to fragile, beautiful little creatures." Waldo halted, as if the statement necessitated a physical pause. "The world has gone mad, Hawke. We must draw those we love ever closer. Do you ever fear for your little girl?"

"Of course I do. Life is precious. I lost my younger brother in the influenza epidemic last year. One day he was perfectly healthy; four days later my mother was picking out his coffin. But I think you're taking a rather extreme position with your daughter. A parent must strike a balance between mindful caution and—"

"Utter suffocation? The kind of suffocation that may lead to asphyxiation of the spirit? And yet I'm certain that Angeline is content to be so thoroughly loved and protected."

"There are schoolchildren waiting."

"Yes."

The two men resumed their walk to the office.

The tour began outside at the loading dock. "It is here," said Archie to the two dozen young boys and girls who clustered closely around him, "that the cream is taken from the wagons of our local dairy farmers. See those milk cans over there?" Nearly all of the children nodded. "We weigh the cans and then take a sample of the milk and test it. Why do you think we must test the milk that comes here?"

One little girl raised her hand and when acknowledged replied, "To make sure that it's clean and pure?"

"That's right. What's your name?"

"Louise."

"Very good, Louise. We will make the cream even purer as we turn it into butter, but we cannot use cream that hasn't been properly handled by the farmer to begin with. Only the best cream for Bridgeman-Russell!"

As Archie signaled the children's teacher to take her pupils inside so that the tour could continue, Waldo leaned over to Archie and whispered into his ear, "Louise is too beautiful for this world. The world can be injurious to fragile, beautiful little creatures."

Archie pushed Waldo away. "What the hell is wrong with you?"

Archie found out what was wrong with Waldo. He spoke to Mr. Kibbee, who answered to the president of the company at its headquarters in Duluth. The meeting took place after work that day, after Waldo had gone home. Mr. Kibbee's office smelled slightly of sour milk, though it was kempt.

"If you ask me," said Archie, "the man should be residing at the Hospital for the Insane. If you like, I can drive him over there myself."

"You're jumping to conclusions, Hawke. Spraig is odd, I'll grant you— very much the eccentric. He took time off from his job to serve in the war. You weren't in the war. There are things you see, things you experience on the battlefield that change you."

"He is obsessed with protecting little girls. But I wouldn't want him anywhere near my daughter."

The old man flattened down the hair that encircled his prominent bald spot. He got up from his chair and walked over to his bookcase. It was filled with volumes about dairying and the creamery business. "Have you tried our ice cream? It's very good."

"I have. And it is."

"We make advertising plates for our ice cream. Have you seen them? Spraig came in here not so very long ago, quite worked up about the children—the little ones whose photographic images grace our plates. 'Why do you pick only the sweetest, most adorable little girls to help sell our ice cream?' he shouted at me. 'Now they'll be marked women. Certain men will see their faces and go looking for them.'"

"Mr. Kibbee, you're proving my point."

"Now hear me out, Hawke. It goes to what I'm saying. He's very protective, that's a fact. It's strange the way he goes on about it, but there is, actually, a logical explanation for his behavior. Would you care to know it?"

Archie nodded.

"There were stories told by the men and women of a particular village in France. Who knows if any of them were true. You never knew if the Boche were actually capable of committing any of the atrocities of which they were accused. We've all heard stories, but *these* stories represented a particularly diabolical brand of depravity. I won't give the details. It isn't necessary to make my point. I should simply say that the stories had largely to do with the most beautiful young women of the villages in that part of France, and how the German soldiers had their way with them, as if the girls' beauty gave the men special license. It's madness, this human propensity for the infliction of so much pain on others, Hawke, but it is nothing new through the course of history, and it goes on around us still, right in this country, even as we try to make some sense out of that war— out of what it was supposed to have done to make us all better human beings. Don't get me started or one of the Palmer men will pop in here and deport me to wherever it is my forebears came from. My point is that these stories had a profound impact on Spraig. And so he worries. He sees a pretty little girl and he imagines her as a lovely young woman and then the sad sickness that has taken hold of his artillery-pounded brain sends his thoughts to a very dark place. No, Hawke, it isn't necessary for Spraig to ever meet your lovely daughter, though—" Kibbee smiled warmly. "Though I do hope that you and your wife and daughter will pop over to have a slice of pie with us at Thanksgiving. Jamestown isn't Plymouth Rock, but our name isn't all *that* slouchy as historical monikers go."

"I will do that, Mr. Kibbee," said Archie, returning the smile. Archie liked Mr. Kibbee. He liked nearly everybody at the creamery. *Nearly* everybody.

The Spanish flu had returned.

No, not really, but rumors of its reoccurrence and the fears ignited by those rumors took hold at Jamestown's Bridgeman-Russell Company Creamery. What was probably nothing more than a galloping seasonal cold epidemic sent half of the employees of the "butter factory" to their beds.

Including—or so it appeared—the creamery's operations manager, Waldo Spraig. In fact, Spraig had been out for a whole week, and his absence had begun to worry Mr. Kibbee, since Waldo was seldom off from work so long due to illness. Mr. Kibbee called Archie into his office. He asked his director of payroll and personnel to go to Waldo's house and check on him.

It was nearly six thirty in the evening when Archie arrived at the Spraig house several blocks north of the creamery. It was Mrs. Spraig who opened the door. Archie identified himself and was asked to step inside. Mrs. Spraig, a woman in her late twenties, spectacled and pleasant but slightly halting and rather vacuous in her demeanor, stood with Archie in the front hall, saying nothing. Just waiting.

A moment later, Waldo emerged from the front parlor off the hall. He was accompanied by a man in his sixties, who wore a clerical collar. "Hello, Hawke," said Waldo. "This is the Reverend Peacock. Pastor Peacock, this is one of our factory men, Mr. Hawke."

"Good to know you," said the minister, cheerlessly. Then, turning to Spraig: "I'll be waiting in the parlor."

As the minister was returning to the other room, Waldo turned to another man who had just stepped out of a room that appeared to be the kitchen. The man was casually gnawing a turkey drumstick. His eyes were on Waldo, who was wearing a sweater and trousers. The man wore the uniform of sheriff's deputy.

Waldo said to the law officer, "I won't bolt, deputy, if you want to have a seat in the kitchen while we wait for the sheriff. The doctor isn't here yet, either. It's going to be a long night."

The deputy sheriff nodded and went back into the kitchen.

"What's going on, Spraig?" asked Archie. "What's happened?"

"Sit, please," said Waldo, pointing to the wooden bench behind him. Underneath the bench was a tidy row of boots and galoshes. The two men sat down. "Now, this is what you must tell Mr. Kibbee: I won't be returning to the creamery. At some point this evening the sheriff and my doctor will arrive. They will confer. They will decide whether I am to be taken to the jail or to the Hospital for the Insane."

"I don't understand."

"Of course you don't. I'll explain. Earlier this week I went to the house of the little girl, Louise. You remember the girl who asked all those questions during our last school tour? I went to the home of that beautiful little girl and tried to see her, but her father and mother wouldn't permit it. I persisted. They telephoned the sheriff. My request was a simple one, Hawke: I wished only to make sure that Louise remained safe, to see that she would be properly protected from those who would later seek to harm her—to violate her as the mademoiselles were so terribly violated, their womanhood sullied by the evil that is man in his true, carnal, sadistic nature. Mignon, my wife, and Pastor Peacock have made me see that my quest has gone to extremity—has become a sickness of its own that must be healed. Either that or I should be put into a jail cell—it is not my choice to make. We have discussed the matter at length and I have agreed to tell my story to those who will either help me or at least prevent me from doing any further damage."

"What kind of damage do you mean? Try to make some sense, man."

And then in that next instant, the clouds began to clear. Standing before Archie was a pretty little girl of six—pretty in her tight blond curls, pretty in her striking cornflower blue eyes, pretty in her whisper of a smile for the visitor who had just come to her house, but ugly in one terrible, terrifying aspect. Her creamy white cheeks had been deeply carved by some instrument of frightening disfiguring capability. The gashes had widened without stitching, and time had created several fat, hideous scars upon her youthful face.

"My daughter Angeline," said Waldo, introducing us. "My angel. My cherub. No man will ever see in her face a reason to hurt her when she grows up. She will remain forever pure. I wish the same for your own daughter, Hawke. And for all the other beautiful little girls of this wicked, wicked world. All should be protected from the evil that is our cursed gender. Come give Daddy a little hug, my angel. He's going away for a while. But at least no harm will come to you in his absence. You will grow up untouched by the depravity of man."

The little girl embraced her father, the expression on her lacerated face quizzical, confused.

1920

FILIAL IN TENNESSEE

He was, at twenty-four, the youngest of all ninety-nine members of the 61st Tennessee General Assembly. He was also among its better-looking gents, his face boyish, smooth-shaven, and really rather beatific. (Although the second of those three attributes was hardly extraordinary in the year 1920; only a handful of the members of that august legislative body still maintained their mustaches, and only four of the Assembly's most senior representatives, Messrs. Rector, Leath, Skidmore, and Oldham, could be categorized as true bearded relicts—Mr. Oldham, a possible lost twin of the famously whiskered former associate Supreme Court justice Charles Evans Hughes.)

Harry was winded. He sat himself down upon the mouse-nibbled, moth-munched upholstery of an overly embroidered chair from the Reconstruction Era and attempted to retrieve his lost breath. Although he hadn't been *literally* chased from the House of Representatives' Assembly Hall, there had been movement of a discernibly angry character in Harry's direction by a number of those upon the floor who sported red roses upon their lapels. Not knowing whether such movement would transform into an overt display of broom-torch and pitchfork-wielding mob vengeance, the young legislator made the snap decision to decamp from the chamber in a great hurry, to climb out of one of the capitol building's third-floor windows, to inch his way along a ledge, and finally to secure refuge for himself under the rafters of that proud Greek revival building where the representatives of the people of Tennessee gathered to make laws.

In the attic, Harry found quiet and solace. He also found Rufus Vester Cawthon, one of the Assembly's two youthful chaplains (Rufus was thirty). R.V., as he was sometimes known, was a minister in the Church of Christ—a gospel preacher still in the spring of a career that would span decades and win him fame far beyond his pulpit at the Mt. Juliet Church of Christ seventeen miles east of Nashville.

Cawthon was standing behind a tattered, upstanding steamer trunk. He had been rehearsing the delivery of his next sermon. For a brief moment, Harry Burn thought he was seeing a ghost.

"Why aren't you downstairs watching history in the making?" asked Harry, coming quickly to realize that his sudden companion wasn't spectral in the least, and was, in fact, a man he knew quite well and even liked.

"Because history will be made whether I choose to be witness to it or not," answered Rufus, stepping out from behind his makeshift pulpit.

As the two men came together to shake hands, Harry remarked that in the summer-long "War of the Roses," the good reverend wore neither the yellow rose of the suffragists nor the red rose of the anti-Anthony amendment opposition.

To which the Church of Christ pastor replied, "The color of one's lapel flower appears to have little bearing upon how one will ultimately vote on granting the franchise to the fairer sex." Rufus poked the air in front of Harry's red-colored sartorial garnishment. "You would not be seeking the sanctuary of this cobwebbed aerie were it not for the fact, Harry, that you have voted against those who also wear the red rose—against your own side. So, I ask you, sir, in my absence and in the presence of our all-seeing God, did you, in fact, just alter the course of history?"

Harry nodded. He sank down into a molting armchair and allowed all of the air in his lungs to take temporary leave.

"And why did you betray those in the cause to which you had already sworn fealty? Are you a traitor to your comrades?"

"I suppose, Reverend, that that is one way to look at it. On the other hand, let it never be said that I was a traitor to *womanhood.*" Harry and Rufus each took out handkerchiefs and patted their perspiring foreheads and the moist necks beneath their wilting collars. It was the middle of August, after all, and the attic was but minimally ventilated.

Rufus pulled up an antique hassock, which was losing its horsehair stuffing in three of its corners. He sat with his legs splaying out, his large ears giving him the appearance of a spindly-legged, floppy-eared creature of the East Tennessee forest.

"You searched your soul. So much was at stake. If the legislature had voted down the Anthony amendment today, the cause would eventually be won, I have no doubt, but most of the women of America would have to wait until 1924 for the chance to cast their first presidential ballot."

"You sincerely believe, then, Reverend, that the amendment would have won its final statehouse ratification whether I switched sides or not?"

Rufus nodded. "Connecticut's legislature has yet to vote on it, as you must surely know. Vermont's is also waiting in the wings. And one of the southern states that has already rejected it could always put the matter up for a vote of reconsideration."

Harry laughed. "You sound as if there might be a yellow rose tucked inside your jacket pocket."

"And a red rose in the other pocket. I'm chaplain to all ninety-nine of our state representatives, Harry—not just the ones professing allegiance to the cause of universal suffrage. So the margin of victory: was it really only one vote—*your* vote?"

"It was my vote."

"Boy, you amaze me. That took much courage, I'm sure."

"Some, perhaps. Of course, I subsequently fled the hall like a hunted animal."

Harry reached into his striped seersucker suit jacket pocket and took out an envelope. He pulled from it several handwritten pages. "It's from my mother back home in Niota."

"And given all the events of this tumultuous day you haven't had time to read it. Let me leave you, then, to your private letter."

Rufus started to rise. Harry stayed him with a fluttering hand. Harry's eyes browsed the several pages of the folded letter. "She's unhappy about the rain. And here she's talking about a visit from Uncle Bill and Mr. Bushnell. They came in the Ford. She asks if I'll be home for Labor Day. Oh, and here she tells me something that she figures I have forgotten: how very much she dislikes politicians and how very much she doesn't want her own son to be one. And no, Reverend, I have not completely made up my mind as to whether I will run for re-election this fall, although if I choose to run, I do stand to pick up a few female votes as reward for my male apostasy, don't you think?"

Rufus smiled. "How can you not?"

"And here it is—the part of the letter in which my mother pointedly asks me to vote for women's suffrage. She tells me not to forget to be a good boy and to help Mrs. Catt with her 'rats.' Mama is making a joke, you see."

"Yes. Carrie Chapman Catt. Ratification. Your mother is quite the clever one."

"College educated. Mama has never understood why an illiterate field hand on our farm has more of a right to vote than she."

"So your mother *told* you to vote for the amendment."

Harry nodded.

"And do you always do what your mother says?"

"Every good boy obeys his mother, Reverend. Isn't that one of the commandments?"

"The Bible tells us to *honor* our mothers—our mothers *and* fathers."

"I honored *her* by changing my vote." Harry swallowed against the nervous lump in his throat. "And now they're going to tar and feather me."

"Cooler heads will prevail, Harry. Try to relax. You made your mother both happy and proud. And Mrs. Catt with her giddy lady rat."

Rufus and Harry waited a while before they crept back downstairs. There were no feathers, no cauldron of soupy tar. Only hundreds of celebrants and members of the press who had been searching all over Nashville for the suddenly elusive, history-making boy legislator. Someone procured for Harry a single yellow rose and pinned it prominently to his jacket.

The Tennessee War of the Roses was over. In a little over a week, the Secretary of State would certify the adoption of the latest amendment to the U.S. Constitution: number nineteen.

Later that year Harry T. Burn won re-election to the state assembly from his district in rural southeast Tennessee. But he would not run for the seat again, although twenty-eight years later a far more mature Harry did run for and win a seat in the Tennessee State Senate. Over the decades that followed the passage of the amendment, the dozen states that had either rejected it or had postponed voting for it until after Tennessee's own decisive vote fell in with the majority. The forty-eighth and final straggler, Mississippi, blushingly ratified the amendment named for Susan B. Anthony in the spring of 1984. Four and a half years after that anticlimactic vote, something quite remarkable took place in Harry Burn's hometown of Niota, Tennessee: six women—four of them running as write-in candidates—won election to the Niota City Board of Commissioners, one of them elected as mayor. The six women won international recognition as the only all-female City Commission in the country.

This, too, would have made Harry's mother happy and proud.

1921

COMPOSED (?) IN OREGON

Percy Llewellyn knew Aaron Francis before he became famous. They had met when the two were young musicians playing under the baton of John Philip Sousa. Though Percy's musical instrument in those days was the cornet and Aaron's was the trombone, both men, in quitting Sousa's tutelage, decided to devote the next years of their professional lives to the piano instead—as well as to the fine art of music composition. It should be noted that neither man ever wrote a march. Each was sick to death of marches.

Yet by the age of forty-four, Aaron Francis had written a great deal withal: five symphonies, three operas, four theatrical overtures, two symphonic suites, and concerti for four different instruments (none of them, it perhaps goes without saying, in the brass family). In the fall of 1921, all of the music above was still extant. What had been lost, however, were several other large works of no small importance, including a symphony (Symphony Number Three, to be exact), a tone poem, and a ballet. Aaron had burned the original manuscripts while in the depths of destructive depression.

There were no copies.

Aaron's friend Percy, far less accomplished in his own efforts at composition, understood depression, for he was similarly afflicted, though his episodes were less frequent and far less intense than those of his friend.

It took several years for each man, private in his own way, and not given to opening up so easily, to own to the disease of the mind and spirit that had twice prevented Percy from walking down the matrimonial aisle, and kept Aaron from essaying even a single marriage proposal, though both men, being of strong sensitive natures, fell easily in love. The world to each was a beautiful place that was all too often clouded by dark, obsessive, punishing thoughts—like a resplendent orchestral rhapsody marred by the sudden appearance of a roguish Sousaphone.

For the last several years, the friends had spent one week out of every summer tramping through Crater Lake National Park together. They took long hikes around the caldera, negotiated the "Pinnacles," and climbed Mount Scott like seasoned alpinists. From the mountain's summit they could gaze down upon the verdant panorama of peaks and glens that had first called them from their boyhood homes in the Eastern flatlands.

On their sojourn this year they bared an even greater portion of their souls, feeling cleansed and renewed in the process. Still, each continued to feel imprisoned by his nature. Aaron, in particular, though heralded as his generation's Edward MacDowell, worried that, like his predecessor in the field of celebrated music composition, he might also come eventually to lose his mind.

"That's a rather strong statement to make, chum," said Percy, having first stopped for a moment to catch his breath, and then to put the distant snowcapped crown of Diamond Peak into the viewfinder of his Number 2C Brownie.

"You don't wonder sometimes if *your* hold on reality might start to slip away?" asked Aaron earnestly.

Percy shook his head from behind the little box camera. "I do, however, get depressed from time to time. When that happens, I want to lie down and never get up again."

Aaron speared the friable soil with the end of his alpenstock. "Then you and I are different in that way."

Percy pulled the camera down from his face. "How so?"

"I have created a different persona for myself. First you have 'Me,' who answers as well to 'I.' It is I who works twelve hours a day on his Oregon Symphony commission so that it should be ready to premiere in the spring. It is I who may climb a mountain in the company of a good friend and colleague and breathe the fresh air and pronounce life to be very much worth living despite its shortcomings. And then there is 'Myself.'"

"'Myself,' I take it, is someone entirely different from 'I' and 'Me.'"

Aaron nodded. "And different in quite a disturbing way. Myself will do things that I would never do. He *has*, in fact, done things of which 'I' and 'Me' have been egregiously ashamed."

"Is he the one responsible for the destruction of your Third Symphony? Is he the one who put to flame your all-but-completed score for the *Little Dorrit* ballet?"

"The very same one. Sad, really, my inability to tell Mr. Denton with the Oregon Symphony that my Concerto for Ukulele and Orchestra is in no danger of immolation when 'I' am around. Only when 'Myself' comes calling."

Percy sat down upon the wind-smoothed top of the prehistorically tumbled boulder behind him. "If I were that nervous maestro, I would have taken the very same precautions. Who has the manuscript at this moment?"

Aaron sat down as well. He began to unlatch his knapsack, the two companion mountaineers coming to a silent understanding that the time had arrived for a midday collation. "Rafferty. He's in the employ of the Symphony. The man has a pinched face and pinched demeanor to match. I can't compose with him sitting there watching me all hours of the day and night—not that he should ever wish to spend the best years of his youth observing me work—so he shares his duties with two other exigently hired collegians from the neighborhood. One is distractingly female. Now it is the daily occupation of each of the three, in some manner of prearranged succession, to come in the morning with the box containing the full score and at day's end to take it all away, so that I am never left alone with it."

"And what if you choose to write at night?"

"I write at night quite often, Perce. Upon mutual agreement all new pages must be surrendered to Rafferty or to one of his associates and put into the box the very next day. We have it down to a perfect little science, I think."

Percy took out his sandwich and began to remove the wax paper that enwrapped it. "Has 'Myself' made an appearance during the many months you've been working on the new concerto?"

"Once or twice late at night. I dare say that if the full manuscript had been at hand, he would have tossed it into the hearth fire."

"Why?"

"Because Myself finds my work to be absolute shit, not worth playing or being heard. He also came once on the eve of a visit by the soloist, Mr. Edwards."

"Otherwise known as 'Ukulele Ike,'" Percy offered with a grin.

Aaron nodded, his mouth filled with ham and cheese sandwich. "He wanted to see how things were coming along. Just prior to his visit, things had not been going well. I was inclined to burn every measure I'd written and start again from scratch. I didn't do it, as luck would have it—as the thoughtfully provident Music Director Carl Denton would have it—because one of my keepers was there: Miss Julie. Miss Julie was there with her luscious lazuline eyes, which twinkled while seeming to whisper to me, 'I see it in your face, Mr. Francis: the self-doubt. But I feel compelled to warn you that if you cook even a single page of that manuscript in your new Hughes Electric Range oven, there will be consequences too grim to even imagine.'"

"And did that snap you out of it, my friend?"

With a nod: "I was well aware of what one of those consequences would be, and it was grim indeed: that my gainly guardian should go, and then I should die the death of a thousand wistful sighs."

Percy took a sip of still-hot coffee from his vacuum flask and asked his friend about his mother, for whose benefit Aaron had purchased the new stove. "How long do you anticipate that she'll be staying with you?"

"Perhaps indefinitely. Certain recent episodes of queer behavior on the part of dear Mother have demonstrated the infeasibility of her continuing to live on her own. I'm sure that I inherited my demons from her. Psychological derangement seems to be the family curse."

"If it is a curse that must be borne alongside your incredible gifts for music and whimsy—gifts that are making possible the world's first concerto for ukulele and orchestra, dear chum—then you must learn to bear your cross with dignity, and yes, even with some measure of gratitude."

Aaron nodded. Then he said soberly, "But you haven't met 'Myself.' And I would never wish it, most especially upon my best friend."

When the stay at Crater Lake had concluded, Percy Llewellyn returned to his piano lessons, and to his instrumental participation in various local concert and dance bands, and to playing the organ for Douglas Fairbanks adventures and Fatty Arbuckle comedies. And he returned to his lonely bachelor suppers at the Rex Café, and to falling in love (vicariously speaking) with every pretty new piano student above the age of sixteen and every beautiful woman who would catch his eye from across the dance floor. And the cloud of depression would periodically roll in and Percy would take to his bed for a brief season. Life went on thusly with little variance.

Several miles west of Medford, in Jacksonville, it was a different matter for the great American composer Aaron Francis, who dared with a smirk of mischief to give the world its first concerto for that Hawaiian instrument presently finding its way into hundreds of new works of popular music. A month after Aaron's trip to Crater Lake National Park, he was visited by the maestro himself, Carl Denton, who had come to check on the progress of the concerto, to see how things were going with his sometimes beleaguered overseers, and even (an organist virtuoso, he) to play, on a whim, the "Mighty Wurlitzer" in accompaniment for *The Sheik*, starring Rudolph Valentino, at a local movie house.

Denton was especially taken with Aaron's mother Mamie, a woman of noticeably good breeding, a fine cook, and one who loved her talented son even through the frequent fogs of her own cyclothymic cycles.

During his last night in Jacksonville, over dinner, the permanent conductor of the Oregon Symphony apologized to Aaron. "Now you must forgive me for treating you so criminally, Francis. This commission is very important for raising the profile of our new symphony orchestra. The fact that one of the best Vaudevillian musicians and arguably the best ukulele player in the country has been engaged to play an Aaron Francis premiere necessitated my taking great care to prevent any sort of setback. Your history of destroying concert scores in which you've lost faith is legendary. And it's not the kind of legend I'm happy to bruit about. You understand, don't you?"

"So when I return with you to Portland tomorrow to meet the members of your organization, into whose custody will we place the score?"

Denton thought about this. "Since you've refused my offer to have either a hand or photostatic copy made of the work in progress, we shall have to find *someone* to whom to entrust it."

"I'd be happy to keep an eye on it," volunteered Mrs. Francis. "Or am I not to be trusted?"

"I have no reason not to put my confidence in you, dear woman," said the conductor. "Mr. Francis, do you agree?"

"Since I do not wish to share the work with members of your orchestra prematurely, and because Rafferty and Miss Julie and the perpetually drowsy Mr. Snopes would all be happy to have a two-day holiday from staring at me like a watched pot for ten or eleven hours a day, I can devise no better solution."

It was decided, then, that the manuscript should remain behind in the care of Mrs. Francis.

That night, as Aaron was packing his smallest suitcase for the brief trip, his mother came into his dressing room and said, "When you played some of the piece for Mr. Denton and me on the piano this afternoon, I was thinking that it should be livelier, much happier in its tone. Ukulele music, by its nature—why, it's supposed to have some pep to it, isn't it? Since when has music from the islands ever moved a listener to uncontrollable melancholia?"

"What I played for you—it moved you to melancholia?"

"It did, Aaron. Should I iron these trousers for you?"

"They're fine. Who would have thought it?"

"Thought what?"

"My concerto to be anything but exultant. Mother, I believe that you are the exceptional case."

"I'm quite certain that I am not. Don't forget your razor strop."

"Well, what do you want me to do about it? You don't have to come to the performance in March. In fact, I'd rather you *not* be there if the music is only going to depress you."

"I won't be singular in my view. You'll see. There will be people who will hear it and imagine that the Hawaiians have become just as morose as the Scandinavians."

"I've never heard such flummery in all my life. Is this why you agreed to come and live here, Mother? To spout nettling inanities about my work whenever you take the notion?"

"You'll see."

"Stop saying that." Aaron closed his suitcase and cinched the straps around it. "I've asked my cook and housekeeper, Mrs. Cutberth, to stay with you while I'm gone. For your own safety."

"Like mother, like son."

"I don't know what you're talking about."

"But you do, Aaron. I know that you do."

Mrs. Cutberth had very little to do. Mrs. Francis was offended each time the cook got herself anywhere near the new Hughes Electric Range Oven, though Aaron's description of his mother's psychological infirmity gave the older woman to imagine Mrs. Francis putting her head into the oven—not necessarily to asphyxiate herself (it not being a gas appliance) but to burn herself up like an over-crisped roast chicken.

The cook/housekeeper, having kept Mrs. Francis under an eagle eye, finally submitted to the importunity of sleep and laid herself down for a nap as Mrs. Francis was preparing their dinner—a baked ham with pumpkin and cheese. As the house grew quiet (Mrs. Cutberth had been listening to phonograph records—all songs that Mrs. Francis didn't particularly favor), Aaron's mother wiped her hands upon her apron and went to her son's work alcove, which was dominated by his grand piano, its lid closed and supporting a clutter of music notation paper, each page filled with the musical calligraphy of his profession. "Leave it to my boy Aaron to make a ukulele sound gloomy," she muttered between tuts of parental judgment. The full in-progress score of *Concerto for Ukulele and Orchestra, a commission for the Oregon Symphony under the direction of Mr. Carl Denton, by Aaron Francis, Esq.* was tidily stacked an inch and a half thick within a box on the piano bench.

Mrs. Francis picked up the box and carried it into the kitchen.

She stared at the oven, wishing in vain that it had an open flame. She went into her son's library and gazed upon the cold and empty fireplace, not yet engaged for the season. Finally, she went out into the backyard, found a shovel, and buried the concerto in the ground.

When Aaron returned two days later and couldn't find the manuscript, Mrs. Francis admitted without guilt that she had gotten rid of it, but she wouldn't say how she did it. "You would have come to your senses eventually and done the deed yourself, dear," she said. "Just as you destroyed those other manuscripts, each penned by the dark hand that your melancholic mother has passed along to you through the curse of inheritance. For we are so very much alike, you and I. We kill the things we love. We just can't help ourselves."

Within hours, Mrs. Francis was gone. Aaron never saw her again.

Upon their trip to Crater Lake the next year, Aaron Francis related to his friend Percy Llewellyn in great detail all of the particulars regarding the loss of the concerto (except how it was that his mother had disposed of it, for she would never tell), and how the loss had brought him to the important decision of ending his career as a composer of serious music—or *any* music, for that matter. "I therefore pass the baton, willingly, to you, chum."

"And I take it and will cherish it in my dilettantish hands, but forever will I mourn the end of your famed musical life, doomed as it always seemed."

"Please don't weep for me, comrade," said Aaron, who smiled along with his friend, both men remembering that the word "comrade" was used by German soldiers in the Great War to signal a desire to surrender. Aaron Francis was surrendering to the inevitable. Talent alone cannot assure one of professional success. There are other factors at play—some of which are beyond one's control. Once Aaron realized this important fact, he was able to accept his fate with equanimity.

And this is the story of Aaron Francis, the most brilliant composer you've probably never heard of.

CODA

The above is the rough first draft of a story that I wrote in early 1970. Both Aaron and his friend Percy had been long dead by then, but both men's diaries were available for me to draw from. I was inspired to tell the tale by a discovery my son made out in our backyard one day. We hadn't had the Francis house for very long, and Robin, my wife, hadn't had time to restore the flowerbed, which had reverted to grass and weed after being neglected by its two previous owners. My nine-year-old Stevie had created a moonscape there for Major Matt Mason (Mattel's NASAish astronaut) and his miniature lunar rover, and in the process of digging out a crater, he'd struck the long-buried box with his trowel, its contents fairly well preserved during all those years of undisturbed entombment.

I took the unfinished music score to the Oregon Symphony. There was little interest in finding someone to complete it so that the concerto might someday be performed. Ukulele Ike, otherwise known as Cliff Edwards (and more familiarly known to me as the voice of Pinocchio's Jiminy Cricket), having passed away, I tried to contact the only other ukulele player I knew of—Tiny Tim—to see if he might be interested in doing anything with it, but he was preparing for his televised wedding to Miss Vicki on *The Tonight Show* and didn't have time (although the idea intrigued him).

It saddened me to think that the work might never be finished, might never be performed—this potential masterpiece by a now largely forgotten American composer. Over the succeeding years, Robin would sometimes catch me staring at the box on the shelf, wondering if there was anything that could be done to honor the memory of the talented Mr. Francis.

"You could do him the biggest favor of all, Steve, by returning the poor thing to its grave. Let it rest in peace. Let *him* rest in peace."

This I resolved reluctantly to do.

We had a funeral of sorts—Robin and Stevie and me. Stevie played a plucky dirge on the little Mickey Mouse ukulele we'd given him when he was in kindergarten. Then I put the box back into the ground. As I was about to cover it with dirt, Robin stayed my hand. "I've changed my mind, honey," she said. "I'd like to put a rose bush here. Let's bury the concerto someplace else."

It didn't matter to me. And then, several minutes later, it came to matter quite a bit. Because the place in the backyard that my wife had selected was already occupied. Aaron's mother was there. She had apparently been buried in the spot by Aaron himself. I pictured Aaron, spade in hand, a smile upon his once melancholic face, making this valediction by the light of the Oregon moon: "You're right, Mother. We *are* alike. We do kill the things we love. I'll leave you now, Mother. I suspect that you'd like some privacy while you decompose."

1922

CINEASTIC IN ARKANSAS

Abel Adamson never regretted his father's sense of humor or the fact that his mother hadn't a veto over the name his father had chosen for him. There was undeniable clerical whimsy in a Methodist minister bestowing upon his second-born the name of Adam's own, with a convenient reference to Adam himself in the surname. The name was an especially appropriate choice given the fact that the son decided to follow in his father's ministerial footsteps. At many an annual conference did Abel's fellow pastors and the district superintendents and even the bishop himself josh him about his name or, more affectionately, draw the obvious respectful comparison between Abel, the Old Testament shepherd, and the Reverend Abel Adamson, shepherd of his own two-legged flock.

Abel took great pleasure in his chosen profession. He enjoyed serving as spiritual leader of the Second Methodist Episcopal Church of Blytheville, Arkansas, a medium-sized church in a medium-sized town. He never worked too hard, nor, contrariwise, did he consider himself slothful in any way. And there was much for a Methodist minister of a medium-sized church to do: deliver sermons on Sunday morning and Sunday night, lead a more informal "prayer meeting" service on Wednesday night, make appearances at meetings of the Epworth League, the Junior Epworth League, and the Ladies Aid Society (each visit pointedly brief so as to not get himself too much in the way). There was the occasional wedding and funeral to officiate, and pastoral calls to make.

Abel Adamson prayed frequently. His were largely prayers of supplication on behalf of members of his congregation and thanksgiving on his own behalf. Because Abel had much to be thankful for—satisfaction in his job, good health, and a fine family comprised of Julianne, who was wife, lover, companion, and partner in the salvation of Blythevillian souls; and Matthew, his much-beloved son, who, in the summer and fall of 1922, was thirteen.

A quiet boy who kept largely to himself, Matthew liked nothing better than the chance to go off fishing alone on warm summer mornings and brisk Saturday afternoons in autumn, almost always returning home with an empty creel due either to poor luck or to the bequeathing of his piscatorial gain to a poverty-stricken widow and her hungry children who just happened to live along Matthew's path to and from his favorite fishing hole.

At least this is what Matthew told his father, and because Matthew was a boy who had never before been caught in even the whitest of lies, Abel Adamson had no reason not to believe that what his son said was true.

Of course, Abel Adamson could not have been more wrong about his son.

The truth came to him one Saturday afternoon in September. This was the Saturday Abel was scheduled to drive to Jonesboro and meet with the district superintendent and others whose charge it was to plan a choir festival that would enlist all the district's M.E. church choirs and would be, in the words of the superintendent, "so joyous a lifting of voices as to put the Welsh to shame!"

The location of the meeting was an hour's drive away, and though Abel could easily have made the trip on the train connecting the two towns, he enjoyed the sweet solitude of driving his second-hand flivver along tranquil country roads. The trip offered Abel the opportunity to collect his thoughts in the midst of a beautiful cottony-white landscape, evidential of the hand of both God and man at his most agrological, while commanding a machine that rarely questioned his authority (except upon those rare occasions when it overheated) or argued for a different path than the one that Abel, in all his directional wisdom, had chosen for the two of them.

The meeting lasted two hours. Perhaps because Abel had a good voice and often sang with the tenors in his own church's choir, he was made co-chairman of the committee, and, exercising his endowed leadership, was successful in convincing the committee to program a nice mixture of both the hymns of old and those newer songs of praise that had of late gained popularity among the more urban churches—hymns that injected a little pomp and collegiate muscularity into the songful portion of the worship service.

Abel had been forced by a busy market day to park his Model T several blocks from the large church in which the meeting was held, a spot not too far from the majestic Empire Theater, which added an element of architectural sophistication to this somewhat unsophisticated block of downtown Jonesboro. Abel had parked so close to the theatre, in fact, that upon returning to his car he found himself within easy sight of the bill for that weekend's fare; the picture was *Grandma's Boy*, starring Harold Lloyd. It looked to Abel like a fun picture and he wished he could disregard his own pulpit repudiations of Hollywood decadence—repudiations that took the form of exhortations against the attending of any cinematic performance—and slip inside. This movie, in particular, seemed far from decadent and was perhaps even morally instructive. Was that not the warmest and most chaste of familial embraces depicted upon the poster? Was not the bespectacled Mr. Lloyd both affectionate and properly deferential toward his aged, loving grandmother (who resembled several of the septuagenarian members of Abel's own congregation)? "But I'll resist the temptation," said Abel to himself as he slid behind the wheel of his Tin Lizzie. "For that which is not inherently evil may in giving the *appearance* of evil divert the mind nevertheless from thoughts both spiritual and pure."

On the other hand, the motion picture *did* look to be quite funny. In fact, were not those patrons presently emerging from the darkened theatre, squinting in the bright afternoon sun—were they not smiling and laughing and elbowing one another in fresh recollection of some of the photoplay's more amusing scenes? And look at that boy there! marveled Abel. He hasn't even a companion, and still he laughs heartily to himself in private merriment.

That boy who bears a remarkable resemblance to my own son Matthew.

That boy who is, in fact, my own son Matthew!

Father and son sat upon stools at the pharmacy fountain counter across the street and sipped and slurped from their tall glasses of orange phosphate. "And what is it you usually do with the fishing pole?"

"Oh, I ditch it behind the train depot."

Slurp.

"I see." Abel nodded his head in the manner of the contemplative pastor, assaying all the facts before pronouncing an ecclesiastic verdict. "Please make note, son, that our sitting here partaking of refreshment with one another shouldn't be construed as a reward for your misbehavior."

"I know that, Dad."

"I'm actually quite displeased with you for going to the pictures without seeking my consent first."

Matthew wiped his mouth with his napkin. "But if I'd asked your consent, Dad, you would have said no."

Abel thought about this for a moment—thought so long, in fact, that his son felt it necessary to put the supposition to him again: "*Wouldn't* you have?"

Abel rubbed the tendons running up the back of his neck. "I suppose I would have."

"And *then* if I went, I would have been disobeying you. This way, I'm not disobeying you because I never asked you in the first place."

Abel marveled at his son's impeccable logic.

"But you know how our church feels about moving pictures. It is our denomination's studied opinion that most of them are products of the Devil's handiwork."

"Do you really believe that, Dad?"

"Well, I—"

"Gee willikins, Dad! They don't *all* have Rudolph Valentino or Gloria Swanson in them!" Matthew took another long drink of his phosphate. "Next month they're playing *Clarence*—you know, from the Booth Tarkington story. And then *Robin Hood* with Douglas Fairbanks. *Douglas Fairbanks*, Dad! I really want to see it. And now I suppose I'll have to ask you for permission, and I suppose you'll say no because somebody might find out."

"If *I* found out, Matthew, don't you think the possibility exists that *other* people from our church might see you going in or out of that theatre? Our congregation isn't small and our members do venture into Jonesboro on occasion."

"*Robin Hood*, Dad! He does good works for the poor just like Jesus did."

"Yes, I know the story of Robin Hood, son."

Matthew scowled. "Sometimes you act just like a Baptist."

"Stay your tongue, boy." Abel cleared his throat. "On the other hand, I'm not an Episcopalian either—and neither are you. Being, in fact, a careful and deliberating Methodist, I shall think about it. I may even do a little praying on it."

Father and son grew silent.

Abel finished his orange phosphate and poked the bubbles at the bottom of the glass with his spoon. Then he said, "It's a clever picture? The one with Harold Lloyd and his grandmother?"

Matthew nodded.

"Would you like to see it again?"

Matthew nodded again, a big grin brightening his previously fretful face.

That Saturday afternoon the Reverend Abel Adamson of Second Methodist Episcopal Church of Blytheville, Arkansas, and his thirteen-year-old son Matthew watched *Grandma's Boy*, starring Harold Lloyd and Mildred Davis.

Over the weeks that followed (on those Saturdays for which the pastor had no visitation appointments) the two sat together in close companionship, father and son, in Jonesboro's Empire Theater, and enjoyed, as well, *Tom Mix in Arabia*, *Brawn of the North* starring the German Shepherd Strongheart, *Clarence* with Wallace Reid, *Robin Hood* starring Douglas Fairbanks, *Oliver Twist* featuring Jackie Coogan in the title role, and *The Prisoner of Zenda* with Lewis Stone and a newcomer to the silver screen named Ramon Navarro. There was sin and bad behavior in every picture, but every transgression was properly punished in the end.

It wasn't until the next year, with their attendance at a showing of *The Covered Wagon* (starring J. Walter Kerrigan and Lois Wilson), that the two were finally spotted by a member of Abel's Blytheville flock. The inadvertent sidewalk interloper was Cleo Summers, a deaconess and head of the church's women's Bible study class. She spied her minister and his son going in to view an afternoon screening, and though the movie commanded a higher ticket price than usual due to the fact that it was very long and quite sweeping in its story of transcontinental migration, Miss Summers paid the price and marched with a sense of strong moral purpose into the darkness, where she planned to ambush her pastor as soon as the lights came up.

She did not.

Instead, Deaconess Summers confessed to Abel and Matthew over a cherry phosphate that she simply couldn't help loving the film. Having grown up in a Nebraska sod house when the American West was still wooly and wild just like in the picture (and "couldn't you almost hear the whoop of those Indian savages when they launched their attack upon that caravan of pioneer wagons?"), there was little in the picture to criticize and much to applaud.

Deaconess Summers didn't tell a soul whom she had seen and *what* she herself had seen (with immeasurable delight), except for members of that secret society of two dozen or so from her Blytheville church who had been making similar surreptitious excursions to the Jonesboro picture shows (just like those morally bankrupt Catholics and Episcopalians!), and who later came to share their enthusiastic assessments with one another in a more organized fashion at the soda fountain counter—a band of the most exuberant Methodist cinephiles, together with their own Reverend Abel Adamson serving as honorary chaplain.

When, several years later, internecine disharmony in the Baptist community of Jonesboro rose to the level of injury, death, and the calling in of the Arkansas National Guard by the governor to restore order— the events of those tumultuous years dubbed by Arkansas historians "The Jonesboro Church Wars"—the Blytheville Methodists withdrew themselves to the safe confines of their own cohesive Methodist community (founded, in fact, in 1879 by a Methodist minister named Blythe). Concomitantly, the open secret of movie attendance by Abel and Matthew and Abel's congregants lost its semblance of sin, and Blytheville's own movie theatres became more commercially fruitful and multiplied.

It was also about this time that the Reverend Abel Adamson and his son Matthew stopped going so often to the movies.

They went fishing instead.

1923

CONSPIRATORIAL IN NORTH CAROLINA

Emory Jones was cold. He stood next to the radiator to warm up. Two other jurors were doing the same—a man named Sykes and another named Fogleman. Albert Sykes was an insurance salesman. Horace Fogleman worked for Vick Chemical. Fogleman was telling Sykes what went into his company's popular Vaporub. He was rattling off the list of ingredients using his fingers like an abacus.

"Oil of eucalyptus, menthol, oil of juniper tar, camphor."

Albert Sykes nodded. "You can certainly smell that camphor and eucalyptus."

"Then you got your oil of nutmeg and your oil of turpentine."

"You put turpentine in your Vaporub?"

Fogleman nodded.

"Never ever thought to check the ingredients on the label. My sister, she slathers that stuff all over my two little nieces—you know, when they get a mite croupy. Clears that congestion right up. You married, Horace? Got kids?"

"No and no. But it's probably for the best. I spend sixty, sometimes seventy hours a week down at the Vick laboratory. Why, this courthouse is the first place I've spent any time at all outside of that plant and my rented rooms at Mrs. Harvey's."

The two jurors who'd been in the washroom now emerged and joined the other men. The man whom the other eleven had designated as foreman, an older gentleman by the name of Dean Tuttle, had been waiting for them to finish up. He now called all of the jurors back to the table.

Tuttle was a district manager for the Southern Life and Trust Company. There were three insurance men in the room, Greensboro being, arguably, the "Insurance Center of the South." All three knew each other; the insurance community was tightly knit. There were three textile men present as well. White Oak Cotton Mills, which employed both Emory Jones (beamer operator) and another man, Wesley Lowermilk (dolpher), was the largest denim mill in the world. (Inarguably.) In fact, each of the twelve men serving as Superior Court jurors at the Guilford County Courthouse that week came quickly to realize that they were on a first-name basis with at least three and sometimes four or five of their juror brethren. Enoch Voss, who ran the Piedmont Café downtown, actually knew, on sight, every man in the room.

The fact that there were so many threads of acquaintance woven throughout this group of men wasn't all that unusual for a city the size of Greensboro; at 43,500 residents it still felt more like a big small town than a bustling metropolis. The jurors' paths crossed in a variety of ways. And there was something else that linked them—something of which only one of them was presently aware. Something fairly important.

Tuttle, who sat at the head of the table nearest the door, cleared his throat. "How would you like to proceed, gentlemen? Shall we discuss the case first or would you care to take a preliminary vote?"

The jurors responded with silence. A couple of the men shifted uncomfortably in their chairs. It wasn't the kind of case that lent itself to easy discussion. The details surrounding it would never have been bandied about in mixed company, and because of this, each of the twelve men was grateful that the administrators of the court hadn't yet capitulated to pressure by women's rights advocates to bring members of the gentler sex into the jury pool. In this particular case, the charge being aggravated assault with a deadly weapon, and the defendant being a woman, it would, of course, have only been fair. Technically speaking, this was not a jury of Lorene Wimbish's peers. None of the jurors wore a dress.

At least, not in public.

In simplest fact, Mrs. Wimbish had walked in on her husband in the midst of a sexual act with someone who was, obviously, not his wife. She had stormed from the room and then returned with a gun and a retaliatory gleam in her eye. She had fired upon the two, striking Burley Wimbish's lover in the side. The bullet had missed all the internal organs and spared its target (or was the target Burley? Mrs. Wimbish had testified at one point that it was her husband she wanted to see dead) the deadly complications of peritonitis.

Because Mr. Wimbish's lover had survived the assault, Lorene Wimbish had the good fortune to escape a murder indictment. Instead, she was being tried for firing a gun at her husband and at the man he was blithely mounting from behind: one Marcellus Teague, an assistant paymaster at the Orange Crush Bottling Company. It was a case of such a scandalously prurient complexion that the *Greensboro Daily News* and the *Greensboro Daily Record* and the *Greensboro Patriot* didn't know how to cover it without giving offense to sensitive female readers, and Lord help the child who happened to steal a peek at the morning paper before Papa had quarantined it. The *North Carolina Christian Advocate*, a weekly published in Greensboro, avoided the story as if it were the pox.

Those who did venture an opinion—the prating pickle-barrel crowd down at Richardson Grocery, for example, or the pundits and opinionaters who held forth at the town's two Arcade barber shops, or the check-jacketed salesmen who sold the Studebakers on East Market (and gawked at French nude photographic cards when business was slow)—were nearly unanimous in their defense of the defendant, a wronged woman if there ever was one. Why, it was bad enough for a wife to discover that her husband was cheating on her with a woman, but it was sin and perversion of Biblical proportion to discover that he was having congress with another man!

An open-and-shut case of marital self-defense, of moral retribution— so decided those who allowed their feelings to be known where such feelings could be safely aired. The woman had married a freak. To think that there were such men as this in their fine town! Were the children safe? How about the farm animals?

Yet in this particular jury room, with this particular set of jurors, it wasn't open and shut at all.

Foreman Tuttle tried again: "Shall we vote, gentlemen, or shall we *talk*?"

"*I'll* talk," said Jesse Cates, a young man who took all the baby pictures at Harrell's Cute Photo Studio. "The law is the law. She shot at both of the men and wounded one of them, and it isn't our place to consider the moral rectitude, or lack thereof, of her victims."

"Yet how can we not?" asked Wiley Shube, who worked as an underwriter for the George Washington Fire Insurance Company. "Because—like it or not—there was another crime being committed in that room. Fourteen-dash-one-seventy-seven in the state penal code. A

Class 'I' felony carrying a presumptive penalty of two years imprisonment. Both gentlemen should be grateful that the district attorney's hands are tied here; the only witness to this second crime, this 'crime against nature,' is the easily impeachable defendant in *our* case."

Bob Weaver, who worked as a napper operator for Revolution Cotton Mills, now spoke up: "You're suggesting, therefore, that we should take the fact of that other crime into consideration when arriving at our verdict?"

"Not necessarily. I'm just laying everything on the table. Each of you is free to do the same."

The room grew quiet except for the hissing and sphygmoid clanking of the room's radiator. Emory Jones looked out the window. The dark January sky augured snow.

"May I—may I say something?" he asked, turning back around. There was a catch in his throat. He was nervous. He had every reason to be. Emory Jones, before entering the employ of White Oak Cotton Mills, made his living as a supervisor of telephone operators (both local and toll) at the Southern Bell Telephone Company. He was a man who had never married and who had never even asked a single one of his equally unmarried female operators out on a date. He was generally scrupulous in his behavior, even in his mannerisms and the way that he spoke, lest he be thought to be partial to "crimes against nature" himself. It was not an easy way to live and Emory prided himself on his efforts. Even so, there had been two occasions in which he had surrendered to the inclinations of his true nature, taking no small risk as a result.

The previous summer, Emory Jones, now in his late thirties, had finally given in to a lifelong desire to be with another man. He had found himself in a dangerously frank and flirtatious conversation with a young, strikingly good-looking waiter at the O. Henry Hotel Café. There was an instant affinity between the two men from which Emory would have formerly shrunk away. Yet the young man, whose name was Tracy—Tracy Sprowl—was genial and witty and knew how to put Emory at ease. Tracy was also a dead ringer for a young man Emory had seen in an Interwoven Socks advertisement. The man had taken Emory's breath away with his square-jawed, collegiate good looks. Emory had torn the ad from the magazine and secreted it away in one of his bureau drawers. It shared space with other choice print advertisements featuring fine-looking young men wearing Knapp-Felt hats, and Arrow collars and shirts, and Kuppenheimer "Good Clothes," though the athletes in the Kuppenheimer pictures weren't, in truth, wearing much clothing at all. It seemed as if there were some secret legion of magazine ad men in New York and Chicago who knew that their job was twofold: to sell items of men's clothing to the male reading public, but also to feed the fantasy appetites of men of Emory's persuasion.

Emory Jones knew that there must be others like him, men aching with unspeakable desires, men yearning to enlist in that covert society the laws of the land told them was wrong—wrong to the tune of two years of hard labor, or worse. Emory knew this as Tracy led him up to the fifth floor of the O. Henry Hotel and he knew it for certain when, after spending an hour doing things with Emory that seemed both wrong and right at the same time, his new friend complimented him by saying, "You're the best I've had all week."

"You bring other men up to this room?" asked Emory, lacing his shoes with nervous fingers.

"I do. It's a hobby of mine. I'm very selective, Jones, so consider yourself quite lucky." Tracy winked. "Yes, I'm also vain as hell, but wouldn't *you* be vain if you looked like me?"

"So you—you have an arrangement with someone here in this hotel?"

"A nice and tidy arrangement, but then I told you that already. Ain't you been listenin', honey chile?"

Emory nodded and then he said, "Will you bring *me* up here again?"

"If you're good and eat your spinach," Tracy laughed.

True to his word, Tracy took Emory up to the room again. This visit didn't go as well as the first. Emory could hear noises coming from the room next door. The noises reminded him that he and Tracy weren't off on a desert island somewhere frolicking naked in the tropical sun; they were in the middle of a city of over 43,000 other people. These people were always close by, always liable to find out about him and report his illicit behavior to the proper authorities.

It took him out of the mood.

"Not to worry, my buddy—" And then Tracy interrupted himself to sing a line à la Al Jolson from "My Buddy," one of Jolson's recent hits. "You're a fine looker and a real trump and although I can't give you the key to my heart, here's the key to this room: 505. Someday, if you find your own sheik and want to take him to Araby, you can bed that Bedouin right up here. I'll give you the nod down in the café to let you know the room's available."

Tracy handed Emory the room key. "Gotta fly, Hot Lips. See you in the funny papers." And with that, Tracy Sprowl, the most handsome man Emory had ever known, and the *only* man Emory had known in the Old Testament sense, poked his head out into the hallway, and, finding his escape route conveniently unpopulated, flew down the back stairs to the café, where he was already late for his Saturday afternoon shift.

Emory sat dazed in the chair next to the bed, holding a key that had the potential to open up his twilight world in ways that he could never imagine, though he never found the nerve again. A year and a half had passed and opportunity failed to present itself. Emory concluded that there weren't many like Tracy or himself in this town—men willing to take a chance and taste forbidden fruits. The pun was a dreadful one, he had to admit, but it always made him smile with guilty satisfaction.

In spite of this, Emory never left his rooming house without the key. Just knowing that he had it with him made him feel special and less alone.

"Go ahead. Say whatever you like, Jones," said Wesley Lowermilk, who knew Emory from the cotton mill. Wesley, a handsome young man whom Emory nicknamed "Zorro" from his resemblance to the hero of the 1920 swashbuckler picture, *The Mark of Zorro*, was close to Emory's age, had been married—unhappily, by Wesley's own confessional account—and was now waiting with great anticipation for the woman's return from Reno. Not that he ever wanted to see "Xantippe Redux" again, but he was eager for that happy day when he would know for certain that the divorce was finalized and he had at last been set free.

Emory had always had a crush on Wesley, who reminded him of the cleft-chinned movie actor Bryant Washburn.

"I agree with Mr. Cates and what he said about upholding the law," Emory began, nervous but determined to put his point across. "And my initial vote will reflect that fact. But should I then find myself on the wrong side of the sentiment in this room, I promise not to be an obstinate holdout. You all seem good and decent fellows and will not, I trust, hold this principled stand against me."

"On the contrary!" exclaimed the normally soft-spoken chemist Fogleman. "We commend your stand. At least *I* do."

"My only wish," contributed Hampton Womack, a barber at the National Midway Shaving Parlor, "is that I shouldn't miss the vaudeville show at the Grand Opera tonight. I'm taking my mother for her birthday and they're box seats. See?"

Hampton had taken the tickets from his wallet. In the process of drawing them out, a key was disturbed. It dropped upon the table with a little clink.

Emory knew this key. He had one just like it. Hampton and Emory exchanged a look. But Emory wasn't the only man in the room scrutinizing Hampton and his key.

A long moment passed, a moment that would ultimately determine whether or not Mrs. Wimbish had the right to punish her husband and his secret lover for what she discovered them doing on that day—for what they had, no doubt, been doing for quite a number of days or weeks or even months. Not in a guest room on the fifth floor of the O. Henry Hotel but in the Wimbishes' own colonial revival in the still fashionable Gilded Era neighborhood of Fisher Park. There was wrong there, one would suppose—adultery is always wrong, is it not? But did the act warrant the kind of visceral revulsion that had induced legislators the country over to exact such sharp penalties of moral retribution? Did it warrant such repugnance and distaste among the "upstanding" citizens of Greensboro that, even decades later, homosexual men of that town would find themselves rounded up and sentenced to highway gangs in what became infamously known as "The Gay Scare of 1957"?

Earl Stutts was the second man to lay his key on the table, and he placed it there deliberately. Earl was a butcher at Nicholson Meat Market. Like the other key, his was imprinted with the number "505." It had also been painted yellow. The O. Henry Hotel painted all of its keys—a different color for each floor. "To help guests remember what floor they're on," was the manager's explanation. As if simply having the room number on the key wasn't enough.

Hampton slid his key across the table to keep company with Earl's. The two keys were quickly joined by a third key—this one from Captain (retired) David Bishop, a recruiter for the U.S. Navy. If the other men in the room hadn't been making such concerted efforts to keep their faces solemn and unrevealing there might have been a few private smiles, given that some of the men were quite familiar with the legendary penchants of certain of Uncle Sam's sailors.

In quick succession, identical keys were produced by Bob Weaver, then Dean Tuttle, then Jesse Cates, then Horace Fogleman. Emory hesitated, waiting for just the right moment to unite with his brothers in their mutual admission. That time came after Wesley dropped his own key upon the jumble. The two men smiled at one another and shrugged. To have worked in such close proximity and to have never known...

To Emory, the world had suddenly become a very strange place. Strange and really quite fascinating.

Eleven keys now taken from wallets and pulled from pockets and detached from key chains to be put upon the table, each bearing the room number 505. Eleven men now revealed to be members of the 505 club, Tracy Sprowl, its president and CEO, in absentia. The only man left in the room who had not joined his fellow jurors in this joint avowal of secret fraternity was the insurance salesman for the Gate City Life Insurance Company, Albert Sykes.

Every eye was now on Sykes.

"I don't have a key like that, I'm afraid," he finally said. "Nor have I any inclination to possess such a key. But I know what it all means. You see, gentlemen, I'm a good friend of Marcellus Teague, in whom Mrs. Wimbish deposited her nearly fatal bullet. Well, to be perfectly honest, we were once very much more than friends, if you understand my meaning. Marcellus knew, as did Mr. Wimbish, that should Mrs. Wimbish be acquitted, charges would in very strong likelihood be swiftly brought against my friend and his paramour Mr. Wimbish under the statute that our friend Shube here has just reminded us of. It was important to the two men that Mrs. Wimbish be found guilty so as to destroy her viability as witness in the other matter. And it was important to find the right men to do it—men who would not be put off by what Mrs. Wimbish saw.

"No, I don't have a key, gentleman, nor will I ever have need of one, since I anticipate no future need to break the heart vows that I have made to a gentleman with whom you are all quite familiar: Elliot Curry, the jury clerk for the Superior Court of Guilford County. Mr. Curry has put his job on the line by handpicking, with Mr. Sprowl's assistance, the jury pool from which we were all selected. And if you will all be so good as to keep this rather large secret to yourselves so as to save his job and preserve his liberty—because he'd be certain of a conviction for the grave crime of clerical malfeasance— then Mr. Curry and Messrs. Wimbish and Teague and I will be forever in your debt. Now, Foreman Tuttle, shall we have that vote?"

There was a vote. It was unanimous; Mrs. Wimbish would be required to pay for her crime of passion with *her* liberty. Subsequently, the keys were reclaimed, hands were shaken and cheeks kissed (and not just in the duple-Continental way).

It wasn't until the landmark Supreme Court case *Lawrence v. Texas* in 2003 that sodomy laws were invalidated in the fourteen states that had not yet seen fit to overturn them on their own. One of those states was North Carolina.

Emory Jones did not live to see that day. Nor did he ever pay another visit to Room 505 (though a good many of his fellow jurors kept up the practice for many years thereafter). He kept the key, though. He put it in the drawer with the clippings of all of his favorite magazine advertisements. Many of the handsome male models in the ads were smiling, rident with celebratory youth. Now and then, Emory Jones found himself smiling, too, knowing that he wasn't alone—that there were others quite like him.

Like a certain good-looking divorced coworker named Wesley Lowermilk, with whom Emory became—let us put it in the safe vernacular of the day—*very* good friends.

1924

DOUBLE FAULTED
ILLINOIS AND D.C.

One of the two teenagers was fourteen. The other was sixteen. One was the son of a millionaire Chicago financier; the other, the offspring of a sitting United States president. One died quickly, within a matter of minutes. The death of the other boy took eight days.

Bobby Franks died on Wednesday, May 21, the victim of cold-blooded, premeditated murder. Calvin Coolidge Jr. died less that seven weeks later on Monday, July 7, the victim of an era that had yet to experience the medical miracle of antibiotics.

The deaths of both of these young men came, indirectly, from a love of tennis.

* * *

"Bobby, you want a ride home?" Dickie Loeb stuck his head out of the passenger-side backseat window of the blue Willys-Knight touring car he and his friend Babe Leopold had just rented. Babe owned a Willys-Knight touring car himself, but both nineteen-year-old Babe and eighteen-year-old Dickie thought it would be better to rent a car for what it was they needed to do. So Babe picked the car he liked best: one exactly like his own.

> "Cal . Hurry up. It's getting late. Let's play."
> "Have you seen my socks?"
> "What am I? Your valet? Let's skidoo."
> "I'll play without my socks."

"Whatever suits you, Cal. Get your racket. Or have you lost that, too?"

The younger of the two Coolidge boys found his racket and raced his brother out to the White House tennis court.

"I'd just as soon walk, Dickie."

"Come on, Bobby. Get in. I wanna ask you about that tennis racket you were using at our court last week. I was thinking about getting one just like it for Tommy."

Tommy was Dickie's brother and one of Bobby's best friends. Bobby and Tommy both playing with the same kind of racket: that sounded to Bobby like a swell idea.

Babe held the door open for Bobby to climb into the front seat. Bobby didn't know Babe. Dickie introduced them.

"I have to stop playing, John. I've got a blister."

Calvin sat down on the court and pulled off his shoe. The big toe on the right foot was inflamed and tender to the touch. He put the shoe back on. He thought no more about it as he hobbled inside. He had other things to do, other things to think about. For a sixteen-year-old, life is a busy, crowded place.

The idea was to hit Bobby in the head with a chisel and knock him out. Babe and Dickie had seen it done this way in the movies. Then once the boy was unconscious, they'd take him to a place Dickie had come across during one of his bird-watching rambles. There was an inconspicuous culvert-drain pipe there. There the two teenagers would strangle the unconscious boy, each pulling on different ends of the rope to share in the responsibility for the crime. Once the killing was finished, Babe and Dickie would stuff Bobby's body into the pipe.

Unfortunately, the first blow didn't quite do the trick. The result was nothing like what generally happened when Charlie Chaplin did it to Mack Swain in the movies.

"What's wrong, Calvin? Why are you limping?" The President of the United States set his paperwork aside and motioned the younger of his two teenage sons into his office.

"I've got a blister. I think it's gotten infected."

"Let me have a look at it."

President Calvin Coolidge examined his son's foot. It was in bad shape; a serious blood infection had set in.

"Stay here. I want to get Dr. Boone's opinion."

Dickie Loeb struck Bobby again, and then again, holding his hand firmly over the boy's mouth to muffle his screams. Babe Leopold cringed. Dickie was putting strong force behind each of the blows, but Bobby was still conscious, still struggling for his life. "This is terrible," Babe muttered. Then the words came with more volume, with even more horror: *"Oh, Dickie! Oh, Dickie, this is terrible!"*

Blood flowed freely from the growing wound on Bobby's head, the spot where Dickie was concentrating his assault. The back of the front seat was now bathed in blood.

Finally, Bobby stopped squirming. He stopped screaming. He began to moan. Bobby Franks was, at long last, losing consciousness. With Babe pushing and Dickie tugging, the boy was brought over the seat and into the back of the car. Dickie stuffed a wad of cloth into Bobby's mouth.

Bobby, as luck would have it, was now bleeding all over the rental car.

Calvin was delirious with fever. He imagined that he was a young boy again. He was leading his toy soldiers into battle. Dr. Boone, now attending the teenager at Walter Reed Hospital, watched as Calvin played out his fevered fantasy with weakened hands. His body was tense, battle-ready. And then Calvin Coolidge Jr. relaxed.

"We surrender," he said in a hollow whisper.

"No, Calvin," replied the doctor. "Never surrender."

But the second son of the president wasn't listening. He had lapsed into a coma.

Dickie Loeb wrapped the boy—who had been his young friend, his neighbor, his second cousin, his tennis companion, and was now his murder victim—in a blanket and put him on the floor.

"Is he dead?" asked Babe.

Dickie looked up at his partner-in-crime. Babe's face wasn't handsome like Dickie's. The eyes were like a lemur's, and the lips too fat for the size of his mouth. Babe didn't have Dickie's personality, either. Dickie made friends with everyone. He had charm. It masked his sociopathy.

Was the deed done? Was that thing which the two had planned to do— Babe and his friend, his lover, his idol, Dick Loeb—was it finished at last?

The sun was bright on this warm spring afternoon in Chicago. There was approval in the air. Had they actually pulled it off: the perfect murder? An "inferior" life brought to an end simply because they—two Nietzschean Übermenschen—wished it so?

"Let's see if he's still breathing," said Dickie, with casual, biology-lab curiosity.

At 10:00 in the evening, the other attending physician at Walter Reed, Dr. John Kolmer, prepared the patient's father for the inevitable: the second son of Calvin Coolidge, thirtieth president of the United States, was slipping away. The president's son was dying from an infected blister he had acquired while playing tennis on the White House tennis court with his brother.

Racked with grief, giving voice to a species of parental anguish that defied his famously solemn, quietly wry character, Coolidge jumped from his chair and took his dying sixteen-year-old child into his trembling arms. Through a voice raw with pain and emotion, Calvin Coolidge invoked his religious faith in his address to his son. He cried, "I will soon join you in the Great Beyond. Tell Grandmother." He placed into his son's hand a medallion that had belonged to his mother—a woman who had succumbed to tuberculosis when the president was only twelve.

Babe and Dickie drove the rented, blood-drenched car around until night fell. While they waited for the imminent cover of darkness, they stopped to have hot dogs and root beers with the lifeless body of fourteen-year-old Bobby Franks lying cocooned on the floor of the car. Babe tried to get a better hold on his emotions. Dickie made jokes.

Richard Loeb was cool. He was calm and collected. He and his friend Nathan Leopold had just committed the perfect crime, notwithstanding all the blood that they would have to figure some way to get rid of before they returned the vehicle to the rental agency. (Who knew that there would be so much blood?)

And notwithstanding the fact that Babe's eyeglasses (there were only two others sold in the Chicago area that had the same hinge) had fallen from his coat not far from the remote culvert where they deposited the naked, hydrochloric-acid-doused body of their young victim. It would be a matter of only a few hours before the body would be found—and the eyeglasses as well.

Calvin Coolidge Jr.'s body was brought back to the White House. It lay in state in the East Room, attended by an honor guard. When the wake was over, the boy's father went downstairs, wearing his dressing gown. He stood next to his dead boy for a long time, smoothing down his hair with a tender hand. He was later to say that the power and glory of the presidency died with his son.

It was most difficult, from that point forward, to get himself even to look at it—the tennis court.

The Loebs had a tennis court, as well, and this is where Bobby Franks had come to play. There were no courts at the prison in which Richard "Dickie" Loeb spent the remaining eleven and a half years of his life (his sentence of life imprisonment made possible by what was generally considered the finest trial speech of Clarence Darrow's long and illustrious legal career.) On January 28, 1936, Dickie Loeb died in the Stateville Penitentiary of wounds incurred when he was attacked in the shower by a razor-blade-wielding fellow prisoner. Nathan "Babe" Leopold, the model prisoner, lived to see his freedom. He was released from prison in 1958. He moved to Puerto Rico, married a widowed florist, and became a lab and X-ray assistant.

His remaining years clouded by depression, "Silent Cal" Coolidge suffered a fatal heart attack at the age of sixty on January 5, 1933, in his Northampton, Massachusetts, home. His surviving son, John, died on May 31, 2000, at the age of ninety-three, having outlived his younger brother by almost seventy-six years.

It is not known if John ever picked up another racket.

1925

ACROPHILIC AND AGORAPHOBIC
IN PENNSYLVANIA

Tillman Hopper, the oldest of the three, was regarded as the "almost normal brother." He left home at eighteen, lying about his age to get into the Great War, and enlisting, as luck would have it, literally one month before the signing of the Armistice. Mustered out with swift military expedience, he moved to Scranton and took a job with the Scranton Button Company, first stamping out shellac buttons, and then coating Braille sheets with shellac to protect the pips from recklessly indifferent speed-readers. During this period, Tillman taught himself to read Braille and sat up late at night in the darkness of his boardinghouse lodgings laughing at jokes from a Braille humor magazine similar to *Captain Billy's Whiz Bang*. It was called, with journalistic brilliance, *Captain Billy's Biz Whang*.

In late July of this year, with the sudden emergence of the latest craze of this half cocked decade, flagpole sitting, Tillman spent a delightful Sunday afternoon in neighboring Wilkes-Barre standing next to its downtown flagpole and conversing with "Shipwreck" Gail Hoyt, a young woman of about Tillman's age from Galveston, Texas, who was perched upon the top of the pole. The two had a long and lively conversation that ended with a jesting proposal of marriage by Tillman and an equally fatuous riposte of feigned interest on the part of the impetuous daredevil flapper, Miss Hoyt.

When ordered to come down from the flagpole later that evening by the city fathers due to the fact that William Jennings Bryan had just passed away and an American flag would have to be flown at half-mast upon it to respect his passing—this coupled with the fact that Shipwreck Gail was wearing an ape suit to commemorate with devil-may-care frivolity the recent verdict rendered in the Scopes "Monkey" trial (which had been Bryan's unintentionally harlequin courtroom valediction)— Gail shimmied monkey-style down the pole and joined Tillman for a late dinner in Scranton.

Gail was famished; there hadn't been any food up on that flagpole.

Over hamburgers and Coca-Colas, the two discussed other stunts for which Gail had become semi-famous, including dancing the Charleston on the wing of an airborne Curtiss Jenny biplane and playing tennis with famed wing walker Lillian Boyer, also while buzzing the clouds.

"Are you a barnstormer, as well?" asked Tillman.

"No, but someday I'd very much like to learn to fly. But that's enough about me, Tillman. Tell me something about yourself. What is it in a man that makes him want to stand for three hours in the hot summer sun just to gaze up at a crazy woman in a gorilla costume?"

"It's not such a strange occupation, I should think. I was almost certain that there was a pretty girl under all that pithecoid pilosity and I'm happy to see, now, that my assumption was correct. What brings you to central Pennsylvania all the way from Texas, Miss Hoyt?"

"I can never quite say just how it is that I wind up in the places I do. My life, you see, has no purpose other than shrugging off these earthbound traces whenever possible, and taking wing."

Tillman smiled. "I like a girl who soars—one who plays by her own rules. You must know, though, how hard it is to set yourself apart from the crowd these days. Everybody's trying to gain attention for themselves. Ten years ago there was no such thing as an exhibitionist and now the country's teeming with them."

"Is that what I am? An exhibitionist? Is that a bad thing to be, Tillman?"

"Not when you do what you do with such skill and panache. Now what is it that I can say about *myself*? I'm in shellac. I hail from Williamsport, where I grew up with two slightly younger brothers, both very odd. Even though they don't play tennis on the fly or hang from the wings of inverted Jennys, I'm sure you'd find them strange beyond facile description."

"Intriguing. And your parents?"

"Our father died of influenza and our mother presently resides in a sanitarium in Arizona."

"Tubercular?"

"*And* insane."

"I'm sorry to hear that. I'm an orphan."

"For how long?"

"Since the Galveston hurricane swept my parents out to sea. I'd like to meet your brothers. I never had siblings."

"I must warn you, Gail, they're a panic. And not necessarily in a fun way."

"I'll gird myself for the occasion."

A moment of silence passed. Gail savored her last bite of hamburger. Tillman watched with affectionate eyes as she licked the residual mustard from her fingers. "Are we falling hopelessly in love, Tillman Hopper?" she asked simply.

"What do *you* think, my dear cloud-ape?"

Gail tossed her napkin at Tillman teasingly, and then asked if the two of them might leave. The still-intact trousers portion of her ape suit was really starting to itch.

Tillman's youngest brother Palmer was tenting.

The other brother, Hezzie (short for Hezekiah), noticed upon entering his brother's bedroom that Palmer had gotten himself into a state that, given the size of his member, could not be so easily ignored. "You're flagpoling, brother," said Hezzie. He was wearing the prototype of his latest invention: a life preserver with attached propellers ("When simply floating and waiting for rescue isn't a viable option").

"Of course I know this. You don't think I know this?"

"The question then becomes *why*? Or perhaps, *what*? What has happened to put you in such a state of arousal, dear brother?"

"*That!*" said Palmer, pointing to the film projector set upon a nearby table. "Here I am, brother—the diligent, *innocent* correspondence-course student—a fully committed matriculant of the National School of Visual Education. Here I am studiously—and did I happen to say, quite innocently—viewing one of the instructional films being projected by my leased De Vry motion picture machine, learning everything I need to know about how to run a radio switchboard and/or electrical substation and/or fully operational, maximum-output power plant, when suddenly without warning, the quite engaging animated step-by-step process for repairing a cracked Alexanderson 200 kilowatt motor alternator is suddenly replaced by the image of a French woman taking off the top of her Chinese pajamas and rubbing lotion on her bare breasts."

"How do you know she's French?"

"I just assumed she was French. Do American women embrocate their bare supple breasts with skittering, lambent fingertips?"

"Our mother rubbed motor oil all over herself and then admitted that trying to join that minstrel show was only a convenient afterthought."

Palmer released a wistful sigh. He missed his mother.

"What caused it, brother? The tenting, I mean. Was it the application of the lotion? Was *that* what did it?"

Palmer groaned. "It was *everything*, brother. It was the lotion. It was the glistening nipples. It was the naughty come-hither look on her ooh-la-la face. The way her bee-stung lips contracted themselves into that little dime-sized 'O' that you know always seems to get my gonads dancing. And now I'm flagpoling and nothing I can think of is furling me back to flaccidity. What time did you say Tillman was coming by with that new girl of his?"

"You have until four o'clock to subside. Perhaps you should think about slugging that weisenheimer who thought he'd be clever and put that come-to-life French postcard right into the middle of your instructional film."

"I should. I should invite him over and let him have it."

"That's good. Keep thinking those angry thoughts. I've got to go straighten up the parlor. Here's something else you can park your brain on: think of Aunt Melvina without her clothes, trying to confine all that naked avoirdupois to a single chair."

Palmer nodded, then shuddered.

Tillman and Gail arrived at four o'clock on the dot. Hezzie was wearing the best suit he had: his heat-generating electric suit. But because the short circuit still hadn't been found and fixed, he left it unplugged. It wasn't necessary to plug it in anyway, it being a warm summer's day, and so the unplugged electrical cord was left to trail behind him like a limp tail. It wasn't too much of an inconvenience, except when he turned to acknowledge the entrance of his brother Palmer and the cord got wrapped lasso-like around one leg.

"How long has it been, Tillman?" Palmer asked his oldest brother, all grins and no flagpole.

"Too long, little brother," replied Tillman, grinning back. "Hezzie tells me you're taking a correspondence course that involves watching instructional films."

"Among other things, yes. They say that the day will soon come when we'll all be learning how to be electricians and plumbers and barbers and whatever you please by watching educational movies in the comfort of our own homes. It's the way to go. Especially for those of us who don't wish to ever *leave* our homes."

Tillman nodded. He frowned sympathetically. "You too, Hezzie?"

"As of October 8—" Hezzie directed this to Gail, who sat next to Tillman on the sofa, "it will have been nine years since either of the two of us has stepped outside the ol' family manse."

"Goodness!" exclaimed Gail. "Who brings your food? What happens when something comes up that demands your presence elsewhere?"

Palmer and Hezzie both shrugged at the same time. "It hasn't happened yet," said Hezzie. "I write my funny pieces for *Grit* and Palmer helps me with my inventions. He's a very able assistant. As for foodstuffs, we have longstanding arrangements with the various purveyors in town to deliver all that we require to our front door step."

"But it encourages me," said Tillman, "that you're learning a trade, Palmer. Something that will eventually take you out into the world."

Palmer nodded. "Someday I *do* hope to find the courage to leave. I'm certain that my brother Hezzie does as well."

Hezzie nodded.

Palmer turned to Gail, whose eyes were now watering from involuntary commiseration with the two brothers' plight. "Have you ever met anyone like us?"

"One of the wing-walkers I worked with one day couldn't find the courage to leave the cockpit of the plane. In her defense, she had just seen a flock of geese knock another daredevil right off the wing and into the arms of Jesus, so I can't blame her. But no, I've never known two men who together couldn't find the wherewithal—let's not use the word 'courage'—to leave the house they've lived in since…I take it you've both been here since adolescence, would that be correct?"

The brothers nodded as one.

"Now. Hezekiah," Gail went on, "Tillman tells me that you've been an inventor for quite some time now. Would you like to introduce me to some of your little brainchildren?"

Hezzie was happy to take his brother's new girlfriend down into his basement laboratory/workroom, where he entertained her with demonstrations of the propeller-affixed life preserver, a cigarette holder with built-in ashtray, a "timesaving" motorized toothbrush, a machine designed to indent dimples into the cheeks, and an umbrella-shaped shield against inconveniently directed grapefruit squirts. Gail found it all delightful and then, in a blink, her smile evaporated. She shivered. "I'm sorry, but I don't do well this far underground. I don't even much like the *ground*, for that matter. Tillman, take me up to your roof. I'd like to sit up on your roof for a while and catch my breath."

While Tillman and Gail were climbing up to the rooftop of the old Grampian Hills mansion where all three boys had grown up, Palmer and Hezzie sat downstairs pronouncing Gail Hoyt a gentle, beautiful soul with a pert little Colleen Moore mouth and a funny, engaging disposition, and "brave beyond every known definition."

"For not only does she come and go at will from edifices that would hold men like you and me in a form of torturous psychological imprisonment," said Palmer with both admiration for his houseguest and rancor over his present situation, "she has walked the circus tightrope and played tennis on the wings of aeroplanes. Our future sister-in-law drinks in deep draughts from the elixir of adventure and the fully realized life. Perhaps, brother," and now Palmer hesitated, "perhaps she can work that miracle of all miracles for *us*."

"And just how would she do *that*?" asked Hezzie. "Merely opening the front door so as to more efficiently aerate the house will, on occasion, nearly put me into a faint."

"What's wrong with us, brother?" returned Palmer. "There are creatures among us who soar above the clouds and yet we can hardly move upon the ground. We're plankton, brother, or something to be found among the anchored constituents of the phylum Mollusca."

As the two brothers were bemoaning their burden of shared agoraphobia, something unfortunate was taking place up on the roof. A deer hunter on the forested hill behind the house missed his target and sent his projectile with blistering speed right into Tillman Hopper's left shoulder, knocking him from the pitched roof. Gail, attempting to stay his tumble, did something that had only happened to her once before (and since she was only a baby at the time, she had no recall of it): she lost her balance and fell earthward as well. Both of the lofty lovers landed upon the grassy front lawn, the impact leaving them in a state of temporary unconsciousness.

Together Tillman's two younger brothers stood before the front parlor window and absorbed the scene before them: Tillman and his new girl Gail, lying tangle-limbed next to one another on the green lawn. "Someone will surely motor by and see them there and call for an ambulance," said Palmer.

Hezzie shook his head. "They're hidden from the street by that large hedge. Don't you see?"

"Then we should telephone the hospital immediately," said Palmer.

Hezzie shook his head again. "But we can't. This morning I borrowed the electromagnet from the telephone receiver for my combination electric hair rejuvenator and radio helmet."

"Then remove the components, brother, and put them back into the telephone."

"The process would take time—time which we don't have. One of us will have to go and seek help from a neighbor."

"It would be death to me," said Palmer, his expression transmogrifying itself into a look of abject terror.

"You think that only *you* would die were we to leave this house? I believe it to be true of myself as well, Palmer. But could it be—could it be, brother, that our brains are playing a terrible trick on us, the way that Mother's brain made her go into that delicatessen and fill her purse with scrapple and headcheese when the butcher wasn't watching?"

Palmer shook his head, confused, frightened, impotent, and self-loathing.

Finally Hezzie said the thing that his brother was wholly receptive to hearing: "All logic says that we will not die. It is only mindless *illogic* that requires us to remain within this house. And yet regardless of the outcome with regard to our own survival, do we not love our brother enough to put our lives on the line for him—for the girl he loves who climbs flagpoles and walks on the wings of aeroplanes? Has he not allowed us to live here in the house of our birth, to draw from the family accounts as needed while he must work in Scranton and demean himself by making buttons to keep himself financially solvent?"

"Yes to all of your questions," said Palmer reverently and with an effusion of affection for his oldest brother that knew no bounds.

"Then we must risk our lives for them. We will do it together. Together we succeed or together we perish in that noble essay. Are we partners in this endeavor, my little brother?"

Palmer threw up. He took out his handkerchief and wiped away the bits of half-digested bread and pimento loaf that clung to his lips and chin while nodding his consent. "Let's do this," he said.

For the first time in almost nine years the two young men opened the front door and stepped over the threshold and out onto the front porch of their house. With a high-pitched ululation born of their great fear and with hesitant geisha-like patter-steps, they crossed the porch and descended the stairs to the front lawn. The screams of mortal terror subsided. A soft summer breeze caressed their faces. There was the smell of honeysuckle in the air, of something else floral and lovely that their gardener had planted when he wasn't mowing their grass and trimming their hedges and running the illicit craps game that went on right under the brothers' noses in the backyard toolshed. Hezzie knelt beside his older brother Tillman. He glanced up at Palmer. He took up Tillman's wrist to feel for his pulse.

"He's dead," Hezzie said dolefully.

"I'm not dead," snapped Tillman, his eyes still closed.

"He's not dead," said Hezzie, exultantly.

"I'm not dead either," said Gail. "But I think we've both sustained some broken limbs, and someone in the woods who apparently doesn't like to see people sitting on roofs has shot your brother in the shoulder."

Palmer ran for help.

"The two of you—you did it! You have broken free of your personal Bastille!" said Tillman to Hezzie through various stabs of pain.

"By jingo we *have*, brother," replied Hezzie. "Will you look at that beautiful blue sky? Can you hear the birds?"

"Is their song any different from what you might have heard through an open window inside the house?" asked Gail, who first thought it was her right leg that was broken but was now convinced that it was both of them.

"Gloriously different! Thank you, Gail. Thank you, brother."

"For what? For falling off the roof?" asked Tillman.

"For coming here to see us. For believing that we *aren't* freaks after all."

The oldest of the three brothers kept his eyes closed. In the temporary darkness he had made for himself, he sought Gail's twisted hand and clasped it tightly. "You know that you'll never be *completely* normal, Hezzie," he said, matter-of-factly. "It's the family curse."

"Yes, I know," said Hezzie. "I have patents for forty-seven inventions that I've never been able to sell."

"I'd like to take a closer look at that life preserver with the little propeller attached to it." Tillman opened his eyes. The world was a blur, indicative of damage, he feared, to the optical nerve. "Now that you are out and about, Hezekiah, you should really sell this house and move away from Williamsport. It's time for you and Palmer to give your lives a fresh start. Perhaps the three of us should go into business together."

"Yes, I would like that."

"Do you think Palmer would go for it?"

"Let's run it up the flagpole and see if he salutes it."

"Yes. Let's."

1926

BETWEEN THE HAMMER AND
THE ANVIL IN KENTUCKY

My parents divorced in 1928. Divorce was not as commonplace in that year as it would later become, especially in the small town of Winchester where we lived. Looking at my mother and father people have shaken their heads and clucked their tongues and commented in low voices about how much Mama and Daddy must have despised each other to come to this difficult decision. But I know that through the remainder of their lives (my father died in 1946 and my mother in 1962) there was never an ounce of hatred between them—only profound sadness over the fact that tragic circumstances had led inexorably to the end of their union. Each naturally blamed the other for what happened, but they must certainly have come in the end to the conclusion that they were both in part to blame—my mother for what she did and my father for not trying to understand why she did it.

It has been many years since I've been back to Winchester, and though it rips my heart to do so, I'd like to tell the thing that I've been carrying around for all these years. My name is Margaret Leach and I am an old woman with a very good memory.

In 1926 my aunt Kitty lived in Harrodsburg. She was several years younger than my mother. As far back as I could remember (I was twelve that year) Aunt Kitty had come to stay with us for several weeks in the summer. Mama was very close to her baby sister, and Daddy was fond of her as well. Kitty adored my two younger brothers and me, and I looked forward with great eagerness to each of her annual visits.

My aunt graduated from the Western Kentucky State Normal School and Teacher's College in 1924 and got a job teaching geometry and algebra at a high school down in Harrodsburg. She would usually come for her visit in July, but in 1926, the second summer after her move, she showed up on our screened-in front porch in early June, right after school let out for summer vacation. She wore an all silk mosaic blue flat crepe dress with chenille hand embroidery, and the hat she had on was geranium red and dramatically wide brimmed (she told me she hated snug-fitting cloches— they gave her a headache). I was almost positive I'd seen Gloria Swanson wearing the very same hat in a picture that had come out just a couple of weeks earlier!

There was something very different about Kitty on this visit, which would be the last time that she would ever stay with us. She appeared older, more sophisticated than I remembered her from the previous Christmas, when we had all gathered to spend the holiday in Lexington with my grandmother. She also seemed anxious, noticeably preoccupied. Even so, she gave my brothers and me a big kiss, and she couldn't wait to give each of us the presents she'd brought: for Mama, a big box of butter cream candy; for the boys, a mechanical train set; and for me, the best gift of all: an absolutely adorable Mayflower Pearl-on-Amber toilet set in the most beautiful sateen-lined gift box. My father (who got a "safety-first" bright red deluxe hunting cap on account of the fact that he had almost been shot during deer season the year before by a nearsighted fellow hunter) wondered aloud how a young woman like Kitty, fresh out of college and living on her own on a meager teacher's salary, could afford such nice things for us.

Kitty just laughed. She said that the value of all the gifts hardly equaled how much it cost my father to feed and house her during her lengthy summer stays, and besides, she had made a little extra money helping a friend sell Djer-Kiss beauty products for most of the spring. Daddy remained skeptical, but Mama nodded as if the explanation had put the question to rest.

I knew that my toilet set had cost at least eight or nine dollars. I knew this because I had priced a similar set in the Sears, Roebuck catalogue.

That night, as was always the case when Kitty came to stay, I was tucked into the little trundle bed that pulled out from under the shared bed in my brothers' room. Kitty got my room. Of course, that never stopped me from creeping back down the hall after the house had gotten quiet and right back into my own bed, where my favorite aunt and I would talk and giggle until she started feeling guilty (for denying me my "beauty sleep"). My nocturnal visits were special, and I looked forward to catching up with her that first night. But this year, circumstances wouldn't permit it; Mama, long aware of my late-night bed-switching, forbade me. Aunt Kitty had been tired out by her trip, said Mama, and needed her rest. "And besides, Margaret, you're getting much too old for such silliness, and your aunt simply doesn't have the heart to tell you."

Feeling hurt and bewildered by what my mother had said, I lay in the trundle bed and listened to my brothers' sonorant breathing and to the low, whispered voices of my mother and aunt in the next room. This being the first Friday of the month, Daddy was off at his lodge meeting, where he would be until nearly midnight, so Mama and Aunt Kitty had a long time to talk.

I thought of going out into the hallway and putting my head up to the door to hear what they were saying, but I was too afraid that I'd be found out. Still, I knew that what was being discussed must have to do with the reason that Kitty had come to us bereft of some of her customary cheerfulness and good nature. There was a seriousness to their voices even if I couldn't discern the words.

The next day, a rainy Saturday, my brothers, Willie and Enos, played with their new model train set while I read *The Triumph of the Scarlet Pimpernel*, a book Mama would never have allowed me to read had she been home that afternoon. (She contended that it was "beyond the comprehension of my young years.") But Mama was out with Aunt Kitty, and Daddy, not being much of a supervisor in her absence, spent most of the time out in his workshop building a birdhouse. (Not that he would have raised objections to my reading the book anyway, since he probably thought that the Scarlet Pimpernel was some sort of bird and *not* the daring rescuer of threatened aristocrats during the French Revolution!)

I didn't see my mother or my aunt when they returned very late that afternoon. While I had been in the kitchen making peanut butter sandwiches for my brothers and me (Daddy had totally forgotten that growing children required three meals a day), Mama took Kitty directly up to my room. When Mama came down much later, she told us that Kitty wasn't feeling well and that we were to be very quiet, and that under no circumstances whatsoever were we to go upstairs and disturb her. This last warning was directed especially at me.

Aunt Kitty didn't come down for supper, but Mama made her some broth and took it up. I didn't understand how someone could take so terribly ill so quickly, for she had looked perfectly well on her arrival the day before.

Later that night, after my brothers had gone to sleep, I heard quarreling in my parents' room. Determined to know what was going on—for my mother and father seldom exchanged unkind words with one another, even behind closed doors—I crept out to the hallway and put myself beside their door.

"I really wish you'd talked to me about this," my father was saying.

"And *if* I'd talked to you, you would have stopped her. And it wasn't your place to do so," my mother replied.

"I don't see how you could possibly have allowed Kitty to take such a gamble."

"*I* took that gamble. *Twice.* And both times I pulled through."

"Both times you nearly *died*, Cora. The man is a dangerous menace. He should be thrown in jail."

"And where does a girl like Kitty go, then?"

"She shouldn't have gotten herself in that way in the first place."

"The insensitivity of that remark silences me."

I returned to my trundle bed but couldn't sleep. I finally got up and went downstairs to see our cat, Mittens, who always welcomed my wee-hour visits with her in her favorite sleeping chair on the porch. As I was walking past my room, I could hear the sound of soft, muffled crying coming from behind the shut door. I wanted so badly to go in and comfort Aunt Kitty, but I remembered what my mother had said.

Downstairs, I petted Mittens and listened to her grateful purrs for perhaps fifteen minutes, and then I crept back upstairs. I stood outside the door to my bedroom. It was quiet now. I felt that I should open the door to make sure that Aunt Kitty was all right. I didn't see how merely taking a look into the room could disturb my aunt, so I turned the knob and slowly pushed the door open. It gave only the slightest squeak from its dry hinges. Aunt Kitty was lying doubled up in the bed. She was awake.

Perhaps the light from the hall sconce, which now creased the darkness of the room, signaled my presence. She turned immediately and looked up at me, her face half obscured in shadow.

"Hello, Maggie Girl," she said in a hushed, tired voice. "I've seen so little of you since I got here."

"I'm sorry that you aren't feeling well, Aunt Kitty."

"Now don't you worry. I'll be back to my old self in no time at all." Aunt Kitty tipped her head in the direction of the oscillating fan that had been set upon my vanity table. "It's a hot summer night, yet I'm very cold," she said.

"Do you want me to turn it off?"

"No, sweet angel, I want you to climb into bed, as you always do, and I want you to put your arm around me to warm me up."

I couldn't believe that my Aunt Kitty wanted me with her. I was overjoyed to be needed in such a way. I climbed into bed and pulled the covers tightly around us, placing myself next to her. She purred—not unlike my little cat, Mittens. "You are so good to me," she said groggily, and in no time at all she was fast asleep. I stayed awake for a while longer attending to my job of keeping my favorite aunt warm and safe and helping her to heal from whatever terrible illness had suddenly befallen her.

When I woke in the morning, Aunt Kitty was still lying next to me, but her body was cold. And the bed felt very wet and my skin felt sticky. Perhaps it is perspiration, I thought, for it had been a very warm night for me. But there was a smell there that I couldn't identify—an acrid, metallic smell.

I blinked. Harsh morning light invaded my room through half-opened curtains. I looked down in the brightness of this light to discover the true reason for the dampness all around me. The sheets were stained dark red. Dirty, scarlet red. I drew back. I said my aunt's name, and receiving no response, I touched her, then shook her shoulder. She didn't move.

I screamed.

I screamed as I had never screamed in all of my moments of childhood terror, most of those moments being silly and largely self-inflicted.

And I couldn't stop shaking.

Mama rushed in and swept me up from the bed. As she held me tightly in her arms, she kept saying, "Oh my darling little girl, my poor, poor little girl!" Mama kept me from looking as the doctor came and formally pronounced Aunt Kitty dead. I was sent, along with my brothers, to a neighbor's house while police officers interviewed my mother and father in our own home.

Someone had broken the law. Someone had done this to my aunt and it would be several years before either Mama or Daddy would impart the details to me, before my questions received answers. By that time I had already figured most of it out.

What I didn't know yet was that there was a man in Harrodsburg who was married, who could not leave his wife, but neither could he stop seeing Kitty. And giving her things. One thing that he gave her she couldn't keep. And such a thing—and I cannot easily bring myself to call that which was growing inside my aunt a *thing*—could not be allowed to *be*. Aunt Kitty would have lost her job if she had chosen to carry the baby to term. Once word of it got out, no one would have hired her to do that which she so loved to do: teach.

What I also didn't know was that it was Mama who had talked Aunt Kitty into going to the man—the man who had spared Mama not once but twice from giving birth to a child that she didn't want. He had not been so lucky with Aunt Kitty. The autopsy revealed that she had died from a rupture in her uterus.

My mother blamed society for putting herself and her sister between the hammer and the anvil. My father blamed my mother for sending Aunt Kitty to such a dangerous man—one who did what he did without medical training, with callous disregard for the health and well-being of the women who came to him, and only for the money.

When a death comes between a husband and wife, some things can never be mended. I lost both of my parents the week that my Aunt Kitty died, although two years were to pass before the fissure was formalized by divorce.

And I lost the beautiful toilet set that Aunt Kitty had given me, which I knew that I could never bring myself to use—the dainty comb and brush, the smart little hand mirror. I gave it all away to a little girl at my school who wept with joy over my unexplained generosity.

1927

ASSISIAN IN MASSACHUSETTS

I met her at the Majestic Restaurant downtown, although I'd seen her earlier that day in the Union Savings Bank. The restaurant isn't there anymore. Most of this part of town burned down in February of the following year when the crew that had been hired to demolish the recently shuttered Pocasset Mills accidentally turned the job over to a far more efficient agent of destruction.

The 1928 fire was the most destructive in Fall River's history. The Union Savings Bank was among the worst casualties. Not even the contents of its safety deposit boxes were spared by the conflagration.

Union Savings was Andrew Borden's bank. You know President Borden, I'm sure. He was the poor fellow who was allegedly given forty-one whacks by his daughter Lizzie. Except that it wasn't forty-one. It was actually eleven, and that very first whack had probably been enough to send him to his Maker. It was Lizzie's stepmother Abby who, in fact, got the greater number of blows: eighteen or nineteen. They say that Lizzie despised her stepmother, who was bent on directing most of her husband's fortune to her own family. There was more than sufficient motive for the indictment. But Lizzie, as you probably know, was acquitted.

Alice Rose Carteret had brought a flask. Two, in fact. It was the sort of thing you'd see in a speakeasy or some low-end dive: a woman brazenly fortifying her Coca-Cola with something puissant from her stocking. However, Alice Rose Carteret wasn't anything like your typical speakeasy habitué. She was rich and respectable and ridiculously philanthropic, having devoted no small portion of her time and money to the Fall River Animal Rescue League, which she helped to found.

She'd been stood up.

A man was to meet Alice Rose at the Majestic that night and he didn't show, and she reacted not by hanging her head in disgrace over the public snub, but by doing what any other thoroughly modern woman of the thoroughly modern 1920s would do: she repaired her assaulted pride with bootleg hooch. Soon finding herself both potted and pot-valiant she beckoned me, also dining alone, to join her. And I did—not even knowing at the time what a remarkable confession awaited me.

The encounter began with small talk: mindless banter about the weather, the movies. She took out her compact and recoiled from the image in the little mirror, proclaiming that the room's harsh lighting made her look like one of the waxworks at Madame Tussaud's. I contested this observation. I also suggested (with some delicacy) that we might decamp to a little watering hole I knew of a few blocks away: a murky, smoky establishment where I violated the Volstead Act on a regular basis.

She took to it immediately.

We settled into a booth. Her flasks now empty, she and I ordered from the menu. My stomach protested the resultant incursion all the next day.

"Do you know who died last week?" she asked. Alice Rose had not yet begun to garble her words, though her manner was casual, and she touched me often upon the arm with impromptu familiarity and eventually laced her fingers through my hair, this last encroachment upon my person accompanied by an invitation to share her bed that night. I perhaps owe it to you to note our respective ages in that ancient year of 1927. I was twenty-five, a reporter for the *Globe* (although nothing I was about to hear would she permit to be published—at least not until now, following her recent death). I supposed that Miss Carteret was in her mid-to-late fifties in 1927. She had been twice married. (Her biography served as prologue to the revelations that were to come.) But she so despised her two former husbands that she refused to perpetuate their surnames.

"Of course I know who died last week," I said. "Emma Borden. Older sister of Lizzie. And Lizzie just the week before."

"Do you find that odd? Two spinster sisters so estranged—both by distance and by the heart—dying in such quick succession?"

"I would think it *somewhat* odd."

"And yet I'll have you know that it isn't odd at all."

"Why do you say that?"

Alice Rose's finger beckoned me to come close. We leaned forward across the table and nearly touched foreheads.

"I killed her."

"Emma?"

Alice Rose nodded. "Right after Lizzie's demise. She always preferred to be called 'Lizbeth' in those years that followed you-know-what, but I never could make the change. Anyway, shortly after Lizzie's death, I took the train to Newmarket, New Hampshire, where Emma was living. Of course I knew that she would have already heard that her sister had died—from complications arising from that botched gall bladder surgery. Don't you think that certain doctors ought to be strung up for their incompetence? But that's a topic for some other night. I went to Newmarket to speak to Emma, to tell her—no, let me be honest—to *demand* from her a certain thing. Lizzie had toyed with me and it will probably be years before her will is probated, not that I have any doubt what we will find therein. I was not going to let Emma off so easily."

"Alice Rose, I have to put you on notice here: I'm getting drunk. You're going to have to start making some sense very soon or you're going to lose me entirely."

"Young man, I have every intention of telling you with absolute clarity what has been eating away at my very soul for all of these past four—what is it—*five* days. But I must exact a double promise from you in exchange."

I made my face as open and amenable to hearing the proposal as possible.

"That you should first tell no one what it is that I intend shortly to impart to you, and that you should at a later hour make passionate love to me in the manner of that gorgeous, soft-spoken cowboy Gary Cooper in that new western picture *The Winning of Barbara Worth.*"

"So as I am to understand it, you'll be Miss Worth and I am to be the cowhand who will 'win you'?"

"Oh, you have won me already, dear boy. We must now simply consummate the transaction."

In my gin-clouded head this sounded like a fair arrangement. For a woman of a certain age, Alice Rose Carteret was youthful in nearly every aspect.

Or I was perhaps even more intoxicated than I thought.

Our drinks refreshed and the Negro chanteuse on the gin-mill's little stage having switched from bawdy Black Bottom jazz to a quiet, introspective, "he-done-me-wrong" torch song, Alice Rose leaned back in her chair and asked in a playful, not unmelodious voice of her own, "So, Blue Eyes. Do you think she did it?"

"The jury acquitted her," I answered matter-of-factly. "It took them scarcely an hour, didn't it?"

"How closely have you studied the case? The judge was notoriously biased in her favor. All of that incriminating inquest testimony was disallowed. *And*, as I recall, no one seemed to care. The whole town *wanted* her acquitted."

"I wasn't alive then, and I haven't studied the case very closely."

Alice Rose effected stupefaction. "You live in Fall River and don't even know the details of the double murder trial that made the town world-famous?"

"I suppose what I'm saying is that I know the case just as well as most, but unlike some of my colleagues at the *Globe*, I don't make revisiting the minutiae of it a lifelong obsession. Are there facts that have come to your attention which you'd like to share with me?"

"I should say so. I maintained a healthy acquaintance with both of the sisters, you know. We had a bond—our love of animals. Both Lizzie and Emma were very supportive of the Animal Rescue League. I sought to make them even more supportive. Here was my thinking, cowboy: neither woman married. They were richer than Croesus from that sizeable inheritance they received from their father. Remember that it was the stepmother who was hacked to pieces first, so her pre-decease put every penny of that miser's fortune directly into the scrabbling hands of his two surviving daughters. They both died quite wealthy. I have no idea to whom they have left the lion's share of their many thousands, but I suspect that the Animal Rescue League will get only a fraction. Despite all my best efforts."

"What efforts are you talking about?"

The singer on the stage had now begun a special rendition of Fanny Brice's "My Man." I commended her with an unsteady bow and salaam for classing up the song by returning to the original French.

"Am I to compete with this Negress singer?" asked my suddenly indignant companion.

"She's distractingly good, but I'll try my best to give you my undivided attention. To what efforts are you referring?"

"There was a party that was given by Lizzie at Maplecroft back in '05. Lizzie's lover was there—let's just call a spade a spade. Lizzie Borden and Nance O'Neil were lovers. And the house was filled with all of Nance's intemperate theatre friends, and Emma, who was a good nine years older than Lizzie and was quite *temperate* by *her* nature, didn't much care for Nance and her unruly companions. And so they were having themselves a little sisterly spat just outside the library, where I was sitting primly and patiently waiting for Lizzie. You see, she was supposed to come in and sign a petition I was circulating on behalf of the superannuated draft horses of Fall River—"

"Do you ever take a breath?"

My loquacious companion smiled. She inhaled and exhaled compliantly, then barreled ahead with renewed vigor. "My sweet, dimpled Adonis, you simply would not believe it: I am sitting in that library and I am hearing everything that is said between the quarreling sisters in spite of the pounding of the Ragtime piano and the squeals and screams of those theatrical debauchees. Here is what I hear. I am no actress, so I can't give you the sort of performance that Nance O'Neil might give, but I'll do my best. Garçon! Garçon!"

"Is that Lizzie Borden you're imitating or her sister Emma?"

"Neither. I want another drink."

The story was temporarily suspended for the waiter to bring us both another drink. I watched as the Negro singer surrendered the stage to a jazz quartet featuring a Beiderbeckian cornetist of no small talent. With musical accompaniment more appropriate for her purpose, Alice Rose began her little play.

"'Lizzie, I want all of these drunkards and dope fiends out of this house immediately. Their presence here is an absolute scandal!'

"Now you must imagine that I am laughing rudely and raucously, for this is how Lizzie proceeded to laugh in that next moment. Then she crowed, 'Emma, you forgetful old fool! If you feel that this harmless little gathering constitutes a scandal, then how would you characterize what Maggie and I did, under your perfectly planned orchestration?'

"'Apples and oranges, Lizzie. One is hardly harmless, for it disturbs my peace and the peace of everyone on this block. The other comprises a chapter of ancient history in which, in the opinion of the law and of this community, we played absolutely no part. Do you understand the distinction?'

"'The only thing I understand at the moment, Emma, is that there is a letter on my desk in the library of which you should take serious note. It bears a Montana postmark.'

"'Is it from the murderous housemaid, our very own Maggie?'

"'Who else? She asks for more money.'

"'What of it? We'll send her more money. She's greedy, but we have more than the necessary funds to accommodate her.'

"'I don't like the little hussy blackmailing us like this.'

"'Then take the train to Montana and hack her up.'

"'No, dear sister, I think it's *your* turn.'

"'This isn't funny, Lizzie. Pay her what she wants and then destroy the letter. Where did you say it was?'

"'On my desk in the library.'

Returning to the role of narrator, Alice Rose said (as she caressed my elbow with a silken hand), "But, of course, my little handsome cowpoke, they *didn't* find the letter on the desk in the library, for it was now in *my* reticule, where I had hastily deposited it, knowing how very valuable such a letter could be to me."

"And *has* it turned out to be valuable to you?"

"Oh, goodness, yes. Generous contributions by both of the sisters have allowed my animal-loving colleagues and myself to found the Fall River Animal Rescue League. Of course I wanted more for our abandoned kittens and puppies and those poor, spavined old workhorses than what we were originally able to give them. I was determined, therefore, that with that letter in hand, which indicts both sisters and the family maid, I should exact even more money from the Sisters Borden for the benefit of *all* of my furry friends."

"Why did you not use the money for your own gain?"

"I have enough money of my own. The man who stood me up this evening was after my money. I suspect that the adventurer chanced upon some dowager with an even fatter purse, or you and I wouldn't be sitting here tonight. Anyway, I made it clear to the two sisters that if the first to die didn't leave the bulk of her whole fortune for the benefit of the neglected animal population of Fall River, Massachusetts, I would publicize the revelatory letter to the detriment of the surviving sister. Prior to her death two weeks ago, I went to Lizzie, knowing her to be in her last extremities due to that terrible surgical infection. I asked if she remembered my request from several years previous.

"She merely laughed at me, as best as one can laugh through the throes of abdominal agony. 'You have figured this all wrong, Alice Rose,' she said, with bite. 'While I share your love of animals, I have no love for my sister, and it should give me no greater pleasure, in whatever afterlife awaits me, than to see Emma finally implicated and brought to late-life ruin. It was always *I* who had to suffer the indignity of that dreadful schoolyard rhyme, and it was *I* who in time lost the support of nearly all friends and family. The consensus now is that I *did* do it—I alone. Whether out of obsessive hatred for my father and my stepmother, whether in some fugue state of menstrual epilepsy. Whatever the reason, the jury of public opinion has now reached a contrary 'what-say-you.' They say nothing of Maggie, who sits fat and financially secure with her smelter husband in Anaconda. And they are deafeningly silent as to what part Emma may have played in the scheme—Emma, who, in reality, dreamt it all up in the first place; Emma, who placed herself conveniently out of town at the time of the murders so that I must do the work of cleaving my father's skull as he lay napping, and Maggie the far more satisfying job of hacking away at the witch. So here is my revenge, beside the point that I plan to leave her not one thin dime in my will—that if she should die first, I will be protected under the constitutional defense of double jeopardy. And if I should go first, which seems the more likely, you may reveal her complicity—no, no, her mastermind brilliance for all the world to know, for I plan to give the Animal Rescue League only $30,000. Which is no small sum, I might add. Oh, and you may have my shares of stock in the Stevens Manufacturing Company."

"Which I assume, my loverman, is the exact bequest that we should expect to see when the will is ultimately probated," Alice Rose concluded.

"And what of Emma? It seems that her fast-following death kept you from carrying out your plan to get all of *her* money into the hands of the Rescue League."

"Yes and no." Alice Rose smiled mischievously. "When I went to tell her what it was that I was now compelled to do, courtesy of her sister's long-nursed hatred for her, Emma suffered an attack of nephritis and then fell down her back stairs."

"And died there as you stood watching?"

Alice Rose shook her head. "A couple of days later. But I cannot help attributing the demise to my threat."

"Are you pleased with this outcome?"

"I'm not pleased with the fact that I was unable to wring more money for the Animal Rescue League from the two sisters, but I'm quite satisfied that two of the three most notorious murderesses in the long chronicle of

New England criminality are now gone from this Earth. And the third—
that Bridget, whom Lizzie and Emma insisted on calling Maggie, probably
because their previous maid was named Maggie and they couldn't be
bothered to learn a new name—would receive a personal visit from me
if there were profit in it. Alas, there is not, and I fear for my own safety,
besides, since the maid has already demonstrated that she will not hesitate
to use a hatchet when the situation requires it."

"And what happens to the incriminating letter?"

"I plan to sell it to some future biographer for a kingly sum."

"No doubt to the benefit of the Fall River Animal Rescue League."

"That very charity."

"And where is the letter now?"

"Safe and quite secure. I have just this morning placed it in my safety
deposit box in the Union Savings Bank. That was Andrew Borden's bank,
you know."

1928

MISDEEMED IN INDIANA

Two things crossed Amelia's mind when she woke that morning. First that she was married. At long last. At the ancient age of thirty-one. When no one in her family thought it should ever happen. Here she was, wed for life to a handsome man, a prosperous man, officer in the local Kiwanis, a man who loved every little thing about her—even the fact that she wasn't from Richmond and wasn't (horrors!) even a Hoosier.

The second thing that crossed Amelia's mind was that the marriage, only one month old, was a mistake—a terrible, grievous mistake. For all his William Haines/Ramon Navarro boyish good looks, for all his charm and bonhomie, for all the respect that he commanded in this very odd community that had welcomed Amelia with, if not open arms, then at least with arms that were not blatantly closed, she should not have wed Chester Bream.

Richmond, Indiana, in the year 1928, was a Midwestern dichotomy of Quakers and non-Quakers; of men who wore white collars and those who wore blue; of men whose collars, in fact, were hidden under white hooded robes, and those men and women who were the object of their disfavor. This last group included Negro jazz musicians like Louis Armstrong and Joe "King" Oliver and Jelly Roll Morton, who recorded with the town's Gennett record label and were earning Richmond the impressive nickname "The Cradle of Recorded Jazz" in spite of all the Klanimosity.

Richmond had colleges. It had a large artistic community, and a full orchestra. But it also had factories that made farm machinery and lawnmowers and school buses. Amelia's new husband Chester was employed by Wayne Works, where the school buses were put together. He headed WW's national sales department. Chester, thirty-eight, had come a long way from his early years as stock boy at Knollenberg's Department Store, elastic-stitcher at the Atlas Underwear Company, and assistant to the chief ivory procurer for the Starr Piano Company.

Amelia wondered where her husband was this morning. She wondered if he'd gone to work as usual. The night before, as he was stalking out of the house, she'd asked where he'd be spending the night. He said he was going to the Rex Hotel. He packed a large suitcase. This made Amelia think that it might be a while before he ventured back home.

Amelia wanted to go home. Back home to Ohio. She wanted an end to the marriage, an end to this ill-begotten sojourn in Richmond. She didn't like Richmond. She'd made only one friend since Chester moved her here after their brief three-day honeymoon in Chicago. The woman was a neighbor. Her name was Lurelle. Lurelle was thirty-three and married to a fireman who spent over half of each week at Hose House #3 (on North A between 15th and 16th Streets). Lurelle's husband Gaines felt guilty for being away from his wife and three daughters for so long at a stretch. He easily agreed to Lurelle's demand that her kitchen be rewired and fitted with multiple outlets so that she could have as many electrical appliances as her lonely heart desired. On Amelia's first visit to drink coffee and exchange gossip about people whom Amelia neither knew nor had any desire to know, Lurelle showed off her new electric table grill, her electric corn popper, her flat-top toaster, her no-burnout iron, her electric waffle iron, and her shimmering, newly minted Nicalume four-piece percolator set with gold-plated creamer and sugar bowl.

Amelia woke at seven thirty. Thirty minutes later she was still in bed. She was looking at the roses that climbed the trellis outside her window. At eight fifteen she put her face into her pillow and cried. At eight thirty she studied a robin that had perched upon her windowsill. At eight forty she cried. At eight fifty-five she rose and put on her robe and went into the bathroom and prepared herself for a day filled with uncertainty.

Having dressed and having had some tea and a boiled egg that she cooked with her non-electric New Perfection Oil Cook Stove—or rather *Chester's* oil cook stove, because it was, after all, Chester's house—Amelia was roused from her reflective nibbling of a slice of buttered toast by a knock on the front door.

Was it Chester? Had he returned? Had he forgotten his key? And how did she feel about his coming back?

It wasn't Chester.

The young man at the door was Ichabod gangly. He had an Adam's apple protruding from his stringy neck that looked big enough to be an Adam's grapefruit. His suit looked to have been recently purchased, and ill fitted a man of his height and long pipe-stem limbs, giving too much of a view of his socks. It wasn't necessary for the slightly nervous young man to explain the purpose of his visit. He was holding it next to him. It was a vacuum cleaner—a new, self-contained, self-adjusted, dust and dirt-proof, lubricant-packed, ball-bearing-motored Greater Energex life-lasting cleaner, and it could be Amelia's for only $24.95.* (*Without attachments.) The young man, in spite of his greenhorn appearance, was salesman enough to have said all of this to Amelia before she was even able to return his "good morning."

As he finally took a breath, she wedged in. "Are you always this talkative so early in the morning?"

"Is it early?" He glanced at his wristwatch. The watch was easy to see since his cuffs and sleeves were nowhere in its vicinity. "It's after nine thirty."

"Then let me say that it's early for *me*. Moreover, sir, I'm not in the market for a vacuum cleaner."

"Perhaps you would change your mind, madam, if I told you that it's the best vacuum cleaner in its price range. It has several truly astonishing features. Are you familiar with the 'Airizer'?"

"No. And I haven't really much of a desire to be."

The man flashed a smile that said that he was all but certain Amelia's statement was only a passing jest. "The Airizer is a marvelous new way to air your blankets, pillows, woolens, and baby's things. It forces fresh air through every thread and fiber by vacuum. So, you see, our product not only sucks, but it also airs with sanitary precision."

With a sigh: "Yes. That is truly astonishing."

"May I step in and demonstrate our wonderful new product?"

Amelia shook her head. "This isn't a good time."

"Perhaps I may come in for a few minutes only? I'm eager to have you hold the easy-grip, ebonized wood handle. And we have three different brushes, each of which is earning the praises of thousands of housewives just like yourself."

"I really don't think—" Amelia shook her head. Tears began to well up in her eyes.

"I'm sorry. I didn't mean to be so pushy." The young salesman pulled a handkerchief from his shirt pocket and offered it to Amelia. "Please…"

Amelia took the handkerchief and dabbed at her eyes.

"The fact of the matter is that my husband bought me a new vacuum cleaner just last month. We were married in early June. I'm sorry to say that it isn't an Energex. It's a Hoover. He even bought me a Hamilton Beach carpet washer—the industrial kind that professional carpet cleaners use. He wants me to be very happy in our new domestic life together. But I'm not."

"I'm sorry to hear that."

"Would you like to come in for a cup of coffee? I would love to have someone to talk to, provided you don't try to sell me a vacuum cleaner I don't need."

"I don't suppose one cup of coffee would put me too much off my schedule. And I *have* been feeling a little draggy this morning."

Amelia held the door open for the man to enter. "Oh," she said, patting her eyes again. "What's your name?"

"It's Ray. Ray Gurson."

Ray set all of his demonstration equipment down on the floor near the front door and followed Amelia to the kitchen. Over her shoulder, Amelia said, "I also have some muffins. I made them yesterday. Do you like muffins?"

"I do, madam. Very much so."

"You may call me Amelia."

While Amelia was making coffee she spoke of her husband. "Do you know him? Chester Bream. The Breams have been in Richmond for three generations."

"I don't know too many of the non-Quaker families."

"You're a Quaker?"

"I grew up a Quaker. I don't know what I am now—just a vacuum-cleaner salesman, I guess."

"I don't know anybody in Richmond. Except a woman who lives down the street. Her kitchen is an electrical fire hazard, but that's all right because her husband's a fireman. And of course, I met some of Chester's family and friends at the wedding."

"That's a beautiful Hoosier cabinet."

"Chester bought it for me. He loves me very much. That's the problem. I wonder if I can ask you a question. You're a man."

Ray nodded.

"And I don't get to talk to too many men who aren't my husband, as a rule. I didn't have any brothers. And my father was shy—wasn't very comfortable discussing certain things."

"Certain things?"

"Don't you love the smell of brewing coffee? It infuses a room with such a wonderful aroma. I drank tea earlier. I don't know why. I don't know what I'm doing these days. Now may I ask you, Ray—you seem like a man of the world—is it a natural thing for a husband to want his wife to urinate on him?"

Ray blushed. And choked. "I beg your pardon?"

"My new husband. He has this proclivity. He didn't speak of it before we were married. But then afterwards—just last night, in fact—he asked me if I would squat over his stomach and pee all over him. He said that a lot of men enjoy this sort of thing. Is it something that *you* enjoy, Ray?"

Ray remained speechless for a quarter of a minute.

"I'm sorry. I've embarrassed you. Well, there's my answer, and I thank you for it. I knew he was a freak. I held out hope that maybe I was just a little behind the times. After all, it took me a while to acquire a taste for bathtub gin. And I very much like my hair long like this. I didn't see why I should bob it. But it just seemed to me that a husband asking a wife to pee on him was something very much outside the norm."

Ray stood up. "I should be going."

"You think I'm joking? I'm not joking. I threw my husband out of the house last night because of this. The very thought of it. Disgusting. And that awful way that he begged for it."

Amelia closed her eyes and shook her head.

Ray took a step away from the table.

"Before you go, I really would like you to tell me: Is this the sort of thing you would ever ask of your wife? I don't see a ring on your finger, so I'm speaking in terms of your *future* wife. Would you ask her to empty her bladder all over you? Would that excite you?"

Ray shook his head. Then he said emphatically, "No, it would not."

"Just as I thought. You've been very helpful, Ray. Are you sure that I can't talk you into staying for that cup of coffee? I promise to change the subject."

Ray shook his head again. "I really must go."

"I'm sorry if I offended you."

"Please. Give it no more thought."

Amelia was going to walk Ray to the front door, but he fled too quickly for her to keep up with him. In his haste he dropped the cleaner's library brush attachment (for the cleaning of portieres and draperies) and Amelia had to call after him and have him return momentarily to retrieve it. Then she watched him run down the street as if someone were chasing him.

She sighed.

It had felt very good to give voice to it. It felt even better to see Ray's appalled reaction. So her equally appalled reaction the night before *hadn't* been unreasonable! This gave her a warm sense of vindication.

Amelia went into the bathroom and sat down on the toilet and relieved herself. She had been holding her wee for hours, knowing that once she released the urine that had been stored for so long inside her, the image of her husband would appear in her mind's eye, writhing happily beneath her. And it would disgust her anew and make her question once again why she married a man who turned out to be so strange, and strange in such a repellent way.

Yet as she sat and urinated, the feelings of repulsion seemed to be receding. It was a most amazing thing. In that moment Amelia came to recoil from her husband and his proclivity just a little less. She even considered, for argument's sake, the logic of his position. That micturation was a natural act, and if he took delight in this natural act, especially when it involved the exclusive participation of his new wife whom he dearly loved, could not the case be made for there simply being those things that exist in this world in which some may find delight that others do not fully understand?

Amelia Bream spent the remainder of the day giving additional thought to her husband's position. It was a messy thing that he wanted her to do and he would be fully responsible for the cleaning up that it required, even if that cleaning necessitated the use of her brand-new industrial Hamilton Beach Carpet Washer. But Chester was a good man, a handsome and prosperous man, an officer in the Richmond Kiwanis, a man who loved every little thing about her, even those things that he had yet to learn.

Such as the fact that she liked her toes sucked. Licked and sucked hard—like the heavy-duty suction of a Greater Energex vacuum cleaner.

That evening Chester returned. Amelia greeted her spouse with loving arms. Then she whispered sweetly into his receptive ear, "I want to pee on you, Chester. And then I want my toes sucked. And later we'll have raspberry cobbler. I baked it for you this afternoon."

1929

TAKING A DIM VIEW IN MICHIGAN

Leonora Wallace was going blind. Glaucoma. Her mother knew this. Her friend Amanda Squalls knew this as well. Amanda worked in the Detroit Police Headquarters Building in Greektown. She was a file clerk in the Traffic Division.

This story is only partially about Amanda Squalls. But it is important to know where she worked. Were it not for Leonora's weekly trip to meet Amanda for lunch at New Hellas Café and eat saganaki and drink wine— Detroit had for the last several years flouted the Prohibition statute with near impunity—were it not for a friendship that included weekly luncheons of flaming cheese and lively gossip and Amanda's acicular opinions on the subject of how her forty-one-year-old friend Leonora should spend the second half of her life—the benighted half—there should be no story.

Leonora lived with her mother in Redford Township west of Detroit. Although the two were very close, Leonora enjoyed the time they spent apart, especially her visits to the Kunsky Redford Theatre not far from her house. The Kunsky was a beautiful new movie palace with a colorful Japanese garden motif, and Leonora was one of its most frequent patrons.

Sound was coming in. And sound movies couldn't happen too soon for a woman who was fast losing her eyesight.

Leonora worked as a sales clerk for C.S. Smith Hardware, a vocation that guaranteed she'd soon be unemployed. She was the store's first lady sales clerk, hired for her "chromo-smarts." Leonora sold house paint. She was exceptionally adept at guiding her customers through the lengthy catalogue of available hues: Beaver Brown, Chocolate Brown, Colonial Yellow, Dove, Fawn, Terra Cotta, Pea Green, Nile Green, Golden Green, Emerald Green, Willow Green, Pearl Gray, Mother Goose, Cremnitz

White, Brickdust, Sauterne, and American Vermilion (for firehouses). This is only a partial list.

"I'm going to miss it," said Leonora to her friend Amanda over lunch during one of those Tuesdays in October when the nation, though faced with an unstable stock market, was still gay and prosperous, and most of its citizens' problems could still be solved without jumping out of windows.

"Miss what?"

"Color. All the color in the world. I know the name of every color there is. And if a color doesn't have a name, I'm quite good at making one up."

"Such as?"

"Hmm. See the ribbon on that woman's hat? The cloche with the turned-up, scalloped brim? What color would you say the ribbon is?"

"It looks yellow."

Leonora shook her head. She smiled impishly. "That isn't just yellow, Mandy. It's yellow with a slight cast of white. I would call it Canary in the Snow."

"You would, would you?" Amanda laughed and took of sip of her thick, muddy Greek coffee.

The waiter came by to see if the two women would be having their usual dessert: baklava.

"We're so terribly drab and boring, aren't we, Pavlos?" said Amanda with a wink. "But the baklava is so sinfully good that I don't ever want to try anything else. What about *you*, Leonora?"

"Baklava," said Leonora with authority.

The two women watched the handsome and hirsute young waiter walk away.

"I want to have his baby," confided Amanda. "How about *you*, my dear?"

"That train has already left the station, love."

"I have no idea how you could possibly have reached the advanced age of—what is it, darling? Are we at the mid-century mark for you now?—without your ever having had a taste of—"

"I am forty-one," snapped Leonora. "But regardless, that window has closed, and I've made my peace with it."

"Oh, I don't believe that for a *minute*! You haven't *lived* at all. You've let the parade pass you by. And now..." Amanda bit her lip. She closed her eyes and leaned forward in her chair, wanting very much to say something her sensitivity to Leonora's feelings would not permit.

"Just spill it, Amanda."

Amanda pulled a cigarette case from her pocketbook and fumbled with the clasp. "And what is it you think I want to say?"

"I think, sweetheart, that you want to say that I have defied all the bookmakers' odds. I have lived and worked in a city, or rather very *near* a city of *men*. Of every sort of he-man steelforger, shipbuilder, carmaker— every sweat-dripping, brawny-limbed, big-shouldered, woman-hungry man that there could possibly be and for some reason known only to God, I have not had the good fortune to bring any of them permanently into my life. *Or* into my bed. And now I must live with the conse—"

"Sweet Jesus, Leonora. You've never been to bed with a man? Please tell me you're joking!"

"I'm not."

"What about the doughboy?"

"You mean Adam, with the reproductive wound?"

"Or the Glidden salesman. What was that handsome young man's name?"

"It was Vincent. Vincent liked colors even more than I did. He liked other pretty things as well. He collected lace."

"Poor, poor girl. And now you're going blind. And you won't even be able to *see* what it is that you've been missing."

"That was beyond cruel."

"It's true. Have you ever seen a man without his clothes on? Even if by accident? Your father?"

Leonora shook her head. "What's more, I am uncomfortable with this conversation."

"But surely you must know what a naked man looks like."

"I am not a nun, Leonora. I've seen pictures."

"My heart is breaking."

"It's my cross to bear. Let's change the subject. I may decide not to come for lunch next week if you don't turn off the pity faucet. *And* you're being rude. Not to mention lewd."

Leonora was forced to suspend her reproach of her friend; Pavlos had returned with dessert and Leonora's eyes were now level with his crotch, the perimeter of darkness in her narrowing glaucomatous field of vision fortuitously irising in on the waiter's groinal contours, both to Leonora's temporary delight and to her ultimate gloom and despair, for this was yet another reminder of what would be lost to her once her eyesight disappeared altogether.

But there was truth to what Amanda said, and Leonora knew it.

By the following week, Leonora had come to an important and rather bold decision that she felt she should share with her best friend. She could not—*would* not, it was now clear—lose her eyesight without having seen a man in the flesh, in *all* his flesh, an image that would create a lasting visual memory through all the years she would spend in darkness. She had reached the apex of this decision while watching *Coquette*, featuring a one-hundred-percent chattering Mary Pickford and the ruggedly handsome football-player-turned-screen-actor Johnny Mack Brown, whom Leonora would very much like to have glimpsed showering in some stadium locker room during his gridiron days.

It would be asking a lot of Amanda, but Leonora wished to enlist her best friend in soliciting some kind of viewing for Leonora's transitory pleasure and permanent retention. Amanda knew men—men of sufficient build who might agree to give Leonora a free look. Amanda knew Detroit coppers, both those who carried guns and those who wore gloves and directed traffic with balletic grace. She knew tough-as-nails, square-jawed federal agents, some of whom chased rum runners with patriotic zeal and others who were on the take but no less sthenically appealing. Amanda might even be able to entice a strapping young Canadian Mountie to ford the Detroit River from Windsor and remove every stitch of his uniform and undergarments (while keeping the Stetson securely in place). Leonora was sure that Amanda, after some initial sniggering, would agree to her odd yet desperately articulated request.

Tuesday came and Leonora found herself sitting in a chair in the Traffic Division of the Detroit Police Department waiting for Amanda. Her heart was pounding. Leonora had never in her life attempted anything so impetuous. And yet, Leonora's lifetime of prudence and circumspection had brought her to a point she was not proud to admit to. Men had shown interest in her. She had politely turned them down. Men had sought to bed her—she was sure of it. But she had been afraid and somewhat put off. *Is this all that men think about?* Leonora didn't believe herself to be priggish, and yet their advances—the advances of most of the men she'd met—seemed boorish and sloppy and presumptuous, and she would have no truck with them.

That was the old Leonora. The new Leonora wanted to see a live naked man in all his muscular glory before time ran out.

There was a man sitting next to her—a man perhaps in his mid-thirties—a good-looking man with curly black hair, a smooth-shaven face and half dimples that revealed themselves when his ear caught the punch line of a joke being told by another man a couple of chairs away. The good-looking man said hello to Leonora when he sat down and tipped his homburg brim politely before removing the hat altogether.

The clerk at the window called his name. It was James. James Touliatos.

"Aren't *you* next?" said the man, turning to Leonora. "You were here before me."

Leonora shook her head. "I'm just waiting for a friend. She works here and we're having lunch together."

The man—Mr. James Touliatos, who bore a slight resemblance to Pavlos the waiter, but was, thought Leonora, even better looking—got up from his seat and carried a sheaf of papers over to the window.

Leonora could hear snatches of his conversation with the clerk. Since the clerk had the louder voice, she got only half of the exchange: "Here is the application for certificate of title. Fill this out. The fee is a dollar. Have you owned a car before? Are you aware that the receipt of registration must be carried in the car at all times? What kind of vehicle is it? No reason. I just like cars. Except Fords. Don't tell them that in Dearborn or I might find myself out of a job." The two men laughed. Leonora thought that Mr. James Touliatos had a friendly, engaging laugh.

Amanda came out. She said that she couldn't get away. Someone from the Secretary of State's office was coming over for a meeting and they needed a stenographer. She was very sorry, but perhaps they could see each other over the weekend. She'd come up to Redford and they could go to that new musical picture, *Applause* with Helen Morgan. Cities were banning it all over the country, so it had to be good.

Amanda returned to her office. James had overheard the conversation. He approached Leonora. "You've been stood up for lunch. If I might be so bold, given that I'm a total stranger to you, how would you feel if *I* took you to lunch?"

"I would say, sir, that you *are* total stranger to me and *no*."

James nodded. He ruminated. "I wouldn't be a stranger to you if you got to know me. My names is Touliatos, by the way. I'm a welder with Great Lakes Engineering Works in Ecorse. I help to put freighters together."

He helps to build freighters, thought Leonora. *He has large arms. He must have a nice physique. I'll say no again as any proper woman would,*

but if he persists, I will pretend that he has worn down my resistance and
agree to have lunch with him.

She said no again. The man put on his hat, tipped the brim, and walked out.

Leonora died a little inside. She didn't get up. She sat for the next
moment ruing her decision. Then something miraculous happened. Mr.
James Touliatos returned. He walked straight up to Leonora and said, "I'm
going to ask once more, not because I'm a rude s.o.b., but because you
seem like a very nice woman, you've been stood up for lunch, and I feel
just a little sorry for you. I also note from the absence of a wedding ring on
your finger that you aren't married, and I happen to think that you might
be a charming and stimulating table companion."

"Sir, you have won me over," said Leonora with relief, and with a
sudden feeling of reckless abandon that took her by surprise.

James had a favorite restaurant he wanted to recommend. The New
Hellas on Monroe.

The two ate and drank and talked for over two hours. James loved his job,
but he was getting ready to move to upstate New York and try his hand
at farming. His life was a series of discrete chapters. He said this made it
interesting. He had been married, but the marriage hadn't worked out. He
saw his young daughter in San Francisco twice a year.

Leonora talked of her job, a little of her mother (trying her best to
couch her impatience with her mother's all-too-mothering personality in
gentle, non-critical terms), and then over baklava and American coffee,
she confided to James that she was going blind.

She didn't happen to mention the other thing.

James had a sister who was blind. She lived there in Detroit. James
wanted Leonora to meet her. James asked if Leonora might wish to go to
his sister's apartment and say hello.

"That would be nice. I mean, having someone I could talk to—someone
who could give me a sense as to what to expect."

"My newly registered car's just down the street. I'll drive us over."

"You mean right now?"

"Why not?"

Leonora shrugged. A jolt of happiness shot through her. It mattered less
now, her original mission. Just to know someone who could help her now that
the lights were rapidly dimming—what an unexpected gift that would be!

*

James rang the bell. The sister was not home. "I have a key. We'll go up and wait for her. She's probably out shopping."

Leonora grew suspicious.

"It's all right. She won't mind."

It was Leonora who minded. It didn't feel right. Although James had been funny and warm and kind, Leonora didn't trust people easily. But this had to change. Because life is difficult for a blind person who is incapable of putting trust in those whom she meets—those who have the benefit of sight. The blind man who asks for help crossing the street, isn't the request usually made of a total stranger? A balance must be struck. A balance between commonsensical caution and faith in the good intentions of the majority of human beings—even brash young men who don't take "no" for an answer.

James took two bottles of Pepsi-Cola from his sister's icebox and poured them into glasses of chipped ice. The two talked for a few minutes before James excused himself to use the bathroom, closing the door between the sitting room and the intervening bedroom behind him. He was gone for several minutes. Leonora felt awkward. Then Leonora felt a little afraid. She questioned why she was there, sitting with a stranger in a strange apartment. She wondered if she should leave. She even started up from the sofa, but then sat back down again.

And then the door opened and James appeared. He was naked. Completely naked. His body had been perfectly sculpted from years of manual labor. He was Michelangelo's David, but with greater muscularity (and no Victorian-appended fig leaf). All the colors of James's body sang out to Leonora: the Copenhagen Blue of his eyes, the Rustic Brown of his lips and Ebony Black of his wiry hair. The French Tan of his sun-kissed forearms, the more muted Cinnamon Heather and Velvet Brown of his upper arms, shoulders, chest, and legs. The Oyster White of his exposed buttocks and groin, the Autumn Brown of his scrotum and shaft, the Blush Pink of his peeking glans. It was all magnificent to Leonora. She didn't turn away. She got up from the sofa and walked up to the naked man she hardly knew and touched him, ran her hands all over him, absorbing every inch of muscle and sinew and appendage. Memorizing his body with both her eyes and her hands.

"How did you know?" she asked.

"Amanda's a good friend of mine. She knows that I'm a nudist. I'm joining Mr. Barthel's League for Physical Culture. He's starting a group in the Hudson Highlands in New York."

"Your body is beautiful."

"You're beautiful, too, Leonora."

"Amanda told you to say that."

"She did. I won't deny it. So now I'll say it again, because *I* want to say it. I find you very attractive. I want to get to know you better. How about I get dressed now and the two of us take a nice walk through Belle Isle Park?"

Leonora nodded. "Is there a sister and is she really blind?"

"Yes. We'll meet her later. Oh, and I really *did* have to register my new car. Funny how things work out sometimes."

Leonora watched as the proudly naked James Touliatos turned and went back into the bedroom. Regardless of what happened between James and her from that point forward, she was enormously grateful to her friend Amanda for having brought the two of them together. And she didn't know how she could ever thank her.

But she tried nevertheless. That next week she bought Amanda's lunch. You know where.

1930

WITHOUT APRON STRINGS
IN DELAWARE

The woman lived in an old ramshackle boardinghouse two blocks from the boardwalk in Bethany Beach. Her eyesight was failing and she had to squint up at the balding middle-aged man standing before her. She was sitting with another woman on a bench in front of the weather-beaten clapboard building. At first she doubted what the man had said when he introduced himself, but then she saw something in his eyes that reminded her of a man she'd known when she was young.

Jerome.

She had always believed Jerome to be the father of her second child, whom she had given up as an infant. The stranger's eyes now confirmed it. The eyes spoke. They asked things of the woman. Jerome had been persistent in his bedroom advances. It was easy to see how his son would be persistent in his search for his mother.

"Would the two of you like some privacy?" asked Mrs. Grosbard. "I can make a pot of tea and take it up to your room."

"I think I'd like to stay out here, if the young man doesn't mind." Sadie Craddock turned to the man she now knew to be her son. "This is my favorite time of year. The breeze is so cool and the ocean so kind."

Mrs. Grosbard smiled at the man and got up. She turned and climbed the stoop and disappeared inside, the click of the screen door's latch punctuating her departure.

A seagull landed on a grassy patch of sand nearby. It looked about for some stray morsel to eat. Sadie Craddock patted the wooden bench where she wanted her son to sit.

It was an old bench and seemed out of place in front of the boardinghouse. Harold wondered if it had once sat bolted to the boardwalk and then been replaced by something newer and shinier. He wondered if it had been brought here to end its days in the company of creatures equally old and only slightly more ambulatory.

Harold sat down. The sun, which had been bold, now retreated behind a rack of clouds. Harold took off his hat and brushed his brow with the sleeve of his shirt. His forehead was dry, but it was force of habit. Harold worked out of doors as a railway traffic inspector.

"How did you track me down?" she asked after he had settled in next to her.

"Aunt Emily said she'd heard that you'd moved to the Delaware coast a couple of years ago. She thought you'd become a Disciple of Christ. Isn't this where ocean-loving Disciples of Christ wind up?"

It was hard for Harold to look at Sadie while sitting so close to her, but he wanted very much to do so. He had wondered for years what she would look like if he ever found her. Instead he looked at the sliver of seascape tightly framed by the two buildings across the street. The boardinghouse was near enough to the ocean that Harold could hear the cadence of its surf—near enough to smell its salty, fishy scent.

"How is Emily? It's been years since I've seen your aunt."

"She's well. She lives in Plainfield, New Jersey. So you aren't denying that I'm your son?"

Sadie took up Harold's left hand and sandwiched it between her own hands, each age-spotted and osseous. "You have your father's hands. Strong hands. He's dead, isn't he?"

Harold nodded. "When Aunt Emily told me who I was a few years ago, we talked a lot about you and about my dad—the way he'd come and go when I was young—checking in with me, I suppose, seeing what I was to become. And then he stopped coming. I was fifteen, sixteen by then. I knew what it meant. I knew that the drinking had finally done him in."

"All the men I lay with drank. That's one of the reasons I wouldn't marry them." Sadie released her son's hand. He allowed it to lie limp and unattended upon the wooden slats of the weathered bench.

"How many children did you have?" he asked.

"Four. By four different men. Three girls and you. You went to the finest couple I knew: Jerome's sister Emily and her husband Ennis. They couldn't have children of their own. They treated you well, I imagine."

"Very well," said Harold. "You're a Disciple of Christ now. Have you mended your ways?"

"I have. Most whores do when they reach a certain age. It's either that or death by drink or injection." Sadie swept her hand through the air to indicate the tiny sea town around her. "Not so terrible a place to pass the remaining years of one's life. Quite churchy, but very quiet. Even in the summer. Not like Rehoboth and Ocean City. So, you see, I haven't come to a tragic end. I'm relatively happy in my final chapter."

Harold pulled back. He wanted to take in every crag and wrinkle upon his mother's face, to see his own reflection in her eyes.

"Do you want to know anything about *me*?" he asked.

Sadie shook her head. She watched the seagull take wing to seek scraps at some other doorstep. "Whatever good has happened to you in your life will only make me regret the fact that I wasn't there to share it. Whatever bad will only make me feel guilty that I couldn't offer support in your times of difficulty."

"So you feel guilty? I mean, about having given me up?"

"Some days I feel terribly guilty. But the feeling doesn't cloud my every hour. I was a selfish woman, Harold. I wouldn't have made a very good mother. This was for the best. At the same time, I'm not the worst creature that God has ever placed upon this Earth. I've had my charitable moments. Some might say that my giving you and your sisters up was a charitable act in its own way."

"I didn't come here to judge you. Only to meet you."

"And what will you take away from our visit, Harold?"

"This won't be my only visit. I'd like to see more of you, with your permission."

Sadie shook her head. "Let's limit ourselves to this one time, shall we?"

"Why?"

"I brought you into this world. And then I sent you away. That was my choice. I reconciled myself to that choice many years ago."

"And do I have no choice in this? It's *my* choice that I should see you again. I choose as well to find my sisters and give them the chance to meet their mother while she's still among the living."

Sadie laughed. "A man of purpose. What do you do for a living, Harold? Are you a politician of some sort?"

Harold shook his head, his cheeks mantling over the precipitancy of his outburst.

There was music now, coming through the window of Mrs. Grosbard's second-floor lodgings. It was a song that had been made popular by the Brox Sisters several years earlier. Mrs. Grosbard had put the record on her Victrola. Mrs. Grosbard could not possibly let this momentous encounter between long separated mother and son go without appropriate musical commentary.

The three songbirds from Tennessee sang in sweet harmony:

Tie me to your apron strings again.
I know there's room for me.
Upon your knee.
Bring back all those happy hours when
You kissed my tears away…

"Mrs. Grosbard has slightly missed the mark," said Sadie with gentle amusement. "That song. It's about a child that leaves its mother but then comes back again. There's a history there—a history that you and I don't share."

"I'd like to see you again. I live in Philadelphia. I'm not so far away."

"And what if I don't wish to see *you* again? What if to me you are only a reminder of something I'm ashamed of?"

"Are you ashamed of *me*?"

"Only of having given you up."

Please take me back tonight,
Where I belong.
Sing a cradle song to me and then
Won't you tie me to your apron strings again?

There had never been apron strings. Harold knew this.

The final matter to be decided was whether there should be a parting embrace. Sadie put her son's mind at ease. She wrapped her arms around him and kissed him on the cheek. There were tears in his eyes as he walked away. He wanted to turn and look back but he held himself steady and did not.

Late that night Sadie walked in the moonlight to the ocean's edge. She stood before the lapping sea and then stepped into it. She moved slowly through the waves and finally disappeared beneath them.

The ocean was kind.

Harold would return. That was certain.

She didn't want to be there when he came back.

1931
AWED AND WONDERING IN CONNECTICUT

Let's start with that actor with the big ears. Clark Grable or something like that. He played a gangster in *A Free Soul* and he slapped Norma Shearer, who played his girlfriend. And then there was that other gangster picture *The Public Enemy*. And James Cagney is sitting at the breakfast table in his pajamas and he smacks Mae Marsh in the face with a grapefruit, just like it's the most natural thing in the world to be doing first thing in the morning (although she seems pretty shocked when he gives her the business). And just last spring there was that big dinner at the Metropolitan Club in New York where Theodore Dreiser slapped Sinclair Lewis in the face. *Twice*. He probably would have done it a third time if somebody hadn't intervened. And I just read about this thirty-hour face-slapping competition they had in Kiev just a few weeks ago.

Seems like everybody's slapping everybody else's face this year. It's an absolute mania. So the fact that I slapped Hank's tonight shouldn't have been any big stop-the-presses kind of surprise. But you couldn't tell that from the way he looked at me with those "Say it ain't so, Joe" droopy peepers of his—giving me the kind of hangdog look that can nearly tug a person's heart right out of her chest.

I stared right back at my husband, my hand still hanging in the air like I just might do it again, just like that talented yet pugnacious American novelist, Theodore Dreiser.

This is when Hank calmly took my hand and brought it down to my side, using his other hand to rub some of the sting out of his cheek.

"Well, why'd you *say* it?" I asked matter-of-factly, my rage having fled just as quickly as it came.

"You asked me a question and I answered honestly. Why'd you ask it if you didn't want me to give you a truthful answer?"

Hank walked over to the icebox. He took out a bottle of milk and held it up to his cheek.

"I didn't hit you that hard. Are you trying to make me feel bad?"

Hank shrugged. He got a glass from the cabinet and poured himself some milk. He returned the bottle to the icebox and sat down at the kitchen table. He stared at the glass of milk and I stared at him. The window was open, and through it we could both hear Eddy Cantor's crooning voice wafting down from the Petersons' new Atwater Kent upstairs. It reminded me of our own RCA Radiola 60 Super-Heterodyne tabletop, which my parents bought us for Christmas last year, but which we had to sell through the want ads this past summer when Hank lost his job with Merchants' All-Risk.

Generally speaking, I like Eddie Cantor's voice, but now for some reason it grated on my nerves. I closed the window.

I sat down across from my husband. "I suppose I asked you that question because I was expecting you'd answer a different way."

"And when I didn't, you slapped me."

"It wasn't so much an angry slap as a slap of awe and wonder."

Hank mumbled the words "awe and wonder," then took a drink of milk.

"Do you want some of that cake?" I asked.

"Is there any left?"

"One more slice. You can have it. I couldn't eat anything right now."

As I was getting the last slice of cake for Hank, he turned to me, droplets of milk clinging to his Warner Baxtery moustache. "I can't find another job. I don't know *when* I'll find another job. For good or bad, you're the sole breadwinner right now, Frances. We can't afford for you to get yourself fired as well."

I sat back down. The last slice of chocolate cake was larger than I'd remembered. I brought two forks.

"You answered very quickly, Hank. You answered as if there was no need to even think about what this means."

"It means, honey, that I'm giving you permission to commit adultery with your boss. If I were a better husband, I would put my foot down. I would defend your honor and our marriage. I'm not a better husband. I am a failure as a provider. Ergo, I am a failure as a husband. When it comes right down to it, I'm probably also a failure as a human being. I have been thinking about jumping off the Bulkeley Bridge. I know it isn't very tall, but if I hit the water just the right way it might slap me so hard I'll get knocked out and then I'll drown."

"Oh, shut up, Hank."

I took a bite of cake. It was delicious. Rosemary Peterson makes the most delicious cakes in Hartford. And why shouldn't she? Her husband's a chef.

The Petersons have a good marriage, by all appearances. Tom works at one of the nicest hotels in town and their little girl Peggy just won the Baby Clara Bow lookalike contest. Hank and I have been trying to have children for five years, and it's probably for the best that we haven't succeeded since things have gotten so difficult for us as of late, financially speaking.

This morning I went in to ask my boss at the railroad yard for a raise, and he said, "Well, of course not," but that he was glad that I came in, and "please sit down" and "I have two letters to dictate, Frances, and then a question I need to put to you." And he dictated his two letters and then he asked the question, which required a slight preface: there are a lot of out-of-work secretaries out there, Frances, times being tough for *everybody* these days…

And here he gestured out his window and toward the yard, where, with exquisite timing, one of his yardmen was in the process of chasing off two hobos with obvious hopes of securing free passage and gratis accommodations on one of our empty outgoing boxcars that afternoon… so would I consider continuing to be his secretary between the hours of eight and five, and then after hours and on weekends doing some things for him that his wife was unwilling to do?

"Errands?" I asked naïvely.

"You're very beautiful, Miss Hellmann."

"*Mrs.* Hellmann, Mr. Gaither. I am married."

"I like to think of you as *un*married, Miss Hellmann. Unmarried and willing to do those things for me that my wife, who is not an adventurous woman—who really is not much of a woman at all, but a fleshy cow, a Marie Dressler sort of foghorn-throated, muscle-bound sort of—I will just put it right out there, Miss Hellmann—*gorgon*. The marriage is all but—well, this is certainly beside the point, I'm sure. The point is that your job now depends on whether or not you will be able to meet my new requirements for keeping the position. I'll give you until tomorrow to make up your mind. Should you decide against my proposal, I'll have no choice but to let you go."

"Oh." I looked out the window. One of the hobos was being clubbed by the yardman. I turned away. "I'll have to talk it over with my husband."

"Your husband? You're pulling my leg."

I shook my head. "I'd really like to speak with him about this. He may not like it."

Mr. Gaither exhaled rather noisily. He ran his hand over his mouth with some exasperation and a little bit of pity, as if I were too stupid to see that talking his proposition over with Hank was something that only an imbecilic woman would do.

"And if he doesn't like it, where does that put things? You're out of a job *and* you could be out of a marriage. Do you want that, Miss Hellmann?"

"*Mrs.* Hellmann, Mr. Gaither. And I will consider your proposal. I will. But I really have to speak with Hank about it. It is only right. We took vows. I don't want to break my vows to him without his permission."

Mr. Gaither shook his head. He wore a grimace that said that he was more than a little put out with me. I think the look also said that he didn't believe I was going to speak to Hank. I was bluffing, testing him. And if this were true, if he called my bluff—well, where was the risk in having ever asked such an audacious thing of me? Whom otherwise would I tell? What person of consequence would believe that he had actually used this awful economic depression to compromise me in such a way? I had no avenue for appeal or redress. So testing him like this could only be a stupid move.

"Ask him if you wish, Miss Hellmann, but if you do, don't bother to come to work tomorrow. It should not be my desire each time we embrace to be on silent alert for the approaching footsteps of a cuckold with a gun."

"Hank doesn't have a gun. He does have a very sharp fishing knife, though. The kind you gut the big fish with."

Mr. Gaither lost a little of the color in his face.

Hank laughed when I told him this. And I told it all to him in between forkfuls of Mrs. Peterson's Dutch chocolate cake (did I mention that Monday was my birthday?) and stolen sips of Hank's milk. I always tell my husband everything. Just as he tells everything to me. We are very open and honest with one another. Which has made the difficulties of the last several months all the harder to bear. Night after night we have lain in bed and discussed the bleak uncertainty of our joint future. Night after night Hank has held me close to him as we have yearned in a single voice for things to get better, for the Depression to end, for Eddie Cantor to sing again to us in our very own living room, and not through the open kitchen window.

"But did you really mean it, Hank? That you would have actually agreed to what that lecherous old man was asking?"

"Well, *yes*. On practical grounds, of course. Look at the alternative. Me selling apples on a street corner and you taking in laundry." He added, "And you're not even very *good* at laundry."

I felt like slapping him again. Hank had surprised me. No, it was something stronger than surprise. It was utter stupefaction. Total awe and wonder. To think that he would give me up in such a way, regardless of the guaranteed return. I felt a little sick.

After a long moment, I said, "Well, your answer shouldn't matter so much at this point. Because I'm fired."

"Maybe I should call him. Maybe we could work something out."

The second slap came even harder than the first. I had a little of Mrs. Peterson's cake on my fingertips and they left parallel streaks of chocolate frosting upon his cheek. I was like Norma Shearer in that other movie—the one she made early in her career—in which *she* got to do the slapping. It had the most appropriate title you could think of—that is, for a movie in which there is no shortage of face-slapping going on: *He Who Gets Slapped*. She slapped Lon Chaney, who played a clown.

That was my husband to a T. My Hank. The slappable clown.

But the clown had one final antic to put across before he left the stage. "There's something I haven't told you, honey," he said, keeping his face straight and solemn, though I could feel that there was mischief just below the surface. "Your boss Mr. Gaither called before you got home. I think he started to get nervous about you spilling the beans to me. He said he called to tell you that he'd decided to give you the raise you asked for. No mention of his having thought about firing you, by the way. Seeing that I had lost my job and we needed the dough, the raise was something he was glad to do. Besides, you were a good secretary. Of course, he conveniently left out the *real* reason."

"And what was the *real* reason?" I asked, tenderly wiping the chocolate smudges from my husband's reddened cheek with my moistened index finger.

"That he didn't want me to come down to his office and gut him like a fish."

I leaned back in my chair in a state of joyous awe and wonder. My husband has the most darling smile. He's the best husband. To think that he'd even kill for me!

1932

FASCISTIC IN D.C.

They brought the troops over from Fort Myer in trucks, and the ones from Fort Washington, why, they came up the Potomac in a steamer. I suppose that was an improvement over what had happened on July 14. That was the day, you see, that Vice President Curtis got tired of watching all of us unemployed veterans marching back and forth outside his office window on Capitol Hill, and called out the Marines. Curtis's successor John Nance Garner once called the job of vice president "not worth a bucket of warm spit." Well, Vice President Curtis, he must've felt a little different, because that Kansas Big Chief used the leverage of his office on the fourteenth to summon a whole contingent of Marines all the way from the Navy Yard just to help improve his view of the Capitol Grounds.

They came in streetcars. For true. In full gear, bayonets fixed. And a lot of good they did. Police Chief Glassford was fit to be tied. He called the vice president a "hysterical meddler." And some of the veterans knew some of the Marines besides and it ended up being like Old Home Week at the U.S. Capitol.

July 28 was different. Nobody was smiling. Tar-paper shacks in all the little rag-and-tin-can villages throughout D.C. were going up in flames. The tanks were rolling and the tear gas grenades were flying. People who didn't have nothing to do with anything were coughing and tearing up in the eyes and cussing the president and cussing his chief of staff, Douglas MacArthur, who was leading the charge. And I was hightailing it back to Anacostia Flats, where the largest of all the encampments had been set up. (The biggest Hooverville in the country, it was said.) Trying to get myself back by my own cardboard and packing-crate cottage (the one with the egg-carton roof) to snatch up what few belongings I had in the world before the troops put a match to them, the way they was doing over by Camp Glassford.

We gave our camp the name of Camp Marks—named for the commander of the city's Eleventh Police Precinct, Sidney J. Marks, who was with us from the beginning. See, it was Marks and Glassford who saw us all coming and did right by us—giving us a place to bivouac and finding food for us when the federal government would have turned us all away at gunpoint on Day One. Some of those sons of bitches who said we was all Communists, why, they used the camp name to prove their case. They spelled it Camp Marx. For true.

I came from New Orleans with my colored pal Odell. We been friends since we was kids together in the bayou, me and him. And I only mention he was colored to make a couple of points here: that we *both* served in Uncle Sam's army. I was in the Battle of Belleau Wood, where I took shrapnel into my hindquarters, and Odell, not being among them coloreds who got to serve with the French Africans, got hisself put on kitchen and ditch-digging duty until the signing of the Armistice.

But there was no Jim Crow here in Camp Marks. You find this hard to believe? Believe it: black men and white men—all veteran soldiers of the United States of America, eating and sleeping (making dodo, me and Odell calls it) and rising together at reveille and parading side by side and visiting the Sallies together at the Salvation Army hut (what a collection of little cuties they were, in their doughnut girl bonnets!)—puts a fellow in mind of being at liberty in France back in the day, except there was no Red Cross here in Anacostia. The Red Cross wanted nothing to do with the Bonus Expeditionary Force.

But white and black, it made no never mind, and that's probably one of the reasons that the government thought we was all Communists. These caps would come into the camps and you could tell they was spies and snitches because of the way they'd give a closer eye to the Negroes and the Jews. But it wasn't nothing like the Soviet brotherhood of man that put us all so warm and friendly with each other; it was just plain old-fashioned *American* brotherhood. You see, we had a lot in common. We'd all served under the American flag and now our country had turned its back on us—every one of us. And it was time to demand our due, all in one loud voice.

Me and my soap box. I would've voted for Roosevelt if I'd been able when the election come up later that year—wanted more than anything to see this country taken out of the hands of the damned plutocrat Republicans and Mellon-aires who got us into this fix. But I was back to riding the rails by then. Me and Odell. Wondering if we was ever going to see that bonus for service in the Great War that was promised to us in 1924 and then deferred for twenty-one more years out of pure political meanness.

Me and Odell was over on the north banquette of Pennsylvania Avenue when that Little Caesar sends in his Cossacks with the tanks and the guns and the gas masks, and we was watching the men scatter and listening to the frightened screams of the mothers and their boos. (You'd be surprised how many of us former doughboys brought our wives and babies along. Sometimes they just had no other place to go.) And I walk up to this one fuzz-faced soldier boy who's fixing to put on his gas mask and do his dirty business with the tear gas, and I say, "*I* used to wear one of dose, too, chief. Of course I was fighting the Huns, not my fellow Yanks."

And the boy—'cause I grant you he was nothing more than a boy, no more than the age *I* was when I went off to fight the Kaiser—he gives me such a sad-ass look, and he says with hardly any volume to his voice at all: "I'm just doing what I've been ordered to do."

"Uh huh," I say. "And dat man over dere, the one on the ground—" says I, as me and Odell are looking over at Shorty, who came with us to see if there was any truth to the rumors about sending in the cavalry against us. Shorty's on the ground from where one of the cavalrymen swung his saber and sent him tumbling. His banged-up face and arms were K&B purple. "Dat man dere was three times decorated."

The soldier boy said he had to throw his tear gas grenade now and we'd best be moving on down Pennsylvania Avenue if we knew what was good for us, and then he put on his gas mask, and Odell and me, we shot off running.

All the way to Camp Marks.

Here was our crime: We came to Washington, D.C., to ask for help from our government. It wasn't like what some of them politicians was saying—that we was asking for special treatment just because we'd been soldiers. But we came back from a war that had filled the pockets of our civilian brothers and was an especially good thing for their bosses on account of all the profiteering. And a hell of a lot of us veterans had a hard time finding work. The jobs we had when we went "Over There" weren't waiting for us "Back Here." And there wasn't a lot of hiring going on elsewheres neither. Some of us eventually landed on our feet, but then the Depression hit and we lost our footing all over again. Millions of us. And the country was supposed to do right by us and compensate us for putting ourselves in the trenches in service to the American flag. But they reneged.

And we got mad.

Some folks gave a listen to us. Some fed us. And the chief of police looked the other way when we built the saddest junk-pile testaments to this damned Depression you ever saw, right within view of the Capitol building, of the White House, right there in the shadow of the Washington Monument. For true.

But there were them others who wanted us gone. As of yesterday.

That afternoon in Washington, D.C., one man lay dead and another dying. The city, it was turned mightily on its head. But General MacArthur was ready for whatever might come. And he was dressed to the military nines. I hear tell he sent one of his aides back to Fort Myer to fetch his polished riding boots. For true. The general was ready to vanquish his foes with all the horses and all the men and all the Goddamned firepower he could muster. Forgetting exactly who those foes actually were.

I was one. And Odell was another. And there was Shorty with all his medals, crawling on the ground like a thrice-kicked dog. All this came back to me when that son of a bitch MacArthur got his insubordinate ass whipped by Truman in '51 and I remembered it again when I wrote the son of a bitch to tell him why he'd best not think of running for president the next year. That he wouldn't get the veteran vote—at least not the World War I veteran vote, because there was a hell of a lot of us doughboys still around in '52 and we had real good memories about how he turned the American army against its own during the bloody summer of '32.

I also reminded him what me and Odell saw in the middle of that wide Pennsylvania esplanade while his troops was pushing us all farther and farther south.

He was sitting in his limousine and talking to the reporters and photographers.

"Point down to the troops, General," the photographers said, trying to pose him.

And he grinned and obediently pointed.

"Now give us a salute, General."

No grin. Just a face of utmost seriousness for the cameras. And the salute.

"Now get out and stand beside your horse."

Someone fetched the general's horse. Standing next to his mount, he soaked up every ounce of that limelight for the cameras. It was probably the best day he ever had, in my humble Cajun opinion, until 1944 when he sloshed through the water on his triumphant "return" to Leyte, with his speech all typed out nice and proper and ready to be delivered to the grateful Filipinos.

Odell used to ask me, years later, about my hatred of that corncob-pipe-smoking Napoleon, when the two of us were settled back down, him with his Vera and all those "chillren," and me with my Peggy, who dared to take a chance on a forty-three-year-old confirmed bachelor with a little shrapnel still left in his ass and an itch to go off and fight in this new world war—an itch that was never going to get itself scratched. And I'd remind him that when the historians got out their pens, and the Hoovers (I'm also referring to that Commie-obsessed FBI squirrel) and Deputy Chief of Staff Moseley and Major Patton (Eisenhower, I think, was always embarrassed over the orders he had to follow on that sad day) got all their Communist-uprising bullshit knocked down by the truth of who it was who actually lived in those crowded mud-caked camps during those rainy weeks of June and July, 1932—when all was said and done and everybody knew the whole truth, folks would be reminded that it was Douglas MacArthur who deliberately disobeyed the president's order not to send his avenging army across the 11th Street Drawbridge and upon the boggy fields of Anacostia that night. It was Douglas MacArthur who ignored a presidential order for the purpose of his own bastard glory. Sound a little familiar, don't it?

Camp Marks. Where Odell and me had hardly any time at all to stuff what little clothes we had into our beat-up grips, and tuck away our official discharge papers and our meager souvenirs from our occupation of a land that belonged to us by right of American citizenship.

We retreated alongside the thousands of other impoverished veterans of the War to End All Wars, and their wives and their children. And the stories began to circulate about the boy who wasn't allowed back into his soon-to-be-ignited hovel to get his pet rabbit, of the Negro bayoneted in the foot for evacuating too slowly, of the babies hospitalized from the gas, of the woman who wasn't permitted to pick up all of the things that had spilled from her gunnysack and a moment later everything she owned was trod under a cavalry horse's heavy hoof.

It seemed like Belgium all over again. Except that unlike the Flemish facing the invading Germans, we'd hardly offered up any resistance at all. And when it was over, where was our Herbert Hoover, the man who had headed the Belgian relief effort? Why, hunkered down in the White House, that's where! No longer the brave humanitarian. Just a frightened, cowering little man, sorely inconvenienced by the audacity of our presence. They say we'd made him a prisoner in that place, and that in the end, we'd kept him from getting hisself re-elected.

President Hoover must have stood at his window and watched Washington burn, just as Odell and I watched the flames from the hills above Anacostia, surrounded by the huddling mothers putting wet cloths to the tear-gas-stung eyes of their whimpering babies.

This was the America I had fought for?

Yet I knew in my optimistic heart that better days were coming. Because there was one thing that struck the heart of every visitor to Camp Marks that summer. It was the presence of all them American flags. Every state's bivouac had its own Stars and Stripes, you see. Men marched with them held aloft, waved them, saluted them on every occasion. And in the smoking aftermath of the attack upon the camp, there was one flag upon a pole that stood alone, untouched, rippling through the smoke of that night's terrible fires. All was smoldering, jagged rubble around it. Yet the flag was still there.

For true.

1933

LETTING GO IN MISSOURI

"When did you know?"

"'Seems like I've wanted to be an iceman as far back as I can remember. I think about the times when I was a kid and Ma and Polly and me were living at the Broussard place just a few blocks east of here. There'd be these hot summer days when the landlady would forget to take the ice card out of the window from the time before. And the iceman, he'd see the card and climb those two flights of stairs with that dribbling, fifty-pound block of ice on his back, and Mrs. Broussard would realize her error and make her hundred-and-one apologies, but he'd be damned if he was gonna play Sisyphus's cousin and haul that ice all the way back down to his wagon, so you know what he did?"

"Chucked it out the window?"

"Raised the sash and pushed it right out."

"That sounds like a reason *not* to want to become an iceman."

"There's an upside to the story. That big block of ice—it would hit the concrete in the courtyard below and shatter. And the kids in the neighborhood, they'd hear the noise and all come running over to grab up those frozen chunks to cool themselves off with. I wanted to be the guy who made all the kids happy. What time is it?"

Ralph Morris looked at his wristwatch. "Ten till."

Garth Kordel clucked his tongue in wonderment. "Did you have any idea so many people would show up?"

Ralph shook his head. "Let's get out of the car. I feel like a federal agent on stakeout."

The two men, both in their mid-thirties, stepped out of Ralph's Ford Deuce coupe. Ralph leaned back, planted a foot on the running board, and lit up. Garth took in the gathering crowd. It was mostly men, a few women, even a kid or two in tow. A man and little boy walked by.

"Isn't it a little past his bedtime?" Garth called after them.

The man stopped and turned. His look was open and friendly. "Brother, I've been waiting thirteen years for the chance to wet my whistle legally. This is a historic moment and I want my boy to remember it."

The man and the boy moved on.

There was an electrical current running through the crowd. A brass band was assembling near the front entrance to the Anheuser-Busch brewery. Word was that they'd begin playing right at the stroke of midnight.

The new president, Franklin D. Roosevelt, planned to keep his campaign promise to repeal Prohibition. In the meantime he'd gotten Congress to amend the Volstead Act, thus allowing 3.2 percent beer in localities that were happy to have it. St. Louis, home of both Anheuser-Busch and the Falstaff Brewing Company, would most certainly have it. Ralph and Garth were among the hundreds who had gathered to be the first to taste Busch's "near beer." Nobody was getting drunk that night, but it was a welcome taste of what was to come. In just four days, Michigan would take the first step toward getting rid of the bane of Prohibition forever. Its state convention would ratify the 21st Amendment (proposed by Congress only six weeks earlier) by a walloping three-to-one margin.

America wanted desperately to be wet again.

Ralph and Garth had claimed their spot a couple of blocks from the brewery about an hour earlier. They had invited their wives to join them, but both women preferred to stay home. Ralph's wife Vivian didn't like crowds; she had a delicate and retiring nature. Garth's wife Caddy didn't like *Ralph*. She found him arrogant and overbearing.

The two men had become friends at a young age. Garth was poor. Ralph's family was in the ice business. When he reached his majority Ralph inherited Morris Ice. Ralph brought Garth on as a deliveryman, then later promoted him to the job of icehouse foreman. The friendship remained intact, but Caddy had always seen the cracks in the ice. It's hard for one friend to be Gebieter (in the parlance of Garth's German heritage) over another. Sometimes Ralph had to make decisions that didn't benefit his employee Garth. Garth tried to be understanding. Caddy didn't try quite so hard.

Over the previous hour, the men, both football fans, had discussed the sordid details of the recent death of Dr. Fonsa Lambert, who had won fame for formalizing the rules of the game. He had been shot by his seventeen-year-old son Samuel, after the boy had walked in on Lambert trying to choke his wife (Samuel's mother) to death.

The song had said that "happy days" were here again, but there was too much evidence to the contrary. At a time of national economic troubles, the U.S. Navy had come under fire for putting thousands of precious tax dollars into the construction of helium-filled airships. Despite improved building methods, the aircraft were difficult to fly and often perilous to land. Earlier that day there had been a somber press conference held for the national news services. The only three survivors of the crash of the USS *Akron*, a steel-framed "flying aircraft carrier," were brought out to give their account of the tragedy. The dirigible had gone down in rough winds off the coast of New Jersey two days earlier. Investigators would later conclude that the crash couldn't have been helped, although having life jackets on board for use by its seventy-six passengers and crew—most of whom perished by drowning—might have somewhat mitigated the tragic outcome.

The whole country was talking about the accident, along with the pending legalization of three-two beer, and FDR's recently declared bank holiday. The *Akron* disaster was front and center, though. It represented, for Ralph, just another star-crossed attempt by the government of the United States to try to turn the impossible into the possible at great cost. "You take Prohibition, Garth. This idea that you can lead a man to abstinence through constitutional fiat—it was asinine from the very start, and look at all the havoc it's wrought. And you can't put balloons up in the air and pretend like they're gonna do anything but bounce around like balloons. Every one of these dirigibles has been trouble. The *Akron*'s had one deadly mishap after another. Why, they killed two men just trying to land the Goddamned thing last year."

Garth nodded. People had started to form themselves into a line.

"Should we be lining up, too?"

"No need. There's plenty of beer in there for everybody. Besides, I'm tired of watching this country lining itself up: bread lines, unemployment lines. As a nation we're always queuing ourselves up for one sorry reason or another."

Garth licked his lips and winked. "But this is a *good* reason."

"Now you take that accident last year," said Ralph, who never had much regard for clean conversational transitions, "when the *Akron* tried to land in San Diego."

"They said the sun heated up the helium too much—made the ship too buoyant."

Ralph nodded. "You see the newsreel footage? They got this landing crew of inexperienced Navy men trying to hold the thing down with trail ropes. Then all of a sudden she starts to rise up into a nose stand, and they've got to free the mooring cable from the mast. In all the confusion most of those boys let go of their lines. But four sorry saps hang on."

"One let go pretty quick, though, right?"

"Yeah. Maybe fifteen feet off the ground—the kid breaks his arm, I think. But the other three—they *don't* let go. I mean, Garth, the *Akron's* drifting higher and higher and those three boys—they're still dangling from the ends of their ropes like maybe they're hoping that ship's gonna miraculously come right back down again. Jesus!"

Garth was well versed in the details of the story but pretended not to know too much about it. He knew that Ralph preferred it this way.

"So at about one hundred, two hundred feet, two of the kids just can't hold on any longer and guess what happened to *them*."

Garth shook his head, dutifully feigning ignorance.

"Splat, splat!" Ralph slapped the palm of his hand twice upon the roof of his car. "But the other kid—he ties himself in, and two hours later they're able to reel him up into the ship. Man was not meant to fly by helium or hydrogen, Garth. Those German zeppelins are powder kegs just waiting for somebody to light a match."

The crowd was getting boisterous. Both men, who had hardly been out of their teens when the legal spigot got turned off, edged a little closer to their fellow celebrants.

Ralph crushed his cigarette under his shoe. "When I heard that the 'Queen of the Skies' had gone down for good on Tuesday, I started thinking again about that kid Cowart—couldn't have been more than eighteen— the way he hung on, the way it takes either a special person or a mighty dimwitted cluck to stick it out when a situation gets desperate like that. The rest of us—and that's pretty *much* all of us, Garth—we reach points in our lives when we have to make those same kinds of fish-or-cut-bait decisions. Do we hang on, keep persevering in a bad situation, or do we cut ourselves loose and take a life lesson from the experience? That first boy did the sensible thing: he let go early. Broken arm, sure, but his whole life still ahead of him. Two sailors are dead because they *didn't* bail out when they had the chance. That fourth kid, Cowart, is only alive because he was one lucky son of a bitch."

"It isn't because he knew how to tie himself in? That isn't luck, Ralph. That's rope smarts."

"You're missing my point."

"Just what *is* your point, Ralph? What's the story?"

"I'm shuttering the business, getting out of the ice-selling racket. It isn't profitable anymore. I never got into the coal delivery line. I never diversified. I sell ice. Just like my father sold ice, and just like his father before him. But nobody's buying ice these days. They're buying refrigerators. I don't blame them. Hell, Vivian and I just got a Frigidaire ourselves."

"There will be people who won't want to give up their iceboxes, Ralph."

"But not nearly enough of them to keep me in the black."

"Do you have a buyer?"

Ralph shook his head. "Just where would I find such a person? They gave the ice industry last rites two or three years ago. I'm selling buggies, Garth, while the country's buying Duesenbergs. So I'm walking away while I've still a little something left in the family piggy bank. I owe that to Vivian and the kids. She loves the big house. And we both want the boys to go to college. I'm not gonna bleed myself dry just so a handful of Mrs. Broussards can hang onto their iceboxes for old times' sake."

"When did you make this decision?"

"I've been mulling it over for a few months now. Finally got off the pot and talked to Vivian a couple of nights ago. She agrees that it's the right thing to do."

"What am *I* supposed to do, Ralph?"

"Look for a job like everybody else."

"You know what that means."

"So let me get this straight: I'm supposed to keep losing money every Goddamned day just to keep you and Preston and Jibbs and all the rest of you fellas off the bread lines? And what happens when the company finally goes belly up and my bank account's totally wiped out? I get to take my place in line with you? My father and grandfather were successful businessmen, Garth. They passed a thriving business down to me. It stopped thriving. But I'm still a Morris man. I don't know the words to 'Brother, Can You Spare a Dime?' and I've got no intention of ever learning them."

Garth didn't reply. The band was tuning up. The oompah-oompah of the tuba reminded Garth of Oktoberfest. He glanced at Ralph's wristwatch. A minute till midnight. He looked at his friend.

"Caddy thinks you've always been this way," said Garth. "I tell her: 'No, baby. I can remember a time when we were both kids and we looked out for each other.'"

"My back's against the wall. Can't you see that?"

"Here's what I see: You should have gone into fuel delivery. Your competitors did. You didn't because you aren't half the businessman your father and grandfather were. Caddy wanted me to get into another line of work, quit Morris Ice ages ago, back when I had a few prospects. I stuck with my friend. This is how I'm being repaid."

"Now you wait just a minute there, Garth—"

"I don't think I want to, Ralph. I think I want to get me a beer."

Garth turned. As he started to walk away, the band began to play. Seconds later the sound of "Happy Days Are Here Again" was drowned out by the blare of steam whistles and the squall of sirens from the brewery. Several people honked their car horns to add to the festive cacophony. Garth took his place in line. It was a much different line from the one he'd be standing in a few days later.

He closed his eyes. He tried to imagine what that first swallow of beer would taste like. He tried to imagine, as well, what his life would have been like if he'd left Morris Ice when he had the chance. How much better things might be for Caddy and him now.

Or not. It was the Depression, after all. Who's to say that he wouldn't have lost that other job, too?

Garth glanced back at the car. Ralph was pulling out of his spot. He was going to have trouble getting his coupe through the dense crowd. But he'd come out of it all right; Garth had no doubt. Ralph was a Morris, after all.

1934

ADULTEROUS IN ILLINOIS

The first conversation took place between Norman and Patsy inside the Amos and Andy rocket car of the Century of Progress Exposition's Sky Ride. Their conversation was low-toned, almost whispered, and went virtually unnoticed by the other thirty-two passengers in the car, some of whom oohed and ahhed and nudged one another with glee and wonder, while others recoiled with a shiver, as still others bravely pressed their noses against the glass in hopes of getting a better view of the fairgrounds decked out in all its Art Deco splendor 215 feet below. The Sky Ride was the signature attraction of the World's Fair, which had opened the previous year and was now bringing in tens of thousands of new visitors in its second successful season.

Chicago rolled the dice in the middle of the Depression and had come up a winner.

"What is that?" asked Patsy, removing her official guidebook from her purse as she peered down. "The Hall of Science or the Hall of *Social* Science? I always confuse the two."

"Did you hear what I just said?"

"The colors were different last year. Remember? Bolder. I liked it, but I read somewhere that they were giving people headaches—all those gigantic exhibition buildings in brilliant blues and golds and reds. The fair got complaints, so they toned it down. It's all so muted now. Almost drab in places."

Norman, who had been looking at the side of Patsy's face, turned to take in the panorama below. It was still very colorful, he thought. What was Patsy talking about? Why was Patsy trying to change the subject? They had twenty minutes—twenty-five minutes at the most—and then they would meet up again with John and Shirley at the Mayflower Doughnut Restaurant next to the Havoline Thermometer. The Havoline Thermometer, standing at a height of 227 feet, was the largest thermometer in the world. It overlooked Admiral Richard E. Byrd's South Pole ship moored in the South Lagoon.

"What is there to say?" said Patsy. "We both agreed we would drop the bombshell. I told you to pick the time and place. If you want to talk to them about it over doughnuts, that's fine with me. Prohibition's over, though. I thought you might like to get our spouses liquored up first."

"Shirley is unpredictable when she drinks. I don't want to take a chance on a dramatic overreaction."

Norman looked up into the sky. Several others on this side of the Amos and Andy rocket car did the same. Some pointed. "The Goodyear blimp needs a little more lift or it's going to hit the transport bridge."

Patsy took a breath. "The pilot knows what he's doing."

The next conversation took place among Norman and Patsy and Norman's wife Shirley and Patsy's husband John. Both couples were in their early forties and lived not far from one another in Kenosha, Wisconsin, where Norman worked as a mid-level manager for Nash Motors. Nash had one of the more popular attractions at the fair: an eighty-foot-high plate-glass tower with sixteen 1934 model Nash automobiles stacked one on top of the other like compartmentalized slices of pie at the Automat.

John was a podiatrist. He knew Dr. William M. Scholl personally and had spent part of that morning visiting his friend at the Scholl Manufacturing Exhibit in the Hall of Science.

Although John had wanted more than doughnuts and coffee, he consented to the late-morning snack with a promise by the others of a full luncheon in Midget Village a couple of hours later; the guidebook had assured him that the portions served there would be filling for a man of normal stature.

"How was the ride?" asked Shirley of her husband and her best friend. "I still can't see how you could go up in that thing."

"The view was spectacular," answered Patsy, chewing on a cuticle.

"I went to see the Incubator babies," said Shirley. "I cried. Everyone around me was wiping their eyes with handkerchiefs. The guide said that the survival rate for these itty-bitty babies is very high. It's a miracle of science. Forget your television and your what-have-you, *this* is technology that makes a difference. One of the babies weighed less than twenty-four ounces. Can you imagine?"

Norman shook his head. "Patsy and I are having an affair. What's more, we have no desire to end it."

John stood up. It was a sudden move, and his chair nearly tipped over backward. "What the hell are you saying, Pomeroy?"

"Sit down, John," said Patsy. "Don't make a scene."

John sat down.

Patsy took her husband's hand and spoke in a dulcet tone, after detaching a large crumb of glazed doughnut from the corner of her mouth with her blood-red-polished fingernail. "Neither of us wants a divorce. We are both quite happy with our marriages and all of our lovely children."

The lovely children were promised a visit to the fair in the company of their parents next month. But this particular trip was just for their parents. There was to be dancing and drinking and Sally Rand and her naughty feathers. The two couples were slightly more sophisticated than most of the other couples of Kenosha, Wisconsin. The question, however, was whether this level of sophistication extended to the concept of companionate marriage.

John removed his hand from his wife's grip. "You're asking Shirley and me if we will allow the two of you to sleep with one another right under our noses."

Norman nodded. He dunked his doughnut with a nonchalant flick of the wrist and then took a sloppy bite.

Now Shirley spoke. She was upset. When Shirley got upset, her voice jumped into a high register like that of a beset schoolteacher. "If you don't love me, Norman, why don't you simply ask for a divorce? I'll take the children and we'll go to Reno."

"Because I don't want a divorce. I want to stay married to you. I still love you, Shirley. But there's someone else I love as well."

Shirley began to cry. She pulled out the handkerchief that was already damp from seeing the squirming preemie babies.

"You think I'm that *evolved*, Norman?" she asked between sniffles.

"We're not evolved at all," added John. "We're like those dinosaurs out there. I'm a Sinclair brontosaurus. I'm not a mastodon."

"I cannot believe you would do this here at the fair," said Shirley to her husband Norman. "When we were all having so much fun. Why didn't you wait until we got back home?"

"Because we can't live the lie another minute," said Patsy without much animation.

"We've been wanting to level with you two for some time," said Norman.

"Would you like some more coffee?" asked the waitress. She wore a spiffy little felt hat that had the words "Mayflower Doughnut Restaurant" stitched on it.

John did not even wait until the waitress had left with her coffee pot to say that he and Shirley had already suspected the affair. They weren't born yesterday, or in the Pleistocene epoch, for that matter.

Shirley nodded. Then she tightened her brow and said to her husband and her best friend, "I had hoped that your rocket car would come loose and the two of you would plummet to your deaths."

The third conversation of the day took place between Shirley and John in the McKaycraft Lounge. The McKay Company of Pittsburgh, Pennsylvania, made spring-action, chromium-plated metal furniture for porch, lawn, and solarium. Shirley and John sat on a glider and drank from bottles of Coca-Cola. Next to them a woman spoke to her friend in a muted voice about a woman she had met in the Kraft Mayonnaise Kitchen in the Foods Building, who had just the night before dipped her dress in the blood of John Dillinger as he lay dying on the sidewalk in front of the Biograph Theatre. "Everybody was dipping something into that puddle of blood," said the woman with squeamish delight. "And the G-men were letting them do it. Like the 'G' in G-man stood for 'Go right ahead and get your liquid souvenir.'"

Shirley held her handkerchief to her mouth as if she might throw up a little. Then she turned to John and said, "I didn't see this coming. I knew all about the affair. I know you did, too. But I thought that it would either run its course or they would come to their senses. At the very worst, I thought they'd come to us asking for divorces. But *this*." Shirley shook her head, her hands poised limply in the air.

A smartly dressed woman with fashionably large epaulettes and a disc hat that clung to the side of her head as if it were glued on came up and asked if Shirley and her "husband" would like to know about some of the features of the McKaycraft porch furniture.

John shook his head politely. "It's very *chic*, though. Very *moderne*. And comfortable, too."

"Take this brochure with you," the woman said. "Thank you for visiting the lounge."

After she moved away, John looked at Shirley and said, "You want to fuck each other?"

Shirley stared at John. It took a full fifteen seconds for her to reply, "I'm not attracted to you."

"Really? Not even a little bit? I give a damned good foot massage. Dr. Scholl taught me."

Shirley swallowed and then put her hand to her throat as if it were tightening up.

"Well, I thought I'd ask. We both seem to be in companionate marriages now."

"Yours may be like that, John. *Mine* isn't. I wasn't brought up that way."

"So what do we do now?" John pulled a chrome-plated ashtray stand over to his side of the glider and lit up.

Shirley shook her head wearily. Then she let her chin fall, the tears flowing freely.

"We should really just, you know, go somewhere and fuck," said John "You and me. That'll show 'em."

Shirley stood up. She had forgotten that there was a purse in her lap, and when her lap disappeared, the purse tumbled to the floor and everything spilled out of it. She got down on her hands and knees and began scooping everything up. A woman came over to help and Shirley waved her away with her compact. John crouched down next to her.

"This is happening to *me* too, you know."

"It all seems like one big joke to you."

"It isn't. I don't know what to do, either."

"I can't find my lipstick."

"Here it is." John handed Shirley the lipstick, which had rolled under the glider.

"I can't go back to the Blackstone. I can't face him. The two of us alone in that hotel room. I just can't do it."

"Then let's not go back. Let's not meet them at the Midget Village. Let's make them worry about us. Do they think of us? Have they thought of us at all?"

Shirley shook her head. John helped her to her feet. "Take me to Italy," she said. "Then I want to go to Belgium. Norman says the Belgian village looks just like the one he visited during the war."

John nodded.

"Did you know that Patsy wasn't visiting her mother last year? Did you know she was here with Norman?"

John nodded.

"Were you never going to say anything to me?"

"What could I have said?"

Shirley brushed the dust from her hands. "This means the affair has been going on for over a year."

"Maybe two."

John took Shirley's hand. He led her out of the McKaycraft Lounge.

The fourth conversation of the day took place on a bench in Midget Village. Nearby, two Little People—both middle-aged men—were shaking their tiny fists at one another over some small thing that one had allegedly done to assault the dignity of the other. It was of no large concern to Norman and Patsy, just slightly annoying.

Norman looked at his watch. It was nearly two thirty. Norman and Patsy's spouses were supposed to have rejoined them at two. "I suppose they aren't coming," said Patsy.

"I suppose you're right," answered Norman.

Patsy sighed. "The colors were much brighter last year," she said quietly. "They're quite muted now. They almost seem to be fading."

The two looked at one another, each knowing the same thing: that by this time next year there'd be no fair, and thus, no color left at all. And what then?

What then?

1935

PERSEVERINGLY TERPSICHOREAN IN WASHINGTON STATE

The two women hadn't started out as friends. In fact, they weren't even acquaintances in the beginning. But after a couple of days of polite nods and another three days of courteous verbal greetings, Mrs. McLatchy took the plunge and invited Mrs. Trestle to take the empty seat next to her in her box. It was positioned on the opposite end of the ballroom from the bandstand and the stage. Here one could see the full breadth of the competition area.

The Century Ballroom on the "Seattle-Tacoma Hi Way" was less than a year old but had already earned a name for itself not only for its size—it boasted an impressive twenty thousand feet of floor space—but for its strange design: it looked, upon first glance, like a Martian mausoleum, the subtlety of its Art Deco design origins getting somehow lost in architectural adventurism. This hadn't stopped Guy Lombardo and his brothers from performing there a few weeks earlier and bringing over twenty-five hundred fans in out of the rain.

Mrs. Trestle lived in nearby Fife. Mrs. McLatchy came from Tacoma, a half-hour's drive away. The distance didn't discourage Mrs. McLatchy from attending the "Walkathon" (as the dance marathon's promoters chose inexplicably to denominate it) just as often as Mrs. Trestle. Both women came twice a day with rigorous regularity—first for several hours in the morning and early afternoon, and then again for several more hours in the evening. In between their two daily visits, they dashed home to feed their respective pets and to read their respective mail, Mrs. Trestle to dust and mop and add the spic to the span of her little widow's cottage, and Mrs.

McLatchy to make sure that her maid was doing all of the above in addition to putting Johnson Wax wherever Fibber McGee and Molly on the radio told her to. Mrs. McLatchy was wealthy; Mrs. Trestle was not. This mattered not at all to the two sexagenarians, who became fast companions as the Walkathon plodded on, hour after hour, in the great Martian ballroom.

In the quiet mornings, when there wasn't much to see, Mrs. Trestle brought her knitting. The dancers were much more subdued at this early hour and appeared to be saving their strength (what little of it there was) for the evening, when the ballroom boxes and grandstands would swell with those who came from as far away as Seattle to see what had been banned both there and in its companion metropolis, Tacoma. Arbiters of morality in both cities branded dance marathons cruel and indecent, and attractive to only the riff and raff of society.

The dance marathon attended by Mmes. McLatchy and Trestle in the Century Ballroom of Fife, Washington, was not so different from any other. Most of the spectators came to see the live drama of bedraggled human endurance—to take voyeuristic pleasure in witnessing hardship and peril from a safe distance, and to thank their lucky stars that it was not they out there on that punishing dance floor. It was a ghoulish thing. But this was not the reason that Mrs. McLatchy and Mrs. Trestle came. They came to cheer on their favorites.

Each woman had selected two couples early on for whom she would root—*two* so that if one dropped out or was purposefully eliminated from the competition, there would still be a couple left to pin her hopes on.

"47 and 93," said Mrs. McLatchy, pointing out her favorites to Mrs. Trestle with one of the latter's unemployed knitting needles. "And you?"

"Numbers 13 and 62."

"Why those two?" asked Mrs. McLatchy, who did not like to knit, and so was in daily possession of crossword puzzles instead. As Mrs. Trestle considered the question, Mrs. McLatchy plucked up a crustless cucumber sandwich from the little picnic basket resting on the floor at her feet. There were crackers in there as well, and a little cool stainless steel tub of some sort of pâté that Mrs. Trestle couldn't identify.

Finally, Mrs. Trestle replied: "I looked them all over on the first day. I can spot the professionals—the ones who make money from dancing. I don't like it that they let the professionals in here. The specialty acts are always entertaining, but I know for a fact that many of these dancers are vaudevillians who are being paid on the side."

Mrs. McLatchy, who did not know this, cocked her head in edified amazement.

"So I seek out the ones who look hungry, who look down on their luck. I study the clothes they wear. Are the girl's dresses faded? Are the boy's trousers tattered and torn? Is there a hollowness to their faces? Are their eyes sunken in their sockets, as if retreating from all the pain they've seen? I choose to put my faith in those who seem the most deserving."

"Your two couples are quite young."

Mrs. Trestle nodded. "They're just babies."

"Mine are older, as you can see. I'm looking for the two couples who seem to have the best chance of winning. It's just like sizing up thoroughbreds in the enclosure before a race. Take Couple Number 38 over there, for example. I very nearly picked them. See how they're moving like stiff corks bobbing in the water? They appear to be conserving their energy."

Mrs. Trestle nodded. "You can tell that they've been in marathons before. But they don't look very hungry."

Mrs. Trestle didn't like it that the crowds in the evening came to see blood. When the sun went down, the Walkathon became all but gladiatorial. On some nights there was the "sprint." "One fall and they're both out!" the emcee would bray into his microphone. On other nights, there was the "grind": continuous dancing without the customary fifteen-minute rest period every hour. The couples danced on and on until one member of a partnership dropped from sheer exhaustion. And the unfortunate dancer need not even make full bodily contact with the floor to be disqualified, along with his companion; a single knee touching the floor was sufficient to send the pair home.

"I sometimes feel guilty watching it," confessed Mrs. Trestle during a particularly long-lived "grind." It was nearing the five hundredth hour of the marathon and there were still fifty-one couples remaining on the dance floor. No one seemed fatigued to the point of imminent danger but all seemed painfully, wearily beaten down—even more so than usual. "I feel that I *shouldn't* be watching, that I ought to turn away. There is so much suffering inside this hall."

"Now, my dear," said Mrs. McLatchy, setting down her pencil and crossword puzzle, having been stymied by a four-letter "tool" containing the letter "z." "They'd be dancing here day in and day out whether we're present to watch them or not. And, darling, you know that I have a great deal of money and I take every opportunity that is given to me to add my coins to those generous silver showers. I'm sure that's why many of these young people have entered this competition, my dear. To win the top prize, well, certainly—but also to take *some* money home with them even in defeat. And I speak for the professionals as well. Vaudeville is dead. Where else has a dancer to go? The radio? And Hollywood is such a terribly difficult place to make a—"

Suddenly, something caught Mrs. McLatchy's eye. Something awful. One of her two couples, Number 93, was in the soup. The woman, whom Mrs. McLatchy had come to know familiarly by her given name, Velma, was slipping through the arms of her partner, Antonio. Velma had bright red hair with only the remnant of a Marcel wave. Her build was slight—as slight and willowy as Antonio's was solid. Yet Antonio was having trouble keeping her aright. Velma had sunk into the deepest recesses of sleep at just the moment that Antonio's strength had begun to fail him. Mrs. McLatchy rose quickly to her feet and began to shout, "Hold onto her, Antonio! Don't let her fall! For God's sake, don't let her fall!"

Antonio let her fall.

Velma lay on the floor, still fast asleep. Antonio dropped to his knees and wept. Mrs. McLatchy and Mrs. Trestle knew their whole story by now. He worked at the sawmill—the one where the strike was taking place. They had two little girls. Once, early in the Walkathon, Velma's mother had brought the girls to see their mother and father compete. But the chastened grandmother was strictly forbidden ever to bring them back.

Two days later, one of Mrs. Trestle's two favorite couples was also eliminated: Couple Number 13. They were the losing pair in the heel-and-toe derby. Unlike Mrs. McLatchy's Couple, Number 93, Jake and Angeline weren't married. But they had planned to wed as soon as the marathon was over, as soon as they won the $1,750 cash prize. Mrs. Trestle had shared in their high hopes. The duo often danced over to visit her at the box. Mrs. Trestle knitted a sweater for Angeline. Angeline had two deep scars on her face that she never talked about. They seemed invisible to Jake, who sometimes kissed her right on the cicatrix tissue.

Jake got a charley horse. It brought him down like a crippled pony. There was a pile-up on the track where he fell. Someone kicked him in the head. An athletic shoe came down hard upon his right shin. Mrs. Trestle found it difficult to watch.

The emcee encouraged the crowd to throw money at Jake and Angeline as Jake was being carried away on a stretcher. Angeline stayed behind to collect all the coins. Mrs. Trestle asked if Mrs. McLatchy would send them a silver dollar. The heavy coin hit Angeline in the head, but she smiled when she saw it on the floor and blew the two women a grateful kiss. Then she shambled off, the show smile having been replaced by a look of deep, hopeless despondency. Mrs. McLatchy wondered aloud if there would ever be a marriage.

It was over eight hundred and fifty hours into the competition that Mrs. McLatchy's second couple met defeat.

It was a terrible thing.

Stella of Couple Number 47 went "squirrelly" upon her cot. It was "Cot Night," in which the dancers took their hourly rest periods upon cots that had been pulled out in full view of the audience. Mrs. Trestle had overheard someone, tongue loosened, no doubt, by too much beer, remark that the dancers' only bodily function still left to the audience's imagination was taking a shit. His companion had cynically replied that public shit-taking generally came after hour one thousand.

Stella began hallucinating. She was seeing the sky. A bird-congested sky. At first the sight of the imagined birds fascinated her. She stood upon her cot and pointed and stared and smiled. But as the sky turned black with them, she became frightened and began to scream. She woke all of the other contestants, all thirty-one other couples still left in the competition. All watched the trainers and the nurses try to quiet squirrelly, screaming Stella. Her partner, Dermot, vaulted over the rope that separated the men's public slumber quarters from the women's, and hurried to her side. It was quite some time before she could be sedated by a doctor's hypodermic; it took no time at all, though, for the contest managers to expel Couple Number 47 from the marathon.

Mrs. Trestle put her hands over her eyes while it was happening. "Poor, poor dear. Oh, poor dear."

Mrs. McLatchy patted her friend on the knee. "The whole thing has become barbaric, Lydia. I'm not sure if I have it in me to come back tomorrow."

"Is it also because your other favorite couple is now out of the competition?"

Mrs. McLatchy bridled. "No, my dear. I should certainly stay and root for your Number 62. But I just don't know if I have the willpower. I agree with you that it's become very hard to watch. You can take your hands down now, Lydia. The girl has been removed. All is quiet again. Have a Crackerjack."

Mrs. Trestle pulled her hands from her eyes. She pushed the Crackerjack box away. "I would break a filling."

The next morning Mrs. Trestle came and claimed her seat in the first row of the box she shared with Mrs. McLatchy. She took out her knitting and got to work. She waved at Gloria and Tom, the remaining couple on whom she had staked her hopes. They waved back. Gloria and Tom looked very tired. It had been a long night. It had been hard for them to sleep well during the rest breaks with so many eyes on them.

For over two hours Mrs. Trestle looked for her friend, having not quite believed it when Mrs. McLatchy said she might stop coming. Mrs. Trestle wondered if she should telephone her. Why should the two of them limit their friendship to only watching the Walkathon together?

The next day Mrs. Trestle did that very thing: She called Mrs. McLatchy. The maid who answered the telephone said that Mrs. McLatchy was unavailable and would call her back.

She never did.

Four days later, sitting by herself, Mrs. Trestle watched as Tom of Couple Number 62 was stabbed in the shoulder by Pavel of Couple Number 88. Pavel had convinced himself that Tom had made a pass at his wife Katrina, also of Couple Number 88. It wasn't true. Pavel had only imagined it in a sleep-deprived brain that often played tricks on him these days. Mrs. Trestle would have been happy to explain to Pavel that Tom would never have done something like that. Tom and Gloria were good kids. She would have been happy to have them for her own children. Tom collected stamps. Gloria lived with her sister, who was a beauty operator.

The following evening Mrs. Trestle came back. Both of her couples were out of the competition now, but still she returned. There were nineteen pairs barely moving on the dance floor. After that evening's grind there would be eighteen. The couples stumbled and staggered. The sight of it saddened Mrs. Trestle. She didn't know why she'd come.

Later that night, someone sat down in the chair next to her. It wasn't Mrs. McLatchy. It was the girl, Gloria, previously of Couple Number 62.

She came with her sister Lulu. Lulu, standing next to Gloria, was wearing her beauty parlor smock. Gloria gave Mrs. Trestle a hug. "I came to tell you that Tom will be okay. They're hoping to send him home from the hospital in a couple of days. I thought you'd like to know."

"I did want to know. Thank you so much for telling me, honey," said Mrs. Trestle, who was touched by Gloria's thoughtfulness.

"So this is what it looks like," said Gloria, studying the couples still left on the ballroom floor.

"Yes," replied Mrs. Trestle.

Lulu bought a bag of popcorn. The three women munched in silence and watched the show. The band was playing "I Won't Dance" by Jerome Kern, Dorothy Fields, and Jimmy McHugh.

The bandleader had a sense of humor.

1936

SHABBY-GENTEEL IN CALIFORNIA

The older of the two women set the tea tray upon the table.

"Oh, it's right lovely!" exclaimed the younger, who was a guest of the older.

"The set was my great-grandmother's, and it was passed down to me. I made sure to pack it very carefully when we moved west. As you can see, not a single piece was chipped."

Lois held up her cup and turned it slightly to give it a full inspection. There wasn't a chip or scratch anywhere on it. Nor were any of the other porcelain pieces damaged in any way. Arrayed between the two women was a teapot, sugar bowl, and creamer, each with the same colorful, hand-painted design as could be found on the teacups: violets and ferns set off against an almost perfect white background.

"Not a scratch," said Lois. "And the tea—it's very good. Did you bring it with you from back East?"

"Yes. I can find nothing like it out here. It's a special English blend that my family has been drinking for years." Millicent took a sip of tea, the steam rising up from the cup and half-clouding her eyeglasses. "Where are *you* from, dear?"

"Booker and I come from Arkansas. He says he's got folks in the state that go back to the original Arkansas Traveler. I guess you can say me and Booker and the kids, we's the Arkansas Travelers now."

Millicent picked up a serving plate upon which she'd placed several diminutive slices of shortcake. She held it out to Lois.

"Thankee," said Lois, taking the slice resting on the top.

"Lois, my dear, how long have you and your family been here in California?"

"Not long at all," replied Lois, shielding her mouth with her hand as she spoke, since there was masticated shortcake in there. "I reckon it's been about two weeks."

"And do you like it here? Do you think you'll put down roots?"

"It's awfully purdy. All them orchards and vineyards. I ain't never seen a place as purdy as Californy. But it all depends on where Booker can find work."

Millicent patted Lois's dormant hand. "I'm sure everything will work out for you, dear. You didn't think you'd be attending a tea party today, now did you?"

"No, ma'am, I didn't." Both women took a sip of tea.

"More tea?"

Lois peered into her teacup. It was half drained.

"A splash perhaps—warm it up a little?"

Lois smiled. "That would be right nice."

As Millicent poured, she said, "Clarence and I have traveled quite a bit. We've been to Arkansas. The mountains are lovely there. Everything so green."

"We lived in the southern part of the state," said Lois. "It's purdy flat. We had us a cotton farm."

"Did you lose your farm, dear? I'm hearing that some of our farmers these days are losing their farms from all that wind and dust. You can't grow cotton or anything else, I'd imagine, in fields of dust." She smiled, then sighed contentedly. "Of course, there's no dust out here. Smell how clean the air is. You just toss a seed over your back, and voilà! An orange tree sprouts up just as easy as you please. Have you ever had a California orange, dear?"

Lois shook her head.

"Juiciest, tastiest orange there is." Millicent licked her lips and closed her eyes. "I wish I had orange slices to put out today, but they aren't quite in season yet. Have you ever smelled an orange blossom, Lois?"

"No, ma'am. I don't reckon I ever have."

"Most luscious scent in the world. How many children do you have?"

"I got the two boys, Oren and Les. They's six and eight. And then a little girl, Viola. She's five."

Millicent bent slightly forward in her seat, intrigued. "Is she that new little girl I've seen running around—the spittin' image of Miss Shirley Temple?"

"Some folks say Viola looks a little like Shirley Temple, though I cain't quite see a hard resemblance."

"If that's the little girl I'm thinking of, she's just as cute as a button. You and your husband ought to be very proud. And while you're here in California, you should try to get her seen by one of the studios."

"Studios?"

"*Movie* studios. I'm sure that's what Miss Shirley Temple's mother and father did—just marched her right up to the gate of Twentieth Century Fox and said, 'Well, here we are. Open up that gate, if you please!'"

Millicent chuckled. Lois laughed along with her. "I'll talk to Booker about it. Be nice not to have to worry about money for a change."

Millicent's expression suddenly turned solemn. "Has the Depression been hard on you and your family, child?"

Lois nodded. "We don't need much to get along, but it's a real trial tryin' to get along with *nothin'*."

"Poor dear." Millicent patted her guest's hand again.

"Well, I best be gettin' along now," said Lois. "Booker'll wonder what's happened to me if I'm not around when he gets back." She stood up and reached out to shake Millicent's hand. "It was very nice. It was the nicest tea party I ever been to."

"I'm glad you liked it. We should do it again." Millicent poked her cloth napkin at the corners of her mouth.

"I'd like that, but I don't think we're gonna be here much longer. If Booker comes back and says there ain't no work in these parts, we'll have to be movin' on to someplace else."

Millicent nodded. "Lots of places need good pickers these days, I understand."

"Booker's got to get work soon or I don't know what we'll do."

"You wait right here. I want to give you something."

A moment passed. In Millicent's absence, Lois quickly snatched up three of the remaining rectangles of shortcake and slipped them into the pocket of her dress. It was a floral print dress, dirty and frayed. She was ashamed of it and at first didn't want to accept her hostess's invitation on account of not having anything better to wear. But she'd given her hair a good combing and had taken a water bucket and scrub-rag to her soiled face and arms and legs, and made herself halfway presentable, given the circumstances, and Millicent had welcomed Lois to her tea table without even batting an eye over her appearance.

"I want you to have this," said Millicent on her return. "It's my lucky half dollar."

"Oh no, Miss Millicent. I cain't possibly take your lucky coin."

Millicent opened Lois's right hand and placed the fifty-cent piece on her palm. Then she closed Lois's fingers around it. There was dirt beneath all the nails. Lois's fingers were thin and withered like those of an old woman.

"Goodbye, Lois, and good luck."

Once outside, Lois opened her hand to look at the coin. It was a 1920 "Walking Liberty" and it glistened in the bright, afternoon sunlight. A moment later, Lois felt a hand upon her shoulder. "I been lookin' for you," a man said. "You weren't around the tent. Who's lookin' after the children?"

Lois turned to peer up into the face of her husband Booker. It was ruddy from the sun. He had been out with three other migrant men driving through the valley looking for work, and had returned without prospects.

"Mrs. Jordan, from the tent next to ours—she said she'd keep an eye on 'em 'long with her own young 'uns."

"Where'd you get that half dollar?"

Lois tossed her head in the direction of the structure behind her. Its sides were constructed of sheets of rusty, corrugated iron and strips of tattered roofing paper. The "roof" itself was made of old canvas, as if cannibalized from a tent that had been ripped apart and put to slightly less transient use. For a door there was a hanging gunny-sack. Likewise, there was a paneless window next to the door, curtained by flour sacks. In front of the makeshift house were two crates (for "night sittin'"). Between them was an improvised flowerbox containing field flowers. The tiny shack looked as if someone—in all likelihood, Millicent—had tried her best to make of it something tidy and pleasant. There was even a welcome mat of sorts made from automobile floor carpeting.

"What are you doin' takin' money from folks just as bad off as we are?" asked Booker, pocketing the coin that had been offered to him by his wife.

"She wanted us to have it."

"Why?"

"She likes me, I figger. We had a nice visit. We had a tea party."

"You had a what?"

"A tea party. I ain't never been to no tea party before and it was right nice."

Booker thought about this and then said, "I heard about her, that Mrs. Tengle. Met her husband. He's got his hands full. She's a might tetched."

"She didn't seem tetched to me a'tall, Booker. She seemed *refined*."

"Well, don't you go takin' no more of her money. Not that you're gonna get much of a chance anyways. We's heading out tonight. Couple of the fellas said there's better chance for work farther north."

"Are the Tengles comin' too, do you reckon?"

Booker shook his head. "Tengle, he says they'll stay here a mite longer. He's still got stuff of his wife's he can sell. She's got family things worth a bunch of money."

"I hope she don't have to sell her tea set."

The two started back to their tent. It was little more than tarpaulin stretched down to the ground in lean-to fashion from the raised side of the back of their truck—a 1926 Hudson Super-Six sedan conversion. The children were waiting for them next to the tent. Each was barefoot, the two boys dressed in torn shirts and patched blue jeans held up by single suspenders. The girl wore a faded plaid school-day dress with a trace of what had once been a frilly white collar.

"We's hungry," said Oren, the oldest boy and spokesman for the trio.

"I'll boil up the rest of them potatoes," said Lois to her husband. "Oh, I almost forgot—" She pulled the crumbling pieces of shortcake from her pocket and divided them among the children.

Booker chuckled a little to himself.

'What's got you so tickled?" asked Lois, handing the water bucket to her son Les. "You take that down to the creek and hurry right back, y'hear?"

"Yes, ma'am."

Booker reached over and kissed his wife on the forehead. "You goin' to tea parties and all. Woulda never believed it."

"I couldn't rightly believe it neither. But it was nice, Booker. It was so very, very nice."

1937

DEPILATED IN OHIO

Dewey and Florence Hurd adopted the girl from nuns when she was three. Joanna was the illegitimate daughter of a woman who had worked in Chillicothe in one of the town's shoe factories. Joanna's mother fell on hard times at war's end and began to sell her body and dissipate herself. She eventually left Ross County under a cloud of shame and disgrace, and ended her life in a fleabag hotel in Los Angeles in 1930, an empty morphine-injecting Pravaz at her side.

Joanna had been grateful that the Hurds, who had no children, had taken her in and brought her to live as their daughter in their simple cream-colored century-old rectangular stone house, which stood embowered by white oaks and black walnuts on the Cincinnati Pike west of Chillicothe. The house and surrounding farm were situated in the valley of Paint Creek, within easy walking distance of hills thickly wooded by hickories and beeches and ashes. It was during all those solitary sylvan rambles that Joanna grew into the shy young woman of sixteen she had this year become. And it is to these woods that Joanna fled when her adoptive father and mother flung their angry barbs at one another in each new chapter of that all-too-familiar tale of protracted marital discord to which the girl was daily witness—evidence of a rocky union that would not be dissolved, for neither husband nor wife could afford to live without the other in a devil's pact of prolonged mutual destruction.

Dewey Hurd had been an English professor at an Indiana college when he inherited the farm from his uncle and decided to have a go at the agrarian life. Florence had once worked as a children's advocate in New York City, loving every child that she discovered hungry or ill-clad or homeless or unloved, though once a child—in this case, her own adopted daughter Joanna—was rescued from the dire vise of societal neglect, it was nothing for her to show (as it was with her husband) that side of herself that was not compassionate, but grasping and snide and brutally competitive, as evidenced by participation in a marriage that was nothing if not a daily rivalry of biting wit.

At times Joanna felt that her two parents were competing for her exclusive endorsement. At other times, she was the invisible child, hardly noticed when it came time for an exchange of the harsh, bitter words and sly machinations that defined and defiled the marriage.

Aside from the metaphorical storm of hymeneal strife that blew in regular gusts through the simple stone house beneath the oaks and the walnuts, the weather in its truer meteorological sense had been especially unkind to Ross County, Ohio, over the past three years. In 1935 a flood had left the corn crop and the garden choked out by rampant Johnson grass. The winter of 1935–36 had sent temperatures plummeting to twenty-two below, killing the winter wheat and rye. The drought that arrived the following summer was one of the worst on record, and when it was over, all that was left for the Hurds was a harvest of scarcely a single bushel of corn nubbins and a field of defiant wild cornflowers. Sometimes Joanna thought of herself as the cornflower surviving in the midst of the ugly landscape that was her tempestuous family.

For Joanna was very pretty indeed. She had beautiful long, tawny hair that she allowed to cascade luxuriously down her back. But where was the defiance, the filial insurgence?

In those moments in which mother and daughter found temporary tranquility in the company of one another, putting up vegetables in the cellar, for example, or making a pie, or together gathering the eggs in the henhouse, all was well and good, and Joanna felt only love for her second mother. Likewise, there were times that left Joanna alone with her father and there was commensurate tenderness and quiet bliss between these two as well. The morning in late April on which the sheep-shearer was to come for his annual visit was not, however, to be counted among those times. In fact, the morning brought one of the worst rows between her parents that Joanna had ever witnessed.

Mr. Hurd had risen earlier than usual to get the milking and other morning chores out of the way. He had looked in on his small flock of eighteen ewes, which he'd penned together at dusk the night before so that they would be ready for shearing when Mr. Talbot arrived. It had rained in the night and the upper doors of the shed had been left open and several of the sheep were now wet. Who had opened the doors?

Mrs. Hurd confessed. It was too stuffy in the cramped shed, she said, and she didn't think that close confinement would be too healthful for the animals, whose fleeces had grown uncomfortably thick over the previous hard winter.

"It's quite apparent to me that it's only the wool you care about—having enough to sell to the Cooperative," Florence railed from her new electric range, which she was still struggling to learn to use. "But if those sheep should all drop dead from heat exhaustion, where will you get your wool to sell then?"

"I'll have to ask Talbot to return on some other day," Dewey muttered in reply as he pushed his plate of ham and badly charred biscuits away. "Or else we'll have to write off the fleeces of all those ewes who took an unexpected shower last night thanks to your thoughtlessness."

"Why can't you simply dry the drabbled fleeces on the floor of the corn crib after they've been sheared? Didn't you have to do that a couple of years ago—the time that *you* left the upper doors open?"

"I'll do what I have to do. And I'll do it without breakfast. You burned the biscuits again. When are you going to learn how to use that new stove you forced me to buy? The stove we could hardly afford?"

Florence swung around to face the stove so that her husband couldn't see her cry. Her hand fell on the handle of the frying pan. She wheeled back around, her reddened eyes burning with fury. "I should be like one of those hardened women who live in the shacks in the hills. I should take this iron skillet to your head and be done with your constant carping and cruelty."

"Just try it," dared Dewey, frostily. He buttoned his threat with a quick gulp of coffee. "It's cold," he pronounced.

Through all this, Joanna had been sitting at the kitchen table, staring down at her own blackened biscuits. She'd been sitting as she always did, silently, painfully, wishing that the hard words would stop. But this morning Joanna would not remain silent. This morning Dewey and Florence Hurd's adopted daughter did something she had never done before: she made a threat of her own. "If you don't stop this, I'm going upstairs and cut off all my hair."

Joanna's parents stared at her for a moment in awe. Then her mother said, "You will do no such thing."

"I will," said Joanna. "Stop it, or I intend to cut off every strand."

Now it was her father's turn to speak. "If you cut off even one filament of that beautiful hair of yours, Joanna, you will be swiftly and roundly punished. Do you hear me?"

"She has ears," said Florence. "She heard you."

"You can put down the goddamned frying pan now, Florence, unless you intend to use it, and then I'll return in kind with enormous pleasure."

The husband and wife glared daggers at one another, while their abashed daughter reverted to her former plate-staring posture. Like a whale unexpectedly breaching the surface of the water and then submerging herself again, Joanna disappeared, dropping down, down, down into the depths of her customary depression.

Dewey Hurd rose from the table, his look now redirected to the window across the room. "Talbot's pulling in. Come with me, Joanna. I'll spare you having to sit here and listen to your mother disparage me for the rest of the morning."

Talbot was a large man in his middle years. As was his sartorial wont, he wore a western hat and overalls over a flannel work shirt. He trimmed sheep the same way his father and grandfather had trimmed them: with hand shears. He was very good at his job—the best in the county. It was impossible not to nick the ewes now and then, but when the job was over, there were very few cuts upon the sheep he'd sheared that were not small and easily healed by the wool grease, which contained a natural antiseptic. Talbot explained this to Joanna as he trimmed. He was fond of the girl, who reminded him of his three daughters, each now grown and moved away.

There had been three wet sheep and Talbot saw no need to return on another day after the fleeces had dried out. Nor would his busy schedule have even allowed it. "The wool can dry just as easily off the sheep as on."

"How much do you think we'll get this year, Talbot?" asked Dewey as the professional shearer went about his business.

"I'm guessing these ladies are good for about seven, maybe seven-and-half pounds a coat. That's around 130 pounds all told. Not bad for the Shropshire-Hampshire cross and not bad at all for one of the smallest herds in the county. When are you going to decide to go all in as a sheep man, Hurd?"

The question being largely rhetorical, Dewey shrugged. He liked keeping milch cows too.

The sheep presently being trimmed was the smallest of the flock. Talbot had set her easily upon her rump on the shearing platform, holding her in place with his left knee and upper arms. Joanna watched, fascinated, as he worked his way down and out from the animal's right ear, taking the coat off one piece at a time. Talbot was fast, but he was also good at holding the ewe still while keeping large sections of the wool intact.

It took about three hours to get all the sheep sheared, and Talbot took a few extra minutes to help gather the wool pieces and tie them all up, inner side out, into tight balls with paper twine. Joanna assisted with this as well, though her interest lay, as it did each year, in making sure that the waiting lambs were properly reunited with their respective mothers. Stripped of their wool jackets, the ewes all looked alike to the worried, bleating young ones, each of whom had to wait until her mother, through diligent rump-sniffing, claimed her. This day's reconciliation went smoother than in previous years and made Joanna think of her own birth mother and the fact that she would never have the chance to reunite with *her*. Instead, she was now fixed by law to a woman who, no doubt, loved her in her own way, and a father who showed affection often enough to keep her from hopping on the next freight train to try her luck elsewhere.

Still, Joanna was far from happy and quite serious about her threat. Had her mother and father not already defied her request by keeping up their hostility toward one another in spite of her warning? Did they not believe her when she said that she would cut off all of her beautiful hair? And yet she didn't want to be punished. The punishment would come out of anger, she had no doubt, and would be severe.

Joanna watched from the window of the shed as Talbot trudged back to his truck. Her father had gone to take the bundles of dry wool to his own truck behind the barn. It was at this moment that an idea came to her. She tore away from the sheep shed, running as fast as she could to catch up with Talbot before he drove away. She succeeded in reaching him just as he was climbing into the cab.

"What's the matter?" he asked.

"There's something I'd like you to do for me," she said, slightly breathless.

"Something that you—" He faltered.

Talbot knew that the Hurd household was a troubled one. He had spoken more than once with his equally sympathetic wife about how hard it must be for a child to have to grow up in such a noxious environment.

He worried in that moment that the girl might be preparing to ask him if he would take her home with him—let his wife and him be her new parents. He had heard stranger requests.

But this is not what Joanna sought. What she wanted was simply this: "Would you take your shears, please, Mr. Talbot, and cut off all my hair?"

"Cut off—"

"All of my hair."

"I don't understand."

"I can't do it myself. My parents have forbidden me. But they haven't said that someone else couldn't do it."

"Good God, Joanna. I can't cut off your hair. Not unless your parents asked me to, and even then, it would be a crazy thing to cut human hair with these things. You take scissors to hair. Have you never been to a beauty parlor?"

Joanna shook her head. "The last time my hair was cut I was just a little girl." Joanna looked down. It would be difficult for her to say what needed to be said while she looked at him. "Mr. Talbot, they won't stop. I've asked them to stop. I've told them what I will do if they don't. But then they would punish me. They won't punish me if *you* do it. They *can't*. Cut it very short, please. I want them to know that it's their hatred of one another that's made me look this way—like, like Joan of Arc. Like *Joanna* of Arc!"

"You want to martyr yourself to bring peace to your family."

Joanna nodded.

There followed a long silence. The silence was broken by the sound of Mr. and Mrs. Hurd's raised voices inside the farmhouse. Talbot watched what the anger-laced words did to the girl—how they made her flinch and shudder, made her retreat inside herself. He took out his shears.

Over the phone that night, Dewey Hurd said he would have Talbot arrested.

"You arrest me, Hurd, and you'll have to find another shearer. Nobody in this county does as good a job as I do for the price that I charge. You'd be an ass and a fool to do it."

Dewey didn't call the sheriff.

Even stronger words were leveled against Joanna, who sat on the sofa in the front room of the simple stone house looking very much like Joanna of Arc but looking not saintly at all.

"We told you that if you cut off your hair we'd have to punish you," said Dewey. Florence nodded. It had been a long time since the two had been in full agreement about anything.

"But I *didn't* cut off my hair," said Joanna matter-of-factly. "Mr. Talbot did it. You didn't say that I couldn't have someone *else* do it."

"But you knew the *intent* of our warning!" screamed Florence.

"Yet that isn't what you said. You should really try to be more specific in the future, Mother."

Florence Hurd wasn't accustomed to such insolence from her daughter. For a moment she said nothing in response. Then through growing tears: "Just look at yourself. How in the world can we let you go to school on Monday looking like that?"

"You made your bed," said Joanna in a low, severe voice.

The next night, after Mr. and Mrs. Hurd had had time to think and had time to talk with one another in this brief holiday from mutual hatred— to examine their feelings and actions toward one another and how these actions had affected their now embittered, bald-headed daughter—they sat the sixteen-year-old again upon the sofa to take up the matter, this time in softer, more conciliatory tones. Joanna wore a scarf, which had the effect of making her parents feel strange and guiltier still. Dewey spoke first. "We've decided not to punish you, because if taken to the letter of what we said to you, you *didn't* cut off your long, lovely hair. Instead, you asked someone else to do it, and Talbot, the son of a bitch, has obliged you."

Now Florence Hurd spoke. "But let us be clear from this point forward, darling girl—and especially after your hair has grown out and you begin to resemble our beloved daughter again, and not some mannish aviatrix— that you are forbidden ever again not only to cut off your hair while still beneath the roof of this house, but to ask anyone else to do it for you."

Joanna nodded. It was a simple request and one that she vowed to keep.

There was peace of a sort in the house for several months thereafter— all the time that Joanna's tawny locks were growing by leaps and bounds from living on a farm and ingesting ample protein and other healthful nutrients at every meal. When the circumstantial truce inevitably ended and Mother and Father were back at each other's throats with a vengeance that made up for lost time, Joanna once again weighed her options.

There was a lice epidemic in the grammar school, and great platoons of young schoolchildren were being sent home to have their hair shorn and pediculicides applied. She could easily find a little boy who could rub his pretreated head against hers. She would not have to ask anyone to cut her hair; it would simply be done as a part of prescribed medical procedure.

She had also heard of a female worker at one of the Chillicothe shoe factories who had gotten her hair caught in a leather strip-cutting machine and was thoroughly scalped. Should Joanna take this course, it would be the machine itself—a non-human entity—that would do the deed. Scalping seemed an extreme measure for Joanna's purpose, but she remained open to the idea of it.

Joanna Hurd had become a determined young woman.

1938

JIVING IN NEBRASKA

Dear Miss Allie (Gator):

Greetings from the great American plains, where it might be cold but boy are these cats playing hot! Goodman's Carnegie gig beat it down, and the jitterbugs at Harvest Moon kept me swing-happy for days, but it ain't just New York and L.A. where the cats are sending and the jitterbugs are flittercutting, and it ain't just New York and L.A. where you and me and the rest of the whackies can watch all those boys and girls posing and pecking and grinding the apple. They're sending here too, Allie. Right here in North Omaha.

There's a place here called the Dreamland Ballroom and they've got this cat, Lloyd Hunter, who formed his own band back in the mid-twenties, and this kid saxophonist Preston Love who lets it ride—oh my good woman, does he LET IT RIDE! And weekends, Allie, this joint is one o'clock, two o'clock, three o'clock jumpin'! Makes me a little ambivalent about coming back to New York, when everything I need is right here.

Which is what we've got to talk about. The old man's after me to hire on with the company he works for. He's an insurance man with Mutual Benefit Health and Accident Company. Pop's wacky for the insurance game but I never gave it much thought. Me, your favorite alligator, pushing a pencil all the livelong day? I guess it beats pushing a broom, not that pushing a broom's an easy thing to do from a wheelchair. The old man's laid down the law, though. His crippled son's got to start pulling his own weight. The years of me living off Daddy's dough in my ground-floor Greenwich Village rabbit warren have come to an abrupt end.

I'm going to call you long distance on Sunday night and you be close to the phone, ya hear? You remember that question I popped a few weeks before I headed west to spend some time with the folks? Remember how I wouldn't take your answer without giving you some time to think it over? Well, Allie, your Icky's going to ask it again and now I need to know where you stand. Could you possibly see your way to spending the rest of your life with a hopelessly lovestruck one-legged future pencil-pusher here among the cornhuskers and the insurance actuaries and all of Father Flanagan's orphaned delinquents? (You saw *Boy's Town* with Mickey Rooney and Spencer Tracy last month? Flanagan's place is right down the road. My parents always threatened to send me there if I didn't keep my nose clean.)

If your answer is yes, you'll make me the happiest man on one leg. If your answer is no, Allie, and it's maybe because you could never imagine yourself living anywhere but Swing Town, U.S.A., then I'll just give the old man the brush-off (I've done it plenty of times before) and figure out some way to pull down a few simoleons of my own in the Big Apple. I don't want you to have to support the two of us on your stenographer's paycheck. It's not that your Icky don't got a head on his shoulders, right? And who knows just what might turn up?

But I do think you could really like it here. The first night I got up the nerve to take myself up to the colored part of town (I like the chance to get out of the wheelchair and back on the crutches now and then), I could hear the Ballroom jump-jivin' all the way down 24th Street. I thought I'd just stand out there on the sidewalk and let the music groove 'round my eardrums, but this colored cat, he taps me on the shoulder and asks if I want to come up. (Dreamland's on the second floor.) So jive on this, baby: the guy carries me all the way up the stairs—just lifts me up like I was a sack of potatoes or something, with some other fella minding my crutches.

I was the only white face in the joint, but that was copacetic. I get set up at a table, baby, and Basie and Goodman and all the rest of them New York cats, why, they got nothing on Omaha. These fellas rode me right out of this world, and Allie, honey, you have never seen such dancing—not at Roseland—maybe, just maybe at the Savoy. The band played hot all night and the jitterbugs were organ-grinding, Susie Q'ing, shagging and truckin'. They were peeling the apple like Whitey's Lindy Hoppers, and the whole room, it was airborne, baby!

Now, I'm not saying this is the only reason you ought to be here in Omaha, but what I AM saying is we don't have to give up why it was the two of us whackies got together in the first place. And sooner or later the whole country's bound to go jitterbuggy, so I figure Omaha's just as good a place as any to get swing, swang, swung.

I'll call you at eight o'clock your time.

Your Icky

Dear Icky,

You got off the telephone in such a hurry, I felt like you didn't give me the chance to fully explain myself. Like I said on the phone, Icky, I'm very fond of you. You brought me out of my shell, and I'm so grateful for that. And I never minded that you were a cripple. These days cripples can do almost anything. They can end up as President of the United States! But there's one thing that you can't do, and I can't help myself, Icky—I want to dance. I just can't sit still and watch everybody else cutting a rug any longer, knowing I've got a couple of perfectly good legs that I'm having a devil of a time keeping still these days. There's this guy, Salvatore, whose been teaching me the moves. I'm getting pretty good. He nearly broke my neck with an over-the-head throw the other night, but I couldn't pick a better way to sever my spine! (A little gallows humor, forgive me.) Of course it means I live a double life: oh-so-proper and terribly retiring stenographer by day—daredevil, flittercutting, apple-grinding daughter of Terpsichore by night. And oh, Icky, how I'm loving it!

You want me to do this, right? You wouldn't want to bring me there and have to wait and wait and wait for all those white cornhusker kids to get wise to the jive. I'd go buggy, Icky, I surely would! And how would you feel having to watch me dancing with all those other guys every night anyway?

Now here's the thing I didn't have the heart to tell you on the telephone last night: I'm not sure that I could ever love you the way you need to be loved. Gosh oh git-up, Icky, you know how fond I am of you, just like I said, but it's more like a brother-sister kind of feeling if I can be perfectly honest with you. Fact is, I just couldn't give myself 100% to somebody with one leg, to somebody who could never cut even one inch of that rug, and that's just the plain truth. You can make me out to be the villainess in your heart if you have to, but I have to be honest. Maybe I'm selfish—well, of course I'm selfish—but don't you think I've got a right to a few things too? And I'm getting to find out what kind of a dancer I'm going to be, and, Icky, I really think I'm going to be one hell of a jitterbug. I can just feel it. Because I feel the music, I'm in the groove, but not just with my soul. I'm swing-happy with my whole body, Whackie-poo!

Take good care of yourself, and if you ever make it back to New York, come see me dance at Roseland. You'll be very proud of me, I know you will.

Your Allie

Dear Laurence,

I haven't heard from you in several weeks, so I thought I'd write, since I don't have the telephone number for your parents. (The long-distance operator says there isn't a listed telephone number that goes with this address.) I just wanted to make sure you're okay. I know I threw you for a loop. Write me when you have the chance and tell me how you're doing.

Vanessa

Dear Vanessa,

I'm sorry it has taken me so long to write. My parents wanted to go down to Florida for the holidays and I decided to join them. I don't go to the Dreamland Ballroom anymore. It isn't that I'm not welcome—there are actually more and more white people going there to hear the music—I just don't feel like doing it anymore. Nowadays I listen to my parents' favorite music programs on the radio: the NBC Symphony, the Voice of Firestone, and The Carnation Contented Hour. You wanted to know how I'm doing? I'm actually fairly contented myself. I met a swell girl in Florida, and we've been corresponding. She may come up to Omaha in the spring to see me, or I might go back to Florida, if the Mutual Benefit Health and Accident Company gives me a few days off.

I wish you well, Vanessa, and trust that you and your partner Salvatore are extra careful with those throws. I read just the other day about a girl in Chicago who got flipped on her head. Now she drivels like a dog and speaks only through grunts. I also understand that jitterbugging is very hard on the knees. You'll regret all the abuse to your fragile patellas when you get old.

Now I must close. Several of Mom and Pop's friends are coming over for bridge tonight, and Mrs. Hennigan's husband is home sick. I will have to be Mrs. Hennigan's husband for the evening. Paul Whiteman is on the radio tonight. Mom and Pop and all of their friends love Paul Whiteman. He doesn't play swing, though. I don't think he likes it.

Come to think of it, I don't much care for it either.

Sincerely,
Laurence

1939

GALACTOPHOROUS IN VIRGINIA

Paulette leaned into the radio and smiled. "What's new?"

Both Paulette's husband Prentice and the man in the suit said "huh?" in near perfect unison.

"'The song: 'What's New?' So wistful. So subtly elegiac. And doesn't Kathleen Lane have a sweet voice?"

"Nice enough," said the man from MGM—the man who had come all the way from California to sit and talk to Paulette about the movie adaptation of her bestselling novel, "but when it's over, could you be so good as to…?" The man from MGM, whose name was McCubbin, mimed switching off the radio. Next to him, Paulette's father sat upright in Prentice's ample armchair, snoozing away. The fifth occupant of the room, Paulette's similarly slumbering mother, lay luxuriously draped out among the throw pillows on the sofa.

Paulette wondered at that moment if the song was permeating her mother's dream world. Madeleine Gammond sometimes had troubled dreams about the San Francisco earthquake; thirty-three years later, her memories still haunted her.

When the song was finished, Paulette obligingly turned off the radio. It was the first time it had been off all day. Paulette frowned at McCubbin. "My parents come up to Falls Church every other month. This is their day. They come up to listen to the radio because they can't get a good broadcast signal where they live in the mountains. You burst in here like gangbusters—like some overstrung G-man—and it's rude, Mr. McCubbin. It's really off-putting. *And* counterproductive. If I were to fashion one of my characters after you—let me tell you—he wouldn't be very popular."

Michael McCubbin, who was bald and smelled to Paulette like an ashtray, didn't back down. "Be that as it may, I have to catch a train to New York in a few hours. Moreover, I was tasked, while I was in the vicinity, with attending the special midnight premiere screening of *The Women* at Loew's in D.C as a favor to Mr. Mayer and to report back on audience reception. It now being 12:40 in the a.m., I could not do that now even if benefited by the world's fastest autogyro."

Paulette's husband, Prentice, sat up in his seat. He stubbed out his cigar. "Am I to understand, McCubbin, that you're blaming my wife for your poor time management skills?"

"Well, of course not." McCubbin inhaled. Pushing his words through the exhalation that followed, he said wearily, "I'm only saying—what I am saying, Mr. Fedderson, is that this day has been unlike any I've ever experienced. I had hoped to come here and sit with you and your wife and have a calm and reasonable discussion about why Mrs. Fedderson should accede to my simple request that—"

"*Mr. McCubbin*," interrupted Paulette Fedderson, her hands firmly on her hips in the traditional stance of female disdain, "you have been neither calm nor reasonable since you got here."

"Then I apologize. I have every good excuse. All day long I've had to compete with that damned electric squawk box over there—the morning soaps, the Senators and Indians game in the afternoon, then Amos and Andy and Joe E. Brown in the evening. Mr. Brown, who is not in the MGM firmament, could not be of any less interest to me."

"Apology accepted. I'm going to make more coffee." Paulette started out of the room. "Would you gentlemen care to join me in the kitchen?"

As both men were rising none too lithely from their chairs, Prentice said, "Your report to Mr. Mayer, McCubbin—it doesn't have to be *entirely* dismal. You can, for example, tell him that the orchestra on Joe E. Brown's show tonight performed a fine version of that song, 'Something, Something, the Witch is Dead,' from your new picture *The Wizard of Oz*."

"And wasn't Judy Garland singing 'Somewhere Over the Rainbow' on Arthur Godfrey's show this morning?" added Paulette, her voice trailing off into the kitchen.

"And don't forget that we all heard that adenoidal girl singing it on Major Bowes only a few hours ago," said Prentice. "The whole country is going nutty for *The Wizard of Oz* and you have the proof right here in the suburbs of our nation's capital, McCubbin. Mr. Louis B. Mayer should be very pleased."

As the two men were pulling out chairs to sit down at the kitchen table, McCubbin replied, "It isn't that simple. Now I'll admit it, Mrs. Fedderson: you aren't the only reason I was dispatched to the East Coast. I've got three days of meetings scheduled with Nick Schenck and the other MGM lever-pullers in Manhattan. Everybody's nervous about *Gone with the Wind*—the cost overruns, the whole Cukor mess, and may I say, between you and me and the lamppost, what a terrible decision it was to cast Leslie Howard as Ashley Wilkes? The man is forty-six years old and isn't even *attempting* a Southern accent. And now that Britain's at war, we may have to contend with even more of these English milksops coming over here and limeying up our red-blooded American movies."

"Spoken like a true Fenian," groaned Prentice with a roll of his eyes. McCubbin and his host and hostess for this long day—now coming mercifully to its end—had reached a level of uninhibited appraisal of each other. The sort of appraisal that usually comes after a long period of intensive imposed intimacy. Positions had been staked out early in the day, and through all of the ensuing hours, neither party had budged.

It had, in fact, been a most remarkable day. That morning, McCubbin had come to the door of Prentice and Paulette Fedderson's small wood-frame house in their Falls Church, Virginia, neighborhood, just west of Arlington, to discuss Paulette's wildly popular novel of Old San Francisco, *The Milk of Human Kindness* and its forthcoming film adaptation *View from Potrero Hill*. MGM's 1936 blockbuster *San Francisco* had led the studio heads to believe that they could repeat their success with Paulette's book. The story was also set in 1906 'Frisco, and would be fortified by a scintillating screenplay by the gifted Miss Anita Loos (who had also contributed to *San Francisco* and, coincidentally, to *The Women*). The film, which was slated to go before the cameras in the spring, was to be given a budget that would nearly rival that of *Gone with the Wind*, with the entire picture being shot in glorious and decadently expensive Technicolor.

Everything was set. There was only one small hitch—a hitch that was visited and revisited repeatedly throughout the day, each visitation fraught with numerous interruptions. These interruptions in various forms related to Paulette's monthly reunion with her parents, originally from San Francisco and now living on the family's ancestral farm in the Blue Ridge Mountains of central Virginia, and to the audio wallpaper of WJSV radio's broadcast signal. WJSV, a CBS affiliate, infiltrated every moment of the day in a sometimes welcome, sometimes intrusive manner, through the speaker of Paulette and Prentice's tabletop cathedral-styled radio, disrupting, along the way, nearly all thought and conversation through, for example, importunate offerings of Arthur Godfrey and *Pretty Kitty Kelly* and *Life Can Be Beautiful* and *The Romance of Helen Trent*, and the Goldbergs, and President Franklin Delano Roosevelt. The president, as it so happened, had chosen September 21 of all days to make a joint address to the Congress to urge, in light of the recent invasion of Poland and the beginning of the Second World War, the repeal of the arms embargo provision of the Neutrality Act of 1937.

Paulette's father, Dilby Gammond, had demanded absolute silence during the speech, and Michael McCubbin had sat obediently, though restlessly, mum. It was an important day in history (the Romanian prime minister Armand Călinescu had just a few hours earlier been assassinated by members of the pro-Nazi Iron Guard, this fact representing just one more inconvenience to Metro-Goldwyn-Mayer's chargé d'affaires). He had come to Falls Church for one purpose only: to ask that the author's contract by which *The Milk of Human Kindness* would be turned into *View from Potrero Hill*—a contract which had been especially structured to give Paulette nearly unprecedented script approval—be altered to reflect the following: that when it came to the matter of whether a female character, for the first time in the history of the much-strengthened Hays Code of Hollywood self-censorship, could or could not be seen suckling a child at her breast, MGM would have the definitive last word. And that word, obviously, would be "no." No baby in any American movie was to be fed by anything but a bottle, given that the cinematic guardians of American morality felt that the presentation of the female mammary gland in any form or fashion (including that function for which it was expressly designed) was patently lewd and vulgar.

"I think," said Prentice, picking up the topic that had been picked up and then dropped repeatedly throughout this day of false starts and frustrating distractions and an outright presidential coup de théâtre, "that you will have to do a much better job of explaining to my wife and me why she must sign off on an ending that would most assuredly subvert the primary intent of her story, when the whole matter of a woman feeding a child in the way that God intended isn't even addressed in the Hays Code. I'm looking at it right now."

He was, in fact. A typewritten copy of the code, formally titled, "The United States Motion Picture Production Code of 1930," all one page of it, was laid upon the table so that Prentice could stab it with his forefinger to make his point. "See? Nothing here about a mother nursing her child—"

Paulette interrupted from the coffee pot: "Not *her* child, dear—her *friend's* child. That's the point of the climactic scene: a wall has collapsed upon the crib holding her own baby, killing it. Her friend has sustained an injury to the breast that prevents her from nursing her own child, so our heroine volunteers her own milk to feed the other woman's little girl in the name of sister love and Christian compassion."

"It's a moving story," said McCubbin. "I wept when I read it. But you can't show a tit on the screen—or even anything suggestive thereof— however high-minded your purpose. Mr. Mayer would shit a brick. If this entire matter got before the press, can you just imagine the firestorm? All the advance publicity for *Gone with the Wind* would be drowned with the bath water as this whole country got to arguing the pros and cons of wet-nursing on the silver screen. And I can tell you from experience, Mrs. Fedderson: that Puritanical subset of the film-going American public won't sit still for it. Besides which, it isn't even relevant these days. It's a rarity, is it not, to find the mother of an infant who feeds her own baby in such an outmoded way?"

"It wasn't a rarity in 1906, Mr. McCubbin, and that's when my novel is set. It is also the year in which your movie will be set. And it was a good thing that women *did* feed their babies in the natural way back then, because otherwise all those nursing babies that survived the quake and the fire would have starved."

McCubbin picked up the piece of paper with the Hays Code typed upon it and put it back into his briefcase. He folded his hands on the table before him. "I'm afraid, then, that we have reached an impasse. Because as lofty as our purpose might be in putting this on the screen, we remain forever at the mercy of the puerile imaginations of our audience. And I make this guarantee to you, Mrs. Fedderson: there will be those who will elbow one another and snicker—a few who will guffaw outright. The gravity and sobriety of the scene will be undermined by a schoolboy mentality in this country that is inescapable. The effect will not be what you'd wish. And those Americans who are not crass, my good woman, they are morally parochial. It is our job as purveyors of American culture to uplift them all, to educate and elevate them whenever possible to some higher, loftier sensibility. We simply cannot do this by giving them, *ahem* …knockers."

Paulette Fedderson tutted. "It's so typical of your male-dominated industry to take something so beautiful and so natural and turn it into something ugly and indecent. My story must suffer because of the prurience of the American male moviemaker. It sickens me. And it saddens me deeply, sir."

Paulette sat down and held her head momentarily in her palms.

"I didn't make the world the way it is," responded McCubbin.

Paulette looked up. "Nor have you any right to rewrite my own life."

For a moment Michael McCubbin didn't speak. He turned to look at Paulette's husband, who confirmed what his wife had just said with a commiserating nod.

Finally finding his voice, Michael said, "I knew that there had to be some autobiographical component to your book, but are you telling me the baby that lived—that was you?"

"Well, she certainly wasn't the one crushed by the brick wall," quipped Prentice.

"Mr. McCubbin—Michael," said Paulette, her voice softened by the sudden serious turn in the discussion, "how could you possibly change the story without hiding the truth of what this woman did for me?"

"In the only way that Hollywood will permit us. That in *our* story, the mother will die at the same time as her friend's baby and that the surviving child should then be raised by the woman who took it to her surrogate breast. We won't see the, um, nursing, obviously, but every bit of maternal feeling will be there in the fade-out: the woman holding the orphaned child in her arms, knowing that she will now become the little girl's new mother."

Paulette shook her head. "In spite of the acceptable sentiment, it doesn't tell the story the way that I want it told."

"And is that a no, Paulette? Because you know that this is the deal-breaker."

Before Paulette could answer in the affirmative, thereby delivering the death blow to the multimillion-dollar Technicolor adaptation of her bestselling novel, a project that David O. Selznick had already been champing to get his mitts on, Paulette's mother Madeleine, who had just stepped into the kitchen, interrupted with, "I thought I smelled coffee brewing," and then, "Paulette, dear, I'd take the offer if I were you. It's the best that you're going to get. Fifty years from now perhaps things will be different, but we live today in a world that doesn't make a lick of sense—a world that is far from fair. You've been hearing what's happening in Europe right now. And things are only destined to get worse. This movie will be about two women who come together in love and self-sacrifice. Depiction of such a relationship can only help to redeem this sullied world."

Paulette was about to reply, but her mother silenced her with a raised hand. "I'm not finished. There's another reason why your father and I are encouraging you to allow the change that the studio wants. It's because the story that MGM wants to tell *is*, ironically, the valid one."

"I don't understand, Mama."

"Your actual birth mother died in the quake. My birth child and your birth mother—they both perished in those terrible pre-dawn hours. I was that other woman, and your father and I—we adopted you. We'd always meant to tell you, but after a while it stopped mattering, because you had become such an integral part of our lives. And I could not be any prouder of you and your wonderful book than if I had given birth to you myself. The story you wrote, and the story that Mr. McCubbin would like to bring to the screen—the world needs more stories like these. And now I've had my say and I'm going to lie down on a bed. That sofa has lumps, honey. Wake me before nine. Your father and I want to hear one last episode in the thrilling life story of the "Golden-Haired Irish Girl," Pretty Kitty Kelly, before we head back home. Do you listen to *Pretty Kitty Kelly*, Mr. McCubbin? Since you're Irish, I thought you might."

Michael McCubbin shook his head. Madeleine Gammond went to her daughter, kissed her on the forehead, and said, "I continue to be enormously proud of you. Your other mother would have been equally proud." Then turning to McCubbin, she said, "Paulette's birth mother was more stubborn than this one here. Consider yourself lucky not to be dealing with *her*." Madeleine laughed. "Oh, and please let the record show that Paulette was very much correct in one thing I heard her say: if I hadn't offered my own breast milk to feed this little girl during those horrible first few days before the city could pull itself back up on its feet, she *wouldn't* have survived. That part of the story is very much true. Goodnight, all. Or should I say 'good morning'?"

Madeleine woke her husband with a gentle hand and led him back to the spare bedroom Paulette had fixed up for them. Lying in bed, Dilby Gammond asked his wife how their daughter had taken the important news of her true parentage.

"It will take her some time to come to terms with it, I'm sure," answered Madeleine.

"Do you think she'll go along with MGM?"

"I don't know. She's very hard-headed. Very much Ellen's little girl." As Madeleine thought about her long-deceased friend, she ran her fingers slowly and affectionately through her husband's thinning gray hair, his head pillowed snugly upon her large, warm, nourishing breasts.

1940

AU FAIT IN COLORADO,
NEW MEXICO, AND CALIFORNIA

George and his wife Dahlia Heyman couldn't find their son Todd. They had just finished breakfast in the dining car, each ordering and very much enjoying the Santa Fe French toast which had been recommended to them by the woman in the room next to theirs. The woman was a successful Hollywood hairdresser. The Atchison, Topeka and Santa Fe Super Chief, which sped with minimal stops from Chicago to Los Angeles two days a week, was the train of choice for many of the well-to-do of Tinsel Town. Not that George and Dahlia and their missing son Todd had anything to do with Hollywood themselves. They were taking the train for two reasons: to see Dahlia's sister in Pasadena and to celebrate Todd's fifteenth birthday.

Todd loved trains. He was especially enamored of the ATSF, one of the country's oldest and most beloved railroads. Todd would become slightly perturbed whenever someone asked why the Atchison, Topeka, and Santa Fe Railroad, its sleek *Streamline Moderne* locomotives emblazoned with the familiar, almost iconic, red-yellow-black pin-striped Indian "Warbonnet" paint scheme, did not, in fact, pass through Santa Fe, New Mexico. Without variation, Todd would explain that the civil engineers who had laid the track realized that they couldn't surmount the mountains around Santa Fe, so they built the railway through the small nearby hamlet of Lamy instead. A smaller spur line was later constructed to take Santa Fe-bound passengers the final few miles of their journey.

Todd knew everything there was to know about the ATSF (excepting technologically abstruse engineering and design specs, and facts of a strictly proprietary nature). At the same time, Todd had been slow in certain areas of his social and psychological development. George and

Dahlia had no name to give their son's condition, unaware as they were of Hans Asperger's groundbreaking research being conducted at the time in Vienna. Todd's uncle Johnny merely called his nephew, with breathtaking insensitivity, "the idiot-genius."

"I'll search the front end of the train and you take the rear," suggested George to his wife. The boy had excused himself to use the washroom as the three were finishing breakfast in the company of a gentleman who made his living selling microscopes for classroom application. Once Todd came to realize that their table companion knew absolutely nothing about the Super Chief beyond those items that pertained to his own traveling comfort and convenience, Todd retreated into his ATSF Railway System Time Table and only looked up to note to no one in particular that by his personal railroad chronometer (his most prized possession) the train was pulling into the La Junta, Colorado station (an operating stop only) a good one minute early.

Dahlia agreed with her husband's plan and turned to initiate her half of the search. Both parents, though concerned, remained calm. Furthest from their minds was any possibility that Todd would have left the train even if he'd wanted to; it wasn't due to stop again until 4:35 that afternoon (another operating stop with no discharge or receipt of passengers permitted) in Albuquerque.

As she reached the passage door, Dahlia stopped and turned back. "And we should meet back here, don't you think?"

George nodded.

"Oh, and George?"

To which a porter, coincidentally placed between the two, replied, "Yes?"

"I beg your pardon. I was speaking to my husband," explained Dahlia. The porter, who was trained to respond to the name "George" as tribute to the Pullman company's founder, smiled indulgently.

Dahlia continued: "If you're the one to find him, George, don't scold him. I'm sure he doesn't think he's done anything wrong."

"I don't scold the boy. I never scold the boy." Then, addressing the porter: "Our son Todd has wandered off. If you find a boy unattended, would you ask him to return to our room?"

"Yes, Mr. Heyman," answered the porter. "But he isn't a *little* boy, if I recall. He's a great *big* boy."

"He is," said George, "and getting bigger every day. Todd isn't like other children. But, of course, you've probably noticed that already."

The porter nodded. "He asked me if I'd ever worked the 'El Capitan.' And 'did the ATSF need Pullman porters on trains without sleeping compartments?' That's an 'all chair' car, don't you know. 'Why,' I said, 'every train needs a porter. There are lots of things that we porters got to do.' He said if he couldn't be an engineer, he'd be a porter. The boy loves trains."

"That is a fact," said George.

"And he ain't the only different sort of boy on this train. Mr. Bergen's riding with us on this trip. And he's got his wooden boy Charlie with him—got the little top hat on and everything."

Dahlia raised her eyebrows and said, "Ahh!" She and her husband loved the *Chase and Sanborn Program* with Edgar Bergen and his giggly sidekick Charlie McCarthy, and Todd was especially fond of Charlie after he heard him say on the radio how much he liked going places on trains. "I'd love for Todd to get the chance to meet him."

Neither Dahlia nor her husband George was aware that their son was doing that very thing at that very moment. Both Todd and Messrs. Bergen and McCarthy were in the train's observation car. Bergen's impromptu performance for the occupants of that convivial car had been suddenly and effectively co-opted by Todd's arrival, by the sudden entrance of a teenaged boy who, dead set on meeting his friend Charlie, had proceeded without attendance to proper railroad passenger etiquette, toward a bold introduction of himself.

Here is what Dahlia Heyman saw when she walked into the observation car eight minutes later:

"Aren't you one smart cookie!" pronounced Charlie McCarthy through his ventriloquist Mr. Bergen.

"I'm not a cookie. I'm a boy."

"Well, bright boy, let's see if there's *anything* you don't know about this railroad." Charlie turned to a thoroughly engaged woman wearing a blue suit with pleated skirt, her long blond hair curled into a sausage in the back. "Care to play 'Stump the Choo-choo Genius', my dear?"

The woman nodded enthusiastically, her morning Bloody Mary sloshing a little out of her highball glass. "I want to go from Lawrence, Kansas—I'm originally from Lawrence, Kansas—to Flagstaff, Arizona. I absolutely *adore* Arizona!"

Todd took hardly any time at all to deliver his response. As his mother looked on from the lounge door, he said, "You could take the Number

Three—that's the 'California Limited.' It makes a flag stop in Lawrence at 10:13 in the morning. But it's a flag stop. I'd recommend the Number Nine, the 'Navajo.' It stops in Lawrence at 1:48 in the afternoon. It gets into Flagstaff at 9:25 the next evening. The 'California Limited' arrives in Flagstaff at 6:05 the next evening. But Lawrence is a flag stop. You take your chances with a flag stop."

The man who was seated with the woman carefully conned the timetable in his possession and then looked up in amazement. "The kid's right. He's exactly right."

Charlie had been doing all the talking up to this point, but now it was Mr. Bergen's turn. "There's a new show on my network, NBC, that I think you'd be perfect for, son. What's your name?"

"Todd Heyman."

"And how old are you?"

"I'm almost fifteen."

"Good. You're under sixteen. They want boys and girls under the age of sixteen. You live in Chicago? The show broadcasts out of Chicago."

Todd nodded.

"What's the name of the show?" asked Dahlia, making her way through the car. "I'm Todd's mother."

"Did you know that your son is a veritable genius? Don't you agree, Charlie?"

Charlie nodded his wooden head and said, "He's a regular Casey Jones Einstein."

"It's a summer replacement show for Alec Templeton, Mrs. Heyman. It's called *Quiz Kids*. I know the producer. I'll talk to him."

Back in their room, Dahlia shared the good news with her husband.

"What a kick!" he said. "And it'll shut my brother Johnny up for good— my own kid on the radio. What do you say, champ?"

"Will Charlie be on the show too?"

"No, honey," said Dahlia gently. "Charlie McCarthy is on *Chase and Sanborn* with Mr. Bergen."

"Oh," said Todd, turning his dog-eared timetable over in his hands. He looked out the window. "Coming back, of course," he said quietly to himself, "that lady would have to catch the Number Ten in Flagstaff at 5:40 in the morning. That might be too early. Yes, yes, that just might be a little too early."

Todd sat and continued to ponder the blue-suited woman's predicament as the sun-burnished mountains of northern New Mexico began to crowd the tracks of the Atchison, Topeka, and the Santa Fe Railroad.

Mr. Bergen's show was on summer hiatus. It had been replaced during the vacation months by a new detective show, *The Bishop and the Gargoyle*, about a crime-solving retired Catholic bishop and his ex-con partner. Mr. Bergen was performing at a nightclub in Hollywood and invited Todd and his parents to come and see the show while they were in the area.

Dahlia asked if her sister Lily in Pasadena could come too.

"The more the merrier," said Charlie McCarthy in his funny voice.

Mr. Bergen performed with all of his friends: Charlie, and the dim-witted Mortimer Snerd, and the geriatric man-chaser Effie Klinker. After the performance, after Bergen had deposited his fellow performers in his dressing room, he joined the Heymans and Dahlia's sister at their table. Bergen reported that his discussion with the producer of the new quiz show for hyper-intelligent child contestants had gone well, and the man was eager to meet Todd once he got back to Chicago. Todd asked about Charlie. Was he coming back out later?

Bergen chuckled. "Charlie needs his rest, son." Massaging his throat, he added, "We *all* need our rest." Everyone but Todd nodded and laughed. Dahlia laughed the hardest; she was giddy with thoughts of her son's impending career as a radio "whiz kid."

"Not *whiz* kid, honey," George corrected his wife. "*Quiz* kid."

Todd excused himself to go to the washroom.

When Todd still hadn't returned after five minutes, George said he would go and look for him. "He's probably gotten himself into a long-winded discussion with the washroom attendant. Especially if the man used to be a railroad porter."

Everyone laughed.

Ten minutes passed. George returned ashen-faced. "He isn't in the washroom. I've looked all over the club."

"Let's check my dressing room," said Mr. Bergen.

George and Dahlia accompanied Edgar Bergen to his dressing room. The door was open. There was Todd sitting on the floor next to a still and lifeless Charlie McCarthy, whom Mr. Bergen had draped over his divan. Next to him lay Mortimer and Effie, equally mute and motionless. Todd, his hand resting on one of Charlie's stationary, dangling legs, was crying. These were not soft tears, but great sobs of nearly hysterical anguish.

Todd turned and looked up at his mother and father through reddened eyes. "He won't talk to me! Charlie won't talk to me!" And then to Mr. Bergen: "Is he dead? Did Charlie die?" As his cries grew louder and more intense, Dahlia rushed to put her arms around her son.

"Don't be dead, Charlie!" cried Todd, now hugging both of the dummy's legs. "Please don't be dead!"

"But he can't be d—" Edgar Bergen did not finish his sentence.

"Todd," said George. "Look at me, Todd." George's voice was even, the words delivered in a placid, demulcent tone. Todd looked at his father.

"Number Sixty-six, Todd."

There was family ritual in the words; they had been said before.

"What?"

George took a step toward his son. Then another. "Number Sixty-six. Fort Worth to San Angelo."

"Charlie's dead."

"Number Sixty-six, son," said the father.

"Dry your tears, baby," said the mother.

"Train Number Sixty-six," said Todd in a mechanical monotone. "Fort Worth, 11:05 p.m. Primrose, 11:33 p.m. Flag stop. Winscott, 11:40 p.m. Flag stop." Todd choked back his tears, his voice becoming quieter now as George laid a comforting hand upon his shoulder. "Cresson, 12:01 a.m. Chapin, 12:09 a.m. Flag stop. Waples…"

1941

UNDER FIRE IN HAWAII

The Day That Hawaii Was Attacked
by Lisa Chapman
Miss King's Class

My name is Lisa Chapman. I am eight and a half years old and I live with my mother and father and baby brother in Makalapa. That is a hill that Daddy says was lava but now it is hard and you can live on it. On Sunday Mama was making oatmeal for my baby brother and me. His name is Jeff. He has the same name as my father. But my mother and me have different names because her name is Frieda. Daddy calls her Val because they were married on Valentine's Day and she is his Valentine. Mama was making eggs and bacon for my father. We heard some loud noises. Daddy was reading the paper. He got mad because he said they were probably blasting the lava rocks to make room for some more houses and they should not be doing this on a Sunday morning so he threw his paper down and went out on the lanai to see what was happening. Mama and Jeffie and me and Fumiyo who is our maid and cook went out too. Pearl Harbor is burning up!! cried my mother. She was pointing at the ships which you can see down the hill from our backyard. There was smoke coming from some of the ships. Daddy was pointing to the planes in the air. He said fixed landing gear. I didn't know what he meant. Daddy said this meant that they were Japanese planes. It was Japanese fliers that were dropping bombs on the harbor.

Go get my binoculars said Daddy. When Mama came back with the binoculars, Daddy looked down at the harbor. He said I have to get down there with my men. Don't go said my mother. She was still holding the fork she was using for the bacon. Mama doesn't like Fumiyo to make the breakfast because she doesn't know how to make an American breakfast. Fumiyo has only been in Hawaii for a couple of months. She tries very hard but Mama says she still doesn't know the American ways.

I have to go says Daddy. Lock up the house and stay inside. We all went inside. In no time at all Daddy was dressed in his uniform. He kissed Mama and then he kissed my little brother Jeffie then he kissed me. Do what your mother says.

After Daddy left some planes came flying low over the house. We all got scared and Mama said Jeffie and Lisa stay close beside me. Fumiyo was standing at the window watching the planes. Get away from the window Fumiyo says Mama. Fumiyo does not always understand what we say to her. Mama pulled Fumiyo away from the window. She said she saw anti aircraft shells going up to the planes but they were not hitting them. Fumiyo looked very scared. There was a loud knock at the door. Don't open that door!! yelled Mama to Fumiyo. Mama told Jeffie and me to go and get in hall closet. Then we heard who was at the door. It was Mrs. Hicks who lives next door. Mrs. Hicks and her husband don't have any children. He is a navy captain like my Daddy. Let me in!! Let me in!! It's Mabel said Mabel Hicks. Mama unlocked the door and let Mrs. hicks come in The first thing Mrs. Hicks said was Their invading the island!! Turn on the radio!! Mama turned on the radio. While it was warming up Mrs. Hicks said that she had a gun. She showed it to us. Do you have a gun, Frieda? she asked my mother. She said that we have to protect ourselves.

We have a gun but Daddy took it Mama tells to Mrs. Hicks. Push all the furniture against the door!! Push all the furniture against the door!! Mrs. Hicks shouted. We did what Mrs. Hicks said. We have to keep low and stay away from the windows. They can shoot you through the windows. Jeffie started crying he was so scared. I wanted to cry to but I tried not to. I have to be strong for my mother and brother. On the radio there was just music playing and a man was singing I don't want to start the world on fire. That man is NOT Japanese!! said Mrs. Hicks. She was laughing in a hateful way. She was looking at Fumiyo while she was laughing. It was like she just now noticed she was here. Then my brother Jeffie threw up on the rug. He's just scared said my mother. What did that Jap maid of yours feed him?? said Mrs. Hicks. I fed him said Mama. She sounded mad at Mrs. Hicks. Then Mrs. Hicks said They are going to poison us. Mama said WHO is going to poison us, Mabel?? All the Japs on this island. This is what they do. Mama said I don't think this is what they do. And Fumiyo will not hurt us. How do you know?? said Mrs. Hicks. Make her leave this house Frieda. Mama looked worried. She was looking at Fumiyo. Fumiyo was wiping up Jeffie's throw up with a towel. Mama said Where will she go?? She lives here with us.

Mrs. Hicks said I don't care where that dirty Jap goes. Her people are the cause of all this. My husband could be killed. Make her go or I will shoot her.

Mama did not know what to say. She made her lips move like she was going to speak but no words came out of her mouth. Then there was a loud explosion outside. It rattled all the walls of the house. Mrs. Hicks went over to the window. We all went to the window though Mama said we should not. The eucaliptis trees were on fire and the big pineapple field down the road. Mrs. Hicks said We cannot stay here. It isn't safe because they will come here. A man's voice came on the radio. He said that all doctors and nurses and defense workers should report for emergency duty. He said that Hawaii was under attack by the Japanese nation. Mrs. Hicks talked to the man on the radio. She said to the man Tell me something I don't know. Mrs. Hicks said Let's go. But Mama says Where do we go?? Then Mrs. Hicks said There are some caves in the hills we'll go to them. Mama says to Mrs. Hicks Jeff wants us to stay here. Mrs. Hicks says Frieda you are a fool. Please listen to reason. But Mama just kept shaking her head.

Mrs. Hicks said that Fumiyo will slit our throats as soon as she gets the chance. She will slit our throats in our sleep. Jeffie started to cry again. And I started crying I was so scared. Fuyimo looked very scared too. Mama pointed to the door and said Get out of here Mabel!! Mrs. Hicks said You should at least keep this gun. There will be a time when you may have to use it. Then Mrs. Hicks said in a quiet voice I mean use it on yourself and the children.

Mama gave Mrs. Hicks a look I have never seen before. It was a face like you make when you smell something very bad. I thought that it was the smell of the throw up that was making mama look that way. But then I figured it out. It was the way that Mama felt about Mrs. Hicks. It was because she was scaring us so bad. It was the things she was saying about Fumiyo.

I looked at Fumiyo. There was water going down her leg. I liked Fumiyo. She made puppets for Jeffie and me when she wasn't working and let me wear her kimono to see what it felt like. It is very pretty and has very big arms. Now Fumiyo was wearing her sleeping kimono but it was all wet from pee pee. Mrs. Hicks left. She took her gun. We all sat down on floor and listened to the sound of the planes and the guns. The radio went dead. It got quiet for a while outside but then the planes came back and started to drop their bombs again. Mama had her arms around Jeffie and me. Fumiyo was sitting next to me but she wasn't sitting very close. Finally the planes went away and Mama told Fumiyo to go and get herself cleaned up.

Later a truck came down the street it had a loudspeaker telling people to go the YMCA or the college. Fumiyo looked at Mama. She said I go too? You go too said Mama. Mrs. Hicks is a nincompoop. These are men who bombed us. You are a girl. You are not the cause of this. Mama held Fumiyo's hand. Fumiyo was shaking.

We went to the YMCA. There were other families there. There were other Japanese cooks and maids and gardeners there. They were part of the families too. The bad things that were happening were not their doing Mama said looking around. But some people gave the Japanese people bad looks. Mama says this will be the way it will be until the war is over. She said for me to be extra nice to Fumiyo. I made her a necklace made of pretty ribbons that a nice lady gave me to play with. Fumiyo cried when she put on the necklace.

This was written all by me Lisa Chapman but my mother made the words spell right.

1942

CERULEAN IN WISCONSIN

That first morning, the two men went deep into the forest. Wheaton's father-in-law, Vester, took him into a new-growth stand planted a few years earlier by the Civilian Conservation Corps. "Most of our forest primeval was logged right out of existence," Vester explained. "There's good and bad to that, I suppose. We've got some beautiful young maples and paper birches down this path."

Where Vester discerned a path, Wheaton saw nothing so distinguishable in the cluttered carpet of leaf and branch beneath his feet. "The muskeg where Dack got himself trapped when he was about twelve—I'm sure you've heard the story—it's a mile or so in *that* direction. I'll take you there on our loop back. It's an unearthly, diabolical place. The ground is like sponge cake, except where there's water underneath. Then the earth seems to ripple like something vital and alive. The Chequamegon Forest is a smorgasbord of anomalies of nature. Fascinating. Makes me sometimes regret going into the paper business instead of natural sciences."

Vester Ostrum was in his late fifties; his son-in-law, Wheaton, in his early forties. Wheaton was too old for the draft but wouldn't have been able to serve anyway. As a teenager, his arm had been crushed in an automobile accident. Wheaton was a quiet man. He preferred to listen to his father-in-law and comment only with a smile or a comprehending nod, or the occasional "you don't say."

Vester settled himself down on a mossy nurse log to catch his breath. "I get winded romping through these old woods," he wheezed. "Not a kid anymore. And the two packs of Lucky Strikes a day don't help much."

Vester lit up.

Wheaton nodded as he pulled out his own box of Camels for a smoke.

As Vester was giving his son-in-law a light he said, "I can't thank you and Monica enough for coming up here. I noticed you got a B sticker on your car. You can get yourself all the way up here and back on just an eight-gallon allotment?"

Wheaton shook his head. "But I figured we'd be here at least a week, so that's another eight gallons to send us back to Appleton."

"Whichever of those dry-as-dust grammar schoolteachers of mine said I'd need all that arithmetic in my later years, I'd like to give *her* the gold star. With every goddamned fill-up at Drummond's pump down the road, I've got to calculate everything I've got to do and how many gallons it's gonna take to do it. And it's hardly a fair arrangement. The OPA ought to give a little special consideration to those of us who have to drive twenty-five miles just to buy our weekly groceries."

Wheaton nodded.

"You haven't asked about Ann," said Vester.

"Monica told me some things."

"Did Monica, when she had *your* two—did *she* get that way?"

Wheaton shook her head. "She lost a little sleep there in those first few months. We both did. It made us both a little, you know, *cranky*, but it wasn't anything like what Ann's been going through."

"I still think it's because Dack hasn't been here. Christ, think of it: my boy's got a two-month-old boy of his own he's never even seen. It's a hard thing for a woman to have a baby when her husband's off at war. And *I'm* no good—an ornery old coot like me. More like a Dutch uncle to the poor girl than a proper father-in-law."

"It's good that Monica and Ann are getting to spend some time together."

"It's a Godsend, really. Especially after what happened last week."

Ann and her sister-in-law Monica sat at the kitchen table drinking lemonade. The weather had turned warm (about as warm as it generally got in woodsy northern Wisconsin), and the screen door was letting in a nice breeze. It fluttered the pages of the Flambeau Paper Company's 1942 calendar pinned to the wall next to the icebox. Ann's father-in-law Vester worked at Flambeau as a bleaching engineer. Ann hoped that her husband Dack's job as pipe fitter at the mill would still be waiting for him when he got back from Europe at the end of the war.

Ann and Monica had known each other since childhood. It was Monica who had set up her brother Dack and Ann on their first date five years earlier. Park Falls had always been a fairly small town. Everybody knew everybody else, but after Ann's emotional depression settled in, she stopped seeing her friends. She even kept her father-in-law at arm's length. Vester didn't know what to do. He wrote to his daughter and asked if she'd come and spend some time with Ann. Maybe Ann would open up to Monica, even though she wasn't opening up to anybody else.

"With each day," said Monica after patting her lemonade-sticky lips with a napkin, "does it get a *little* bit better at least?"

Ann looked over at her other son—her two-year-old. He was playing with a toy dump truck on the kitchen floor. Ann shook her head. "Most days it's just the same as it was the day before."

"And you don't think at least part of this has to do with Dack not being here?"

Ann shrugged. "I felt like this after Dack Junior was born. But it wasn't nearly as bad. I don't know. You could be right. I feel so alone sometimes, but it's—Monica, it's more than that. It's hard to put into words."

"Is it a kind of a sadness, Ann? Or are you afraid? Does it make you afraid?"

"I do get scared. I get very scared. But other times I just want to walk out that door and keep going. I think maybe I'll get to someplace where I won't feel so empty anymore."

"And how do you feel right now, Ann?"

"It's good that you're here. I should be happy. But there's nothing there. I look at Little Dack or at the baby and I know I'm supposed to be filled with a special kind of mother's love, but it isn't anywhere inside of me. That's what worries me the most."

"Can we talk about what happened last week? Would that be all right?"

"I should talk about it, I know. I'm sorry for what I did to Little Dack. I'm sorry for what I put Vester through. I can't defend it."

The two men were walking again. "The cranberry bog's over there," said Vester. "And that glade over there: blueberries and raspberries. I'm sure Monica's told you stories about what it was like to grow up in these woods. I hated it when she went off to college. I knew that as much as she loved this place she wouldn't be coming back here to live again."

"It'll be easier when the war's over and we can drive up to visit more often."

"I was suspicious of you. From the very beginning."

"How do you mean?"

"So much older than Monica. Taking her away from me the way you did."

"My work has always been in Appleton."

"Yes, I know. And I know you do good work with that Lutheran aid group." Vester pointed and lowered his voice. "See. I told you we'd see a cardinal before too long. I'm not much of a birder myself. I'm generally only on familiar terms with the ones that get roasted and put on a plate— the wild turkeys and pheasants and ruffed grouse. But we do get our share of binocular folk here in the warm seasons. There." Vester pointed again. "That's where I found Dack Junior. Right over there in that clearing."

"What do you mean, 'found him'?"

"Where she left him. Last week. I was out in the barn working on that old Essex coupe Dack bought a couple of years ago. That's when she wandered away with my grandson. She must have left the baby napping, but he started wailing not long after she'd gone. That's what brought me inside. I see the baby in the crib, but there's no Ann and there's no Little Dack. It doesn't add up, her going for a walk with Dack and not telling me to keep an eye on Steven. I get Goldie to come over to stay with him and then I go off looking for them."

Ann took a loaf of bread from the breadbox and set it on the table. Monica was cutting slices of ham for sandwiches. "So you sat him down and just walked away?" asked Monica. The question wasn't casually delivered. There was serious concern written on Monica's face. The whole topic was making her quite uncomfortable, but it was important to get to the truth of what had happened. Monica now realized that there was an even more important reason for her being here: to talk Ann out of ever doing such a thing again.

"He had a little cattail. He was sweeping the cattail across the ground like a broom. I stepped back and took a good look at him. He seemed so happy, so perfectly content. I wondered if I would ever be that happy again. I backed away a little more. He looked up at me. He didn't call my name. He didn't reach out for me as he often does at home. He didn't need me at that moment. It was odd. Both of them, Little Dack and Baby Steven—always needing me, holding me fast, cutting off my oxygen. But now it was as if Dack was giving me permission to go.

"The air smelled fresh and clean. The breeze felt so cool. There were loons conversing on the lake. The sky was blue and filled with ravens. I walked toward the alder thicket. Little Dack became smaller and smaller in the clearing each time I glanced back at him over my shoulder. With each step I felt more free. A peace settled over me. I stopped looking back. I just walked. I don't know that you'll believe me, Monica, but it was as if I wasn't myself anymore. I wasn't a mother of two needful boys, I wasn't the abandoned wife of a soldier husband. I was no longer that hollow, useless person that I had grown to hate. I was something else—a creature of the forest, existing for no one but herself. It sounds daffy. I didn't want to tell you."

Monica set her knife down on the table. She looked at Dack Junior, who seemed to bear no emotional scars from having been left by his mother to fend for himself in the middle of Chequamegon National Forest. She got up from her chair and placed her hand upon his silky-haired little-boy head. He smiled up at his Aunt Monica. "How long did you leave him, Ann? How long did you walk?"

"Until I got to the muskeg. My feet started sinking. I felt as if the ground wanted to swallow me up. That was all right. Being swallowed up was something that I was prepared to accept."

"You need to see a doctor, Ann."

"What can a doctor do? My own mother suffered from depression after the birth of each of her four children. With each child it got worse. She endured it. They say when it comes you're *supposed* to endure it. They say that it eventually passes and that things get better. That's what happened with my mother." Ann sat down. She spread her hands out on the table, palms down, leaving space between each of her fingers. She looked at her hands as if seeing her mother's hands in their place. "My mother was strong. I'm not as strong as she was."

"I'm sure that circumstances were different for her."

Ann nodded. "But I can't think of *any* circumstances in which Momma would have walked away from one of her children." Ann picked up the knife. She got up from the table and carried it to the sink. She placed it carefully into the basin of the sink.

"When I finally found my way home, the baby was crying. Goldie Larson gave me a look. She didn't want to give Stevie up to me. Ten, fifteen minutes later Vester walked in with Dack Junior. I couldn't bring myself to look at him—the shame of what I had done."

*

The two men, both hungry, were coming home now. There would be ham sandwiches and coffee waiting for them. There would be talk of Monica staying on for a few weeks. Monica's husband Wheaton would be okay with that. These things were temporal, he had heard. These things eventually worked themselves out. But it was good to have a woman there.

"I didn't know how to help her," said Vester to his son-in-law as they tramped across a thick, overgrown field.

"Would *Dack* have known what to do?" asked Wheaton.

"Who knows? Maybe not." The two men walked on in silence. After a while, Vester said, "A quarter mile in that direction is the lake where I caught that giant muskellunge I was telling you about. I noticed the rod in your car. We'll go fishing tomorrow—give the girls some more time to themselves."

Wheaton nodded. Then he said, "The female muskellunge remains near her eggs after she spawns. But only for a short while. Then she goes. She swims away. This is the way it is with the muskellunge."

"Makes you wonder why," said Vester, wisps of smoke curling about his head. "A real puzzlement."

Back in the kitchen the knife lay in the sink. Ann tried not to look at it.

1943

TELEGRAPHIC IN IOWA

Someone called him the Angel of Death. Which wasn't fair…or even true. Technically speaking, Angels of Death choose only the doors of those whose lives are coming to an end on which to rap with skeletal knuckles. They do not deliver telegrams to next of kin. This was Billie's job.

Billie Smaha worked for the Western Union Company. The gangly sixteen-year-old reported each morning to the company's office in Red Oak, Iowa, the small office right next to the Hotel Johnson. He'd wait on the delivery bench until there was a telegram to go out, and then he'd hop on his bike and deliver it to whomever it was addressed. After school, Billie put in a second shift.

Billie Smaha never had to wait long on the bench, because in 1943 there were a good many telegrams that needed delivering. 1943 was the year that the war came home to this farming community of 5,600 in southwestern Iowa. This was the year that forty-five of its young men, all members of Company M, 168th Infantry Regiment, 34th Infantry Division, along with hundreds of their fellow GIs, were vanquished by the German army in the catastrophic Battle of Kasserine Pass, the first major meeting of American and German forces in the war. There were heavy casualties.

March 6 and 7 of that year were especially grim for the residents of Red Oak. On those two days, Billie needn't have even brought his bicycle along. The families were assembled for the sake of convenience at the hotel next door. Upon its long portico, a solemn vigil was held. One by one the telegrams arrived, each new telegram nearly identical to the last: *"The Secretary of War desires me to express his deep regret that your son has been declared missing in action."*

"Missing in action. What exactly does that mean?" asked one of the anxious mothers.

"It means what it says," replied her equally worried husband. "That they don't know yet just what's happened to him."

How could that be a good thing?

Yet it actually *was* a good thing. Two months later word came that most of members of Company M had, in fact, survived the battle. They had been captured by the Germans and were now being held as prisoners of war.

They were still alive.

The war raged on. Billie rode his bike all over Red Oak in service to the Western Union Company.

He stopped wearing his Western Union cap. He did this in an attempt to soften the looks of apprehension that registered with those who observed his approach. The looks were hard for Billie to bear. Fewer telegrams came to Red Oak in those days in the innocuous form of congratulations or birthday greetings or baby announcements. They were replaced by the little yellow envelopes which bore the three stars that every home-front wife and parent had reason to fear.

Billie was not the Angel of Death, but with him came news of a life cut short, a life mislaid, or a life crippled on some foreign battlefield by the vicious instruments of war.

I will not say that the citizens of Red Oak, who had already tasted too much the bitterness of military conflict during the Civil War and the First World War, hated Billie. How can one hate a boy who is only doing his job—a job that few of us would wish to do? Yet Billie's sudden presence upon a porch or portico; his knock upon a door after all had sat down to supper; or his unbidden appearance early in the morning when the father had already left for work and the mother had begun to wash the breakfast dishes—it was never a welcome occurrence. It was never without pain, a pain that Billie could not help but feel.

Mrs. Harold Simpson's face turned white when saw that it was Billie ringing her bell. She had the envelope half-open before Billie could say those few words with which he sought to prepare her: "It isn't good news, Mrs. Simpson."

Of course it wasn't good news. Because it was Billie who delivered it. It was Billie Smaha of the Western Union Company who had rung her bell.

Billie watched as the woman's two young children crept with cautious curiosity into the room. "Your daddy is dead," Mrs. Simpson said softly to them. Only this.

"Is there anything I can do?" asked Billie. The sincere request was often made, but seldom did it elicit an answer in the affirmative. What, in truth, could Billie do? He was the messenger. He had delivered his message. He had done his job.

Mrs. Simpson shook her head. She continued to shake her head just as some of those who mourn will rock back and forth, the grief made palpable in the throbbing motion.

No one shut his door against the boy. All met his or her own darkest fears bravely, with painful resignation.

There were over one hundred telegrams in all. So many doors to be knocked upon, so many doorbells to be rung. Sometimes the recipients of the telegrams weren't home. Billie had to go and look for them.

He tracked down gray-haired Martin Jentoft at the Burlington Station. Martin was an engineer on the Hamburg-Red Oak run. His boy Tom was dead, the yellow piece of paper said. The young man was killed just off the Gilbert Islands.

No one was home at the Doggetts' house on Eastern Avenue, either. Billie went instead to the Red Oak Creamery, where he was told Mrs. Doggett could be found doing her marketing. Mrs. Doggett's son, Clair, had died in the Battle for Cassino in Italy. She read the wire that Billie had given her, read it without emotion and then set it down. "Clair is with his God," she said evenly. Like Billie, Clair had been a delivery boy. Instead of telegrams, he had delivered newspapers—issues of the *Red Oak Express*.

Billie knew Clair. He knew his story. He knew many of their stories. Clair had wanted to be a football player, but he had a small build. Billie flashed on the night the high school football coach had put him in as a substitute. Clair had run the ball for sixty yards before being tackled, and tackled hard. Clair had broken his leg, but he'd gotten his moment of glory. Another moment of glory—his last—had come several years later and many miles away.

Theresa Tinkham was eating breakfast alone when Billie came. She was thinking of her husband Darl. Through the window she watched Billie ride up. The morning sun was shining brightly. The sky promised a beautiful day. Billie's arrival turned the page of her life. She entered a new chapter on that bright morning—the morning that was to become the darkest of her life.

Billie decided that he wanted to study psychology when he went away to college. He had watched the wives, the mothers and fathers, the sisters and brothers who were left behind. He had studied them—not unfeelingly—and yet it was hard not to quantify, to clinically categorize the different reactions that his news elicited. There were those like Mrs. Simpson who had no time for shock—who donned sorrow in that instant as if it were a cloak hanging conveniently nearby, simply waiting to be worn. Others, like Mrs. Johnson, were not ready yet for grief. Because the unreality of it pushed everything to the side: losing her first son when his B-29 crashed on maneuvers, and then a second son in Belgium—two sons, in defiance of the odds, sacrificed to this hungry war.

Once, Billie had to read a wire to one of his classmates. It told of the death of the boy's father. Billie didn't know what to say. It is difficult to bring news of death to one much older than yourself. It is harder still to tell it to someone your own age, someone you josh around with, someone whose own life has just gotten started.

"I never get used to it," Billie told his mother one night when she had sought the reason for his pensive withdrawal to his room. She found her son sitting at his window, gazing up at the clear, star-stippled sky. The radio in Billie's room was turned down low, the voice of the man who was giving news of the war both distant and ever present. "But I feel like—well, it's like it's something I'm supposed to do. Everybody's got some lousy job in this war, Ma. I guess this is mine."

One morning in December of 1944, Billie was handed a telegram that seemed different from all the others he had delivered. It was directed to the town's mayor. There was another one that got put into Billie's hand, this one going to the editor of the *Express*. When all was said and done, Billie walked out of the offices of the Western Union company with several separate wires to be delivered, each destined for a different elder in the community and each carrying news that for one bright and happy morning in this town which had for its size given more of its blood and sinew to the fight against fascism and for liberty and for American ideals and for everything else that Kate Smith sang about on the radio—that for one bright and happy morning there would be no death, no hometown casualty of war, no miserable imprisonment to be conveyed through the clipped, economically worded language of telegraphy. What was being conveyed was this: a ship had been commissioned, a ship that had been launched on November 9. It was given the name *Red Oak Victory*, in honor of the town's extreme sacrifice: its young men—both those who would come home crippled and scarred and forever changed by the war, and those whom the Secretary of War—through the good offices of Western Union—reported would not be coming home at all.

There are Red Oak boys buried all over the world.

It was a nice change for Billie—the chance to deliver telegrams that put smiles of joy and pride on the faces of their recipients. And upon his own face as well. But such a smile doesn't have a very long shelf life. The next day would come yet another yellow envelope, followed by another, and then another. Each would bear the requisite three stars, and each would need Billie Smaha to make sure that the proper person received it. Billie was a conscientious boy who never shirked his duty.

Stop.

1944

SEQUESTERED IN NEW MEXICO

Trust is an important thing in a marriage, and it was especially important in ours. I uprooted her from her parents and from her sister and from all of our friends in Berkeley and flumped her and the boys down upon this windswept mesa in one of the remotest reaches of northern New Mexico. And then I said—not to put too fine a point on it—"I can't tell you why."

He thinks I didn't know. Not until the Trinity test in July of '45. That's what's so funny. And the wind and the dust and the mud and all the daily inconveniences were a true test, I'll grant you that. But there were also consolations in the unearthly beauty of the place—the gorgeous strata of color in our sunset skies: the orange and lavender and scarlet, the shimmer and glow of cottonwood and aspen gold in autumn—even the exquisite native pottery that fills our house to this day. I remember, as well, all the lasting friendships we made there. It was a special place and a special time, and I felt privileged to be a part of it. In theory. Though what came from it has always troubled me.

It had to be done.

My husband's right. Somebody had to do it. Philip was a physicist—one of the best. He was young and talented and the war had to be won. He didn't tell me, but I knew.

You say you knew. You always say you knew, and yet I never mentioned any of it to you. I was careful in everything I said.

And yet. And yet. Philip, dear, please give me credit for being a halfway intelligent woman. I have a master's degree. I was well aware that it wasn't a submarine you men were building up there, though you got some mileage out of that nutty canard. And then there was that disastrous attempt at putting forth that bit of fiction about some kind of electricity-powered rocket. As if Flash Gordon had suddenly taken up residency in Los Alamos and we were all girding ourselves to fight the axis of Hitler and General Tojo and Ming the Merciless!

Whatever you knew or didn't know, you were a trooper and a trump through it all, and I loved you for it.

Did I have a choice? Oppie asked you to come and you came. And you brought your wife and your two boys with you, and what a time we had. We were certainly in the thick of it by 1944, weren't we? Everything good about that place had revealed itself and everything bad, excepting the water crisis the following year—

Our water tower failed us. The pipes froze. Things got pretty grimy.

Well, my point is that by and large we were tested and we passed the test with surprising resilience and ingenuity.

But with some complaint.

Of course I complained. We all complained. We were civilians and that's what American civilians do. We came here out of patriotic duty to assist the United States Army in winning the war for the Allies. And here in this secret, isolated community of soldiers and scientists—lovingly deemed by General Groves "the finest collection of crackpots the world has ever seen"—we made a life for ourselves and our families. It was a life unlike any that had ever been or probably ever would be.

In Washington we were called "Manhattan District," in Santa Fe, "Site Y." To anyone who ever wanted to write to us (and you will remember this, honey: all those letters you could never reciprocate without the censor breathing down your neck), we were known simply by our post office address—one address shared by all: P.O. Box 1663.

There upon the mesa we referred to our home as "Los Alamos," which is Spanish for cottonwood trees. Although I would have believed you if you'd told me the words also meant "Phantom Town." We were all spooks and spirits, weren't we, dear? Occupants of a shadow world. Officially, we weren't there, yet our neighbors over in Santa Fe and the men and women who came up from the pueblos to clean our homes and sweep the grit from our porches and do all those jobs that the Army couldn't or wouldn't do— they obviously knew we were there. We were flesh and bone to them. And though they didn't know why we'd come, they had to have suspected that it was for some vitally important purpose.

We were building a submarine.

Who said that my husband doesn't have a sense of humor?

Let me tell you about Betty. Sit back, Betty. I'm going to embarrass you. My wife was a regular dynamo. She looked after our two boys and worked part time in the Tech area as a secretary. She even put in a few hours every week at the high school and the hospital. The older kids in town were near delinquents and needed taming, and the hospital was forever filled with newborns, all of our fertile young wives dropping litters like estral she-dogs.

Dear, that was absolutely disgusting. You'll make them think that all we did up on this mesa was build bombs and make babies.

I recall that we also did a little skiing and played some cards. But you have to admit that there was a hell of a lot of baby-making going on.

Once a month my husband would reward me for all my hard work by letting me drive down to Santa Fe and stuff the trunk of our car with everything I couldn't find in our little hamlet on the hill, which was a very long list, if you want the truth of it.

Of course there was a definite ulterior motive behind my wife's monthly shopping spree: Betty's four o'clock gin Rickey at the La Fonda hotel—always in the company of several other similarly shopping-sapped expatriates from the land of government-imposed deprivation.

While you and Oppenheimer and Fermi and Teller nudged your neutrons and accelerated all your cyclotronic particles, it was Peg and Kitty and Mici and all the rest of us "significant others" who were required to keep the home fires burning, or in the case of those damned furnaces from hell, keep those ultra-efficient monsters from turning every Quonset hut and apartment house on the mesa into Finnish saunas. And it was we who stood up at the community meetings and bewailed the non-functioning Black Beauty stoves that converted all of our kitchens into various versions of the Museum of Ma Kettle, and vegetables that arrived at the commissary so spoiled or wilted that even the Three Little Pigs wouldn't have taken them for slop. With your head in the clouds of vaulted scientific theory and your hands doing the hard work of practical experimentation, you never seemed to notice the wind and the sand and dust of spring and early summer, or the mud of the late summer "monsoon." You took Oppie's word that this was going to be our very own Southwestern Shangri-La, when it was Oppenheimer himself who left the grid off the plat, and all of our houses and duplexes and apartment buildings—each the same lovely, unvarying shade of army green—being scattered without rhyme or topographical reason. And God help the husband who sought his own home in the dark night after he'd tied on one too many.

I was well aware of everything you just itemized. Didn't I try my damnedest to get you a house on Bathtub Row?

You did, dear. And I'm grateful for the effort, futile though it ultimately was. When we thought we might have a chance to move into one of those lovely old boys' camp homes, I dreamed of jasmine-scented bubble baths for several nights in a row. And then, alas, the bubble burst and it was back to the showers. But I do credit you for trying, and for getting me an Indian maid for three half-days a week, and you always spent time with the boys on the weekends, and didn't embarrass me at any of the parties or chase after any of the other wives.

I was quite satisfied, as it turned out, with the wife I had.

Thank you for that, dear.

It was a strange time.

And 1944 was the strangest year of all. It was the year that we settled in and looked all around us and the utter surreality of that place would sometimes stop me dead in my tracks.

You say you knew. How did you know?

I'd like to say, dear, that I overheard you talking in your sleep, but you never did. Although, one night I could swear you were sing-mumbling "Ac-Cent-Tchu-Ate the Positive."

Some of the guys had been singing it in the lab—the obvious protonic reference, of course—and it was locked inside my head.

Some of us girls were singing it in the commissary too when the milk delivery didn't arrive and we had to stay ourselves from riot. Darling, I figured out that you were here to build a great big bomb through process of elimination and through all the hundreds of hints that were dropped in front of those of us who were kept out of Oppie's Inner Sanctum. Why else would you have dragged Tommy and Philip Junior and me up here? You were worried that Hitler's scientists would get the jump on us. You boys had to come up with it first. And if all your theories found the practical application you were hoping for, the U.S. Army was going to drop that bomb and change the world forever.

You never spoke of any of this.

And why should I? Why should I give my poor overworked husband something else to fret over? I remember the grave look you used to carry on your face. I noticed the looks of serious purpose on the faces of all of the men who worked with Oppenheimer. General Groves couldn't be bothered with our petty grievances about wilted lettuce and paper-thin walls that afforded us all so little privacy, and electricity that seemed to come and go willy-nilly. He couldn't be bothered, darling, because he was overseeing something that would turn the page in the book of humanity. Never before had man been capable of creating a weapon of such exponentially superior destructive power. The door was opening now on that possibility. You and the other scientists were prying it open not quite knowing what you would find on the other side. My doors, dear—my doors were inconsequential.

They had hinges with missing screws. They had pencil marks on them from charting the growth of our boys. My world, my darling, was domestic, plain, and quotidian. But it was that world which you and Oppenheimer and the others were trying to save.

And that next year the sky lit up over southern New Mexico and all those little things that you boys had been blowing up on and off the mesa gave way to one big, blinding explosion that took the shape of a giant Alice in Wonderland mushroom. And then three weeks later, hell on earth was visited upon the residents of those two unfortunate Japanese cities.

And with parched lips and dirty faces, because the water still hadn't been restored upon the mesa, we packed our bags and moved back to California, our job here done, my job as helpmate to one of the men who built "the bomb" having come to an end.

I detect ambivalence in your feelings—about why we came to Los Alamos and what was accomplished there.

Haven't you the same ambivalence, darling? You've seen the newsreels. Pandora's box now has no lid.

I try to eliminate the negative and latch on to the affirmative. My wife is still here at my side and my two sons are safe and grown to sturdy manhood. It was a murderous madman in Germany who brought this horror upon the world, and generals in Asia who kept the Pacific in flames. I did what was asked of me with every good intention.

I hope we've told you what you wanted to know. We've got to get to our grandson's Little League game.

Did you know? They play baseball in Japan now.

1945

HYPERNATREMIC IN
THE PACIFIC OCEAN

"I heard it was one hundred thou the Cubs paid for him."

"My aunt's ass. No team in baseball's got that kind of dough to throw around."

"You don't think he's worth it? He's ten and five this season, and if they hadn't cancelled the All-Star game this month, you know he would've been back on the mound for the American League."

"So why you think the Yankees agreed to cut him loose?"

"Beats me. Beats me why these big league owners do *any* of the things they do."

"How'd Borowy get his draft deferment? He's what, twenty-eight, twenty-nine?"

"They say there's some kind of important off-season work he's doing at one of the war plants. Sounds a little fishy to me. Sounds like the important work he's doing might have less to do with putting bombs together and more to do with a certain high-pitch fast ball."

"I wonder about some of these guys—you know, the ones who get to stoke the home fires while the rest of us Joes rally 'round the flag. Take the 'Voice' for instance. What's kept that bony boy crooner in permanent civvies?"

"Something wrong with his eardrum when he was born—got punctured or something."

"This sun's killing me."

"Huh?"

"The sun. The heat. I'll take the cold. Just make that goddamned sun go down, Hillard."

"Don't think about it. Let's try to think about something else."

"What time do you think it is?"

"I don't know. Three, four in the afternoon."

"Oh."

"You ever seen him? Sinatra? You ever seen him sing?"

"Went with my sister. He was performing at the Waldorf. Show was in the Wedgewood Room, I think."

"Tell me about it."

"I got a big sore in my throat. Hurts a little to talk."

"Ask me if I care. Tell me about Sinatra. How does a string-bean kid like that get every thirteen-year-old girl in America to wet her pants just to look at him?"

"He does have a good voice."

"Good as Crosby?"

"How should I know? I grew up in a house full of Rudy Vallee records."

"Couple of weeks ago, they bring out this picture, *Anchors Aweigh*. Two sailors on leave in Hollywood: Sinatra and I forget the name of the other actor. I'm thinking: *I* never got shore leave in Hollywood. Did *you* ever get leave in Hollywood?"

"I didn't even get leave in Guam. I was sick in bed with stomach flu."

"How are you feeling now, Tork?"

"Oh, I'm over the flu. I've just got this little problem with being half out of my mind from thirst. Oh, and there's this other little thing with the upper half of my legs—you know, where they got scalded in the explosion. They still feel like they're on fire sometimes."

"At least you can still feel your legs. I lost all feeling below the waist several hours ago. Anyway, they say salt water's good for skin shit. Good for a lot of things, I hear. Just don't fucking drink it."

"I'm afraid I'm gonna flip my wig and start to hallucinate like some of the other guys."

"What other guys?"

"Heard Boyd and DeMornay a couple of hours ago—when they floated by. They were talking about going down to the Geedunk and getting themselves a big drink of water out of the fountain. Talking like they were still on the *Indianapolis*."

"Maybe they were just kidding around."

"Uh-uh. Dead serious. Rory, sometimes I think we're dead. I think we died already and we're in some kind of purgatory because I can't believe I deserve to be in hell."

"Here's how I know we aren't dead, Tork: because hell can't be half as bad as *this*."

"Makes no fucking sense."

"No fucking sense, you got *that* right."

"Two days we been out here. It just doesn't add up. They were expecting us in Leyte. You know there had to have been distress calls. How come nobody's shown up?"

"I don't know. I've thought about it and thought about it and I just can't figure it."

"What time do you think it is?"

"You asked me that already. What am I, a floating grandfather clock?"

"I was just wondering because—"

"What did Sinatra sing? I mean, at the Waldorf?"

"I don't remember. And it didn't matter anyway. Where my sister and me was sitting, you couldn't even hear him."

"Why's that?"

"Huh?"

"Why couldn't you hear him?"

"Did you hear that?"

"It was nothing."

"It was something. You heard it. Don't say you didn't."

"Some fellow napping—woke up yelling from a bad dream."

"You know that wasn't it. It's late afternoon, Hillard. They get hungry in the late afternoon. Then they feed through the night."

"Why couldn't you hear what Sinatra was singing? Was there a problem with the microphone?"

"No. The microphone was working fine."

"Look at me. Turn around and look at me. Talk to me about Sinatra."

"He's a singer. Now he's a big movie star—movie-star sailor. Movie-star sailor-crooners don't get torn to bits by sharks, so don't look for him out here. He makes a million dollars a year. That's what I read. A million dollars a year, and you can't even hear what he's singing because all the bobby-soxers are yelling so fucking loud. Yelling right in your ear. Like you aren't even there. Why don't they know we're here, Hillard? For Chrissakes, why isn't anybody coming to get us? The ship had nearly twelve hundred men on board. How can you totally forget about a ship with twelve hundred men on board?"

"You rest your voice now, Tork."

"Yeah, I'll need it for when the shark pulls me under—the shark out there with my name on his fin."

"They'll be here. They've realized their error. They're on their way."

"We don't deserve to win this war—a navy this incompetent."

"Don't talk that way."

"I'll talk any way I fucking want to. We're all going to die—we're dying one by one already. Couple more days there won't be any of us left."

"I don't see it that way."

"The sun's killing me. I'm going to the Geedunk. Gonna get me a cool drink of water. Then I'm gonna get me a big vanilla ice cream cone. Sound good, Rory? You wanna join me?"

"No. I wanna stay right here. And you're gonna stay right here with me."

"Why?"

"You saved my life. I owe it to you to—to look after you."

"Save your life? All I did was push this potato crate over to you. What's the big deal?"

"I want us both to live, Tork. I want us both to get out of here and get married and have kids and tell the story to our kids and our grandkids about how we survived."

"How *did* we survive, Rory? You tell me. What did we do so special? We just hung on and waited."

"And kept our wits by talking. I don't care if your throat hurts. You keep talking. If you start to sound a little screwy like all that hooey about going down to the commissary, I'll pull you out of it. You do the same for me. Okay?"

"I don't—"

"Okay? You tell me it's okay, Tork—what I'm proposing. You say it's okay or I bean you with this potato."

"It's okay or I bean you with this potato."

"First-class comedian we got here."

"How that elephant got into my pajamas, I'll never know."

"You wanna lick a potato?"

"Throat."

"Just lick it. Think of it as an ice cream cone."

"Sure."

"Good."

"It's hot as hell out here."

"Try not to think about it."

"Did you hear that?"

"I didn't hear nothing. Who was it liked Rudy Vallee so much—your mother or your father? Tork, are you listening to me?"

"Yeah. I'm listening. It was Ma. Ma was crazy for Rudy Vallee."

"Your mother—now where were *her* folks from?"

"Uh. Kansas. Little town in west Kansas."

"Born there?"

1946

ENNEADIC IN IOWA

Barend Kleerekoper taught mathematics at Coe College, a small college in Cedar Rapids. He was a good teacher and a favorite among his students, though he kept largely to himself and had no close friends. Dr. Kleerekoper had immigrated to the U.S. in 1934 from the Netherlands. When he lost his job teaching at the University of Groningen after the school experienced a severe drop in enrollment during the Dutch economic depression, the faculty of Coe's mathematics department worked to bring him to their campus. The professors had long been admirers of his renowned achievements in irrational and transcendental number theory. They were happy to welcome him to their friendly town of solid, common-sense Iowa values, leavened by the kind of gentle, self-deprecating humor emblematized by native son Grant Wood's popular and iconic *American Gothic*.

When Kleerekoper moved to the U.S., he left his whole family behind: his mother, father, and younger brother in Amsterdam, and his older brother and sister and their respective families in Rotterdam. A confirmed bachelor, Barend had never married.

The fate of the professor's extended family was tragically sealed when the Netherlands fell to the Nazis in 1940. His sister and her husband died in the bombing of Rotterdam. The rest of the family was rounded up and sent to the death camps of Sobibor, Buchenwald, and Auschwitz. None survived.

By the end of the war, well-kept Dutch civil records confirmed exactly what had happened to each of Kleerekoper's loved ones back in Europe. In the wake of this news, the professor was rarely seen outside his classroom. During the winter break between '45 and '46 he holed up in his tiny apartment near the college, only emerging to buy groceries once a week and on one occasion to visit a doctor. His eyes hurt him. The physician diagnosed eye strain and prescribed more rest. More shut-eye, the doctor said. Kleerekoper didn't crack a smile; some American idioms still eluded him.

Kleerekoper's fellow faculty members reached out to him during those long, dark months of mourning. He rejected their attempts to envelope him in the warmth of their holiday collegiality and cheer. Kleerekoper had always been a semi-solitary man. Now, his solitude seemed to have become permanent.

For this reason, Nancy Fairfax had hesitated going to him. It was her brother, Eli—who'd taken a couple of classes from the professor before the war—who talked her into it. Dr. Kleerekoper was the perfect candidate, said Eli, to tutor Nancy's son in junior high math. It was the week between Christmas and New Year's, and Nancy's husband was still needed in Europe. Nancy operated a granulator at the city's Quaker Oats factory (which made Cedar Rapids smell, on blustery days, like cooked oatmeal). Her son, Jim, wanted a career in military intelligence like his father, but first he had to pass eighth-grade algebra. Nancy wanted only the best for her son.

The best was Barend Kleerekoper.

She didn't phone. Instead, she showed up at his door on the morning of December 26, 1945.

Still dressed in his pajamas and a tatty house robe, he at first tried to ignore the repeated sequence of knocks. He hoped that whoever it was would simply give up and go away. It was early. He hadn't even opened the *Gazette*. Kleerekoper had been closely following the news coverage of the Nuremberg trials and was especially invested in learning the fate of the Netherlands' murderous Reichskommissar, Arthur Seyss-Inquart (who several months later would be found guilty of crimes against humanity and sentenced to hang).

His visitor didn't go away. When Kleerekoper finally opened the door, he found a woman several years younger than his forty-seven years standing with chattering teeth in the unheated hallway.

"Hello," she said, holding something round and flat upon the palm of her hand in the manner of a waitress. "My name is Nancy Fairfax. You taught my brother Eli several years ago. He's spoken very highly of you ever since. Here's a pie. It's a Christmas pie. I know you're Jewish and you don't have to eat it, but I brought it anyway."

"Why?"

"May I come in?"

"No, you may not come in. Why did you bring me a pie? Because I taught your brother several years ago? That isn't logical."

"If you want the truth, Dr. Kleerekoper, my son, Jim—he's in the eighth grade. He needs a tutor. He's going to fail math if he doesn't get help."

Barend Kleerekoper slammed the door shut, although he wasn't entirely impolite about it. As the door was closing, Nancy heard the "Happy" part of "Happy holidays."

He didn't take the pie.

The pie did, however, find its way into his apartment later that day, when he stepped out to put his garbage into the chute and found the pie, reposed within a twined baker's cake box, waiting for him on the thin square of footworn carpet that served as his welcome mat. He ate two slices that night. It was the first American Christmas pie he'd ever had—strawberry-rhubarb—and every bit as good as the eierkoekens and kruimelkoekjes he'd enjoyed as a boy in the Netherlands.

The professor discovered a box of homemade raisin and oat cookies in front of his door the next morning. Everyone ate raisin and oat cookies here in Oat Town, but these were especially good. "You can send me all the sweets you like," he said to the baker in absentia, "but I have better things to do with my time than tutor a fourteen-year-old mathematical illiterate." He put a forkful of the half-finished strawberry-rhubarb pie into his mouth and almost smiled. Pie. Pi. If only Mrs. Fairfax knew the unintended appropriateness of that first culinary bribe.

No one knew, in fact, how Professor Kleerekoper spent his solitary hours, because he saw no reason to share details of his private masterwork with his colleagues. Perhaps some might find merit in it, but he also risked exposing himself to ridicule from others.

Pi. A mathematical constant whose value is the ratio of any Euclidean plane circle's circumference to its diameter. Arguably the most fascinating and most celebrated of irrational numbers—that is, numbers whose value can't be expressed as a fraction m/n, where m and n are integers—its representation in decimal positional notation never ending and never repeating as a whole. Despite the fact that pi need only be taken to the tenth decimal point to give the circumference of the Earth to within a fraction of an inch (that point reached by Madhava of Sangamagrama late in the fourteenth century), mathematicians (both those of the professional stripe and rank pi-loving amateurs) have throughout the ages been calculating pi to as many decimal places as their abilities and the technological sophistication of their calculating hardware permitted.

Kleerekoper, in joining (though hermetically) this longstanding cerebral pastime (one that in only three short years would be removed to the realm of eye-popping supra-achievement through application of the electronic computer), found in his efforts both the solace-granting satisfaction and the calculative sanity necessary to combat his deep depression. Working with his mechanical desk calculator, he permitted the numbers to order themselves in that lackadaisical way that affirmed his belief that the universe was randomness writ large. That the guiding hand of God was the stuff of fairy tale. That loved ones were put to death by madmen only because good and evil were cards played out of the same deck of chance, and in a chaotic universe everything is possible, even the unimaginable.

Dr. Kleerekoper had heard Christians speak of God's will. What God, the professor would have liked to have asked them, would ever countenance the genocide of millions? But he would not ask it, nor could he even allow himself to think it—to allow such musings to crowd his calculating brain cells. Only the day before—the day that Nancy Fairfax had come to his door to distract him with an errand of advocacy for her son—he had reached the 761st decimal place in the infinite number pi. He was certain that it was a world record, far surpassing the previous publicized record set in 1873 by an amateur mathematician in England by the name of William Shanks: 707 decimal places. And Shanks' wasn't even a valid record: both Kleerekoper and a fellow mathematician by the name of Ferguson, using similar mechanical calculators in 1944, had discovered that Shanks had erred at the 528th decimal place. Every digit thereafter was wrong and had to be corrected before his record could be bested.

It was all hard work. It required time. Time was something that Kleerekoper had in great abundance. This is what pi looks like taken to the 761st decimal place:

```
3.1415926535    8979323846    2643383279    5028841971
6939937510    5820974944    5923078164    0628620899
8628034825    3421170679    8214808651    3282306647
0938446095    5058223172    5359408128    4811174502
8410270193    8521105559    6446229489    5493038196
4428810975    6659334461    2847564823    3786783165
```

```
2712019091    4564856692    3460348610    4543266482
1339360726    0249141273    7245870066    0631558817
4881520920    9628292540    9171536436    7892590360
0113305305    4882046652    1384146951    9415116094
3305727036    5759591953    0921861173    8193261179
3105118548    0744623799    6274956735    1885752724
8912279381    8301194912    9833673362    4406566430
8602139494    6395224737    1907021798    6094370277
0539217176    2931767523    8467481846    7669405132
0005681271    4526356082    7785771342    7577896091
7363717872    1468410901    2249534301    1654958537
1050792279    6892589235    4201995611    2129021960
8640344181    5981362977    4771309960    51870721134
```

Kleerekoper planned to reach the 800th decimal place by the end of summer. He would celebrate his accomplishment with a dish of creamy Dutch Advocaat. He wondered if Mrs. Fairfax had ever tried it.

He was thinking of her.

He was thinking of her because she was at that moment on this third morning getting out of her car, which was parked right in front of his apartment building. Her son was with her. The woman was like a Dutch Shepherd Dog with a bone. He was the bone. It rankled him. He was curious about what tasty dessert she'd brought along this time, but still, it rankled him.

It was cake, as it turned out. A sweet, citrus-smelling, frosting-drizzled lemon pound cake.

His resistance was shattered.

Within minutes of Mrs. Fairfax's arrival Kleerekoper had agreed to tutor the boy twice a week. He had wanted, in spite of the cake, to tell the woman and her son to leave him alone now and forevermore, but there was an earnestness about the boy that touched him. Jim seemed willing to really apply himself. He didn't have a head for numbers, but that wasn't his fault. Kleerekoper's own head was *too* filled with numbers, he sometimes thought. Because they were his refuge. Pi was his refuge. He wondered how he should go on living if he didn't have something to occupy his empty hours. Only so much of his time could be given to his undergraduates. And during the long winter break, there weren't even any of them around.

"Twice a week," Kleerekoper repeated. "Ninety minutes a session. Make note that I plan to work you hard."

Jim nodded.

The first two tutoring sessions went well. Jim learned things. He retained important mathematical concepts imparted to him by an excellent teacher. Kleerekoper had never had a child, had spent very little time around children or adolescents. This was something new for him—working with the boy, guiding him, helping him to understand the simple things that Barend had mastered in early childhood.

The third session found Jim unfocused, distrait.

"What's the matter? Why can't you concentrate?" asked the teacher.

"I've been noticing: there are no pictures on your walls."

"No. I'm not an aficionado of the visual arts, of *any* of the aesthetic arts. Seeking beauty in an ugly world is, to me, a fairly unavailing occupation."

"I mean, Dr. Kleerekoper, that there aren't any *photographs*—no photographs of people on your walls. Or anyplace else."

The boy was restless. He wandered around the room, touching its naked, empty paneling.

"My family is dead. I choose to remember them only through my memories."

"My mother told me this—about your family. Last night."

"What else did your mother say about my family?"

The boy sat back down. "It doesn't matter. I'm having trouble with problem number four. Can you help me with number four?"

"I'll help you with number four if you'll tell me why the subject of my family came up last night."

Jim took a moment to answer. When he spoke, he withheld his gaze. It was hard to look at Kleerekoper as he said it. "We saw pictures of some of those men in the camps. The ones who survived. They looked like skeletons."

"Yes. That's right."

"My mother prayed last night with me. She prayed to God that He won't let this ever happen again."

Kleerekoper sat down at the table next to Jim. He put his palm under the boy's chin and raised his face to look at him. "I regret to inform you, James, that her prayers are in all likelihood falling on nonexistent ears."

"You don't believe in God?"

The professor allowed the question to answer itself.

"I sometimes wonder if there's a God myself," said Jim. "I haven't told my mother."

"It's best to keep such musings to yourself. James, I want to show you something." Kleerekoper got up from his chair and fetched a folder from his desk across the room. "You're the first to see this," he said, opening the folder. "I spoke of pi the other day. Do you remember?"

"It's a number that has no end. It goes on and on like eternity."

"That's right. I've calculated this unending number to the 761st decimal place. See?"

"Why?"

"Why what?"

"Why do you calculate a number that has no end?"

"I happen to derive some measure of satisfaction from it. Why do we do *any* of the things we do?"

"Are you looking for something, Professor?"

"What do you mean, 'looking'?"

"Numbers that continue on and on like that, at some point something has to happen, right?"

"I still don't get your meaning, boy."

Jim wriggled slightly in his chair. "I don't know how to say it. You say they're just a bunch of numbers that don't make sense. What if they *did* make sense? I mean, all those numbers—they have to be coming from *somewhere*."

"They're coming from *nowhere*, Jim. They're already here. I just want to find out what they are. I'm inquisitive. Most mathematicians *are*."

"What if God put them there?"

Kleerekoper smiled. "I thought you weren't sure if there *was* a God."

"I'm playing the devil's—what?"

"The devil's attorney, I think it is. Yes, you are, James. But there *is* no God. Show me the proof of God's existence against all evidence to the contrary, my boy, and I will engage you further in this discussion. But for now, we must return to our far less fanciful discussion of binomial coefficients. What's giving you trouble about problem number four?"

Two weeks later, Barend Kleerekoper took pi to the 762nd decimal point. The number was 9. A week after that, he calculated pi to the 763rd place. Another 9. He'd seen double 9s before. Nothing unusual here. School was back in session. The next decimal place wasn't reached for another couple of weeks: a third 9. Interesting. There had only been three previous appearances of numerical triplets up to this point: a trio of 1s, then 5s, then 0s. A week and a half later, very early in the morning, Dr. Barend Kleerekoper made a rather startling discovery: a fourth 9. Quadruplet 9s! The very first appearance of a numerical foursome. He celebrated his discovery by eating a whole plate of brownies left by Mrs. Fairfax when she picked up Jim the night before.

It wasn't over.

Place number 766 was also a 9. Astonishing. Remarkable. Five 9s in a row! How far, Barend wondered, would this phenomenon extend itself?

Farther still, it turned out.

Place number 767 was a 9 as well. Six 9s all lined up together. It was beyond remarkable. It was unbelievable. Kleerekoper calculated the odds of any chosen number sequence of six digits occurring this soon in the decimal representation of pi at 0.08 percent. "Quite unusual, yes?" he put to Jim with a level of giddy animation the boy had never seen from him before.

Jim nodded and grinned. "Do you think the nines will keep going on and on?"

"I rather doubt that."

"But what if they do?"

Kleerekoper thought about this. He shook it off. "Nonsense."

It was nonsense. The next number wasn't a 9. It was an 8. Still—all those 9s—a sextet of identical numbers appearing so early in this seemingly random sequence of digits that was supposed to go on and on and on into infinity...

Like God.

"Pi is God?"

"That's not what I'm saying, Professor." Jim looked at the number, which Kleerekoper had typed up on a piece of paper and put before him. Kleerekoper had circled the six nines and underlined them, had even put an exclamation point beneath them.

"Then what are you saying? And what have I told you about speaking clearly and precisely? There is no room for ambiguity in our discussions."

"Pi isn't God, Professor. But I think God is there. Those six nines—I think that was God, um, *winking* at us."

Barend Kleerekoper smiled and scratched his head. "Interesting deduction. So this God of ours—he sets the universe in motion, and then he steps back and allows what will happen to happen, except that…"

"Except that sometimes He, well, *winks*. To let you know He's still there."

"Absolutely ridiculous and end of discussion," said Kleerekoper with finality. "Let's have a slice of that cake your mother left. Why do they call it 'pineapple upside-down cake'? It looks right-side-up to me."

At some time between 1961, when an IBM 7090 computer in New York City calculated pi to the 100,265th decimal point and 1966 when an IBM 7030 computer in Paris calculated the number to the 250,000th decimal point, the important decimal place of 193,034 was reached. It is important for this reason: it is the point at which the next sequence of six identical consecutive numbers finally makes its long-delayed appearance.

You may be interested to know that this second set of sextuplets also happens to be…nines.

Wink.

1947

RACIST IN TENNESSEE

There were three men in the room. The oldest was in his late seventies. The other two were significantly younger. The old man sat behind a desk. The other two men, having just entered the room, gravitated to the window.

It was a fine view.

The three men were meeting on the top floor of a building which, while not the tallest skyscraper in town (that would be the twenty-nine-floor gothic-deco Sterick Building), did happen to distinguish itself in its own way. It was white. Shimmering white. And its architectural design was derived from one of the most famous skyscrapers in the world: the Woolworth Building in New York City. (Though it stood not nearly so tall as its five-and-dime Manhattan inspiration.)

"Either of you boys been up here before?" the old man asked casually. Both men shook their heads. "You ever heard of Irving Block Prison?"

One of the men nodded. The other shook his head. The old man answered as if both had replied in the negative. "Stood right on this spot. Irving was the Union Army's military prison after the city's capture. One of the reasons for the second Battle of Memphis was to free the Confederate sympathizers whom the Yankees had locked up here. Of course, the attack on the prison didn't go nearly as well as General Forrest would've liked."

The old man didn't mention that the building from which the two visitors were presently enjoying their exalted twenty-second-story vantage point had been built by the very man whom they had come to see: Lloyd T. Binford, president of the Memphis branch of the Columbia Mutual Insurance Company. Appropriately called the Columbia Mutual Tower, the downtown structure housed not only the Memphis offices of that large, esteemed insurance firm, but the headquarters, as well, of the Memphis Censor Board. As it so happened, the insurance company president was also the head motion picture cop for the Bluff City.

Lloyd T. Binford was a man who loved movies. Except for those movies which he, well, *didn't* love.

And that's why the two men were here. They were emissaries of Memphis's downtown movie houses—beautiful buildings in their own way: ornate movie palaces whose seats sometimes sat nearly empty. It wasn't that Memphians didn't like to go to the picture show. It was just that Lloyd T. Binford sometimes made it hard for them to see the movies they wanted to see here. In Memphis. They'd usually have to leave town— go to West Memphis, Arkansas, for example. West Memphis sat on the other side of the Mississippi River, just west of a broad, empty floodplain. West Memphis theatre owners did land-office business exhibiting all those movies that Mr. Binford had banned in Memphis.

"I take it you boys didn't just come for the scenery," said Mr. Binford with a pleasant, avuncular smile. The smile came with some effort: Binford's face drooped a little in its lower half as was its wont, partly from the gravitational pull of the aging process, but also from the tug of his permanent declivitous pout. "Nor do I think that you're here to get me to reverse my decision on *Curley*."

"No," said the taller of Mr. Binford's two visitors, though his head was nodding affirmatively. "If all the powers that be at United Artists can't induce you to change your mind about that picture, I'm sure my inconsequential little Princess Theatre could do no better."

The taller man moved to take one of the two empty chairs positioned on the other side of the desk.

"But surely you must understand my reasoning," said Binford, tapping a forefinger on his desk's blotter. "Have I not made myself perfectly clear on this?"

The other man, who was Jeff to the first man's Mutt, answered for his partner: "It's the usual, isn't it? The picture's got colored kids sitting side by side in a classroom with white kids. It's because the picture's integrated."

Binford leaned forward, scarcely dropping a shadow on the great expanse of oak. "Which Memphis isn't."

"We aren't here to discuss *Curley*, sir," said the first man. "That horse has already left the barn. We're here to talk about all the horses still inside."

"Gentleman, let us not waste time rehashing my feelings about black folk on the screen. Memphis doesn't recognize social equality between the races, and that goes for children, too. As head of the Censor Board, I do my very best to give the people of this city what they feel comfortable with."

The second man—the short and dumpy one—now sat down next to his companion. "But Mr. Binford, if they aren't comfortable with these kinds of pictures, why are they all getting in their cars and driving out of town to see them? And that's the point of our coming to see you today. Mr. Seale and I represent the interests of nearly every theatre owner in Memphis. We've been losing money to theatres in West Memphis and Desoto County, Mississippi, for years—ever since you got appointed head of the Censor Board. 'Banned in Memphis' is big business for our out-of-town competitors. At the risk of giving offense, sir, these interdictions of yours—and your fondness for taking the scissors to movies with scenes that you don't like—it's all very bad for local folk in our line of work. And, to put it, if I may, into civic terms, it reduces taxable revenue for the city. So on behalf of all concerned, we implore you and the rest of the Censor Board to demonstrate a little more lenience when it comes to the films you may wish to ban or expurgate." Turning to his companion: "Did I say 'implore'?"

"You did, brother. You said 'implore.' I second the motion."

Binford now stood. He placed both hands palms down on his desktop. "I *do* take offense, Mr. Cantor. I take offense because the board doesn't make its rulings arbitrarily. Its members think long and hard about how a film will be received by the movie-going citizens of this movie-loving town."

"Two years ago," pursued the man named Cantor, "you banned *Brewster's Millions* because you said that the servant character played by Rochester—by Eddie Anderson —you said he was treated too well. What does that mean, Mr. Binford? 'Treated too well'? I saw the picture in West Memphis, and this is by no means a remake of *The Admirable Crichton*."

"I don't know *The Admirable Crichton*. Does it have Niggras in it?

"No, it doesn't. You're missing my point."

Mr. Cantor's partner in logic took up the cause: "Last year, Mr. Binford, your busy Censor Board cut Lena Horne's number out of *Ziegfeld Follies*."

"The whole setup was unpalatable, sir. She was fighting with another Negress over a man in a bar."

Seale sighed. "You banned *Curley* because of harmonious interaction between colored children and white children. You snipped out Miss Horne for a reason that goes to the opposite extreme. I submit to you, Mr.

Binford, that you don't much care to see colored people appear in white movies in any context at all, other than perhaps a wholly subservient one."

Binford nodded. "There is no good reason to put a Niggra in a Hollywood picture, unless the Niggra's wearing an apron or toting a bale."

"And acting appropriately servile," added Seale.

"I didn't make the world the way it is, gentlemen. We have black folk and we have white folk, and by the way, I happen to like Niggras. I've got a soft spot in my heart for *old* Niggras especially. They remind me of the servants we had down in Duck Hill. But I don't believe in a mingling of the races and I don't believe in putting forth this mendacious idea that Niggras have the smarts or the innate capacity to be anything more than domestics and day laborers."

"I think the lawyers down at the NAACP might beg to differ. By the way, Mr. Binford, is Charlie Chaplin colored?"

"Now don't you go and get my temperature up about that limey guttersnipe—a demonstrable enemy of American decency and virtue."

"Mr. Binford, you don't even allow cowboy pictures to play in Memphis if there's a train robbery somewhere in the story."

"Train robberies are frightening to young children. And I should know; I was on the receiving end of one that turned deadly when I was a boy. There isn't a child in this city who'd derive benefit from seeing a Western picture with a vicious train robbery in it."

The old man pounded his fist to drive home his point. It was an anemic act and hardly made a sound.

Binford's two visitors passed a look of defeat between them.

"When do you plan to retire, Mr. Binford?" asked Mutt.

"Next year, perhaps?" sought Jeff.

"Now you'd just like that, wouldn't you?" retorted the old man, easing back down into his chair. "You'd like me to remove myself as guardian of the morals of the citizens of this fine town, so that you can bring communist pictures in here and pictures with chesty harlots like that there Jane Russell piece of garbage, pictures where gunslingers go about their nefarious business of robbing trains and shooting innocent railroad clerks and giving them lifelong nightmares. You'd like that pretty darn well, *now wouldn't you?*"

"No, Mr. Binford," said Seale evenly. "We're just trying to make an honest buck in this town—that's all. And you, sir, have been tying our hands mighty tight."

"That's what the miscreant did who robbed the train I was clerking on. But I didn't dissolve into a Jell-O cup of quivering cowardice, no-siree. I held my chin up high and looked my captors brazenly in the eye. And I can tell you as sure as I'm sitting here that from the looks of those black-eyed felons, they had Niggra blood, all right. No doubt about it."

The two men walked away from the refulgent white Columbia Mutual Tower, built by a white man who had done well in the insurance game. Their stroll took them down Main Street and to their respective movie houses, where all the best pictures of the day played, except for those that featured Charlie Chaplin and train robbers and any character of African American descent who didn't know his place.

Neither man registered the passage of a garbage truck moments earlier. There were two men in the cab. The driver was a young white man. Riding shotgun was an African American man. His name was Tom Lee. The next year Tom would retire from the job he had held for over twenty years—the first African American to be hired by the City of Memphis's Department of Sanitation. He would be stricken with cancer and die in 1952. Posthumously, he would be honored by having a downtown park named for him. Tom Lee was a hero to the people of the city of Memphis. He had rescued thirty-two people—both white and black—from the turbulent waters of the Mississippi when a steamboat, the *M.E. Norman*, flipped freakishly on its side in 1925.

In the last two years of Mr. Binford's life, he would look down upon that park from the pinnacle of his glistening white tower—look down and scratch his hoary head.

To think that they'd named a whole park after a Niggra! It mystified the hell out of him.

1948

HAUNTED IN CONNECTICUT

Ramona found her husband looking out the window at the end of the couple's narrow galley kitchen. He had pulled a chair in from the dining room and sat there in his bed robe, the window sash raised, a cool waft of night air stroking his face with delicate, invisible fingers.

"Dana?" she said softly in the darkness.

He didn't start. He had already felt her presence, felt her standing there watching him, worrying about him. Somewhere along Second Avenue a taxi honked its horn. Somewhere in the courtyard that separated his boxy monolithic apartment building from its boxy monolithic neighbor one block north, someone was playing a radio. Or perhaps it was the noisy jukebox in the bar on Second Avenue, where Dana sometimes stopped to get a drink on the way home from his job as an advertising copywriter.

"Dana, dear, would you like some warm milk?"

Dana Darby shook his head.

"Come to bed, then. We'll get everything worked out with the architect. I told you, it's not worth losing sleep over."

"I wasn't thinking about the new house." he said.

Ramona Darby knew not to ask. She knew that her husband rarely shared his war memories with anyone, even the person he was closest to in the world. They were too painful. Dana was generally good at keeping them at bay during the daytime. It was during the quiet, empty hours of the night that they crept back in the form of dark, intrusive recollection, or returned in full assault in the form of brutal dreams.

Bataan. The death march. The camps.

Dana Darby liked to pull a chair up to the window in his kitchen and stare out into the night, to behold the twinkling, geometric cityscape of Upper Eastside Manhattan, its steel and masonry little resembling the Philippine jungle of his nightmares. He liked to remember that in large American cities like New York, crime is generally an isolated act of selfishness perpetrated for want of money or the need for illegal drugs. Or it is an expression of jealous rage or interpersonal rivalry. If there is an element of inhumanity to it, it is nothing compared to that which Dana had seen and experienced first hand on the Bataan Peninsula. What happened to his fellow POWs, to the interned Jews of Europe, to all the victims of that war only recently ended left him with a gaping wound in his soul that would not heal. That man was capable of such unconscionable acts against other men. Against women. Against defenseless children. It was difficult even to contemplate.

"I want you to come to the bedroom. I want to show you the colors I was thinking of for the new house."

Dana rose heavily from his chair. He closed the window. "You're already picking out colors? They haven't even laid the foundation yet."

"You know I like to plan ahead. Come sit with me." Ramona took her husband's hand and led him to the bedroom. She often mothered him. He never complained. On nights like these, nothing mattered. Ramona could do or say whatever she liked, and she often did, to coax from Dana something that resembled a smile.

Tonight Ramona went over the colors for the paint and shared with her husband some ideas she had for wallpaper. She did this in a variety of funny voices. She succeeded in making Dana laugh in spite of himself. And then she put everything away and tucked him into bed, reminding him that he needed his rest. Dana was supposed to get up early the next morning to drive up to the five pristine acres he and his wife had just purchased a few months before—acres that, thanks to post-war inflation, had cost them twice what they had intended to spend. Tomorrow was the day that the drilling company was supposed to come. They were going to dig the Darbys a well.

Dana and Ramona knew that after years in the city, it was time for them to move out, to situate themselves in the peaceful Connecticut countryside. Where the nights were long and quiet. Deathly quiet.

Oh how Dana was looking forward to *that*.

Dana didn't reach the property until midmorning. The drilling operation had been in full swing for at least two hours. There were friendly waves from the father and son and the other two men who were involved in the laborious business of extracting water from the hard rock that lay beneath Dana's property. The men couldn't be interrupted at the moment; the early part of the operation was the most critical and labor intensive. A great hole had first to be dug. Once the digging was completed, the men had to jack the drill up, secure it and level it. Dana watched as the son began to set up an onsite blacksmith shop, complete with anvil and bellow, sledge, coke pile, and water quench. The young man found a nice shady spot under a couple of tall elms. Dana thought this might be a good time to introduce himself. From a distance, the four men were a blur of hats and heaving shoulders and active hands. He'd hoped it wouldn't take weeks to find water, but odds were they'd be on a first-name basis by the time the well was completed, and Dana was nothing if not a friendly employer.

The son had stopped his work in the makeshift forge to watch as his father and the other two men guided the five-hundred-pound drill bit into place. Both he and Dana stood silently, observing the twisted steel cable being threaded through the pulley of the rig's tower, and then being looped under a pulley in the walking beam, and finally pulled back to a drum from which it could be released foot by foot into the deepening hole. A few minutes later the young man turned to Dana, pushed back the brim of his hat, and wiped his right hand on his overalls. He walked over and, smiling amiably, reached out to shake Dana's hand.

Dana shook it, even as all of the color left his face. He looked into the cheerful countenance of the driller's son, into his dark brown eyes, the skin slightly creased below. He took in the hard jawline, the recessed cheeks, a shock of dirty blond hair escaping from beneath the hat. The man, whose name Dana knew to be Larry Anders Jr. was a perfect replica of a young man whom Dana had known seven years earlier. Like Dana, the man had worked with the 27th Materials Squadron at Nichols Field—a pursuit and operations base—on Luzon in the Philippines. He was a flight mechanic, Dana a crew chief. Within weeks the two men were moved to the Bataan Air Base and then in April, 1942, were surrendered along with 75,000 other Americans and Filipinos to the invading Japanese forces. The young man was his friend. Was his *best* friend.

"Are you all right?" asked Larry.

"Yeah—I'm—you look like somebody."

"I get that sometimes. That actor, right? Who does the Pete Smith 'Specialities'? He was also in that crazy—that *Reefer Madness*. He was the dope fiend who kept yelling—now what was it he kept yelling?"

Dana interrupted: "No, I mean in the war. A guy I knew in the war."

"Where'd you serve?"

Dana was getting lightheaded. He backed himself into a folding chair and sat down. "I was in Bataan," he said softly.

"That's a long way from where Uncle Sam put *me*. I was over in France for most of the—you want I should get you something to drink?"

Dana shook his head. "Just let me sit here for a second."

Larry squatted in front of Dana. "I look that much like him?"

Dana nodded. He swallowed. He didn't feel well. Brett Freuer. Incarnate. Resurrected. The resemblance was more than uncanny. Even the voice was similar; it had a slight drawl. Brett grew up in Arizona. Dana wondered if Larry and his dad were also from the Southwest.

Dana felt like an idiot. He felt like a little old lady with the vapors. For Christ's sake, he'd survived the Bataan Death March and then spent over three years in dehumanizing captivity. Brett didn't even survive the march. A lot of men didn't. There was no rhyme or reason to which men would crap out, would succumb to the lack of food and water, to tropical disease, to the murderous whims of their Japanese captors. Or was there something in his mettle, in his desire to survive that gave Dana the advantage? And if so, where was that fortitude today?

Dana spent the rest of the afternoon listening to the loud drone of the rig's motor, watching the walking beam rise and fall as the cable went from taut to slack each time the bit hit the bottom of the deepening hole. He rescued himself from the Bataan Peninsula ten, twenty, fifty times that afternoon and put himself in the here and now of rural southwestern Connecticut, upon his five pristine acres, in the presence of the men who were drilling for the water that would allow him and his wife to escape the heat and congestion of the city and live a cooler, quieter, less chaotic life. And yet Dana's gaze repeatedly returned to his dead friend's twenty-something-year-old doppelganger.

Dana left before any of the men in the drilling outfit did. But he didn't go home, didn't drive right back down the turnpike to the City. He found a neighborhood tavern in nearby New Canaan, a place where he could get a beer before all the thirsty working stiffs from the area filed in, hot and tired from their long day of manual employment. Dana sat in the friendly watering hole nursing his pint, popping peanuts into his mouth, listening to a couple of regulars discussing the at-bat pyrotechnics of Musial and Williams and Kiner and Mize.

He didn't even notice when the Anders, both father and son, entered the place and slid into a booth. Was totally oblivious to their presence until Larry Jr. excused himself from his father and claimed the stool next to him.

"Play it faster! Play it faster!"

Dana turned.

Larry was grinning. "That's what the character says in that crazy marijuana flick, *Reefer Madness*. He's yelling it to some girl playing the piano. I guess when you're hyped up on reefer, you want your music hyped up too." Larry signaled the bartender for his usual and then said to Dana, "That friend of yours you mentioned earlier—he's dead?"

Dana nodded.

"Christ. Sorry. He was your best buddy, right?"

"He saved my life."

"You mind telling me how?"

"I—um."

"Sure. Sure. Okay."

The two men sat quietly. Then Dana said, "How much are you and your dad going to cost me when all of this is said and done?"

"Depends on whether we have to go below three hundred feet. Three hundred feet, the price takes a big jump. But you probably already knew this."

Dana nodded. Yes, he knew.

Dana had three beers. He was a little fuzz-brained from having skipped lunch. "You want that I should drive you to the train station?" Larry asked. "You can pick up your car tomorrow or the next day. I know the owner of this bar. He'll let you keep it parked out back if you like."

"No. I think I'll be all right."

Larry walked Dana out to his car. He put him behind the wheel. Then he said, "Don't move. I'll get you some coffee. We'll have a little coffee until you feel sharp enough to head home."

Dana was about to decline. Something stopped him. Something in Larry's solicitous look. Something in his concerned voice.

The two men sat drinking coffee as darkness began to settle in.

"You had to keep moving," said Dana without preamble. He was looking straight ahead, staring at the middle distance and seeing nothing but the jungle. "You fall down, you go for water to slake your thirst, you slip off to take a crap, they shoot you, or slice your throat open. Those of us who couldn't keep up, who moved a little too slow got picked off by the buzzard squads. I didn't have a helmet. The sun was burning my brain. Brett was next to me—we'd been right next to each other the whole time. Brett was from Tucson. He said he was used to the heat. Me, from Jersey, the sun was going to be my death. He watched me fading. I started stumbling, my legs pretzeling up. He gave me his helmet. He didn't need the helmet, he said. He was from Tucson. I revived. Brett revived me, kept me moving forward. The last two days we're walking like the dead—one foot in front of the other. Little food, little water, but there's something that keeps me going. It's how much Brett *wants* me to keep going. In the midst of all the death, I represent life to him and he represents life to me.

"We get to San Fernando and they put us into boxcars. And we're packed so tight in there we can't sit down. We're in that boxcar from early in the morning until late that afternoon. Pushed up together like—I've got nothing to compare it to. You stop thinking at a time like that. Your brain just shuts down. It gets taken over by a practical need to survive, to keep taking in each new breath. I'm pushed against Brett. Pushed up so close I can feel his heart beating against my back. We're all just organs and bones at this point—came into this march already half starved to death after those last grueling weeks in Bataan. I can feel his heart. The heart of the man who saved my life.

"And then..." Dana stopped and took a deep breath, willing himself to finish the story. "And then I don't. Just like that, Brett's dead. He's a standing corpse. One of many. But I don't think about the others. I've seen death fifty times over. I think only of Brett. How he did something for me to keep me alive, but I couldn't do anything for him. I just stood there and let him die."

Dana swallowed the last of his coffee from the cardboard cup, shook his head.

"Just let him die."

Dana grew silent as Larry stared out the window, thinking. Then Dana tried to say something. He struggled to form the words. He was like a stuttering boy unable to get even the first syllable out of his mouth. Finally, it came: "Are you Brett?"

Larry didn't answer for a long moment. Then, as if it were the most natural thing in the world for him to do, he nodded.

"Where you been, Brett?"

"Been away."

"How you doing, Brett?"

"Doing good, Dana. Doing good."

In the darkness Dana wept. He leaned his head toward Larry. He put his right ear against Larry's chest. "I can hear your heartbeat."

Larry laid his hand upon Dana's convulsing head.

"Do you forgive me?" asked Dana, his voice slightly muffled against the fabric of Larry's work shirt.

"Ain't nothing to forgive, pal. But if that's what you want—"

"It's what I want."

"Then I forgive you. Let it go, buddy. Let it all go."

Tears moistened Larry's eyes. He'd also seen men die. Men who were his friends.

Larry kept his hand on Dana's head until it was time to send him home.

A week later, at a depth of one hundred and forty feet, Larry Jr. and his dad hit an artesian vein with good pressure and a great flow.

1949

BALL CHANGING IN MISSISSIPPI

It was one of the middle Saturdays of the month—I can't remember which one—that my mother, just as she did every Saturday, dropped me off at the Dixie Theatre at Broadway and Main to compete in our local radio station's weekly Kiddie Talent Show. The contest took place during the hour just before the start of the Saturday morning matinee, up on the theatre's stage. The broadcast went out all over Yazoo County. Each of the contestants who participated got a complimentary ticket to that day's movie bill (which usually included a cowboy double feature, one chapter of an adventure serial, and a Disney cartoon).

But there was something *different* about this particular Saturday, which is the reason that it has always remained so clear and fixed in my head. Let me just start off by saying, simply: a few things happened. I'll tell you one of them right off the bat: Carthy McCharlie fell into the orchestra pit.

Now, it wasn't a real orchestra pit. It was just a narrow recessed space between the first row of seats in the picture show auditorium and the raised lip of the stage. And a good third of that pit was filled up with Mrs. Vonda Taliaferro's upright piano. It had been put on cement blocks so Mrs. Taliaferro could better see the stage from atop her sheet music. Not that Mrs. Taliaferro was one to ever use sheet music. She played all of her songs by ear and sometimes she would inadvertently change key in the middle and you'd have to make the necessary adjustments if you were singing along with her or else you'd end up sounding hopelessly off-key.

Tilted at a jaunty angle upon Mrs. Vonda Taliaferro's curly bob was a perky moss-green straw hat. It was flat on the top and had hardly any brim at all. It looked—as did all of Mrs. Taliaferro's millinery confections—fairly ridiculous. But to the little undiscerning girl I once was, it was quite charming. Unfortunately, Mrs. Taliaferro's special Kiddie Talent Show hat rarely stayed on her head for the whole show. It had a habit of flying right off whenever she was required to play a lively Broadway show tune or a dramatic march that involved some measure of bodily attack upon the keys.

Maryanne and Piddy and I didn't have to worry about Mrs. Taliaferro's adventures in the wilderness of piano key changes. Because we were dancers. We tapped as a trio, Maryanne and Piddy and I, and we made our teachers, Hiram and Helene Odell of Hiram and Helene's School of Dance and Loveliness, punch-proud.

The competition was stiff that Saturday. There was a little girl named Sue Ann McGeorge—also a student of Hiram and Helene's. She was their star pupil, in fact, and could generally be expected to tap rings around all the rest of us. If I'm remembering correctly, this particular Saturday, she sang and danced to "Ma, He's Making Eyes at Me," ending her routine with her usual audience-pleasing leg-split. Several months later, when the whole country was humming songs from South Pacific, Sue Ann would dance to "I'm Gonna Wash that Man Right Out of My Hair," and she'd trade her signature sequined top hat for a sequined bathing cap.

There was another girl a little older than us whose name was Geneva Abdoo. Geneva sang "Aloha 'Oe" while doing a hula dance. You couldn't take your eyes off of Geneva. You see, she was exotic. She was half Italian and half Lebanese—part of the large Lebanese and Syrian community in town. Geneva had coal-black hair, rich olive skin, and big black eyes. She wore a grass skirt and a man's floral Hawaiian shirt that she tied off just north of her belly button to show a little of her olive-toned midriff. Her undulating arms helped to tell the story she was singing.

Anyway, Carthy McCharlie was the name that Johnny Humphries gave his dummy, who was, as you can probably guess, the department-store version of Mr. Bergen's monocled, tuxedo-wearing sidekick. Johnny was a fourth grader, and as far as we second graders were concerned, old enough to go off and join the army or father children or something. Fourth graders didn't stoop to talk to second graders unless they were related to them, and that's why I didn't say anything to Johnny when he set that dummy on the chair in a way that looked dangerously tottery while he ran off to get the glass of milk his mama was holding for him just offstage. Johnny brought out the glass of milk to show that he could drink it while Carthy kept talking, although sometimes he would get so nervous that he'd forget just who was supposed to drink the milk, and end up pouring it down Carthy's shirtfront.

Carthy had lost an eye from a pop gun, so there was a patch over the eye that didn't have the monocle, and sometimes his leg would fall off in the middle of Johnny's routine from being so roughly handled by a rambunctious nine-year-old boy. And Johnny, who was usually prepared for just such a possibility, was at the ready with a line like, "Hey, Carthy! Looks like somebody's been pulling your leg!" One time he said "durn leg" and he got in a little trouble with his mother, who was a Sunday School teacher in the Baptist church and thought that substitution words like "durn" and "dang" were just as bad as saying the real thing because the thought was there, and God knows what is in our thoughts.

So, like I said, I would have told Johnny that he was setting Carthy McCharlie on that chair in such a haphazard way as to invite disaster, since the chair sat so close to the edge of the stage, but I decided it would probably be best for me to keep my mouth shut. Especially since it was a rule—largely applied to me alone—that when Maryanne and Piddy and I were just offstage getting ready for our number, I was supposed to keep my thoughts to myself and my flapping lips buttoned up tight. And it was a true challenge because of how much of a little chatterbox I was. So anyway, I watched in delicious horror as Carthy slid off that chair and then fell forward right into the orchestra pit, and when Johnny came back to find that his dummy was gone, he started looking all around in a panic, as if Carthy McCharlie had gotten right up and walked off by himself, bad leg and all.

Right after asking Avis the custodian to go down into the pit with Johnny to rescue Carthy, Mr. Jones, who owned the theatre and emceed the talent show, pointed to Maryanne and Piddy and me, which meant it was our turn now to come out on stage and to position ourselves as close to the microphone as possible so the people listening to their radios could hear the sound of our taps. And nobody thought there was anything odd at all about doing on the radio something that was best beheld by the eyes, the radio being an exclusively sound medium. They just listened to the tattoo of our tap shoes as they struck the wooden floor (more thuddy-thunk than clickety-clack) and tried to picture in their heads what our feet and legs and arms could possibly be doing. After all, tap dancing on the radio made just as much sense as ventriloquism on the radio.

And while we're on the subject of talents that don't translate too well via the radio medium, a listener couldn't see Geneva's hula arms and hips either. And they also couldn't see Nora Gibson's demonstration of how best to pack a picnic basket, although she got better over time as far as offering a running commentary on what she was doing. "Now I am laying the toasting forks next to the other utensils. Make sure when you do this at home that you keep them all pointed in the same direction so as to avoid injury upon retrieval." (I know good and well that Nora's aunt, Miss Gautreau, our librarian, wrote everything out for her to say because Nora's instructions sounded just like some of the handmade signs that Miss Gautreau had hanging around the library. For example, in the little girl's room there was a sign that said, "No one is too rushed not to flush. Please read this sign twice.")

So anyway, while Avis and Johnny Humphries were bumping around down in the orchestra pit, the three of us who matriculated at Hiram and Helene's School of Dance and Loveliness were hastily ushered out onto the stage by Mr. Jones' pretty assistant, Miss Lighthouse. And Mr. Jones introduced us with his peppy, cheerful voice—a voice that always made you think that there was absolutely nothing wrong in the world that couldn't be fixed by listening to his talent show on the radio. Not war or poverty or hunger or even the dreaded plague of unionization.

The song that Maryanne and Piddy and I danced to was the one that Shirley Temple and Bill Robinson tapped up and down the stairs to in *The Little Colonel*. We had learned our steps to the tune of "Yankee Doodle Dandy," but Mrs. Taliaferro said it was better to be Yankee Doodle Dandies around the Fourth of July and only Kate Smith was permitted to be patriotic all year round. Mrs. Taliaferro gave us the tempo of the new song and said everything would be fine. It would be just like falling off a log.

Hiram and Helene Odell's "Dancing Trio" stayed with the music and kept in sync with one another pretty well, I have to say. It helped that this was the tenth or eleventh or twelfth time we'd danced in competition together. Up until this point we'd never won, though. Geneva did a couple of times, but more often it was Corinne Lester who took home the big prize. Corinne liked to deliver dramatic readings in which she would punch the air with her fist at a predetermined climactic moment, and sometimes she would recite inspirational poetry with clear rounded vowels and some degree of urgency. We always thought that Corinne Lester was good enough to go to Hollywood, but I don't think she ever tried her luck there. The last I heard—and this was years ago—she was a shoe buyer for a department store in Jackson. I heard that she personally sold a pair of snakeskin slingbacks with five-inch heels to Eudora Welty, who brought them back the very next day after the shoes made her fall down in a restaurant. The only time that Corinne didn't win or at least take second or third place was when she recited "Invictus." The judges (who were Mr. Jones and Miss Lighthouse) were complimentary of Corinne's impassioned delivery, but couldn't in good conscience give her an award, since the poem was generally regarded as atheistic and the Dixie Theatre was a Christian movie house.

But this was the Saturday that we thought we had a good chance of winning, because there'd be a little something special about our performance that day, which was our teacher Miss Odell's idea, but which we liked just fine: we each got to wear little tiaras on our heads.

"You look so much like little princesses," said Miss Odell, "you make me want to genuflect. You do. Right here. Right now." This is what Miss Odell had said at our dance lesson the afternoon before. And her bachelor brother Hiram, overhearing her from the front office of their dance studio, shouted his enthusiastic concurrence. Then, for a reason that was not clear to me at the time, Miss Helene Odell began to weep. She spent a long time after that in the powder room while her brother had us doing fondus and pliés while he sang "That Old Black Magic," and "You Make Me Feel So Young," and finally, "Chi-Baba, Chi-Baba (Bambino Go to Sleep)," which had been popularized a couple of years earlier by Perry Como.

"The only thing that will make it official," said Miss Odell, finally emerging from the powder room while blotting her eyes with a wad of toilet paper, "are sparkly little rhinestone diadems. One for each of you. Let me get you each a tiara and then I defy Mr. Jones not to be enchanted and enchained."

"Enchanted and enchained!" repeated Hiram in grinning agreement with his sister, who had never married and whose womb had remained fallow.

So Miss Odell went back to her storeroom and came out with three glistening tiaras, a perfect fit for our little seven-year-old heads, and we could not have been more pleased with the way they made us look as we crowded around the mirror in the powder room. But as we were gathering to get a good look at ourselves, Piddy's tiara came loose from her hair and landed in the sink and snapped in two. After an attempt to glue the pieces back together failed ("I told you that Elmer's was only for paper and cardboard products, Hiram!"), there followed some debate as to whether or not we should wait a week to reveal our new look so that Piddy could get herself a new tiara. But Piddy, who was going through an insistent phase, would have none of this. So she and Maryanne and I ended up dancing with our new tiaras on our heads, and Piddy kept both of her hands fixed to her own head to hold the disjoined tiara in place. I know that we lost points with the judges because of Piddy's stiff and limited arm movement. But in the end, we were happy that we didn't have to wait a full week to enchant and enchain Mr. Jones and Miss Lighthouse.

As Mrs. Taliaferro got the signal to bring our number to a close, we noticed that Johnny Humphries and the movie palace custodian Avis had finally rescued Carthy McCharlie. It was a sad sight, though, because the dummy was broken up into so many different pieces. Even his head had come off. Miss Lighthouse went to Johnny and whispered something to him. She was asking him in her gentle, motherly way if he might like to wait until next week to perform the rest of his ventriloquist routine after Carthy had been put back together again. But Johnny, like Piddy, seemed determined to go on and bring his act to a proper finish.

We were supposed to all troop down and sit with the rest of the audience when our number was over, but I wanted to see what was going to happen with Johnny and Carthy from a backstage perspective; so I planted myself just offstage next to Mr. Jones, who heaved a heavy sigh and then turned to me and said in a doleful voice, "Just look at that poor dummy—he's only a shadow of his former self."

Johnny sat in the chair and held Carthy's head and all of his detached body parts in his lap, and then, as if stricken with sudden genius, began to pretend to the listeners throughout Yazoo County that Carthy wasn't in several pieces at all, but fully restored to his old self (this being radio and the listening audience being none the wiser). This ploy upset the in-theatre audience of nine-, ten-, and eleven-year-olds who began to boo and hiss. One boy yelled, "You big bamboozler! You flimflam merchant!" (which the boy had probably heard his father say more than once about President Harry S. Truman). Johnny responded by throwing Carthy's head at the boy as if it were an angry football. Then he fled the stage in tears.

They gave third prize (a pity prize, I'm sure) to Johnny. Third prize was a coupon for a free bag of popcorn. And first place—a month's worth of free tickets to the kiddie matinee—went to a boy who had never competed before named Mitch, who talked his way through the story of "Old Shep," but was so shy that he never looked up from his shoes, as if he were telling the story to his feet. And believe it or not, we Tiara Girls came in second place! It was all because Piddy had shown courage in the face of adversity by going on with the show wearing her broken tiara, and Mr. Jones, as he was awarding us our coupons for a free Coca-Cola and a free box of Jujubes at the concession stand, said that we were an inspiration to all the young people of America because we had shown the kind of grit and determination that had made this country great! And then he interrupted himself to scold two boys in the audience who were playing catch with poor Carthy McCharlie's disconnected head.

1949 was a long time ago and I'm an old woman now and quite amazed that I can recall it all in such detail. But they always say it's the earliest memories that get retained the longest and maintain the greatest clarity. I've lost touch with nearly everyone I knew in those days—with Maryanne and Piddy and Sue Ann and Geneva. The town where we all grew up, having fallen on hard times, is now, to borrow from Mr. Jones, only a shadow of its former self.

In some ways the world has become a much more sensible place; today we would never accept the isolated sound of little tapping feet on the radio as any conceivable form of entertainment. Yet what has been lost that was with us back then, I think, even with a world war only four years past and the atomic bomb casting its ominous shadow all about, is that longing for childlike simplicity and innocence. We didn't have it then—not really. But still we yearned for it.

Today we don't even seem to yearn anymore.

1950

POIKILOTHERMAL IN WEST VIRGINIA

"For a steel town, Weirton's got her charm." Mr. House was standing at the window next to Russell, his daughter's latest "gentleman friend," whom she brought home for Thanksgiving weekend. The two men were watching the flakes start to fall. "Has Trudy taken you around?"

"I'm supposed to get the grand tour tomorrow."

Mrs. House stepped out of the kitchen. She wore an apron with a big cartoon turkey on it. "Don't be so sure about that, Russ. Can I call you Russ? We're supposed to get a half-foot of snow by tomorrow."

"I hope they don't have to cancel the Ohio-Michigan game on Saturday," said a suddenly worried Mr. House.

"Not of snowball's chance of *that* happening, Dad," offered Trudy's brother, Bud, looking up from the *Pittsburgh Post-Gazette*. "Even a blizzard ain't gonna stop *that* game."

"*Isn't*, not *ain't*," Mrs. House corrected her college freshman son as she pushed through the swinging door back into the kitchen.

"Say, Russell—or can we call you Rusty?—who are you putting *your* money on—Michigan or Ohio State? Or do you care? Trudy says you're from Pennsylvania."

Russell turned from the window to face his teenage inquisitor. "I'd rather see Ohio State go to the Rose Bowl, but they played pretty lousy against Illinois last week. Moving Janowicz to quarterback was a good move, but Fesler's probably on his way out the door and you just gotta wonder if his heart's really in it. The Wolverines are looking good. I'd go with Michigan."

"How long will you and Trudy be staying with us?" asked Mr. House, patting his pockets for his tobacco pouch.

"The plan was to finish up the trip in Erie to see my mother," said Russell, "and then turn around and get back to Cleveland before Monday."

"*If* the weather cooperates," appended Mr. House.

"A little snow doesn't bother me," said Russell.

It snowed all through the Thanksgiving feast. The Fergusons—Arnold and Bet—who broke bread with the House family every postal holiday, got nervous, and even though they lived only a few miles west of Weirton in Steubenville, they didn't wait around for pumpkin pie. "Arnold doesn't like to drive in the snow," explained Bet through buckled, apologetic lips.

"And Bet doesn't drive *at all*," added Arnold as he inserted his wife into her coat.

The Houses grilled Trudy about her new "man," and Trudy, agreeably accommodating, said everything about him that she adored and nothing about him that she didn't, for there was, in truth, very little that she *didn't* like about Russell. He had a good job as an aeronautical engineer at the Lewis Flight Propulsion Laboratory. The two had met at a party and hit it off immediately. Now, without a formal engagement but clearly headed in the direction of marriage, Trudy was bringing Russell "home to meet the folks."

Gathered around the fireplace in the Houses' rustic stone manse (containing such familiar American colonial revival accents as interior wooden shutters, pewter mugs suspended from the mantel, and an early American spinning wheel that had, by all appearances, never been touched) the Houses and Trudy's "young friend" Russell toasted marshmallows that had been left over from the candied sweet potato casserole and drank cocoa (which went well with the marshmallows) as the snow fell...and fell. The conversation orbited around Trudy and her brother Bud (as children) and Harry S. Truman (as president) and developments in the Korean War (or, rather, "police action"). Mr. House was a union man and his politics leaned more to the haw than to the gee. Mrs. House was a New Dealer in theory, just as her father was, but, unlike her father, had a moralistic streak that led her to say a few unkind things about Ingrid Bergman, who earlier that year had given birth to Italian director Roberto Rossellini's "love child."

"And to think that she had just played Joan of Arc!"

Russell spoke vaguely of his childhood in Erie and his war service in Italy, and did not happen to mention (as he had never mentioned to his potential future wife Trudy) the fact that often, before he met Trudy and nearly as frequently thereafter, he would go out late at night and put a gun to the heads of a total strangers and make them beg for their lives. Eventually he would let his victims go, and then on the way home he would try to remember exactly what the persons had said in their moments of fear and quiet hysteria, and he would write it all down in a notebook and read it now and then while masturbating.

The snow didn't let up all the next day. Russell took Trudy aside that afternoon to say that perhaps they should try to make it back to Cleveland before the weather got any worse, so that they wouldn't find themselves snowbound either here or in Erie.

"If you miss a day or two from work, will it be the end of the world?" asked Trudy, pinching her boyfriend's nose with playful affection. "You really should see your mother, and aren't you having a good time here?"

"I love my mother. I like your family. I don't, however, enjoy the thought of being trapped. Anywhere. I'm already feeling antsy."

Trudy put on her pouty face. "My family has been nothing but open and hospitable since we got here. How can you be antsy?"

"I just am. I get a little claustrophobic in situations like this."

"Daddy would be happy to lend you his snow boots. You can go out and crump around all you like."

Russell nodded. He closed his eyes and tried not to imagine the walls closing in on him. That afternoon, under the pretext of checking to see if the local supermarket was still open so he could get Mr. House some Pall Malls—because his possible future father-in-law was almost out of smokes and was in a near-panic of his own over the fact that he hadn't stocked up before the storm—Russell braved the snowstorm that was increasing in intensity and that had all the makings of a "doozie," as Mr. House called it. Russell took deep breaths—though the air was arctic-frigid and punishing to his lungs—to calm himself.

It seemed to work. He felt better that night—at least for a while. But as the family gathered around the fireplace anew, after having just eaten the turkey tetrazzini that Mrs. House had whipped up (with Trudy's help), Russell became restless again. The feeling that the walls were closing in returned with a vengeance. But there was another feeling too—a longing to take his Colt .32 pocket pistol from its hiding place in his suitcase and go out into the night and find someone who could weep and beg in ways that Russell had not heard before.

Later that night, in the room he shared with Trudy's younger brother, he waited until Bud had gone off to sleep and then he went over to the suitcase on the stand and he pulled out the notebook that he kept with him at all times. He went into the bathroom and locked the door, put the lid down on the toilet and sat and read the transcriptions of several of his encounters from over the last three years, none of which had led to an arrest or even a single suspicion, since Cleveland was a large city and Russell made sure to venture only into neighborhoods far from home or work. Reading from the notebook made him feel temporarily better.

By the next day, the snowstorm had transformed itself into a blizzard of historic proportions. And though in Columbus the Buckeyes and the Wolverines managed to do something that looked a little like football in the midst of near whiteout conditions, and Michigan to do it slightly better than Ohio State, the snow brought several states from the Great Lakes across the Ohio Valley and throughout the Alleghenies to a near standstill. And while the two-foot pileup upon the roof of his house made Mr. House worry about a cave-in, and while high drifts *against* the house made Mrs. House fear that they might soon be trapped within— this particular fear also resonating with Russell, who volunteered to keep the porch and front walk "semi-shoveled" (because full shoveling in a blizzard is a bootless activity)—Russell kept his head. He kept his head by shoveling and drinking.

Trudy explained to her parents and to her brother that Russell wasn't ordinarily a drinker, but given the trying circumstances, surely they would excuse him, and Mr. and Mrs. House and Trudy's younger sibling understood, even though Mr. House regretted seeing some of his best bourbon disappear right before his eyes.

That night—officially the third night of the powerful blizzard—and with the snow still falling like some grand meteorological joke being played on the Tri-State area, which was bearing the brunt of the storm, Russell tranquilized himself with gin (the bourbon whiskey having now been fully expended) and fell asleep on the ruffle-skirted black-and-white plaid colonial sofa where he had sat feigning politeness and equanimity and sanity earlier in the evening. At precisely two o'clock, he awoke. It was the chiming of the Houses' faux colonial table clock announcing the hour that had disturbed his hard alcohol-abetted slumber. He felt woozy. His head was pounding. The house was quiet. He walked to a window. A nearby streetlamp illuminated the snow, its flakes still falling fast and thick.

Russell counted up in his head how many nights had passed since he had last been able to practice his unique hobby. Was it eight? Maybe it was nine. Russell had never felt that it was an addiction. Hadn't there been periods in the past—three, four, five weeks at a time—that had gone by without his having terrorized even a single person?

And yet he missed it terribly, longed for the thrill of holding the lives of total strangers in his hands. Because the gun was always loaded. Because the safety was always off. There was power and authority in Russell's trigger finger—a power and authority that stimulated and excited him both in the moment of the potentially deadly encounter and later in the sordid, orgasmic recall of it.

Tonight he wanted desperately to go out and yet he could not. Quietly, he opened the front door. What faced him was the white wall of a snowdrift, like something out of a cartoon.

He stepped back from the imposing barrier. He closed the door and stumbled to Bud's bedroom. Trudy had turned down the sheets for him, perhaps thinking that he might later regain consciousness and want a more comfortable place to spend the balance of the night.

He stripped down to his underwear and slipped under the sheets. The house was cold. Trudy's father liked to turn the thermostat down at night. Miraculously, the electrical current to the house hadn't gone out. The power lines were still holding their own against the brutal assault of snow and ice. Just in case, though, Mr. House and his son had gone out that morning and brought in more wood for the fireplace. Russell had volunteered to help, but Mr. House knew that his guest had worn himself out trying to shovel the front walk, and declined the offer.

Russell closed his eyes. He wanted this night to be over. He tried to think of anything that might relax him. He remembered the last man he had engaged in the night. The man had been an especially timid fellow and there was a pitiful dog-like whimper to his voice that sometimes, when Russell was alone, he liked to try to emulate. Russell wished that he'd had some way to record those pathetic, yet thoroughly entertaining pleadings from his victims, so that he could listen to them over and over again the way one replays a favorite record.

"Please don't kill me."

"You'll have to do better than that, milquetoast. Your life is in your own hands. Beg or die. Beg or die, little man."

"*Russell?*"

Russell opened his eyes. At that same moment the lamp on the little table between the two single beds clicked on. Bud was sitting up in bed. He had Russell's notebook.

"What is this?" Bud was holding the notebook by one corner as if he were pinching the tail of a dead rat.

"Just some of my scribblings. May I have it?"

"Why do you write this stuff?"

"The better question is, why are you in possession of something that doesn't belong to you?" Russell grabbed for the book but Bud jerked it out of reach.

"This is twisted shit."

"You had no business reading it."

"Does my sister know that you write this kind of stuff?"

"No. And why don't you be a good little brother and not tell her? Look, my head is killing me. Give me the book and let's go to sleep."

Bud shook his head. "Is this for a movie? Are you writing a movie script?"

"Yeah. I'm writing a movie script," said Russell with sere sarcasm.

"I don't believe you."

"Believe whatever you want to."

"I found the notebook under your mattress. I found *this*—" Bud pulled the revolver out from under his pillow. "—stuffed in the back of your suitcase. What are you doing bringing a loaded gun into my parents' house?"

Russell didn't have an answer. Even if he could concoct some halfway plausible explanation, his head was too cloudy to be able to deliver it successfully. He was caught. He had to fess up. Maybe the kid was like him. Maybe Bud had an interesting dark side of his own. Some people did. Sometimes Russell thought that maybe *everybody* did. He remembered the old man he had stopped near the lake in Euclid. Right behind a noisy polka palace. "Beg for your life," he had told the man, whom he feared at first was too intoxicated to effectively play the game. But the man was sober. Cold sober. "Go ahead and kill me, hoodlum," the old man spat. "I was about to drown myself in the lake anyway. You'll save me the trouble." Russell had ended the encounter with a few murmured epithets. "I should have obliged him," he thought as he walked away. Then he laughed to himself. "'Hurt me! Hurt me!' cried the masochist. '*No!*' returned the sadist with a leer."

"I'm not going to ask you again," said Bud in a voice suddenly devoid of all youthful innocence.

"I use the gun, Bud. I put the muzzle to people's heads and I make them think that I'm going to kill them. It's a game I play."

"Why do you play this game?"

"It excites me. Aren't there things that excite *you*? Things that you keep to yourself? Everybody has their dark corners, their little pockets of depravity."

The gun had been resting on Bud's palm. Now he took it into a proper grip so that he could aim it at Russell's head.

"Have you ever killed anybody with this gun?" asked Bud.

"Not with that gun or any other gun. I just told you: it's only a game."

"If it's just a game, why is the gun loaded?"

"It heightens the stakes. It makes it more exciting." Russell swallowed. "Is that what you want to do, Bud? Do you want to play the game with *me*?"

"I don't want you marrying my sister. I don't want you to even *see* my sister again. You need to be put into a padded room."

Russell licked his lips nervously. "I've thought that myself, on occasion."

"All those people out there. I've read in your little book what you make them say. They're going to carry this around with them for the rest of their lives."

"You're very perceptive for a kid."

"I'm not a kid. I'm a freshman at Carnegie Mellon."

"All right. Point taken. Just—could you just point that thing away from me?"

"Why?"

"Because I don't want you to shoot me."

"But I'm not like you, Russell—or should I call you 'Stark Raving Lunatic'?"

"You can call me whatever you want to. And I've come to the conclusion that you are in no way whatsoever like me."

"That's right," said Bud. "*You* never pull the trigger." Bud fired. The discharge was loud and seemed to shake the walls of the small bedroom. "*I* just did."

The bullet lodged in Russell's left arm. There was a great deal of blood for Trudy (who assumed full responsibility for the mess) to have to clean up. It took a long time to get Russell to the hospital on account of the severe weather.

Trudy later confessed to her parents and to Bud that she had no idea that the man she thought she loved was a…was a…

"Was a stark raving lunatic ," said Mrs. House helpfully. She was sitting with her daughter, running loving, maternal fingers through her hair.

"As insane as he was," said Mr. House, "at least he never killed anybody. So far as we know."

Everyone agreed with a nod. The House family was gathered around the fireplace drinking cocoa. The storm had finally let up. The Thanksgiving Blizzard of 1950 had come to an end. The long dig-out was about to begin.

"Did you *mean* to shoot him, Bud?" asked Trudy of her quiet and reflective brother.

"In that moment I did. I guess your lunatic boyfriend was right. We've all got a little something screwy about us. For example: I put several hundred dollars on Ohio State."

Mr. House nodded sympathetically. "I did too, son. I did too."

1951

PSITTICINE IN PENNSYLVANIA

"It was hard going there at first."

"To Mrs. Lyttle's apartment, you mean?"

"That's right. But over time I got used to it. Would you like another Ladyfinger?"

"No, no. One hand is my limit. I really must be off. Sometimes I say that to Arthur and he goes, '*Must* be? Why, Pearl, you've been 'off' since the day I met you.' Did James ever talk to *you* like that?"

"Not very often. I think he was afraid that since I wasn't able to see his face I wouldn't know when he was kidding. But I could always tell by the tone of his voice. Shall I see you to the door?"

"'See you to the door.' Do you say that to all your guests?"

"The ones who might think it funny."

"I'll let myself out, honey." Pearl Patz kissed her blind friend Leonora Touliatos on her forehead. "Oh, and I'd stop going over there if I were you. I still don't see how a person could ever get used to something like that."

"It's not her fault. It's very hard to censor a parrot, Pearl—especially one that was once owned by a salty-tongued merchant marine."

"But honey, don't you still cringe to hear all that potty talk?"

"A little, yes, but I really do like Nancy Lyttle. We've spent some very nice evenings together."

Pearl took her coat from the back of a chair near Leonora's front door. There was an antique mirror by the door, for which Leonora had no use now that her son Tim was off at college, but Pearl leaned into it to check for bits of pecan in her teeth, which might have taken up residence there from the pecan coffee cake her friend Leonora had served with the tea. Her panties had bunched up a little, and she pulled at the elastic, appreciating the convenience of having a blind friend who would not be aware of such rude adjustments to her person.

"Goodbye, my dear," said Pearl, donning her hat. "I'll see you next week."

"And I *won't* see you!" tittered Leonora.

After hearing the front door to her apartment close, Leonora rose from her sofa to put away the tea things. She turned on the radio to listen to some music. She had heard somewhere that television was going to replace radio. All of her favorite programs would be gone, and she'd have to be content with a medium that was not kind to the visually compromised. "I hope, at least," she said to herself, "they'll still let me have my music." Rosemary Clooney was singing "Come On-a My House." Leonora stopped for a moment to allow the silly song to make her smile as it always did. She wondered if her late husband would have liked it. It was also a favorite new song of her friend Nancy Lyttle.

Leonora and Nancy were neighbors. Like Leonora, Nancy lived in the E line of their Philadelphia apartment building. Her apartment was only two floors above Leonora's. The two women had met on the elevator one day and had taken an immediate liking to each other. Nancy had begun to invite Leonora to "Come On-a My Apartment" for supper every Friday night. Nancy was Roman Catholic and always prepared a different fish dish each Friday, and Leonora, whose father had been a professional fisherman on Lake Huron, loved fish as well.

Leonora agreed with her building's superintendent Mr. Wachsel that Nancy Lyttle was an odd duck. She didn't seem to make friends easily and was stingy with gifts to the buildings' employees on holidays. She was also a very private person, and Mr. Wachsel was amazed that she allowed Leonora into her apartment. "*I've* never been inside. Even when her kitchen sink backed up into her bathtub. She had a cousin or somebody come in and fix it."

"Maybe she makes an exception with me because I'm blind, Mr. Wachsel. Did you ever think about that?"

Mr. Wachsel chewed thoughtfully upon his lower lip as he nodded his head.

Leonora went on: "You know that she has a parrot, don't you? It belonged to her brother. That parrot is quite a prattling polly. Do you ever hear him from the hallway?"

"No. But I'm not on eight very often—not since we replaced all the valves on the risers and radiators on that floor."

*

Friday came and Nancy greeted her friend Leonora at the door with her usual ebullience: "Oh my goodness, Leonora—we are having the most divine meal tonight: steamed sole with tomato-leek sauce. I hope you like dill. It's my favorite herb. Isn't it my favorite herb, Meshak?"

"Blow it out your ass."

"You remember Leonora, don't you, Meshak? Won't you for once show some courtesy to our favorite guest?"

"Blow it out your ass."

"It's going to be one of those nights. I'm so sorry, Leonora. I fear that one of these times you're going to say enough is enough, and just give up on me entirely."

"How long do parrots live?"

"Well, cockatoos can live to be over fifty."

"How old is Meshak?

"Touch my cock! Touch my cock!"

"I'm not certain. Perhaps he's thirty."

"Blow it our your ass!"

"I can put him in the other room if you like, Leonora."

"You said he doesn't like to be put away when I'm here."

"That's true. Believe it or not, he *does* like you. He doesn't know the meaning of the words he says. He just gets excited when you're here and says the things that my naughty brother taught him to say."

"You fucking whore!"

"I have cheese and crackers for our appetizer. And I bought some Chianti. I know it doesn't go with fish, but it's very good. Let me have your hand. Isn't this a lovely wicker cozy the bottle came in?"

Leonora rubbed her hand along the bowed contour of the bottle holder. "It's nice. Nancy, I'm curious: the other guests to your home—does Meshak talk to *them* this way?"

"Oh good mercy, Leonora! He most certainly would. That's why I can't have anyone over. You are the only one. *You* understand. I'm not sure that there's anyone else who would stand for it."

"You fucking whore! Touch my cock! Touch my cock! You fucking whore!"

The fish was delicious. Nancy Lyttle was an excellent cook. After dinner, the two women listened to their favorite music programs on the radio over cups of Sanka. Nancy was happy to report that Meshak had fallen asleep. But when it was time to go—Nancy always accompanied her blind friend home late at night, even though Leonora could easily navigate the halls and elevator to get herself to her apartment door without assistance—the parrot was apparently awakened by the rustling and the sound of voices nearby.

"Eat shit, bitch!"

"Goodbye, Meshak. Nancy, may I pet him?"

"Just a gentle pat on his back. He doesn't like to be handled by anyone but me."

Nancy guided Leonora's hand to the soft feathers. "That's a good bird," said Leonora. "Can you say, 'I'm a good bird deep down'? 'I'm a good bird deep down.'"

"Fuck you and the horse you rode in on."

Leonora laughed. "I'm not giving up on this old bird. Maybe you can't teach an old dog new tricks, but I might be able to teach Meshak to be just a little more respectful."

"Amen to that! Let me get you home now, Leonora. It's past both of our bedtimes."

"Blow it out your ass!"

Several days later, as Leonora and her friend Pearl Patz were walking across her apartment building's lobby so that Pearl could take Leonora to buy a new toaster at Wanamaker's—her present one had a slightly frayed cord and Pearl was afraid that Leonora might accidentally electrocute herself—the building's superintendent Mr. Wachsel called out to Leonora.

"Yes, what is it, Mr. Wachsel? Pearl, this is my super, Mr. Wachsel."

"Hello there. If I might have a word with you, Mrs. Touliatos. It's about Mrs. Lyttle in 8-E."

"Is anything wrong? I just saw her last Friday night."

"Well that depends on how you define the word 'wrong,' Mrs. Touliatos."

"Has the bird—has Meshak, her parrot, died?"

"Yes, Mrs. Touliatos. But not recently. The bird I saw when I had to make an emergency visit to the apartment this morning has been dead for quite some time. He's stuffed, Mrs. Touliatos. It looks like he's been stuffed for years."

"Stuffed, you say?"

"That's right."

"Oh."

For a moment Leonora got very quiet. Finally she asked if everything was all right. "What kind of emergency was it?"

"An overflowing toilet. Your upstairs neighbors, Mr. and Mrs. Carter, had themselves a little bathroom waterfall courtesy of Mrs. Lyttle."

Leonora's hand flew up to her mouth. Then she pulled it away to say, "Is Nancy—is Mrs. Lyttle still at work?"

"I would imagine. I had to use the passkey. If I had waited, the whole E line would have gotten flooded out—your bathroom as well. I took a minute to look through the rest of the apartment. There is no other bird. Just the stuffed one."

"Oh my," said Leonora.

Leonora didn't speak to Nancy until she arrived at her door at the usual time the following Friday night. Nancy had prepared pepper-honey salmon steaks. There was no wine this night, but a nice pitcher of limeade Nancy had made from fresh-squeezed limes.

Leonora was not feeling herself. Each time the "parrot" spouted his depravities, she would cringe a little inside, but she tried her best not to let it show. She must have succeeded in hiding her concerns, because Nancy never said anything.

As the two women were making their way toward the front door at the end of the evening, Leonora said, as she always did, "Goodbye, Meshak." Then she said, "Nancy, may I pet him?"

"I don't think he'd mind. He didn't seem to mind last week."

Leonora held out her hand so that Nancy could take it and place it in the vicinity of the bird. Leonora felt for the feathers and then suddenly took gouging hold. She yanked the stuffed parrot from its perch and threw it to the floor. Then she stomped all over the floor, hoping to trample it.

There was a long, deadly silence. Then Leonora said, "It looks like I've killed your goddamned bird."

Another silence. Then: *"You can't kill me that easy, you crazy blind bitch."*

Leonora went home unescorted that night.

1952

DOUBLY UXORICIDAL IN COLORADO

I'm not sure if it was Charlie who saw Bob first, or Bob who spotted Charlie. It probably doesn't matter. It wouldn't have been long after sitting themselves down at separate tables in the dining room of the Golden Lantern for each man to have gotten squarely into the other one's line of vision, and neither man was simply going to ignore what he saw. Fate required that the two should meet. Fate and their own impetuous and curious natures. Because it isn't every day you chance upon someone who looks exactly like you.

Neither man had been to Denver before. Charlie was there to meet with owners of a small company that was preparing to bring out their own automatic ranch gate. Charlie managed a construction supply company in Brooklyn—a company that didn't want to get left behind in the automatic ranch gate boom. Bob was a freelance photographer who was just wrapping up a trip to the Colorado Rockies. He'd been taking nature shots for an iron lung-bound artist colleague who'd grown tired of painting objects in his room.

Let's say that it was Charlie who made the initial approach. Let's say that before he'd even placed his order with the waitress, he got up from his seat and crossed to Bob's table on his own initiative. (Both were dining alone.) Without saying a word, Charlie, let's say, sat down and the two took themselves a long silent moment to fully digest what each was seeing—to completely dismiss the possibility of hallucination.

Even though Charlie may or may not have made the first move, it was Bob who broke the ice with the following observation: "Mom told me about you. I never quite believed her until now."

"What are you talking about?"

"My mother. My adopted mother. She sat me down one day. I was a pretty big boy at the time—maybe twenty-two. She told me that there was something she'd never told me before—something about my adoption. I had a twin, you see. Our birth mother put us both up for adoption before she croaked from whatever street drugs had eaten that big hole in her brain. Why my adopted mother told me this, I don't know. I really had no desire to go looking for you. I knew the odds were slim that I'd be able to find you, even if you really existed. Who knew that dumb luck would do all the work for me?"

"So you think we're twins?"

"Can it be anything else? Separated at birth, my friend. Why? I don't know. It would have been nice to have had a brother all those years."

Another silence passed, each man studying the face of his biological mirror image. Finally, Charlie reached out his hand and said, "I'm Charlie. Charlie Towers."

And Bob took the hand and said, "Bob Fletcher."

And then the waitress interrupted to ask if Charlie would be returning to his table, and Charlie said no. "I didn't think so," replied the waitress. "What happened? You two brothers have a fight and now you're making up?"

Bob didn't answer. Charlie smiled. "Making up. Yeah, that's it. My brother and I are making up…for lost time."

Bob handed the waitress his menu. "I'll start with the Seafood Louis cocktail and the apple-marshmallow salad—whatever the heck *that* is. Then give me the pork tenderloin with the whipped potatoes."

The waitress shook her head. "No potatoes."

"It's on the menu."

"Well, there still aren't any spuds to be had, so I'd recommend the buttered new peas and the creamed coleslaw. You get double vegetables without the potatoes."

Bob sighed. "I miss potatoes."

Charlie nodded. "Me too. But look on the bright side: they say the shortage will be over when the new crop comes in. This isn't the Irish potato famine we're talking about here…*brother*."

As Bob was left to consider the marvelous implications of that wonderful word, Charlie placed his order and the waitress disappeared and the two long-lost siblings got down to brass tacks. Bob didn't know much more than what he'd already said. Charlie didn't know anything at all. The two thirty-five-year-old brothers, both a little guarded with one another initially, soon began to relax, soon began to open themselves up to discovering how very different they were in terms of the life paths they'd chosen for themselves, but also how very similar certain aspects of their lives had turned out to be.

Both men, for example, had insufferable wives—grasping harridans (their own words) who refused to grant their longsuffering husbands divorces out of spite, or rather because of the presence of the prettier, newer, much less insufferable model who waited impatiently and amatively in the wings.

"I've been thinking a lot about that Hitchcock picture that came out last year: *Strangers on a Train*," said Bob. "How convenient it would be to find some stranger to do in the little woman. Now just what if the stranger you happen to meet ends up being your very own identical twin brother? What an additional convenience *that* would be!"

"How do you mean?" asked Charlie, digging his spoon into the syrup-glazed mound that was his butterscotch sundae. "I mean, how's that going to work—the stranger I get to kill my wife looks just like me? Would you consider this one of your better ideas?"

"Wait, hear me out. Say, let's blow this place. Where are you staying?"

"The Brown Palace."

"Good. We'll go there. I'm at a bedbug motor court on 85."

The two men went to the Brown Palace. They held up in Charlie's room in the company of a fellow named Jack Daniel who had long been a friend to them both.

For the first three hours of that long, sleepless night, the men traded stories from their own lives—from the life of the twin who was the shrewd and calculating businessman with hopes of some day taking over his uncle's construction supply house, and from the life of the artist with a camera who created works of beauty on Kodak paper when he wasn't taking incriminating snapshots of adulterous spouses and their future divorce court corespondents.

The rest of the night was spent plotting the murders of the women who held them back—the women who carped and whined and pinioned their husbands unmercifully.

Because what had started out as mere whim had, in that long night, transformed itself first into distinct possibility and then into glorious reality.

The key element in the planning was the creation of high-profile, indisputable alibis for each of the two brothers. Just as it was proposed by the character of Bruno in *Strangers on a Train*, each man would be committing the other man's murder. (Under some sort of disguise, of course, bowing to the slim possibility that one or both of the brothers might be seen going to or coming from the scene of the crime.) But here was the beauty of the entire setup: each brother would be quite some distance from his wife at the time of her murder, with a perfectly engineered and strongly corroborative alibi.

It seemed like a perfect plan. All of their adopted parents were dead. No one else knew of their true biological origins. Charlie's friends and relatives were as ignorant of his roots as he had been. Bob was certain that his younger sisters in Philadelphia had never been told about Charlie. Why should they have been? Bob's mother hadn't seemed all that eager to tell *him*, and the confession had come almost as an afterthought from her deathbed. ("Be good to your sisters, don't spend your inheritance all in one place, and, oh, you're adopted.")

Charlie's alibi was this: a birthday party for a country club chum. It was a party which Charlie's wife Edna had no desire to attend. She loathed the man. She even hated his parvenu wife. The to-do was scheduled for Friday night, March 28, at the country club. The murder (strangulation was thought best; Edna had a pencil-thin neck that wouldn't take much torque to successfully wring) would take place during the party. At least thirty people who knew Charlie would see him there at the time of the murder.

Knowing that in spite of the soundness of the alibi there might be need by the police authorities to keep Charlie from leaving town for a few days (even suspects with rock-solid alibis can remain persons of interest), Bob would have to wait until sometime in the summer to have his own wife, Mitzi, cross-dispatched by his brother. There was simply no way to commit the murders simultaneously or even within a few days of each another, and Bob lost the draw.

The first murder went off without a hitch.

As predicted, the air had cleared by midsummer. In fact, by the date of Bob's own agreed-upon alibi event, the 1952 All-Star Game at Shibe Stadium—a game that Bob was set to attend with several of his baseball buddies, some of whom had yet to see Jackie Robinson play—the air had cleared quite nicely. Thanks to Bob's inspired decision to open a box of

Kellogg's Cornflakes over his murder victim's head, police psychologists rapturously surmised that Edna's strangler was signaling his intent to kill again and again. *Cereal killer*—therefore—*serial* killer.

On July 8 in Philadelphia, it rained off and on. Bob sat in the sodden stadium with his sodden friends, wondering if the All-Star Game would be cancelled.

Bob was lucky. The game started late, and though it went only five innings, that was more than enough time for Charlie to slip into Bob's row house in South Philly and slit the throat of Bob's wife, Mitzi. And besides, regardless of the length of the game, Bob and his pals almost never went home right after their baseball outings. By custom they usually gathered at some agreed-upon drinkery and wet their collective whistles with a couple rounds of beers first. As Bob was listening to his buddies argue the merits and demerits of various Philadelphia-area saloons, the conversation taking place in the middle of the torrent that would eventually put an asterisk next to this particular All-Star Game in the stat books, he couldn't help smiling. To think that it was now done. Bob and his brother Charlie, having successfully deconcatenated their respective balls and chains, were now free to marry the women they were always meant to wed. For Charlie, this meant the shapely bookkeeper for his company, and for Bob, a fellow artistic free spirit with a penchant for bedroom acrobatics.

At least this is the way it was supposed to go.

Bob kept smiling. And then in that next instant, he stopped smiling. Few of the All-Star fans had left the stadium. Most were waiting for the rain to let up a little before trooping out to their cars. Like Bob and his baseball buddies, people stood huddled in small groups under awnings and overhangs. One man in Bob's line of vision stood alone. His look was familiar—frighteningly familiar. Because he looked exactly like Bob. And, by natural extension, Charlie.

"Double cross" was the first thing that insinuated itself into Bob's thoughts. That he had held up his end of the bargain while his brother had reneged. And reneged in a big way. And for what reason? Blackmail? Bob had no money. It was Charlie who had the fat income, the country club membership, the big house in Riverdale. (Bob knew the house well. He'd strangled his sister-in-law in the largest of its four bedrooms.)

With rising anger, Bob Fletcher stepped away from his rain-drenched companions. He pushed past all the people who stood between him and the object of his ire. The man noticed Bob coming toward him. He smiled.

He smiled in the same way that Charlie had smiled when the two brothers first discussed the possibility of ridding themselves of their unwanted marital appendages.

But that man wasn't Charlie.

The man who wasn't Charlie was still smiling as Bob reached him and grabbed him roughly by the arm. "What are you doing here? You're not supposed to be here."

"Where am I supposed to be?" asked the man, his smile dissolving into a look of genuine perplexity.

"Did you do it? Or did you come here to tell me you *couldn't* do it? Answer me!"

The man didn't seem to know what to say. He looked at Bob, disconcerted, helpless.

Bob seemed equally helpless. "I beg you. Go. Get out of here."

The man, as if wishing to be accommodating, took a step back, and then another, but had he wished to leave, circumstances would not have allowed it. Because at that moment Bob's friends joined him, and one in that group did not hesitate to exclaim, "Bob, you ol' son of a bitch—you never told us you had a brother."

"A twin brother!" marveled another.

"He isn't my twin brother," said Bob, all color having left his face.

"He's right," said the man. "We aren't twins. We're part of a trio. *Triplets*." And turning to Bob: "Have you met up with our other brother yet? My adopted mother told me I was one of three. I never quite believed her until today."

I know this story well, because I am that third brother. I didn't want to speak of myself in the first person until now, so as not to spoil the ending of the story. And of course, to be fair, the logical ending to this story should include my attendance at the executions of my two brothers for the insensate, cold-blooded crisscross murders of their respective sisters-in-law. But as I write this, two years after my chance meeting with my triplet brother Bob at Shibe Stadium (I can still hear the crack of the bat that sent Jackie Robinson around the bases), my brothers' convictions are still working their way through the appeals process. So they're both still very much alive. And I get to pay them visits every now and then. That is, when my wife lets me out of the house. Should I tell you about that smothering, nagging shrew? Oh, please don't make me.

1953

PHARISAICAL IN WYOMING

Everybody laughs when Billy Sherman, the dentist's boy, nudges his friend, one of the Hollis twins—I think it's Casper, although it could have been Jasper—and points to one of the Abernethy ranch hands who are in town on some errand or another for his employer and goes, "Shane! Come back!"

Shane has just opened at the town picture show and everybody just has to see it because it's set on the high plains over by Jackson Hole, though somebody said most of the movie was actually shot in California—which isn't anywhere near Wyoming. Anyway, it has Jean Arthur in it and Cornelius (that's my dad) likes Jean Arthur, and so Cornelius and I have seen it twice already, which means that Cornelius laughs harder at Billy's little *Shane* funny than anybody else.

It's Cornelius and me and the two boys and Mrs. Sherman and Mr. Reese, who has the sugar beet farm south of town, and then a uranium man I don't know, and an evangelist who's in town for a tent show that nobody's been going to, because Riverton folks don't much go in for Bible thumping and holy rolling.

The evangelist's name is Proctor.

So it's all of us standing in line at the Riverton Bank and Trust, and two tellers in their cages, and Mr. Lanell, the bank manager, and Mr. Lanell's secretary, Miss Philpot, and the security guard whose real name I don't know, because most everybody just calls him Pops.

It's about twelve-thirty in the afternoon and everybody's in a good mood because the weather's started to warm up and everything's budding and blooming, and another devil-hard Wyoming winter has been happily put out to spring pasture.

The preacher named Proctor says, "That's a good one!" to Billy Sherman, although he was probably preaching just last night, in fact, about the "sin" in today's "*cin*-ema." Then, not to be outdone in the way of comical observations, Reverend Proctor starts singing his own version of "Shall We Gather at the River," which starts off:

> *Shall we gather at the RivertonBankandTrust.*
> *The beautiful,*
> *The beautiful*
> *RivertonBankandTrust.*
> *Gather with the depositors at the RivertonBankandTrust*
> *That sits in the middle of town.*

Everyone laughs politely. Even the two men who have just stepped inside the bank unnoticed by anybody but me. They laugh and then almost in the same breath they order us all to drop to the floor because, you see, they aim to rob this bank. Pops the security guard goes for his gun and the younger of the two men cold-cocks him with his revolver, and Pops is put temporarily out of commission right on the spot.

We drop to the floor as we've been instructed to do, and the older of the two bank robbers motions for all the employees to come join us, so within a couple of minutes we're all spread out mostly face down on the floor while the younger robber goes to empty all the tellers' cash drawers.

Well, one of the tellers must have pushed the silent alarm button, because all of a sudden we hear the sound of a police siren (I guess there's no such thing as a silent police siren), and the older robber gets the bank manager up and has him lock the door and then he reminds the rest of us to stay right where we are if we know what's good for us. The younger robber is at the window now and he goes, "We're surrounded," but the older robber doesn't seem all that upset. The phone rings and it's the police chief and he wants the bank robbers to know that there's no way that the two of them are going to be allowed to leave the bank with both the money and their lives *and* they had best give themselves up.

The older robber smiles and scratches his itchy forehead with the muzzle of his gun and says that he has a baker's dozen worth of hostages, and just like something out of a Humphrey Bogart picture he makes it clear that he'll kill every one of us if the cops storm the building. So don't try anything.

On hearing that she's a hostage, Billy's mother starts shaking like she has the St. Vitus lay-down dance and one of the tellers tries to comfort her and the evangelist starts to pray over her.

"That's good," says the older bank robber, whose name is Cutler. "You pray for *all* these folks, because they're gonna need God on their side if they're ever gonna see the outside of this bank building with living eyeballs."

Whatever that means.

"And what if God *ain't* on their side?" asks the preacher, fairly conversational in his tone.

"What do you mean?" asks Cutler, who seems a little put out over having to deal with a problematically philosophical man of the cloth.

"I *mean*," says the preacher, pulling himself up into a seated position, "if it comes down to negotiating over which of these poor innocent children of our good Lord get to go free and which must remain behind as your human bucklers, who are you gonna release? Those who live by the word of the Lord or those heathens who deny Christ's love and habitate in the province of sin?"

The two bank robbers share a look with one another that says neither has ever considered criteria for which hostages should get their freedom and which should have to stay behind, other than the usual setup that says women and children and old men in need of heart-saving nitroglycerin pills should get first dibs.

I study the face of that revival preacher to try to understand for myself if he's working a plan to get us all released under the general umbrella of Christian mercy, and I get to wondering, even in my own far-from-developed fourteen-year-old brain, if there might be brilliance behind his piercing blue-eyed gaze, the kind of God-given gaze that people farther east who care a little more about such things would be slightly more susceptible to.

"My father was a preacher himself," says the older robber named Cutler, "and he taught me a thing or two about the prerogatives of strong faith." The strangely well-spoken bank robber interrupts his confession by boot-kicking poor Pops, who had just begun to rouse himself from his temporary stupor. "And the rewards that come to he that lives a good life in the spirit. So I say this unto you, Parson: If you want to use the faith and spirituality of your fellow captives here to decide who gets out of this place alive and who gets to stay behind and share my fate and the fate of my partner Codges here, by all means you go right ahead. Why don't you start your assaying with that bank officer over there? He looks like a Jew."

The preacher looks over at the bank manager, Mr. Lanell. "You, sir: are you a Jew? Are you a denier of the divinity of Christ Jesus?"

Mr. Lanell shakes his head. "I'm not a Jew."

"But do you deny Christ, nonetheless?" asks Proctor.

"Of course not. I accepted Christ as my personal savior when I was eleven."

"And what a joy it is to hear it," says Proctor as the telephone begins to ring. The younger robber Codges answers it.

Codges says, "Yeah, yeah," into the phone and then turns to Cutler and says, "The police chief wants to know if we can send out a couple of the hostages in a show of good faith."

"It's *them* who oughta be showing *us* good faith!" the older bank robber rails. "What kind of back-asswards cowboy town *is* this?"

"A Christian town," offers Miss Philpot, the bank manager's secretary. "We're all Christians. I know all these folks except for that uranium man over there. We're every one of us good Bible-believing Christians. Except for that uranium man, whom I don't know."

"So what *are* you?" inquires the preacher of the man in coveralls who works for an out-of-town uranium prospecting outfit.

"I'm a—a Christian Scientist," the man admits in a slightly stuttery voice, his head barely raised from the floor.

The preacher puckers his lips in thought. "Those Christian Scientists are a good bunch. They got faith all right. But I don't much trust 'em."

The uranium man emits a pained sigh.

"Come to think of it, I don't much trust *any* of these folks to be dyed-in-the-wool followers of our blessed Lord," Proctor continues, "until they show me their religious bona fides. I'm gonna need a little time to talk to these folks and find out what kind of Christians they are. I haven't seen a single one of them at my tent revival."

The younger of the two female tellers raises her hand. "I was at your tent show—last Friday night, in fact."

"You were?" Proctor smiles, pleased.

"Reverend Proctor, we really don't have time for—" Cutler taps his foot impatiently. "I need to give up two hostages, and as soon as possible, if you please."

"Well, naturally, my lifelong journey down the highway of righteousness," replies Proctor, "should dictate my inclusion, although I would leave it to you to make the final decision in that regard. But allow me to cogitate for a moment over which of these lovely young women deserves that second spot." Proctor turns to the young female teller. "Were you really there, missy? Why didn't I see you? I hardly ever forget a face as pretty as yours."

The frightened, yet undeniably beautiful, blond-haired teller whose tasseled leather vest, a uniform of sorts for this cowboy bank, does little to restrain her large Tetonical breasts, answers in a high, tortured register: "I was there. I was sitting in the third row. I can tell you all the hymns we sang: 'Softly and Tenderly Jesus is Calling,' 'Old Time Religion.' I can hear them now in my head. The memory of them fills me with the wonder-working spirit!"

"But why didn't you come down during the invitational? Why did you not rededicate your life to Christ at that most blessedly opportune moment, my darling girl?"

"I was shy, I suppose," peeps the teller.

"Honesty, child. Your mind wasn't on the Lord, now was it?"

"It was on the Lord, Reverend." And then with a glance over at the two bank robbers and their guns, "*Oh for the love of all that's holy was my mind on the Lord!*"

Proctor clucks and shakes his head. The security guard is shaking his head at the same moment, trying to bring himself back to full consciousness. Cutler kicks him again hard with his boot, right in the left temple, and returns him to dreamland.

Codges shakes the phone receiver in the air and cries, "We simply do not have all day!" His older partner Cutler nods in agreement.

"Reverend," says Cutler, "my colleague-in-crime reminds me that we need to deliver a couple of hostages to the police A-S-A-P. Now if you can't make up your mind whose faith is worth a get-out-of-bank-free card, we'll just have to go back to the old standby: women and children and old men with heart ailments first."

"My heart! My heart!" cries Mr. Lanell, dramatically clutching his chest.

"Oh please, I beg you!" weeps Mrs. Sherman, both her son Billy and the Hollis twin pulled protectively to her sides. "Let it be women and children first!"

"Spoken like a true Latter Day Saint," hurls the other teller, Mrs. Witemeyer, a woman in her fifties with Mamie Eisenhower bangs. "Let it be known here and now, gentlemen, that Mrs. Sherman is, in point of fact, a Mormon. She calls herself a Christian, but she's a Mormon, all right. And Mr. Reese over there is, in fact, a worshipper of the Pope, and Cornelius McIntire and his daughter—" She's looking straight at Cornelius and me now. "They aren't any kind of believers at all. I think they're either atheist or Buddhist or something else Asian and heathen. I'll tell you who the true Christians are. I'll put them in any order you like, and I can be fast about it. Just let me get some paper and a pencil. Don't leave it to this tent preacher to decide. He doesn't know us. I know every hostage here except for that uranium man over there, and good Heavens, you already know he's a doctor-denying Eddyite. Give me some paper."

As the younger bank robber goes looking about for some paper, the uranium man, who is on the floor not far away, suddenly grabs the young man by the ankle and jerks him off his feet. The young criminal named Codges fires upon the uranium man and wings him before his gun goes flying out of his hand. At the same time Pops, the security guard, having come once again to his senses, draws his own gun and puts a fatal bullet into the back of the older robber Cutler. Codges' gun, by luck or miracle, lands within a couple of feet of me and I roll right over to it.

Then, I don't know—maybe it's mischief or maybe it's rancor over the fact that Mrs. Witemeyer had called my father and me atheists, I aim the gun at Mrs. Witemeyer and shoot her in the knee. Then I draw a bead on the revival preacher who had clearly manipulated our dire straits for his own benefit, and I plug him in the arm. I've been shooting tin cans and barn rats since I was six; a runny-mouthed Pharisee's a pretty easy target.

There are several of us either dead or severely wounded when the police, having heard the various shots, come storming in from the back offices of the bank and take Mr. Codges into custody, and various ones of us away to the hospital (or in the case of Mr. Cutler, to the morgue)—even the uranium man, who protests the medical attention.

I spend six months at a camp for juvenile delinquents and learn to rope calves and how to release my bean farts for optimum dramatic effect. I don't regret what I did for a second.

Amen.

1954

FAMISHED IN TEXAS

Tessie was in her slip. Her ten-year-old daughter Regina stood next to her. "I won't wear the jumper if I can't find the belt," Tessie said to her daughter. "What do you think about these Bermuda shorts? Are they too casual?"

"It's a barbecue, Mom. It's *supposed* to be casual."

Regina handed her mother the purple cinch belt that went with the purple jumper.

"Where have you been hiding that? Go check on the au gratin." Tessie laid the matching cinch belt and jumper on the bed. She crossed to her dresser and looked at her image in the mirror. She gave gentle pats to her Maggie McNamara pixie cut, which was probably too young for her by about ten years. "Go on, Regina. I don't want the cheese to burn. Where's your father?"

"I think he's out on the patio."

Tessie went to the bedroom window as Regina left the room to look in on the spaghetti-broccoli au gratin.

"Rory! Rory!" Tessie called through the window screen. "Can you come over here?"

Tessie stole back to the bed to set her violet print blouse against the cotton jumper. "I don't like this," she said to herself. "It doesn't look insouciant. I want to look insouciant. Like Audrey Hepburn in *Roman Holiday*. Where is that sundress with the bib halter front?"

"Are you talking to me?" asked Rory. He was now standing just outside the bedroom window, holding his grill brush.

"This won't do," said Tessie, taking up the jumper and blouse. "I'm going to wear my salmon floral print sundress. Any of our guests who think I look *too* casual will just have to keep it to themselves."

"What did you want, Tessie? I have to finish scraping the grill."

"You should have done that already. I want you to promise me you'll keep the TV off. It will absolutely ruin the party if everybody goes into the den and starts watching the hearings."

"The Army–McCarthy hearings aren't held on Saturdays, Tessie. Weekends is when the whole country gets a break from the ravings of the 'Distinguished Senator from Wisconsin.'"

"Well, I don't want you even *talking* about those awful hearings. I want this party to be a success. I don't need rancorous political debates over my broiled fish with celery sauce or your vermouth-basted sirloin steaks."

"Translated, Tessie: you don't want me to do anything that will bring even a moment's discomfort to our new neighbors. I know how important membership in the River Oaks Country Club is for you. I know how much you've been aching for a recommendation, regardless of the fact that your husband—your husband, the *butcher*—has absolutely no interest in hobnobbing with the Hobbys and the Hoggs."

"You have no interest in doing *anything*," said Tessie with a frown.

Rory didn't reply right away. Then he said, "I'm in the bowling league." Another silence.

"I have to finish cleaning the grill. Then I need to go pick up your Aunt Irma."

"Why? I didn't invite Aunt Irma."

"*I* did."

"Without asking me?"

"She's your only aunt, Tessie—your only living relative, not counting Regina and me."

"You know she doesn't mix well with our friends. And Dr. Crowley and his wife are an unknown commodity. What if she's in one of her *moods*?"

"What if Vivian Crowley is in a mood, for that matter? What if your new patio furniture catches fire from one of Maddie Jorgenson's foot-long Fatimas? What if Russia drops a bomb on our house right in the middle of the angel cake and plum ice cream?"

Tessie turned away from the window. "I can't talk to you anymore. You go out of your way to make my life a daily trial."

Rory finished brushing and scraping the backyard grill and then drove across town to pick up his wife's aunt Irma.

Irma Chambers was in her early sixties. She had never married and lived alone in the small house she'd inherited from her mother. Irma had once been a schoolteacher but had to retire after a couple of years because of her nerves.

Rory had seen her only three days before, when she came into the Piggly Wiggly supermarket where he was employed as head butcher. He had caught her out of the corner of his eye in the pet aisle, holding a can of Ken-L-Ration dog food.

Aunt Irma didn't have a dog.

"Howdy, Irma. How are you?"

Irma quickly returned the can to the shelf. "I'm doing well. It was a lovely morning so I thought I'd do my marketing."

"How's that old Chevy Clipper of yours getting on? Time to put her out of her misery?"

Irma shrugged, then shook her head. Her skin was pale; the over-application of rouge to her cheeks gave her a slightly clown-like appearance. She wore a scarf over her hair, which looked upon the margins as if it hadn't been washed in a while. This was a woman who didn't expect to be bumping into her nephew-in-law, or anyone else she might know, for that matter.

"Is she still running?"

"No. I think the battery's dead."

"I should come take a look at her. How'd you get over here?"

"I walked. It isn't far, you know."

Rory glanced at the cans of Ken-L-Ration dog food lined up on the shelf. Then he nodded in the direction of the meat department. "We just got in some really fresh ground chuck."

"Did you think I was going to *eat* that?" asked Irma, pointing with a slightly quivering finger at the dog food cans.

"They eat horse in Europe," said Rory matter-of-factly.

Irma didn't respond. Rory looked down at her grocery cart. It held a small carton of milk and some over-ripe bananas that he was certain Irma had gotten from the "reduced" produce bin. "Let me get you some of that chuck. It's on sale. In fact, we got a new thing here at 'Mr. Pig.' Ground chuck is free to family members of employees every other Wednesday."

"Thank you, Rory, but I wouldn't feel comfortable with that."

"Then at least come to our house on Saturday. We're having some friends and neighbors over. I'm grilling some prime-cut T-bones and sirloins, and Tessie's making something with broccoli and cheese she got out of *McCall's*."

Irma's response was another shrug. She seemed tired. What she seemed even more, though, was weak.

Weak with hunger.

"No ifs, ands, or buts, Irma. I'm picking you up at one." Then, with a sly wink: "And you're taking that ground chuck."

It was one o'clock. It took a full two minutes for Irma to come to the door. She was still in her robe. The robe looked old and unwashed. Irma herself looked as if she hadn't had a bath in weeks.

"Is everything all right?" asked Rory. Irma didn't invite him in. In fact, she seemed to be blocking the door in case he had a mind to come in on his own. "Are you sick?"

Irma nodded. "I'm not feeling well." Irma's face seemed even paler than it had on Wednesday at the Piggy Wiggly. And there was a skeletal angularity to it. Formerly the face had appeared rounded, even doughy.

"Is there something I can pick up for you at the drugstore?"

"No. I'll be all right. I just have to rest. Tell Tessie that I'm sorry I can't come to your barbecue. Maybe next time."

At just that moment Irma's knees began to buckle. Rory caught her as she collapsed. He carried her into the house and laid her down on the sofa in the living room. The room was tidy, but everything within it seemed tattered and faded, as if it contained nothing that had been purchased in the last thirty years. At first glance it appeared to be the room of someone who was not only poor but had given up on trying to be anything else. Although they had Irma over to their house two or three times a year, it had been quite some time since either Rory or Tessie had visited *her*—years, even, since they had seen what had become of Tessie's grandmother's old house.

"Do you have someone who can come and stay with you?" asked Rory. He had pulled up a chair and sat down next to her as she lay slightly jackknifed upon the threadbare sofa.

"Oh, I don't—" Irma shook her head.

"Then you're coming with me. We'll put you in our guest room until we can figure all this out."

Irma shook her head again. "I don't want to leave my home."

"You can't stay here, Irma." Rory started to get up. "I'm gonna go look in your refrigerator and cupboards."

"Don't."

"Let's get your things."

＊

Tessie stared at her husband in horror. "She's *where?*"

"I put her in the guest room."

"But we have guests coming."

"It's June. Nobody needs a coat bed. She's not doing well, Tess. I'm going to have Dr. Vickery come give her a look on Monday. Or would you rather have your Dr. Crowley check her out when *he* gets here?"

"You're too funny. Besides, Dr. Crowley wouldn't be right for her. He's a pediatrician. With the new children's hospital. I thought you knew that. What do you think is wrong with her?"

"I think your aunt is starving to death."

"What?"

"That's my diagnosis."

"That's ridiculous."

"She has no money, Tessie. On Wednesday, I came upon her right as she was about to put a can of dog food into her cart. I wasn't going to tell you."

"I wish you hadn't."

Tessie sat down in one of the patio chairs. She and Regina had been putting decorative paper tablecloths over several borrowed card tables. Regina was in the kitchen at that moment cutting cucumber and tomato slices.

"She's our responsibility, Tessie. She's family."

"I knew the day would come when I'd be saddled with her. I cannot believe this is happening to me. What if she comes out of that guest bedroom and has one of her *episodes?*"

"You act like she's Olivia de Havilland in *Snake Pit*. She has nervous spells, Tessie. She wrings her hands and bites her lips and then eventually she gets hold of herself and everything's okay. If you can't live with *that*…"

"What do you mean, 'live with that'? Are we taking her in?"

"If she's no longer able to take care of herself, we may have to."

"Over my dead body. I'm not going to have her here. People come here. People who shouldn't have to see her; people who wouldn't *want* to see her. You don't put someone like Aunt Irma on *display*, for crying out loud! What are you trying to do to me?"

Regina was standing in the doorway to the kitchen. She'd heard everything that her mother had just said.

"Regina," said Rory calmly, "make your Great-aunt Irma a sandwich. There should still be some of that chicken salad in the fridge. Put the sandwich back in the fridge for when she wakes up. She'll probably be okay for a while. I got her some soup at the diner on the way home."

Tessie turned to her husband. She scowled. "Is that what took you so long? We have people coming over in less than half an hour and you're stopping off at a diner with my batty aunt?"

"Go on," said Rory to his daughter. Regina was still standing in the kitchen doorway.

"Hurry up, Regina," said Tessie. "We've got a hundred things to do before our guests arrive."

Regina opened the door to the kitchen. She turned and said, "When I'm done, I want to go and sit with Aunt Irma. She always likes it when I sit and talk to her."

Rory smiled. "You do that, honey."

Tessie sprang to her feet. "The Crowleys haven't even met you yet. What am I supposed to say if they ask where you are?"

"I'm sure you can think of something, Mom." Regina went into the kitchen.

"She takes after you," muttered Tessie, glaring at her husband, who had begun to busy himself at the grill.

"And I thank God for that every day," replied Rory, flipping over a large sirloin steak in the basting tray and splattering the grill with sweet vermouth basting sauce.

1955

AGITATED IN ALABAMA

The bus was empty.

The two middle-aged white women took their seats on the starboard side of the first row of forward-facing seats. Patty set her shopping bag down on the seat in front of her and nested her purse in her lap. Harriet put each of her two shopping bags down on the floor near her feet.

Harriet had a car and often drove her friend Patty when the two went shopping together or had themselves a lunch out. Patty had never learned to drive. Patty had a colored man who took her where she needed to go when he wasn't deadheading her flowers or raking leaves or doing any of the many repair jobs that Patty and her husband Roland's antebellum mansion required. There was less for Lucius to do in the winter, but Roland Sprinkle kept him on at full salary. Patty's husband Roland was a lawyer. But he was also half-owner of two launderettes, each in a colored neighborhood. Though Roland Sprinkle was a founding member of Montgomery's White Citizens' Council, it was important for him to show the Negroes of this very segregated southern city that he wasn't a racist. He simply believed that black people and white people got along best when they kept their interaction to a minimum.

It was Roland who suggested to his wife that perhaps she and Harriet should take the Cleveland Avenue bus to the Montgomery Fair department store downtown. Harriet had wanted to go to Loveman's at the new Normandale Shopping City. Harriet had been there the week before and had set her eyes on an absolutely divine Lassie Maid wool and cashmere camel-colored balmacaan coat that she now wanted to buy; she was also looking forward to trying Francis Cafeteria's new veal sauté. On the other hand, Patty's husband Roland felt that it was important, given the fact that the Negro leaders of Montgomery had decided to prolong what was originally supposed to be only a one-day boycott, for the city's white citizens to patronize the bus line as much as possible to keep its drivers—most of them good, hard-working family men (all of them white)—from losing their jobs.

A full week had passed since a seamstress by the name of Rosa Parks (who coincidentally worked at Montgomery Fair) refused to give up her seat to a white man. Mrs. Parks had been sitting dutifully behind the "Colored Section" sign, but when the bus began to fill up with white passengers, the driver had gotten up and moved the sign to the row behind her and then asked that she give up her now white-designated seat. When Mrs. Parks defied him by staying put, the driver called the police and had Mrs. Parks arrested for failing to abide by a city ordinance that gave city bus drivers the authority to maintain segregation upon their vehicles through whatever means they saw fit. She was also charged with disorderly conduct.

Up until now, Harriet Jacobs and her friend Patty Sprinkle had avoided discussing the boycott. It troubled Patty to think that law and order was breaking down in the city of her birth. That the peace and security of this quiet and stately southern capital was now being disturbed by Northerner-led foment and general unrest. Even the Negro preachers were setting their Bibles aside and preaching hatred of the white man. This is what her husband Roland told her, and it chilled her to the bone.

In spite of all this, Patty had vowed to keep her opinions to herself, even as she stared out the bus window at the hordes of colored folk crowding the downtown sidewalks, deliberately avoiding the buses and hoofing it to wherever it was they needed to be. Because it would be several more days until the newly formed "Montgomery Improvement Association" created carpools and independent taxi services to ferry their black brothers and sisters around town.

Yet, try as she might, Patty couldn't keep her thoughts and her fears to herself, and so in that next moment she unleashed a great rant that took her friend Harriet by surprise. "It's just—I'm sorry, Harriet—it just isn't right. Roland and I—we've gone out of our way to do right by Lucius and his family and our maid Wilma and all of her kids, but it just isn't enough, is it? Not for them, not for any of these Negroes. You give them an inch and they take a mile. I'm sick to death of it. Just sick."

"How are Lucius and Wilma getting to and from your house?"

"I don't know and I don't care. This city has a fine bus system for them to use, but they refuse to use it. They listen to that Reverend King and that Mr. Abernathy and all those other rabble-rousing ministers who only want to stir the pot, and I couldn't care less if Lucius and Wilma have to walk twenty miles to get to my house. It serves them right. Of course, your situation is different because you've always taken your maid back and forth like she was the Queen of Sheba."

"Lollie lives too far from a practical bus route."

"Well then, I suppose she's sitting pretty now."

Harriet moved her bags away from her legs to give herself more room. With no other passengers on the bus, she could put the shopping bags right in the middle of the aisle if she wanted. "I don't think she's sitting pretty. Her daughter is sick."

"That isn't what I meant."

"I wouldn't want to trade places with a single colored person in this city, Patty. Would you? What do you mean my maid is sitting pretty?"

"It's a figure of speech."

"Well, I'd really rather not talk about this."

Patty snorted. "I can't help it." A quiet moment passed. The bus squealed to a stop at a traffic light. Twenty-five to thirty black people appeared in the crosswalk, all of them staring at the nearly empty bus. A young Negro man in blue coveralls, denotative of his employment at the long-integrated Maxwell Air Force Base, fleered cockily at the driver. Patty saw it. She trembled with rage. "I have to say it. I wasn't going to say anything about it, but now I have to. Beverly said that yesterday she saw you driving down her street with four or five colored women in your car."

"Yes, I saw her. I was wondering if she was going to mention it to you."

"Have you started your own taxi service for the help?"

"Lollie was afraid that her friends would lose their jobs if they couldn't get to the houses where they worked."

"They can take the bus."

"No, they can't, Patty. They have a right to their principles. Even you have to grant them that."

Patty stared out the window. "What principles?"

"The right to not always have to sit in the back of a bus." Harriet swept her arm at all the empty seats behind her.

Patty frowned. "*Somebody* has to. I suppose you think we ought to put all the black people in the front and the white people in the back. How much sense would *that* make?"

"It's segregation that doesn't make any sense." Harriet said this softly. A part of her hoped that Patty hadn't heard it. The words were provocative.

"I just know you weren't always this way," said Patty.

"You mean before I married 'the Jew'?"

"I didn't say that."

The bus pulled up to a stop. The front doors opened and an old black woman drew herself up with difficulty onto the bottom step and then, gripping the horizontal bar to her right, hoisted her frail body up onto the raised floor of the bus. The process of boarding was labored and protracted. At no point did the bus driver offer a hand of assistance.

"Good for her, taking the bus," mumbled Patty. "At least there are a few sensible colored folk left in this town."

The old woman paid her fare. Then she turned away from the driver.

"Don't make her—" said Harriet almost inaudibly, the words intended for the bus driver but only in apostrophe.

Dismounting the bus seemed to be equally difficult for the woman since there was a big drop-off between the floor and the bottom step and another drop-off from the step to the ground, and she would have to try very hard not to lose her delicate balance and fall. "Hurry up or I'll leave you," said the bus driver, poking at his teeth with a toothpick.

Once upon the street—for the bus driver had left the woman too much room to step easily down upon the sidewalk—the woman scurried to the rear door, which the driver had opened for her. This was the rule for the black passengers of Montgomery's city buses. They were expected first to enter the bus through the front door to pay their fare, then exit the bus and re-enter through the rear door to take their seats. It respected the long-observed custom of black servants only being permitted to enter the house where they worked through the rear or side kitchen door.

The old woman now struggled to pull herself up the bus's back steps. The driver revved his engine. Harriet rose from her seat and went to help the old woman. Once on board, the woman took a seat in the next-to-back row. Harriet returned to her seat next to Patty. There were now three passengers on the bus: Harriet and Patty in the first row of the forward-facing seats, and there in the back, an old black woman who, for whatever her personal reason, found it necessary to ignore the boycott and take the bus on this particular day.

Harriet turned to make sure that the woman was comfortably settled into her seat. Although the old woman had thanked Harriet at the time of her assistance, she now thanked her again with a grateful smile.

"I was afraid that he was going to leave her," said Harriet to her friend Patty.

"What?"

"The bus driver. Sometimes they take a colored passenger's money, and then while the person's walking around to the back door, the driver pulls away.

"I don't believe they do that," snapped Patty. "But if they do, it's wrong, and they should be reprimanded."

"Considering the fact that very few Negroes are riding the bus this week, the drivers should let those who do sit in the front."

"That would be against the law."

"It isn't against the law, Patty. Drivers can implement segregation on their buses any way they see fit. And I feel sufficiently segregated from any black person who might like to sit in that front seat." Harriet pointed to the side seat just behind the driver.

"You're being ridiculous, Harriet. Is this what you and Abe talk about every night over dinner?"

"Yes, Patty. We talk about injustice. And what do you and Roland talk about—I mean, when he isn't watching Nat King Cole on television?"

"Roland doesn't like—well, aren't you funny and clever? I can safely predict that tonight Roland and I will be talking about how you've started driving colored maids all over town like Montgomery's very own Eleanor Roosevelt. He'll get a kick out of that."

Harriet didn't respond. It was almost Christmas and her attention was suddenly captured by a Salvation Army Santa Claus standing on a street corner shaking his bell. The very white Santa was using his other hand to pat the head of a little colored girl who, it appeared, had just dropped a coin into his pail. The scene defused Harriet's anger. She was able to say to Patty in a very calm voice, "Patty, to be very honest, I don't like you very much."

Patty looked as if she had just been slapped.

"*Or* your husband. We wouldn't even be friends if the men we're married to didn't happen to be partners in the same law firm. Or—for that matter— if I hadn't always been so willing to drive you around like a white female version of your man Lucius. I think it's time that we stopped seeing each other. I hope this boycott lasts for months. I only hope that nobody gets hurt. People in this town—white people—have a tendency to play dirty when they don't get their way."

Harriet stood. In a raised voice she said to the bus driver, who was giving her a stony look through his overhead mirror, "And I could not care less if you lose your job. You're the one who had Mrs. Parks arrested, aren't you? She didn't have to get up. My husband has read me the ordinance. It clearly states that no person, and I emphasize the phrase 'no person,' has to relinquish her seat to another person should the bus be crowded and no other seats available. You have twisted the law for your own autocratic purposes just as the judge who sentenced her *ignored* the law. My friend Patty here sees things much differently than do I. Her husband sees things so differently that he's joined the Montgomery White Citizens' Council. I am now going to sit in the colored section of this bus. I have decided to make it my mission to see that the elderly woman with whom I will be sitting makes it safely off this bus and that you don't try to run her over while she's disembarking. Arrest me if you like. Goodbye, Patty."

With that, Harriet Jacobs picked up her Montgomery Fair shopping bags and moved to the back of the bus. She sat down next to the old black woman. The woman seemed confused.

Patty Sprinkle had lots to talk to her husband about that night. He had lots to say as well. There was a faction of men who shared Mr. Sprinkle's views who were exploring ways to punish the black leaders of the boycott for that they had done. There would be arrests and convictions for violation of state statutes that banned boycotts "without just cause." Local automobile insurers would be coerced into canceling coverage for those who enlisted their vehicles in the carpooling efforts. Taxi drivers who lowered their fares to match the bus fare would be subjected to a re-animation of an ancient city ordinance that set a minimum on taxi fares—a minimum that most black folk in Montgomery couldn't afford to pay. Later would come the retaliatory house and church bombings. These, though publicly disavowed by the ostensibly upstanding members of the white community, were always effective in drumming up the requisite amount of fear among the black citizenry.

1955 was ending but 1956 promised to be an even more difficult year for Montgomery, Alabama, in the area of race relations. Harriet Jacobs spent that year driving maids to and from their places of employment, and avoiding contact with almost all of the women she had once considered friends, including the woman who was a friend only by the broadest definition of the word. Patty Sprinkle, without a car, and without the ability to drive one even if she had one, spent the year largely at home berating her maid and yardman, and agreeing with everything her husband said, no matter how racist, no matter how venomous.

Three hundred and eighty-one days after the boycott began, the federal judiciary of the United States agreed with Rosa Parks and the boycotters, and put an end to segregation on all modes of public transportation nationwide.

In April of that year, the singer Nat King Cole, native of Montgomery, was brutally assaulted in the middle of a concert ninety miles up the road in Birmingham by members of the Northern Alabama White Citizens' Council.

During the boycott, Patty Sprinkle would on occasion go downtown to shop. The bus was almost always either empty or nearly so. She told people that she liked it that way. She told people that it suited her just fine.

1956

DISCREETLY SILENT IN MONTANA

The deputy sheriff and the emergency room physician had been friends since childhood. Their familiarity with one another often placed them into situations of like-minded understanding, obviating the need for long explanations or even drawn-out disagreement. There were occasions, in fact, in which each man knew exactly what his friend was thinking. This was such a time.

The bodies of two dead teenage boys lay on examining tables at one end of a long corridor, its white walls alternately strobed and obumbrated by two flickering, dying overhead fluorescents. At the other end of the corridor were the boys' families and friends: two fathers and two mothers, one grandmother, five siblings, four friends, and one solicitous neighbor. It was two-fifteen in the morning and several of those who waited anxiously for word on the boys drank from cardboard cups of coffee. The men smoked. The grandmother prayed. The two youngest children slept curled upon the waiting room divans, their heads resting in mirror symmetry upon their mothers' laps.

Over the fluorescent tube's importunate hum, the deputy sheriff said, "When are we—?" He finished his question by jerking his head in the direction of the waiting room.

"I thought we should talk first," replied the doctor. "You'll tell me what you and your men saw when they reached the scene?"

The deputy nodded. "We should be on the same page, though, about what the families need to know."

"Yeah, right." The doctor pulled a package of Salems from the pocket of his scrubs. The mentholated cigarette was new. "I don't get all the hoopla," he said, offering one of the smokes to the lawman. "Tastes exactly like Kool."

The two men started walking together down the corridor. They passed an empty gurney, then an abandoned candy striper's hospitality cart. The doctor exchanged nods with a bustling night shift intern.

The doctor led the deputy into a small hospital conference room. Sometimes families were brought into this room to discuss options for the care or, in some cases, the termination of care for their sick or dying loved one. The room was spare, more formally arrayed than the waiting room. It was a place where the families, many of them ranchers from isolated parts of Lewis and Clark County, could think more clearly and less emotionally about what needed to be done. Of course, there was no need to bring the families of the two dead teenagers into this room tonight. There was no decision to be made—only information to be conveyed: that the lives of two young Helena men had ended too soon, had ended in a terrible automobile accident on a darkened highway a few miles east of town.

And yet.

And yet, there was also that other matter.

The lanky deputy sheriff settled himself into a chair. The rock-faced doctor half-sat, half-leaned against the edge of the table a few feet away. The deputy ran his hand through his thick, dark brown hair. He was in his late thirties and the gray had only just begun to sprout at the temples. The doctor, who was only a few months older than the deputy, was still blond, but his hair was thinning. Crow's feet had begun to form in the outer corners of his eyes, squinting now in the room's bright unnatural light.

"As you know, both boys arrived DOA," said the doctor. "Though the Findley kid—"

"Died in the ambulance," said the deputy, his voice solemn. "We'd hoped that…" His voice trailed off. He shook his head.

"So both were in the car when you got there? Neither of them had been thrown?"

The lawman nodded. "The Findley boy was still behind the wheel. Chest staved in. From the steering column?"

The doctor nodded. "Where was the Robinson boy?"

"On the floor."

"At the time of impact?"

"My guess: half on, half off the seat. When we found him his head was down by the other boy's feet."

"What do you think, Gavin?"

"You want me to say it?"

"I need you to confirm it."

"I didn't wipe it all off?"

The doctor shook his head. "Not completely. There was still some residue of semen on the right cheek."

"But that wasn't the only thing that would have given it away."

The doctor scooted off the table. He pulled up a chair, turned it backward and sat down next to the deputy.

"The kid's pants," the deputy went on, "the Findley kid's—they were pulled down to his ankles."

"The BVDs too?"

The deputy nodded. "Merton and I figure that the wreck could have been attributed to any number of things. All related. The booze, obviously. Diminished attention to the road on the part of the teenager getting fellated. Merton thinks it could also be partly due to the Findley boy's pants getting tangled up with the accelerator pedal. They were both barefoot, you know. They were coming back from their senior class's big bonfire at the lake. Neither of the boys had apparently bothered to put his shoes back on."

The doctor leaned forward in his tipping chair. He rubbed his knuckles absently against the two-a.m. stubble on this chin. He drew in a deep breath as he thought. His lips rounded to blow out the air in slow, measured release. "So what do we say?"

The deputy looked down at the floor. "Whatever we decide, it needs to be the same thing coming from both of us, okay?"

"And Merton too?"

The deputy nodded. "Merton knows what's going on here." The deputy closed his eyes. "The families—they don't have to know. It just adds shit to all their grief."

"I agree."

The deputy continued: "The boys had had too much to drink. Two pals went for a drunken joyride and didn't make it home."

"So nobody had any idea that they were…?"

"Merton knows Findley—knows him pretty well. He'd never mentioned any suspicions about his son." The deputy sighed. "Of course, that's not the kind of thing a father would be all that eager to talk about."

"You're right." The doctor scratched the top of his head. "We'll never know *what* the parents know. We're just going to have to assume that they don't know *anything*. That's usually the way it is, right?"

The two men sat for a moment in the quiet, brightly lit conference room, each processing his own thoughts while waiting for the other to say something that would put the whole matter in a more personal light.

"Some boys grow out of it," said the deputy, finally.

"Some boys *have* to," said the doctor. The doctor came very close to touching the deputy's hand. The deputy moved his head as if he would shake it, as if he would negate that impulse that the doctor suddenly wished to act upon.

Obligingly, the doctor retracted his hand. The deputy slipped two fingers of his own hand into his jacket pocket and pulled out a small, colorful rectangle of paper. "Merton and I went through the boys' pockets and their wallets. Didn't find anything on the Findley kid. But this was on the Robinson boy. In his wallet."

It was a photograph of Sal Mineo, the actor. It had been carefully cut from a magazine. The size was a perfect fit for a wallet.

"For what it's worth—" said the deputy.

"Huh?" The doctor was studying the picture.

"For what it's worth, the car—the Findley boy's car. Well, it was a '49 Mercury coupe. Just like the one James Dean's character drove around in that movie last year."

"The boys—they were playing something out?"

The deputy sheriff shrugged. "Looked pretty real to me."

The doctor got up. "I don't like to put this sort of thing off. Worst part of my job. Yours too, I'm guessing. We shouldn't keep the families waiting any longer."

The deputy nodded. "Merton's been staying tight-lipped on my instructions."

Both men left the room, the doctor switching off the light on his way out. The corridor was empty—the bright illumination was again broken by the pop and flash of another fluorescent rod in its death throes above their heads.

The deputy reached over and touched the top of the doctor's hand. The doctor turned his hand around, hungrily grasping the deputy's hand, palm to palm.

After a couple of seconds, still alone in the corridor, the men broke their clasp. The doctor squared his shoulders. The deputy cleared his throat a couple of times.

Each man prepared himself to deliver the sad fact of the teenage boys' deaths and then the lie that went along with it. It was the same lie that the doctor and deputy sheriff would have wanted told if they had found themselves in the same situation.

It was the lie that permitted the boys to take their secrets to the grave.

1957

LOYAL IN UTAH

Sanpitch Academy was founded in 1875. Located one hundred miles south of Salt Lake City, it sat in the dead-eye center of the state. Its twenty-five-acre, sixteen-building campus lay in the scenic Sanpete Valley, where alfalfa grew in abundance, sheep grazed in fat, fleecy flocks, and thousands of farm turkeys, it was said, tried very hard not to think about Thanksgiving. A boarding school, it was built by Mormons in the largely Mormon town of Mount Pleasant. In 1957, most of its day employees (that is, locals who didn't live on campus) were Mormons. Most everyone else—its administrators, its teachers and students—were Gentiles   (as western Mormons in 1957 referred to non-Mormons, that latter group even including the school's music teacher, Julius Lafer, who was, in fact, Jewish). The school was affiliated with the Presbyterian Church, and a good many of its teachers and students were more than just non-Mormon; they were Protestants, and more specifically, Presbyterians.

This is somewhat important when one considers the political leanings of Sanpitch. The eighty-seven-year-old boarding school had a racially integrated student body (remarkable for the time). It boasted a student organization devoted to debating issues of international import (this in an era of monochromatic Cold War politics). Even more controversially, it used the recently published Revised Standard Version of the Holy Bible in its religion classes—a bold move that generated no small protest from parental proponents of the King James (penned, it has been said, by God's own hand). While Boston was banning the Everly Brothers' Top 100 single that autumn, "Wake Up, Little Susie," it was played with defiance and impunity in Sanpitch's Tiger Den snack bar, the kids agreeing with most of their contemporaries that "Susie" wasn't about teenage fornication at all, but told the rather benign story of a teenage couple who happen to fall asleep at the drive-in because the movie was so boring.

In the same way in which its teachers and students lived a soundly insular and familial existence (weekends as observed at Sanpitch were Sunday and Monday, so that its male students would have less opportunity to interact with roughneck townie youths), the school was allowed to go its own way in terms of policymaking and day-to-day operations. There was a governing board that oversaw things from a distance, but the board rarely involved itself in matters that onsite school officials—the superintendent, the director of academics, the separate deans of boys and girls, and the pastor and director of Christian education—could handle.

On Monday, December 16, shortly before the Christmas break, that changed. As it did twice a year, the Board of Oversight met in the conference room of the school's administration building to review the first few months of the school year and to be apprised of what to expect in the months that lay ahead. It was also time to gather up signed contracts for the next semester.

Three new members had joined the board since its last convocation— members not so willing to remain hands-off, members far more conservative in their political ideology. What came out of the meeting was a dictate that was perceived as both intrusive and, well, apocalyptic.

"There have been mumblings and grumblings," said Vince Sprawley, the youngest and most vocal of the new troika, "about your decision this year to replace the King James with the Revised Standard. Though most of us have had misgivings about it, we—the board—have done, I think, a rather good job of mustering support for your decision, Tim."

"And I thank you for that, Vince," replied the superintendent, who was sitting next to the school's pastor, Howard Claxton, both men tensely clinching their shoulders with mention of this potentially contentious matter and then instantly relaxing them when the matter was defused in a single breath.

"This board continues to believe," Sprawley went on, "in the importance of preserving Sanpitch's autonomy in all matters of religious instruction and identity, especially given the minority status of Presbyterianism in this state. Good citizenship, however—now that's a cat of a different breed."

Superintendent Timothy Grimm cocked his head. "I don't quite get your meaning, Vince."

"I think he means rendering unto Caesar and so forth," interposed the Reverend.

"Not exactly." Sprawley casually leaned back, intertwining his fingers behind his neck. "This country being a democracy and not an empery. As you've no doubt noticed, these are difficult times. Communism is on the rise, sirs, both outside our borders and within. Senator McCarthy's committee demonstrated that—"

The only woman at the table, Wanda Showalter, an outspoken member of the board for nearly twenty years and one easily annoyed by such things as being negligently designated a "sir," interrupted: "Mr. Sprawley, I must caution you against invoking the name of the late senator to make any sort of point regarding national fealty."

"My point, good lady, and I will gladly detach Senator McCarthy from it, is that institutions and organizations throughout the U.S., from the federal government all the way down to your local PTA, are asking their employees and constituent members to sign loyalty oaths these days—oaths that affirm one's allegiance to this nation by taking a pledge to protect and defend it."

"You mean a pledge not to *overthrow* it," explicated Mrs. Showalter with an attendant groan. "The board has drafted the oath and we've voted on it. Please be honest with Superintendent Grimm and the others as to its meaning and intent."

"May I see it?" asked Grimm. "You say the oath has already been approved?"

Sprawley nodded. "As a condition for renewal of your employee contracts for the spring. It will be incorporated into the language of Sanpitch's biannual employee agreement. By signing the contract, your teachers, and all of your non-teaching staff, as well, will be agreeing to uphold the tenets of the oath."

"Or *affirmation*," added the Reverend Claxton. "Some of our teachers do not 'swear.'"

Sprawley nodded again as he handed a copy of the oath/affirmation to Grimm. Claxton peered over Grimm's left shoulder to read along with him. Director of Academics Roger Rainwater looked over his right.

Nonetheless, Grimm read the pertinent paragraph aloud. "By affixing my name to this contract, I promise that I will not advise, advocate, or teach the overthrow by force, violence, or other unlawful means of the Government of the United States of America. I further promise that while I am in the employ of Sanpitch Academy, Mount Pleasant, Utah, I will not become a member or become in any other way affiliated with any group, society, association, organization, or party that does not uphold and respect the laws of the United States and all of its constituent governmental units."

Grimm looked up. Mrs. Showalter was poised to speak; she waited until his eyes met hers before saying, "What I continue to find incredibly troubling, and the reason that I didn't vote for this oath in the first place regards the wording 'which does not uphold and respect the laws of the United States' and so forth. That's all well and good for keeping any of our male employees who happen to be members of the LDS Church from taking a second or third wife, for old times' sake..."

"Don't be disrespectful of our Mormon brethren, Wanda," said one of the other board members, a former Presbyterian minister named Dorrell.

"I apologize, Gordon, to all of our Mormon brethren who may have been within hail and taken offense. Now let me make my point. There are some of us here who don't believe every law in this country to be sacrosanct and inviolable. Witness what is happening in the American South right now—massive protests against unjust laws that discriminate against our colored citizens—laws that no good Christian in his right mind should ever 'uphold and respect.' The wording in your oath is problematic and unrealistic, especially for those of us who happen to care about effecting positive change in this country."

"So I take it, Wanda," said Sprawley, narrowing his gaze on the long-opinionated former schoolteacher (ten years at Sanpitch), "that you would be fully supportive of the oath were we to strike that offending second sentence."

"Only in your dreams, Vince. The whole thing is ludicrous. Asking teachers to promise that they won't advocate the overthrow of the U.S. government—it's an insult."

"And yet," said Grimm, with a lugubrious expression that well suited his name, "at least five of the nine of you went along with this. I'd be interested to know which of the *longstanding* members of the board were persuaded that this oath was in the best interest of the school."

No one spoke. The vote had been taken by secret ballot, and so the secrecy would remain...for a while at least.

The board broke for lunch. Afterward came the presentation of a special program of student music performance, recitation, and declamation in the school's auditorium. It was thought best by Superintendent Grimm and the school's twelfth-grade English teacher, Miss Greene (and at the very last minute), to remove from the program Danny Worley's five-minute oration, "Jesus, the Original Liberal." There followed a tour of improvements to the campus, which was led by the deans of boys and girls and assisted by the dormitory supervisors. The tour was mapped so that by its end, the board would have had an opportunity to visit with nearly every one of the school's adult employees, as well as make passing acquaintance with a good number of its most promising students.

Superintendent Grimm, who was supposed to go along with the tour, delegated the responsibility to his second-in-command, Director Rainwater. Grimm sat in his office with the Reverend Claxton, the two discussing whether or not to mount a protest against the loyalty oath. Such a protest might do little good and could only alienate the three new members of the board, each of whom had won his seat due to generous (and ongoing) financial contributions to the school. Future donations might very well be imperiled by administration contumacy.

"There are members of this faculty who will refuse to sign it," said the pastor. "I can name four right off the bat. I assume you'll have to terminate them. It's going to get very messy, Tim."

"I know," said Grimm. "Here's the rock and there's the hard place. I got spoiled, Howard. All those years of minimal oversight. Occasionally we screwed up, but what got broken we fixed, and in some ways we even made it better than it was before. It's not easy, as the board certainly knows, shepherding all these kids twenty-four hours a day, nine months a year—not only teaching them but feeding them, keeping them healthy and safe, tucking them sometimes literally into bed at night. The parents of these kids have always put a great amount of trust in us because they know how committed we are to this school. Most of them could not care less whether we've ever entertained thoughts of insurrection against this government. They just want their children to grow up to be decent adults, good citizens who love this country but aren't afraid from time to time to point out ways in which she could improve herself. I wish I knew who those board members are—the ones Sprawley got to. I thought I knew the old timers better than that."

"I can tell you who they are," said Miss Taylor. Sharon Taylor was Grimm's secretary. Because everyone at the school shouldered multiple responsibilities, she was also dorm mother to the sophomore girls. "They asked me to count the votes. I don't mind spilling the beans. I hate the whole idea of a loyalty oath. I had an older brother who died in the Battle of Okinawa. I have another brother who was injured at Inchon. Swearing an oath presumes you aren't patriotic to begin with. It galls me. I almost altered the votes on a couple of the ballots. But I knew that God was watching."

Miss Taylor shared a smile of spiritual affinity with the Reverend Claxton.

"Anyway," she concluded, "it was Dorrell and Cummings."

Grimm nodded. "Just those two. That's good news, at least. Dorrell I suspected. His heart hasn't really been in this school since his wife died a couple of years ago. I can see how he might go that way. Cummings is a surprise. You're sure it was Augie who went along with Sprawley and the others?"

Sharon was about to explain that she easily recognized Augie's blocky handwriting when a new voice—a deep and cavernous voice—entered the conversation: "Why don't you ask him yourself?"

This from Augie Cummings in the flesh—a large, burly, ham-fisted sheep rancher in his fifties. Augie was the only board member who lived in Sanpete County (earning his seat because of his militant Gentile status: he was an outspoken Baptist in an overwhelmingly Mormon county). Augie had been listening outside a door that Sharon had inadvertently left slightly ajar. Now the door was open and Augie had stepped fully into the room.

"And you're aware, Miss Taylor," he appended, "that what you just did could result in your dismissal from this school."

"I would fight that effort tooth and nail, Cummings," responded Grimm.

"Do you want me to leave the room, Tim?" asked Sharon.

"No. Stay. Sit. Augie, I don't get it. By your single vote you've put me and the rest of this school in a terrible fix. I don't understand how you could go along with it. Your politics have never run toward platitudinous spread-eagleism."

"The school's getting a reputation, Tim. I happen to like what you're doing here, but perception is changing: we're not just some college-prep boarding school for the kids of boondock ranchers and National Park rangers anymore. The word now is that Sanpitch is becoming a lefty school—like one of those Greenwich Village little Red schoolhouses. Look, I hauled myself thirty miles across the county to cast my vote for Adlai Stevenson both times, even though I knew that he didn't have a prayer when it came to winning this state, so don't question my own progressive credentials. But the Westerners who send their kids here—they may be a live-and-let-live bunch, but they aren't Wobblies, and if Sanpitch starts to get known as the place where Rocky Mountain Reds board their Marxist brood, the other parents—the kind who've been the backbone of this school from the beginning—they're gonna start yanking their sons and daughters right out of here. This loyalty oath is going to make a lot of those parents feel better."

"What happens to my teachers—the ones who won't sign?"

"Well, you'll just have to *make* them sign, Tim. You have to explain to them why it's important for them to swallow their pride and do what in the end is really the best thing for the school."

"Can you at least get the second sentence taken out?"

Cummings nodded. "I think I could even get Dorell to go along with it."

Grimm thought for a moment. "So I really have no other choice, do I?" This question was posed to his friend, the Reverend Claxton.

"To be human is to compromise, Tim. Only Jesus Christ was allowed to stick unwaveringly to his principles."

"I think," interjected Cummings, "that you'll be surprised how few of your teachers would be willing to sacrifice their jobs for a principle."

"Or how many would choose to stay simply because of their affinity for *you*, Tim." The reverend was smiling warmly at his friend.

In the end, after much handwringing and soul-searching, only one teacher refused to sign the contract, which was tantamount to agreeing to the loyalty oath. It was Mr. Gage, who taught junior high mathematics. The fact that in the end he was the only one to object to the point of taking a hard stand came as a surprise to both Superintendent Grimm and to his right-hand men, the Reverend Claxton and Director Rainwater, in spite of what had been speculated on board review day. Grimm decided to talk to Gage. He could always be called upon to speak his mind and he had a reputation for not holding back, regardless of the circumstances.

"It isn't what you think at all, Tim," said Gage, as the two men strolled through the darkened campus on the night before the students would be released for their much-anticipated winter break. "I'm almost sixty. I've spent nearly two-thirds of my life as a teacher here at Sanpitch. Excepting service in the military, there is no other job in this country that demands as much of one's time and attention as being a boarding school teacher. Right now as we're walking and talking I'm wondering in the back of my mind if my eighth-grade boys are really all asleep or have a few of them stolen down to the common room to trade Lash LaRue comic books and watch John Wayne on the late show. And this being the last night in this term, I have a mind to be intentionally negligent and creep right off to bed without checking on them."

Harley Gage chuckled over the recklessness of his contemplated dereliction.

"Lookit, Tim—I wake up in the morning thinking about these boys, about *all* of our kids, and I go to bed at night praying that they get all the good breaks when they grow up and leave this place. This school has been my life and I've been quite blessed. It is all that I've had and all that I've ever wanted—to make some kind of small difference in these youngsters' lives. I do hate sometimes the direction this country is headed, but I know that we're raising kids who will be equipped to help make it better.

"Do I advocate the overthrow of this government by force or other unlawful means? What a question! And how terribly inconsequential when set beside those things that really *do* matter. But it's important for at least one of us to send a message on behalf of all of the rest of us."

Men in 1957 rarely showed the kind of physical affection that would come so much easier to their grandsons over fifty years later. But on that night, beneath a spangled late autumn sky in the Sanpete Valley of central Utah, two men shook hands in a way that more-than-adequately expressed the strength and solidity of their friendship—a friendship cemented by serious shared purpose. And John Wayne, with Mr. Gage's blessing, fought the outlaws and the Apaches into the wee hours of the morning with no small number of rapt eighth-grade boys as witnesses.

1958

EXPLOSIVE IN SOUTH CAROLINA

2212, 03/12/58

Doris Daltry makes her husband Air Force Lieutenant Kenneth Daltry a Scotch and soda. It's late. He's tired. He's also jittery and needs to relax.

"Did you collect all the pieces?" asks Doris, massaging her husband's tight shoulders through his t-shirt.

"By the hardest. There was one little boy who really dug in his heels—wouldn't give up any of what he'd found. His father really had to work on him. Pretty uncomfortable situation. The kid's crying, the mother's standing there giving me the evil eye." Kenneth groans at the memory. Then he moans, this time with pleasure. "Ah, that knot right there. Really dig in, honey."

As Doris kneads harder, she asks, "Have they finished combing the area?"

Kenneth shakes his head. "They'll be going over it for a week at least."

"Remember what I said to you on Monday morning?"

"Something about a nightmare you'd had the night before. Hiroshima. I'd told you Sunday night to put Hersey's book down and stop reading it right before you went to bed."

"And I asked you that next morning—"

"Not if anyone could ever drop a bomb on us, but whether we might ever accidentally drop a bomb on ourselves."

Kenneth turns around and kisses his wife. "In light of yesterday's atomic bomb mishap, I'd say your question was a pretty timely one."

BEFORE THAT:

1724, 03/12/58

Lieutenant Daltry is sitting in the living room of Mr. and Mrs. Caleb Flowers. Caleb Junior is crying.

"Caleb," says Caleb Senior, sternly, "go and get your atomic bomb fragments and give them to Lieutenant Daltry. They aren't yours to keep."

"The other kids got to keep theirs."

"I'm afraid that isn't true, Caleb," says Daltry, the fatigue of the long afternoon beginning to wear on his even-tempered, spit-and-polish military mien. "I've visited the homes of all of your friends and they've turned over everything they have. You're the last one on my list."

"Molly Greaney said she was going to make an ashtray out of the piece she found."

"Well, that would be a little hard now, son."

"As if the Greaneys need another ashtray in that house," opines Mrs. Flowers with puckered, judgmental lips. "That den of theirs is like an ashtray museum."

"Go and get the pieces of the bomb you found," says Mr. Flowers. "Give them to the lieutenant so he can go home. He has a long drive ahead of him. You have a long drive back to Savannah, am I right, Lieutenant? Be a good patriot, son."

As the boy goes reluctantly and with residual sniffles to bring his bag of shiny metallic shrapnel from the Mark 6 30-kiloton bomb that was accidentally dropped on his neighborhood only the day before, Mrs. Flowers sighs and says, "I was reading the book *Hiroshima*, which I checked out of the library last week. I was wondering if someday a bomb might be dropped on *us!*"

"By accident?" asks her husband.

"No. On purpose. I would never have believed that a bomb could be dropped by *accident.*"

BEFORE THAT:
2152, 3/11/58

Lieutenant Daltry receives orders to drive to Mars Bluff and assist in securing the area. There have been reports that children who live near the blast have been taking fragments of the bomb home as souvenirs. It will be his job to see that all fragments are collected, even if this means going door to door to confiscate them.

Daltry asks his commanding officer if it has been established that the area is free of radiation contamination. He is told that nothing has registered beyond the level of normal background radioactivity.

Daltry sighs with relief. Just the morning before, his wife had related the horrors of radiation poisoning that she had read about in *Hiroshima* by John Hersey.

BEFORE THAT:

1618, 3/11/58

Bill Gregg is out in his workshop building a bench with his son. His wife Effie is in the house, sewing. Their two daughters and the couple's young niece are playing in the yard. Bill hears a plane overhead, then seconds later the detonation of a 7,600-pound bomb right in his back acreage. The concussion makes his ears ring. The walls of the workshop shake. The air becomes a maelstrom of dust and smoke. He runs out into the yard to search for the rest of his family. Huge clods of earth hurled high into the air from the bomb's impact with the ground start their raining descent. One-hundred, two-hundred-pound soil boulders come crashing down on the house. Smaller chunks pelt the girls as they run and scream in terror. A gash is ripped in Bill's side; large plaster patches from the house walls come crashing down on Effie.

A mushroom cloud rises up from the instantaneous crater—a crater that measures seventy-five feet wide and thirty feet deep. Several nearby homes and a church are struck by the falling debris. A state trooper, forced off the highway by the blast, shields his head as he rushes to the scene.

The bomb carries no fissionable material. This is not a poisonous mushroom cloud. The bomb is atomic in name only, but the TNT that provides its explosive charge wreaks havoc nevertheless. The Greggs, all of whom survive, find that several of their free-range chickens have been vaporized.

BEFORE THAT:

1616, 03/11/58

Co-pilot Charles Woodruff is having trouble with his bomb's locking pin. Unlocked by regulation mandate during takeoff, the bomb must now be secured. The B-47's commander, Captain Earl Koehler, suggests that the bombardier, Captain Bruce Kulka, try to seat the locking pin by hand. Because the bomb bay isn't pressurized and the plane's altimeter now reads fifteen thousand feet, the three crew members must strap on their oxygen masks.

The entrance to the bomb bay is too small to allow for both a man and his parachute, so Kulka goes into the bay without it.

Kulka can't find the locking pin in the bomb-release mechanism. After twelve minutes of fruitless searching, the bombardier pulls himself high up in the bomb bay, where he thinks the pin might be hiding behind the bomb. Unfortunately, he uses the emergency bomb-release mechanism for his handhold. The bomb drops from its shackle. For a brief moment, it and Captain Kulka come to rest together on the bomb bay doors, Kulka straddling the bomb like a rider on a bareback horse. The enormous weight of the bomb forces the doors open. Kulka grabs hold of something—he doesn't know what—which keeps him from plummeting earthward with the bomb.

Hunter Air Force base doesn't understand the coded message the crew sends. Captain Koehler is forced to radio the civilian airport in Florence to ask that they communicate to Hunter the fact that they have lost a "device."

BEFORE THAT:
0800, 03/11/58

A specialized loading crew consisting of two men work for one hour and seven minutes to implant a bomb in Aircraft 53-1876A. The bulbous, blimp-shaped weapon bears a strong resemblance to the infamous Fat Man that was detonated 1,800 feet above Nagasaki, Japan, a dozen years earlier. The plane is scheduled to participate in "Operation Snow Flurry," part of an important "Unit Simulated Combat Mission and Special Weapons Exercise" programmed for later that day. The purpose of the mission, in which the plane would be accompanied by three other B-47s from the 375th Bombardment Squadron, is to transport a nuclear bomb to Bruntingthorpe Air Base in Great Britain and pretend to release it somewhere over that country.

The loading team has trouble with the bomb's steel locking pin. They ask the weapons-release systems supervisor for help. He has the weapon removed from its shackle and put into a sling. Then he futzes around the pin with a hammer until it's seated. The bomb is returned to its shackle. The two crewmen decide not to take the locking pin through its engage/disengage cycle; time is running out. They have to be finished by 1000 hours.

BEFORE THAT:
0715, 03/10/58

Lieutenant Kenneth Daltry and his wife Doris have finished breakfast. Each is indulging in a second cup of coffee before Daltry has to drive to

Hunter Air Force Base for the day. Doris mentions the nightmare she had the night before.

"I wish you wouldn't read that *Hiroshima* book before you go to bed."

"I was thinking about that midair collision last month, Ken. The plane was carrying a nuclear bomb. They dropped it in the water, but what if it had hit Savannah?"

"I think you look for things to worry about. The bomb didn't have nuclear capability. Do you know what the odds are that something like that could happen again? Give me a kiss. I'm late."

BEFORE THAT:
1558, 02/05/58

An Air Force B-47 Stratojet leaves Hunter Air Force base and shortly thereafter collides with an F-86 Sabre. The B-47 is carrying a Mark 15 hydrogen bomb. The pilot of the crippled bomber (the fighter's pilot ejects as his plane goes down) makes three attempts to land the plane at Hunter, with its nuclear bomb on board. A safe landing cannot be assured, given the condition of the craft. It is decided that the bomb, its nuclear explosion triggering capsule believed to be safely absent, should be released to allow the compromised craft to land. The weapon is jettisoned in the Wassaw Sound off Tybee Island and doesn't detonate upon impact with the water. The plane lands safely.

MANY YEARS AFTER THAT:

In 2004 there will be renewed interest in finding the exact location of the ejected bomb. High levels of radiation and unusual magnetometer readings will pinpoint a spot just off the southern tip of "Little Tybee." This will indicate the possibility that the bomb contained a nuclear capsule after all. On the other hand, the Air Force will report in 2005 that the high radiation reading could most likely be attributed to monazite, a kind of radioactive sand.

One hundred and seventy miles away in South Carolina, a different, terrestrial bombsite exists now only as a shallow depression in the ground, overgrown with vegetation. There were once hand-lettered signs that directed the curious to the spot, but they have been stolen.

Perhaps they were taken as souvenirs.

1959

TIGHT IN NEW YORK

"You're starting early," said Janice, turning around so her husband could zip her up in the back.

Cliff set his highball glass down upon the blonde-wood buffet next to him. "No earlier than usual."

"It's going to be a long evening, Cliff. No one goes to a New Year's Eve party with any expectation of leaving before one or two in the morning—even when the party is as boring as Marilyn and Gilbert's parties usually are." Janice glanced up at the aluminum sunray clock hanging from the dining room's grass cloth wall. Its rays were spiny and looked like something that lived at the bottom of the ocean. "It will be 1960 in less than five hours. I cannot even imagine it. 1960. We met in 1949. We're entering a third decade together."

Cliff finished with his wife's zipper and retrieved his glass. "So what are you suggesting?"

"That you don't show up at the Powells' drunk. How will that look? Aren't you expecting Gilbert to move all his business over to you next year?"

Cliff nodded. Then he sighed. "I'll stop. It's seven fifteen. I should go pick up Miss Stillwell. Has Rosalie left yet?"

"She's clearing the children's dinner plates and then she'll be off."

"Why couldn't *she* babysit Judy and Dicky tonight?"

Janice rolled her eyes, annoyed. "It's New Year's Eve, Cliff. Rosalie's going into the city. That would have been mean, don't you think—making Rosalie stay home on a night like this?"

"*I* wouldn't have minded it—I mean, if it meant we didn't have to go to Powells'. Pop open a bottle of bubbly, snuggle up on the couch with Guy Lombar—"

"You can't snuggle on that couch. I hate that couch. I hate Danish Modern. I don't know what I was thinking. It's so *sterile*."

"That's *your* bailiwick, baby. I'm quite content with my Herbert Hoover armchair in the study."

"You're sloshing," said Janice, pointing to Cliff's glass. "You're very drunk. Now what are we going to do about Miss Stillwell? We can't get her a taxi. Not tonight of all nights."

"I'm fine. I've driven far more intoxicated than this."

"That's supposed to set my mind at ease?"

"You need to learn to drive, Janice. It's almost 1960, as you've already noted. Women drive these days, maybe you've heard."

"I've told you already that learning to drive is my New Year's resolution. Go on. Be careful. Westchester County is probably swarming with highway patrol officers just looking for people like you to give tickets to. Or worse."

"I'll go slow. Miss Stillwell's only ten minutes away."

Janice Fredericks had called Miss Stillwell, whom she knew from their work together on the Tarrytown Library Committee, in early December to make sure that she would be available for New Year's Eve. Janice knew that babysitters in Westchester County were a valuable commodity on the last night of the year, and even more so on this *particular* New Year's Eve. The 1950s were about to bow out, to have their place taken by a decade that held great promise. At least this is what Americans were told. Wasn't the New York World's Fair's "Futurama" exhibit, which Janice had seen as a girl in 1940—wasn't it all about 1960, about that portal year to all the glories and wonders of an enterprising, utopian future?

Janice thought about this as she watched her husband go out to the garage. She thought about all the little model cars she'd seen in the World's Fair exhibit. She wondered if there had been any tiny drunk drivers in any of those tiny cars—especially drivers like her husband, who seemed to do a fairly competent job of keeping his Eldorado on the pavement, despite obvious mental impairment.

Miss Stillwell answered the door. She was a little more smartly dressed than Cliff anticipated. It was New Year's Eve, after all, even though she expected she'd be spending it first playing Candy Land with a five-year-old and seven-year-old, and then sitting alone in front of the TV and watching the crowds make noise at Times Square thirty miles away.

Miss Adelaide Stillwell used to be a schoolteacher. She was retired now, but she still enjoyed being around children. Adelaide volunteered at the library; she read storybooks aloud during story hour. And, of course, she babysat. Adelaide had made her peace with spinsterhood a long time ago. (Although she would forever detest the designation "old maid.")

"How are you tonight, Miss Stillwell?" Cliff affably inquired.

"I'm doing just fine. Let me get my purse and my snacks."

Cliff waited on Adelaide's porch while she fetched her purse and tray of snacks and then locked the front door. He let her go ahead of him down the brick walk that bisected the neatly trimmed front lawn of her small, fairytale stone cottage. Halfway down the walk, she heard a scraping, scuffing sound, an "oof!" and then a "damn!" She stopped and turned.

"I'm okay," Cliff said, tipping slightly to the left. "I just got tripped up by one of your bricks."

"I don't see how that's possible. My bricks are all fairly even."

"Well, at least one of them wasn't. But it's all right. I don't think I did any damage. Not to me or to the bricks."

"Have you been drinking?" Adelaide moved in closer so she could smell the air in the vicinity of Cliff's mouth.

"A cocktail before I left the house."

"You've had more than a single cocktail, Mr. Fredericks."

"Does it matter? I'm a better driver tight than most men are sober. I've been behind the wheel since I was twelve."

"A drunk man praising his driving skills." Adelaide whistled her disbelief. Then she folded her arms and straightened up her lower back to show resolution. "You've been drinking. I have a hard and fast rule about not being driven by people who've been drinking."

Cliff frowned, his brow narrowing. "Is this a *new* rule? Because I can name at least a half-dozen times I drove you home after you babysat for us when I was nowhere near sober and you clearly knew it. And may I add, Miss Stillwell, that I got you home in one piece each and every time."

"It's a recent rule, I'll admit, but I'm sticking to it."

"Why this rule all of the sudden?"

"Apparently you don't read the local papers, Mr. Fredericks. That young woman who was killed right before Christmas—the man who put that car right through the trunk of that tree—*he'd* been drinking too, and drinking heavily. He'd been to a party—just as you are *going* to a party. She was his children's babysitter, Mr. Fredericks. Just as I am *your* children's babysitter."

"Miss Stillwell, it isn't necessary for you to speak to me as if I'm still in the third grade."

"I'm simply trying to make you understand. I won't brook it. Not ever again. It's irresponsible for a man to get behind the wheel of a car when his eyesight and his reflexes are encumbered by strong drink. I sincerely hope, Mr. Fredericks, that you are not in the habit of endangering your wife and children in this manner."

Cliff sighed and slumped. "I assure you, madam, that I do not. I generally only drink during that one hour that conveniently falls between 'Hi honey, I'm home,' and 'Dinner looks great!' Oh, and I have a few beers on the weekend. I'm not the dipsomaniac that you paint me."

"I wasn't painting you in any such way! I was merely asking if you would in the future—"

"All well and good, Miss Stillwell. All well and good, but what about tonight? I am taking my wife and myself to a New Year's party given by a very important potential client. It isn't a party that we can afford to miss. I believe that Janice secured your services for this evening several weeks ago. That's how important it is that we have someone to babysit our children tonight. If you decline, you'll be putting me in a terrible bind. *And* you'll be in breach of our oral agreement."

"Every agreement carries certain unspoken expectations, Mr. Fredericks. One of these expectations is that both parties will act in good faith. This isn't good faith. You tripped on my front walk because you're sozzled. I will not ride with you. I'll be very sorry if you happen to miss your party, but you should have used better judgment before you left the house."

Cliff thought for a moment. "May I come in and use your phone? I'll see if I can get you a cab."

"Certainly."

Cliff knew before he began to dial the various cab companies that covered this section of Westchester County that it would be a lost cause. But he still had to try on the outside chance that he might get very lucky. He didn't even care if the companies wanted to gouge him. He'd pay whatever they asked. This was an important party. He had told Gilbert Powell that he and his wife were looking forward to it. He cursed Janice now for never having learned to drive. And why didn't Miss Stillwell drive? Did she just sit around like royalty and expect people to ferry her to wherever she needed to go? It was infuriating. But he tried his best to keep calm. Keeping calm might help Adelaide Stillwell to change her mind.

After striking out with the fifth cab company he phoned, Cliff turned to look up at Adelaide, who was standing next to the little phone table. It was a heavy table—Stickley maybe. Miss Stillwell wouldn't be caught dead with a house filled with Heywood-Wakefield's Contessa Danish Modern, thought Cliff. She was practical. She was sensible. Miss Stillwell didn't even get into a car unless she knew that the ride would be safe. "No dice," he said.

Adelaide tutted. Forever the school marm, thought Cliff.

"Any chance you might reconsi—?"

"Absolutely not."

"May I have some coffee?"

"I'll be happy to make you a cup of coffee, Mr. Fredericks, but studies have shown that simply drinking a cup or two of coffee doesn't magically sober a person up." She cleared some phlegm from her throat. "If that's what you're aiming at here."

"And just how long *do* you think it will take for me to sober up, Miss Stillwell?"

"It depends on how many drinks you've had. Will you be honest and tell me that, Mr. Fredericks? And would you also take a guess at how strong you made each one of them? Or was it Janice who made them?"

"No, no. I mix my own drinks. I think I had two. I got home a little late and I had to shower and dress for the party. Two. I'm sure that was it."

"It smells like more."

"I can't help what it smells like. I'm telling you two. How long for two drinks, Miss Stillwell? How long before you think I'll be clearheaded enough to drive you the six or seven miles to my house?"

"Two hours, I should think. One hour for each drink. Yes, I'm fairly certain I'd be comfortable riding with you after I was sure that you hadn't been drinking for two hours."

"I suppose we could be late. I could just say that something came up with one of the kids. Yes. That might be doable. Can I use your phone to call Janice and tell her?"

"Of course."

Cliff called Janice and explained where things stood. "So, I'll come on home and wait there and then in a couple of hours—"

Adelaide interrupted. "Not acceptable. How do I know that you aren't going to treat yourself to another drink once you get home?"

Cliff snorted. It was actually a half-snort, half growl. He spoke into the phone's mouthpiece: "She doesn't trust me."

"Yes, I heard her," said Janice.

"Can't you promise her that you'll keep me on the straight and narrow?"

"I can try."

Cliff handed the phone to Adelaide. "Hello, Adelaide," said Janice.

"Hello, Janice. I hate to be so difficult, but you know what happened to Dot Sparrell last week."

"Yes, I do. It was so tragic. She was going to be a nurse."

"Janice, I would certainly trust you to keep an eye on Cliff, but that isn't the only issue. When he drives in this condition he puts other people at risk besides himself and whomever happens to be in the car with him— other motorists, other passengers, innocent pedestrians. It's best, I think, that he stay here with me until he sobers up."

"You're probably right," said Janice. "Maybe you could feed him while he's there. He didn't eat much for dinner. It's no wonder the alcohol went straight to his head."

"The alcohol went straight to his head because there was a great lot of it, Janice. Let's not kid ourselves. I made myself a little New Year's Eve hors d'oeuvres platter to take with me to your house tonight. He can have some of that. Do you want me to put your husband back on the line?"

As Janice was saying that it wasn't necessary, Cliff was shaking his head as well. Adelaide returned the phone receiver to its cradle and placed her hands on her hips.

"Well, little man, let's get you some coffee. I have Eight O'Clock coffee. That's the A&P brand. Would that be all right?"

"It'll be eight o'clock soon. Why not?"

Cliff sat at the kitchen table drinking coffee and reading a Red Smith sports column in the *New York Herald Tribune*. Adelaide sat across from him. She pushed the hors d'oeuvres plate a little closer to him. "Are you sure you wouldn't like a canapé?"

"Well, hell, why not?" Cliff picked up a cracker with a thin slice of prosciutto on it and popped it into his mouth.

"You like it?"

Cliff nodded.

"Have another. I can make more." She sat back in her chair and studied Cliff.

"What is it? Am I *chewing* recklessly?"

She shook her head. "You look like a boy I used to know."

"When was this?"

"Oh, years and years ago. He died in the Spanish flu epidemic. We were engaged to be married."

"I'm sorry."

"It wouldn't have worked out. He drank." She looked embarrassed. "That was rude. I'm sorry. I'm sure you aren't nearly the drinker he was. It's terribly ironic—the fact that he died so close to the start of Prohibition."

"People drank during Prohibition. You should know. You lived through it."

"You're right. You're quite right. Try one of those little mushroom thingies."

"You made all this just for yourself?"

"I was going to give Judy and Dicky a taste. But most of it is pretty rich, and I didn't want them to get a tummy ache."

"Smart. It's good. The mushroom thing. It's all very good. I should pay you for this tray and take it to the party. Never much care for the spread that Marilyn Powell sets out."

A silence passed, Cliff turning desultorily through the pages of the newspaper while taking an occasional bite from the hors d'oeuvres tray, Adelaide puttering around the kitchen. "Do you mind if I turn on the radio?"

"Not at all."

Adelaide tuned her kitchen radio to big band music. "I usually can't find anything but rock and roll these days," she pronounced.

Cliff grunted agreement.

After another couple of minutes, Adelaide turned the music down and said, "Cliff. Is it all right for me to call you Cliff?"

"You can call me whatever you like, Miss Stillwell. Just don't call me a cab, because you won't have any luck." Cliff's little joke was chased by a glimmer of a smile.

"There's something I haven't told you. Something that I *should* have told you."

Cliff, whose head had been largely in the paper, now looked up. "What?"

"I can drive. I even have a car. I let my brother borrow it. He wanted to drive down to Atlantic City for the weekend."

"You can drive? Since when can you drive?"

"Since I finished my lessons last month."

"Why didn't you tell me this? You could have driven *my* car! Why did you put me through all this?"

"You shouldn't drink and drive. I was trying to make a point that would stick."

Cliff could feel his face turning red. "You know, Miss Stillwell, this really shouldn't be any of your business."

"I disagree. You're going to kill somebody one of these days—if not me, then your wife or one of your children, or somebody you meet coming around one of those curves on Highway 119. *Or* yourself."

"So you've been teaching me a lesson."

"I suppose I have."

Cliff got up. "So can we go? You know, of course, that I don't intend to pay you for all the time that we've wasted here."

"I wouldn't expect you to. Let me get my purse. Can I have your keys? Be a dear, if you would, and carry out my hors d'oeuvres platter."

As the two were walking out to the car, Cliff stopped. Adelaide, who was walking next to him, stopped too. "Just going to take a wild guess here, but your boyfriend didn't die in the Spanish flu epidemic, did he?"

Adelaide shook her head. "It was a car crash. Late one night in Trenton. I lived in Trenton then. That crash last week just brought it all back to me. Of course, I think of him other times, too. Like when I see you. I can't help myself. The way your hair recedes slightly at the temples just the way his did. And you have a similar smile. You really should smile more often."

"Give me a good reason, Miss Stillwell, and I'll smile as big as you like."

As Adelaide was sliding in behind the steering wheel, she said, "Now I have to warn you—I'm a very slow driver. I'm quite night blind, you see."

Cliff Fredericks didn't drink again that night. He wanted to be teetotaler-sober for later—when the time came to drive Adelaide home. For all Cliff knew, night blindness had played a role in the car crash that had killed Adelaide's boyfriend; he wasn't taking any chances.

1960

SMILING IN CALIFORNIA

It was a very simple plan. It should have taken only one sentence to explain. But Forrest was expressive, and he gave it five. This is what he wrote on the piece of paper that he then left on the top of his bedroom chest of drawers:

> *Today I plan to walk to the Golden Gate Bridge. If, along the way, I meet anyone who feels compelled to smile at me, I will not jump. I am tired of watching the best men and women of my generation eviscerated by insanity, stripped bare of soul, crawling through dirty, ebon gutters at break of day, ravenous for the needle or the spliff, consumed by cancerous loathing. Will there be a smile to supplant the anger, to dispel all the loathing? If you are reading this, the answer is "no."*

Forrest Wilton was twenty-four. He lived in his parents' Edwardian painted lady in the affluent San Francisco neighborhood of Pacific Heights. Only recently had he gotten the idea of jumping from the Golden Gate Bridge, the most popular suicide destination in the country. His life, which had held promise (he had worked for a couple of years on the city desk of the *Examiner* and had even been engaged for a couple of months to a girl who did, in the beginning, truly love him), had now hit a wall. He wanted to write professionally, but he didn't feel he was good enough. He stood on the outside of the Beat movement, peering longingly through breath-fogged windows, unworthy, insignificant.

Two weeks earlier, on May 13, Forrest had watched San Francisco police officers blast heavy jets of water from fire hoses at protesting college students. He had witnessed the officers dragging students bruisingly down the front steps of City Hall, while William Mandel, a left-wing radio broadcaster, sat inside spitting figuratively into the faces of the members of the House Un-American Activities Committee who had gathered to figuratively string *him* up as a Communist sympathizer in this "Marxist City by the Bay."

The country was going down the toilet in one fast flush. Richard Nixon was poised to become the next president come November.

And in the midst of it all—amidst all the madness and the anger and the hysteria that, unknown to Forrest, was ushering in one of the most turbulent decades in our national biography—there wasn't, in his pessimistic estimation, even a glimmer of a smile. Not one single smile of hope, or of happiness or joy writ personal, or humanity or compassion writ large. There was only Moloch, who fed on hope and despair and robbed mothers of their children. Hell, thought Forrest, was that place— or that time—in which the child in each of us dies.

Could it be that Forrest Wilton wanted to end his life because he couldn't return to the innocence of his childhood? Or was it simpler, even, than this? That all he needed was a smile—one single, redemptive, life- changing, life-*saving* smile to keep him among the living.

Her name was Ying. She'd moved to San Francisco ten years earlier from Taiwan. She was the Wiltons' housekeeper. Mr. and Mrs. Wilton had just been summoned to Boston to be at the side of their daughter—Forrest's older sister—following a difficult delivery. They'd hardly had time to pack before flying out the door. Ying usually came on Thursdays, but Mrs. Wilton asked in parting if she'd come the next day instead—Tuesday. The house was such a mess, you see, and it would only get messier with the Wiltons' slovenly son left to his own devices.

Forrest left for the bridge at eleven. Ying arrived at the house at eleven fifteen. Ying discovered the note on the chest of drawers at around eleven thirty. Her English was good; she'd studied the language for years as a student in Taipei. It was unclear to Ying as to whether this constituted a suicide note or not. If there was truth to the statement, the law of averages dictated that Forrest would meet someone along his long walk to the southern reach of the bridge who would smile at him.

But then again, what stranger had ever smiled at *her* in the ten years she had lived in San Francisco? People she knew—they smiled, of course. Ying had many friends in Chinatown. But she could remember no stranger who had ever opened himself or herself up in this way. Was it not this way to a great extent in every big city—the building up of walls to keep ourselves from the harm that may come from those whose hearts we don't know? Ying remembered how it was when she was a girl in Taiwan. She was taught—indeed, all Chinese children were taught—to be cautious of those they didn't know. Wariness kept the face set, unrevealing, unsmiling. San Franciscans must be very much like the Chinese, thought Ying.

Poor Mr. Wilton, thought Ying. Poor, troubled, brooding Mr. Wilton. He will see no smiles this day. He will go to the bridge that beckons him in all of its majestic, International Orange-colored, Art Deco splendor, beckons him to come and climb over its low, four-foot safety railing—a railing that invites thoughts of the seemingly unthinkable. Ying had been on that bridge. She had strolled along its walkway. She had seen its thirty-two-inch-wide beam, where jumpers made their now-or-never decision to let go.

Ying knew nothing of the many people who had ended their lives by plummeting the 245 feet into the waters of San Francisco Bay below, but Forrest did. He had helped to gather research for a newspaper story about the bridge and why it was such a popular place to kill oneself. It seemed to Forrest at the time that the view from the bridge should have been so breathtakingly beautiful as to give the potential jumper a renewed appreciation of life and all of its glorious promise. And yet, according to one of those whom Forrest had interviewed for the piece—a member of the tiny privileged fraternity of those who had beaten the stiff odds and survived the jump—"There is god-awful poetry in that plunge. As you seek to invisible yourself beneath the water below, you become part of something far greater than yourself."

That's right, Forrest had thought cynically to himself; you become part of the Golden Gate Suicide Club—the sane need not apply.

The man had described to Forrest the feeling of the seventy-five-mile-per-hour, four-second drop—a drop that seemed to put one into a state of protracted abeyance. Here was the intersection between life and death. The man had made it sound almost romantic. Of course, a majority of jumpers end up thwacking the water like it was hard concrete—the insides of their bodies torn apart with a force of fifteen thousand pounds per square inch. Upon impact, ribs snapped, tearing into internal organs; vertebrae shattered; often the liver ruptured. If the jumper was lucky enough (luck being a relative term here) to survive the fall, he would more than likely drown, sucked under by a powerful current, or else die from hypothermia, his body becoming food for sharks or crabs, the latter of which especially loved the taste of human eyeballs.

Forrest's interviewee had hit the water in the only way that allowed for the remote possibility of survival: feet first, with a slightly angled entry. And he was rescued almost immediately thereafter.

The interview, combined with the facts and figures assembled for the newspaper piece, opened Forrest's eyes to the drawbacks of this popular form of suicide. But none of that mattered to him now.

Ying had seen him in this state. During her weekly visits, she had watched him as he grew more and more emotionally distant. She had wondered how his parents could be so oblivious to their son's pain.

Ying left the house in a great hurry, clutching the note in her tremulous hand. He had said that he would walk. This was to her advantage. She would take the bus.

It being a beautiful, fogless day, there were clumps of tourists moving up and down the pedestrian walkway. They were snapping pictures of Angel Island, of Alcatraz, of Treasure Island in the distance, and taking panoramic shots of the colorfully cluttered, contoured hills of San Francisco. Ying chose a spot where she would wait. And pace. At one point a bridge worker approached her. She couldn't believe what he said: "You're not thinking of— *you know*." He made a diving motion with his hand.

"No, I'm not," said Ying brusquely, after she had collected herself. "I'm waiting for someone."

The bridge worker nodded, though there was skepticism in his look. Recently, there had been a rash of suicides. There was a campaign underway to put up a safety barrier, but it would be expensive, and there were engineering and aesthetic challenges. Most people didn't want it. "If we stop them here, they'll just find some other place to do themselves in," was the general refrain. "After all, there's always the Bay Bridge. Ugly as sin, but quite serviceable."

An hour went by. Ying began to think that Forrest had changed his mind entirely. Now there existed the possibility that he wouldn't be coming at all. She relaxed. She took in the view. She snapped pictures for those who handed her their cameras: tourists wishing visual records of their visit to one of the best-known bridges in the world.

Then, after letting her guard down, she noticed him. He walked slowly. He didn't see her—not from a distance, nor even, finally, up close. Was she invisible to him?

Having no other recourse, as he came close enough for her to reach out and touch him, she spoke his name. Startled, Forrest stopped and turned.

"Ying?"

She nodded. "There was no one?" she asked. "Not a single person who smiled at you?"

"You read my note?"

"How could I miss it? Your room—it was very much in need of a cleaning."

"I thought that a girl was smiling at me, down there, at the end of the bridge. But I was wrong. She was smiling at her friends and I happened to get in the way. The smiles of the young are frivolous and inconsequential, anyway. Why are you here?"

"To keep you from jumping off this bridge."

"Why do you care?"

"Life is precious."

Forrest didn't answer. He was looking over the rail. He was looking down at the water far below. Four seconds is a long time to fall, he thought to himself. When he turned his head to look at Ying again, she was smiling. It was a big smile—almost cartoon-like. It was the picture of the woman in the dictionary next to the word "smile."

"What are you so happy about?" he asked.

"I'm not happy. I am smiling to keep you from jumping into this bay. Or does my smile not count either?"

In a soft voice, almost a whisper: "It counts. Of course it counts."

"Then I can stop smiling now? I look foolish."

Forrest nodded. The two started down the walkway, heading south, back to San Francisco.

"I lost my father and brother in the 228 Massacre. In 1947. Do you know of it?"

"The Tawainese uprising."

"Yes. The White Terror. I lost many other family members and friends then. They said we were Communists, but we weren't. We were proud Tawainese who protested too loudly what the Mainland Chinese were doing to our land and our people."

"You came to this country to escape all of that?"

Ying nodded. The two passed a gaggle of Japanese tourists taking pictures of each other taking pictures. She lowered her voice. "Life was better under the Japanese occupation." She paused. "But *all* life is precious. Mr. Forrest Wilton, you put too little value on your own life."

They walked on in silence. As they were leaving the bridge Forrest said, "I'm hungry. My feet hurt. I have money for a taxi."

Forrest was about to direct the driver to his parents' house when Ying made a suggestion: her cousin's restaurant in Chinatown.

"You'll like it," she said to Forrest. "All the waiters smile."

1961

UNLITERATE IN NEW HAMPSHIRE

"We have a whole house full of books. My husband and our two kids are big readers." This is what Josephine heard the woman say—the woman whose house this apparently was. And there was no reason to doubt her; half of the items for sale in the driveway or overflowing upon the lawn were either books or magazines. There were full sets of Childcraft and Colliers encyclopedias and the usual stacks of non-sequential *National Geographics*. Josephine, who was an amateur chef, was most interested in the small cache of cookbooks she discovered in a box that sat appropriately upon a child's miniature play oven. The woman of the house casually leaned against the oven, almost touching Josephine with her shoulder as she and a female neighbor talked about the yard sale.

"Lyman said the beginning of May was too early in the season for a yard sale. He was afraid that people wouldn't come out if the weather was nippy. But we really didn't have a choice. It was either this or Goodwill. I think this is a good turnout, don't you?"

The neighbor nodded. "*I* was thinking you might lose some customers from all the foofaraw about yesterday's flight, but it doesn't look like it's kept *too* many people away."

The two women weren't the only ones talking about what Derry's native son Alan Shepard had accomplished just the day before. There were two men, standing among boxes of tools and other hardware, who appeared to be discussing the details of Shepard's historic flight into space. The younger of the two, whom Josephine assumed to be the husband of the first woman (he was drinking coffee from a kitchen cup and wearing bedroom slippers) was making arching gestures with the plane of his hand as if demonstrating the trajectory of the Mercury astronaut's spacecraft.

The man's wife noticed Josephine looking through the box of cookbooks. She pointed to the box and said, "Do you like to cook? I'm a terrible cook. I haven't even opened half of these."

"I *do* like to cook," said Josephine. She picked up an early edition of *The Joy of Cooking*. "This could be a first edition," she said.

"I couldn't possibly care," said the woman flippantly. "I just want them all out of here. Lyman and I are moving to Portsmouth. I refuse to cart all this stuff with us."

Josephine nodded and smiled. "To quote Thoreau, you are 'driving life into a corner and reducing it to its lowest terms.'"

"To quote who?"

Josephine's guess that her purchase might be a rare first edition was confirmed a couple of days later. The book was actually quite valuable— one of only three thousand copies self-published by Irma S. Rombauer, a St. Louis mother and housewife, back in 1931. Mrs. Rombauer's husband had committed suicide the year before and left her struggling to make ends meet. The author had taken the unusual publishing route of engaging the printing services of a company that made labels for Listerine mouthwash.

"I can't believe that crazy woman would let this go for seventy-five cents," Josephine said to her husband Quentin. "I know the right thing to do would be to take it back to her."

Quentin looked up from the television. He was watching *My Three Sons* for personal reasons; like Fred MacMurray's character Steve Douglas, Quentin used to be an aeronautical engineer. He had worked in St. Louis for the McDonnell Aircraft Corporation, and small world that it was (though this fact would never be known to him) he and his wife, during their ten-year sojourn in "the Lou," had lived not so very far from none other than Irma S. Rombauer herself.

"For once," said Quentin over his shoulder, "*don't* do the right thing. Didn't you say the woman didn't care if it was a first edition or not? Keep it. Do something nice for *yourself* for a change."

"All right. I will. Don't have a heart attack from the shock."

Quentin laughed.

Josephine sat down at the dining room table where the light was good. She was almost as bad as the woman from whom she'd bought the book; she'd hardly even opened it herself, so busy was she visiting the local library and a couple of book dealers in Manchester and Nashua to try to figure out how much it was worth. Josephine already owned a later edition of the cookbook, published by the commercial printing house Bobbs-Merrill Company. It was the book dealer in Nashua who encouraged her to spend some time with the first edition. "It's very conversational in tone, really quite quaint. My dear, there are recipes for preparing raccoon and squirrel in there. I kid you not."

In looking for the raccoon and squirrel recipes, Josephine happened to open the book to the dessert section, specifically to a recipe for something called "Jelly Tots" (otherwise known as Hussar Balls, Jam Cookies, Thumbprint Cookies, Deep-Well Cookies, and Pits of Love). But she couldn't give much of her attention to the recipe. Her gaze was drawn to a small envelope taped down upon the page.

The Scotch tape was old and had lost most of its stick; the envelope came up easily. On the outside was written in a delicate hand, "To my favorite niece: Surprise! And now you can make Jelly Tots just like your Aunt Sue. (Because this is where I got the recipe!) I hope that you'll enjoy this cookbook in the first year of your marriage just as much as I've enjoyed it in the last years of mine. And there's a little something else, which you'll find inside the envelope. A wedding gift that should help you and Lyman build yourself a beautiful kitchen in that new dream house of yours. With love, Aunt Sue. March, 1946."

Josephine opened the envelope.

"*Quentin?*"

"Just a minute, hon. Bub's about to—I still can't get used to seeing William Frawley without Vivian Vance. It's like Ethel never existed."

"Quentin, get over here. I want you to see this."

Quentin pulled himself from his recliner and lumbered into the dining room. "See what?"

"It's a check."

"Where'd you find it?"

"In the book, Quentin. Where else would I find it?"

Josephine handed her husband the slightly yellowed check. He tipped up his glasses so his nearsighted eyes could give it a closer look. "It's for fifteen hundred dollars."

Josephine nodded.

"Who's Bette Merkel?"

"She's the woman I bought the book from. Merkel's probably her maiden name. This check was a wedding present. She never cashed it."

"Well, she probably didn't cash it because she never saw it."

"Because she never even opened the book. Now here's what *I* think. Sit down."

Quentin minded his wife; he pulled out one of the dining room chairs and sat down.

"I think this aunt must have made these—what are they—these *Jelly Tots* for her niece and now the niece is all grown up and about to get married and the aunt's passing the recipe down to her. But it's not some family secret—it's in *The Joy of Cooking*. Anyway, the recipe was Aunt Sue's way of surprising Bette with the fat check."

"But how could Bette be surprised if she never saw it?" asked Quentin, scratching his chin.

"There's a bigger question than *that*, honey. Why didn't the aunt tell her the check was in there? I mean, after she didn't figure it out on her own. That's a lot of money."

"Of course it's a lot of money. Too much money to give to a niece who doesn't appreciate you enough to even look inside a book you gave her, whether she liked to cook or not."

"You think that's it?"

"That would be my guess."

"I really need to know for sure."

"No, you don't."

"I wonder if Aunt Sue is still alive. I wonder if she lives around here."

"Josephine, how are you going to find her? And let's say you *do* find her—what are you going to say to her? This isn't any of your business."

Josephine pushed the check back and forth across the table as she thought. "Do you think I should just give it to her? To Bette? It *is* hers, after all."

"I don't know. It might just stir things up. There's a reason that the aunt didn't break down and tell her niece where to find it. Something soured the relationship."

"I wouldn't be surprised. She didn't give me a very good feeling last Saturday. She was very flip, very dismissive. I didn't like her."

"Let it go, Josie. Tear up the check, and let it go. Can I get back to *My Three Sons* now?"

"All right."

As Quentin was heading back to the TV alcove of the couple's living room, he said, "Hey, make something fun out of that cookbook for dinner tomorrow night."

"All right. I'd already decided to make those infamous Jelly Tots for dessert."

"Whatever those are."

Josephine didn't tear up the check. She couldn't. She had never been the kind of person to let go of something that gnawed away at her. And there was so much that was gnawing at her. There was a story here she was dying to know. Hadn't the aunt called Bette her "favorite niece"? And then, suddenly, something must have happened to permanently erase that special status. Could it be exactly what Quentin surmised: a niece's lack of interest in a book her aunt obviously treasured? Josephine had to know. She'd never tell Quentin, but she absolutely *had* to find out.

Josephine knocked on the door, even though it was already open. A truck was in the driveway and there were moving men lifting a bedframe into the back of its large, capacious trailer. "Hello?" she called into the house.

The husband appeared. He was dressed in a soiled sweatshirt and jeans and he looked tired.

"Is your wife—is Bette here?"

"She's around here somewhere. You're not selling anything, are you?"

"Oh, no. I came to your yard sale last week."

"Well, everything we were going to sell's already been sold." The husband disappeared into the house. "BETTE! THERE'S SOMEBODY HERE TO SEE YOU!"

Josephine waited.

At last Bette appeared. She wore knockabout clothes like her husband— an old sweater and Capri pants with a patina of dust on them.

"Hi. I'm Josephine Charles. I was at your yard sale last week."

"Yes. I think I remember you. You bought some baby clothes, didn't you?"

"Um. No. I was looking at the cookbooks."

"Oh, okay. I guess you can tell that we're just a little busy here. Is there something I can do for you?"

"I'm sorry. Do you want me to come back?"

"If you like, but I won't be here. We're leaving tomorrow morning."

"Well, I—" Josephine was interrupted by the muscled passage of two uniformed moving men going through the open door. Both women had to step back to keep from getting body-checked.

"Come inside," said Bette. "We've still got the couch for a few minutes."

The two went to sit down on the tarpaulin-covered couch.

"Sorry that I don't have anything to offer you to drink. We just finished up the lemonade. Lyman was supposed to go out for sodas and sandwiches, but I don't know when *that* will be."

"That's all right. I won't keep you. I wanted to tell you something about that book I bought from you—*The Joy of Cooking*."

"Oh, you were *The Joy of Cooking*!" Bette said with a grin. "My friend Naomi gave me such a hard time about letting that go for six bits. She said it's got to be worth twenty dollars at least."

"At least," said Josephine, cryptically. "Bette, I came to tell you about something I found inside. It's—well, here it is. It's from your Aunt Sue."

Bette took the envelope from Josephine. She read what was written on the outside and then looked inside and pulled out the check. She didn't gasp, but her hand went up to her mouth as if she had. "I can't believe this," she finally managed to say.

"I guess you would have seen it if you'd—well, it was taped to the page that had the recipe for Jelly Tots."

Bette smiled at a memory. "Jelly Tots. Oh, that's funny. That's rich."

"I don't know if your aunt is still around or even if you want to say anything to her, but I thought you should know that it was in there, in case, you know—"

Bette's smile evaporated. "In case what?"

"I don't know. If it were me—"

Bette's look suddenly turned hard. "If it were you, what? You'd go to her and apologize for never taking the time to look inside the wedding present she'd given you?"

"Well, the book was only *part* of the gift. There was also, as you can see, a check for fifteen hundred dollars. So you and your new husband could build a nice kitchen for your new house."

"Yes, I read that. I'm fully capable of reading, though I *don't*. Lyman and the kids, they're the readers in the family. You want to know why I didn't open the book? That's why you came here, right—to find out why I didn't know this check was in there? Well, I'm going to tell you, even though you're a nosy bitch."

Josephine shrank back.

"My aunt had a lot of money. Lyman and I—we weren't poor, but every cent we were making was going into saving for a house, our very own house. I asked my aunt for a loan to help speed things along. She'd always said I was her favorite niece, and now she had the chance to prove it. But when we asked her, she said no. I couldn't believe she could be so cruel. Lyman said she was probably waiting to give it to us at the wedding. I bided my time. We got a lot of wedding checks—everybody knew what it was we *really* needed going into this marriage. Not Aunt Sue. From Aunt Sue, I got a book. A lousy cookbook. She knew I didn't like to cook and that I had no intention of learning. I threw it away. It was Lyman who pulled it out of the trash. He said it needed to be on the shelf in the kitchen in case Aunt Sue came to visit. Do you know what I said to *that*? When am I going to invite that selfish old crone over here? Well, I never got the chance not to invite her, because she died only a few weeks later. She didn't leave me anything in her will. She never told me about the check and she didn't leave me a stingy dime."

Lyman stepped into the living room. "You need to finish sealing up the boxes in Leiza's room. The movers are asking for the rest of the boxes."

Bette nodded.

"What's wrong?" asked Bette's husband.

"I'll tell you later."

Lyman walked off.

"I don't think you told me your name," said Bette.

"I did actually. It's Josephine."

"I'm sorry I lashed out at you like that, Josephine. I'm not mad at you. I'm mad at myself. I don't blame my aunt for what she did. I probably would have done the same thing in her position. To be perfectly honest, I don't know why Aunt Sue was ever fond of me. She was always a very quiet woman. I'm, well, *not*. When things bother me, I speak up. Some people don't like that. Witness the fact that both my son and daughter live in southern California—just about as far as they can get from their mother without leaving the continental United States."

"The continental United States would also include Alaska."

"I wish I read more often. I wish I read, period. And cooked. My aunt made the most delicious Jelly Tots."

"I baked some last night. They're in the car."

1962

THROWN A CURVE BALL IN NEW YORK

My stepfather Harvey and I were both enjoying our birthday toys. Our birthdays were only two days apart in early April. *My* present was a transistor radio that Harvey and Mom let me pick out at Brach's downtown. I remember going out to my stepfather's brand new Volkswagen Beetle parked in the driveway, knowing that I'd find him inside, sitting in the driver's bucket, patiently waiting for the game to start. Harvey was listening to Frank Sinatra on the car radio as I got inside, my new leather-slipcased radio in hand. A thick, sweet cloud of smoke nebulized by his Tiparillo hung in the air.

"We can listen to the game on my new radio," I offered, holding up my birthday present. (I think it was the rule in 1962 that eleven-year-old boys were supposed to be given transistor radios for their birthdays—especially in families that had qualms about BB guns.)

Harvey took a puff from his slender plastic-tipped cigar, which had just come on the market. He shook his head. "Save the juice in your 9-volt, Scoots. We'll listen to the bug radio."

My stepfather knew a thing or two about batteries. He worked for Schenectady's big General Electric company. He and his fellow scientists and engineers were in the process of inventing the world's strongest superconducting magnet. Harvey's team was competing against Bell Telephone Labs for an impressive prize: several cases of top-shelf Scotch—to be sent by the losers to the winners. Harvey probably didn't tell the Bell folks that he didn't drink Scotch. His potable of choice was Rheingold, the official beer, as it turned out, of the New York Mets, whose very first game we were about to listen to on station WGY, courtesy of WABC out of New York City.

Harvey was from St. Louis, and a little conflicted. The Mets were playing the Cardinals in Busch Stadium, and Harvey had always been a big fan of Stan "The Man" Musial. On the other hand, he'd lived in New York for the last twenty years and was just as fixed in his belief that the state deserved a National League team—after the demoralizing departure of the Dodgers and the Giants—as the most adamant of Gotham's born-and-breds. In fact, it was the tragedy of losing those two powerhouse teams and all the sentimental feelings lingering in their wake that played a big role in the Mets acquiring one of the worst teams in baseball.

"A real Geritol bunch—all these former Dodger and Giant coots," my stepfather joked when he found out whom the team had signed. And he made a similar assessment that day in the car, as one of the broadcast's three announcers, Bob Murphy, presented the lineup for his radio listeners. Each name elicited either a chuckle and a shake of the head or the designation "Gramps" or "Methuselah" or "No Spring Chicken by any Goddamned Metric." Harvey didn't watch his language when it was just him and me. He smoked. He drank his multiple bottles of Rheingold (close at hand this day in a little ice chest on the back seat). He gave me a taste every now and then, so long as I didn't tell Mom. "Gil Hodges has got to be pushing forty!" he exclaimed when the first baseman's name was announced. "And Richie Ashburn's not that far behind him. Oh, good Christ, did I ever tell you the story of Richie and that poor Mrs. Roth—the wife of the sports editor down in Philadelphia?"

I had heard the story before. It's not a story you forget, but I pretended that I hadn't and shook my head.

"It was back in '57, when Richie was playing for the Phillies—he hits this foul ball right into the stands, and wham! The unlucky bastard breaks the poor woman's nose. And this equally hapless Mrs. Roth, they're getting her all laid out on the stretcher and the game picks back up again and—sweet Jesus in a hammock—Ashburn beans her *again*, right there on the goddamned stretcher! It's like the gods of misfortune just aren't gonna be happy until the poor woman gets sent up to that disabled list in the sky."

Although I already knew the answer, I asked anyway: "And was Mrs. Roth—did she end up being okay?"

"Oh, sure—sure. I think she and Richie even became friends after all that."

Murphy announced that Don Zimmer would be playing third base for the Mets. "Now you talk about your bad luck. Did I ever tell you about Zimmer's shit-for-luck magnet head for wild pitches?"

"He got hit in the head too?"

"Right in the temple, back in '53, when he was playing for the minors in St. Paul. Put him in a coma for two weeks and they had to drill a bunch of holes into his head—to relieve the pressure, I guess. I think he wears a steel plate to this day. Anyway, they told him he was finished in baseball, but he proved them all wrong. Came back stronger than ever so he could get himself beaned again in '56 in Cincinnati—broke his motherloving jaw."

As Murphy was announcing the Cardinals' lineup, Harvey sat up straight. I knew he was listening for Musial's name and once he heard it, he couldn't hold back a big grin. "Busch, Sportsman's Park—whatever the hell it is that we're supposed to call it now—it's one of the best parks in the majors for left-handed hitters like Musial. Babe Ruth hit three homers in two different World Series games back in '26 and '28."

"Harvey, how is it you know so much about baseball?"

"I know so much about *everything*. You think your mother married me for my looks?" Harvey grinned even bigger than before and chucked me under the chin. Then we both got quiet and listened to the opening innings of the inaugural game of the New York Mets, which was also the first game of the 1962 major league baseball season. New York City was thrilled to finally have a second team. There was to be a big parade down Broadway in Manhattan the next day. A special ceremony with Mayor Wagner was scheduled for City Hall.

Today's game had been postponed from the day before because of rain. The outfield was soggy and the fielders had to wear football shoes to get any traction. The Mets' pitcher, Roger Craig, struggled against the Cards in the early innings, but for everything that had been said about Gil Hodges and his advanced years (in baseball terms, that is, and only by my stepfather Harvey—Murphy and Ralph Kiner and their broadcast booth colleague Lindsey Nelson being far kinder), the first baseman knocked the ball out of the park in the fourth inning (his 362nd career homer).

"Gil, you son of a bitch!" my stepfather howled, and then turning to me: "I take back everything I said about that old geezer." To punctuate his mea culpa, he took a big swig of beer and passed the bottle to me. "Yeah, I'm a bad influence. Sue me."

Harvey laughed, his whole face radiating happiness. Then suddenly the joy evaporated. He turned the volume knob of the radio so that Kiner's voice dropped to a mumble and the crowd noises were reduced to a hum. The spell that had been cast over us by the game was now broken.

There is something about listening to baseball on the radio, something indefinably gratifying, that has stayed with me well into my later years—past that disastrous first season for the Mets, in which they won only one out of every four games they played (and finished the season 60 ½ games behind the Giants) and even beyond their redemptive Cinderella year, 1969. Even today I can still close my eyes and picture myself at the ballpark, first the Polo Grounds and then the spanking new Shea Stadium. I imbibe the vocal restlessness of the fans—supportive, forgiving, but this being New York, always displaying a kind of ballsy bluntness, a sort of tough love for a team that stumbled just as often as it walked or ran. If I listen close enough, I can even hear the cries of the hotdog and peanut vendors: the perfect ambient embroidery to the drone of that vibrant crowd.

But there is something related to that experience that isn't so gratifying. It's the reminder of what happened next on that first day of the 1962 baseball season, as I sat beside my stepfather in his brand new Volkswagen Beetle.

"There's something I need to talk to you about," said Harvey. "I promised your mom I'd do it today."

Harvey put out his Tiparillo. Years later, whenever I saw an ad for the little cigars or heard the company cigarette girl's catchphrase, "Cigars? Cigarettes? Tiparillos?" I would think back on this conversation with a welter of feelings.

"Your mother wants a divorce."

"Oh." It took me a few seconds to pull myself out from under this ton of bricks. "How come?"

"She doesn't love me anymore."

"What did you do?"

"Maybe I'm not so easy to live with, Scoots. I drink. I smoke. I swear. I buy Nazi cars. Maybe I'm not so good for you and your sister to be around. Your dad moved out, and what does your mom do? She takes in the first fleabitten old mongrel that shows up on her porch. Like that Mrs. Payson who owns the Mets—she doesn't go for a young husband like your father, she gets one with maybe a little too much mileage."

"Gil Hodges just hit a home run."

"And Don Zimmer's playing third with a metal plate in his head. I'm not saying I'm worthless, kid. Hell, I'm designing conducting coils for the strongest magnet mankind's ever put together. I'm just saying your mom and I—we had some laughs, and now it's time for me to chug off in my little insect car and quit corrupting the kids, you know?"

"You aren't corrupting me. I'm eleven. I can take care of myself."

Harvey didn't say much after that. He turned up the volume and together we listened as the Cardinals piled up the runs. The final score that day would be 11–4. It was to be the first of nine straight losses for the Mets. They wouldn't catch a break until they faced off against the Pirates twelve days later, on April 23.

During a commercial for Rheingold Beer sung by Vic Damone, I turned down the volume and asked my stepfather when he was moving out.

"Couple of days."

"Will Connie and I get to see you again?"

"I won't be a stranger. In fact, your mom says once I get my own place, you can come over and listen to the games whenever you like. And your sister can come too. I have a feeling I'm going to start missing her linguine real fast."

I rested my head against the glass of the passenger window. Even with the pervasive smell of the cigar smoke and the beer, I could detect the distinct rubber and vinyl scent of a virgin car. I liked the smell. New cars reminded me that change isn't always bad. I tried to see my stepfather Harvey's departure this way. Harvey knew how much I had grown to love him and look up to him, even though he was a good fifteen years or so older than my mother and obstinately set in his ways (as he would be the first to admit). He had taught me everything I knew about baseball and cars and technology and science, and had been, in truth, over these last two years, much more of a father to me than my own.

I think Harvey knew this and I think it made having to tell me about the decision he and my mom had reached a hard thing to do. Harvey had been married only once before, many years ago for a few months after he got out of the Navy. He never talked about his first wife and I didn't ask. He never had kids. Connie and I were the closest he was ever going to come to having kids.

Harvey turned up the radio. But a moment later there was a knock at my window. It was my older sister Connie. I rolled down the window. "Is the game over?" she asked.

"Bottom of the sixth," said Harvey.

"I'm making linguine."

"Did your mom talk to you?"

Connie nodded. I could tell from the puffiness of her eyes that she'd been crying.

"You two want to come in and listen to the game while we eat? Mom says it'll be okay."

I gave my stepfather the same hopeful look as my sister. "I got my new transistor radio," I said, holding it up, as if he hadn't been with me four days earlier when I picked it out.

"Sure," he said. He turned off the radio and picked up his nearly empty third bottle of beer. Connie looked at the bottle and then looked at me. "Have you been drinking too?" she asked.

I nodded. "But don't tell Mom."

"I won't tell Mom if Harvey gives *me* a pull."

Harvey held the bottle up for Connie to reach in and take through the window. "You see why your mother's kicking me out, don't you?"

We had Connie's linguine, which was seasoned with an ungodly amount of oregano (just the way we all liked it). My mother and stepfather were civil, almost friendly to one another at the table, and when the game was over and the injury of defeat was patched up with positive thoughts from the broadcasting trio on the future of the franchise, Harvey took me aside. Quoting the famous Yankee and future Mets player and manager Yogi Berra, he said, "When you come to a fork in the road, take it."

Then he handed me a fork he'd lifted from the table, and turning his face so I wouldn't see it, went out onto the back porch to smoke another Tiparillo. I didn't follow him. He had a lot of thinking to do about his next inning.

1963

ESTIVATING IN NEW JERSEY

Adrian Martini took out his handkerchief and wiped the beading sweat from his forehead. It was late September but it felt like late July.

"Are you allowed to call it Indian summer when summer never really left?" asked Benny Baum, the other salesman working the floor that afternoon at Landis Avenue Appliances. Benny took a swig of his Coca-Cola, the third bottle he'd plucked from the frosty commercial cooler that afternoon. The cooler was put there by the store's owner for the refreshment of his customers, especially those who had stepped into the un-airconditioned south Jersey appliance store and then seemed immediately desirous of stepping right back out again. The reason was this: in spite of meteorological evidence that argued against it, the owner had a seasonal habit of turning off his store's central air conditioning unit the day after Labor Day. Nobody—not Adrian or Benny or Sophia, who worked in Accounts (and had come to work this day wearing more bath powder than Blanche DuBois)—could talk him out of it.

"Was that a real question or are you being rhetorical?" replied Adrian, sticking his now soggy handkerchief back into his trousers pocket.

"Doesn't matter. Just making conversation," said Benny through a half-yawn.

Adrian was only barely listening to his sales colleague. He was watching the two kids presently situating themselves on the linoleum floor in front of the store's new Magnavox 330-square-inch console. Anticipating their arrival, Adrian had turned on the set and made sure it was tuned to Channel 6. Adrian did this every afternoon he was in the store, and every afternoon he was in the store the girl and boy could be counted on with almost clocklike punctuality to show up between 3:50

and 4:00. This meant that every weekday afternoon of every week, Landis Avenue Appliances got a ten-minute helping of *American Bandstand* rock and roll, leading into the main attraction: *Popeye Theatre*, hosted by Sally Starr. Thursday was Adrian's day off. But he knew that the girl and boy came to watch Popeye and the Three Stooges and cowgirl Sally Starr on Thursday, too (along with the Dick Clark appetizer), because Benny told him so.

The girl, who looked to be about nine, and the boy, who looked to be about seven, had started making their afternoon visits about two months ago. Adrian and Benny figured that the kids didn't have a TV at home. Mr. Poitras, the store's owner, didn't mind. In fact, he liked to think of the kids as props in a sort of real-life diorama about home and hearth and family togetherness—the hearth, the pot-bellied stove, if you will, of twentieth-century America being a sparkling new 330-square-inch Magnavox American Traditional, Normandy Provincial, or Danish Modern console television. *(And nobody beats our competitive prices!)*

Benny took another gulp of Coca-Cola. He pushed the cool bottle against his hot cheek. The store was bereft of customers. Both men were feeling lethargic in the heat. "Who sends their kids to an appliance store every day?"

"What's that?" asked Adrian. The show the girl and boy had come to see had just gotten started. The volume was turned up and Adrian was listening for Sally Starr's daily salutation: "Hope you feel as good as you look, 'cuz you sure look good to your gal Sal!"

"I mean, we're not talking adolescents here," Benny went on. "My Rebecca just turned eight. I wouldn't let her cross the street by herself, let alone come all the way down to Landis Avenue without some kind of chaperone."

Adrian shook his head slowly. "Beats me. Maybe someday I'll sit down with them and get the story. They always seem so engrossed in their show, though; I don't have the heart to interrupt."

Fortuitously, his opportunity came ten minutes later, when the power went out. It wasn't a long outage and Benny attributed it to all the people cranking up their air conditioning at a time of year when the grid wasn't prepared for the extra demand. Not that Landis Avenue Appliances was making much of a contribution to the temporary electricity crisis; except for the lights and a couple of TVs and the refrigerated Coca-Cola cooler, Mr. Poitras's store was hardly pulling any watts at all.

"The TV's broken," said Kirk, the seven-year-old, looking up at Adrian.

"It ain't the TV, pardner. Power's out all over the store. See? No lights." Adrian called Kirk "pardner" in deference to the boy's cowboy hat. Kirk's older sister Angela was wearing a Western hat too, hers very close to the design of that of the "Philadelphia Annie Oakley," Sally Starr.

"When do you think it'll come back on?" asked Kirk, his fretful expression betraying the degree to which both Kirk and Angela depended on Sally Starr for their afternoon fix.

"Soon, I'm sure," said Adrian. "Somebody at the power station probably just has to flip a switch. Would you like a soda?"

Both Kirk and Angela nodded. Kirk's tongue licked one corner of his mouth in eager anticipation.

Adrian signalled for Benny to come bring the kids a couple of Coca-Colas. "And get me one too," he added.

A couple of minutes later, Adrian and Kirk and Angela were sitting on the floor of the half-darkened store, drinking sodas and talking about Sally Starr and her favorite horse and Popeye and Olive Oyl and Larry, Curly, and Moe, and the incongruity of a rootin' tootin' Old West cowgirl being friends with an animated sailor and three violently bellicose slapstick comedians from urban America. Kirk pointed out that Popeye—at least the full-sized cutout of Popeye that adorned the set of Sally's show—was dressed like a cowboy. Case closed.

While the three were sitting and chatting and enjoying the "Pause that Refreshes," a middle-aged couple came into the store to look at the new television models, finding no problem at all with the fact that they would have to do so in the minimal lighting offered by the store's sunlit front display windows, and Benny Baum, the consummate appliance salesman, finding no problem at all in their finding no problem.

Eventually Benny and his customers wended their way over to the dormant Magnavox American Traditional. "Wish you could see the picture on this new 2-MV357 model," said Benny. "I'm thinking of trading in my very own RCA for this technological marvel."

"What kind of wood is this?" asked the woman, reaching over Angela, who politely scooted out of her way. The woman ran her hand over the grain of the cabinet top.

"Hold on to your hat, madam—it's mahogany! And even though we don't have one in stock yet, Magnavox also puts out a Far Eastern Contemporary model similar to this one in *ebony*."

"I like ebony," said the woman, who was holding an all-black clutch. Addressing Adrian, who was still sitting Indian-style on the floor, she said, "Are these your children? They're quite well behaved. My grandchildren would be running all over the store, sword-fighting with the rabbit ears."

"No, these aren't mine," said Adrian, smiling politely.

After Benny and his customers had sauntered off, Adrian looked at both Kirk and Angela and said, "Whose little ones *are* you?"

"We live with our mother," answered Angela.

"No father?"

Angela shook her head.

"We don't have a daddy, but we've got a bunch of uncles," offered Kirk.

"Not really uncles," corrected Angela. "Mama has a lot of boyfriends." This last statement came out as simple fact—neither brag nor censure.

Adrian wasn't sure if he should ask the question that next begged to be asked. But the kids had been forthcoming up to this point, and it was about time, he thought, to get a better sense as to why Kirk and Angela spent ten hours a week being babysat at Landis Avenue Appliances by Adrian and Benny, Sally, and Popeye the Sailor Man. "Is this when your mother's boyfriends come to see her?"

Angela nodded. It wasn't an eager admission, and yet something in her look told Adrian that she might be willing to elaborate. Unfortunately, the conversation was cut short by the return of an electrical current to Landis Avenue Appliances. Kirk jumped up and turned the television back on.

"You're in good shape, kids. Probably just missed some cartoon you'd already seen." Adrian pulled himself up from the floor. He was still a youthful thirty-four, but his legs protested. Restored to his feet, he tousled Kirk's short-cropped brown hair. "Say hello to Sally for me," he said, walking away. Kirk and Angela both nodded, their eyes fixed on the screen, waiting for the cathode ray tube of the Magnavox American Traditional console to charge back up and Sally to miraculously appear out of the ether.

The next day, Adrian's day off, was devoted to errands: the bank, the post office, a visit with an old high school buddy turned insurance agent who had been after Adrian for months to buy a term life insurance policy, even though Adrian wasn't married and had no other beneficiary to speak of, except for a mother in Red Bank whom he would no doubt outlive.

The highlight of the day was to be lunch with a woman he'd met at a party thrown by a friend of a friend in Bridgeton. Adrian recalled the woman as having been funny and smolderingly beautiful—a hot fudge sundae cross between the cool of Jackie Kennedy and the heat of Mamie Van Dorn. Adrian and his impromptu date for the evening had spent very little time talking about themselves, the preferred topic of their increasingly intoxicated, flirtation-larded colloquy being the differences between the primetime intern Dr. Kildare and the primetime surgeon Ben Casey, though Adrian never once mentioned that he might know a little something about television programming since he sold TVs for a living. Like Adrian, the woman lived in Vineland—only a couple of blocks from the appliance store, actually—and after Adrian offered to drive her home that night, she had been all over him with her Yellow Page–walking, bright-red-polished talons while he labored heroically to keep the car on the road. ("Why," he wondered to himself in the midst of her hungry advances, "couldn't women be just as deliciously horny sober as they are when they get tight?")

She didn't invite him in. "Complications," was her explanation.

Now Adrian was curious to know if the woman, whose name was Claire, would be in an equally libidinous mood over club sandwiches and glasses of alcohol-free lemonade.

She was. Which was not exactly what Adrian had been expecting, though he couldn't say he was disappointed. He knew she wasn't married—at least that is what she had told him. And he wasn't married. And this was his day off. And after all, he hadn't—he would be ashamed to admit—been with a woman in almost four months: a record dry spell that he was eager to break without having to resort to paid companionship.

"There's a nice motel over by the Delsea Drive-in," said Adrian, "if you don't find that kind of thing, you know—"

Adrian fumbled for the word, but Claire found it: "Tawdry. But you see, I *like* tawdry. I like to be *bad*. And I like to be with men who *want* me to be bad."

"But we hardly know a thing about each other," he teased.

"Like that matters," she said with a wink, and then pinched Adrian's nose. "And that's the way I like it. Two ships, you know, fucking in the night. Except in our case, it's the afternoon. Buy me a drink, Adrian. After that—well, forget the motel. Let's us drive right on over to my place."

"How's about we drive on over to your place right now?" asked Adrian, who suddenly could think of nothing he'd rather do than hop into the sack with this sultry woman of mystery.

Claire shook her head. Her whole torso seemed to wriggle, her faux pearl necklace whipping against her heaving, taunting chest. "No can do, Adrian. The kiddies come home from school at three-thirty and they're not out of the house until close to four. From four to six you can have me all to yourself."

Adrian sat forward in his seat. "Where do they go?"

"*Who*, sweetie?"

"The kids. Where do they go at four?"

"I really don't know. Our neighborhood is lousy with kids for them to play with. Some days I think they walk over to the appliance store and watch Captain Kangaroo."

Adrian didn't respond. Not right away. Then he said in a voice modulated by the sudden deflation of his libido, "Captain Kangaroo comes on in the morning. More than likely they'd be watching Sally Starr."

"Sally who?"

"Sally Starr. She wears six-shooters and is on a first-name basis with each of the Three Stooges."

"What difference does it make?"

Adrian shrugged. He shook his head. He dreaded asking the question that logically came next, but he had to know the answer for sure. "Your kids—how old are they?"

Claire exhaled. Angrily. "What's with the third degree? Hey, wait a minute—*I* get it; you don't get yourself involved with women with kids, is that it? Look, buster, I'm not asking you to take me down the aisle. I'm only talking about a fucking four o'clock roll in the hay. Look. Forget it." She stood.

"I didn't ask about them because—"

Adrian was stopped short by Claire's suddenly piercing glower. She gave her dress an upward yank, covering up a few inches of her munificent décolletage. The show was over—or, rather, the coming attraction for a show that just got cancelled. "My kids are my own business. And none of yours. And if you have a problem with that, which it looks like you do, then let's just nip this thing in the bud. I've got somebody else I was hoping to see this afternoon anyway."

There was nothing else to be said, but Claire said something all the same: "I got a girl, Angela—she's nine and a half. I got a boy, Kirk—he just turned seven. They're good kids, but I got no desire to play June Cleaver every fucking minute of every fucking day. I thought you were bright enough to see that."

Adrian didn't go home. He sat for a long time in the restaurant, reading the paper, drinking coffee, waiting for the end of *American Bandstand*. Benny would be surprised to see him on his day off. Angela and Kirk would too. They knew that he wasn't supposed to be in the store on Thursday afternoons. They would be unprepared for what he intended to do there. Today he would sit down and watch Sally Starr with them. The whole two hours. And then he'd walk them home. He wanted to make sure they got home safe, this day and every other day they might happen to show up at the store.

The days were getting shorter. Someone needed to be there for them in the dark.

1964

NEARLY INTERRED IN ALASKA

It was my younger sister Debbie who looked out the window and said that Marina, our babysitter, had just fallen into a hole. I didn't know what Debbie could possibly mean and didn't have time to give it much thought. I was trying to hold up the china cabinet, which wanted to come crashing down to the floor, and I was also far too busy yelling at my younger brother Dirk to get away from the television, which seemed about to bounce off its stand.

Dirk had been sitting in front of the TV watching *Fireball XL5* when the earthquake started. The booster rockets on Colonel Steve Zodiac's World Space Patrol spaceship had just ignited when the picture went out and Dirk, being six, was having trouble disconnecting what had just happened on the screen of our family's Zenith black-and-white television from the first few seconds of the most powerful earthquake to hit North America in recorded history.

"Debbie!" I cried, as loudly as my twelve-year-old vocal cords could manage. "Grab Dirk and get out of the house! Where's Marina?"

"I told you! She fell into a hole!"

Debbie went for our brother. Walking was difficult. The floor was rolling like something in a funhouse. I was losing my battle with the china cabinet and had started to worry that in my defeat, Mama's proudest possession—inherited from her grandmother, along with all the fine china inside—would fall right down on top of me and flatten me like a pancake.

I had been helping Marina make spaghetti. Dad, who was an SFC with the Alaska Army National Guard, was supposed to go straight from Fort Richardson to pick Mom up at the J.C. Penney's store, where she was buying some new shoes for Easter, and then they were going to celebrate their anniversary, first by having dinner at the Red Ram and then going to see *The Fall of the Roman Empire*.

I told Mom and Dad that it was humiliating not being allowed to babysit my own brother and sister when my friends were already babysitting *other* families' kids, but Mom said she didn't like the idea of the three of us being left by ourselves so late into the night. *The Fall of the Roman Empire* was supposed to last more than three hours.

So who did she choose? Somebody only four years older than me, who was probably the worst babysitter in all of Anchorage. Mom chose somebody who, when the floor starting rolling and the TV went out, and all the telephone poles up and down Beech Street started whipping from side to side and power lines started snapping and throwing sparks all over the place—somebody who, when the world seemed to be coming to an end (and not in a fun way like with the Roman Empire), got out of the house quicker than you could say "boo" and left her three charges to fend totally for themselves. Nice work, Mom.

And now Debbie said that Marina had fallen into a hole.

I watched as my younger sister grabbed our brother just as the television came crashing down on the floor, right where he'd been sitting, and then, fearing for my own safety, I stepped away from the china cabinet and looked on in horror as it toppled over and smashed to bits all the things my mother held dear. In the kitchen, the pan of spaghetti sauce flew off the stove and splattered the walls and floors with blood-red splotches, while all the cans in the pantry knocked themselves off the shelves and started rolling all around like the way things do on ships in stormy seas.

Alaska's worst babysitter had left the front door open, and I watched as Muffles, our tabby, went dashing out. Once I'd gotten Debbie and Dirk outside, I pulled them away from the house, which seemed to be shaking itself into something that we probably wouldn't even be able to live in anymore, and Dad's Oldsmobile Vista Cruiser station wagon, which he couldn't drive until the transmission got fixed, started looking like Colonel Steve Zodiac's space rocket ramping itself up to blast right off. What surprised me the most, though, was what the ground around the house was doing. It was cracking right open just like it did in that movie, *The Last Days of Pompeii*, even though my teacher, Miss Sabatini, said that earthquakes aren't supposed to make crevices big enough for people to fall into. I later learned what my eyes had already told me: earthquakes of 9.2 magnitude can rip the ground open like a can opener, and this one was doing just that, as Debbie and Dirk and I hung onto the big tree in the front yard and waited for what seemed like an eternity (four minutes is a very long time for an earthquake to last) until everything got still and quiet again.

Once it stopped and I could hear the sound of my own voice, I said to my sister, "What hole?"

Debbie pointed to the obvious choice: a five or six-foot-wide trench that had suddenly appeared in the front lawn.

"You stay right there." I'd read about aftershocks that could be almost as strong as the original quake. (What I didn't know at the time is that the '64 Alaskan quake would be followed by an almost record number of them). I walked with unsteady legs over to the trench and looked down into it. It was eight or nine feet deep and there, sitting at the bottom, was Marina. She was rubbing her knee and looking up at me.

"Are you all right?" I asked.

"I think I broke my leg."

"It's broken?"

"That's what I just said. Can you go find somebody to get me out of here? I think I have to go to the hospital."

I didn't say anything. As upset as I was from the terrible quake, I was enjoying seeing this World's Worst Babysitter (who I hated more than anyone in the world—and that includes Soviet Communists, who my dad says are going to overrun this country someday and steal our liberty) sitting at the bottom of a big hole. In fact, I was enjoying it so much that I almost smiled. This was where she deserved to be. Why? Because she had abandoned the three children SHE WAS BEING PAID GOOD MONEY TO TAKE CARE OF just to save her own sorry self.

"Why are you just standing there looking at me?" asked Marina. I hated that name: *Marina.* It wasn't a name for a person. It was a name for a boat basin.

"I just wanted to say, Marina, that you wouldn't be in this predicament if you hadn't abandoned your post. What if this had been an attack by the Siberian Communists? Debbie and Dirk and I would be taken prisoners by the Red Guard and you would be entirely to blame."

"What does that have to do with anything?"

"You're irresponsible." I folded my arms. Debbie and Dirk, in spite of my orders, now came over to look down into the hole with me. I wondered if my brother and sister thought that Marina looked as stupid as *I* thought she did.

"If you don't get somebody to come and pull me out of here, Darlene, you are going to be in the worst trouble of your life. My parents are probably worried *sick* about me right now, and they don't even know that I'm sitting underground with a crippled leg."

"I'm not going to go and get you help, Marina, unless you tell me why you ran out on the three of us. We lost my mom's china cabinet because of you, and the TV set almost fell on top of Dirk."

"I was scared."

"That doesn't cut it, missy."

"You can't talk to me like that."

"You're a terrible, rotten babysitter. You talk on the phone to your boyfriend for hours and hours and your spaghetti tastes *awful* and I don't think you *deserve* to get rescued."

Marina fumed in silence for a few seconds while she rubbed her knee. Then she started moaning. "Can't you see I'm in pain?"

"I could be *dead*, Marina. That china cabinet must have weighed a ton."

"Suit yourself. I can only imagine what kind of punishment awaits you for leaving me down here."

I was about to say some other things that Marina did and didn't do that got my goat, when my little brother Dirk picked up a clod of dirt and threw it at Marina. It hit her in the shoulder and she cried out, more in surprise than in pain.

"Don't throw dirt down on the babysitter, Dirk," I reprimanded him.

Now Debbie picked up a handful of soil and dropped it down into Marina's lap. She screamed again.

"Enough of that, Debbie," I said in a mature, responsible voice—the kind of voice I would naturally have used if my parents had done the right thing and entrusted to me the care of my two younger siblings, instead of bringing in this awful teenage girl.

"I think my brother and sister want to bury you alive, Marina. What do you think of that? Because they happen to agree with me that you're perfectly awful."

"Please get me out of here." Marina wasn't whining anymore. Now she sounded genuinely distressed. Maybe she was thinking just what *I* was thinking at that moment: that there might be a bad aftershock that would close up the fissure and bury her alive. "You've had your fun," she pleaded. "Now please help me!"

I turned to Debbie and Dirk. "What do you think we should do? Do you think we should get Marina some help, even though she only thinks of herself and her boyfriend and John and Paul and George and Ringo?"

Dirk shook his head. Then he picked up a handful of dirt and threw it down on Marina's head so quickly that some of the hard perma-frosty soil got in her eyes. She cried out and I felt really bad for her. I felt bad again when Debbie picked up a pinecone and threw *that*. It missed Marina's arm by a few inches but it might as well have hit her for how much she shrieked.

"You need to stop doing that," I said to my brother and sister. I looked around to see if anybody was coming to check on us. I figured that somebody would show up soon, but for the time being we were still on our own. It looked like I really would have to go and get help. "You two promise me that you'll be good and if the ground starts shaking again, you'll go over there and hold onto that tree?"

Dirk and Debbie nodded. Then Dirk kicked some more dirt into the hole. I remembered that Marina had said that Dirk couldn't watch *Fireball XL5* until he'd cleaned up his room, and then the time came for the show to start and his room still wasn't straightened up, so there had been a shouting match and Marina was just about to go and turn off the set when the earthquake started and she felt a sudden need to run like a dastardly Communist right out of the house.

I went to the Chigniks' house next door, but nobody was home and I figured that they were either lying crushed beneath their own china cabinet or were off at Good Friday services. I was about to go to the Pottersons' house across the street, but at just that moment a young woman came up to me. She was wearing a stewardess's uniform and looking frightened. She said her name was Miss Dunston, and that she worked for Flying Tiger Airlines. She said she was on her way to the hospital to see if they needed any help, since she had some nursing experience, and I explained that our babysitter had slipped into a crack in the ground and could use her help if the stewardess really wanted to make herself useful.

"I don't know if I'm strong enough to pull her out, but I'll come and survey the situation," said Miss Dunston in that polite way that stewardesses have, though her voice cracked a little from the unremitting fear in her heart. Miss Dunston and I walked briskly back to our front yard, and Miss Dunston got a good look at Marina, who was now partially buried under dirt and rubble. There hadn't been another tremor—not yet—so this was clearly the doing of Dirk and Debbie. Marina was screaming hysterically, and luckily Miss Dunston hadn't put two and two together thanks to my younger brother and younger sister wearing their most angelic faces.

"I need to get someone with a rope or pulley or something," said Miss Dunston with some urgency as she ran off.

I gave Dirk and Debbie a disapproving look and they both shrugged as Muffles the cat, having just pooped in the grass next to our very own front yard crevasse, kicked some dirt and a little something extra into that big hole in the ground.

Ten minutes later Miss Dunston returned with a couple of our neighbors, and the worst babysitter in the history of the universe was rescued.

I didn't learn the extent of the devastation or the death toll from the quake and the tsunami that followed until later that night. Ahead lay weeks of anguish and hardship as the citizens of Anchorage and Valdez and Kenai and Turnagain by the Sea all mourned their losses while struggling to restore their lives to some semblance of normalcy. (To this day, I can't stand the smell of Clorox, which we used to disinfect the boiled snow that was for several days our only source of drinking water). It would be a long time before Dirk and Debbie and I would return to our old selves again, but we did relish this one brief moment of fine revenge, while denying every word of Marina's allegations.

I guess looking back, Marina wasn't that horrible of a babysitter, and I suppose I feel a little guilty now, in my later years, over what Dirk and Debbie and I did to her. It wasn't her fault that she got scared and ran out of our house. I didn't know this at the time, but *everything* frightened Marina. And it got much worse as she got older. Before giving birth to her first baby in 1971, she was so traumatized by the idea of it that she ran out of the delivery room and even out of the hospital. Her family found her at a McDonald's eating a Big Mac and trying to ignore her contractions.

Although she didn't fall into any more holes, she did once *almost* step into an open manhole in Seattle. She missed it by a few inches. And then she turned to her husband and said, "My life isn't that ironic."

And that's my unironical Alaska earthquake story. Take it or leave it.

1965

MISTRYSTED IN NEW YORK

"Two ad men walk into a bar…"

"Oyster Bar."

"Right. Okay. Two ad men walk into the Oyster Bar at Grand Central Station."

"Grand Central *Terminal*. Grand Central *Station* is a post office."

"What are you, the language police? Two ad men walk into—"

"Two Y & R men."

"Important point. Y & R."

"Begging your pardon, what are 'Y & R' men?"

"The gentleman to my right wants to know the meaning of Y & R men."

"Account execs from Young and Rubicam: the crème de la crème of New York City ad agencies."

"I see. Thank you for the clarification."

"As I was saying—two ad men walk into the Oyster Bar. And then they walk right out. Why do they walk right out?"

"Because the lights went out. But that's no punchline. It's just a fact."

The two Young and Rubicam ad men, both in their mid-thirties, one named McCluskey and the other Selman, sighed, nearly simultaneously. Next to them, a man in his late sixties or early seventies, with a London Fog coat folded neatly in his lap and an umbrella at his side, sighed as well. His sigh came out as a melodious hum. The two ad men to his left, both well-versed in ethnic stereotyping, failed, nonetheless, to register the cliché: a man with a British accent carrying a London Fog coat and an umbrella. All that was missing was the bowler.

"I say, gentlemen, if the entire city is without power and you have no hopes of taking your commuter lines up to Peekskill and Scarborough—

Scarborough, now that has a nice English ring to it, doesn't it?—may I ask why you have deposited yourselves here upon this most uncomfortable bench, rather than do that which I've noticed a number of other young executives doing: attempt to secure livery transportation just outside on 42nd Street?"

"Thanks for the suggestion, Pops," said the man named Selman, "but my colleague McCluskey and I tried that very thing for almost an hour after getting thrown out of the Oyster Bar. Looks like we're stuck in Manhattan for the rest of the night with all the rest of you stiffs. So we've staked our claim to half of this bench for the duration. As—I notice—you have too."

"I'm rather in the same boat, it seems. I've rung up the friends with whom I'm stopping in Croton-on-Hudson and successfully dissuaded them from trying to motor down into the city tonight to rescue me. I survived the London Blitz. I can certainly survive one night on a wooden bench in Grand Central Terminal. Alas, though, my conscience may force me to relinquish this berth."

The elderly British gentleman now dropped his voice to a whisper and leaned over to speak confidentially to his circumstantial companions. "I note, as certainly you must as well, a preponderance of stranded, wiltingly bedraggled working girls eyeing this bench with looks of the most heartbreaking longing."

The dapper old man, who bore an uncanny resemblance to the British actor John Williams (forever typecast as proper butlers and proper police inspectors), was right. There were hundreds, perhaps thousands of New York commuters—their faces made flat and garish by the emergency police flood lamps that had been rolled in to light the main concourse—sitting, standing, or milling about. The large knot of those who had earlier stood at the information booth and demanded to know when the trains would start running again (only to be answered with apologies and shrugs) had long broken up. The terminal had since settled into placid communal acceptance of the inevitability of the great Northeast power blackout of November 9, 1965, the largest blackout ever to hit both the United States and Canada.

"You'd be a good ad man yourself," said Selman to the old man. "How deftly you played that guilt card. McCluskey, we're going to do the right thing and surrender our half of this bench to the ladies. But now the big question: *which* ladies? I don't want to invite a female fistfight here. This isn't a sale at Ohrbach's."

McCluskey chuckled. "Ohrbach's doesn't have sales. Get yourself married, Selman, and learn a few things about the female species and its natural habitats. Your housewife-loving clients at General Foods will be especially appreciative."

McCluskey's searching gaze caught the eye of a shoeless secretarial type. The young woman was carrying her pumps in one hand and a purse and Macy's shopping bag in the other. He signaled her with an undisguised "come hither" look while stroking the seat that he was in the process of vacating. The woman's face radiated gratitude.

"Oh, you are a lifesaver!" she gushed as she sat down. "My feet are absolutely killing me!" She referenced her bag with a nod. "I was right in the middle of Macy's when the lights went out. I paid for all this, by the way. I didn't loot it in the dark."

Selman got the same appreciative reaction when he gave up his spot on the bench to an older woman and little girl. "How do you like my twofer?" he boasted.

The Brit rose last, and as he was doing so, motioned for a nun in full habit to take his place.

"I think you have us both beat," laughed McCluskey.

"I did hesitate for a moment," confided the old man. "I'm Church of England, after all. But in a time of crisis, one sets all religious differences aside. The name's Leister, by the bye. John Leister."

"Not Niles or Beverly or, um, *Jeeves*?"

Leister shook his head. "Just John."

"Let's drift," said Selman. "Maybe we can find a nice, quiet corner for our next encampment."

The three men meandered over to the clock, which was actually one clock with four different faces, each presenting in a different direction. The faces were opalescent, the whole unit set in a brass stand that rose from the top of the information pagoda situated right in the middle of the vast main concourse. Perched on one of the pagoda's counters was a young woman working a crossword puzzle with the help of those lolling in front of her. "I need a five-letter word starting with L. A synonym for 'vertical column.'" The woman spoke loudly so that anyone within projected earshot might render assistance. At least two dozen people, enlisting themselves in her challenge, cudgeled their brains, both individually and cooperatively.

A few moments later a man called out, "Lally."

Selman turned to his cohorts. "What's a 'Lally'?"

"I think it's a kind of vertical column," answered McCluskey with a mischievous wink.

Among the sea of tourists and suburban New Yorkers set adrift by the blackout was a nice-looking, fifty-something-year-old woman with graying red hair who didn't seem to be killing time at all. She maintained a stance that was rigid and attentive. Her look was one of obvious anxiety. She glanced up at the clock—a futile act since the electric clock's quadruple sets of hands remained frozen in time, the great timepiece suspended in its chronometry at precisely 5:27.

The two younger men in the trio caught sight of the woman at the same time. They traded glances that bespoke sympathy but did not indicate a desire for personal involvement. However, a moment later, Leister took full notice of her himself and made an immediate, albeit cautious, approach.

"Begging your pardon, madam," he said, "but there appears to be something troubling you. I wonder if I may be of some assistance."

The woman smiled. Leister's accent was disarming. "I'm fine. I'm just a fretter."

"I don't know when the power will be restored, but I'm nearly certain that everything is being done to make that outcome an eventuality. In the meantime, it's heartening—don't you think?—to see the city behaving itself so well on this most Cimmerian night."

"This *what*?"

Offering his hand: "The name's John Leister. I teach philology. Historical linguistics. Across the pond. That means the U.K."

"Hello, Professor. I'm Carole Adams. I teach second grade. Across the plains. That means Kansas. Wichita. Although I'm actually from Grand Island. That's in Nebraska."

"These are my new boon companions, Messrs. McCluskey and Selman. They work in advertising."

The two ad men shook the hand of the fretful Midwestern schoolteacher.

"May I ask," continued Leister, "if that which is troubling you could in some way be mitigated by any or all of the three of us?"

"You're so kind. You're like the Three Musketeers. I'd be happy to tell you. Over a nice cold Manhattan. It's been a very difficult few hours. But for a while longer I really feel that I can't leave this spot."

"And why is that?" asked Selman. "Just how long have you been standing here?"

"I got here at about five fifteen."

Selman glanced up at the clock. "Only twelve minutes. Not a bad wait."

McCluskey groaned.

"And why have you been standing in this spot since this afternoon, Miss—is it *Miss?*—Adams?" asked Leister.

"It's Miss. I used to be a Mrs. But now, by choice, I'm back to being a Miss. I've been waiting for someone. It's an involved story. It's now become a potentially embarrassing one. I'd tell it to you, but—"

"But what?" asked McCluskey, grinning. "But we don't have the time? Miss Adams, we have nothing *but* time."

Carole Adams laughed and nodded. Her story was this: that she had met a man on a visit to New York twenty years earlier. He worked for a war orphans relief organization and was killing time in the city before steaming off for Europe. He had two days left to his Gotham sojourn. Carole had come to New York to spend a few days with an old girlfriend who was traveling secretary for a Hollywood bond tour. "Come to New York while I'm there," the friend had written her. Carole had come, but then the tour was rerouted through New England at the last minute. Carole now found herself alone in the city, although this wasn't necessarily a bad thing; it was nice to be on her own after a dozen years in a crowded classroom, and more importantly, a dozen years in a bleak, loveless marriage.

It was 1945. 1945 was about trains and ships and everybody on the move. It was about going places and doing things that one had never done before—taking risks, not knowing what the next day might bring.

The man's name was Nick Gombert. Like Carole, he had also been in his mid-thirties back in 1945. Like Carole, he was also married. And like Carole, he was also *unhappily* married. Nick and Carole tumbled inexorably into an impetuous two-day whirlwind romance—a romance that coincidentally included a night at the movies. The movie was *The Clock*, a story which, though dissimilar in many respects to the story of Carole and Nick, had two things very much in common: a time-compressed love affair and a climactic rendezvous beneath a clock.

"Is this *your* fated rendezvous, my dear?" asked Leister, who, like the Y & R men, had been thoroughly captured by Carole's tale.

"Well, I don't know. I think I'm going to sit down now. I'm very tired."

Carole's new friends moved with her to a spot on the floor next to the information booth. The woman who had been publicly working her crossword puzzle, having now apparently completed it, sat cross-legged on the counter flipping languorously through a copy of *Harper's Bazaar.* Once Carole was settled, the three men sat down in an improvised crescent in front of her.

"Our agreement was this: that if after twenty years we had been successful in detaching ourselves from our respective unbearable marriages, and if we were not attached to someone else, then we would come to New York and, like Judy Garland and Robert Walker, meet under a particular clock."

"*This* clock?" asked a middle-aged woman who'd been standing within earshot nearby, and who now plopped herself down on the floor next to Carole. "Hello," she added. "I'm Sylvia."

"Hello, Sylvia. I'm Carole."

"Carole lives in Kansas," added Leister. "She's come to see if her war beau is conveniently unattached and willing to pick up where the two of them so poignantly left off. Their very own real-life version of *An Affair to Remember.*"

The woman named Sylvia gasped in slow motion. "You came all the way from Kansas on the *chance* that he might be here waiting for you under this clock?"

"Not *this* clock. The one in Penn Station. That's where they met: Judy and Robert. There was *another* clock where they rendezvoused later in the movie. It was at the Hotel Astor. But Nick and I—we both liked the idea of meeting under that beautiful suspended clock at Penn Station, because it's close to where *we* met. At the Chock full o'Nuts only a couple of blocks away."

"But honey," said Sylvia in a strong Flushing Meadows accent that had apparently followed her up to Westchester County, "the old Penn Station building isn't there anymore. They tore it down."

"I know. That's why I thought he might come *here* instead."

"That's a lot of 'might,'" said Selman with a sympathetic frown. "He *might* be divorced. He *might* not have remarried. He *might* still want to see you again. He *might*—like you—substitute the Grand Central clock for the one in old Penn Station. If this was Belmont, sister, I wouldn't place even a two-dollar bet on *that* horse."

"But if I hadn't come, I would have spent the rest of my life wondering if he *had.*"

Everyone nodded. Sylvia went, "Mmm-hmm," while the Englishman said softly, "Yes, I see. You're so right. And unlike Irene Dunne and Deborah Kerr, you haven't been hit by a car. You just happen to have found yourself in the middle of a blackout." Leister smiled. "And perhaps your beau is similarly inconvenienced."

Carole's face brightened. "I've thought about that. Do you think that could be it?"

"Honey," said Sylvia, taking out a pack of gum, "the poor schlimazel could be trapped in the subway for all we know." There was one stick left; she gave it to Carole.

"Of course, it's probably best not to build your hopes up," said McCluskey.

Carole nodded, her jaws beginning to work on the fresh stick of spearmint gum. "Who has food? I'm famished."

Food was procured. The Oyster Bar was all but giving away seafood at their door because of concerns that it would quickly spoil without refrigeration. The quintet on the floor in front of Grand Central's information kiosk feasted on fried oysters and tartar sauce, fried whole Ipswich clams (also with tartar sauce) and cultivated Maine mussels steamed with white wine and garlic.

Because Carole did not wish to leave her post, her four companions kept her company for the rest of the night.

When the power came back early in the morning and the trains started to run, there were awkward goodbyes exchanged among the kindred strangers: Sylvia and her two new friends, McCluskey and Professor Leister, departing for points north, and Selman returning to his office, where an important client presentation waited for no act of man or God. Carole left for her tiny room in the Taft Hotel, having decided to catch the first available flight back to Kansas, her faith in romance and the triumph of the human heart severely shaken both by the blackout and by the strong possibility of other human factors equally beyond her control.

When at the end of day the exhausted ad man plodded back down to the great Beaux Arts terminal to head home, he noticed someone waiting beneath the famous clock, which had been reset. It said 5:30 upon all of its four faces, and below it was the face of a man in his mid-fifties anxiously searching the crowd.

"What the hell," said Selman to himself.

He walked over. Without shaking hands or even introducing himself, the Y & R account executive accosted the concerned-looking man with, "You're a day late. You were supposed to meet her here on the ninth, not the tenth."

"I beg your pardon?"

"Aren't you Nick Gombert?"

"Yes, but—wait a minute. I'm almost positive it was supposed to be the tenth."

"Okay, so then *she* got it wrong."

 "Where is she?"

"On her way back to Wichita, if she's not there already."

"You got her address?"

"Uh huh. We got her address."

"*We?*"

Selman threw his arm around Nick's shoulder. "Long story. Long night. Let me buy you a drink at the Oyster Bar and fill you in."

"She came." A private smile. "I can't believe she came."

"An almost perfect happy ending. So tell me: where were *you* when the lights went out?"

"Trapped on a subway train. On my way over *here*, if you can believe it. I wanted to come a day early to see the clock where I'd hoped the two of us would be meeting today."

1966

OUTRAGED IN IDAHO

The Sound of Music was released in 1965. It was enormously popular and succeeded in yanking its studio, Twentieth Century Fox, back from the brink of bankruptcy after the disastrous cost-overruns of the obscenely expensive *Cleopatra*, a film which, to add insult to injury, was then only tepidly patronized by a public that, unknown to the studio, had become bored with toga cinema.

By 1966, *The Sound of Music* had entered the world's cultural consciousness. Its songs were covered by hundreds of popular singers. Community theatres throughout America were mounting productions of the movie's original stage version. Story-wise, there was very little difference between the two versions. You had your seven Austrian children, who discovered that they could sing. You had your widowed father, a navy captain. And there was this nun with a guitar and a fine voice of her own. For a musical about singing songs, it is interesting to note that not all of the songs from the musical play are to be found in its Hollywood incarnation and vice versa.

It's more than interesting, actually. It's the reason for this story.

Besides being a sixth grade teacher at Eisenhower Elementary School in Pocatello, Idaho, Carla Willard was music director for the school's annual Autumn Evening of Song. Carla had loved musicals since at sixteen she saw Judy Garland in the 1954 film musical *A Star is Born* sing about being born in a trunk in Pocatello, Idaho. Carla imagined herself being born in that same trunk right next to Judy, whose name in the movie was first Esther Blodgett, and then, thankfully, Vicki Lester, which didn't sound as much like somebody throwing up.

Carla had seen Mary Martin play Maria Von Trapp on Broadway. She had delighted in Julie Andrews' interpretation of Maria in the film.

Delighted in it thirteen times, actually—all in the span of a month. Carla was understandably thrilled when Gilbert Greene, Eisenhower's principal, agreed to allow Carla to pay tribute to *The Sound of Music* by having each of the school's fifth- and sixth-grade classes sing a song from the musical for the autumn concert. She was even more excited to be given creative control over what songs would be sung, especially since this meant that she could choose in smorgasbord fashion songs from both the stage and film versions of the musical.

"So there's a difference?" asked Greene, when Carla met with him in his office one morning in early October to go over her plans for the November concert. "I don't understand."

Carla took a sip of her Tab. Whereas most of her teaching colleagues had a cup of coffee or tea in the early morning to steel themselves to face their sometimes unruly pupils, Carla preferred the soft drink Tab, though her brother, a college chemistry professor, told her it contained cyclohexylamine, a known chemical toxin. ("When they take it off the market, I'll stop drinking it, Wade. Right now it gives me a lift.")

"Most of the songs are the same, Gil," she explained to her principal, "but there are three in the stage version that are different from the film. And after Oscar Hammerstein died, Richard Rodgers wrote a couple of new songs for the movie."

"Why can't you just have the children sing the ones that everybody knows?"

"Because there are at least two absolutely gorgeous songs from the stage version that got dropped when they put the movie together, and I plan to right that wrong—at least with regards to *one* of them."

Carla respected the point that her principal made, but she didn't respect it enough not to choose a song from the stage version that very few members of her audience would know. It was called "No Way to Stop it." It was sung mostly by Captain Von Trapp's socialite girlfriend, Baroness Schräder, and the captain's impresario friend, Max Dettweiler. Through the song the Baroness and Max try to convince the captain to show his support for the oncoming annexation of Austria into the Third Reich, because it would make things easier for him. The gist of the song is this: there are things that happen in this world that can't be stopped, and it is easier to simply accept this fact than waste time fighting the inevitable. It was a philosophy that Carla didn't necessarily comport with, but she liked the catchy tune. It made her smile. In 1948, the city of Pocatello had passed a law making it illegal not to smile. Including the song in the program, she circuitously reasoned, would help make her audience more law-abiding.

Carla's brother Wade, the chemistry professor, didn't necessarily dislike the tune when his sister played the song for him, but he took strong issue with its message.

"The sentiment's pretty loathsome," he stated without qualification over dinner that night.

"Still, I think it would be perfect for Mrs. Roesler's class. They're the mischief-makers among the sixth graders, just like Max and Baroness Schräder in the movie."

"So what are you saying to those students, Carla? Accept everything that comes to you as ineluctable? Don't bother trying to make any kind of difference in this world?"

"You're overanalyzing, Wade. Should I stop Mrs. Beamer's students from singing 'Sixteen Going on Seventeen' because not a single one of them is over the age of twelve?"

"I'm curious: are you putting 'No Way to Stop It' before or *after* 'Climb Every Mountain'?"

"First of all, it isn't 'Climb *Every* Mountain.' It's 'Climb Ev'ry—*Ev'ry* Mountain.' Two syllables to fit the meter. Secondly, I haven't come up with an order for the songs yet, and does it really matter?"

"I'll say it matters. 'No Way to Stop It' is a cynical piece-of-shit song, so you'll need something like 'Climb Ev'ry Mountain' afterwards to get the bad taste out of everybody's mouths. See, the first song says, 'Some things, like the Nazi plan for world domination, as evil as it was, are simply too big to fight.' On the other hand, the old nun tells us in the other song to never stop climbing mountains and fording streams in the pursuit of our dreams."

"Hitler had a dream too. It was pretty awful. So what's your point?"

"My point is to put the fucking inspirational song after the fucking accommodationist song. Hell, Sis, I don't know why you've got some of the kids singing 'No Way to Stop it,' anyway. There aren't already ten good songs you could use?"

Carla shook her head. "Just nine. And there might just be eight if half of Mrs. Drexel's class continues to refuse to do 'Lonely Goatherd.' She says the boys won't sing it because she's asking them all to pretend to be marionettes. The boys say they would rather eat fried monkey testicles than have to dance around on stage like they've got strings attached to their arms and legs."

"The teacher gave them that choice?"

"You think this is funny, but it's just making me depressed. We start rehearsals next week and Mr. Greene is sure he's going to get calls from some of the parents of Mrs. Roesler's students."

It was worse than that. Several of the parents gathered together in Mr. Greene's office on parent-teacher night a couple of weeks later to voice their objections in person. Mrs. Roesler, the teacher of the sixth-grade class whose children had drawn the short straw while other fifth and sixth graders were, for example, analyzing the problem that is Maria and listing all of their favorite things, was there as well. Even though Mrs. Roesler had only a single working eye, one got the uncomfortable feeling that the other eye—opaque and stationary though it might be—was still honing in and making critical judgments.

Mrs. Roesler had strenuously opposed putting her pupils (and their parents) through this indignity, but there was not much else she could do. All of the songs had now been assigned. None of the other teachers would trade with her, and Mr. Lipe, one of the fifth-grade teachers, noted with glee the irony of Mrs. Roesler protesting the inexorable imposition upon her students of a song that was about *not* protesting inexorable impositions.

"I don't like it one bit!" howled Mr. Hambert, the father of Melissa Hambert, a straight-A student who chewed her hair. "Why has my daughter's class been singled out in this way?"

"It was simply the luck of the draw," said the beleaguered principal, who had come to parent-teacher night looking forward to showing off the new gym, which was very nearly finished except for the fact that its ceiling had yet to be sprayed with protective asbestos foam.

"*There's* the woman you ought to be talking to!" volunteered another one of the distraught parents. She was pointing at Carla, her finger jabbing the air as if she were implicating a suspected witch in colonial Salem.

"Are you the one?" asked another woman, who spoke in a softer voice, but who seemed no less concerned. "Was it *you* who saddled my daughter's class with this awful Nazi song?"

Before Carla could answer, a man spoke up. He wore a grease-stained auto mechanic's jumpsuit and must have come straight from work. "Do you believe our children to be selfish and whatchacallit—self-centered?"

Carla shook her head.

"Because that's what the song's telling these kids," the man went on. "Don't look out for nobody but yourself. That isn't what our kids are getting at home, and it isn't what they're getting in their Sunday school classes, and if you ask me, it smacks of communism."

"What it *smacks* of," said Mr. Hambert, "is submission and subordination. You're teaching our children to go beyond simply respecting authority and obeying their elders. You want them all to grow up to be brain-dead automatons without the necessary tools for critical thinking. I'm not one of these conspiracy-minded people, Miss Willard, but I don't think this is the way we ought to be raising our children."

The other parents in the room concurred with nods and under-voiced statements of strong agreement.

"That isn't why I picked it," said Carla, exasperation creeping into her delivery. "I just happen to like the tune. It's bright and breezy."

No one bothered to deliver a retort. Carla now knew where things stood. It had become quite evident to her (a teacher whose own pupils were having a grand time meeting the difficult polyphonic challenge of singing "Maria" against the vocalise counter-melody of the "Wedding Procession") that she had failed both herself and everyone else in not paying more attention to what the song was saying. There was a reason, which she now understood, why the song hadn't made it into the movie. It is true that negative sentiments have just as much right to be put to music as positive ones, but a lyricist often runs the risk of having his words taken out of character and situational context, especially when they are sung on the radio, or, let us say, on a cafetorium stage in a Pocatello, Idaho, elementary school.

"So what shall we do?" asked Principal Greene. This was Greene's customary modus operandi in meetings such as these: stating the problem and then entertaining various solutions before coming to a consensus. "Do we leave Mrs. Roesler's class out of the Evening of Song this year?"

Heads shook. One woman blurted, "Oh, *God* no." She, too, had apparently come straight from work, because she was wearing her beauty parlor operator's smock. It was stained with little red blotches, which looked very much like blood. Carla, when she thought about this later that night, wondered what in God's name the salon was doing to its customers.

There was only one thing worse than singing about Third Reich worldwide hegemony at Eisenhower Elementary. It was *not singing at all.* Greene retreated. "I'm aware, of course, that this is probably the least desirable of the remedies."

The woman who liked to point, whose name was Barbara Calbi, suggested combining Mrs. Roesler's class with another class.

Mrs. Roesler sighed her objection. "The other teachers wouldn't have it. Because their *students* wouldn't have it. My children have metaphorical cooties, you see. It's common knowledge that we are the untouchables of Eisenhower Elementary."

"Well I never!" exclaimed Mrs. Calbi.

"Children can be hateful little buggers," said the auto mechanic. "When I was in the sixth grade, a bunch of juvenile delinquent sons-of-bitches stuck my head in a urinal and made me kiss a deodorizing puck."

Several of the women drew back in revulsion, while Mrs. Calbi gagged involuntarily.

"May I then make a third suggestion?" offered Principal Greene. "It's unprecedented, but in the end it would probably do the least amount of harm." Greene was looking at Carla as he said this. It was *her* approval that would count the most.

It was agreed by nearly everyone present in the principal's office that night—including Carla Willard—that this was probably the best solution, the one that would draw the fewest objections. Mrs. Roesler's sixth graders would sing a different Rodgers and Hammerstein song—one not from *The Sound of Music.*

The text of the mimeographed program went as follows:

Welcome to Eisenhower Elementary School's Seventh Annual Fifth and Sixth Graders' Autumn Evening of Song. Tonight we honor, for the most part, **The Sound of Music** *by Rodgers and Hammerstein.*

Performances will proceed in the following order:

Mrs. McNutt's Fifth Graders will entertain us with: "The Sound of Music."
Miss Schulty's Fifth Graders will enliven us with: "I Have Confidence."
Mrs. Beamer's Sixth Graders will charm us with: "Sixteen Going on Seventeen."
Mrs. Holiday's Fifth Graders will delight us with: "My Favorite Things."
Miss Jackstraw's Sixth Graders will enchant us with: "Do-Re-Mi."
Mrs. Drexel's Fifth Grade Boys will sing: "The Lonely Goatherd."

Mrs. Drexel's Fifth Grade Girls will dance the Alpian marionette dance.
Mr. Lipe's Sixth Graders will touch our hearts with: "Edelweiss."
Mrs. Domanian's Fifth Graders will inspire us with: "Climb Ev'ry Mountain."
Miss Willard's Sixth Graders will enthrall us with: "Maria" and "Processional."
Mrs. Roesler's Sixth Graders will elevate us with "You'll Never Walk Alone."

The last song, which Carla remembered Jerry Lewis ardently rendering two years earlier during his telethon (suggested to him, he said, by a disabled child who was, no doubt, Broadway savvy), concluded the evening and left many in the audience elevated to the point of tears. Audience members were brought to their feet when on the line "Walk on, walk on, with hope in your heart," the untouchables of Eisenhower Elementary stepped off their choral risers and literally walked down from the stage, each child then seeking out his or her grandmother and grandfather to embrace in a gesture that, while it had nothing to do with the song, was much appreciated by its recipients.

Those who were unfamiliar with the full repertoire of songs from *The Sound of Music* thought that this was the song that the Von Trapps must have sung as they were hiking the Alps to freedom. Those who knew better still commended the selection as the perfect inspirational finish to the concert.

Carla told no one—not even her opinionated brother—that her first choice (quickly dismissed) had been *Oklahoma!'s* "It's a Scandal! It's an Outrage!"

Few knew what a wicked sense of humor Carla Willard had.

1967

GOING THE VOLE IN NEVADA

Life's a gamble. I learned this in '46 when I married Lorna and took on her three kids by her former deadbeat husband like they were my very own, and voilà! I'm an instant dad and everything that goes along with that drops itself heavily into my inveterate bachelor's lap, and whether or not I am up to the task is anybody's guess. But it's like Nescafé coffee. Some people try instant coffee and they like it, you know, *instantly*. Me, it took a while. But the kids did start to grow on me over time—Jed especially. Jed was born in 1938, the same year as the Nescafé company and the same year as this little convict-in-embryo who grew up down the street from where we lived in Butte, Montana: Robert Knievel. (More to come about Bad Boy Bobby.)

Now if you don't know Butte, I'll probably be doing you a terrible disservice by trying to sum it all up for you in a few sentences, so please forgive me. Butte from its earliest days was a wild and wooly mining town—one of the most notorious of the copper boomtowns. But Butte was luckier than most boomtowns, which seem to have an annoying habit of eventually going bust. The reason: Butte was diversified. She had zinc and manganese and lead and molybdenum and silver and gold and brothels. Big business, those bawdy Butte brothels.

That's where Jed's wife Babs was born. An unwed sporting lady by the name of Sicilian Cicely (most of the "soiled doves" of The Line, Butte's red-light district in those days, had clever, geographically suggestive nicknames) was her mother, and it's anybody's guess who the father was, although I'd put my money on a favorite customer of hers named Bingham, which, coincidentally, is also the name of a copper boomtown in northern Utah that hasn't fared nearly as well as Butte. Its ever-expanding open pit has literally been eating the town alive for years. And in 1971, the two dozen or so folks who were still left voted to disincorporate and get the hell out. It's a bona fide ghost town now.

Jed didn't mind that Babs, whom he married in 1958, was the daughter of a whore, and it wasn't something that Lorna and I would ever hold against a person. Like I say, Jed was my favorite among my three stepkids (although I know that dads, and *step*dads, for that matter, aren't supposed to play favorites).

Now, I was talking about boomtowns, so I should make mention of Deadwood, South Dakota, which is where my stepson and his wife Babs moved in late '58. Deadwood, as you might know, had a gold rush (1874—boom) and then a smallpox epidemic (1876—bust) and then a fire that wiped out nearly the entire town (1877—double bust). And that boom and bust pattern persisted into the twentieth century, as well. Right after Jed and his new bride got there—Jed was offered a job by a building contractor friend—there was a second big fire (1959—another blazing bust) that destroyed much of the town and sent the couple off on an interesting road trip. From 1959 into early 1962 they must have lived in about ten different western communities, Jed the itinerate laborer and Babs taking part-time secretarial work where she could get it. Their luck changed in 1962 when they wound up on a ranch outside of the little north Texas town of Summerfield, which coincidentally used to be called—I am not kidding—*Boom*. Jed worked construction and punched cattle, and Babs was employed as a receptionist for a dentist in nearby Hereford who took early retirement in late '66 in large part because Hereford's water supply has a high level of naturally occurring fluorine, and so few of the residents had much need for a dentist.

Still, the couple was able to save about twenty thousand dollars during the four years they lived in Texas, and Jed and Babs were now convinced that their conjoined life had strong aspects of boom and bust to it, and since they seemed to have just gone boom (the success of the last four years) and now bust (Babs losing her job and a heifer stepping on Jed's right foot and crushing three of his toes) they believed they were due for a change of fortune, and this is why Jed planned to take every penny of the twenty thousand they had in savings and put it down on either red or black at one of the Vegas casino roulette tables. (Since Deadwood wouldn't be legalizing gambling for another twenty-two years, a Nevada casino was their only bet.)

The big decision: red or black?

"That's all we need, Pops," said Jed. "Just tell us: red or black?" Lorna and I had driven down to Las Vegas from Butte in early March to take a break from the harsh Montana winter, with hopes of using the additional face time with my stepson and stepdaughter-in-law to talk them out of this potentially ruinous idea.

The four of us were having dinner at the Dunes' Dome of the Sea restaurant. Lorna had the veal kidneys Berrichone. Jed and I had steaks frites and Babs had the quiche Lorraine, which she said tasted just like the bacon and Swiss cheese pie that a prostitute friend of her mother's—Betty, the Natural Irish Reddie—used to make in the Dumas brothel kitchen in Butte.

"You wanna gamble?" I asked. "Take a hundred dollars—take *two hundred dollars* to the table. That won't cut too much into that nice little nest egg the two of you've built up. Don't you want to have children? To buy a house somewhere?"

"We can't have children," said Babs. "There's something wrong with me down there."

"There's *nothing* wrong with you down there that *I* care about!" said Jed, looking lovingly and a bit hungrily at his wife's crotch.

"Oh, they love each other so much," sighed Lorna, holding a bite of veal kidneys Berrichone in midair. "Mike, isn't there something that Jed can do with State Farm?"

"Selling insurance would be like a death sentence for me, Mom," Jed burst out. "Sorry, Pops, but I have to be outdoors. If I'm not building or wrangling something, I go buggy. You're the same way, aren't you, Punklin? Didn't working for Dr. Edder have you crawling the walls?"

Babs nodded. "Although some of the children had interesting stains on their teeth from the dental fluorosis."

"I don't just want a house, Pops," Jed continued. "I want a ranch—my own ranch. *Our* own ranch," he corrected himself while looking into his wife's blue eyes, and then slightly down at her crotch again, and then back to her eyes. "I can't buy a ranch for twenty thou. Not around Butte at least, which is where we want to wind up. Now *forty* thou—that puts us a heap closer."

"What about *zero*, son?" I persisted. "Because there's *that* possibility, too. How many years do you think *that* would put you away from achieving your dream? Why do I have to tell you this? You've got a good head on your shoulders."

"Everything in life is a gamble," said Jed, looking at his watch. "The show's about to start. Let's go see the show, okay?"

The "show" was the Dunes' Casino de Paris Review starring Rouvaun, a thirty-five-year-old singer who was virtually unknown only a month before, but was now headlining a one-hundred-person extravaganza that sold out at every performance. (Career: boom!) I didn't know at the time that Rouvaun wasn't European—though his stage name gave one to imagine Caruso or one of the other continental greats. The "Vocal Vesuvius," as he was later dubbed, was born Jim Haun in Bingham, Utah. That's right: boom-and-then-bust Bingham, Utah.

As the four of us sat listening to Rouvaun singing the hopeful "Somewhere" from *West Side Story* while a bevy of sequined, extravagantly fledged showgirls strutted and dipped behind him, Jed leaned across his mother to whisper into my ear, "Peace and quiet and open air wait for us…on the Montana plains." A moment later, Babs, who had imbibed one too many Blue Hawaiis, summoned the attention of one of the dancers on the stage, whose name she told us was Siam Pam. According to Babs, Pam had once worked with Babs's mother at one of the Mercury Street bordellos in Butte. "It's a small world after all," marveled Babs.

The next morning over breakfast, Lorna and I tried one last time to talk Jed out of putting all twenty thousand dollars down on either red or black at the roulette wheel. We also appealed to Babs, but she was no help. Her head was killing her and even though she admitted that of course she didn't want her husband to do such a foolish thing, he had his heart set on it and she loved Jed more than she loved money, and by the way, had we decided yet whether he should go for red or black?

"Why should *we* be the ones to make that decision, dear?" asked Lorna of her son. "That would be a lot of guilt for us to have to carry around if we happened to choose wrong."

"Still," said Jed, "I trust the two of you more than anybody."

"That doesn't make any sense, Jed," I replied in exasperation. "It's all chance, whether I'm picking the color or you are. Life may be a series of choices—choices based on knowledge or experience or skill—but life is also made up of a number of haphazard events over which a person has absolutely no control. Zero. Zilch. This is such an event. Boom or bust doesn't apply here."

Jed thought about this for a moment, and then he said, "I understand. I'll just have to ask somebody else. I'll ask a *bunch* of somebody elses. Excuse me. I'm going over to Caesars Palace and stand by the big fountains and pose my question to folks who walk by."

This he actually did. He reported back that afternoon that twenty-three people had said "red" and twenty-five people had said "black." He discounted three of the people who had said black since they were, racially, black, and obviously exercising a prideful ethnic bias. He discounted another man who said "black" when he admitted that "red" to him carried Communist undertones. A different man, the professorial type, corrected the question: "You mean *The Red and the Black*. Stendhal's 1830 psychological classic. An excellent read, my boy." This man's companion was equally unhelpful; his answer to the question "Red or black?" was "Red when I play checkers, but I do like my coffee black." The final adjusted count was Red: 23, Black: 21. Red it was.

At first I was torn. I wanted to be there to support Jed, but I knew that it would probably end up being the most difficult couple of minutes of my life. Lorna couldn't bear it. Neither could Babs. They escaped that evening to Sultan's Table to hear Arturo Romero and his Magic Violins. I couldn't leave Jed to face this life-altering event alone, so the decision was made for me.

We approached the table. There were a couple of busty blondes there who were all smiles and apparently doing well, and a glabrous-globed older gentleman who looked choleric and probably wasn't doing well at all. I told the croupier what my stepson wanted to do. The man summoned the pit boss and the two spoke for a moment with backs turned. The pit boss ended up shrugging. Looking right at Jed, he said, "It's his money." But I could have sworn that he said, "It's his *funeral*."

I had every intention of trying one last time to talk Jed out of it, but I couldn't muster the energy. Every muscle of my body ached from having tightened up so tensely in anticipation of this moment I had been dreading.

Jed paid for his chips. The audacity of the several towering piles in front of him drew in a small crowd. The two blond women looked intrigued, almost aroused.

The croupier called for bets. Jed pushed all of the chips over to red.

A wise guy behind us cracked, "I would have gone for black."

I wanted to slug him. If only I'd been ten years younger…

The roulette wheel began to spin, the ball deposited. "No more bets," said the croupier. Everyone leaned in. Everyone stopped breathing. The clockwise spinning of the roulette wheel, the counter-clockwise circling of the ball—it seemed to go on forever. And then the ball began its skip and skitter among the number slots as the wheel slowed, finally settling into its final numerical resting place. The number wasn't red. The number wasn't black. It was green. A zero. Zero was the house's number—one of the two numbers (the other, the double zero) that helped the casino to make a profit in this game of otherwise pure chance. It was easy to calculate the payout that Jed would have received had he put all his chips on the house's zero rather than red: seven hundred thousand dollars. Enough to buy several Montana ranches in 1967. But I would have blown up the building before allowing him to put all of that money on a thirty-five-to-one shot.

What did my stepson do in that next moment? He smiled, he shrugged, and then he said, "That's what you call a bust, Pops."

Several months later, Robert—otherwise known as Evel—Knievel, of Butte, Montana, played even longer odds when he convinced the CEO of Caesars Palace to let him (at the time only a *semi*-famous daredevil) jump over the casino's fountains with his motorcycle. Knievel came up short, lost control of his bike, and ended up with a crushed pelvis and femur, several fractures, and a concussion that kept him comatose for almost a month.

Nor was the "Vocal Vesuvius" immune to the vagaries of boom and bust, although his bust was of the permanent variety. After an eight-year career as a popular vocalist and recording artist, Rouvaun, a.k.a. Jimmy Haun of Bingham, Utah, erstwhile boomtown, now vacated ghost town, died suddenly in 1975 of a rupture to the esophagus from all the strain he'd been placing on his Vesuvian vocal cords.

My stepson Jed and his wife Babs won the California SuperLotto in 1993 (boom!) after years of struggling to come back from the Dunes Casino loss. The lottery, which has much in common with the casino game Keno (which was born in Butte, Montana's Chinatown), awarded the couple enough money to share a little with Jed's aging parents (such a good boy) and to pay for a trip to Las Vegas, where Jed and Babs and their adopted daughter Tian planned to stay at the famed Dunes Casino hotel (for old times' sake).

Unfortunately, the casino, having been out-razzle-dazzled by the bigger, better-capitalized newer generation of casinos, was due for demolition on the weekend of their visit. They stayed at Treasure Island instead, and, along with two hundred thousand other spectators (who were there for the biggest show the Dunes had ever put on), watched with wide-eyed wonder the deliberate imploding of the casino that had taken twenty thousand hard-earned dollars from them back in 1967. There were fireworks and "cannon blasts" from Treasure Island's pirate ship, and then the Dunes' North Tower came down in fittingly dramatic fashion.

Jed held his wife tightly around the waist as the crowd gasped and squealed and hooted with delight and Tian covered her tender teeny-bopper ears. Then Jed smiled at a thought which he later shared with his grizzled old man—the stepdad label having long been replaced by dad-in-full: "The Dunes was the first casino on the strip to offer showgirl tits (literal bust). And when it went out, it went out with a big ol' bang (literal boom)!"

I'm telling you—you just can't make this stuff up.

1968

HIERATIC IN KANSAS

Nearly every Saturday night for the last five years, Father Mullavey had driven from his parish in Kansas City, Missouri, across the Intercity Viaduct Bridge, and into the Strawberry Hill neighborhood of Kansas City, Kansas, to visit his childhood chum and fellow altar boy, Herman Klar. The two men, both in their late forties, drank Schnapps and sometimes Scotch whiskey, and if the priest drank too much, Herman and his wife Jelena would play chauffeur and even tuck him into bed in the rectory—ever so quietly—so that Mrs. Davies wouldn't wake and give him a dressing down the next morning for his shameful un-priestlike inebriety.

Father Mullavey was fond of the widow Davies and would have married her if the Roman Catholic Church ever came to its senses on this whole celibacy matter. This is what Herman's wife Jelena believed. Jelena was of every sort of opinion under the sun, including how to make the world a better place on her own terms. She was in her mid-forties, the mother of twin daughters, each recently returned to college in Ohio on this early September weekend. The daughter of Croatian parents, Jelena Lisinki Klar had grown up in Strawberry Hill among Croatian meatpackers and their bustling, garrulous wives. Jelena inherited her big hands and large frame from her father and her assertive tongue from her mother. There was no debate to be brooked on the decision to buy the little gingerbread house on Thompson, which sat on a bluff overlooking the Kansas River. Because Jelena's roots were there.

And she wanted her roots back.

The two men sat on the back porch, cocktail glasses in hand, itemizing aloud all of the things that over the years had rolled down the steeply sloping backyard and into the river. "The girls had a beach ball when they were four, five years old," Herman recalled with a chuckle. "JELENA! COME OUT HERE FOR A MINUTE!"

Herman's wife stepped out onto the ancient wooden porch that she and her husband and their two girls had shared for over fifteen years with intermittent colonies of termites and intermittent tank-sprayer-armed employees from the Smithereen Exterminating Company. "I was about to pop up some Jiffy Pop, Herman. *Miss America* starts in ten minutes."

"They were b-burning bras this afternoon," said the priest. He peered off into the distance as if focusing his gaze on the Boardwalk in Atlantic City, the site of that day's acts of undergarment mischief.

"Who?" asked Herman. "The contestants?"

"Of course not. The—the—the protesters. The women's libbers."

Jelena put her hands on her hips and tapped her foot. "What did you want, Herman?"

"That beach ball we used to have—whose idea was it to leave it in the backyard so it would roll down the hill?"

"I don't know, Ljubavi," said Jelena, employing her favorite Croatian term of endearment for her husband. "How can I remember something from that far back? And they didn't burn their bras, the protestors. The police wouldn't let them. They said the fire would engulf the whole boardwalk. It's made of wooden boards, you know."

"Why would they want to burn their bras anyway?" asked Herman.

"Do you mean that, Herman? Do you mean that question? Tell him, Father. Tell my husband, who is still stuck in the year 1946, why women would protest the Miss America pageant."

Herman stood. He teetered, grabbing the arm of the Adirondack chair he had bought at a yard sale for only four dollars because there were two slats missing in the back. Herman was drunk and a little dizzy. He drank only with his friend Pete the priest, which meant he drank only once a week. The alcohol always went straight to his head. "Sometimes, honey, I wish this was still 1946—when it wasn't so hard for men and women to figure out what was expected of them, I mean, genderly speaking."

"I said 1946, Ljubavi, because that was the year we married. Of course, now that I think about it, it was also the year that most of us female factory workers got our walking papers."

"How else were we veterans supposed to find jobs if Rosie the Riveter didn't give up her—her *what*, Peter?"

"Her air hammer," supplied the priest. He took a sip of his Schnapps and made a small vocal exhalation that sounded halfway between a satisfied "ahhh" and the release of steam from a metal riser. "Tell me, Jelena," said Pete, "if you endorse what these women are doing—what it is that they—they—they stand for, why are you so fired up to go sit and watch—"

"And watch with your Jiffy Pop," interjected Herman, settling himself back into his wooden Adirondack chair with the two plastic lawn chair replacement slats.

"Watch the pageant," finished the priest. Peter Mullavey stared out at the dramatically sloping backyard and whistled, and then said, "You could break your neck cutting that grass, Herman. How do you do it?"

"I use a cylinder mower with an extra-long handle," answered Herman, matter-of-factly.

"If you *must* know—" said Jelena.

"How do you—excuse me, Jelena. How do you keep from losing it, Herman? Losing the mower?"

"If you *must* know—" said Jelena with growing impatience.

"Sometimes I don't. I've lost three. That's why I stopped using an expensive gas mower and got me one of those old hand-propelled jobs from the Iron Age."

"I am watching the pageant," pursued Jelena in service to an answer whose related question had long been forgotten by her husband and his equally toasted sacerdotal best friend, "because there is a girl who's competing this year who grew up with the cousin of a friend of mine. You remember Alana, who lived down the street from us in Overland Park? Well, she knows the girl—she's met her. She's in the pageant this year. She's Miss Illinois."

"Sit down," said Herman, pulling his wife down upon one of the wide, flat arms of the Adirondack chair.

"I can't. I have to make popcorn." Jelena squirmed but she didn't get up.

"It's a beautiful night," said Herman. "I feel like we live on the edge of the world. You should see the sunrises from this back porch, Petey. You're never here for the sunrises. I know why all those Croatians came here with their Dalmatian dogs and their plum wine. They came for the sunrises and the—do you smell that, Petey? Do you smell that smell?"

"It wasn't me."

"No, no, Petey. It's the smell of American enterprise. The smell of American meat. Of ground round and sirloin and brisket and chuck."

Jelena pushed her husband away and rose from the chair. "I have to see how Alana's friend does. I owe it to Alana after she volunteered to give me a kidney after the car wreck. My point is this: that there's something about the pageant that seems a little old-fashioned in this day and age—with all the changes going on in the world. I'll admit it. All those women being asked to parade around like—"

"Mooooo!" said Pete the priest and both men chortled and some Schnapps escaped from Herman's nose.

Jelena ignored this. "And women have a right to protest it. Just as women have a right to *participate*, if they want to."

The priest sat up in his chair. The chair wasn't from upstate New York. It was a traditional rocking chair that stopped rocking after it was nailed down following an incident in which a visitor to the house—a neighbor with a restless nature—rocked herself off the porch and tumbled down the hill like Jill of the familiar nursery rhyme. "Excellent p-p-point, Jelena. But here's what—what—what I want to know, if you'll be so kind as to—there's the Folly Theatre across the river. It's a burlesque house and there've been religious groups—none of them Catholic, I don't think, although I think I saw a nun with a sign. And—and—and they—they have been protesting. Which is apparently what people are doing this year. It's the—the—the thing *this* year—all this protesting and th-throwing smoke bombs and people burning their—their—draft cards and burning their underclothes and what have you. And my question to you, Jelena, is this: a woman has the right to do what she wants with her body, with her—her *life*, does she not?"

Jelena nodded. She had begun to tap her foot again. She had missed her chance to pop her corn before the parade of states. Now she'd have to do it during a Toni Home Permanent commercial or the big spangled musical production number in which pageant host Bert Parks made his annual attempt to sing and dance.

Pete went on: "Even as she is being assaulted from all directions. By the women's libbers with their—their—their anger, and the uptight evangelical Bible-huggers with their—their what?"

"Their anger," said Herman, to be helpful.

Jelena nodded. "And the point is that no woman should have to answer to another woman for *anything*." Jelena took a breath. "Or answer to a man either, for that matter" she concluded, eyeing her husband.

"What is this? Have I ever *once* told you what I thought you ought to be doing? The world may be in flames right now, but please note:

nothing's on fire in *this* house. We have a very good marriage, do we not? I may be a stick-in-the-mud sometimes—I'm sorry. That's the way I was brought up. But I love you, and I respect you, and you wanted a house in your old neighborhood, and I agreed that you should have it, even though the smell of the meat coming from those packing houses— it used to make me—"

"Just a moment earlier you called it the smell of American enterprise."

"I'm drunk. I don't know what I'm saying. So listen now to what I'm saying—"

"My show's almost on. I'm going to miss seeing Miss Illinois. They say she has a good chance of winning."

"What does she do?" asked the priest. "For her talent, I mean. What's her ta-talent?"

"She's a trampolinist."

"What is that?" asked Herman. "Is that what I think it is?"

"Yes, Herman. She jumps up and down."

"Is she chesty?" asked Herman, looking up, a little expectantly, at his wife.

"For the love of Mike, Ljubavi! I'm going inside."

"I'm coming in too. I want to see Miss Illinois jump up and down. This is what she wants to do and we will honor her choice. Are you coming, Petey?"

Peter Mullavey shook his head. "I think I'd like to sit here for a little— a—a—little while longer."

"You sure you don't want to..." Herman had stepped away from the doorway to give the priest room to come inside.

"Just for a few minutes. It's nice out here."

"You're thinking about her, aren't you?"

"No, I'm not. I mean, who do—do you think I'm thinking about?"

"You and I both know. Your Mrs. Davies. You're thinking about the two of you, huh? Cozied up together on the couch with your bowl of Jiffy Pop, watching Bishop Sheen together."

Pete looked out at all the twinkling lights of Kansas City, Missouri. One of those lights represented the rectory where the priest slept and ate and prayed and kept a chaste distance from the woman he had loved since the day she had come to be his cook and housekeeper. "*I'd* like to liberated someday."

"Don't blaspheme, Petey. You always get irreverent when you've had a nip too many."

"I've got nothing against God. Or the church, for that matter. It's men who—who did this to me. You—you—you talk about women telling other women what it is they ought to be doing." The priest lowered his voice. "But my problem is with *men*. It's men who put me here. It's the men of my faith who s-say I'm not allowed to worship God while seeking a different kind of Heaven in the arms of a beautiful woman. What r-right have they to tell me this, Herman? What right?" Pete Mullavey grew silent, thoughtful, yearning, then mournful. Herman held his vigil beside the door. He could hear the opening music of the 1968 Miss America Pageant starring Bert Parks and fifty-one of the finest examples of American womanhood. "*There she is…*" There they were.

"I'll call you in when Miss Illinois climbs up on her trampoline, Petey. Go easy on the booze. I don't want you to fall down and break your crown and wind up in the Kansas River."

Peter Mullavey nodded. He sighed. He leaned back in the stationary rocker and closed his eyes. He saw Mrs. Davies sitting in the front pew of his parish church, smiling supportively through his slightly stammered homilies. He imagined the curves of Mrs. Davies in her house frock, standing with her back to him in the early morning light, frying up his sausage and eggs. Sometimes he pretended that they were married—happily married like his friends Herman and Jelena.

Peter Mullavey and his oldest friend and fellow altar boy Herman Klar and Herman's opinionated, longsuffering, long-loving wife Jelena inaugurated a new annual ritual that year. On a particular Saturday every year in early September, the three popped popcorn and poured Schnapps and Scotch whiskey, and watched *Miss America* together. In fact, it was during the 1976 broadcast that Father Mullavey suffered the stroke that incapacitated him for the next year and a half and resulted ultimately in his retirement from active ministry. The causal arterial embolism occurred while Bert Parks, backed up by three young bobble-headed male dancers in tuxedos, sang the pop hit by Paul McCartney, "Let 'Em In."

Mrs. Davies was there at Pete's bedside at the hospital and then every day at the rectory to assist him in his daily rehabilitation therapy. Every morning she was up early to fry his sausage and eggs. One morning he reached up as she was setting the plate in front of him, reached up and touched her cheek with the fingertips of his right hand—the good hand—touched her soft, warm cheek sweetly, achingly, ever so briefly.

1969

PARENTAL IN ARIZONA

The first year it was a Spartan, and Yellowstone and the Tetons; the next year a Vagabond, and the Badlands and the Four Faces. Last year we bought a used Airway Zephyr and flew like the wind up and down the California and Oregon coastline. This year we went to Bryce and Zion and the Grand Canyon. I don't know why it took us so long to get to the Grand Canyon. There's simply no way to describe it—like nothing we've seen in all of our four years of vacationing out west. Especially when you're vacationing in luxury in a brand-new Avion thirty-one-foot, two-and-a-half-ton Imperial. As the name implies, it's the biggest travel trailer the Avion company makes.

My husband has, over the last several years, become a master rig hauler. He's a man of many talents, that's for certain, and I never doubted that he would get so good at "travelcading." Although Clint inherited quite a bit of money from his father, he didn't simply plop himself down upon his family windfall and proceed to a life of self-indulgence. We have taken a good deal of the Dinkman's Pastries fortune and given it to a number of charities and organizations whose causes we believe in. (Only a small portion of the inheritance actually finances our extensive summer travels through the Great American West.)

Clint has learned to play the violin and he's writing a book about General Custer. I am a gourmet chef. You wouldn't believe the meals I can whip up for my husband and our two hungry road puppies using that Avion butane range with bifold top and broiler. I should have mentioned our road puppies sooner. Robert Joseph—known as R.J. (he's eleven)— and Lisha (she's nearing ten) couldn't wait to get out of school and hit the road for two and a half glorious months of scenic adventure with Mom and Dad. From day one we were like one of those families in the 1950s travelogues, waving and mugging at the camera as they insert their car through the hollowed-out trunk of that Wawona giant sequoia in Yosemite—something that we would have liked someday to do (unhitched, of course) had a heavy snowfall not toppled that majestic Old Man of the Forest just last winter.

Clint and I have a good life, which is made even better by our annual ten-week road adventures with the kids, who are usually game for anything their nutty trailer-touring parents want to do. No, we have never surmounted Pike's Peak with any of our various rigs in tow, but we have crossed the Continental Divide several times, rig intact, and never burned out a single automobile engine.

No one has ever questioned our taking the kids along—even though it removes from them the opportunity to enjoy the kinds of summer activities usually associated with children their age. Well, no one questioned us, that is, until we paid a visit to Clint's two half-sisters in Flagstaff last August.

It was inevitable that we would see them after our visit to Grand Canyon National Park. Clint hadn't been in communication with either of them for almost ten years. Gabby and Gertrude, twelve and fourteen years older than him, respectively, were never close to Clint. In addition to the age difference, there was also the fact that it wasn't the phenomenally successful prune danish and chocolate bear claw magnate, Overell Dinkman, whom they shared as a parent, but Dinkman's second wife, Alfreda, who came into the marriage with two daughters in whom stepdad Dinkman could not have been any less interested.

It also made sense for reason of proximity. Flagstaff is simply too close to the south rim of the Grand Canyon for Clint to have avoided a visit with his spinster sisters. And that was that.

I really wish we hadn't gone.

We'd spent three weeks at the Grand Canyon, making sure to keep the hiking to a minimum for several reasons, not the least of which was the oppressive summer heat. Still, R.J. got enough of a taste of the place to say that he was seriously considering becoming a park ranger when he grew up. Lisha, who loved horses, spent a lot of her time volunteering as a girl-groom at the stables. She worked very hard, and some days she returned to the trailer more tired than others, but overall she amazed us with her stamina and little girl vitality.

It had probably been our best summer trip, and R.J. and Lisha and I fought back tears as we stood watching Clint turn off the butane tanks, disengage the lines, unblock the wheels, fold the jacks, and then open the backseat door to our red-on-red grin-grilled workhorse of a rig hauler—our 1964 Cadillac Deville convertible 429—so that the kids could climb in and we could hit the road. I could tell from their long faces that they were reluctant to leave the trailer park, which had been their happy home for twenty-one blissful days and nights.

"What do you say to your father and me for bringing you here, children?" I asked, with a catch in my voice.

"Thank you, Mom. Thank you, Dad," said the two in cheerless unison.

I could not simply leave it at that. I reached into the car and smothered each of my road puppies with maternal hugs and kisses. "You're most welcome," I said between snuggling smooches.

The plan was this: we'd stay in Flagstaff for three days and then begin the final leg of our journey—east on Interstate 40, north on I-25, and then east again on I-80 to get us, one week later, back where we started: South Bend, Indiana, where our lives would once again settle into their customary off-season routines, and the summer, now behind us, would shimmer in the glow of warm recollection. (For the most part.)

It took Clint no time at all to back the trailer up Gabby and Gertrude's concrete drive so that we could easily uncouple the car for use around town during our stay. The two sisters had stood with folded arms and expressions that anticipated disaster to the flowerbeds and shrubbery flanking the drive. But Clint, with expert aplomb, harmed not a single bloom or branch. We'd embraced each other a little tentatively in the yard upon arrival and noted how long it had been since we'd last seen one another, but postponed any extended catch-up conversation for later. Both of the women, now in their fifties, had cocked their salt-and-pepper heads at R.J. and Lisha and seemed, from their curious looks, set to ask questions that Clint's insistence on getting the rig out of the street did not permit answering.

The car and rig now neatly situated, we were all ushered into the house, which resembled, as did many of the homes of Flagstaff in the sixties, a mountain villa: lots of wood and a steeply pitched roof to discourage accumulation in any appreciable amount of the hundred or so inches of snow the city received each winter. Gabby, as her name implied, was the far more talkative of the two sisters. She was also the energetic one—pouring iced tea and spooning sweetener and plumping throw pillows to make everyone comfortable.

It made me tired just to watch her.

"We didn't know you had children," said Gabby, finally sitting down in a chair. All the sitting furniture in the room was grouped around the large stone fireplace, which, this being summer, sat cold and tomblike. The placement of the television at the opposite end of the room made me wonder if the two sisters watched their favorite shows over their shoulders. Or maybe the furniture was grouped this way for the express purpose of allowing us to speak to one another comfortably (though "comfortable" conversation would be in short supply this evening).

There seemed to be a formality and a certain exactitude to the way the sisters lived. Gabby worked at the university, in the admissions office. Gertrude was owner and manager of her own gift shop. The town attracted a lot of tourists going to and coming from the Grand Canyon. I'm sure that Gertrude kept that shop immaculate—as cleanly ordered as the large living room in which I found myself sitting stiffly erect, wishing that this visit didn't have to last three days. Wishing, as well, that I could just sweep up the kids and throw them in the car, which now sat unmoored from our currently stationary mobile home, so that we could go tramping around the huge Ponderosa forest that climbed the hills within view of the sisters' panoramic living room picture windows. I would do this while Clint "caught up." While he and his estranged half-siblings said everything that needed to be said between marginal family members. And then we could be relievedly on our way.

It would not be nearly that easy.

"The children," Gabby repeated, pointing at R.J. and Lisha as if they were odd little souvenirs we'd picked up during our travels. "When did you adopt them?"

Clint shook his head. "We didn't adopt them."

Gabby bunched her lips together and gave my husband a hard, penetrating look. "If these are not your children, then just whose children *are* they?"

"They're *our* children. But only for the summer," Clint answered decisively, if not a little elliptically. "This tea is good. Are we eating here tonight or going out? Natalie doesn't eat red meat, so I don't ask her to cook it. I wouldn't mind going out for a steak."

"Whatever you'd like, Clint," answered Gabby. "But I'm still confused. 'Only for the summer.' What do you mean by that?"

"Just what I said," answered Clint. "I would have explained already what it is that Natalie and I do with the kids each summer, but we haven't really made much of an effort to stay in touch, now have we?"

Gertrude, who had been sitting in silence, her brow furrowed, the teeth of her lower dental plate chewing her upper lip lightly but intently, now made a contribution to the conversation. "Am I the only person in this room to notice that these two children are...*colored*?"

"They don't want us to use the word 'colored' anymore, Gertrude, darling," said Gabby to her older sister. "They say 'black,' as in 'black and beautiful.'" Gabby was looking right at Lisha now. "And you *are*, honey. You are both black *and* beautiful. But what *else* are you?"

"What my husband means to say," I broke in, "is that we have not formally adopted these children, but they are ours in every other possible respect. I mean during the summer."

"Natalie," said Gabby, without making any attempt to soften her delivery, "you're making no sense. Where did these two black children come from?"

Lisha traded a look with Clint and me that said she wanted to be the one to answer. "We come from South Bend, Indiana," she said without hesitation. "My brother and I live in an orphanage there."

"You mean when you're not living with my brother and sister-in-law?" asked Gabby.

"That's right," I said. "So tell me about that big fluffy dog out in the backyard, Gabby. He looks like Tramp, doesn't he, kids?"

R.J. and Lisha agreed that the English sheepdog in the backyard, who was pressing his furry nose against the window and wagging his tail, looked very much like Tramp from the TV sitcom *My Three Sons*. And they wanted to play with him.

"Can R.J. and Lisha go out and play with the dog?" I asked Gabby.

"Of course. He's very friendly. But don't leave the backyard." Almost as an afterthought she added, "It's getting dark." As the children were going out, Gabby explained that Flagstaff gets very dark at night because outdoor lighting is kept very low to accommodate night-sky viewing from the city's two nationally renowned observatories.

A moment later, Clint said, "Natalie and I tried to have children of our own for years. When we finally gave up, we made other arrangements."

"Isn't the normal course to formally adopt? Why not these children, for example?"

"Oh, Heavens, no!" exclaimed Gertrude.

Clint looked to me to answer. "There are reasons that we've chosen not to adopt." I watched through the window as R.J. and Lisha fell instantly in love with the dog, whose name, we soon learned, was Dawser.

"What reasons?" persisted Gabby. "You're being awfully mysterious. Why do you come into this house and act so mysterious?"

"I'm sorry," was all that Clint said, his head bowed. I noted that his Keds-clad right foot was nervously pawing the deep shag carpet.

"Well, at any rate," Gabby went on, "I don't think it's a healthy game to play with children—taking them three months out of the year and pretending to be their parents and then putting them right back into the orphanage to spend the rest of the year." The topic had finally been put to bed with this pronouncement. "It's too late to go out. I'll start dinner. You said you'd be here by six-thirty and it's already past eight."

Gabby got up and left the room. "I'll give her a hand in the kitchen," I said to Clint, and followed. Later that night, Clint related to me the private exchange that then took place between him and Gertrude.

There was no prelude: "I don't want them staying in this house."

"Them. The children, you mean?"

"Yes. The nigger children. I don't want them sleeping in my house."

"When did you get to be this way?"

"What way? You didn't tell me that you were bringing nigger children with you—the spawn of some heroin whore in the ghetto. Do you know who the father is?"

"Which father? R.J.'s was killed in Vietnam. And I don't want you using that word again."

"I don't want them here, Clint. This is *my* house."

Clint didn't respond to what my sister-in-law had said—at least not right away. These were words that he'd never heard her say before—words that stabbed him, words that diminished her in his eyes. And the relationship between Clint and his half-sisters had been troubled for a long time anyway. He'd given them money—a lot of money—after his father died, to make up for the fact that Overell Dinkman had left his stepdaughters out in the cold. There hadn't been even a whisper of a thank-you. Clint faulted himself for not doing a better job of maintaining communication, but then again, this was a two-way street—one avoided by both parties in equal measure.

Finally, after a long period of silence, Clint said, "I have one favor to ask of you. That you let me keep the trailer here until the morning. I'll take Natalie and the kids to a motel tonight."

"If that's what you want, Clint," said Gertrude. "But you could just as easily put the children in the trailer and you and Natalie can take the guest room. The bed is very comfortable. It has a new mattress."

"We will eat with you. I'm sure that Gabby and Natalie are already well into preparations for the meal by now, but come tomorrow morning we'll be on our way. What you've offered—to state the obvious—isn't acceptable."

"If that's what you want," Gertrude repeated. "I must say, though, that even if there isn't something, I believe, very much the matter with two white adults gallivanting all over the place with a couple of ni—with a couple of Negro children—it's still very odd, this thing you're doing. Playing house. Is that what it's called? It's a children's game that has no place being played by adults."

"It makes Natalie happy."

"Pretending to be a mother."

"*Being* a mother. And she's a very good one. And I happen to think that I'm a good father. Sometimes life deals you certain cards, Gertrude. But you don't have to take them. You're allowed to discard them for something better."

"Are the two of you—are you molesting those children?"

We didn't stay for dinner.

The kids loved Dawser. They didn't understand why they couldn't stay and play with him.

I hustled them into the car while Clint connected the rig. He didn't like driving around with the trailer at night. Even with our expertly devised pilot/co-pilot navigation system, it wasn't an easy thing changing lanes after the sun had gone down with that freight train behind us, and especially in a city that didn't like to light up its streets at night.

We reached a trailer park just east of town at about 9:30. I boiled eggs and we all had egg and olive sandwiches. After tucking the kids into bed, Clint and I sat outside in lawn chairs and talked in low voices late into the night. Was it wrong, what we were doing? Was there something wrong with *us*? Gabby had been right about it being a game, but it was a game that we all bought into, that all four of us enjoyed, and who got hurt? For ten weeks out of the year—weeks that Clint and I looked forward to with enthusiastic, childlike anticipation—we played that game to the hilt. And for those two and a half months the children had something they hadn't known for a long time, if ever: real, live, loving and giving parents.

In late November, Clint and I made it official: next summer we'd be going to the Payette National Forest and the spectacularly scenic Salmon River in Idaho. And we'd be trading in our Avion Imperial for an Airstream. I'd always wanted an Airstream. I wasn't sure, though, if R.J. and Lisha would be strong enough to make the trip. As it turned out, R.J. died in February. Lisha's own battle with childhood leukemia ended in April.

We will have a new R.J. and Lisha when we set out in June—two new terminally ill orphans whom fate has dealt terrible blows.

We keep photo albums of all of our trips, of all the children we have parented, and loved, and lost. The albums keep me going until the arrival of blessed summer.

1970

SKIRTING THE ISSUE IN WEST VIRGINIA

Starkman's a good listener. Hell, I tell him things I don't even tell myself in the bathroom mirror. He has that father-confessor quality about him that opens me up just like a zippered garment bag. Sorry. I've got clothes transport on the brain. I work on the fashion floor at the Diamond. I'm a buyer in Misses Dresses, Daytime Dresses, and Furs. But on any given day you'll find me all over that floor. And this week, with our big Samsonite sale, I'm like the gorilla in that TV ad, pounding all that hard-shell luggage and all but jumping up and down on it. I swear to the ever-lovin' God of Retail that there are people who are actually buying those suitcases because of my antics, coupled with that saturation ad campaign on TV. And here's the kicker, if you don't know it already: those commercials aren't even for Samsonite! They're for "Strong Enough to Stand On" American Tourister! You've heard of collateral damage, right? This, brother, is what I call a collateral *assist*!

Speaking of monkeys, or rather monkey suits, Starkman works in the men's store on street level. He's been in men's furnishings since he came here in the early fifties. He was a different sort of man back then. He kept things to himself. Now he tells me everything, and I'm not even— what's the word the homosexuals are using now?—"gay." I'm not gay, but I listen to the details of all of his little adventures—the quickies in the men's washroom and the changing rooms and all his assignations with those bright-eyed and bushy-tailed hill-Billys and hill-Bobbys who come to the big city looking for Mr. Right. Why do I do this? I told you already: because he listens to *me*. (Let alone the fact that you'd have an easier time finding a John Bircher on college campuses these days than a heterosexual male in the retail clothing line. I'm one for Ripley's.)

Starkman and I have lunch together two, three times a week—sometimes at Blossom Dairy over on Quarrier, sometimes in the Diamond's cafeteria up on the fifth floor. Some days we even get a cheese ball and a box of crackers from the Hickory Farms Daisy Mays down in the basement and go alfresco.

We like the cafeteria, though. One of the assistant managers is a past boyfriend of Starkman's (whom Starkman likes to keep close tabs on). And, on my side, there's a cashier there that I've had my eye on for a few weeks now. I think she's ready to move beyond the flirting stage, and I'm giving the prospect some consideration, but there's the whole matter of Jillian. What to do about Jillian.

Jillian also works on the fashion floor. She's in Bridal and Maternity, which I always thought was funny and Starkman thought was a royal hoot. "I hope she spends the first half of her day in Bridal and the second in Maternity. The other way around would be downright illegitimate, don't you think?"

He's a funny old fruit, and I love him.

Jillian is twenty-two. She's married to, but presently separated from, a mountain galoot, who she says has the looks and muscular build of Willy Armitage on *Mission Impossible*, but the intellectual capacity of Sergeant Schultz on *Hogan's Heroes*.

Jillian has said she likes my looks. She says I remind her of Darrin Stephens on *Bewitched*. Not the one who's on now—the first Dick. But I wonder about this, because when we're going at it like rabbits in the mannequin storage room on the sixth floor, she's hardly ever looking at me. Apparently her Hoot 'n' Holler backwoods husband never takes her from behind and that's what she likes. That's what she craves.

"Here's what *I* need, Starkman," I said to my friend in the cafeteria yesterday. "I need management to come to their senses about this whole midi thing."

Starkman set down his coffee cup so he could gesticulate with more freedom. "Isn't it *awful*? It's like those Seventh Avenue Hebrews in New York have lost their ever-lovin' minds! I've never seen anything so hideous in all my life. Now I was never a big fan of the micro-mini like *you*, Tommy—"

"You bet I was. The thought of getting my daily peeks of panty put a smile on my mug each and every workday morning."

"You don't have to be delicate on my account, love. Peeks of panty? Peeks of pussy is more like it. You're thirty years old and you've still got the sex drive of a horny college freshman. Why else do you steal away with Jillian two, three, four times a week to make-the-beast-with-two-backs right there in front of poor Marsha and all her friends?"

"Marsha. You're talking about that what—that *Twilight Zone* episode where Anne Francis finds out she's a mannequin?"

"Beauty mark and all."

"How do you—" I lowered my voice and leaned in. We were off by ourselves at a secluded table in the cafeteria, but I was taking no chances. "How do you know where Jillian and I tryst?"

"Oh, honey, just call it by its real name. You *fornicate*. Don't you just love that word? It's so Biblical. I absolutely adore the Bible—Leviticus, especially. It's like reading pornography."

"There's a problem here, Starkman, that you probably aren't aware of."

"And that is…?"

"The midi. The midi! Granted, it's a stupid concept—taking hems down below the knee. Only a few women can pull it off. *Doris Day*. Doris Day can pull it off, because she looks good in boots. The leg is gone. I happen to be a leg man, Starkman. I miss calves. Shapely thighs? Gone with the wind, baby. Midis aren't groovy. They're the *anti*-groovy."

"Is there supposed to be a Jillian connection here?"

I nodded. "A big one. Management has issued its decree. You haven't seen the memo? Well, of course you haven't. You work in the men's store. You're a world unto yourself down there—like the Foreign Legion or something."

Starkman squirmed. "Oh, the French Foreign Legion. Yum. Cute Frenchmen in white kepis!"

"Listen to me. I'm attempting serious discourse here."

"What's the decree, Tommy?"

"The same as what's being dictated in every other department store around the country: salesgirls have to wear the midi. It's become a condition for employment. The Diamond, just like every other department store in America, bought too damn many. And women aren't having them. We pulled our entire inventory of minis, and as a result, our customers are either buying pants and pantsuits in protest or just staying the hell home. The customers aren't *cooperating*, Starkman. Doris Day or no Doris Day. Do you blame them? Put a midi skirt on most women and what's your pleasure: Mennonite housewife or female spy in a bad Russian movie?"

"I'm still waiting for the part where you and Jillian and your frequent appointments with carnality come in."

"I get turned off. I see her walking into that room looking like Natasha Fatale, and suddenly I lose my—lose my—"

"Do you lose your erection, honey? You can say it. You lose your erection. Let's say it together."

I sighed. I try not to lose my patience with Starkman when he gets flip. Because he always gets flip. He thinks he's one of those bitchy characters in *The Boys in the Band*.

"All right. I can't get it up when she wears one of those godawful skirts."

"But doesn't she take it all off once the two of you get down to business?"

"Yeah, but it's still there. She drapes it over the chair and it mocks me. It's like one of those body-smothering pelts I sell in the fur department. People are going to look back on this period and wonder how we ever survived. The Kremlin should just drop the bomb already and put us out of our misery."

"She must know that you don't care a fig for what's she's been made to wear, may our beloved management rot in fashion hell."

"Maybe she knows how I feel, maybe she doesn't. I just get the strong sense that it isn't an issue for *her*. In fact, I think she might even *like* the look. A few women do. She does, after all, have slightly larger thighs than most girls her age, and midis are pretty good at masking that. I don't know; I've tried to analyze it. When I think about it too much it becomes self-defeating in its own way."

"You mean you get flaccid at the mere thought?"

"Starkman, to be honest, I spend the *whole day* deflated. I used to love my job. I used to love to watch the women who come to our store—one of the fringe benefits of working in women's clothing. You probably don't notice such things, but we've got some gorgeous women here in Charleston. But the fashion poobahs have issued their edict, and *Women's Wear Daily* has endorsed it, and all women who want their couture sprinkled with a little hip haute must take heed. I'm thinking of changing professions, my friend. But in the short term, I'm thinking of cutting it off with Jillian. It wasn't going anywhere anyway. And as of late, she's making noises like she might want to get back together with her husband."

"So what's the rub, sir?"

"I don't know. I just—Starkman, I think there's some kind of lesson I need to be taking from all of this."

"What? The fact that you can't get it up with Jillian anymore, or the general shape of things when it comes to you and your otherwise galloping libido?"

"I don't want to be that person anymore. That, that, you know—"

"Lothario? Skirt-chaser? Roué?"

"I'm tired of following the edicts of my, you know, *dick*."

Starkman cocked his head and pulled his glasses down to regard me from over the frames. "My dear Mr. Benson, I do believe that you have finally grown to strapping, responsible manhood. This whole midi thing has been a wakeup call. You have reached the point of questioning why your pleasure center must be driven exclusively by the animal brain. I, of course, *adore* the animal brain and how it warms my cockulls—with or without the kulls—but man was given an *outer* brain too, which is supposed to emancipate him from his baser instincts. My friend Shermy and I, for example, we make passionate man-love, and then we play chess. Do you play chess? You should find a beautiful woman who does— someone who is independently minded, deliberately out of lockstep with the mandated *de rigueur*."

"And might not be so ready to toss out all of her micro-minis?"

"Precisely."

"Have you decided yet if you're going to get that slice of pie?"

"I have, Tommy. Just now, as we were giving your vacuous swinger's life a sense of purpose once more, I decided in the affirmative."

As we were returning to the cafeteria line for our just desserts, I thanked my friend Starkman for his open ear, and for his wise counsel. And he told me in sotto-voce confidentiality that he wished I had been born homosexual. That would have settled matters quite tidily.

Starkman apparently has a thing for guys who look like the husband of Samantha Stephens.

1971

BIBLIOPHILIC IN ALABAMA

Eileen stood in the doorway with her wicker beach basket in one hand and her beach towel in the other. Her chartreuse-colored, wide-brimmed beach hat, circa 1965, revealed only her nose and mouth, and it was a mouth that was turned down and petulant. "It's an absolutely beautiful morning and you're all sitting around here like the Dracula family waiting for the sun to go down."

"Give me just a minute," implored Julia, not taking her eyes from her book. "I want to get to the end of this chapter." Julia was reading the popular horror-thriller, *The Other*, by actor-turned-author Thomas Tryon. Julia kept flipping to the back of the book to look at the jacket photo. He was the best-looking author she'd ever seen.

"Donna? Michael Junior?" Eileen pointed at the beach just outside the motel window. "Are you going to make your poor grandmother sit there by herself like some lonely old lady beach bum? Michael Senior, am I speaking to a wall?"

"A what?"

"A wall, Michael."

"Of course not." Eileen's forty-three-year-old son was lying on the couch with his feet propped up on one of the two armrests. He was reading *The New Centurions* by policeman-turned-author Joseph Wambaugh.

"You're as bad as the kids," said Eileen. "You can't read your book on the beach? Come keep your mother company."

"Sure thing, Mom," said Michael Senior, slapping the book shut and kipping up from the couch. In his most authoritative father-voice he said, "Everybody out to the beach. We came to Gulf Shores for the sun and the surf. Your grandmother's right. We need to feel the grit of sand between our toes and the taste of salt water on our tongues."

"Ugh!" pronounced sixteen-year-old Julia, as her fourteen-year-old sister Donna rolled her eyes with commensurate disgust. Donna had been reading *The Exorcist* by William Peter Blatty, who used to work for the U.S. Air Force's Psychological Warfare Division after selling Electrolux vacuum cleaners and serving as ticket agent for United Airlines. Earlier in the morning Donna had, in the course of reading the horror novel, gasped—audibly—three times, but the sound had registered with no one but her grandmother, who had been sitting at the little table near the motel room's corner kitchenette, reading absolutely nothing, although she had previously skimmed an article on the front page of the Mobile paper, the *Press-Register*, about the death of Louis Armstrong. "Satchmo is gone," she had said softly and plaintively to herself, while recalling her honeymoon trip to New Orleans and all the Dixieland jazz she and her new husband had heard in the Quarter. "Lord, how I want to be in that number," she mused aloud, absently conjuring up a line from "When the Saints Go Marching In"—a song that always reminded her of the now-silenced singer and trumpeter.

Eileen looked at her two granddaughters and at her twelve-year-old grandson, Michael Junior, who was reading *The Lord of the Rings*—specifically, the volume entitled *The Two Towers*. *The Lord of the Rings* was written by J.R.R. Tolkien, who had been, early in his life, employed by the publishers of the *Oxford English Dictionary* researching words that started with W.

"Up, up, book vermin," said Michael Senior, heading off to the bedroom to change into his swimming trunks from his pajamas. "Your illiterate grandmother is feeling neglected."

Eileen allowed her beaked upper lip to disappear altogether beneath the angry bulldog protrusion of its lower companion. "I really wish you wouldn't talk about me that way in front of the children," she called after her son. "I know it's all in fun. But it's disrespectful."

Donna jumped up and shrieked. The shriek had nothing to do with what Eileen had just said.

"This is so gross!" she pronounced, tossing *The Exorcist* onto the armchair where she had been sitting, scrunched into a little ball of intense engrossment.

"Don't you dare say a word!" cried her older sister Julia. "You'll spoil it."

"You already know what it's about," called Michael Junior from the other end of the room.

"But I don't know if the priest will succeed in getting the devil out of the girl or not. We live in a literary era in which there is no longer the guarantee of a happy ending."

"It'd be really cool if he couldn't do it and then ol' Beelzebub goes and possesses the soul of everybody in Washington—even President Nixon!" said Michael Junior, who had gotten very sunburned the day before reading on the hood of his family's station wagon and was now covered with globules of white healing salve.

"Put down the books, kids. We're all going to the beach," said Michael Senior, "and we're going to build sandcastles and play in the waves and pretend to be a totally ambulatory, nearly normal American family. We're all being very rude to your grandmother. She came all the way down here to spend time with us and look how we're treating her."

"I'm sorry we're being so rude, Grandma," said Julia, who got up from her fold-out cot to put her arms around her grandmother's waist.

"I'm not against reading." Eileen returned the hug. "I just think you're all missing out on the best part of being on vacation—getting out, *doing* things. Michael, honey, weren't you going to drive Mike over to the fort?"

"Sure. If he wants to see it. You want to see Fort Morgan, champ?"

"That'd be neat." The enthusiasm in the words was only marginally reflected in the manner of their delivery.

Michael Senior clapped his hands together. "Okay, and this afternoon, you kids are going over to the Hangout and play some Skee-Ball, and then we'll have hamburgers at the Pink Pony Pub, and…"

Eileen sighed. She exchanged a look of frustration with her son. Michael Junior was back in Middle-earth. Julia had returned to *The Other*, and her younger sister, Donna, was creeping warily up to the temporarily abandoned *Exorcist* as if it were something to be conquered through dint of will and intestinal fortitude. Donna had been told by her friend, Sherell, who had already read the book, that there was projectile vomiting in there.

Everyone took to the waters for a few minutes at least and allowed the surf to knock them off their feet—for a bit. Michael Junior tried to build a sandcastle and ended up with a sand hogan with no windows. And later, just as their father had ordered, there were greasy vacation hamburgers at the Pink Pony Pub, and Skee-Ball at the Hangout, and all the tickets dispensed by the old-fashioned Skee-Ball bowling machines were pooled and redeemed for a plastic Hawaiian hula dancer, and this went to Donna because her wildly bowled wooden ball had hit a Coca-Cola clock and knocked the minute hand off and she had been mortified with embarrassment.

That night Michael Senior and his mother, Eileen, and his three children, whose mother lived in London with her second husband, a network television news correspondent, ate fried shrimp and crab claws at the Sea-n-Suds restaurant down the beach from their motel. Each of the three offspring of Michael Cameron tried their best to be glib and engaging at the table, as dinner conversation meandered from New Orleans and the late, great Louis Armstrong to the subject of Jim Morrison, the lead singer for the rock-and-roll band The Doors, who only a few days earlier had been found dead at the young age of twenty-seven in his bathtub. Michael Senior had not been familiar with the details of Mr. Morrison's untimely demise, the actual cause still open to speculation, while Eileen Cameron was unclear as to whom Jim Morrison even *was*, and wondered if he'd ever played the trumpet or sang in a phlegmy voice like Louis.

"And you say *we're* the ones the world is passing by!" proclaimed Julia, her palms up and open in the universal gesture for "so there!"

Eileen began to butter her dinner roll with hard strokes. "I thought one of the reasons for this trip was to get you kids out and interacting with other young people. Why, just last night there was a big weenie roast on the beach, and none of you seemed the least bit interested."

"It wasn't groovy enough for us," replied Donna with gentle sarcasm. "Are you ashamed of us, Grandma? It sounds like you're ashamed of us."

"Of course I'm not! I just wish—oh, pooh. Forget I brought it up. I know my place in this family. As soon as we get back to the motel room, I'm going to pull out my new Miss Marple, and you won't hear another peep out of me." Eileen took a bite of her roll and then began chewing while staring sulkily at the ceiling.

"We didn't mean to upset you, Grandma," said Julia as she placed a conciliatory hand on her grandmother's arm.

Michael Junior's expression now turned solemn. "The old that is strong does not wither. Deep roots are not reached by frost." Michael Junior enjoyed quoting J.R.R. Tolkien whenever a relevant opportunity presented itself.

"How are the hush puppies, sport?" asked Michael Senior, plucking a puppy off his son's plate. "Yum," he said, answering his own question.

*

The Cameron family did not return to the Seahorse Motel. They strolled to the end of a nearby pier and gazed down upon the reflection of the moon on the water. They waited for feelings to come to them that did not derive from the pages of books.

The Camerons weren't alone; a man and woman were there as well. Perhaps they were in their twenties. Perhaps they were on their honeymoon. The woman was sitting on the flat top of the wooden railing, in front of her boyfriend—or husband—who was holding her loosely around the waist from behind. The couple had greeted the Camerons with polite smiles and then returned to their close-contact moonlit cooing.

A moment or so later the woman cried out in pain. "Something's biting me! Something's biting me!" She slapped at her left thigh. Then she jumped to one side so that the clinch with the young man was broken. Then the woman cried, "Ooh! Ooh!" and began jerking and wriggling as if the thing biting her was intensifying its attack. In the midst of all the jumping and squirming the woman lost her balance upon the railing and toppled from the pier.

She fell, screaming all the way down, and hit the dark, swishing water below with an audible smack. Her young companion peered over the rail and then turned and looked at the middle-aged man and the three adolescent children and the mature woman who comprised the Michael Cameron family of Lexington, Kentucky, each member appearing to the distressed man just as horrified by what they had just witnessed as he appeared to them. "She can't swim!" he announced in a terrified voice. "And neither can I!"

A moment later, all of the Camerons, with the exception of Eileen, who though strong and unwithered did not find herself so motivated, sprang into action. In fast succession they slipped off their shoes and leapt from the pier—one, two, three, four—from the opposite side, each allowing sufficient space between them so as to avoid landing upon a fellow family member and inviting additional complications. It was Michael Senior who hit the water closest to the drowning young woman and who employed the lifesaving technique he had read about as a teenager in *The Red Cross Lifesaving and Water Safety Manual*. He received encouragement and support from his three children, who tossed sloshy words of counsel to the young woman along the lines of "You're okay," "Calm down," and "Stop struggling, he's got you," and the literary, though somewhat incongruous, "All's well that ends well."

With the young woman dragged to shore and laid out upon the wet sand, Julia cleared the water from the victim's lungs in a manner she was familiar with from having read about such near-drowning episodes in at least three different novels, one of which led its characters—a lifeguard and office receptionist on holiday—into a serious, long-term Harlequin romance. The operation was so successful that it wasn't even necessary to take the woman to the hospital. It remained a mystery what had bitten her on the thigh, although Michael Junior surmised that it was probably an insomniac sandfly, which he had read about in a book entitled *Predators of the Littoral Regions of North America*.

"I don't know how to thank you," said the woman's boyfriend—or husband—who shook the hands of all the Camerons, including that of the morally supportive grandmother. Eileen felt a burst of family pride that put a long-lived smile upon her face. The young woman was grateful as well, though shaken up and distracted by the itch of the causal bites.

The Camerons returned to their motel room after a long walk on the beach and a lively group recap of their thrilling accomplishment—a team effort, a family activity that diminished all others by comparison.

This was much better than a weenie roast.

After hot showers and the donning of robes and bedclothes, each of the children and their father curled up or spread out—such as the case was—with a book. Michael Senior put down *The New Centurions* and picked up *The Underground Man*, the latest of Ross Macdonald's hardboiled Lew Archer detective novels. Julia returned to *The Other*, while her sister Donna, with fresh groans and assorted expressions of distaste and disgust, revisited the Satan-sanctioned assaults upon the dignity of fathers Merrin and Karras. Michael Junior renewed his affiliation with Frodo Baggins; Frodo's cousins Pip and Merry; the wizard Gandalf; and Legolas, son of King Thranduil.

Eileen, wearing her nightgown and drinking Postum, because it usually made her sleepy, sat at the table in the room's corner kitchenette with the volume on her radio turned low, listening to Louis Armstrong sing "Do You Know What It Means to Miss New Orleans," and then, perhaps because the DJ wanted to lighten the funereal mood, "Jeepers Creepers." Halfway through the song, she happened to look over at her son. He was holding apart the lids and lower folds of skin beneath his eyes to give himself a goggly look in comical reference to the "peepers" part of the song.

Eileen laughed and waved at him to stop. Michael returned to his book.

A sea-scented breeze ruffled the curtain of the open window next to her as night quietly settled in.

1972

PRECIPITATE IN ILLINOIS

Elsie had never seen so much rain in all of her fifty-eight years. It was as if a great spigot had been opened up over Waukegan and nobody knew how to turn it off. Elsie had almost talked herself out of driving to the mall that afternoon because of the weather, but had finally decided to make the two-mile trip because if she hadn't, she was quite certain she would soon find herself climbing the walls of her new apartment like some caged primate at the zoo.

It had been three weeks since Elsie Thompson's arrival in Waukegan. Her son had talked her into selling her house in Muncie—the house she had owned with her husband until his untimely death six months earlier— talked her into leaving her friends and her church and the familiarity of the town where she had spent all of her adult years. Her son thought she would benefit from living near her only child and her only two grandchildren. So he found Elsie a clean and quiet apartment in this town of industry and cool lake breezes and a great big enclosed mall for her shopping convenience. The Lakehurst. The one with the seagull on the sign.

Elsie didn't need much convincing. She *did* want to be near her son, who designed pinball machines in Waukegan, and her daughter-in-law, who taught school in nearby Gurnee, and her two granddaughters, who, at eight and eleven, were just the right ages to appreciate having a loving and doting grandmother close by. Hers was the familiar story of a woman set adrift by sudden widowhood and finding comfort in those loving family members who also remained behind—comfort that was sometimes coupled with sheer, stultifying boredom.

That night on Eyewitness News, the weatherman would report that four inches had fallen on Waukegan, Illinois, that day—a record. Four inches of rain, which collected into myriad puddles and opportunistic ponds in the middle of traffic intersections—shallow lakes, really, so large that Elsie was given to wonder, as her car skidded and splashed and pontooned through them, if nearby Lake Michigan was expanding its shoreline one block of Waukegan at a time.

As Elsie pulled into the large parking lot that encircled the mall (except for one soggy empty field on the south side where, it was hoped, a Sears or Montgomery Ward would eventually go), she was disappointed to discover that thousands of others had also ventured out on this waterlogged Tuesday. In 1972, enclosed shopping malls were still things of relative novelty and innovation. To think that one could now go to a place protected from all the elements and shop for as long as one's heart desired (or at least for as long as one's legs held out)—whatever would these enterprising retailers think of next?

Elsie shook the rain from her umbrella and sought out an unoccupied bench where she could shrug off her raincoat and remove her galoshes to her big plastic carrying bag. Once properly prepared for her afternoon of shopping, she began her exploration of this bright, shiny, modern mall, dry and comfortable and in the perfect frame of mind.

Elsie wandered without purpose. She window-shopped and aisle-browsed. Betty's of Winnetka was having a sale on beachwear, and Chas A. Stevens bragged in big, bold letters about its large inventory of summer sandals, and there were brand new futuristic microwave ovens in the appliance section of Wiebolts for only six hundred dollars. Elsie had a scoop of chocolate mint ice cream at Bresler's, chocolate mint being one of the chain's thirty-three advertised flavors. She tried on a pair of white crinkle-vinyl knee-high boots at Thom McAn and couldn't keep herself from giggling when the salesman sang a couple of lines from "These Boots Are Made for Walking." She even found the courage to steal into the clanging, pinging semi-dark interior of Aladdin's Castle to see one of the pinball machines her son had designed. She identified "Haunted Cemetery" immediately.

Elsie eventually found herself in Carson Pirie Scott & Company, one of the mall's three anchor department stores. She had once visited Carson's flagship store on State Street in Chicago, and wondered if the suburban version would feel as elegant. She was struck by the large contemporary light display above the escalators—great concentric circles of exposed bulbs throwing off muted luminosity in all directions.

As Elsie moved through the store, her interest in the merchandise that surrounded her receded and she began to study the people instead: mothers with preschool children, girlfriends perhaps enjoying a companionable weekly shopping excursion, teenagers lolling away their summer vacation. There were only a few men in the department store, and they were mostly fastidious, nattily suited salesmen. One of the exceptions was a man who looked to be in his early forties. His trench coat was partially unbuttoned and still wet from the rain. The man was slightly overweight. His face was flushed and a little bloated, his hairline retreating. Elsie wondered if he was there on his lunch hour. Perhaps he was picking up an anniversary gift for his wife, since both Elsie and the man were situated in one of the store's women's departments. He did seem, after all, to be looking for something…or some*one*.

Nearby was a little girl. Perhaps she was four. Elsie looked about for the mother. Where was she? Behind that clothing rack? On the other side of that display? Elsie would never have allowed her son out of her sight in a public place at that age.

The man was near the girl. He was looking at her now. Now he was moving toward her. In a brief moment he was crouching down to say something to her. Was it her father? Or her grandfather? If so, why had *he* left her, even for a minute or two? How could people be so irresponsible?

The man was saying something and the little girl was nodding. The man pulled a bag from his coat. He offered the bag to the little girl. What was in the bag? Elsie couldn't tell.

She felt intrusive, staring at the man and little girl like this. Yet something didn't seem right: the way he was looking around, as if attempting to detect if he was being watched. Had he stolen what was in the little bag? Was he a shoplifter? Elsie turned away. She didn't want the man to see her looking at him. When she turned back around, the man and the little girl were gone.

She thought about what she had seen. She walked over to where the man had crouched down in front of the little girl. Just when she thought she had lost them, Elsie caught sight of the man's head bobbing above a rack of sundresses. Elsie picked up her pace. As the man moved out into one of the wider aisles, she noticed the little girl walking next to him. He was holding her hand. The little girl was smiling, all of her attention on pulling something from the bag and putting it into her mouth. She was preoccupied with the act of eating the candy, or whatever it was, and did not seem to be concerned much with who was walking next to her and holding her hand.

Elsie thought she would approach the man to set her mind at ease. Yet what would she say? If he were her father or grandfather, he would not take kindly to her suspicions that he was someone else—someone who had no business taking the little girl by the hand and leading her away.

Elsie didn't know what to do, except to follow—to keep her distance, but to trail the man and the little girl. This she did for a minute or so, until the man and girl left the store and moved out onto the mall concourse.

Now Elsie thought that perhaps the best thing to do to assuage her fears was to go back to the spot in the store where the little girl had been and see if there was someone in the vicinity who was looking for a lost girl.

Yet this was supposing the worst. It was supposing something Elsie could scarcely bring herself to think. And there was a problem with this course of action: if the child was—she would make herself *think* it because the gravity of the situation required her courage—if the child was, in fact, being abducted by the man in the wet trench coat, though it was all well and good that the mother should be informed, what a terrible risk she would be taking in allowing the man and the girl out of her sight. Would she be able to catch up with them? What if they disappeared into the crowd of rainy-day shoppers and couldn't be found again?

Elsie decided that she must continue to follow. She *would* follow. She would watch to see where the man went. She would seek out someone who could help her. She wished she wasn't new to this town. At the shopping center she frequented in Muncie she was always bumping into people she knew. Perhaps she would get lucky and chance upon a security guard. There had to be security guards in a mall like this.

The man and little girl passed a gift shop, then a men's clothing store. The man didn't look at the display windows. He didn't look at any of the passing shoppers. He walked briskly, and the little girl had to trot to keep up with him. She dropped her bag of candy. He stopped and picked it up for her. Elsie hadn't had a chance to study the girl's face until now, and with the face now turned slightly in her direction, she saw something that greatly disturbed her. The little girl looked frightened. She looked confused. The little girl held tight to her rescued bag of candy with her right hand; her left remained within the tight clasp of the stranger's hand. Elsie's heart skipped a beat. The little girl was being kidnapped. Elsie was sure of it now. Something inside her made her want to point and shout to enlist the assistance of everyone around her to stop him. But how would she make her accusation? What words would she use? Elsie was paralyzed even as her feet kept moving.

A moment later she caught sight of a pay phone out of the corner of her eye. It was affixed to a wall down a small corridor off the concourse. She could call the police. This is what Elsie could do. She would have to take her eyes off the man and the girl for a brief moment. It would be risky; there was the chance she might lose sight of them. And how would the police, once they arrived, find the man and the girl? The mall was large, the parking lot even larger, and the lot was now dark under a cover of heavy rain, its mercury vapor lamps doing little but casting an eerie glow over the great expanse of empty, parked cars. Even if she dared to make the call, there was a teenaged girl on the phone. How long would it take to convince this girl of the magnitude of her emergency? How much time would Elsie lose in wresting the phone from the chatty girl? Elsie abandoned this idea.

The three were approaching the mall's center court now. There was a circular fountain there. Hanging from the ceiling was a large silver-colored revolving mobile. The man and girl moved quickly through the center court, headed toward the nearest exit. Elsie felt the words rising in her throat: "Stop that man!" She felt the words fly from her mouth: "That man! Don't let that man get away!" She pointed at the man just as he was passing a group of adolescents splashing each other at the fountain. Those who noticed observed a troubled woman pointing in the direction of clowning, misbehaving teenagers. Was she warning them against the possibility of falling in? Was she scolding them for their bad behavior? One could only guess, because the words of her desperate plea were swallowed up in the acoustics of the large space, their clarity erased by the echoic hum and thrum of the song playing over the mall's loud speakers: "The Candy Man," sung by Sammy Davis Jr., recipient of nearly constant airplay that month.

Elsie couldn't hear the song's words. She couldn't even hear her own voice, although there was someone who did: the candy man. He stopped. He turned and gave her a hard stare—stared at the woman who was not in fact dressing down the playful kids at the fountain—the woman who had the audacity to try to call attention to him.

For a tense moment, Elsie and the man traded cold, freighted looks. Elsie prayed that the man would simply let go of the little girl's hand and run away.

Yet he did not.

There erupted now an expression of angry defiance upon his hard face. Without taking his eyes off Elsie, he yanked the little girl toward him, wrenching her tiny wrist, her eyes wild with terror. She dropped her bag of candy, some of the pieces scattering upon the tiled floor of the center court. Elsie couldn't hear the little girl's cry but she could see the fear in her face.

Now the man was running. He was running as the crying girl tripped and stumbled behind him, still a prisoner to the fate he had chosen for her. Elsie began to run, too.

A salesman was standing outside of Florsheim Shoes on the concourse, smoking a cigarette. This man was watching the other man tearing through the mall's center court, nearly dragging a little girl behind him. He was watching Elsie chasing after the two of them. His gaze caught hers.

"Help me," she mouthed.

The man ran inside and directed one of the other salesmen to call security. Then he raced out of the store.

The abductor was near one of the doors to the parking lot now. The rain was coming down in wimpling sheets, rattling its glass pane. The abductor pushed the door open. The wind seized the door and slammed it shut again. The man fought against the wind with one hand and against the struggles of the little girl with his other hand. Elsie reached the man. She threw herself upon him, maniacal, hating him for what he sought to do, hating him as well for what he had put *her* through. The man fended her blows. He dropped the hand of the little girl, who started to run away, but was caught by the Florsheim shoe salesman.

The abductor pushed Elsie away from him. She stumbled backward. He shoved the door open with both hands and went out. Elsie watched as he disappeared into the billowing blankets of rain. A flash of lightning gave Elsie her final glimpse of the man—less a man now than something umbral and hulking and monstrous scuttling between the cars. She turned back to the shoe salesman. "Go after him. Stop him."

The salesman shook his head. "Catch in my knee," he said, rubbing his right kneecap. The girl was next to him. The shoe salesman wasn't holding her hand but she stood close to him. The girl seemed to know that both he and the older woman coming toward her were there to help her. Still, she wept hysterical tears. The girl allowed Elsie to reach down and embrace her, lovingly, protectively.

"Security's on its way," said the salesman, glancing over his shoulder.

"They won't find him," said Elsie above the sound of the little girl's sobs.

Sammy Davis Jr. was singing about separating the sorrow and collecting up all the cream. The shoe salesman, a young man with long black sideburns and a modified Afro, led Elsie and the little girl, from whom was coaxed the name Lucinda, back to his store. Across the center court, the robustious kids had retrieved the bag of candy from the floor. They passed it back and forth, chewing the soft caramels inside.

Minutes later, the distraught mother of little Lucinda arrived, accompanied by two security guards. She had been looking all over for her little girl. She tearfully thanked Elsie for having found her.

Elsie spent the next day alone in her new apartment. She wanted to be bored. She would have been glad on this day to be very, very bored. But there was too much to remember, too much to play over and over in her head. And there was one thought in particular that held her hostage: *he was still out there.*

1973

VENGEFUL IN MARYLAND

The two women sat in the front seat and the two boys in the back seat. The woman behind the wheel, Darva, smoked a cigarette until her friend Camelia asked her to put it out. The smoke, she said, was injurious to her son's formative lungs. She added, almost as an afterthought, that it was, no doubt, damaging the lungs of Darva's boy as well.

It was below freezing outside—too cold to leave a window down.

"There. I'm putting it out, Cammy," said Darva. "Stop waving your arms. What's that supposed to do?"

Camelia stopped waving her arms. She turned around and looked at her eleven-year-old son, Garrett. He was talking to Darva's eleven-year-old, Kyle. He was telling Kyle about his action figure—the one standing on his knee, poised for action. Its name was Torpedo Fist. According to Garrett, Torpedo Fist used to be a Navy pilot, but he lost his right arm fighting a shark off the coast of Ceylon. Some local Ceylonese fishermen came to his rescue, and then he got a new arm that was telescopic and cybernetic. The arm sprang into action each time Garrett pushed a button on Torpedo Fist's muscular back.

"He's the only P.A.C.K. team member with superhuman powers," said Garrett in answer to a question that nobody asked.

"He's a fag," said Kyle, punching numbers into his HP-35 scientific calculator, which his father had just gotten him for his birthday. "And get that fag doll out of my face," added Kyle.

"He isn't a doll," said Garrett in a small, defeated voice.

"Yeah, he is. And he's wearing a faggot cap and a stripey faggot shirt." Then, when it appeared that Kyle had said everything that he was going to say on the subject, he appended, "And *you're* a fag."

Camelia turned to look at her friend behind the wheel. "Are you going to say anything to your son, Darva?"

Darva turned around. "Kyle, don't call people names—especially your friends."

Kyle couldn't be bothered to look up. He was making the numbers on his upside down calculator spell the word "BOOBIES." "He isn't my friend. He's the son of *your* friend."

"I thought you boys liked each other," said Camelia.

Kyle didn't answer. Garrett kept quiet.

The car in front of Darva's Coppertone Buick Electra pulled forward about a car length. Darva engaged the ignition, applied slight pressure to her accelerator, and moved her car forward an equal distance. Then she turned off the ignition.

"Why don't you let it idle?" asked Camelia. "You probably use more gas turning it on and off like that."

"That isn't what Doyle says. Kyle, tell Mrs. Holley what your Uncle Doyle, who owns his own auto repair shop—tell Mrs. Holley what Uncle Doyle says about idling for thirty minutes to an hour in a long gas line."

"For every minute a car idles," said Kyle in a voice that was half instructional and half smartass, "it uses the same amount of fuel it takes to go a mile. Idling for too long can damage your engine. It leads to a buildup of fuel residue on your cylinder walls."

Camelia sighed exasperatedly. "But, Darva, you must have turned your car on and off ten times since we got in this line. That can't be good for fuel economy either."

Kyle didn't wait for prompting by his mother. Without lifting his eyes from his calculator he continued: "My uncle says that if you're stopped for more time than it takes to sit at a traffic light, you should shut off your engine. It uses less gas to turn it back on than it does to let it idle."

"Kow! Pow!" said Camelia's son Garrett, who was employing his action figure's superhuman fist to vanquish all manner of imagined enemies.

"Fag," said Kyle under his breath as he punched in the numbers 7,7,3 and 4 to give the word "hell" upside down. His father had paid almost four hundred dollars for the calculator. It was just one of the many expensive gifts that Kyle's dad, divorced from Kyle's mother for the last two years, had bought his son.

A silence passed, disturbed only by the occasional honk of a horn and somebody shouting something at somebody else. All in all, though, the motorists in today's gas line—which extended for several blocks down the northbound lane of York Road, in Towson—were fairly well-behaved. There had been no fistfights today, no altercations with the gas station attendants, no frustration-fueled assaults on the pumps with ball-peen hammers. There was just the agonizing, interminable wait. The Chinese water torture stop and start. The silent cursing of OPEC and the oil companies (who were surely somehow playing this gas shortage to their own advantage). The angry look of the attendant when you asked for a top-off. Which was exactly what Darva wanted. She had three-fifths of a tank of gas already but she wanted it full. For peace of mind, everybody wanted it full.

Darva wished that Kyle and Garrett's karate lessons were closer to her house. But at least the dojo was near the mall, and today she and Camelia could finish their Christmas shopping while the boys were chopping and bowing.

Then, as if out of the blue, Camelia gulped. It was very vocal, like the kind of noisy gulp that sitcom characters make.

"What is it?" asked Darva. "What's the matter?"

Even Kyle looked up.

"Behind us. In that Mustang."

"Who? Who's in the Mustang?"

Darva tilted her rearview mirror to get a better look. The boys turned around as well, so that all eyes fell upon a 1973 ketchup-red Ford Mustang convertible with the top up and a twenty-something blonde in the driver's seat.

Darva whipped around to get a better look out the back window. "It's *his* car." She squinted, then nodded. "It's her. I think. Kyle, is that your stepmother?"

"It looks like her."

Camelia tutted and shook her head. "What's she doing with Dave's car? I thought Dave left her."

"I did too. Kyle, do you know why your stepmother is driving your father's Mustang? Have they gotten back together again?"

Kyle hunched his shoulders into a modified shrug.

"What do you know that you're not telling me? Put down the calculator. What has your father done? Has he gone back to her?"

"I don't know, Mom."

"You see him every weekend. Does she come over? Do they talk on the phone?"

"Kow! Pow!" said Garrett, who was using Torpedo Fist's enlarged hand to pound the folds of his gi.

"Garrett, shut up!" shouted Camelia. "Move forward, Darva."

Darva turned the key in the ignition and rolled the Electra forward to fill in the space that had just opened in front of her.

"Has he gone back to her, Kyle?" asked Darva, turning off the ignition. "Your father told me they were getting a divorce. He told me they were incompatible. Does he still love her? Do you know the answers to any of these questions?"

"Mom, I don't want to talk about it."

The Mustang pulled forward.

"If there's something that your father has shared with you that you're deliberately not telling me, I'm going to ground you for a month. And I'm taking away all of your expensive gadgets."

"This isn't a gadget, Mom. It's a calculating device."

"Did he or did he not move back in with her?"

Kyle looked into his mother's angry eyes. There was hurt there as well. The hurt was taking the place of the hope. Hope for a reconciliation. Hope that Darva and Kyle's father would remarry and things would go back to the way they were before Darva's world fell apart.

"Everybody turn back around," said Camelia. "She sees us all looking at her."

But Darva wasn't looking at the woman in the Mustang. Her eyes were focused on her son. "He told me that the marriage wasn't working. He took me to Lexington Market. We had Faidley's crab cakes and he told me it was over. He was going to divorce her. This is what he told me. Did your father lie to me?"

Kyle nodded.

"That son of a bitch," Darva muttered. She settled her head on the steering wheel, then a moment later jerked it back up. "I don't blame her. She's just looking out for herself. I blame *him*. He lied to me." Then louder, the next words directed to her son: "Your son-of-a-bitch father lied to me."

"He didn't *really* lie, Mom. He wanted to leave her. Honest. But he couldn't."

"Why? *Why?*"

"Because she's going to have a baby."

Camelia pointed. A new space had just opened up in front of Darva's car. Darva needed to pull up. "You need to pull up, Darva."

"I'm not going to pull up," said Darva, her jaw clenched, her teeth locked. "I'm tired of moving forward by inches. I'm tired of topping off. I'm tired of being the only casualty in this family. Give me that goddamned calculator."

Kyle shook his head.

"You need to pull up, Darva," said Camelia. "People will start honking."

Darva twisted around in her seat. She yanked the calculator out of Kyle's hand. She rolled down her window and tossed it out of the car. Kyle stared at his mother in horror.

Then Darva turned the key in the ignition. She put the car in gear. A new gear. Reverse. She gunned the accelerator and slammed the Electra into the front of her husband's ketchup-red Mustang convertible with the second wife—the pregnant second wife—inside. Darva put the car in drive, jumped it forward and then immediately back into reverse so she could ram her husband's car again.

The new wife screamed, the sound muffled by the closed windows. She pounded the horn futilely. Camelia's hands flailed at her friend with equal uselessness. People began to jump out of their parked or idling vehicles to intercede—to stop this madwoman from further destruction.

Darva was brought to her senses.

That night, Darva Johnson made the local news. "It just got to be too much for her and she snapped," said her sympathetic and helpfully misinformative friend Camelia Holley, when the news reporter shoved the microphone in her face. "The waiting and the waiting. She just lost it."

There was no mention of the identity of the woman in the deeply dented Mustang. The true story of Darva's descent into temporary madness remained, at least for the present, a well-kept secret.

1974

VICINAL IN TENNESSEE

To borrow from the Bard (with sincere apologies): "Some are born fans of Elvis, some achieve an appreciation of Elvis, and some have Elvis thrust upon them." I fall into the last camp.

I grew up in the mid-century suburban Memphis neighborhood of Hickory Hills in a community called Whitehaven. It was called Whitehaven not because of the fact that it was originally a "whites only" residential suburb (and years later became a largely African American community, making the name more than a little ironic), but because a man by the name of Colonel Francis White owned most of the original property out of which Whitehaven was created.

Graceland was there. Upon that 13.8-acre estate in the year 1939 was built the most recognizable white-columned mansion since Tara. (Given the year of the house's construction, its original owners, the Moores, could very well have been influenced by the movie adaptation of Margaret Mitchell's classic.) Elvis bought the house in the late fifties. Shortly thereafter, my parents built their own far-smaller domicile in the subdivision that sprang up around the house. All of our neighbors across the street used the stone and brick walls encompassing Elvis's impressive demesne for their own rear fencing.

To put it in medieval terms, ours were the serf cottages that looked up at the castle of the King. (Of Rock and Roll.)

I attended elementary school with Elvis's stepbrothers. They had reputations for being rowdy boys, and my mother made me decline their invitations to come swim in Elvis's pool. The closest I ever came to entering the hallowed grounds of Graceland was climbing the wall in a friend's backyard and peering over. I remember scaling this wall in a different spot shortly after Elvis's death. I watched the pageant of mourners snaking up the driveway to view the body. It was an assemblage fit for a head of state. Film-history buff that I was, I couldn't help comparing the turnout to the ridiculously overattended viewing of the body of Rudolph Valentino.

There were great tears and much fainting.

No, I never got to swim in Elvis's pool, though he often rode his motorcycle up and down our street and gave the neighborhood kids—the progeny of the serfs, if you will—a noblesse-neighborly wave.

And on July 12, 1974, I spent an evening with Elvis. I shared the experience with my twin brother Clay.

Coincidentally, it was our birthday.

My sharp recollection of that summer is marked by three enduring memories, all having to do with the movie theatre where Clay and I worked as ushers and general factotums.

1) I ate popcorn. All summer. I never tired of it, because I made it just the way I liked it. I was forever chastised by the manager of the multiplex, Mr. Humphries, for not oversalting it. Oversalted popcorn sold at movie theatres is good for business; it's supposed to make the customers thirsty so they'll want to buy sodas. (Or "cokes," as we called pop and soda in Memphis, regardless of whether it was actually a Coca-Cola or some entirely different brand of soft drink.) I didn't care. Like the koala bear and his eucalypt leaves, popcorn was my mainstay throughout the summer of 1974. And I popped it to suit my own tastebuds.

2) President Nixon's resignation speech. A political junkie at a young age, I was unhappy to discover that Nixon's televised speech announcing that he would resign the presidency the next day was scheduled to be delivered while I was working the evening shift. Mr. Humphries took pity on me and allowed me to take my break at 8:00 and watch the address upstairs alongside the projectionist on his portable black-and-white TV. I have forgotten the name of the man with whom I shared this historic moment, but not his political affiliation. He was no fan of the thirty-seventh U.S. president and hurled frequent animadversions at the televised image of that "goddamned son-of-a-bitch" who would soon be departing, and "none too soon, the lousy crook bastard."

3) Then there was the night of earlier mention that I spent with Elvis, my brother Clay, and all the other monkey-suited male ushers and teenaged candy-counter girls who agreed to stay on after public operating hours ended so that we could help host Elvis's wee-hour private movie party.

Elvis liked to do this every now and then: arrange with this particular suburban multiplex to rent out the whole shebang for the balance of the night, and bring along a few friends and family members for company.

Clay and I called home: "Hi, Mama. Elvis is coming to the theatre tonight. See you at breakfast."

What did Elvis and his troop watch that night? Two fairly underwhelming movies. The first was called *Macon County Line*. It was a low-budget indy written and produced by Max Baer Jr., more familiarly known at the time as an erstwhile Beverly Hillbilly. The movie told the story of a deadly road trip taken by two U.S. Army-bound brothers in the redneck South. Elvis enjoyed this one.

The second film selected by the King to round out the evening's double feature was a George Segal sci-fi stinker called *The Terminal Man*, about a brilliant but dangerously epileptic computer programmer. Elvis slept through this one. I know this because Clay and I—and several other ushers and candy-counter girls, including my own girlfriend Jerri, sat behind him. Just before the movie, Mr. Humphries had asked Jerri if she'd ever dreamed of being kissed by Elvis. Jerri was cute and unquestionably kissable. When she had bashfully answered in the affirmative (Jerri told me later that her mother, who had once flown all the way to Vegas to see Elvis on stage, would have killed her if she hadn't been receptive), Elvis leaned in and gave Jerri a chaste peck on the lips.

Elvis drank.

We were under strict orders not to reveal this fact, since it would undercut the clean-cut image that Elvis's handlers, even in this late season of his life, still wished to put across to the Elvis-worshipping public. And so we all kept dutifully mum. Elvis is human, I thought. What's the big deal?

Elvis was pissed.

At one point in the evening he decided to don the mantle of moral authority and reprimand one of his entourage for either maliciously or mischievously pulling up yard signs (and getting caught) during this, a fairly contentious city primary season.

We were ordered not to speak of Elvis's temper. Elvis has a temper, I thought. Who doesn't?

The evening ended just as the sun began to rise over the mall. Elvis and his sleepy entourage headed back to Graceland, a couple of miles from the theatre, and Clay and I slid into our parents' mammoth green Pontiac station wagon and drove back to our "outer" Graceland hovel, having enjoyed our evening of close proximity to superstardom.

These were the times that I felt the strongest connection to my twin brother Clay. It had been a great summer for him too. If one's eighteenth birthday marks the passage from adolescence to adulthood, then this was the summer—indeed, this was the very night—that Clay and I made that all-important transition.

There are ironies here. Sad ironies. The fact that like me, Elvis was also a twin. His own brother, Jessie, had preceded Elvis by thirty-five minutes but was stillborn. I was also born second, and like Elvis, I also lost my older twin brother. Clay died Christmas week of 2006 of an accidental prescription drug overdose.

Elvis may have wondered what his life could have been like with a twin brother taking the journey alongside him. I didn't have to wonder. Twindom is a queer phenomenon. One goes through life as both an individual and as part of a couple, for even those twins who allow competition or jealousy to poison their relationship cannot deny the kind of bond that in truth can never really be severed.

Even in death.

I often think back on that night in 1974 when my brother and I turned eighteen, when Clay was well on his way to becoming the funny, gregarious hail fellow well met whom he'd be for most of his life. Because that night wasn't just about Elvis. It was about two men, both of whom embraced life with gusto, until life tripped them up and ultimately betrayed them. Both Elvis Presley and my brother Clay met sad ends abetted by serious drug addiction.

Tens of millions the world over mourned the death of Elvis Presley. I saw only a small fraction of them on the sprawling front lawn of Graceland the week of his demise in 1977, but the crowds that turned out were vocal and communal in their bereavement. When Clay died, there were far fewer to mourn his passing.

Several years later, I continue to mourn my brother and to think about him.

Clay was born with a black eye. We joked that it was my fetal fist that delivered the punch. "You boys were fighting with each other even before you were born," our harried mother quipped. And we did fight. All brothers fight. But not in those first few hours of our nineteenth year on this Earth, when the world was suddenly everything it could possibly be and life held every imaginable promise.

Jerri had been kissed by the King of Rock and Roll. And the King had shown that he could drink and cuss like all the rest of us. And George Segal demonstrated that even a good actor can sometimes be hampered by a bad script.

And did I mention how damned good the popcorn was that night?

Clay and I were all smiles on the short drive to Hickory Hills. Once we got home it was hard to sleep. But we had to get *some* shuteye. Our work schedules called for us to report back to the theatre at noon.

Life goes on—at least for as long as fate allows.

1975

PHYSICALLY CANDID IN LOUISIANA

Jake and I had never done any work in the Fairfield/Highland neighborhood before—I mean after I started my own construction company. I'd worked on a couple of remodels there for two other outfits, but this was my first job in the neighborhood since striking out on my own. The house was on Herndon and it belonged to Henry Badeaux, who was well known in both Shreveport and Bossier City.

I figured it was going to be a good three-day job: first day to pull up the old brick terrace that looked to be about a hundred years old from its crumbling condition; then day two lay in a new foundation, and day three put in a new paver patio. I asked Badeaux why he wanted to go with an itty-bitty company like mine (it's just me and Jake and sometimes my boy, Kit, on the weekends, and then there's my hardworking wife Theresa in the office). He said he was drawn to my ad in the Yellow Pages. How do you like that? That little turtle with a toolbelt that my artistically gifted teenage son had drawn for us actually landed us a decent-sized job! And a decent-sized job in old-money Shreveport, for crying out loud.

It was the maid, Callie, who was there the first couple of days we worked. She brought us lemonade (this being Shreveport, and October in Shreveport being just as hot and muggy sometimes as August), and even served us lunch. Every now and then I'd catch her peeking out at us through the utility room window, I guess to make sure that we weren't loafing on the job.

We didn't meet Mrs. Badeaux until very early Thursday morning, Callie's day off, and Mrs. Badeaux's first full day back in town after a week down in the Big Easy to see family. There was a milk delivery van parked in front of the house. I didn't pay it much mind, except to comment that I didn't think people got milk delivered to their homes anymore. Jake suspected foul play: an empty van, a missing milkman. I think Jake watches far too many of those Quinn Martin detective shows.

It was about seven thirty when we got our first look at Mrs. Badeaux. We'd already been working for about half an hour, giving the paver sand one last screed before beginning the next big phase of the operation. Mrs. Badeaux looked dressed and ready to meet the day. I'd say ready to go to work except that a) she didn't work, according to Badeaux, and b) no woman I know would have gone off to work looking the way she did. You'd think she had the starring role in some gypsy movie, for crying out loud. If she hadn't been beautiful (oh, Lordee, was she beautiful, as second wives—or was she his third?—always are), I'd say she looked like a blueberry. That's the color she was wearing—this sort of bluey-purple peasant dress with flouncy sleeves and tassels at the bottom and a pirate-like thick sash the color of the dress tied around her waist, and a long, sinuous scarf that went around her neck and hung down low and then wrapped itself around her head real tight but with just enough of her blond hair poking out in the front to assure you that there was a good flock of Herbal Essences-scented yellow silk under there.

She looked nothing like my wife, and suddenly I felt guilty. Guilty for looking. Guilty for entertaining thoughts that—let's be honest here—I really had no control over.

So this is what rich young women wear when they're lounging around the house, I thought. The only thing missing was bonbons!

I pulled my eyes from her long enough to notice that Jake was looking at her too. Jake's gaze was especially noticeable since he's crosseyed.

"It looks like you're doing a fine job," said the lady of the house, in that distinct northern Louisiana drawl that I'd been familiar with since birth. "Do you put the bricks in today?"

"Yes, ma'am," said Jake and me together, and then I gave Jake a look that said, "I'm the boss here. I'll talk to the woman. You can just keep quiet."

"We got the sand smoothed down and we're ready to lay in the pavers," I went on.

"What are pavers?"

"That would be the brick, ma'am," Jake replied, winking at me insubordinately.

"Oh, I hated the old patio that was here before. I was afraid one of our guests might come out here and trip on the broken stones."

"Then it's a good thing you're getting it replaced," I said.

"Well, you've got a warm day for it. The weatherman says it's getting up into the eighties this afternoon. Now, you boys just give a knock at that door if you need anything. Callie said the two of you got pretty thirsty yesterday."

"We did, ma'am," said Jake, whose eyes were still fixed on the stunning Mrs. Badeaux. I'm sure I was ogling her just as much as he was, but I was doing it a little more subtly.

Jake is constitutionally incapable of being subtle. He's a hard worker and that's why I keep him on, but his life has largely been driven by his various appetites: sex, food, beer, the Saints, and the LSU Tigers (which he calls the "Bengals" after their nickname, the "Bayou Bengals"), and all of it pretty much in that order.

It's always been hard, during our long side-by-side workdays, to talk to Jake about anything other than the above. He doesn't even know the name of the vice president or either of our two United States senators, although both men are Shreveport natives. And his obsession with the Tigers and his hatred for their in-state rival, Tulane, got old after our first week together.

"Green Wave. You gotta be fucking kidding. Who'd name their team after *water*, for fuck's sake?"

By eight thirty Jake and I had staked the retaining edge in place and had started to position the pavers. Jake was pulling the wet saw down from the bed of the truck when Mrs. Badeaux came out "to see how things were going." The scarf was gone, both from her neck and her head. Its absence displayed a mane of luxurious soft blond hair and a smooth, luscious, lightly tanned neck that wanted badly to be kissed and caressed. Jake fumbled with the wet saw and nearly dropped it. His mouth was open in a slight gape—a look that didn't flatter him and probably gave one the impression of a lascivious, crosseyed, mentally retarded man.

"Oh," she said. "So *that's* how you do it."

"Yes, ma'am," I replied.

"I was going to make me an egg sandwich. Would either of you boys like an egg sandwich?" As Mrs. Badeaux said this, the first two fingers of her right hand seemed to be diddling, absentmindedly, the nodule of her left nipple. "And coffee? Would you like coffee too?"

All that I could get out was "Yes."

"Me too," called Jake, half-slobbering, from the driveway.

After Mrs. Badeaux had gone inside, Jake ran over to me and said in an urgent whisper, "Why was she twiddling her titty like that?"

"You could see that all the way from the truck?" I whispered back. "With that Clarence-the-Crosseyed-Lion eyesight of yours?"

"It don't take perfect eyesight to take notice when a pretty woman fingers her zoom, Cortner."

I took a deep breath. "We need to get a hold of ourselves. I'm a married man and you're—just what *are* you, Jake? Has the divorce gone through?"

"Not yet."

"Then technically you're still a married man too."

"And technically, you'd be an idiot, Cortner, to think I gotta have that decree in my hand to make a move on any woman of my choosing."

"You make a move on Mrs. Badeaux, Jake, and you're fired. You're more than fired. I'll make sure that nobody in town ever hires you. I'm starting to get the feeling that Mrs. Badeaux is one of those lonely housewives who isn't getting enough from her husband."

"Well, hell, Cortner! With a Buddha-bellied, squirrel-faced mari like Badeaux, do you blame her?"

"You heard me, Jake. Now get your mind off Mrs. Badeaux. Tell me about that game against the Gators last Saturday."

When Mrs. Badeaux brought out our egg sandwiches and cups of coffee, another item of apparel was missing from her blueberry ensemble. The sash was gone, and her shoes as well (I hardly ever notice a woman's shoes; I'm always too busy taking in everything else). Mrs. Badeaux was totally barefoot, her toenails painted hot pink. Without the sash, she looked even more like a gypsy, the dress flowing every which way. She directed us to the gazebo and served us there.

As we were eating—or *trying* to eat—she stood nearby and talked about some of the ideas she had for landscaping the large backyard. "Henry loves it that I'm inclined that way, though I wish *he'd* care a little more about how this place looks. It's been in his family for four generations, you know." And then, apropos of nothing she'd just said, Mrs. Badeaux pressed two fingers against her lips with a coquette's tease, and then trailed her fingers down her chin and farther south between her breasts, finally withdrawing them just above the land of unearthly delights.

Then she excused herself and went back inside, her floating stride across the green lawn sensuously mesmerizing. Jake and I sat for a moment in a state of suspended animation. I finally found my voice to say, "Something's going on here. I'm not comfortable with it. I don't even know if we should finish the job."

"There's no harm in looking, Cortner. She's playing a game. I want to play. I won't touch her. And we'll both hightail it out of here, no problem, if she decides to make a move on either of us. I'm just saying—"

"I know what you're saying. But I'm weak. And I know that you're even weaker than I am."

"It's a *game*, Cortner. We won't let her win. But for fuck's sake, let's play!"

We kept playing.

At about nine forty-five, Mrs. Badeaux returned to offer us lemonade on a tray. The blueberry gypsy lounging attire was gone. Now she was wearing a pleated skirt that came up high, like cheerleaders used to wear, and a halter top that looked like the kind of tit-sling that sluts wear. It was a very different look—slightly schoolgirl, mostly trailer-park trash. The purpose here, I suppose, was to share with us an exposed midriff that seemed both taut and touchably soft—nothing at all like my wife Theresa's abdominal Michelin pudge, of which she was extremely self-conscious, because it didn't used to be there, but appeared as we both passed the forty mark and my own paunch coincidentally became more pronounced.

"I know what's going on," said Jake after she'd gone back inside. He was so excited that he could hardly get the words out. "She's doing a striptease."

"Strippers don't generally change clothes in the middle of their act."

"Well, there wasn't much under that blue dress. She wasn't even wearing a bra, far as I could tell. You could see the outline of her hard kernels."

"Look, Jake. We need to stop doing this color commentary after each of her appearances. It's only making it worse and it's hard for me to concentrate on getting this patio finished."

"I'm hard too."

"That's not what I said, butthole."

Jake laughed. He was having a blast. I was having fun too—too much fun—but I was also starting to feel a little anxious about the whole thing.

Jake's theory was confirmed with Mrs. Badeaux's next emergence. It was almost noon. She had brought us lunch. She served it to us wearing an all-white two-piece bathing suit. I couldn't call it an itsy-bitsy teeny-weeny because, in truth, it was actually quite modest as bikinis go, but it gave us a much better look at her plump gazungas, and more gam than a gam-man deserved to see.

"I'm going to do some sunbathing over by the pool. You boys know where I am if you need anything." She went back inside, and a few minutes later re-emerged wearing sunglasses and carrying her towel and a couple of magazines and a big glass of something pink and cold and condensating.

By this time Jake and I were ready to fill sand in between the pavers in the section of the patio we'd already laid down. After emptying the third bag over the bricks, I handed Jake a broom, but he wasn't looking at me and the handle end of the broom went into his eye. He held his hand over the poked eye and pointed toward the pool, which was in clear view of the patio we were constructing. Jake could hardly form words. "The— the top is down. The top is down." It took me several seconds to realize what he was saying had nothing to do with automotive convertibles and everything to do with the fact that Mrs. Badeaux had just taken off her bikini top. And she hadn't done it in the way that most sunbathing women do it: tummy down, to allow the sun to bronze their strap-free dorsal regions. She had rolled over completely *upon* her back so that her fully exposed breasts could soak up a little of the early October radiance that had already reduced Jake and me to sweat-drenched t-shirts.

Neither of us could speak. Jake's broom was poised in midair.

And it wasn't over.

Something buzzed from just inside the door. It sounded like one of those house intercom systems that builders put into some of the larger homes in the sixties. Without donning her top, Mrs. Badeaux came bounding inside to answer the intercom. "It's Callie's day off," she remarked as she passed. (This she had already told us.) Who then, I wondered, was inside that house, summoning her? And was this person privy to all the fun that Mrs. Badeaux was having out of doors, clearly at Jake's and my expense?

The top half of Mrs. Badeaux was swinging and bouncing wildly as she disappeared inside. It was as if Jake and I had been unknowingly cast in a comedy sketch from the burlesque-bawdy *Benny Hill Show*— the difference, of course, being that in the TV show the bobbling boobs of Benny's sprinting sexpots were never *fully* bared. Nevertheless, Boots Randolph's lively rendition of "Yackety Sax" played obscenely in my head.

A moment later, Jake and I could both clearly hear her speaking, apparently into the intercom: "How was your nappy, Mr. Milkman? *Now*? Oh my good Lord, you are *insatiable*!"

Almost simultaneously, I said, "We're packing up and leaving, Jake," while Jake said, "Fire me if you like, Tony, but I'm going in there. I can be just as good a lover as any son-of-a-bitch milkman."

As my coitus-crazed assistant made his move to the door, I threw myself upon him. In the ensuing scuffle, pavers were scattered, great areas of smoothed, leveled sand gouged out by our dancing heels. Flashing through my mind was the fact that our tussle had probably added another couple of hours to the job.

If we were to finish the job. I knew now that I had just cause to stop work on the patio. And I had every right to charge Badeaux for all the hours we'd already put in (and for the cost of our materials), though being an extremely successful corporate attorney, Badeaux could have made it hard for Cortner Construction to prevail. Why had Mrs. Badeaux done this? For what possible purpose?

Jake was still struggling as I grabbed the hand tamper to hold him in place on the ground. We remained like this, Jake lying breathless on the degraded sand foundation, me standing equally winded, trying my level best to bring him to his senses.

"Uncle!" he finally cried. "I'll go. Let me up."

I'd hardly had any time to consider whether or not I could trust him when the lady of the house stepped outside.

She was now completely naked.

"*Why*?" was all that I could bring myself to say.

"Why not?" she answered, standing statuesque before us, something out of Greek antiquity in alabaster or marble. "It's all my husband's doing, you know," she tossed out casually, seductively running her right index finger up and down the soft curve of her sunlit right thigh. Jake did a double take, just like a gawking cartoon scamp.

"How can this possibly be your husband's doing?" I asked, having turned my back to the woman so that I could converse with her without distraction.

"Last month, Henry accused me of having been unfaithful—'serially unfaithful' was, I think, the phrase he used—he's such a goddamned lawyer—ever since we married. The accusation was totally baseless. The trust is now gone from our marriage. If he thinks this is who I am, then this is who I will be. I am now officially open for business."

"Do you strip for all the men who come to your house?"

Mrs. Badeaux shook her head. "I got the idea of coming out here like this from that Candid Camera movie that came out a few years ago."

"*What Do You Say to a Naked Lady*," offered Jake. "I saw it more than once."

"I had fun. Did *you* have fun? Would you like to have *more* fun?"

Jake looked at me. His expression seemed to say, "All of my future happiness depends on how I am allowed to answer this question."

I shook my head.

The stunt was over, the prospect for further merriment dematerializing in that next moment. Mrs. Badeaux reached inside and drew out a bathrobe, which she promptly put on.

I loosened my compactor hold on Jake, who immediately began to take deeper and more healthy-sounding breaths. "Get up, Jake. We're leaving now, Mrs. Badeaux. If your husband asks why, I will leave it to you to explain it to him. I'll put our bill in the mail next week."

Mrs. Badeaux looked disappointed to see us go, but didn't try to stop us.

As I was backing the company truck down the driveway, I noticed that the milk delivery van had been joined by a mail truck, sans mailman. "That crazy woman really *is* open for business," said Jake. Then he sighed. "I came *this* close to getting myself a piece of that action."

I boxed his ear.

Over the course of the next couple of weeks, I could not help swinging by the house to see to what additional lengths Mrs. Badeaux had gone to confirm her husband's suspicions of her. The telephone repair truck in the driveway wasn't overtly suspicious, but the pink Mary Kay Cadillac parked two days in a row sent Jake on flights of girl-on-girl fantasy that were hard to rein in.

I knew that the day of reckoning would come, but neither Jake nor I was privileged to witness the denouement to the domestic drama (or comedy) in which we had both played small supporting roles. All I know is that in the end, Badeaux did pay us (though he apparently had to pay someone else, as well, to come in and finish the job), and that two years later we were, astonishingly, invited to put in a bid to convert the house's catacumbal cellar into a modern rec room.

"It might interest you to know that I have divorced and have not remarried," he said. "My days of marital heartache are finally over. I get all the companionship I need from my younger brother, Chad, who moved in with me a couple of months ago."

Badeaux liked my bid and we won the job. I estimated three weeks to get it finished. We met Chad for the first time on Thursday of that first week. He came down the stairs bearing glasses of lemonade. He was wearing purple eyeshadow, a bright red kimono (loosely sashed), and embroidered mules.

We knocked the job out in two weeks. I'm thinking of changing professions.

1976

THROTTLED IN ARKANSAS
AND OKLAHOMA

It was Dr. Key who first suggested the unthinkable: that the two fifty-something-year-old couples should drive to Oklahoma City together.

In the same car.

One sister in the front seat, one in the back seat.

Ladella and Fay in closer proximity than they'd been in twenty-some-odd years.

Ladella said that such a suggestion didn't even deserve a response.

Still, this didn't stop her from delivering one: "I don't like Fay. I don't look up to her. She's nasty and she's selfish and I vowed after that awful Christmas when she went out of her way to put me down in front of our whole family that I would never see her again."

"Well, you're going to have to see her in Oklahoma City, whether you like it nor not."

"I *will* go to Oklahoma and wish my mother a happy eighty-fifth birthday, Cleron, but I intend to avoid even placing myself in the same room with Fay. And I will *not*, in this lifetime or any other, trap myself in the same car with her for twelve ungodly hours."

Ladella and Fay's mother lived with the sisters' younger brother, Marcus, and his family near Tinker Air Force Base, where he served with the 2854th Air Base Group. Neither Ladella nor Fay had chosen to marry military men, though there was a tradition of national military service in their family going all the way back to the U.S. 10th Cavalry Regiment, more familiarly known as the "Buffalo Soldiers."

Ladella and Fay, both nurses, wed medical men instead—both physicians and instructors at Meharry College in Nashville, the largest historically black medical college in the country. Ladella's husband Cleron had won national recognition for his research into the pathology of sickle cell anemia. Fay's husband, Truman, achieved equal recognition for his work in developing treatment protocols for childhood asthma. Each woman felt that her husband was more successful than her sister's spouse, though the husbands themselves remained noncompetitive colleagues. Friends, even.

The rivalry between these two feuding siblings extended itself into all areas of their lives. It was a tragedy that in one instance became an odd blessing when Fay learned that she couldn't bear children. Ladella, who didn't want children, was then released from having to bear and raise a "spite" child, though she had nevertheless given serious thought to going ahead and making the sacrifice for the sake of rubbing Fay's nose in it. Ladella's husband Cleron was forced to undergo a vasectomy to keep the peace.

The rivalry extended itself into all areas of their husbands' lives as well.

While this non-starter conversation was taking place in a neighborhood north of the Cumberland River, which bisects the city of Nashville, a similar conversation was playing out in a neighborhood south of that river, near the college.

"Cleron came by my office this morning with what I think is an excellent suggestion," said Dr. Truman Nicholas to his wife. "He thinks that the four of us should drive to Oklahoma City together. I agreed and volunteered the Matador station wagon."

"Are you insane?"

"It makes perfect sense to me."

"I'm going to schedule an appointment for you with Dr. Eastman."

"Dr. Eastman teaches psychi—oh. You're very funny, Fay. You're a laugh a minute, baby."

In spite of the fact that Dr. and Mrs. Nicholas and Dr. and Mrs. Key would both be headed to the very same place, taking a mostly straight-shot route from Nashville, Tennessee, to Oklahoma City, Oklahoma; in spite of the fact that they would be leaving at roughly the same time on the morning of Thursday, July 29, and arriving at roughly the same time early in the evening of that same day; in spite of the fact that both relatively law-abiding brothers-in-law intended to flout only minimally the double-nickel speed limit leveled against the American motorist by the Emergency Highway Energy Conservation Act signed by President

Richard Nixon on January 2, 1974—in spite of each of these things which strongly argued for a carpooling solution to the problem of how best to transport two women equally fearful of plane travel due to a certain excessively turbulent flight they'd shared in their youth, the two couples set out in their own cars, and that was that.

But it really wasn't. Because fate was to play several mischievous tricks on Fay Nicholas and her slightly younger sister Ladella Key on that trip. The first came at a West Memphis, Arkansas, truck stop both husbands had visited on earlier road trips. Both the Nicholases and the Keys had decided independently of each other to stop there so their vehicles' drivers, in each case the husbands, identically possessive of their respective steering wheels, could quaff down a couple of hasty cups of coffee to keep the late morning drowsies at bay.

It was Truman who noticed his brother- and sister-in-law from across the crowded truck stop dining room and acknowledged them with a friendly wave. Truman and Fay were seated in a booth, Cleron and Ladella at a table across the room.

"Well, look who's here!" marveled Dr. Key to his wife as he waved back. "Fancy seeing the Nicholases so far from home."

"You aren't the least bit funny," muttered Ladella, hiding her face behind her menu.

At the booth across the room, Fay flinched. "I'm going to the bathroom. Knock on the door after they've left."

At the table, Ladella said nearly the same thing.

The upshot was that both sisters entered the restroom at almost the same time, Fay having kept her eyes front and center upon her approach, and Ladella having kept her gaze largely focused upon the vinyl tile floor.

Left alone for the time being, the two husbands gravitated toward one another in the no man's land between their respective dining stations.

"Funny how things turn out," said Dr. Nicholas to Dr. Key. "How long do you think it will take them to realize they've wound up in the bathroom together?"

Cleron chuckled. "We should lock them in there and not let them out until they both promise to be good little girls."

In the ladies' restroom, Ladella had sequestered herself in a stall only a moment before her sister entered. They were the only two women in the room. It quickly became apparent to each that the other was sitting in the neighboring stall, Ladella recognizing Fay by her "Evening in Paris" perfume, which Fay had worn for years, and Fay recognizing her younger sister Ladella by her comfortable, slip-resistant Nurse Mates shoes.

Both sat for a long time in mortified silence. Eventually Ladella said, "All right. I'll go first."

"Yes, go," answered her sister curtly.

At the Stuckey's store outside of Conway, Arkansas, Ladella munched on a pimento cheese sandwich as she strolled through the aisles containing pecan rolls and boxed peanut brittle and pecan divinity. Ladella had pulled the sandwich from the ice chest, which sat on the funky Levi jeans–upholstered back seat of the couple's 1973 Gremlin. Ladella's husband, Cleron, like his counterpart, Truman, liked American Motors cars for their value and a little for their placement a few rungs below the top three automaking giants. Being men of color who had overcome the powerful forces of prejudice and orthodoxy in the medical field, both Cleron and Truman respected companies that tried to break down barriers. The Gremlin, being a funny little car with a sawed-off rear end and blue-jean upholstery, was especially iconoclastic.

Cleron ate a hamburger at the roadside chain's snack bar. Through the window he could see the Nicholases' station wagon pull up. "Katy, bar the door," he said to himself.

A moment later, Ladella joined him. She had finished her sandwich and was holding several boxes of Stuckey's brand confections she wanted to buy, along with a cedar plaque that read, "I don't swim in your toilet, so please don't pee in my pool." (She and her husband had just put in a swimming pool the previous spring.)

Ladella had been standing very near the front door when her sister and brother-in-law entered the store. One of her candy boxes had slipped from her nervous hands and hit the floor with a loud thwack. She had looked at Truman (trying her very best not to give her sister the courtesy of even a brief glance) and said somewhat exasperatedly, "Truman Nicholas—you had to have seen our car in the parking lot. Why didn't you keep on going?"

Before Truman could attempt an answer, Fay shot back, "We have every right to stop here too. You don't own Stuckey's." Fay had said this without looking at Ladella, and then brushed roughly past her to peruse, with serious purpose, a row of roasted nut products.

"What was I to do?" Truman whispered in an apologetic tone to Ladella after his wife passed. "She likes this place just as much as you do."

At her husband's table in the snack bar, Ladella recounted what had just happened. Then she subjoined, "I am going to make my purchases and then go and sit in the car. Finish your hamburger, and don't keep me waiting."

Ladella strode over to the cash register and bought her confections and the plaque with the funny saying on it and then went out to sit in the Gremlin and stew and fume. Her husband Cleron followed a few moments later. He passed Truman on the way out. The two men shook their heads and shrugged. After walking out of the store, Cleron turned and walked back in and then said to Truman by way of afterthought, "I've been meaning to ask you what you think about the curriculum changes for the fall, but we'd better not do it with the women around, or they'll think we're talking about them behind their backs."

Truman nodded and sighed.

After they'd gotten back on I-40, Fay said to Truman, "What was it that Cleron said to you in the Stuckey's?"

"Nothing. Nothing at all."

"You're lying. You men are conspiring in some way. I just know it. And we aren't stopping anywhere else between here and Oklahoma City. If you get hungry, you can eat these pralines."

Truman had every intention of not stopping again, but the gas gauge took that decision out of his hands. Plus, he was hungry—hungry for something in the meat family. Unlike Cleron, he hadn't eaten a hamburger at the Conway Stuckey's. There was another Stuckey's in Checotah, Oklahoma. They could get gas there, and he could grab a sandwich. The Nicholases hadn't packed a cooler like the Keys. Truman Nicholas didn't believe in filling a car up with food from home; that's what roadside eateries were for.

Ladella was sitting at one of the plastic laminated tables in the snack bar section of the Checotah, Oklahoma, Stuckey's store eating pretzels when they arrived. She watched with unmitigated horror as her older sister and her husband got out of their brown Matador and started across the parking lot. "If that doesn't beat *everything*!" she said aloud.

She had hardly finished the word "everything" when a piece of pretzel slipped into her windpipe. She began to choke. Very little air was getting through. Her husband was in the restroom. There was a white couple sitting at the table next to her. They watched, horrified, as she quickly began to claw at her throat. "Help her!" the woman called to the short order cook behind the counter.

"You want me to call a doctor?" he replied stupidly.

Ladella couldn't speak. She couldn't breathe. She was becoming lightheaded even as the adrenaline of fear pumped throughout her body.

Fay saw what was happening as she entered the store. She saw Ladella clutching at her throat with a woman standing helplessly next to her and a man slapping her futilely on the back.

Fay ran toward her sister. She knocked over a display of old-fashioned fruitcake to get there. She pushed the man out of the way, grabbed Ladella, wheeled her around, and placed both of her arms around her sister's waist. With her right hand, Fay made a fist and pushed it against Ladella's abdomen just above her belly button. She grabbed the fist with the other hand and began to make a series of strong upward squeeze-thrusts into the abdomen. On the fifth thrust, Ladella coughed. The piece of pretzel flew from her mouth.

Fay sat her sister down. There was a long silence. Then the man, who had now been joined by Fay's husband Truman, said, "How did you learn to do that?"

Fay didn't answer. She had sat down across from Ladella and was gently patting her sister's trembling hand.

Truman turned to the man and said, "It's a procedure developed by a Dr. Henry Heimlich. He published it a couple of years ago in *Emergency Medicine*—that's a medical journal."

Cleron was out of the restroom now. He hadn't heard any of the commotion and was startled to find his wife and sister-in-law sitting at the same table, looking tenderly into each other's eyes. He turned to his brother-in-law Truman. "Did Jesus just come back?"

"Ladella was choking. In case you were wondering, the abdominal thrust maneuver attributed to Dr. Heimlich apparently works."

The two sisters kept their silence for a moment longer and then Ladella, still looking at Fay, said, "I think you broke one of my ribs." She touched the lower part of her rib cage gingerly.

"You're welcome," said Fay. She pursed her lips, then released them. "Let me feel it. Maybe it's just bruised."

As Fay was touching Ladella's diaphragm, Ladella said, "I probably wouldn't have choked on that pretzel if I hadn't seen you and Truman driving up."

"Do you hate me *that* much, Ladella?" asked Fay, sitting back in her seat and folding her arms across her large breasts.

"No more than you hate *me*," said Ladella.

"But I don't hate you at all," replied Fay. "I just don't like you very much."

"Then why did you save my life? Or would you have saved *whoever* was choking at this table?"

"Well, of course I would have done the same for anybody," said Fay. "But it obviously mattered more to me because it was you. For good or bad, you're still my sister." Fay thought for a moment and then said, "When are we going to end all of this, Ladella? Does it go on like this until we're both dead?"

"Mama always favored you."

"And Daddy always favored *you*."

"The sad truth is that when it comes right down to it, they both probably always liked *Marcus* best."

Fay nodded. "He *is* the only son and he *is* the only one of us to give our parents grandchildren."

Ladella took a sip from the cup of water that the short order cook had brought her. "I never enjoyed any of those years of not having a sister."

Fay agreed with this statement by nodding pensively.

Out in the parking lot, after their wives had gotten inside their respective AMC passenger vehicles, the rent between the two temporarily, perhaps even permanently mended, Truman said to Cleron, "Had we all decided to take you up on your idea of driving out together, this reconciliation might never have happened. The Lord, Brother Cleron, works in mysterious ways."

"Ain't that a fact, Brother Truman. Ain't that a fact."

1977

RECTALLY REMUNERATIVE IN ILLINOIS

The younger men sat around the table in their Tattersall check vests and their Tattersall shirts with buttoned-down collars noosed with silk challis ties—ties that spoke in the muted earth-toned voices of the brown-beige-forest green seventies. The older men wore pinstriped and herringbone double-breasted suits and straight, uncuffed trousers that signified money and prestige (given the venerability of the patricians in the room), while respecting the fashion of the day. Almost all of the men wore tassels on their wing-tipped shoes, which were constructed of soft leather and hardly pinched at all. This being the eighth year of the "Me" decade, the men preened a little, but not too much, because, after all, they were real men, and didn't Anita Bryant remind them every other day how much God loved men who acted like real men and not like fruits?

The conference room—a quarrel of chrome and cherry wood paneling—smelled of incinerated tobacco and Old Spice and Yardley Jaguar and Black Tie and Aramis and little of the Chicago smog which, Sandburg tells us, creeps into a room on little cat feet.

The oldest of the room's esteemed elders sat at the head of the table. His name was Bob Grady Senior, and he opened the meeting by asking where the hell the coffee was. He was reminded that, like every other company that vigilantly attended its bottom line, Grady Enterprises was boycotting coffee until the price came down, to which Bob Grady Senior responded in wonted curmudgeon fashion, "So when the hell are the Brazilians gonna get their act together and do something about the weather down there?"

The men drank tea.

Out of oversized, masculine coffee mugs.

This being an early morning meeting, some of the men drank orange juice, just like Anita Bryant and the Florida Citrus Commission told them to.

A man who resembled a younger version of the older man and was, in fact, his son, stood to address the group gathered around the table, interrupting cluttered cross-talk pertaining to last week's bowl games and the recent death of Mayor Daley (this, again, being Chicago), the closed-door ascension of Michael Anthony Bilandic to that same office (ditto previous parenthetical), and Farrah Fawcett (this being 1977 and Farrah being, well, Farrah).

"Good morning, gentlemen," greeted Bob Grady Junior from his station at the other end of the table. Bob Grady Junior stood against a backdrop of easels and flip charts offering pies and bars in blazing primary and secondary colors. Then, eschewing all other preliminary pleasantries, Grady the younger called his colleagues' attention to sales figures for the past quarter. "If you will please turn to page seventeen in the quarterly sales report, you'll see that I've quantified the figures by product line. Note which of our lines have experienced a moderate decline in sales and which have lost all viability whatsoever in the marketplace."

As Bob Grady Junior directed his colleagues to page seventeen, thirteen of the fourteen men gathered around the cherry-wood conference table sought in concert that page so designated in their own copies of the quarterly sales report, all the riffling fingers creating in the aggregate a soft, susurrant rustle. The fourteenth man—the oldest in the room, whose name you now know to be Bob Grady Senior, founder and pater-emeritus of Grady Enterprises—did not turn his pages, but looked out the window at the City of Big Shoulders and hummed.

"Gentlemen," continued Bob Grady *fils*, whose voice sounded similar to that of Beatrice Arthur but with less of a sandpaper rasp, "please make note that the market share for eight of our ten best-selling products has dropped markedly in the last three quarters. I don't have figures yet for the pre-Christmas sales, but projected earnings are far below those of the last five holiday cycles. I find it necessary at this juncture, poised as we are upon the cusp of our merger with Hawthorne-Hay Industries, to ask which of the following products we can afford to do without. Item." The young Mr. Grady cleared his Maude-ish throat preparatory to placing several time-honored Grady Enterprises staples upon the merchandising chopping block. "Happy Tush Sanitized Rectal Wipes. Fifty-percent drop in sales over the last year. Quite dramatic. Mr. Powers, you wished to—"

"Yes. I wanted to make note of the economic downturn."

"Actually, there was an up-tick," said the man sitting next to Powers. This man's name was Avernell. He was a large man, and he crowded his two neighbors.

"Whether the economy is doing well or not," pursued Young Grady, with a soupçon of exasperation, "I would not consider sanitized rectal wipes to be a discretionary purchase for most consumers of anal cleansing products. Is there anyone here who would dispute this fact?"

A blond-haired man who looked to be in his late thirties raised his hand.

"Yes, Henderson? Are you disputing this fact?"

"No. I just wanted to say that there are at least three other products on this list whose sales have fared worse that Happy Tush Sanitized Rectal Wipes. Granted, the Rectal Appliances Division has taken a hit over the last year, but be fair, Grady. Every marketing study we've undertaken has demonstrated that the Stool-Eaze Anal Caliper Helpmate lawsuit was only marginally responsible for the drop in sales of our rectal wipes and pile balms. In fact, our Do-Your-Doody Extra-Strength Pile Balm and Fresh Booty Scented Sphincter Cream have actually each seen a marked *increase* in sales in the last two cycles."

Bob Grady the Elder now began to hum, inexplicably, "Love for Sale" by Cole Porter.

Another man, Cass Jorgens, a balding fellow with canine-like flues, raised his hand to solicit attention. Without receiving acknowledgement by young Grady, he proceeded nonetheless to pronounce that the advertising agency recently retained by Grady Industries to sell Jorgens' division's products—namely Nip-It-in-the-Bud Nipple Hair Tweezers and the Umbili-lievable Belly Button Irrigation Kit—was confident that its new ad campaigns for each of these products would boost sales far beyond anyone's wildest expectations. "I share their confidence," said Mr. Jorgens, whose temples begat the sweat of a clearly anxious man, his division's very reason for existence having now been placed in jeopardy.

And so the morning's executive meeting went: each division head defending his own products against hard statistics pointing to diminished sales, the usual level of public ridicule, and several nettlesome lawsuits: the vaginal douche, Yes-M'Lady, for example, having promulgated infections when improperly applied, and the Glad Glans uncircumcised penis antiseptic scrub pad, having been the focus of both lawsuits and a boycott after numerous reported chafings from over-diligent application.

Of all the products brought to the forefront in the morning's discussion, only the Wee Fingers therapeutic labia cuff and the Nutty Brother scrotal sling had achieved sales increases, due in both cases to subtle mentions by guests on *The Tonight Show with Johnny Carson*, each constituting an enthusiastic endorsement.

The meeting concluded an hour later than scheduled, with drawn and wan faces accompanying plodding shuffles from the room, the only exception being the hopeful expression and near-prance of Henry Kierbaum, head of the Genitalia Accessories division, whose product line would not be put before the boards of both Grady Enterprises and its future partner Hawthorne-Hay Industries for the purpose of future assessment thanks to the aforementioned glowing *Tonight Show* endorsements by Sylvia Sidney and Sir John Gielgud. The room now having been emptied of everyone but father and son, Grady Junior crept up to Grady Senior, who, seemingly unaware that the meeting had been adjourned, stared wistfully out the window at the hazy Chicago skyline.

"Hey, Pop," said the son, "can I take you back home now?"

"Is it time already?" asked the father.

"I don't know how much you got out of that meeting."

The father turned to look at his son. "Enough to know that this ship is going down in a hurry. I don't know why H-H wants the merger. Unless they're planning to scrub everything and start from scratch. We have a fine plant. I wouldn't blame them." Pivoting back to the window: "Look at all the pigeon shit. Why do pigeons fly all the way up to the twenty-first story of this building just to shit on our ledges?"

When Bob Grady Junior saw his father's face again, there were tears in the old man's eyes. "I built this company from nothing. Just me and my dreams and that oversized rectal thermometer that took off like gangbusters in Greenwich Village and San Francisco, and, for some reason that I still can't understand, Cheyenne, Wyoming. Now we're floundering, Bobby. And I'm no help. I'm put out to pasture, son, like a half-dead horse."

"We're going to turn this company around, Dad. I'll make it my mission to put Grady Enterprises back in the black. I'll make you proud."

Father and son stood at the window, the father's thoughts drifting to memories of his glory days as a young entrepreneur in go-go Chi-town, the son's thoughts wandering to how to improve the Bladder-Guard Antibacterial Urethra Shield. It wasn't long before the father's musings turned once again to pigeons. He thought he might like to be one himself so that he could fly away to a place where people still drank coffee and wanted to buy everything he had to sell, even though they would continue to do so with a blush.

It was a chimerical wish—the impractical wish of a man who could no longer be of service to his company. And the reality of having lost his father to useless senility felt to Bob Grady Junior like a swift kick in the balls. Unfortunately, and to Bob's disadvantage, Grady Enterprises had stopped making Tender Testicle Analgesic Cream a good five years ago.

1978

TRIPLE-TOASTED IN MISSOURI

The three St. Louis men had a number of things in common, some more important than others, and one the most important of all. Dennis, Jock, and Marvin were all well into their thirties. Each hated *Saturday Night Fever* and disco in general and the Bee Gees in particular. It was Dennis, oldest of the three, who took the initiative and barked at the bartender to "please can the disco music. This is a bar, not a discotheque."

Kurt, the bartender, looked offended. "It's four in the afternoon. Nobody's here but me and the three of you, and Old Man Rivers, who doesn't give a rat's ass *what* music I play."

"Well, the three of us *do*," Dennis shot back. "And if you're unwilling to kill 'Stayin' Alive' sometime in the next, let's say, thirty seconds, we're gonna pick ourselves up and go drink our expensive Scotch whiskies in some other Carondelet bar. Capice?"

Kurt turned off the music.

Marvin was laughing. Marvin was drunk. He'd gotten an early jump on his companions. "Ironic, too," he added.

"How's that?" asked Jock. Then the answer came to him like a slap, and he nodded reflectively. "*Kill. Alive.* I get it."

Besides an acquired fondness for Scotch, which put each of the three men on an even footing with their hard-drinking colleagues at the two law firms and one district attorney's office where they worked, there was also a strong interest in the sport of tennis, both as players and fans, over which they had inevitably bonded.

Just the week before, Bjorn Borg had lost the U.S. Open Men's Singles title to American Jimmy "Jimbo" Connors. Jimbo had won handily in straight sets. Marvin, who paid close attention to the minutia of the game, had opined moments before (while raising his voice to be heard over "How Deep is Your Love"), that Borg, who had earlier in the year captured singles titles at both the French Open and Wimbledon, was disadvantaged by his unfamiliarity with the new hard court surface, "DecoTurf," that the recently opened tennis facility in Queens, New York, had laid in.

"He got to the finals, didn't he?" retorted Dennis, who looked a little like Borg: blond and Nordic, a contrast to his booth companions. (One of the *differences* among the three men: none bore even the slightest resemblance to his two companions. Another was Dennis's pedigree: he was the grandson of Pulitzer-prize winning novelist Dennis Bailey).

"The thing *I* read," offered Marvin, who looked a lot like a young Arthur Miller—prominently spectacled and possessed of long vertical dimples that framed his voluble mouth like parentheses, "is that the new DecoTurf favors serve-and-volley players, not a baseliner like Bjorn."

"Your theory's bullshit, Marvin," pronounced Jock, who, having his side of the booth to himself, had spread his right arm across the top of the back cushion as if waiting for an adoring female to slide in next to him. Jock was arguably the least good-looking of the three. He was beef and brawn and proprietor of a hairline that was dramatically receding (a product, he often bragged, of a natural overproduction of testosterone), and a face that perhaps formerly had some nuance of shape to it, but was now lithically hard-set and jut-jawed like a bulldog's.

"Tell me why it's bullshit," said Marvin, enunciating each word carefully to keep from slurring.

"Because this kid coming up through the ranks, McEnroe—he's all volley and serve. It's like he's allergic to ground strokes."

"Or just a fucking hot dog," observed Dennis, who waved his glass to get Kurt the bartender's attention. Some of the remaining Dewars sloshed onto Marvin's arm. "But yeah, yeah, I get your point—Connors cleaned his clock in the semi-finals."

Kurt, detecting movement in the periphery of his vision, looked up from his present task of pillowing Old Man Rivers' toppled head with a couple of folded bar towels, to see Dennis summoning his attention from the booth the three men occupied. "Thanks. I mean the music," Dennis shouted.

"Pegged you three for either Billy Joel or Chuck Mangione," Kurt called from behind the bar. Billy Joel was singing "Only the Good Die Young" over the bar's speakers.

Marvin snickered. "Another irony. The room is awash with them this afternoon."

"Almost creepy," said Jock, sitting forward and setting both arms heavily upon the woody tabletop.

"I like 'Brandy,'" admitted Marvin quietly and irrelevantly. "She's a fine girl. What a good wife she would be."

"It's getting late, fellows," said Jock. "I've got to go pick up Scottie at his school. If I'm not there stroke of five thirty, soon as football practice ends, word gets back to Jill, and bingo! It's like the opposite of that Ozark Air Lines jingle." Jock suddenly became tuneful: "She *doesn't* make things easy for me!"

The men laughed. "Are you saying it's time for the toast?" asked Dennis. "Are you rushing the toast, Jocko?"

"I *gotta* rush the toast. Hey, we've been here over an hour. That ain't bad."

"These reunions get shorter every year," Marvin reflected.

"That's bullshit," said Jock. "Christ, we were here well past the dinner hour last year. You should have heard the earful I got from Jill *that* night."

"I need to be heading out, too," said Dennis. "I don't live under the thumb of my wife like Jocko here, but I've still got my domestic responsibilities." Both Dennis and Jock turned to Marvin. Dennis spoke for the both of them: "Insert obligatory observation here about the advantages of bachelorhood."

"Observation stipulated to," said Marvin, his eyes now rheumy.

"You're taking a cab," said Dennis. And then to Kurt: "Make sure our friend Marvin gets a cab home. Oh, and we're ready for our toast. Black Label, please. Only the best for Tracie."

The bartender nodded and drew his bottle of twelve-year-old Johnnie Walker Black down from the back-bar shelf. The three men could hear the clink of the three ceremonial shot glasses as he plucked them up.

When he reached the booth, Kurt asked, "How long have you three ambulance chasers been doing this? All I know about is the last three years since *I'm* here."

"This is our sixth gathering," said Jock. "And you're wrong about our friend Marvin here. He isn't an ambulance chaser; he works for the people of the great state of Missouri." Then to his companions: "Really sorry about rushing things, guys."

"Perfectly understandable considering the circumstances," said Dennis, taking up his shot glass.

"What a good wife she would buh-eeee," sang Marvin. Then he corrected himself: "What a good wife she *was*."

"That's as good a toast as any," said Dennis, raising his glass high. The other two men met his glass with their own over the middle of the table. "To Tracie, loving wife to us all. God bless and keep her in Heaven's sweet embrace."

"Thanks for not bringing Jesus into this," said Jewish Marvin.

"You have anything to add to the toast, Jock?"

"Uh. Let me see. Nice that we can come together every year and raise a glass to my first wife. *And* your first wife, Dennis. And as luck would have it, yours as well, Counselor Remnick."

"First, last, and *only* wife," added Marvin by way of clarification.

"Arm's tired. Let's get to the summation," suggested Dennis.

"To Tracie with love," the three men said in unison. In the next moment they were each tossing back the drink that had been selected at the very first of their reunions to honor Tracie's Scotch-Irish heritage.

"Funny," said Dennis, licking some of the amber liquid from his lips. "To think that each of our three divorces ended so well. Was Tracie anything but a good friend to you afterwards, Jock?"

"To the day she died," said Jock with a smile, his eyes moving about as he visited a couple of his best memories of the woman who had been wife, friend, and lover too, but never a mother due to her inability to have children and their mutual unwillingness to adopt. "Hell, Tracie even came to Jill's and my wedding."

"Did she bring her stenograph?" asked Marvin, remembering that during the two years he'd been married to Tracie, she would sometimes drag her court reporter's primary accessory to events for which the services of a court reporter would never have been required.

"But of course," laughed Jock. "To get a transcription of our vows for future reference."

Jock stood. The men shook hands. "Until next year," said Jock. "Or around the courthouse—whichever comes first. But this is better, yes? Here we could never be adversaries."

Dennis smiled. "Despite the fact that ex-husbands are seldom on such good terms."

Dennis spent the two minutes that followed Jock's departure trying to convince Marvin to let his friend drive him home.

"Not quite ready to go yet, counselor," said Marvin, looking up at Dennis through half-closed eyes.

"Well, when you *are* ready to go, call a cab, Marvin. I'm serious."

"You sound like Tracie when you say that. She was always looking after me. Maybe that's why she never wanted to adopt. She liked mothering the three of *us* too much."

"Interesting point, Marvin. I'll take it under advisement."

"So what was it we were doing wrong that kept her from wanting to have any of us around?"

"What *I* think—and here's something I *have* come pretty close to figuring out—is that our Tracie fell out of love very easily. She dug the romance, the sex, the custodial duties for a while. But when it all started to get a little old, there wasn't enough of what else we were giving her to keep her from looking elsewhere."

Marvin nodded. Then he asked, "Do you still miss her?"

"Every day, Marv. Each and every day." The two men got quiet for a moment. "Say, it's great to get together and share stories, isn't it? You take care of yourself, okay?"

Marvin nodded.

"And you keep right on putting those Mound City thugs behind bars, Counselor Remnick—present company's clients naturally excluded."

Marvin answered with a wordless salute.

Marvin watched Dennis walk out of the bar. He shifted his focus to Kurt, whose hand was on the bar's sound system, cutting Billy Joel off right in the middle of "She's Always a Woman to Me." Billy had just sung, "She is frequently kind and she's suddenly cruel."

Suddenly cruel. Yes, that was the marriage-jettisoning Tracie all right, thought Marvin.

Now *Saturday Night Fever* was back with "If I Can't Have You," performed for the movie by Yvonne Elliman.

"If I can't have you, I don't want no other, baby," Marvin sang along softly. Then he raised his third glass of Lauder's to the only woman he had ever loved. "You aren't getting rid of me that easy, baby."

Old Man Rivers raised his head from his bar towel pillow to make an unsuccessful (and clearly disingenuous) request for "one for the road." Yvonne kept singing and Marvin kept drinking and remembering and aching.

1979

GOING THROUGH THE MILL IN TEXAS

NO. 23,471

THE STATE OF TEXAS	}{	JUSTICE COURT
v.	}{	PRECINCT NO. SIX
ROBERTINE WINDROW	}{	DALLAS CTY, TX

AFFIDAVIT FOR WARRANT OF ARREST AND DETENTION

The undersigned Affiant, who after being duly sworn by me, on oath, makes the following statement: I have good reason to believe, and do believe, that Robertine Windrow on or about the 29th of October, 1979, did commit the offense of Assault by Contact.

1.) I the affiant was dispatched to 2415 Ector Crossing, Dallas, Texas, in response to a family disturbance.

2.) I met with Gus Windrow W/M, Zena Windrow W/F, and Robertine Windrow W/F.

3.) G. Windrow stated that R. Windrow had threatened Z. Windrow with a coffee pot. G. Windrow said this is not the first time R. Windrow has waved the coffee pot in a circular motion above her head, and on a good many occasions she has ended up hurling it at someone. Z. Windrow stated that this particular evening R. Windrow threw the coffee pot at her twice. The first time it almost hit the dog, Cuddles. Z. Windrow said the second throw struck her in what she believed to be the nape of the neck, although she has never been completely sure which part of the neck constitutes the "nape." I asked witness G. Windrow if he saw where the coffee pot struck Z. Windrow and he stated, "In the kitchen."

4.) G. Windrow stated, further, that R. Windrow is prone to frequent tantrums and has thrown the coffee pot at G. Windrow and Z. Windrow in nearly every room of the house. The victim, Z. Windrow, alleged that on one occasion R. Windrow followed her and G. Windrow to the Spoke and Reins Supper Club and threw the coffee pot at her while G. and Z. Windrow were kicking up their heels dancing the Cotton-Eyed Joe.

5.) Robertine Windrow is the daughter of Gus Windrow and Zena Windrow. Gus Windrow, however, is not her biological father. That would be Arliss Smuell, a W/M who lives in Fort Stockton and breeds ferrets.

6.) After questioning all present, I proceeded to arrest R. Windrow, who then began yelling "Police assault!" at the top of her lungs. When she realized that this was getting her nowhere, she began yelling "Attica!" and then "Fire!" and finally, with less steam, "Taxi!"

7.) R. Windrow was booked into DCJ. At this time she asked the booking sergeant for her coffee pot. This request was denied, though she was commended for her chutzpa.

8.) All the above occurred in Dallas County, Texas, except for the part about Arliss Smuell. He lives in Pecos County.

(signed) Deputy Strawn Birdie
Office of Dallas County Sheriff

SWORN AND SUBSCRIBED TO before me the Affiant on this the 29th day of October, 1979: Morris Morales, NOTARY PUBLIC

CAUSE NO. 23,471

THE STATE OF TEXAS	}{	JUSTICE COURT
v.	}{	PRECINCT NO. SIX
ROBERTINE WINDROW	}{	DALLAS CTY, TX

TO THE HONORABLE JUDGE OF SAID COURT:

NOW COMES THE DEFENDANT ON THIS 30TH DAY OF SEPTEMBER, 1979, AND PLEADS NOT GUILTY TO THE CHARGE OF ASSAULT BY CONTACT, AND REQUESTS A HEARING.

<u>(signed) Robertine Windrow</u>

OPTIONAL: State briefly your reason for pleading not guilty. (This information is requested for statistical purposes only and will not be considered as an adjunct to your sworn testimony.)

I read the affadavid which officer Birdie filled out on last night. I never seen so many lies on sheet of paper in my life. If he gets up that stand and spouts them same lies I'm going to through something right at him head I mean it.

Why did he lie? Why did he lie? I tell you why Officer Birdie lyed. Because my parents payed him. He took there money and lyed. Yes he was bribed. I tried to tell them at the jail. I say look in his pockets. Check the fingerprints on the money in his pockets. You'll find my Daddy's fingerprints. Say she swing that coffeepot round like it was a nunchuck. Here ten dollers. Say she hit in the nape. Here ten more dollers. Say she followed us to the Spoke and Rains Supper Club and through the coffeepot at us while we was kicking up our heels dancing the Cotton Eyed Joe. Here twentyfive dollers because that one was good one. Heh heh.

I'm just sitting there in the den being quite and not bothering nobody. Just watching the Newleywed Game and drinking my cupcoffee. That's all. Just drinking my cupcoffee. And he puts hancuffs on me like I was an animal and halls me off to jail.

It is an outrag.

NO. 14672

PUBLIC INTOXICATION

THE STATE OF TEXAS	}{	JUSTICE COURT
v.	}{	PRECINCT NO. SIX
ZENA WINDROW	}{	DALLAS CTY, TX

AFFIDAVITS FILED IN DEFENSE OF ZENA WINDROW

The undersigned Affiants, who after being duly sworn by me, on oath, make the following statements:

AFFIANT: VIONA HASKELL

My neighbor Zena Windrow has been inconvenienced since the summer of 1959 by her marriage to Gus, who is nothing but trouble in human form, and by their hellcat daughter Robertine, who throws coffee pots at people and watches Bob Eubanks without her clothes on. Zena is a good woman and does not drink as a rule until she is pushed to the limit, and even then, her intoxicated behavior is unobtrusive and almost demure, unlike her husband Gus and that she-devil daughter Robertine, who have been known to get into howling competitions with each other and ululate until at least two in the morning. The fact that her husband was arrested last night for celebrating too noisily the arrest of that sewer-mouthed minx daughter of theirs should have been no cause for arresting of Zena. She was merely a bystander to his antics, although she did hold a can of malt liquor in her hand as if she meant business.

AFFIANT: GINGER CRAMPO

I heard noise out in the street and thought it was Barbara Bel Geddes, who my husband believes comes into our neighborhood to hit garbage can lids together. I looked out to see Gus Windrow hooting and hollering as if he had just won the Irish Sweepstakes and banging garbage can lids together as if he was Barbara Bel Geddes. Zena was pleading with him to stop and trying to pull him back inside though he would have none of it. My husband said that he would call the police if Mr. Windrow didn't go back inside, but he ignored him and then went and peed on one of our tires. Not a tire that was on a car but the tire that I had been using for a raised marigold garden. Zena was NOT the one drinking!

PLAINTIFF'S ORIGINAL PETITION
SMALL CLAIMS CAUSE NUMBER 10212

Filed: October 31, 1979
Plaintiff: Ginger Crampo
Defendant: Gus Windrow

The Defendant is justly indebted to the Plaintiff in the sum of $55.00 for:
(Briefly describe the nature of Plaintiff's demand and claim.)

I am filing this small claims suit against Mr. Gus Windrow for damages that were done to several of my front yard ornaments last night. Mr. Windrow fell onto one of my hedges and trampled a bed of nasturtiums and urinated on my marigolds. What is more, he put toilet paper in my trees and I am not altogether certain that the toilet paper is fresh off the roll. I am enclosing Polaroids of the damage. You will note that in one of the pictures I am standing in front of one of my vandalized trees holding today's newspaper to establish that the vandalism occurred last night and not tonight. This being Halloween, I am certain that ruffians in my neighborhood will deposit their own toilet paper and Mr. Gus Windrow will insist that all of the toilet paper was theirs.

DEFENDANT'S ORIGINAL ANSWER
SMALL CLAIMS CAUSE NUMBER 10212

Filed: November 5, 1979
Plaintiff: Ginger Crampo
Defendant: Gus Windrow

I am contesting this lawsuit brought against me by Mrs. Crampo. I did not put that toilet paper in her trees. I'll admit that I was in a celebratory mood, as my daughter Robertine had finally been placed safely behind bars after spending a lifetime making her mother and me miserable with the hurling of various objects at us and speaking nasty of her mother's cooking, though Zena tries very hard to make good meals for us both in spite of the fact that she has to work two jobs, because I cannot work after an industrial accident that left both of my hands turned backwards.

Who is Mrs. Crappo fooling by standing out in her yard holding a newspaper dated October 31? I know for a fact that she filed this lawsuit on November 1 and gave it the date of October 31 so that I would have to clean up what those tricksters in the neighborhood put into her trees. And what does it mean to hold up a newspaper anyway? I could stand on the grassy knoll and hold up a newspaper from 1963 and you're still not going to believe that I was at Dealey Plaza on the day that JFK got shot, especially since there will be those (such as my wife Zena) who will tell you in all honesty that I was actually in Fort Worth at the time having a boil on my bottom lanced.

Mrs. Crappo blamed me for rolling her yard so she would not have to finger the roughneck boys. That's "A." And "B"—Mrs. Crappo blamed me because she is trying to build a case for having Zena and me evicted because her brother Vance Holman, who owns Holman Properties, wants us out as of yesterday!

NO. 5714

HOLMAN PROPERTIES	}{	JUSTICE COURT
v.	}{	PCT. NUMBER FIVE
G. WINDROW, Z. WINDROW ET AL.	}{	DALLAS CTY, TX

SWORN COMPLAINT FOR FORCIBLE DETAINER

TO THE HONORABLE JUDGE OF SAID COURT:

COMES NOW on November 7, 1979, Holman Properties, Plaintiff herein, and files this action of forcible entry and detainer against Gus and Zena Windrow and all others, Defendants herein, and in support of such action would show the Court as follows:

I.

Plaintiff is Holman Properties.

II.

Defendants Gus and Zena Windrow, and daughter Robertine Windrow, are individuals residing in Dallas County, Texas, and may be served with citation in this case at 2415 Ector Crossing in Dallas, Dallas County, Texas.

III.

This is a lawsuit to evict the Defendants from property located at 2415 Ector Crossing, Dallas, Texas, within the jurisdictional boundaries of Precinct Six, Dallas County, Texas.

IV.

The plaintiffs are on a month to month lease. Notice to vacate was given on September 6, 1979.

V.

Although the defendants have always paid their rent on time, they are not model tenants by any means and reasons for their eviction continue to mount like broken promises from an alcoholic whore. Most recently, a neighbor, one Ginger Crampo, reported that the defendant Gus Windrow ~~urinated on an ottoman in her living room~~ urinated on a tire in her front yard and draped her trees with soiled toilet paper.

VI.

There is also the matter of the daughter Robertine Windrow, who is a menace to the neighborhood, and we understand has just been released from jail so that she can continue on her rampage against the commons. An employee of Holman Properties once saw her through the window of Mr. Pickles' Laundromat taking delicates that did not belong to her from an unattended dryer and then rubbing them roughly against her cheek in an act of lingerie mischief. The employee went in and had a long talk with her. He told her that she could not continue to behave in such an antisocial way, and that she was a menace to the neighborhood. Did she not notice the way that neighbors retreated into their homes when she traipsed by? Did she not see them standing half hidden behind curtains, fearfully brandishing things with long handles and defensive prongs? Furthermore, he explained to her that if she didn't clean up her act, Holman Properties would have no choice but to evict her and her parents from its rental house. She responded by pouring an entire single-load box of Tide upon the employee's head, which released enough laundry flakes into his hair that he was comically nicknamed "Mr. Druff" at that morning's property managers' meeting. (His first name is Dan.)

VII.

Plaintiff prays that Defendants be served with Citations and that Plaintiff have judgment for possession of the premises as soon as authorized by law, and judgment for costs and attorney's fees, if applicable.

Respectfully submitted,
Axel Montgomery
7400 E. Nacogdoches
Dallas, Texas
ATTY FOR PLAINTIFF

CAUSE NO. 76119

THE STATE OF TEXAS	}{	IN THE JUSTICE COURT
v.	}{	PRECINCT NO. SIX
ROBERTINE WINDROW	}{	DALLAS CTY, TX

TO THE HONORABLE JUDGE OF SAID COURT:

NOW COMES THE DEFENDANT ON THIS 21ST DAY OF NOVEMBER, 1979, AND PLEADS NOT GUILTY TO THE CHARGE OF SPEEDING 85/45, AND REQUESTS A HEARING.

(signed) Gus Windrow

OPTIONAL: State briefly your reason for pleading not guilty. (This information is requested for statistical purposes only and will not be considered as an adjunct to your sworn testimony.)

My wife and stepdaughter and I had just been evicted from our house and were making every effort to leave the neighborhood in a timely fashion, but no, it was not fast enough for our neighbors, who were anxious to get their "Finally Free of the Windrows" barbecue block party started, so happy were they to have us gone that their display of joy bordered on the obscene. When some of the younger among them began to throw rocks and beer cans and Eight is Enough action figures at us, I put the pedal to the metal to get off of that street with my family and my life intact. This is why I was speeding. These were extenuating circumstances if there ever were any.

APPLICATION FOR PEACE BOND

STATE OF TEXAS   CAUSE NO 3422

COUNTY OF DALLAS

I, GUS WINDROW, ZENA WINDROW, AND ROBERTINE WINDROW, DO SOLEMNLY SWEAR THAT WE HAVE GOOD REASON TO BELIEVE AND DO BELIEVE THAT A MAN WHOSE NAME WE DO NOT KNOW BUT WHO IS REFERRED TO LOCALLY AS SASSYSQUATCH IS ABOUT TO COMMIT AN OFFENSE AGAINST MY PERSON, TO-WIT:

We are in fear for both our safety and our very lives. It all started when we were evicted from our house and had to go live in a drainage pipe. The pipe looked unoccupied, so we felt that squatters' rights would apply. Unfortunately, the hairy gentleman who does not speak except through grunts, or strange appropriations of the lyrics of songs made popular by Judy Garland, has made it clear that we must pay him (money which we do not have) or he will remove us by force.

"Forget your luggage, c'mon, get outta here! Before I chase all you deadbeats away!" That's from "Get Happy," if you don't know it, and that's exactly what we aren't these days. To have reached such a low point in our life trajectory! How we long for the old days when Robertine was on her Valium and I was on the wagon and we all could sit in perfect peace and contentment and drink our cupcoffee. How we miss that quiet cupcoffee and the close-knit family togetherness that accompanied it.

If we can get the court's protection for one week more, I'll have my disability check in hand and we can move someplace else. Where troubles melt like lemon drops and happy little bluebirds…you get the picture, I'm sure.

1980

RENOVATIVE IN TEXAS

I'd hardly gotten a chance to take a peek at my Batman comic book before he was back from the kitchen and the fuse box and climbing the ladder and telling me in his deep, crusty voice to pay close attention. I think he said this out of force of habit, because I was always paying attention. That's why I was there. That's why I was spending all of my summer vacation that year learning how to put a house back together so a person—in this case, *two* persons, my step-grandparents—could move in, could be comfortable, and in the case of this rusty old burned-out chandelier, could have a little light to eat their dinner by.

"Hold the ladder. Are you holding the ladder, son?"

"I'm holding the ladder."

"First you gotta—hand me that screwdriver, son."

I handed up the screwdriver.

"You gotta unscrew the canopy and pull it down the stem. You see what I'm doing?"

"Yes, sir."

"Once you get—okay, take this screw. No, no. Remind me where I'm putting it. I'm putting the canopy screws in my shirt pocket."

"In your shirt pocket—got it."

"Once you get the canopy down the stem then you gotta unscrew the wire caps from the connections. You wanna get a hamburger at Miss LuAnne's for lunch?"

"Okay."

"You want a grilled cheese?"

"Okay."

"And a Coca-Cola? Where's my tester? You see what I'm doing, Wayne?

I'm touching one of the probes to the black wire connection and the other one to the grounded box. Are you watching?"

"Yes, sir."

"You want a Grape Nehi?"

"Okay."

"You're a choosy one. Now I'm testing the white wire connection. Black wire, metal box. Everything gets checked. No glow on the tester. No juice. That's good. Hand me my water thermos. Throat's dry."

I handed Granddad his water thermos and he took a swig. Granddad's throat was always dry. Just a year earlier he'd had the cancerous part of his esophagus removed. Granddad always had his water thermos with him.

"All right. Now I'm untwisting the wire connections. Can you see?"

"Yes, sir."

"Okey dokey. Hold the light fixture while I take off the whatchacallit— the strap. You got it?"

"Yes, sir."

"I talked to your grandmother this morning—looks like she's gonna come see us next week. Asked her to bring you a sleeping bag so she could have your cot. You okay roughing it with a sleeping bag, son?"

"Yes, sir."

"Okay, I'm putting the mounting strap in my lower right pocket. Screws are in there, too. Now let's get to work replacing those sockets."

We got to work replacing the sockets. Granddad wasn't a licensed electrician, but I always got the sense that he knew exactly what he was doing. My stepfather shared my confidence, although my mother was a little leery.

"Your father's recovering from major surgery, Elvin," I remember her saying to my stepfather. "He probably needs three or four more months' rest. Maybe this isn't the best time for him to be undertaking a major renovation project."

But Mama was outvoted. Dad wanted me to spend the summer with my step-grandfather, and Granddad certainly appreciated the help. We were a team. And we got along pretty well. And even though I was only thirteen, I knew exactly what I wanted to do with the rest of my life. I wanted to go into construction—to be a building contractor. It was important for me to know how houses got put together, from the roofing and the dry wall all the way down to the sockets and the wiring, the mounting straps and threaded nipples.

Today we were rewiring the dining room chandelier. Tomorrow we'd be laying a frame for a new concrete driveway.

Granddad had bought this old house and the acreage around it for a song. Houses used to be pretty cheap in out-of-the-way hamlets like Windom, Texas. (I suspect they probably still are.) But even so, it was a point of great contention between my step-grandparents over whether they should make the purchase. And whether, ultimately, they'd both end up living there.

Granddad didn't say much about all that. In those pre-slumber, lights-out conversations from our cots in the still-unfinished bedroom, we talked about the Texas Rangers (both the baseball team and the law enforcement agency—Granddad's brother was a Texas Ranger of the gun-toting variety)—and we talked about trucks. Oh, how he loved his 1970 C/10 Chevy pickup. Medium gold and white—a real Texas workhorse. We talked about how he'd grown up in Fannin County and about how much he was looking forward to moving back after "way too many years in Big D."

"When the Ewings and all those Hollywood people moved in, I knew it was high time your grandmother and I got the hell out."

I hadn't known my stepdad's father very well. I was told to call him Granddad, and I did. Not having any other grandfather, I had no problem with that. But it wasn't until the two of us started our summer-long construction project that I really began to feel the way a kid is supposed to feel about his family elders. And while I guess you could say it was still in many ways the best summer I would ever spend, it was not without a few wrinkles.

The doctors had carved out the cancer, but Granddad still wasn't a healthy man by any definition. Sometimes a good part of his day would be spent trying to get his mind off the discomfort in his throat. I didn't ask about his prognosis. I just assumed he wouldn't have had the surgery if the doctors didn't plan for him to be around a while longer. And on top of that, I figured he wouldn't have been going to all the trouble of renovating a house and bugging my grandma to come live with him in it if he thought his number was nearly up.

The other wrinkle was that he slept with a loaded gun under his cot. ("A house out in the country like this—you never know who might come prowling around of a night.") This was something I never got used to. In fact, on our first night together Granddad told me I was supposed to wake him up when I had to go to the bathroom, or else he might hear me rustling around, shoot first and ask questions later.

I'd generally hold my pee for the whole night.

I came well stocked with comic books and car magazines, and we had the transistor radio, and I can tell you to this day all the songs that got the most airplay that summer. George Jones' "He Stopped Loving Her Today," Charley Pride's "You Win Again," and Mickey Gilley's cover of "Stand By Me" come right to mind. And Granddad had this honky-tonk station he liked that played the really old twangy stuff that made me think of grizzled men in dirty boots and goat-roper hats wailing through their tobacco chaws.

Sweet Jesus, I never forgot for a minute that I lived in Texas!

But there was something about my adoptive grandfather that I wouldn't come to realize until long after he'd died. And despite his best hopes, the good Lord only gave him another year and a half. That came out to about thirteen months my grandmother had to live in this house Granddad and I put together, far from all of her friends and civilization as she knew it. And it was this: The old man wanted to spend what time he had left in close communion with that place where he grew up. He showed me once where the little ranch house had stood, only about six or seven miles away. He was born there, he said, in a spot now reclaimed by weed and mesquite. This is where his roots were, where he remembered being happy as a boy.

And it's where Grandma got him buried.

Like I said, I didn't know this until after he'd died, the part about why it was he wanted to renovate *this* old house. I probably could have figured it out. If I'd pointed my brain in the right direction. But I was too busy getting my education.

Granddad let me fold the wire connections into the wiring compartment and screw the cover back on. While he held the chandelier, I tightened the mounting strap to the ceiling box and gently folded the wires into place. I slid the canopy up the stem, making sure that it pushed flat against the ceiling. Then I tightened the screws to secure it. We put in the new bulbs and reattached the shades, and he let me flip the switch at the fuse box. I left to him the honor of turning on the light at the wall switch. Even though it was early afternoon and there was sunshine coming in from both of the windows, the room became flooded with light. It was a warm light with a sweet yellow cast, and we did as we always did when we finished another stage in our summer-long project: we shook hands. Smooth palm to callused palm. He was my grandfather—not by blood, but certainly by heart. And I was the grandson he had never had.

After admiring our handiwork for another minute or so, we climbed into the cab of his Chevy pickup and headed to LuAnne's for a grilled cheese and a Grape Nehi.

I can still taste it.

1981

SELF-ANOINTED ABOVE, LET'S SAY, OKLAHOMA

It was the first time I'd ever flown First Class.

And the only time.

There are First Class people, and there are Coach people. Coach people are the great unwashed multitudes of us—young, old, poor, rich (because sometimes First Class gets filled up, and Reginald Kensington, Esq. and his wife Boopsy are denied, by circumstances, their caviar and champagne, and must eat peasant peanuts and drink populist pop with all the rest of us). First Class people aren't just people with money, they're also people with attitude. They're flying on the magic carpet of luxury because God has so ordained it.

I remember once being stopped right at the end of the jetway by a flight attendant who had suspended the boarding process until after all of her First Class passengers had gotten their pre-flight apéritifs. I wrote the airline to complain about this assault on democracy. I told them I was never going to fly them again. But of course I did.

And I flew in Coach. Always Coach, except for that one flight on April 15, 1981.

I was flying back to Cincinnati after having just completed an interview with American Airlines at their headquarters in Dallas. I don't know how things were before or after, but for a period of several years in the late seventies and early eighties, American Airlines jump-seated hundreds, perhaps thousands, of flight attendant applicants from all over the country for the purpose of preliminary group interviews—the only step in the multi-step interview process that I made it through. I thought I'd interviewed well. I contributed to the group "conversation" as well as any of the other girls and the three or four boys who hoped to begin careers in "in-flight customer care." I felt that I had said all the things I was expected to say—all the things that should have moved me along to the next stage in the interview process. (Word to all future flight attendant hopefuls: The most important responsibility of a flight attendant isn't making passengers comfortable—it's keeping them *safe.*)

But I wasn't called back.

They never tell you why, but I think I know what happened: I have a large mole on my chin. It isn't the most disgusting mole you've ever seen, but it's quite noticeable, and a former boyfriend, speaking, perhaps, on behalf of all of my former boyfriends, told me the night he broke up with me that, try as he may, he just couldn't get past it. I don't think the recruiters at American Airlines got past it either.

Anyway, there was an empty seat in First Class, and that's where the airline put me. Maybe I wasn't destined to be a flight attendant, but at least I could return to Cincinnati in style. And after what happened that afternoon, I'm happy I never had the opportunity to go into this line of work. I'm not sure what I would have done if placed in the same situation as the First Class attendant on that flight.

I don't remember her name.

Let's call her Susie.

I sat next to a young man who had something to do with the audio-electronics industry, and he was initially very talkative and friendly, but once he got a glimpse of the other side of my face (where the mole was), he suddenly got very busy marking up something spiral-bound with graphs and flowcharts.

Across the aisle from me were two women. I recognized the one in the aisle seat instantly. She was Tricia Swearingen, the forty-something-year-old televangelical wife of the televangelist Luke Swearingen. Both she and her husband preached the "Prosperity Gospel" every night and twice on Sunday on probably one of the most popular syndicated religious programs on the air that year. And it was apparent that Ms. Swearingen practiced what she and her husband preached, because here she was sitting pretty and prosperous in First Class, and I had to imagine that it was the contributions of thousands of the couple's loyal and generous viewers that allowed them to do this and such other things as keep a fleet of Mercedes-Benzes and live in a house that was beyond palatial (sometimes she and her husband would broadcast their show from the mansion's "great room"). The two were obviously quite proud of their wealth, which God, apparently, wanted them to have for doing His work so well.

My grandmother was a big follower of the Swearingens. When we had to move her to the nursing home and my dad and I were cleaning out her apartment, we found at least six different Bibles in her bedroom bookcase, each personally embossed on the cover and mailed to her, according to the accompanying letter, "as our way of saying thank you for your gracious love offerings to *The Hour of Faith*, hosted by Luke and Tricia Swearingen, and featuring 'The Hour of Faith Singers' and the blind Harpist for Jesus Marietta Gee." I always wondered aloud, when I found myself visiting my grandmother during the hour that the show was on, why it was that Brother Swearingen, who had helped countless crippled people rise up from their wheelchairs or throw off their crutches, and who had healed attendees to his televised services of everything from mild eczema to Hashimoto's encephalopathy—why it was that Brother Swearingen couldn't place his hands over the eyes of blind-from-birth Marietta Gee and give her blessed sight, since it wouldn't have affected the beautiful, angelic clarity of her plucking of the harp strings, and would have kept her from stumbling around backstage and sometimes disturbing the broadcast.

"Because it isn't God's will that Miss Gee should see," my grandmother invariably replied.

I debated whether or not I should introduce myself to Ms. Swearingen, since we had already exchanged pleasant smiles across the aisle, but I was in a terribly unsociable mood. I had come to the painful realization that my chances of being invited back for the next level of interviews were about nil (I think it was the way that the interviewer kept levelling side glances at my you-know-what), and there was that constant reminder of my failure in the person of the über-efficient, preternaturally polite flight attendant, Susie, who did not have a you-know-what anywhere upon her peaches-and-cream countenance. I finally concluded that I should not disturb the handsome yet slightly hard-featured telegenic preacher-woman. She was, after all, reading her Bible.

You believed me, didn't you? No, it wasn't a Bible. It was the latest issue of *Redbook*. And the real reason that, ultimately, I didn't say anything to her was because there was already someone doing just that: the forty-something woman sitting next to her. Because of the jet-engine drone I couldn't hear what that woman was saying to Ms. Swearingen, but it seemed to be a fairly one-sided conversation—the other woman talking, Ms. Swearingen nodding and appearing to be only half listening.

Apparently concluding through Ms. Swearingen's monosyllabic responses and her unsubtle body language (i.e. arms across her chest) that the popular evangelist really didn't wish to engage her, the woman got quiet and turned to look out the window at the billowy cloud shelf. Whereupon Ms. Swearingen mouthed a private "Thank God."

Maybe I should have just let it pass, but I couldn't help myself. "Excuse me," I said across the aisle. "I noticed that you just thanked God. I know who you are. My grandmother—she watches you and your husband all the time."

"Oh, is that so?" Ms. Swearingen pushed a fallen strand from her molded blond do back onto its rigid mound.

"So, if you don't mind me asking, what were you thanking God for? The safe return home of the orbiter Columbia yesterday?"

"Oh, no. Although I do pray for our brave astronauts each and every day. No, I just—" She lowered her voice, though she really didn't have to. It would have been difficult for the other woman to hear what she was leaning over to say to me. "Well, I just sometimes need a little time to myself. My life is very public, very hectic."

"What was she saying to you—if you don't mind me asking?"

"Something about—oh, I just couldn't get the gist of it from the way she was rambling. Something about her daughter. Who knows?"

I nodded. I had an open in-flight magazine in my lap, and I now focused my gaze upon its pages so as to let Ms. Swearingen know that she didn't have to keep talking to me. Seemingly grateful for her release, the televangelist returned to her own magazine, or to her nails—I wasn't going to keep looking at her to know for sure just which it was. All was quiet for about a minute and a half, and then the other woman turned and said something to Ms. Swearingen seemingly right out of the blue that was delivered in transparent anger, and then she pushed her call button, unbuckled her seatbelt, and got up. Susie, now wearing an apron that matched her uniform, emerged from the front galley to meet the woman in the aisle as Ms. Swearingen and I (and even the gentleman of the graphs and flowcharts) looked up. The conversation between the woman and Susie the flight attendant was near enough that I could hear every word.

"Is something the matter, Ms. Smith?"

"I can't sit next to this woman anymore. Can I move to that seat there?" The woman pointed to the empty seat right in front of me.

"I'm afraid that seat is occupied, Ms. Smith. The gentleman is in the lavatory. There are available seats in Coach if you'd like to go back there."

"I suppose I have no other choice. I can't sit here. My sister paid for me to fly First Class to see her, and now I'm coming home. You must do me a favor: please come get me when we land so that I can get off the plane with the First Class passengers, or my husband will worry that something's happened to me. He'll be waiting at the gate, you see."

"Ms. Smith, I'm afraid I can't do that. Once we land, the passengers generally jump into the aisles and there would be no way to get you past them without great difficulty. Won't you reconsider and keep this nice seat?"

Ms. Smith thought for a moment. Then she said, indicating Ms. Swearingen with a presentational upturned palm, "This woman makes my skin crawl."

"How horrible!" blurted the indignant subject of Ms. Smith's sudden wrath. "I've said nothing unkind to this woman. Not a single word!"

"That's right," spat Ms. Smith, "and you didn't say an unkind word to me when I phoned you last year either. You ignored my phone calls and didn't respond to a single one of my letters."

"I have no idea what you're talking about."

Susie placed a calming hand on Ms. Smith's shoulder. The shoulder was bobbing up and down as she gave in to a flood of tears. But she would not go back to her seat.

Ms. Smith pointed at Ms. Swearingen, and, choking back further waterworks, spoke in a voice that was both bitter and achingly plaintive: "My daughter, Cassie—last year she was seventeen. Last year she was very troubled, emotionally unstable. We were trying to get her help—to, to find her a doctor, because things were getting so bad. She was an avid viewer of your show, Ms. Swearingen. She watched it every night. Some nights she'd be on the phone with one of your prayer counselors for nearly an hour after the program was over."

"I hope that we were able to help her."

"You weren't. Prayer wasn't what Cassie needed. She needed a doctor, Ms. Swearingen—a doctor of psychiatry. She was cutting herself, burning herself with the lit ends of cigarettes. Your people told her that God would help her to stop if she only prayed hard enough."

Tricia Swearingen took a deep breath and then blew it all out in one long exhalation. "Yes, I remember that girl. To be very honest, Ms. Smith, our lawyers advised me not to take your calls or to engage in any written correspondence with you. They anticipated that you might be considering legal action against my husband and me and thought that this was the best course to keep the situation from escalating."

"But Hal and I aren't like that. We never even thought about suing you or your show. Even after Cassie wound up in the emergency room."

"I'm sorry, Ms. Smith, but you simply cannot blame my husband or me for whatever has happened to your daughter. Luke and I have always preached that the Lord helps those who help themselves. It is the lynchpin of our ministry."

"You heal people on your show—right there in front of everybody. Cassie believed with all her heart that you and your husband, as instruments of God, could heal *her*—could make her stop wanting to hurt herself. She believed this. She prayed and prayed and waited for these terrible impulses to go away. They never did. She attributed this to the fact that Satan had taken hold of her. One of your telephone counselors told her that there was a battle being waged inside her for her soul. The counselor told her that she must be strong to force the Devil out. Cassie tried to force the Devil out of her one night. In the bathtub. She nearly ended up drowning herself.

"Your people aren't trained to deal with people like Cassie. You're playing with fire. You pretend to heal people who come to your revival services, and those watching—they substitute the wild-eyed faith they see on your program for the scientific care of doctors. And you take their money. You're happy to take the money these people give you."

For a long moment Ms. Swearingen didn't respond. She was trembling. She pulled herself together, and then she said, "There is good that we do. Behind all the theatrics, my husband and I have made quiet differences in the lives of a great many people."

"Whether or not this is true, all I see is the circus."

"Where is your daughter now? What can I do for her?"

"She's in a psychiatric hospital, Ms. Swearingen. She's making progress. We hope that she'll be released soon. They don't let her watch your program there. They don't let any of the patients watch your show. There is a man there. He thinks he's the Messiah. He talks of wonders and miracles. He must be carefully watched. That man is no different from your husband, Ms. Swearingen. He is no different from you."

The pilot announced that the plane would soon be experiencing a little turbulence and all passengers should keep to their seats and buckle up. Susie took this as an opportunity to once again request that Ms. Smith sit down.

"I'll be serving the meal very soon. I've got a wonderful salmon and dill salad for you."

Ms. Smith nodded. Indicating Ms. Swearingen with a tip of the head, she said to Susie, "'Thou preparest a table before me in the presence of mine enemies.'"

"Psalm 23," said Ms. Swearingen numbly.

Ms. Smith nodded. "I neglected to mention that I'm a preacher's daughter. My late father had a country church." She smiled at the memory. "Just like the little brown church in the vale."

Nothing else was said by either of the two women for the remainder of the flight. After deplaning, I remained at the gate and watched as several of Ms. Swearingen's enthusiastic followers rushed toward her with flowers and balloons and signs that read "Welcome Home," "Cincinnati Loves You, Tricia!" and "God Bless Sister Swearingen." A couple of preteen girls shoved pen and paper at her, soliciting her autograph. I watched as Ms. Smith made her way over to a man I assumed to be her husband and the teenaged girl who stood next to him. I guessed that this was Cassie, and that she had just been let out of the hospital. The joy on Ms. Smith's face at seeing her daughter all but confirmed it.

As Ms. Swearingen and her entourage swept past, Cassie looked over at her. At the same time Ms. Swearingen seemed to be making every effort not to acknowledge any of the Smiths—Cassie included. Cassie's parents watched their daughter and then exchanged nervous glances. But their discomfort was quickly dispelled by Cassie's loving smile for her mother and father and the double embrace that followed.

The Swearingens' hold on young Cassie had, apparently, been broken.

A couple of weeks later, during my weekly visit with my grandmother at the nursing home, I asked her casually if she was still a regular viewer of *The Hour of Faith*. She shook her head regretfully. "They stopped healing people on the show last week," she said. "It isn't as much fun anymore. I watch Jim and Tammy Faye now. Tammy Faye's a hoot. She's a real scream, that one."

1982

REUNITED IN MISSOURI

Okay, so it's the end of June, and it's hot and muggy, and I can think of a lot of other things I'd rather be doing this particular weekend than driving all the way down to Kansas City to attend my thirtieth high school reunion, though as secretary of our class, I'm pretty much expected to show up. For Pete's sake, I live in southern Minnesota, not Iglooville, Alaska. I've really got no good excuse not to go.

So Vern and I pack our brand-new white 1982 Celebrity with Pringles and pop and all of our Peter, Paul, and Mary cassettes, and head down I-35. Vern's always such a good sport about this kind of stuff, and that's why I haven't divorced him.

The members of the planning committee are so cheap they decided to hold the main event in the high school gymnasium. I mean, what's wrong with the ballroom of some nice hotel? Or renting out some slightly upscale restaurant in the Plaza? But they say the gymnasium is in keeping with the nostalgia theme. I ask you, what high school reunion doesn't have a nostalgia theme? And besides, it isn't even our gym. *Our* gym was torn down ten years ago along with the rest of the school. Most of us have never even set foot in this new building—a building that, incidentally, wouldn't make a person nostalgic for much of anything unless she's got a thing for bad 1970s architecture. And to make matters worse, they even changed the name. It isn't Harry S. Truman High School anymore. Now it's *Bess* Truman High School, because somebody on the Kansas City school board decided that the former first lady deserved to have a school named after her, even though she isn't even dead yet (she's ninety-seven and could very well live to be ninety-eight). And boy are they proud to be beating Independence to the punch for a change.

Independence always had bragging rights to the Trumans and all those one-man-one-wife Mormons. Kansas City only has the Chiefs and the Royals (excuse me while I yawn.) And strip steak.

So here we are in a strange gym with big pictures of Patti Page and Eddie Fisher and the just-crowned Queen Elizabeth and Lucy Ricardo (holding that bottle of Vitameatavegamin and wrinkling her nose) and Gary Cooper and Julius and Ethel Rosenberg plastered all over the walls among the balloons and the crepe paper, and over the loudspeaker we can hear Frankie Laine and Connie Francis and Tex Ritter and even Walter Brennan singing "Do Not Forsake Me, O My Darlin'." And suddenly it isn't 1952 anymore. It's High Noon and everybody's feeling a little jumpy.

Right off the bat I start to notice some vaguely familiar faces. I say vaguely because—and I'm being kind—we have, as a class, not done a very good job of aging gracefully. Some of the girls I used to lead cheers with now look like their own grandmothers and half the boys on the newspaper staff I used to work with are cueball bald and a little hunched over and beaten down. (Ours was not a very wealthy neighborhood and there weren't a hell of a lot of bootstraps to go around.)

I make the rounds with Vern in tow, and compared to most of the men I meet—some of whom I dated, others of whom I wanted to date, and still others of whom I wouldn't have dated if we were the last man and woman on Earth and had to repopulate the species—Vern makes me proud. He's a couple of years older than this bunch, but I swear he looks ten years *younger*. He's trim and he's nice looking and he has almost all of his hair. I say my hellos and make as much small talk as I can that doesn't start with the phrase "Remember when we…?" and then I see somebody who makes this whole excruciating experience halfway worthwhile: it's Candy Melcori.

Candy was my best friend in the ninth grade and the tenth grade and the twelfth grade, although we hated each other's guts in the eleventh grade. What I've always loved about Candy is her ability to tell you exactly how she feels and not tiptoe around *your* feelings because, "You know, Yvette, life is too short, and patience and me: we just don't play on the same team."

Candy dated Rodney Tomasini during the 1950-51 school year (the year that Candy and I hated each other) and I told her (similar to the way *she* always told people exactly how *she* felt about things) that Rodney Tomasini wasn't good for her because he came from a family of lunatics and was once caught trying to drop a puppy from a tree to see what would happen. Granted, he was six at the time (and he was stopped before he could commit caninocide on a Beagle pup), but there was always something just not quite right about him. Anyway, Candy broke up with him right before the summer vacation between our junior and senior years. And she agreed with me that it was probably a good thing.

But the main thing I can't wait to talk to Candy about is Arnold Mordaunt, who I heard had just been released from prison only a few months before. In fact, I'm not the only person at the reunion with Arnold on her mind. I can hear quite a few conversations about his recent release being whispered all around the gym, which if nothing else has great acoustics. Arnold had been put in prison for the crime of manslaughter, though it was the opinion of most people who knew anything at all about the facts of the case that it was probably no accident at all; Arnold hated his ex-wife's new husband, the brakes were in fine working order, and frozen custard trucks don't just mow people down without some kind of murderous intent behind the wheel. The jury thought differently, though, and believed the expert witness's testimony that brakes will sometimes malfunction even when everything seems to be in good working order, and even someone with the car-handling aplomb of an Eddie Rickenbacker couldn't have avoided such an accident.

"So is he coming?" I ask Candy, while taking a sip of the punch that Vern has gotten for me so I won't have to interrupt Candy's detailed report on everything that's happened to the more interesting fraction of our 161-member class, both the terrible things that were undeserved and the terrible things that people clearly had coming.

"Mary Ellen said he RSVP'd yes. She said he paid both for tonight and for the farewell breakfast buffet tomorrow morning."

"So where is he?" I say, looking around. Almost everyone who's supposed to be here has already arrived.

"He'll be here," says Candy. "But I'm still surprised they even invited him. I mean, he's lived almost half his life in a jail cell. That has got to mess you up even if you *didn't* already possess a criminal brain."

"Do you think he has a criminal brain, Candy? Vern, honey, go make me a plate with the little chicken legs on it, and get me some broccoli with the garlic dip. The garlic dip, not the French onion dip."

After Vern leaves, I draw close enough to Candy to smell her Charlie perfume and the faint whiff of Aqua Net she sprayed on her hair like she was Doris Day and it was still 1961. "Did you go to bed with him?"

"When?"

"In high school. When you were going to bed with every guy on the varsity football team and in the Key Club, and somebody said one week you even stooped to the chess club when you got even hornier than usual."

Candy considers the question for a moment as if weighing whether or not she should dignify it with an answer, when, in fact, she's only counting up her conquests. "Arnold was number six. I thought I loved him. But he was dangerous. I could see it in his eyes, that cold-blooded killer look. You really could tell—even in the darkness of his truck when he's all over you with his hot hands. Killer eyes glow in the dark. Did you know that?"

"No, I didn't know that, Candy."

"I was sure that he was capable of committing murder one day. It ended up being his ex-wife's husband, but it could have been anybody who rubbed him the wrong way. Did you know that he used to throw custard cones at people who gave him a hard time when they put in their ice cream orders? What if he'd decided to remove Rodney Tomasini from the picture? To have me all to himself?"

"Did Rodney know you were going to bed with those other boys while the two of you were together?"

"Oh, I don't know. Ooh. Look at Patricia McCloud, or whatever she goes by now. You could set little tchotchkes on that ass shelf of hers, it's so—"

But I'm not looking at Patricia Last-Name-That-Probably-Isn't-McCloud-Anymore. My gaze is directed, instead, at the ex-con himself: Arnold Mordaunt. He's just walked in and is standing at the registration table. And I'm not the only one looking at him. I'd say the eyes of half of the members of Harry S. Truman High School's Class of 1952 are throwing looks in that direction, as if no one has ever seen a convicted killer before, and why on earth is he wearing that vertical blue-striped shirt, which only serves as a visual reminder of all the years he's lived behind bars as a hardened criminal?

What's he going to do, I wonder. We're all wondering. Why has he come to the reunion? Does he seek revenge on those of us who ignored him in high school because of his limited wardrobe and the fact that his hair always smelled of unwashed scalp, or because his poor grades and lack of motivation relegated him to 155th place in a class of 161? Or is it because we're intimidated by his hot-blooded temper—a temper that ignited several altercations with teachers and coaches and got him suspended on at least three different occasions during our senior year alone?

I picture Arnold behind the wheel of that frozen custard truck, trundling over his ex-wife's brand-new husband—a man who had done him no wrong except that he dared to marry the woman Arnold could no longer possess—and then backing up and running him over again to make sure he was good and pancaked. (That was the story we heard, but it wasn't the one that the jury got.)

Candy and I exchange looks of only slightly veiled apprehension. My stomach does a somersault as he starts to make his way toward us. Why? Why is he coming over here?

"I'm going to the little girls' room," Candy announces with a nervous laugh. "There's Rodney Tomasini over there. See him? The love of my junior year. Damn, he's looking good." And as Cindy backs away from me and away from the fast-approaching ex-con Arnold Mordaunt, she adds, "Maybe Rodney's forgiven me for two-timing him that whole year we went steady. And maybe he's outgrown all that crazy."

"Don't leave me alone with Arnold!" But Candy pretends not to hear me as she accelerates her retreat.

Arnold's eyes have that look—that look that used to send shivers down my spine when he'd get some act of mischief into his head and you could almost see the gears turning as he tried to figure out how he was going to pull it off.

"Hi Yvette!" he says, putting me into a near-bonecrushing bear hug. "Long time, huh? I've been in prison, you know."

"Yes, I know," I mumble, finding it hard to speak in a clear, calm voice.

"But that's all behind me now. In prison I found Christ. A minister I've been in touch with has lined up a job for me with a church outreach program over on Vine."

I relax. I actually start to look forward to hearing how Arnold Mordaunt has turned his life around. And I'm prepared to hear even more of this most inspiring story of faith and personal redemption, but something unfortunate keeps this from happening. Patricia Last-Name-That-Probably-Isn't-McCloud-Anymore announces through a bloodcurdling scream that my friend Candy Melcori has just been strangled to death in the little girls' room by a spectacularly vengeful Rodney Tomasini.

Same ol' lunatic Rodney.

1983

ETCHED IN STONE IN WASHINGTON D.C.

Ari Gregory hadn't slept well the night before. It wasn't the bed; it wasn't anything about his room at the Hotel Harrington. The problem was *Ari*. All day he'd been thinking—first in Wilmington and then on the train down to D.C.—about what he'd been reading about the new "gay epidemic." First the scientists called it "GRID," which stood for "Gay-related immune deficiency." For a while, the Centers for Disease Control had taken to calling it, informally, the "4-H disease," because it seemed to afflict, disproportionately, Haitians, homosexuals, hemophiliacs, and heroin users. Once word got out that prostitutes were also coming down with it, a fifth "H"—"hookers"—was half-facetiously added. Then, just last year the scientific community agreed on the acronym AIDS, the letters standing for "Acquired Immune Deficiency Syndrome."

Ari liked this better, but it didn't make him sleep any easier. Sometimes late at night he entertained wild thoughts—thoughts that never would have entered his head in the clear light of day—that a person didn't contract AIDS because of what he *did* but because of what he *was*. That there might even be some credence to the malignant words of the smug fundamentalist preachers: that AIDS was God's punishment for being gay. Yet, if this were true, thought Ari, what had hemophiliacs done to deserve it? Or Haitians? It made no sense. So little of it made sense.

When Ari confessed this fear to his friend Trevor, the wise British expat didn't bat an eye. "Gay people are paranoid by nature. Society makes sure that we stay that way. There's no reason you *shouldn't* think you could get a disease just because of who you are. There's also no reason that I can't from time to time slap a little common sense into that worrisome puss of yours."

It was June. Seven months had passed since the Vietnam Veterans Memorial was dedicated. Ari put off going until the crowds thinned out. He didn't want the crush of visitors to spoil his pilgrimage. He wanted to see the name of his friend Brad etched into the black granite. He had gone through high school with Brad, and then the two went off to college together—William and Mary. Ari studied colonial history, Brad was pre-law. Ari graduated. Brad dropped out to go to Vietnam, even though nobody—*nobody* was volunteering go to 'Nam in 1968. By 1968 everybody had gotten the memo: this was a fucked-up war, this was a war that couldn't be won. Guys were doing everything they could think of to *keep* from getting shipped out, to get themselves discharged once they got drafted. Even the doyen of broadcast journalists, Walter Cronkite, regarded as the avuncular conscience of the nation, had turned against the war.

Ari had wanted to tell Brad what a mistake he was making. He'd wanted to beg Brad to stay home, to finish college, to be the lawyer he'd always wanted to be. Ari loved Brad. But it was a different kind of love than the kind that Brad felt for Ari. He was Ari's best friend—Damon to his Pythias. The two had run track together in high school, had worked on the yearbook together. But Ari's feelings for Brad ran much deeper. Ari loved Brad more than he'd loved anyone in his life. He had followed him all the way to W & M, for Chrissakes.

After Brad's death in Ninh Thuan in May of 1969, Ari had been shattered. He'd even contemplated suicide. Life was different for Ari after Brad died. From that point forward it was a life only half lived.

Ari wondered if seeing Brad's name on the Memorial wall would help him let go. It was all pop-psychology shit, he knew that, but he was willing to try anything. Fourteen years was a long time to mourn someone who didn't even know you'd been nuts about him.

Because Ari had never given Brad even an inkling as to his true feelings. Because Brad was as straight—as proud a pussy-loving heterosexual as they came. There was a silver lining to Brad's death, Ari would have to admit: that Bradley Patterson didn't live long enough to have to face the day when Ari, unable to contain his feelings any longer, confessed his love and let the chips fall where they may. It could have been messy. It could have been very, very messy.

Today was Brad's birthday.

Ari grabbed an egg sandwich and cup of coffee at a counter-diner in the neighborhood of the hotel and then walked over to the Mall. It wasn't too long a hike—just long enough to give Ari more time to think. And to worry. The world had never been a safe place, especially not for people like him, but things seemed even more precarious now. Several months earlier, Ari's brother and sister-in-law in Lawrence, Kansas, had acted as extras in *The Day After*, a television movie about a nuclear attack on the United States. The movie was set to air in November. While Reagan was busy rattling his presidential saber at the Soviet Union and forming his global shield initiative (dubbed "Star Wars" by a skeptical press), an American embassy was bombed by Islamic terrorists in Lebanon with great loss of life.

Reaching Constitution Gardens just north of the Reflecting Pool, Ari quickly found himself convoyed by several groups of people moving silently—almost reverently—in the same direction. Though referred to as "the Memorial Wall," the monument was actually two walls that came together at a 125-degree angle, both seeming to rise up out of the ground to convey the sense of a great gash—a wound that was now closing up, in the process of healing. People of all ages and ethnicities stood or squatted or bent down before the wall, each relating to the monument in his or her own way. Hardly anyone was speaking. There was a sepulchral hush among the memorial's visitors that was undisturbed even by whispers. It was as if all conversation in this sacred place was limited to telepathic dialogues between the living and the dead.

Ari stopped first at the directory at the west end of the wall. The directory contained the names of the nearly 58,000 dead and missing servicemen and their location on the 144 panels. He quickly located "Bradley Patterson, Panel 25W, Row 81." He walked to the designated panel and then counted down the rows to number 81. There, flanked by a Marvin E. Park and a Washington Pauley, was Bradley Patterson. All three men shared the same death date: May 12, 1969. There were others who'd died on this day as well.

With his fingers, Ari traced the straight lines and the curved contours of the etched letters. Several panels to his left a woman was making a pencil rubbing of one of the names. Ari had no desire to do this. He had other, more meaningful totems by which to remember Brad—snapshots, his high school annuals, the Cream album (*Disraeli Gears*) that Brad had bought when Ari dared him to take a sabbatical from country music and get himself something halfway hip, and which he had ended up gifting to Ari after tripping out one night and ever thereafter swearing off both psychoactive drugs and psychedelic rock.

Ari allowed his fingertips to linger there for a moment longer and then he pulled his hands away. He stepped back. The ground right in front of the monument was covered in flowers and dog tags, teddy bears and toys. Ari was reminded that most of the American men who had died in the war were hardly men at all, so many of them mere teenage boys with mothers and fathers who had many years of life left to mourn their fallen children.

Ari had seen the name he had come to see. He didn't feel like looking at the names of the other men—many of whom, had they lived, would be close to his own age: thirty-five. The number of the dead—his contemporaries—whose names had been forever carved into that wall overwhelmed him. He turned, and in doing so came face to face with a young man who looked to be in his early twenties. The man bore a very strong resemblance to Brad. In fact, the resemblance was so striking that Ari was taken aback. It was as if Brad had been standing behind him, looking over his shoulder for the last several minutes.

The mystery was quickly solved. The young man said, "Are you here to see my brother—to see my brother there on the wall? I noticed you were touching his name. You weren't touching any of the other names."

"Is your brother Bradley Patterson?"

The man nodded. He had long ash-blond hair that he brushed away from his eyes. They were Brad's eyes—the same emerald brown, the same smiling creases in the corners.

"You're Randy, aren't you?"

The young man nodded. "And you're Ari."

"You were, what—six or seven when he died? In my mind I don't think I ever let you grow up."

Randy Patterson shrugged and half-grinned. "But since my name isn't Peter Pan, I didn't have much choice."

"What are the odds that we'd both wind up here on the same day at the same time?" asked Ari.

"Not so bad. This being Brad's birthday and all. I wanted to come early because I have to get back to New York. I go to Columbia."

"What are you studying—no, let me guess. Pre-law like your brother?"

"I don't know. I haven't made a declaration. Right now I'm spending most of my time working for Gay Men's Health Crisis. Have you heard of it?"

Ari nodded.

Randy elaborated: "AIDS is already an epidemic, but they're predicting it's going to get a lot worse before the guys in the lab coats can get a handle on it."

Ari, noticing the close proximity of several of the other visitors, said, "Are we done here?"

Randy nodded. The two men started to walk away from the wall, and toward the lake.

Ari pointed. "Last year they put a memorial on that island. It's dedicated to all the signers of the Declaration of Independence. I thought I'd check it out."

"I remember somebody saying you studied colonial history at William and Mary."

"I did, but who would have told you—Brad? You were a little kid at the time."

"One of my parents, I guess. Later. Maybe years later, I don't know."

"So there was mention of me after Brad died."

"You were my brother's best friend, weren't you? The two of you used to do everything together. Dad said he always knew you were gay, the way you ran after Brad like a frisky little puppy."

Ari stopped. "I didn't come out to anybody until I was almost thirty. Your dad must have had some finely tuned antenna when it comes to this sort of thing."

Randy nodded. He smiled. "Hey, he figured *me* out before I was twelve. I think it was the way I threw the ball during all those Dad-mandated t-ball games. Brad was dead and I was his surviving son, and talk about one father's lousy luck. The dead son was a Vietnam War hero and the live one's a 'fucking fruit salad.' Direct quote. And I didn't come out quietly, either. The shame of it was enough to make him resign as president of the Rotary Club."

The statement had bite. And relevance. Brad's kid brother didn't hold back. His frankness was a little startling, but also refreshing, especially given that so much of Ari's interaction with the world had been so guarded, and far from indicative of who he really was.

"You have to catch a train?" he asked.

"I'll catch a later train. You hungry? Can you look at your 1776 memorial some other time?"

Ari nodded. "A friend of mine recommended the cafeteria at the National Gallery. Don't laugh, but they're supposed to have this really great Southern menu."

Randy grinned. "Do the cooks charm the husk right off of the corn?"

"Yes, Mame. I understand that they do."

The two men had an early lunch of fried chicken, mashed potatoes, collard greens, and cornbread.

Randy remarked that he felt like he was back visiting his grandmother in Oklahoma.

Ari remarked that he had been in love with Randy's brother since the two boys met in the seventh grade.

"What do you think he would have done if he'd known?" asked Ari.

"Probably knocked your block off. From what I heard—and remember that I didn't have the pleasure of getting to know my brother all that well— he probably wasn't, in truth, the paragon of sensitivity and tolerance that you wanted him to be."

"He was good to me. We were pals."

"But he didn't know the real you. I'm not saying he was an asshole underneath whatever it was he put out to you; I'm just saying he was probably just like every other straight guy who grew into red-blooded American manhood back in the sixties. The whole idea of homosexuality was a real brain-fuck to them. Same as today, maybe even worse now. You know what they're saying about gay men these days—that we brought this disease on ourselves. I'll grant you the promiscuity in the gay community is something that's a little hard to defend. But speaking as a bona fide fruit salad, we don't deserve to be marginalized, or worse, *demonized*. Reagan hasn't said a word about the AIDS crisis, and I don't think he's going to. The only time he's opened his mouth about gay people was to remind voters during the election that he doesn't condone their 'lifestyle.' And my mother wonders why I'm an activist."

Ari stood up. "I'm getting more coffee. Do you want anything?'

"No thanks."

Struck by a sudden thought, Ari sat back down. "You think I'm a little nutty, the way I've carried a torch for your brother all these years?"

Randy shook his head. "I know you loved Brad, even if in my lowly opinion there might not have been enough there to sing a torch song over. Don't get me wrong. He was a good man. I loved him too. He was my brother. But he wasn't out to change the world. He wanted to get his degree, get himself hired by some big corporate-ass-kissing law firm, snag himself a blond trophy wife, and sire his two and three-quarters children, just like society expected him to. You fell in love with him—if I can be so bold—because he was one hell of a looker. God, was my brother gorgeous. I don't blame you. But be careful how you lionize him or whatever. He was a guy who—I'm trying not to oversimplify this, but I can't help myself—a guy who just happened to be blessed with very good looks. As you can probably tell, it runs in the family."

Randy winked.

"I did notice that you inherited some of those same genes. But I think you're wrong about Brad. *And* me. I'm not that shallow. There was something else going on there."

"Your homosexual fantasy. What is this masochistic thing we gay men have for straight guys? Hey, I need to get to Union Station."

"Any chance I could—"

"See me again?"

"Well, yeah."

"What? To give me another shot at trying to topple my brother from that pedestal you've placed him on? Or is there some *other* reason?"

"I'll take 'B.'"

Randy shook his head. "Presently celibate. And planning to stay that way."

"Since when?"

"Since I contracted AIDS. You don't want to get mixed up with me, Ari. I wouldn't wish this disease on my worst enemy."

Knocked back by this admission, Ari didn't speak for a moment. Then, softly: "Do your parents know?"

Randy shook his head. "I'll tell them when I have to. Look, I didn't intend to drop this bombshell on you, but given the fact that you sometimes have trouble letting go of people, I thought it best to nip this in the bud."

"You're being awfully presumptuous."

"I can tell by the way you're looking at me. I can tell that you're looking at me and thinking of Brad. And I know that this can only lead to a bad end."

Randy stood and held out his hand. Ari, a little dazed, shook it slowly in a loose grip. "Bye, Ari. You take care of yourself. I mean that in every possible way."

Ari watched as Randy walked out of the cafeteria. Ari finished his second cup of coffee and then wandered through the museum, only half registering the paintings that hung all around him.

Later he returned to his hotel and cried. He cried for a very long time.

And then he went to the Air and Space Museum.

1984

PATRIARCHAL IN CALIFORNIA

Regina appreciated the support. She really did. Because she didn't want another child. No matter how much Guy did. The Chillwaters had four children already—all girls. A fifth kid—that much-hoped-for Chillwater boy—well, look, it just wasn't going to happen. Not if Regina and the couple's four daughters and Guy's sister and her husband and Guy's mother had anything to say about it.

Yet Guy was obdurate, immovable, infuriatingly pigheaded in refusing to give up on his dream of perpetuating the family name through a son. Even though his own mother didn't seem all that broken up about seeing this branch of Chillwaters get an unintended pruning.

Edith Chillwater sat with her daughter-in-law, Regina, and her daughter, Amy Crew, in Pauley Pavilion on the campus of UCLA. They had obtained three hard-to-get tickets to the women's gymnastics competition and cheered on Mary Lou Retton while intermittently discussing Guy Chillwater's obsessive need to have a fifth child—in other words, to get himself a son.

"I think she's going to do it," said Edith to Amy. Both mother and daughter wore sweatshirts emblazoned with the words "red," "white," and "blue," each word displayed in the appropriate color.

"But you're wrong. I can't. I won't," said Regina, in between sucks from her McDonald's soda cup.

"I think Mama's talking about Mary Lou Retton," said Amy. "Isn't she adorable?" Mary Lou was, at present, negotiating the balance beam with pint-sized éclat. "So much spunkiness in such a tiny Italian American body." Amy looked at her McDonald's scratch-off game ticket. "And if she wins, I get a Big Mac."

"We *all* get Big Macs, honey," said Edith. "I think this promotion is going to put Mr. Kroc out of business."

"Mr. Kroc is dead, Mama," said Amy. "He died a few months ago."

"His *people*, then. They must have distributed all these tickets before they learned there was going to be a Soviet-led boycott. Serves them right for betting against the U.S. in gymnastics."

Edith glanced at her daughter-in-law. Regina wasn't even looking at Mary Lou Retton. She was staring at the corded forearms and rippling shoulders of one of the youthful male gymnasts who had taken a seat a couple of rows down. She sighed. "Guy really wants a boy."

"Well, my son should have learned a long time ago that he can't always get what he wants." Edith patted Regina on the leg. "He has four beautiful daughters and he should be pleased and proud and let it go at that."

"He never had a son to toss a baseball with."

"He has Janie," interjected Amy. "Or has she grown out of her tomboy stage like my Tamara?"

"I think Janie will always be part tomboy. But she isn't a *boy*." Regina sighed again. "I'm sorry to have laid all of this on you. You and Evan and your kids have been so wonderful to us. We wouldn't have even been able to come to the Olympics if you hadn't offered to put us all up."

"It's really been no trouble at all," said Amy. "But I could have told you that bringing Guy to a place like this—surrounded by all these strapping Free-World male athletes—was going to get him feeling bad all over again about the fact that he wasn't able to have a son."

Edith snorted. "My son can be a real ninny."

Several days later, Guy Chillwater had a chance to be a ninny with his sister's husband Evan. The two were watching the women's 3,000-meter race at Los Angeles Memorial Coliseum, and had just a few minutes earlier witnessed Mary Decker's dramatic collision with the barefoot South African Zola Budd, and Mary's collective-gasp-inducing stumble and ruinous fall. All eyes were pinned on Zola now to see if she would be able to ignore the chorus of boos that instantly rained down upon her to win the race in the absence of Decker's competitive interference. Evan, however, was taking in the pack in the aggregate. "Do you see these incredible women?" he asked his brother-in-law. And then half under his breath: "Apparently you can become a star athlete even without having a dick between your legs."

"I wouldn't care if my son turned out to be an athlete or not."

"Not buying it, Guy. You have all the makings of one of those 'my-kid-über-alles' Little League dads who heckle umpires."

"Then you have me all wrong, Evan. Do you mind if I watch the rest of the race? I want to see if any more of these athletes who aren't men fall on their female asses."

"That was low." This response came not from Evan, but from the woman sitting on the other side of Guy. She scowled. "I feel sorry for your wife."

Guy sank down—thoroughly emasculated—into his seat. The woman looked Japanese. Guy later told Evan that he had spoken so freely because he thought she couldn't understand English.

Guy Chillwater had a chance to talk the whole matter over with his two oldest daughters—his teenagers Janie and Carol Ann—as the three stood in the audience line, waiting to be seated for a taping of that night's *Tonight Show*. "Your mother says it bothers you two—the fact that I want to bring another kid into this family."

"It does a little, Dad," said Carol Ann, who was seventeen and wise. "Because of how much you want to give us a little brother. We don't need a little brother. Really. It's okay."

"How do *you* feel, Janie? Wouldn't you like to have a little brother?"

Fifteen-year-old Janie contorted her lips and nose into a look of mild annoyance. "Whatever floats your boat, Dad."

"Don't you want someone to carry on the family name? It's not a very common name. It deserves wider distribution."

"It's a strange name, Dad," said Carol Ann. "Sometimes people think I made it up."

"I think it sounds Indian," said Janie.

"You act like that's a bad thing," said Guy.

Janie shrugged. "I'm just saying."

Carol Ann said, "I just think you need to respect women a little bit more, Dad. Men may have had all the power in this country since, like, *forever*, and look at where that's gotten us. I think you need to give the women of the world some credit for trying to change things for the better."

Guy thought about this while he was watching all the women chattering away in front of him on *The Tonight Show* soundstage. Johnny Carson had the week off; the substitute host for that afternoon's taping was Joan

Rivers. Her guests were Mary Lou Retton and Dame Judith Anderson, who was appearing on screens across America that summer as the Vulcan High Priestess T'Lar in *Star Trek III: The Search for Spock.*

Dame Judith Anderson, as Guy's mother Edith would tell everyone that night as the two families and their matriarch gathered in Evan and Amy's TV room to eat pizza and watch delayed broadcasts of the Olympic competitions they'd missed that day, was eighty-seven years old. She'd had a long and imminently rewarding career as an actress. Dame Judith had probably never thrown a baseball in her life, but no doubt made her mother and, yes, her father very, very proud. Edith pictured Dame Judith's father watching her sinister portrayal of Mrs. Danvers in *Rebecca*, mentally tormenting poor Joan Fontaine to the brink of suicide, then clapping his hands together and crying, "A capital performance, my dear girl! You nearly scared the wee out of me!"

Two days later, as two of Guy and Regina's daughters and Evan and Amy's two daughters, accompanied by Regina and Amy themselves, stalked shopping-minded celebrities up and down Rodeo Drive, Guy and his mother sat on a bench in the floral wonderland that was the gussied-up campus of the University of Southern California (and site of the McDonald's Swim Stadium), digging into a single Wendy's Frosty with separate plastic spoons.

"So what's this all about, Guy? You know you can tell me. You've told me everything since you were a boy. Remember when you were twelve and you had that inflammation on your rectum? Other boys your age would have suffered in manful silence, but you came right out with it."

Guy winced. His mother was only sixty-eight, but she had the habit, common among those a few years older than her, of turning the self-censorship switch to the off position when it seemed convenient.

Mother and son could hear, not too far away, the voice of the diving announcer giving the results of the previous hour's finals. Nearby, a large group of Olympics spectators had gathered to trade pins. Guy's youngest daughters, Jackie and Belinda, were among them. Belinda, at the young age of nine, Guy had earlier noted to his mother, was a skilled trader. She had even acquired pins from a couple of the boycotting countries—a commendable feat.

"I just remember Dad telling me once that the proudest moment of his life was the day I was born. Not Amy, I'm sorry to say, but me—his only son. He said it made him prouder than helping to defeat the Nazis. Even prouder than the month he was named top salesman at Holiday Motors."

Edith leaned in and said in a mock confidential whisper: "I've got news for you, scout. It's not such an accomplishment. Ask one of the biologists in that science building over there. Sometimes a man gives the woman he impregnates an X and sometimes it's a Y. It's all chance. There's no skill to it at all."

"I'm just saying that it made him proud to *have* a son."

"Why?"

"What do you mean why?"

"Why did it make him proud, Guy—except that this is the crack brained way the world got set up, and your father was always one to follow the crowd. If there was one thing that I would have changed about him, it was the fact that he let too many other people—*men*—influence how he saw the world. You're different from your father in that way. At least I've always *thought* you were different, because I've always believed that you had a little of your mother's independent streak running through you. So let me ask you: have *I* spent my whole life moping around because I wasn't born with a pud in the place of a Lady Slit? The world is what we make it, scout, and you have four wonderful daughters and a wife who makes me a proud mother-in-law every day of the week, and it breaks my heart that you and she and those lovely girls have to live all the way back in Connecticut and not here in Southern California, where I can dispense grandma-hugs whenever I get the notion. And here's the other thing: Regina's womb is tired. She's almost forty-one. She doesn't need to be having any more babies, just so you can roll the dice again in hopes of getting a boy. You need to give this up, honey, and be proud of what you have."

Guy bowed his head. Without raising it, he said, "Regina and I made love last night."

"Was that what you were doing? I heard moaning; I thought you'd eaten something that didn't agree with you."

"We didn't use protection."

Edith's face fell. "Oh, honey, no." Then Edith thought for a moment. "Let's be realistic. What are the odds?"

The odds, as it turned out, were very good. Regina, still fertile into her forties, got pregnant. Regina said that she didn't think she would—that she was throwing a bone to her husband, whose obsession with having a son was ruining the first really good vacation the family had had in years. Not to mention their enjoyment of the Olympic games.

There was no question that they would have the baby. Regina believed in reproductive rights for every woman; she also believed in her own right to give birth to whatever baby took it to mind to start growing inside of her—be it boy *or* girl.

Guy Chillwater didn't want to know the sex of the child beforehand, so he didn't look at the sonogram. Regina promised that she wouldn't look at the sonogram either.

The obstetrician looked at it, but kept a very good poker face.

A little less than nine months after the closing ceremonies of the 1984 Los Angeles Olympics—in which Guy and Regina, and Guy's mother, Edith, and Guy's sister, Amy, and her husband, Evan, and Guy and Regina's four daughters, and Amy and Evan's two daughters and one son sat in Los Angeles Memorial Coliseum and watched a nearly interminable sequence of fireworks to the tuneful accompaniment of multiple verses of "All Night Long (All Night)" sung by the talented Mr. Lionel Richie— Regina delivered unto Guy a precious little five-and-a-half-pound girl.

Which Guy named Rory, after her maternal grandfather.

1985

SMITTEN IN WISCONSIN AND MINNESOTA

Byron and I met in Madison—at the university—and we never left. We lived in sin for a couple of years, and then, finally bowing to pressure from our parents, we married. Byron got a job with the campus radio station and was recently hired by Wisconsin Public Radio in the programming department. I've worked more jobs than I can remember. This past summer I sold homemade glycerin soaps at the farmer's market at Capitol Square. You would know me if you saw me: I have long, straight hair (like Cher used to have before she entered her lioness phase) and I'm either wearing a patterned t-shirt and hip-huggers or an overly ruffled Mother Hubbard in my periodic attempts to be fashion-subversive (though in this town of subversion-by-default—I think our current nickname is "The People's Republic of Madison"—people tend to wear whatever the hell they want).

But this isn't about me. It's about Byron. It's about the reason that Byron and I aren't together anymore, though he calls me every day to beg me to come back. Our official status: separated, but not yet divorced. Because I'm not sure yet if I want to divorce him.

Is being incredibly pissed and really, *really* weirded out proper grounds for divorce?

It all started with the death of my great-aunt Rue, who departed unmarried and childless but in possession of a house filled with scrapbooks, photo albums, and family keepsakes. Aunt Rue never threw anything out because she felt that she was the keeper of the family flame—the official archivist for her branch of my family, never perhaps considering the fact that once she died, people would have to come together and somehow divide up (or discard) the tons of family memorabilia (mostly crap) she had accumulated over her eighty long, very acquisitive years on earth.

Aunt Rue lived in Mankato, Minnesota. We all—her four surviving siblings, all the nieces and nephews, and a few of us great-nieces and nephews—gathered and grieved for about ten minutes and then rolled up our sleeves and got down to the real reason for our visit to this warehouse-with-a-bed-and-toilet: excavation. I inherited all of her photo albums. Nobody else wanted them. Aunt Rue wasn't a bad photographer, but she didn't edit. I thought Byron was going to kill me when I drove up in the Excel with twenty photo albums on board, all containing pictures of people Byron has never met, with the exception of my seventy-eight-year-old grandmother, whom he had met only once, at our wedding.

But he was pretty cool with it. More than cool, actually. Byron was fascinated with this voluminous photographic record of multiple generations of one Minnesota family. We spent a whole Saturday night getting stoned while he asked me the names of nearly everyone in the pictures, eventually becoming quite proficient at identifying the subjects himself.

He was especially taken with my grandmother.

Let's just give that statement a little breathing room.

Let's just circle around that statement and poke it a little and see if it's as dangerous, as potentially marriage-shatteringly cataclysmic here at the outset as it would later prove to be.

Lingering over her photograph—one of those eight-by-ten studio portraits (I forget the occasion, the college cotillion or something)—he said, and I would not make this up: "She's the most beautiful woman I've ever seen in my life."

"Excuse me. Maybe you haven't noticed that your reportedly beautiful wife is still in the room."

"And now I know where you got every little thing about that face of yours that's always turned me on. That gently sloping nose. Those smoldering eyes."

"You can't say hair, Byron," I said, pointing at the picture. "Nobody's done their hair like that since Gloria Swanson."

"I'm having a transcendent moment. Don't ruin it. Look at her. How many boyfriends did she have in school?"

"I don't know. I just know that she met my grandfather at the university. That's who she wound up with"

"How did *he* get so lucky?"

"I'm not sure that I'm enjoying this conversation, Byron."

"I'm just saying—look, all I'm saying—"

"Is that you have the hots for my grandmother. Although you didn't even hint at this possibility when you met her at our wedding."

"I don't remember meeting her at the wedding. Did you introduce me *before* the ceremony, when I was hung over from the bachelor party, or *after* the ceremony, when I was brain-fucked on champagne and weed?"

"Help me find a place for all these photo albums. They're dusty, and I don't want to have to take another Allerest."

"I want this picture." Byron removed the glamour studio portrait of my twenty-year-old grandmother from the album.

"What are you going to do with it?"

"Can I hang it on the wall? Don't people have pictures of their grandmothers up on their wall?"

I eyed Byron suspiciously, but didn't say anything.

A couple of weeks later I had to drive to Milwaukee to attend a bridal shower for one of my college suite-mates. Because I would be gone the weekend, I left some healthy food choices in the fridge. In my absence, my husband will usually eat only Whoppers and multiple Happy Meals, or fill up on crap at one of the many Madtown brewpubs where he likes to hang out with his friends from the radio station. Byron is such a typical "Madison man" it's frightening: he'll spend an hour Bonzo'ing President Reagan with his equally Republican-loathing, liberal NPR cronies, and then, masculated by beer, he'll shift gears and devote the rest of the evening to trying to out-macho his he-men companions by talking Packers and venison Brats and memorable moments in the annals of female conquest.

But not this weekend. This weekend Byron stayed home and entertained my grandmother.

How do I tell this without throwing up a little in my mouth?

I left Milwaukee early. One of my ex-boyfriends showed up. Not at the shower, but later that night at the motel, not only to see me but to visit with *all* of the women he had balled during that scorched-earth period of my sophomore year when he must have been keeping tally on some wall somewhere. Reliving it all creeped me out and I split a few hours earlier than I'd planned to. I was supposed to be home by Sunday afternoon; instead, I got home early Sunday morning—a little after two in the morning to be exact.

There were lights on.

Good, I thought; Byron's still up. I can score some points by telling him that, faced with the prospect of spending time with a man who now makes my skin crawl, I came home to my husband instead. I opened the front door of the apartment. There were candles on the dining room table that had burned themselves down to the point of gutter-glow. I checked my impulse to call out his name. There were two plates on the table, two wine glasses with a little puddle of wine in each. It looked like someone had used our apartment for a romantic evening out of the Rock Hudson/ Doris Day playbook.

The room smelled of some perfume that I couldn't readily identify— but it was intensely floral and reminded me in a flash of recall of something one of my elementary school teachers used to wear. It was a venerable scent. It was the scent of an older woman with sensible shoes.

I crept to the bedroom, not knowing what I would find there, afraid to open the door that had been left slightly ajar. Had Byron picked someone up? Did he go out and bring a woman back to our apartment? A mature woman? Was the *Falcon Crest* matriarch Angela Channing having an affair with my twenty-six-year-old husband?

I held my breath. I pushed open the door. There was my husband, shirtless in the bed (and I assume naked under the sheet, since this is how he normally slept), and next to him—I will just say it. You will be kind, I hope. There, lying next to him, was my grandmother—my mother's mother—my Nanna-Lou. Not in the flesh. In a special surrogate form especially prepared by my husband Byron. He'd enlarged the face of my grandmother from the picture he'd taken such a liking to, and had pasted it over the face of the blow-up doll he must have gotten at some porn shop.

He was asleep. He was smiling in his sleep. My grandmother was still awake. She was smiling, too. She was smiling and staring at the ceiling of our bedroom, as if she were reliving in happy remembrance the at first romantic, then disgustingly carnal night she had just spent with my husband, her own grandson-in-law.

"Byron," I said. "Byron?"

Two more invocations of my husband's name roused him from what I assumed was blissful post-coital sleep. But the smile disappeared in a heartbeat. My husband stammered. No words came.

I had plenty of words I could have said, but all that came out was, "You're beyond sick." Then I fled to spend the rest of the night with a friend.

When I returned later that morning, Byron had prepared his explanation. "I know that you will find this hard to believe, but I have fallen helplessly in love with your Nanna-Lou."

"Byron, you stupid fuck, she isn't that beautiful young woman anymore. You've created a wild fantasy for yourself, because I'm apparently no longer good enough for you."

"That isn't true."

"You got intimate with a blow-up doll, Byron. A blow-up doll with my grandmother's face on it."

"I only kissed and caressed it. I swear!"

"It's still sick. Nanna-Lou is seventy-eight years old. What would she say if she ever found out that you've been getting off on thinking about going to bed with her ever since you saw her picture in that photo album?"

"Well, here's the thing, baby. I think I want to drive out to Rochester next weekend and see her."

"You are rubber-room insane."

"Hear me out." Byron sat me down on the sofa. He still hadn't removed the dishes from the dining room table.

"Did you pretend that she came to dinner?" I asked, glancing over at the table. "Did you actually put food on a second plate and pour a second glass of Chablis?"

Byron nodded. "She wasn't all that hungry—or thirsty. I finished everything for her. She gently corrected my table manners and reminded me to chew my food more slowly. I think, baby—I think it might help if I spent some time with her. With how she is right now. You know, old. I think it would help me to let go of my fantasy—come to realize that it will never—can never be. Sometimes fantasies are only unfulfilled wishes that quickly dissolve away in the bright light of circumstantial reality."

"How long did it take you to come up with that?"

"Let's go see her. She doesn't have to know about any of this."

"You better hope to God she never finds out."

The next Saturday Byron and I packed the Excel. I made a gift basket of some of my favorite scented glycerin soaps, and we drove to Rochester. My grandmother had lived for many years in Yorba Linda, California. But she moved back to Minnesota after my grandfather died. She also wanted to be near the Mayo Clinic. She said that whenever her sciatica flared up it gave her peace of mind to know that the best doctors in the world were located only a few blocks away.

True to his word, my husband dropped not even the tiniest hint that he had been wrestling with a terrible romantic obsession, said not a word about the fact that he had fallen madly, crazy-ass in love with a woman who, in fact, no longer existed. He came to see, through the course of our visit, that her beauty was different now, and the most beautiful thing about her was her kind and loving heart. I loved my Nanna-Lou. She was a sweet, doting, comical old soul. This is the person whom Byron got to know that afternoon. And my grandmother liked Byron. In fact, she said she had warmed to him at first sight—at our wedding—in spite of the fact that he had obviously gotten himself hammered and had not shown himself in the best light.

We had meatloaf. And Nanna-Lou had baked an apple strudel. She talked of my grandfather, of my mother and my three uncles, and, thankfully, very little of her co-ed days, when she was the campus catch.

Shortly before it was time for our drive back to Madison, I excused myself to pick a bouquet of evening primroses from her garden. When I returned, Nanna-Lou and Byron were seated on the sofa, a photo album between them. My grandmother was pointing to a particular photograph. Her eyes were moist and she was touching the corners with a lace handkerchief.

"His name was Harold Connelly," she said with whispered reverence. "And I would have married him the minute he asked, but he dropped out of school after only a semester to help out at his father's farm. Do you see the resemblance?"

I saw the resemblance. Harold Connelly looked very much like my husband Byron. My skin went cold.

"I have always wondered what it would have been like if he'd fallen in love with *me*."

I sat down next to my grandmother. She was now sitting between the two of us.

"Sometimes when I picture Harold," she said, her words softly and carefully delivered, "he's making love to me. The wine, the candlelight." She sighed. Her gaze was fixed upon my husband. It was as if he, for that brief, transcendent moment, had become Harold.

As Byron and I walked to the car, Nanna-Lou stood behind the screen door watching us. We got in the car. But before Byron could turn the key in the ignition, he turned to me and said, "I just need a minute. There's something I have to—" He didn't finish his sentence. He strode up the stone path to my grandmother's bungalow, climbed the stairs to her porch, opened the screen door and then took her in his arms and kissed her fully upon the lips.

Then he returned to the car. We drove back to Madison in silence, while I entertained thoughts of divorce—thoughts I am still having to this day. Because my two-timing husband is still having an affair with my grandmother, in his mind.

But then, Lord only knows what's going through my Nanna-Lou's head. That hussy homewrecker.

1986

LOCKED OUT IN TEXAS

In June of 1986, a long-forgotten, five-by-eight-foot Remington Rand safe was discovered in an office building under renovation in Doylestown Township in Pennsylvania. A locksmith was hired, the safe was opened, and its contents were revealed before a number of interested onlookers and local historians. Discovered within were various account books and other papers pertaining to the Moravian Pottery and Tile Works, glass photographic plates, copper plate-blocks for printing illustrations of tile designs, and, for those eager for at least something historically idiosyncratic, a few animal bones and birds' nests.

The locksmith, a gentleman named William Kroche Jr., had no trouble cracking the safe.

Likewise, syndicated broadcaster Geraldo Rivera had no problem earlier that year opening up the secret vaults of notorious gangster Al Capone in a live television program appropriately called *The Mystery of Al Capone's Vaults*. What was discovered therein was breathtakingly anticlimactic: several empty bottles. Mr. Rivera surmised that they had once contained bathtub gin.

On August 19, luggage locker number 227 in the Spencer Street railway station in Melbourne, Australia, was opened with minimal effort and that which was discovered inside was exactly what police had been looking for the last two weeks: the stolen and ransomed Picasso painting, *The Weeping Woman*.

On November 25 of that same year, Fawn Hall, secretary to Lt. Colonel Oliver North, unlocked with a simple turn of the wrist a file cabinet in her boss's office, so that she could retrieve confidential papers that she would then smuggle out, conveyed within her leather boots.

Each safe, vault, luggage locker, and file cabinet noted above was opened with relative ease. In keeping with this pattern, you might think that it should be an effortless thing for an old man—entirely naked but for his gym-issue towel, standing in front of his locker in the basement of Town Lake YMCA in Austin, Texas, on the morning of Saturday, December 6 of that same year—to turn the dial of the single-dial Masterlock which dangled before him and gain easy access to his possessions inside.

And it *would* be a simple and easy thing if the old man, whose name was Lester Henderson, could remember the numbers of the combination in their proper order.

But he could not.

As hard as he tried.

The numbers had been there in his head not twenty minutes earlier, when he had put his gym clothes and shoes inside the locker and locked it up and padded barefoot and bare-bodied to the showers. And the numbers had also been there three afternoons before when he had come to the Y— just as he had come today—to lift dumbbells, to punch the boxing bag, and to toss the old-fashioned medicine ball about. All these things he could still do, though there were now things that he could not—things that his wife of forty-nine years, whose name was Audrey Henderson, would no longer permit him to do. Lester could no longer cut the grass, for example, after Audrey had found him standing motionless one day in the yard, the motor of the mower still whirring, either lost in thought, or thinking, more troublingly, of nothing at all.

He could no longer light the backyard grill and attend the flame after it flared up one day and singed his cook's apron.

And he could no longer drive. This was the hardest prohibition to accept. He had started driving when he was thirteen; he had driven the pickup truck on his father's ranch north of Waxahachie. He had taught all three of his own sons to drive.

On some days Lester understood fully why his wife felt it necessary to take these things away from him. He wasn't as sharp as he used to be, he had to admit, and much more forgetful as of late. On other days, however, Lester Henderson raged against his wife for relegating him to a kind of second adolescence—one with restrictions and curfews, and marked by a humiliating lack of trust.

Audrey had driven her husband to the YMCA that morning. He had told her that his friend Charlie would be there. The two men usually worked out on the Nautilus machines and sparred with the boxing gloves and then went for a trot around Town Lake, which was actually a dammed section of the Colorado River overlooked by the skyscrapers of downtown Austin on the north side. But this particular Saturday Charlie would not be there. Lester knew this, but he lied so that his wife would let him come to the YMCA that morning while she shopped. There was very little that she and their grown children allowed him to do for himself these days. At the gym, he could be his own man. He could be the young man that he once was, working his muscles and expanding his lungs. Lester felt invigorated, revitalized there. He didn't feel like the doddering, forgetful person he had become. Not the Alzheimer's victim that everyone else knew him to be.

The numbers had left his head. They had been there only minutes before; he had turned the dial in the correct access sequence—clockwise to the first number and then counter-clockwise past the first number to the second and then clockwise again to the third number. It had always been so simple for him that he could almost do it without thinking.

But now he was forced to think about it quite a bit. The first number was thirty-six…he was sure of this much. But the second and third numbers remained elusive.

The locker room was nearly empty. It was late morning. The early risers had finished their crack-of-dawn workouts and gone home. The young men who came in the afternoon after sleeping off their carousing from the night before had yet to arrive. There was a man at the end of the row of lockers, but he seemed in a hurry to dress and leave, and Lester was reluctant to bother him. There were classes going on upstairs—aerobics and abdominal intensives. He could go up there and find someone, let them know that he was having trouble with his lock, but the towel was small and left a good part of him fully exposed. His was an old man's body, drooping and flaccid and covered with wrinkles in spite of his best efforts to tighten up à la the eternally youthful Jack LaLanne. This wouldn't work at all.

The only thing that potentially *could* work was to sit and think and perhaps the numbers would eventually come back to him. Or he could sit and wait for one of the young YMCA employees to come by—one of the young men who gathered up the used towels and wiped down the exercise machines.

Lester sat. He wondered if he would have to stop coming to the gym. It was important to lock up his clothes. Clothes often got stolen from unlocked lockers. He liked to shower at the gym. The shower at home was over the bathtub. Sometimes he would forget to put down the non-slip bathtub mat and his wife would make a comment. She would say that she was going to start doing it for him, because she didn't want him to fall and break his hip.

Audrey had started to do too many things for him already. Things like chauffeuring him around. Smaller things like going to the grocery store alone when the two had always gone together. It was something they'd done since they were young newlyweds, pinching pennies and eating buttered spaghetti, and rice and beans. He was an undergraduate at the time, studying accounting at the University of Texas on a small scholastic scholarship.

Lester laughed mordantly to himself. As a CPA, he had spent his life around numbers. He had arranged them for specific purposes, subjected them to countless mathematical operations, used them as a form of language to tell hundreds of different stories. Numbers comprised the nuts and bolts of his life. His facility with them had provided a good home for his wife and three sons, had put each of his boys through college.

Now the numbers betrayed him. They left him sitting naked and wet upon a wooden bench facing a locker that would not allow him access because he couldn't crack the elusive code. His world had become inscrutable—filled with things that had stopped making sense to him. He felt helpless. And he hated feeling helpless, hated feeling dependent.

Men would soon come into this locker room in large numbers—young men, vibrant men, men with their lives spread out in front of them—they would come and see him in this compromised state and they would pity him and there would be nothing he could do to win back their respect.

The man at the end of the row had been turned away from Lester but was now clearly looking in his direction. The man's name was Cleve. Cleve was in his early thirties—just slightly younger, he appeared to Lester, than Lester's youngest son Jack.

Cleve closed his locker door and slung his gym bag over his shoulder. He started out of the locker room but then stopped and turned back to focus on Lester again.

"You having some trouble there?" Cleve asked, casually but not mocking.

"A little, yes. I can't seem to get my locker opened."

Cleve nodded. "You got it open before you went into the shower, right?"

Lester nodded. "But it's giving me trouble now."

"Oh." Cleve walked over and set his gym bag down on the bench. He was wearing jeans and a sweatshirt. His hair was wet and combed and he smelled like Dial soap. The smell reminded Lester of his sons, who had often come down to dinner from showering after their late afternoon football and basketball practices smelling strongly of deodorant soap and youthful colognes.

Lester had no trouble remembering the way that things smelled or tasted or felt. Memories of these visceral things had yet to break faith with him.

"What's the number? I'll try it for you."

Lester didn't answer. Nor did he look up to meet Cleve's eyes.

Now Cleve understood.

"Let me go find Manuel," he said. "He's around here somewhere. I'm sure he's got a bolt cutter."

"Much obliged," said Lester. The words were those of his rancher father. He didn't know why he said them. They took Lester back to a time long, long ago—a time that he'd been visiting through his memories more and more often.

Cleve returned five minutes later with Manuel, a man in his late twenties who worked for the YMCA. Manuel was sorry to admit that he *didn't* have a bolt cutter because someone had stolen it. The day before yesterday. He had it on his list to buy a new one, but regardless, he couldn't get to petty-cash until the director came in on Monday. Lester thought that there must be a safe in the office that held the money box—a safe that was just as impenetrable for Manuel as Lester's locker was for him.

"You tried the combination in several different ways?" asked Manuel.

Lester nodded. Cleve took Manuel aside and spoke to him quietly. Manuel nodded in response. His look became sympathetic.

Lester could easily guess what was being said. Such things were always spoken in whispers and with backs turned. People were always talking about him and giving him that same look. It angered him, and yet, was it not true? He couldn't get into his locker because his brain had ceased to retain the numbers that access required. It was a very simple fact—a medical, a scientific fact. Like the clean science of numbers. Numbers don't judge. They just *are*.

"Is there someone who's supposed to come here and get you?" asked Cleve with a hopeful look. The last thing, obviously, that Cleve wanted to hear was that Lester had driven himself—that the keys to his car were also there in the impregnable locker, that special arrangements would have to be made before the problem could be fully resolved.

"Yes. My wife." Lester glanced at the clock on the wall. "She's supposed to be here in a little over an hour. I was going to walk around Town Lake first. It's a nice day, and I was going to finish my workout by walking around the lake just as my friend Carl and I do. I mean Charlie. It's what Charlie and I do every Saturday."

"Well, you can't go and meet your wife wearing just that towel," said Manuel, pointing. "Let me get the lost and found box and we'll find some clothes for you to wear home."

There was nothing for Lester to do but nod in agreement. It was the best plan. It was the only plan. Audrey was shopping. Lester wouldn't be able to reach her even if he'd wanted to. She would pull into the parking lot of Town Lake YMCA, not at all expecting that her husband would not have his clothes with him—that, until Manuel brought the lost and found box, all he would have would be a towel.

A few minutes later Manuel returned with the box. Together, Manuel and Cleve and Lester went item by item through the contents of the box of forgotten or abandoned gym clothes.

"This your size?" asked Manuel, holding up a sleeveless Nike workout shirt.

"That shirt reeks, Manuel!" cried Cleve. "Let's find one that won't asphyxiate him!"

Clothes—halfway clean clothes—were found which semi-fit. And shoes that didn't fit at all, but were only needed to get Lester up to the parking lot to meet his wife's car. Cleve plopped a baseball cap on Lester's head to complete the mismatched ensemble before making his quick exit.

"See you next Saturday, Lester!" he called. "Key lock: that's the ticket. Hang the key dog-tag-style on a chain around your neck. That's what I do. Can't stand combination locks."

Manuel had to go too. He had work to do. Lester thanked him again.

For the next fifty minutes, Lester Henderson sat on the wooden bench in front of his locker. He didn't want to wait upstairs. He didn't like what he was wearing. He looked silly. He had on oversized sweat pants that ballooned out like harem pants, a sweatshirt a couple of sizes too small, and mismatched sneakers. He took off the cap, and then, feeling warmly about Cleve's friendly gesture, put it back on again.

At twelve twenty-eight—nearly the time that Audrey was due to pick him up—Lester rose to climb the stairs to the main floor of the YMCA. He turned and started out of the locker room. He took three steps and stopped.

36 right. 6 left. 10 right. It simply popped into his head. He smiled to himself. And then he laughed out loud.

And then he went to unlock his locker. 36 right, 6 left, 10 right, and the lock released. Humming happily, jubilantly to himself, he took off the borrowed clothes and put on clothes of his own from inside the locker. He celebrated his reborn independence by slamming the locker door shut, the noisy clangor reverberating in his ears.

Lester Henderson was spiking his football.

"I've been parked out here for nearly ten minutes," said Audrey from the driver's side of the front seat as her husband slid in next to her. "I was starting to worry about you."

"Everything's okay."

"Are you having a bad day?"

Lester shook his head. "No, I'm having a good day." He smiled. "A *really* good day. Let's get a burger on the way home."

1987

MOTHERLY IN GEORGIA

The world is a mysterious and often confusing place. Especially for a three-year-old. Nona Connor understood this. She thought of herself as the mother hen and her thirteen little ones as her chicks. But Nona also knew that a three-year-old child should still be allowed some freedom to discover and explore. Every moment carries the possibility of being a learning moment. This was the balance that Nona had learned to strike after nearly thirty years of teaching preschool, or even more specifically, after nearly thirty years of teaching three-year-olds. Always three-year-olds. Less infantile than the two-year-olds (and, praise God, out of diapers!) but more pliable, more trusting than the four-year-olds, who could sometimes be wild and wicked little handfuls.

Nona had her routine down, yet she varied it just enough each year so that she and her assistant, Miss Kalette, would never fall into a rut. There were books and magazines that she browsed for ideas. But a good many ideas came from Nona Connor's own fertile imagination.

Take, for example, the pointer Nona used each morning to lead her little ones through the big felted sentence strips she had mounted upon her classroom wall—sentences that changed each day. Together she would point, and Susie and Christopher and Jason and K'lynn and Sharry and Amber and Jessica and Jamaal and the others would recite aloud with her: "Today is [Tuesday]. Today's helper is [Megan]. This week's color is [green]."

It was the pointer that was special, that was uniquely Nona's. It had a tiny glove on one end of it filled with batting, and Nona had pulled the thumb and fingers together—all of them but the index finger, so that the finger did the work, and the finger even had a little personality going for it.

There was never a dull moment in Nona Connor's classroom of easily distracted three-year-olds. Moving them all about the room from activity center to activity center became a game in itself, each of the areas of her preschool classroom—its dull green cinderblock walls hidden behind colorful pictures and displays, easels and cubbies—catching the eye with chromatic splash and warmth and humor. There was a song Nona and Miss Kalette sang that took the children into Circle Time: "Let us take our little mats and sit upon the floor. Today I am a mighty lion. Tell me how I roar. And *what*, little creatures, be *you* today? One – two – three – who wants to play?"

For nearly thirty years, Nona Connor had shown up for work at a little past eight in the morning, greeting the equally early-risen director of the Buford Baptist Church Preschool, which was only two miles from Nona's house in the city of Marietta north of Atlanta. For nearly thirty years, Nona had prepared her classroom for the day. She'd changed the sentence strips on the wall, set out the puzzles upon the puzzle table, arranged the peg boards and sewing cards and interlocking wooden blocks that tiny hands would soon plug and thread and put together and pull apart with serious purpose. Hands that would someday work factory machinery, take blood pressures, draft contracts and steer heavy highway rigs. Nona was old enough now to be teaching some of the children of her first three-year-olds.

And for nearly thirty years, Nona Connor had led her class in the "good morning song": "Let's *clap* hello for Joshua. Clap hello. Let's *wave* hello to Heather and Billy and Annaree. Let's *smile* hello to Erica and Brock…" And when it came time to lead the children single-file out to the playground, there was even a song that Nona sang which accomplished the task of well-behaved transport with perfect efficiency: "One, two, three. All eyes on me. Four, five, six. Fingers on our lips. Seven, eight, nine. Walking quietly in line. What a funny song we love to sing! *Today's* little helper, take your swing!"

There were routines and there was a schedule, and though some flexibility was always allowed—a trip to the filmstrip room on some days, for example, in the place of Quiet Book time, or a visit to the gym on days when there was inclement weather—Nona Connor liked the routine just as much as the children did. It gave her a feeling of security, just as it gave her little three-year-olds a structure and familiarity with the day that kept them feeling safe in an adult-run world of mystery and confusion.

Long after they had left at noon, Nona Connor thought about her children and how to fix what little problems might crop up—the child who spent too long on the potty and held up the class, the boy who wouldn't let go of his favorite truck, the little girl who always wanted to hold on to Nona's leg. Nona even dreamed about her children, for these were the only children that Nona would ever have.

Except for Cory. Nona Connor had Cory in her life for three years.

In late July, Nona got a call from Deloria Wasson, the school's director. Nona was out and the call went to her machine. Nona found it odd that Deloria should be calling, because the first teachers' planning meeting for the fall wasn't scheduled for another couple of weeks. It was also odd that Deloria didn't give her reason for calling. Nona called her friend, Rosanna Walker, who was in charge of the school's day nursery—"Mother's Morning Out," it was called.

Rosanna didn't have it in her to teach. But she liked taking care of little babies. This job was perfect for Rosanna—so perfect that she had been doing it for the last ten years. During this time, she and Nona had grown quite close.

"So what is it? Do you know?" Nona could hear the sound of Rosanna's television in the background. "Are you watching something? Do you want me to call back?"

"I'm fine. I'm waiting for Genie Francis. She's moved over to *Days of Our Lives* from *General Hospital*."

"Why does Deloria want to talk to me?"

"I'll tell you, but please don't tell Deloria I told you. I promised her I wouldn't."

"Just tell me, Rosanna."

"Holly's not coming back next month. I know she waited until, like, the last minute to tell Deloria, but when has Holly ever done *anything* the right way? Deloria knows a woman who'd be perfect for the three-year-olds but she doesn't have any experience with four-year-olds. She's going to ask if you'll teach the four-year-old class."

"I don't have any experience teaching four-year-olds either, Rosanna."

"You can do anything. You know you can."

"I want my three-year-olds. I'm going to have Skyler's little brother Jared this year. And Bethany Towler's little sister Brianne. I've really been looking forward to it."

"Deloria needs you."

"Deloria will have to find somebody else. Seniority has to count for something. Even in a church preschool."

"She isn't going to like it."

"She'll just have to deal with it."

Rosanna took the remaining two minutes of the phone call to talk about the weekend jaunt to Stone Mountain she had made with her geologist husband, Chase, who said that the two should visit the big carved rock more often and stop taking it for "granite." Rosanna added that her husband should be on Johnny Carson, he was so funny.

Nona had never married. She had a little boy. She didn't *have* him have him. She *kept* him. She started the paperwork to adopt him. He belonged to Nona's younger sister Eve. Eve lived in New York City. She was an artist… and a drug addict. Nona took Cory down to Marietta with her to keep him out of the foster care system. And because he was her nephew. And because she loved him and he deserved to have the mother that Eve could never be.

Until, that is, Eve cleaned herself up. And then took him back. Cory was three. A day didn't go by after that in which Nona didn't think about Cory. He'd be well into his thirties now. Nona had stopped speaking to her sister after Eve reclaimed her son. It was the most painful thing that Nona ever had to do—giving up that little boy.

He was three.

Rosanna didn't know all there was to the story of Cory—the fact that Nona had grown to love him as her own. And Deloria didn't know the story at all. At least not until Rosanna told her.

"We need you to teach the four-year-olds, Nona," said Deloria the next morning in her office. "Maureen can't do it. Maureen's a good assistant, but I'm not at all comfortable giving her full responsibility for that class. This is about that little boy, isn't it? Your sister's son."

"How do you know about Cory?" Nona had tried to stay seated in Deloria's office, but she was too agitated, too fidgety, and was now standing at the window.

"Rosanna told me. I have to be honest, Nona. You're a very good teacher and I see how much you love the children. But it isn't just three-year-olds who need you, and it doesn't make sense that you only want to teach three-year-olds unless you've got some wild idea in the back of your head that someday another little Cory is going to come walking into your room, and, honey, that just makes you sound a little screwy."

Nona didn't take offense. "They're *all* little Corys in a way, Deloria. I can't explain it. I just have an affinity for children that age."

Deloria stuck a pencil in her electric pencil sharpener. She had been sharpening pencils when Nona walked in and now seemed to need something to do with her hands. The pause in the conversation gave Deloria a chance to choose just the right words for what she wanted to say next. She pulled the freshly sharpened pencil from the hole and the sharpener got quiet again.

"Have you seen Cory—I mean, since your sister was granted custody of him again?"

Nona shook her head.

"But why? After all these years, don't you ever wonder about him?"

"Of course I do."

"Do you wonder sometimes if he ever thinks about *you?*"

"How much do *you* remember from the age of three, Deloria?"

"Not that much, I suppose. You don't want to know what happened to him?"

"If I wanted to know what happened to him, I'd call Eve. But it's a call I'm not comfortable making. We haven't spoken for years."

Deloria sat down in a chair near where Nona was standing. Deloria motioned for Nona to take the chair next to her. "Honey, you can't hate your sister for getting better and taking her child back."

Nona sat. She didn't reply for a moment. And then, in a very quiet voice, she said, "I don't hate Eve. I admire her for turning her life around. But Cory wasn't hers anymore. I was with him for three years. I did telephone sales from my house so I could be with him, so I wouldn't have to put him in a nursery. So that people could see that even as a single woman I was fully capable of raising a child, of loving a child. So that there should be no doubt that I was the right person for Cory."

"I'd be curious, if I were you. After all these years, I'd be curious to see him now. To ask him if he has any memories of the woman who was there for him in the beginning."

"I let that go a long time ago." Nona bowed her head almost as in prayer. A moment later she raised up and met Deloria's eyes. "If there's no way around it, I'll teach the four-year-olds. But I want my three-year-olds next year. Is that a deal?"

"It's a deal, honey."

*

Rosanna found him. It wasn't her place to do it. But Rosanna loved a good story—especially one that had the potential for a happy ending, just like Luke raping Laura on *General Hospital* and then Laura falling in love with her redeemed attacker. Rosanna crossed her fingers. This one just *had* to have a happily-ever-after. Nona deserved it. She'd given nearly thirty years of her life to teaching her little ones to say their numbers, to put on their tiny coats one sleeve at a time, to wipe their paintbrushes on the side of the jar before attacking the manila paper on their art easels, to put away their toys prior to Story Time, to make funny heads out of Play Dough with just the right number of orifices, to pledge allegiance to the flag, to wipe their little bottoms like big boys and girls, to think of things that rhyme with "shoe," to make presents for Mommy and Daddy.

He lived in Tallahassee, Florida, and worked in the athletic department of the university there. He didn't even seem surprised by the call. "I know I have an aunt," he told Rosanna. "I know that she and my mother have never gotten along. I thought someday I'd look her up. I know she never married, so I've got no cousins."

"I'm sure she'd like to hear from you," said Rosanna. Then Rosanna took a breath and said, "You don't know, do you?"

"Know what?"

"That she took care of you the first three years of your life."

Cory shook his head. "Mom said I was put in foster care."

"You have no memories of that time?"

"Vague ones. Some nice lady who wore pearls."

"She still wears pearls."

Cory didn't call. After getting the full, true story from his mother, who now ran a gallery in Soho, he drove up to Marietta. And when he turned up on his Aunt Nona's doorstep that Saturday, he had someone he'd brought along with him (with his wife's somewhat hesitant consent).

A little boy. Three and a half years old. He looked just like his father at that age: round face, plump cheeks, long black lashes over bright, brown, wondering eyes.

His name was Brandon.

And he liked trucks.

1988

STOUTHEARTED IN FLORIDA

It was an elaborate scheme—and to think that it was engineered by a girl of thirteen. Lindsey took a risk and no matter how you feel about what she did, you have to admire the courage it took to pull it off.

Lindsey is my niece. She is my mother Hallie's granddaughter. I don't want to confuse you with too many names and relationships here, but if you'll bear with me, I'll make it short and sweet. Mom had two kids: me and my sister, Sybil. Sybil married Gary. I never married. I'm what they call a lifelong bachelor. I seldom clean my apartment. Don't come over.

Anyway, I call Gary "Doc" to get under his skin. He dropped out of UF's med school, and now he does probably just as well selling medical appliances, but he hates me reminding him that he couldn't cut the mustard as a doctor. He, in turn, calls me the family bum, and I suppose that makes us even.

Sybil and Gary have three kids—Donald, Glen, and then the "Afterthought," Lindsey. I would never call her that to her face, and would ask that you don't either, or I will come and do serious harm to you.

So that's the cast of characters with regard to my lovely extended family. But there are a couple of other vital players in this family drama: Winnie—now that's my mom's late-life lesbian lover—and Nurse Gibson. I have no idea what Nurse Gibson's first name is, but she's important to the story because she's the night nurse supervisor on the Intensive Care floor at the hospital, where my mother is a critical care patient, and in this capacity she wields quite a bit of authority.

So I got this call at about five o'clock today, just as I was getting ready to head home. I work at a temp agency, conducting interviews, giving typing tests. It's something any monkey could do, but it keeps me employed, and

I happen to like meeting the beautiful, desperately needy young women who come through my door. I'm still waiting for the floodgates to open after last October's stock market crash, with virtual legions of anxious, out-of-work young temp prospects filing through, but the economic prognosticators still can't agree on whether or not we're going into a full-blown recession. I mean, didn't we just come out of one?

So I pick up the phone and it's my niece Lindsey, and I'm thinking she might have been calling to ask how her Gran is, since my mother has been in intensive care for almost two weeks because of the stroke, and I got the chance to visit with her today and Lindsey didn't. It's been touch-and-go, but over the last couple of days things have started looking a little more hopeful, though Mom still hasn't been given very good odds for long-term recovery. She's responding well and even getting a word or two out every now and then, which my sister Sibyl is attributing to all the prayers being sent up on Mom's behalf by members of Sibyl's church's prayer chain.

I pass no judgment on Sibyl for her religious faith excepting the fact that she and Doc tend to wear their religion on their sleeves like big neon armbands. They have charitable hearts, I grant you that. Through their open-handed love offerings they've pulled probably a half-dozen Peruvian kids off the street and into a church-run orphanage and filled their bellies with nourishing food while bringing them to God. Not the Catholic God of South America, but the Protestant God of North America. I make a special effort to keep my feelings about all this to myself. I just duck my head at family functions and keep quiet.

You see, I'm basically a non-confrontational…okay, I'm a coward.

But not Lindsey. Lindsey, as I quickly find out, is bound and determined to get Winnie in to see her grandmother before things take a turn for the worse. Sibyl has made it clear that our mother is to have no visitors besides family. And of course it doesn't matter that Mom and Winnie have been living together for the last eight years. They even rode together on the Lavender Panthers float in one of those West Coast gay pride parades, for Chrissakes, but this is where my sister has decided to make her stand.

The doctor agrees with Sibyl that, as Mom's daughter, she has every right to ask that the official visitor list be limited to family members only. Not that the hospital doesn't have a similar policy of its own, since access to ICU patients is pretty tightly restricted as a rule.

I would have argued against this position on behalf of Winnie, but again, I am, as I have previously noted, a coward. All I've really been able to do is come downstairs to the main waiting room every other day and report to Winnie how Mom is doing. That's not quite what Winnie needs, obviously. She wants to see my mother. She wants to sit and hold the hand of the person she loves most in the world.

My niece Lindsey agrees.

Let me tell you about Lindsey. She's the conscientious kid who volunteers to take all the classroom animals home over summer break. She's the principled kid who stands up to her classmates, and even sometimes stands up to her teachers when something gets said which she considers disparaging of a particular group. I call Lindsey our family's little "Catcher in the Rye." She's like Holden Caulfield stationed in the rye field, keeping everybody from going off the cliff. It's hard work looking out for *everybody*. Do you think you know a Lindsey? Because I happen to think there isn't another thirteen-year-old girl quite like her.

Well, she calls me up just as I'm about to transition to weekend mode. It's Friday night. It's pizzas and Buds with a couple of the other lifelong bachelors who live in my apartment building. I'm in a hurry to start my weekend R & R. But I sit down and listen. Lindsey says she's going to tell her parents that she's spending the night with a friend of hers, but really she's going to the hospital where they have Gran.

"Aren't they going to check with the kid's parents—the one you're supposed to be having the slumber party with?"

"Are you serious? I spend, like, almost every Friday night at Tiffany's house."

"So Tiffany's in on it?"

"Oh, totally. She's got a really cool lesbian aunt who's going to send her to Europe when she's eighteen."

"What does that have to do with anything?"

"Oh, nothing."

Pregnant pause. Third trimester kind of pregnant.

"I'm a little confused here, Lindsey. ICU visiting hours are over at seven. Besides which, they wouldn't let you see Gran by yourself anyway."

"Duh. That's not why I'm going. And I'm not asking you to go either. It's somebody else who's coming with me tonight."

"Who?"

"I am *so* not telling you. You'll go straight to Mom."

"Why would you say that?"

"I don't trust your generation anymore. Gran and Winnie's generation— they're pretty cool, I think, but I don't know about *you*, Uncle Matt."

"I'm devastated. What team do you think I play for anyway, O-Niece-O-Mine?"

"I soooo need to leave to meet Winnie."

"Winnie."

"Well, duh. I have to take the bus, you know, since I do not happen to drive."

"*I'll* drive you. Would that put me on your team?"

"Oh my God, are you serious? Because that's the reason I called you."

Part B of the plan seemed, at first glance, to be the trickier part. It was making a personal, deeply heartfelt, pull-out-every-stop-in-the-emotional-manipulation-handbook attempt to get the night nurse supervisor, Ms. Gibson, to break two hard and fast rules of Intensive Care patient access: to allow a patient to see a visitor past seven o'clock, and then to allow in a visitor who by traditional definition isn't even a member of the patient's family.

By *traditional definition*, I'm smiling. I've known gay couples who've been "married" for more years than most straight couples of my acquaintance. And of course it wasn't Mom and Winnie's fault they got a late start. Winnie knew all along who she was. Maybe Mom knew too, but she'd always tamped it down. Coming out as a lesbian in the pre-Gay Rights era, especially coming out after you've been "traditionally" married and already raised two kids—that would have to be classified as one of life's most difficult decisions. But, to her credit, she did it. I once asked Winnie how my mother could possibly have taken such a bold step, knowing the consequences. (Sibyl didn't speak to Mom for over a year.)

Winnie didn't bat an eye. "Because she loves me."

Added to the mix was the fact that Nurse Gibson doesn't even come on duty until nine o'clock. Roughly calculating the odds in my head, I gave my niece's scheme about a fifty-to-one chance of success. And that was being optimistic.

We met Winnie at her and my mother's favorite Chinese restaurant over on Second Place. Winnie was worried. She's generally a tough old broad, just entering her seventies, sharp as a tack and very much her own woman. Now she seemed emotionally, well, *fragile*. It had been almost two weeks since she'd seen Hallie. And she was the one who brought Mom to the hospital in the first place, for Chrissakes. By late that same day, Winnie's access to Mom had been totally cut off. I think this was

Sibyl's way of getting back at Mom and Winnie for all the embarrassment she felt they'd caused her. If so, it was hateful and punitive. I should have confronted her that first day.

But in case I haven't said it already, I'm a…*right*.

Winnie poked at her General Tso's chicken. She didn't seem to have much of an appetite. "Lindsey, honey." She closed her eyes. "I admire what you're trying to do. But what makes you think that the head night nurse is going to put her job on the line just so I can spend a few minutes with your grandmother?"

"Because she's, like, one of the nicest people I've ever met. I talked to her one day at Ward's."

I gave my niece a quizzical look. "Based on one brief conversation at the supermarket, you've decided that this is the kind of woman who can make miracles happen?"

Lindsey put her chopsticks down. They had been a struggle for her and I had twice suggested that she be an ugly American diner like Winnie and me and resort to the fork. "I think it's wrong the way my mother has stood in the way of you getting to see Gran." Lindsey was looking at Winnie. Both had tears welling in their eyes. I felt like a heel because I wasn't likewise moved. And besides, I wasn't really involved in this little escapade. I was just Lindsey's chauffeur for the evening. Although, if it ever got back to Sibyl that not only had Lindsey lied about where she was that night, but that I had tacitly approved of the deception, I'd probably get put on Sis's shit-list for a couple of years, at least. I'd have to miss all those great Saturday backyard cookouts with Doc bending my ear about infusion pumps, blood pressure cuffs, and peripherally inserted central catheters. On second thought, maybe being on my sister's bad side wasn't such a bad place to be.

"Hey, it might take a little convincing," Lindsey went on, "but I'm totally not giving up. Is it almost nine?"

Winnie glanced at her watch. "No, honey. It's just a little past eight."

"Really? That's all?"

Winnie nodded. We all picked up our forks and tried our best to eat.

In the main lobby of the hospital, Winnie and I sat down on a couch, while Lindsey approached the information desk.

"General visiting hours are nearly over," we could hear the woman saying to Lindsey. It appeared from all the activity behind the desk that the woman was in the process of closing down her station for the evening.

"I know," said Lindsey, glancing up at the clock on the wall. The clock read 8:55.

"I was wondering if all the nurses who come in for the next shift, if they, like, use that door there, or is there a back door—a staff door or something they might go through?"

"Are you waiting for one of the nurses?"

Lindsey nodded. "Nurse Gibson. She works in ICU on the fifth floor. Does she come in through this door?"

The woman, who was holding her purse against her stomach and looked ready to go, thought for a moment and said, "I *have* seen her come in this way."

"Can we wait for her here—the three of us?" asked Lindsey, indicating Winnie and me with a twitch of the hand.

"If you wish. At some point, though, the security guard will come by and ask you to leave. The emergency room waiting room is the only public space in the building that stays open past nine."

"Yes, thank you," said Lindsey. I noticed that nearly all of the Floridian Valspeak had disappeared from Lindsey's delivery. My niece was determined to succeed in her mission; she'd even created a new persona for herself: the ultra-polite and earnest young woman who would carefully watch every syllable that left her mouth so as not to give offense to those who found the youth of today lexically lazy.

Lindsey sat down between Winnie and me. "She was, like, totally nice."

"Lindsey, honey," said Winnie, reaching over and touching Lindsey gently on the arm. "I just want to let you know that regardless of what happens tonight, I very much appreciate what you tried to do for your grandmother and me."

Lindsey nodded.

"Where did you come from, honey?" Winnie cocked her head. "They don't make girls like you very often."

In the midst of all of her worry, Lindsey allowed a glimmer of a smile to peek through. "Twice, Winnie, Gran's asked for you. Both times was while I was with Mom. One time she just said your name. The next time she said, 'Where's Winnie?' She said it out of the side of her mouth but I, like, understood her perfectly."

"And how did your mother respond, if you don't mind my asking?"

"She lied to Gran. Both times. She said that you weren't able to make it."

There were angry words that seemed poised upon Winnie's lips—words that she would not allow herself to say. But I was under no such self-restraint: "Your mother was dead wrong to say that, Lindsey."

"*Très* wrong," said Lindsey, nodding in sad agreement. Then she said in a half-whisper to herself, "Worst. Mother. Ever."

I should have defended my sister, maybe just a little bit. After all, Sibyl, for all her wrong-headedness and duplicity, does have some good points. I just couldn't remember what any of them were at that moment.

Nurse Gibson arrived a few minutes past nine. Obviously aware of the fact that she was late, she came flying through the front door, a large knitted raffia carry-bag swinging wildly from her bouncing shoulder. Her nurse's hat seemed almost swallowed up in her *Working Girl* big hair—which was both prodigious and somewhat untamed.

She had almost made it to the elevators by the time Lindsey popped up from her seat and called out to her.

Nurse Gibson turned. "Yes?"

Lindsey went to her. Winnie and I both stood. Winnie, generally a tower of composure and strength, seemed a little faint. I wondered if I was going to have to hold her up.

"Hello, Ms. Gibson."

"Hello, Lindsey." Nurse Gibson looked surprised to see my niece.

"I want you to meet someone," said Lindsey. "This is Winnie Habjan. She's, like, my third grandmother."

"Hello, Ms. Habjan," said Nurse Gibson. Walking over to shake Winnie's hand, she added, "I was wondering if I was ever going to have this opportunity."

Winnie looked confused.

Nurse Gibson went on: "Hallie—*Ms. Walters*—well, she asks about you quite often. It was hard for me to understand what she was saying at first, but I got her to use her good hand to write things out for me."

Winnie began to cry. Something with which I wasn't familiar began to form in my throat. A lump. Is that what they call it?

Nurse Gibson pulled out a tissue and offered it to Winnie. "I said, 'Now, Ms. Walters, who is Winnie? She isn't on the family list. Is she a neighbor, a good friend?' I have Ms. Walters' response here somewhere. I've kept the piece of paper she wrote it on."

Nurse Gibson dug around a moment in her oversized tropical bag.

Then she produced the slip of paper. It had jagged handwriting on it. The stroke had immobilized my mother's right side, so it was a challenge for her to write with her unaccustomed left.

In answer to Nurse Gibson's question, "Who is Winnie?" my mother had labored to scratch out the following four words: "*She is my everything.*"

Nurse Gibson smiled. "I've been half waiting for you, Ms. Habjan. Let me go up first and swear my co-conspirators on the nursing staff to complete secrecy. Then I'll be back down for you. As for *you* two—" She was now pointing to Lindsey and me. "I'm afraid you'll have to stay down here tonight. You'll have ample opportunity to see the patient tomorrow."

Winnie dabbed at her eyes with the tissue. "Taking me up to see her— that won't get you into trouble?"

Nurse Gibson shook her head. "Not if we're careful."

Later, when Lindsey and I found ourselves sitting on the front steps of the hospital, both of us having been shooed out of the building by the aforementioned security guard, I asked my niece how it was that she was so sure that Nurse Gibson would do this for Winnie.

"Ohmigod! I totally forgot to mention that there was another woman with Nurse Gibson at the grocery store that day. The way the two of them were looking at each other, you could tell that they were, like, so *totally* in love. Nurse Gibson gets it."

Fer shur.

1989

MELODIOUS IN OHIO

The singing career of the Ludden Sisters lasted roughly a dozen years, from early 1959, when the four teenagers were "discovered" by bandleader Augie Rausch, until late 1970, when the quartet, wishing to devote more time to their husbands and to their growing young families, decided to "retire." Their whirlwind years of appearances on *Augie Rausch's Variety Hour* and tour performances before large, appreciative crowds led to significant fame and no small fortune. The girls—and they *were* just girls when they first started out (the youngest, Brenda, only thirteen years old when Rausch plucked her and her sisters from obscurity)—were the most popular members of the bandleader's "musical family," and as such received more fan mail in a day than all of Rausch's other performers did in a month, mostly from women of a certain age who wished that their own daughters and granddaughters could be more like the adorably wholesome Ludden Sisters.

Three of the four sisters married wisely. Patricia wed a successful railroad attorney twenty years her senior; Janice a popular NFL quarterback; and Brenda, a multiply published author and Yale history professor. On the other hand, Frances Kay married a scheming huckster named Burt Squires, whose most recent claim to fame, after a long series of failed business enterprises, was leg warmers made of Old English Sheepdog fur.

Frances Kay and Burt Squires married in 1971, divorced in 1973, remarried in 1976, and divorced in 1982 after Squires, without his wife's permission, invested every last penny of her large financial holdings in an ultimately disastrous non-alcoholic wine cooler venture. ("Isn't it just, you know, *juice*?") Although Frances Kay continued to receive residuals from her appearances on the syndicated version of *Augie Rausch's Variety Hour* (its network incarnation cancelled in 1971 in the midst of CBS's "Rural Purge," an attempt to clear the network's airways of all programs that appealed to an older, less sophisticated, less urban demographic), and though she received royalties from the re-release in compact disc format of some of the Ludden Sisters' more popular LPs, the third-oldest member of the singing group was, by 1989, struggling financially. She and her physically challenged teenaged daughter Carly Ann moved from their large five-bedroom/three-bath ranch-style in Brentwood to one of Hollywood's more seasoned garden apartment buildings, the Oleander Arms, where the two lived next door to an elderly cigar-chomping character actor named Irv Miller. Irv was best remembered for his hardboiled 1940s newspaper editor roles and for the enduring catch-all catchphrase, "I'm running a newspaper here, not [fill in the blank: the *Ladies' Home Journal*, the Federal Bureau of Investigation, a corn-shucking contest for hoedownin' hayseeds, etc.]."

Frances Kay's three siblings each helped their pecuniarily precarious sister as best they could, but by 1989, with the need for a hip replacement for Carly Ann (who was born with a compromised acetabulofemoral joint), Frances Kay watched as her financial situation became even more dire. Frances Kay's ex-husband, Burt, was of no help; though recent re-releases of the films *Fame* and *Flash Dance* revived customer interest in leg warmers, especially those using non-traditional fibers, none of the income generated by these sales went to Frances Kay, and she had not the wherewithal to seek legal redress.

In early March, the four sisters gathered in Columbus, Ohio, to celebrate their mother's seventy-fifth birthday. The mother, Eunice, lived in a nursing home there. She was not an official resident, however, but only *pretended* to be a resident; Eunice Ludden worked undercover for a watchdog group formed to gather evidence on nursing and convalescent home patient abuse. To protect her anonymity, she never used the last name Ludden, but was, instead, Mrs. *Luden*. Like the cough drop. And she asked that her daughters come to see her wearing disguises that would protect their identities as well, given that one of the most popular programs viewed in the television room of the Olentangy Manor Extended Care Center was the syndicated rerun version of *Augie Rausch's Variety Hour*. The geriatric residents had their favorites among the show's regular performers, who often could not be remembered by their actual names, but were referred to, in the necessity of the moment, as the "Accordion Man," "the Happy Married Couple Who Sing about Jesus," and "The Tap-dancing Negro." But the Ludden Sisters (or "'Those Four Pretty Girls with Angel Voices") were the most beloved and revered among Olentangy Manor's television-viewing inmates.

Eunice greeted her four daughters in the home's dining room, where the staff had baked her a large birthday cake. Frances Kay's plane ticket was paid for by her eldest sister Patricia. (All of Eunice's daughters had flown in.) Frances Kay was especially happy to see her sisters. It had been quite some time since they had all been together, and this was a good thing for another reason: Frances Kay had a proposal to make—something that she had been thinking about ever since Irv Miller first mentioned it.

Infomercials.

According to Irv, infomercials were where it was at, baby. Everybody was doing them. Even he had been offered the chance to pitch the new Flowbee Vacuum Haircutting System, though he was forced to turn the offer down because the concept of using the family vacuum cleaner to trim hair unsettled him. "But late-night infomercials are the way to go, darling. You could do a Christmas album with your sisters and sell it in time for the holidays. You need to get something new out there, something that will put a little dough-re-mi into your pockct, darling. A *little*? Who am I kidding? You'll make a mint! And you can get yourself and that verkakta-hipped daughter of yours into a much nicer place. The Oleander Arms—it ain't for you, darling! You got life in you yet. And such a voice! I hear that voice through the wall when you're singing in the shower or sitting on your commode, and hand-to-God, it's just like an angel came all the way down from Heaven just to take a shit in your bathroom."

The four sisters and their Nellie Bly of a mother ate cake and shared it with some of Eunice's fellow residents. No one recognized Eunice's daughters as the world-famous Ludden Sisters; the disguises, made up of various wigs and funny eyeglasses, seemed to be working. After everyone had wandered away and given the Luddens some privacy, Frances Kay made her move. She explained infomercials, though her sisters had seen them and had a fairly good idea of what they were. She reminded Patricia and Janet and the "baby" Brenda how many people still remembered them and loved them, and how much their fans especially enjoyed the old Christmas shows. Frances Kay was exactly right—Augie's special holiday broadcasts had been ratings gold for CBS. Because of the sisters' popularity, each of the new, original carols they sang on the air shot straight to the top of the charts and quickly earned prominent placement in the holiday canon: "Bless this House on Christmas Day," "Santa and the Manger," and "Merii Kurisumasu," which the sisters performed in kimonos fringed with bright silver tinsel. A comical offering in the early '60s, "Uncle Bob Ain't a Masher Tonight, 'Cuz There's Mistletoe Overhead," was covered by Eartha Kitt, Annette Funicello, Michele Lee, Bobby Rydell, and the Brothers Four.

"It certainly isn't the worst idea in the world, Frances Kay," said Patricia, who was looked up to by her sisters as the voice of wisdom and authority for the foursome, "but we're all retired. I don't think any of us has time to do a new album, let alone try to sell it at two o'clock in the morning. Who's watching television at two in the morning anyway?"

"*I've* seen them," said Janet, who was wearing a particolored clown wig. "Sometimes, when I can't sleep. And remember, Patricia: when it's two o'clock on the East Coast, it's only eleven o'clock in Sun City, California."

"Our fans go to bed at eight," deadpanned Brenda.

"She's right about that," added Mrs. Ludden. "By nine, everybody in this place is fast asleep. Even the nurses. Excuse me for a moment, girls— there's a male orderly at the other end of the room throwing Mr. Rothman into his wheelchair as if he were a sack of potatoes. I must document."

Mrs. Ludden left. Her four daughters grew quiet. Frances Kay, sensing resistance to her idea, kept her eyes on her half-eaten wedge of birthday cake, not moving her fork.

Janet sighed. "Although, it *would* be a kick for all of our fans."

Frances Kay looked up and nodded.

Brenda and Patricia nodded too. Their hearts went out to their sister Frances Kay. All of the sisters were close and it was a hard thing to be cruel to the one who had been the least blessed among them.

Finally, Brenda said, "I serve on the board of an orphanage in New Haven. So many unwanted children, and so, so many of them foundlings. Fetal alcohol preemies. Crack babies. My heart breaks in two every time I have to go there. Let's say we do this holiday infomercial. What if—" Her face brightened. "What *if* during the infomercial we were each to hold one of these sad little babies in our arms?"

"You want each of us to hold a crack baby while we're trying to sell our Christmas album?" asked Patricia, not quite understanding.

"Well, I thought we might sing to them. Most babies like to be sung to, even at-risk ghetto infants."

"You do have a point, Brenda," said Janet, nodding with interest. "What would you want us to do—just *hold* the babies while we sing or should we rock them in our arms and serenade them like we were singing them a lullaby?"

"We'll work all that out," said Frances Kay excitedly.

Janet bunched up her lips and thought for a moment. "I'm wondering, though—crack babies—they aren't *always* shriveled-looking and heart-tugging, are they? If we want to tug a little more on our customers' heartstrings, I think the way to go would be babies with congenital defects—visual ones like harelips and prolapsed eyelids, that are easy to see without having to go in too close with the camera."

"What is it you girls are cooking up now?" asked Mrs. Ludden, who was writing on a little pad: *Tyrell threw Mr. Rothman into his wheelchair with unnecessary force. Check for bruises tomorrow.*

Janet answered for her sisters: "Frances Kay is very serious about this new Christmas album idea and selling it through an infomercial. And now Brenda wants us all to hold special-needs babies in our arms as we're singing carols. Which carols do you think the little deformed babies would like, Brenda?"

"'Have Yourself a Merry Little Christmas' would be nice. It's about having a nice Christmas even in the midst of troubles. For example, let's say you're a baby born without legs or you have Down syndrome or something. You can still have a merry Christmas if the fates allow."

Patricia hummed a few bars of "Have Yourself a Merry Little Christmas" as she pondered what her sister had just said. Then she said, "You can't have just one Down syndrome baby in a setting like that. It pulls focus from the other babies. They should probably *all* be severely retarded, don't you think?"

"Is there a special way to hold a retarded baby?" asked Eunice. "It's been so long since I've held one that I've forgotten."

"When did you ever hold a retarded baby, Mama?" asked Frances Kay.

"Many years ago. Before any of you were born."

"What was the occasion?" asked Patricia.

"The occasion? Well, what *was* the occasion? Let me think about that."

"Anyway…" said Janet, attempting to put the discussion back on track.

"No, I'd really like to know, Mama," interrupted Patricia.

"It isn't important," said Mrs. Ludden in a quiet, hedging voice. Then Eunice Ludden amended what she'd just said. "Well, of course it's important. And I've kept this from you girls long enough. The little retarded girl was your oldest sister."

Absolute silence greeted this announcement. All that could be heard in the room was the sound of two cooks in the kitchen off the dining room rattling their pots under the running sink faucet, and Mrs. Malloy being harshly berated by one of the nurses for having accidentally knocked her juice glass on the floor. Such a thing would have ordinarily sprung Eunice, crusading investigator of nursing home mischief, into action, but now she just sat, looking at each of her daughters with significant solemnity.

Finally she took a deep breath and said, "It's a long, sad story. I'll give you the short version, because it's already cast a terrible pall over me. I dated your Mr. Rausch in college. You probably know that he had a show on the radio back during the war. I knew when everybody was gravitating to television that he would go too. His variety show was perfect for television. I am a farsighted woman. I knew that with your father's good voice and fine looks and my fine voice and good looks, we would have beautiful, songfully talented children. I had no idea that I was destined to have only girls, but girls is exactly what the good Lord blessed Felix and me with. It was my dream to put you on Augie's show and make you famous. There was only one problem: my firstborn was neither beautiful *nor* talented. Nor was she even normal. What we did in those days, dears, was we put damaged little girls and boys in places where they could receive specialized care."

"You *institutionalized* her?" asked Patricia, with unconcealed horror.

"Well, she wouldn't have been any good for Augie's show, and what's more, I didn't have time to see to the very demanding needs of such a child. It was imperative that I spend my time raising normal, healthy children—beautiful little songbirds who would grow up to make Felix and me proud."

"And Daddy went along with this?" asked Frances Kay.

"At first he did," replied Eunice. "But then—well, I must tell you, dears, that when he walked out on us in 1959, it wasn't for the reason that I told you. There was no floozy waitress. There was only your father's profound disappointment over the fact that I had chosen to sacrifice little Frances Kay so that the four of you could become famous."

Frances Kay shook her head, confused.

Eunice explained: "Oh, my firstborn was also named Frances Kay. I so loved the name that I gave it to *you*, dear. I hated to see it go to waste."

Brenda stood up. She was the tallest of the four daughters of Eunice Ludden, and now she towered, imposingly, over her mother. "Is she still alive—our sister?"

"I suppose she is, although I've lost touch. The last I'd heard she was in Des Moines. I'm sure she'd love to see her sisters on television again. She always enjoyed watching you perform."

Mrs. Ludden's daughters got quiet. Something both profound and troubling had just occurred. Although the Ludden sisters didn't realize it fully at that moment, a song in their repertoire had just changed its key from major to minor—a mother's lullaby, the oldest song they knew.

The infomercial was a success, though in the end, the idea of singing to babies—any babies, for that matter, with Down syndrome or otherwise—was dismissed as shameful pandering to the sensibilities of viewers whose hearts were already open and receptive. It *was* the Ludden Sisters, after all! Frances Kay II was able to pay for her daughter's surgery and move the two of them into a charming little bungalow in West Hollywood within view of the famous Hollywood sign.

That Christmas, rather than join their mother in Cleveland (she was now working undercover at a different nursing home, which had been accused of putting its residents in adult diapers and nothing else), the sisters took their children and spouses to Des Moines to spend the holiday with their oldest sister Frances Kay I, or Frannie as she would later be called. Frannie, as it turned out, had long been deinstitutionalized and was now living in a group home with several other mentally challenged young and middle-aged adults. The Ludden sisters were lucky. The day that they became *five* sisters was also the day that they met their father for the first time in thirty years. He was one of the house "parents" who watched over Frannie and the other residents.

"I had to make a choice," he explained, "and this was it. I've followed your wonderful careers from a distance, and I couldn't be prouder—but my place has always been with Frances Kay, and all those others here who need me."

Patricia and Janet and Frances Kay II and Brenda didn't know which parent was the bigger disappointment: a mother who had never intended to tell four of her daughters about their discarded sibling, or a father who had been willing to permanently detach himself from the lives of four of his very own children. It was concluded by Patricia, and seconded by each of her songstress sisters, that as parents, both their mother and father were sadly flawed, but in the end, deserving of some semblance of forgiveness.

It being Christmas and all.

Merii Kurisumasu.

1990

GERONTOCONCUPISCENT IN VERMONT

Cornell Rodgers was eighty-four. He'd been a widower for almost fifteen years. Cornell had become comfortably inured to all that went along with living alone, had come to accept the fact that he would probably be forever after a "me" and never again a "we." He came to forget a lot of what it had been like to be married, to be in love—not the kind of love that comes with fireworks or overwhelms every other aspect of life, but that category of love that settles in for the long haul and feels comfortable and secure and just right.

Cornell had forgotten, as well, what it was like to share his life with another person as the norm and not the exception. His daughter Stephanie was the exception. She flew in from Ann Arbor to see her father dutifully once, sometimes twice a year. And sometimes his grown granddaughters—Stephanie's two girls—dropped in for visits (with or without their husbands), when they could be conveniently appended to New England ski trips. And there were friends and neighbors who came by to see Cornell in his musty Victorian on South Willard, and whom he went to see, including one family in particular—the Ludviks—who lived a few blocks away and had been having him over for Sunday dinner every week for nearly a year.

Cornell liked his life in Burlington. It was cold in the winter, and that was okay. ("As my blood gets thinner, I don't touch the thermostat; I just throw on a heavier sweater.") He liked walking along the lake. He even liked the radical politics of the town and happily stuffed envelopes for Bernie Sanders. More recently, he'd marched with the anti-Gulf War protesters, carrying a sign that said "No War for Oil," when the one first handed to him, the overly prolix "Kuwait: Give Your Women the Vote and

Maybe We'll Feel Better About Saving Your Ass!" didn't quite seem to hit the mark.

A former high school principal, Cornell had been in retirement mode for almost two decades, the comfortable pace of his life needing very little adjustment as he aged. Retirement suited him. Burlington suited him. What he missed, even as his libido had waned, was sex.

The power and passion of male/female coupling—it had long stopped being a component of his sensual life. Cornell's sensual life was in his tastebuds now. It manifested in the goose bumps he sometimes got when he listened to Mozart's symphonies and Bach's Brandenburg concertos. It beheld the rutilant sky of twilight, set against the shimmering turquoise of Lake Champlain, with feelings of warmth and peace and quiet joy. Everything was sensory and above the waist now, none of it seated in the gonads.

And yet sexual longing in Cornell Rodgers, voiceless now and largely rudderless, still maintained a pulse.

How to channel it, give expression to it? Cornell couldn't bring himself to buy adult magazines. Nor did he wish to visit one of the city's adult movie houses. The potential appellation of "dirty old man" unnerved him. He had met women close to his own age—women whom he thought might be open to his advances—but in the end, though companionable, they had not proved all that physically compatible.

Cal was a teenage boy whom Cornell knew. Cal had a girlfriend named Kieran. Cornell knew the boy's family from his long tenure as high school administrator (both of Cal's parents were teachers) and he knew *of* the girl's family (the father had a job with the town's big restaurant equipment company, G.S. Blodgett). The boy was into old motorcycles and so was Cornell, and for a time he had thought of giving Cal his antique 1936 Harley Davidson 61EL—the one with the first "Knucklehead" OHV engine—which had been gathering dust in his garage.

Cornell shared aspects of his long life with the teenagers during their visits to a favorite city park. Kieran was especially interested in hearing how high schools had changed over the years, since she now felt that she wanted to be a teacher. With Cornell, the kids shared the empirical evidence of their young love—or rather lust, because Cal found it hard, even in a public park, to keep his hands off Kieran, who was plump-lipped and New England creamy-skinned and hungry for Cal's every touch.

Cornell sometimes felt like a voyeur, even as the kids sat and talked to him, or when occasionally the three would enjoy a late lunch together. But he needn't have; Kieran had, quite early on, designated Cornell guardian angel of Cal and Kieran's love, and Cal was just fine with that. ("The man knows motorcycles. How could he possibly be a perv?")

In time, Cal and Kieran came to learn that Cornell spent his Sunday afternoons with the Ludviks, several blocks from Cornell's house on Cliff Street. In time, Cal and Kieran, acting on Cornell's toss-away admission that he hardly ever kept his doors locked, began to spend a couple of hours every Sunday afternoon sneaking into the old man's house through his wooded backyard so that they could have sex on the bed in his spare bedroom. Kieran usually brought a blanket in a backpack so that after their departure there would be no evidence that they had been using this otherwise rarely occupied room as a trysting place, or, as Cal sometimes referred to it when alone with his beloved, "the place we go to fuck each other's brains out."

Kieran loved this about her boyfriend: his sensitive, romantic nature.

One September Sunday, Cornell came home from the Ludviks', sated on Cornish game hen and mushroom stuffing and a third, shamefully prodigal glass of Zinfandel, and discovered that his back door had been left ajar. Thinking that his home had been broken into, he moved cautiously from room to room, brandishing an old fireplace popcorn popper. Finding no burglar or prowler about, nor even evidence of there having ever *been* one on the premises, Cornell deducted with some relief that he had apparently left the door open on his last visit to his backyard, whenever that may have been.

It was not until later in the evening that Cornell, having wandered into the spare bedroom to look for a particular missing title from his collection of John le Carré first editions, noticed a certain sloppiness in the way that the bed had been made up. Rumples which bunched up the duvet in the vicinity of the pillows betrayed the bed-making hand of someone even more careless than himself. What's more, when he pulled the duvet and underlying blanket away, there were moist spots upon the sheet. Unknown to Cornell, this was the only Sunday afternoon in their string of secret weekly home invasions that Kieran had been unable to bring along her blanket. The lusty teenagers had first considered copulating on the floor but had grown accustomed to the bounce and plushy give of the bed's mattress. So they took their afternoon delight upon the bed without their protective full-sized blanket condom, and hoped that its only marginally observant octogenarian owner would have no cause to put two and two together and get four-nication.

But he did. In fact, given all his years of forensic experience as the chief investigator of campus infractions, a.k.a. high school principal, he figured it out fairly quickly. Had his eyes failed to glean the evidence, Cornell's sense of smell, still keen at his advanced age, would have told the story, for the room smelled both rankly and fragrantly of the sweat and musk and love liquids of adolescent carnality.

Cornell became lightheaded. Suddenly, the wrong of it became excised from the equation. All that was left was the want and need for it. To be young again, to be young and lubricious and driven by hormonal impertinence to feral acts in strangers' beds, and goddamn the consequences. For the first time in several weeks (the last during a rerun of *Baywatch*) Cornell got an erection—one that did not go away for quite some time.

Through the early part of that week, Cornell found himself returning to the room and staring at the turned-down comforter and blanket. He sat in the armchair in the corner and pictured what went on in the room, from the first hungry kiss to the final bucking, writhing, toe-tingling orgasm. By the middle of the week, Cornell had talked himself out of saying anything to the young couple, even though he knew that he would see them inline skating at the park with other teenagers, or catch Cal playing Hacky Sack with his buddies while Kieran looked on adoringly.

However, by the end of the week, Cornell's thoughts had begun to run to the more prurient and far more sinister. He would do this: He would send regrets to the Ludviks, though he would make sure that he could be seen walking in that direction (because he was certain that his house was being staked out, the two young sex addicts watching and waiting for the coast to clear). Then he would take a roundabout way home— the back way—a way not at all anticipated by Cal and Kieran. Finally, having given the kids sufficient time to invade his house, to place their ravenous naked bodies upon the bed in the spare room, he would enter and catch them—what was the phrase?—*fragrante delicto*. He would not scold the young ones. He would not judge them or punish them for doing what nature and youth dictated. But he would explain that there was still a price to be paid for their youthful skullduggery, and the price was this: that they should continue with their lovemaking with him there, sitting in his armchair, observing quietly from across the room, servicing his own brittle, superannuated sexual needs, but intangibly, at safe distance, in promiscuous peep-show proximity. They would do this for Cornell, or he would report them, if not to the police, then to their parents. Someone would be told—someone they would not want told, for why else did they sneak around so? This would be the deal that he would offer them, and they would have no choice but to accept it.

They came for their clandestine assignation that day, and Cornell arrived twenty minutes later, just as he had planned, ready to ambush them and then to name his extortionary terms. As he crept quietly down the hall toward the spare bedroom, he could hear them in there, could hear the noises of bodily abandon, the groans and moans of unfettered youthful sensuosity. He stopped just to the side of the open door, waiting a moment, not looking inside—waiting another moment and then another—putting off that which in his imaginings had given him intense anticipatory pleasure.

He pictured his own young self in that bed with the first girl he had ever lain with. They had both been frightened, but then lost all of their inhibitions and threw themselves into the act. He thought of how it should feel if someone had stepped into the doorway and revealed himself to be *their* interloper. And an old man—a man whose life would in due time be drawing to an end. A man for whom the incandescent sexual fire that characterized his youth had long burned itself to embers. How would he have felt in the presence of such a pathetic old man? The thought now disgusted him.

Cornell sank to the floor in the hallway, perhaps five feet from the door of the spare room. Here he sat and here he wept. There are old men who never cry—men who have seen enough pain in their long lives to build a carapace around themselves until death—and then there are old men who come to walk with softer steps through the emotional rooms of their lives. Cornell was of that second group, and so he cried for what he had lost and for that hurtful thing he had almost done in an effort to somehow compensate for that loss.

The sounds from the room stopped. A moment later, Cal emerged. He was naked, his penis still hard. Kieran, a couple of steps behind him, was wrapped in the blanket that this Sunday she'd succeeded in bringing along. Rather than demonstrating surprise over finding Cornell sitting upon the carpeted floor of the hallway, blubbering now like a lost child— rather than recoiling in shame and bowing their heads in Garden-of-Eden contrition, the teenaged boy and girl presented expressions of silent pity for Cornell. Cal reached down to help Cornell to his feet.

"We won't do it again if you don't want us to," he said to the old man, almost matter-of-factly. "We figured you'd be cool with it. I mean, we didn't ask on the chance you might not be, but—hey, you're okay with it, right?"

Cornell stared at the naked teenage boy for a moment, not knowing at first just how to answer. Then the answer came, and there was an ease to it that surprised Cornell: "I know you kids have no place to go. You can come here if you like." And then he added: "When I'm out."

Cornell wiped his eyes with the knuckles of both hands. Cal nodded. Kieran nodded too. She was holding the blanket as if it were an oversized sarong, one hand bunching the folds of the fabric together to cover her hips, her buttocks, her vagina, but not the creamy-white, sun-shy mounds of her young breasts.

Cornell stared at the breasts as if he had never seen such things before. And then, with no sense as to what his hand was doing, he reached out as if he desired to touch them. Kieran turned and looked at Cal.

Cal shrugged. He drew his lips together and then pulled them apart to say, "They're *your* boobs, monkey."

Hearing that which she needed to hear, Kieran took a step toward Cornell, placing herself within the vicinity of his outstretched fingers. She allowed Cornell to touch the nutty nipple of her right breast and then to cup his hand beneath it, holding it lightly in his palm. Then he drew his hand away and dropped it to his side.

"How long has it been, old man?" asked Cal.

"A very long time," said Cornell in a near whisper.

Cal nodded. Then he led Kieran back into the room and shut the door. From what Cornell could hear, the two quickly picked up where they had left off. But Cornell didn't stick around to listen. He went into the kitchen to make soup and sandwiches.

They'll be hungry when they're done, he thought to himself. Young people are always hungry.

And he nearly smiled.

1991

FILICIDAL IN MISSISSIPPI

Bianca Toland moved out on the morning of October 12, a Saturday. She had moved out before. Whenever Lloyd's drinking got out of hand, she would pack up the bags and drive up to Southaven with the kids to spend a few days with her sister, Christine, and her brother-in-law, Buzz. This time she told her husband, in a note she left behind, that she meant business. She wasn't going to come home—not she nor their son Shawn, who was eleven, nor Kimberly, who was six—until Lloyd took solid steps to end the drinking.

Buzz knew about a clinic up in Nashville. He had been there himself. As a recovering alcoholic, he was familiar with all of Lloyd's tricks. He knew the ways that Lloyd was playing Bianca. He and Christine advised Bianca to give Lloyd this ultimatum and only to come back after he'd gotten the kind of serious help that could truly turn things around.

Bianca's note to her husband, magneted to the refrigerator, said that since their two kids were presently visiting Bianca's parents at their house in Germantown, she would have to come home on Sunday to pick up their clothes and other things. What Bianca didn't realize, though, was that Grandpa Naughton hadn't gotten the word that he was supposed to take Shawn and Kimberly to Southaven and drop them off with their mother and aunt and uncle. He took them instead down to Coldwater and left them with their father.

Lloyd didn't seem himself when the old man and the two kids walked in. He was holding Bianca's note in his hand, but he didn't tell his father-in-law what he'd just found out.

Ned Naughton drove away thinking that Bianca was at K-Mart.

"Where's Mama?" asked Shawn after his grandfather had gone.

"She's moved out again." Lloyd was sober. He was seeing things in the clearest way possible. He was weighing his options.

"Are we gonna stay with Mama and Aunt Christine and Uncle Buzz for a while?"

Lloyd shook his head. He crumpled the note from the refrigerator into a wad and threw it in the kitchen garbage pail. "This time you're gonna stay with me."

Shawn sat down at the table. The Tolands lived in a large circa-1980 two-story log house that was laid out just the way Lloyd and Bianca wanted it. The kitchen had a raised ceiling, which, just like the living room, went all the way up to the roof. Large skylights brought the afternoon sunlight cascading down onto the table.

Kimberly jumped up into the chair nearest her brother's. "Can we have pizza tonight?" she asked.

Lloyd didn't answer. The phone was ringing. He walked over to the wall and unhooked the receiver. It was Bianca.

"I thought you said everything you wanted to say in that note you left this morning—the note you left while I was down in Senatobia."

"Daddy was supposed to bring Shawn and Kimberly here. Did he go there by mistake?"

"Yes."

"So you have them there with you?"

"I have them."

"Will you bring them up here?"

"No."

"I don't want them staying with you, Lloyd."

"I'm sober."

"For now."

"If you want the kids, you can come get them. But we may not be here. Kimberly wants pizza. I was thinking I might take them to Pizza Hut."

"Go to the one in Southaven and I'll drop by and pick them up after they've eaten."

"Or maybe we'll go someplace else."

Shawn was watching his father. He was studying his father's face, examining the way his dad looked when he gave Shawn's mom a hard time. Lloyd always seemed to be playing a game with Shawn's mother, but there was never any fun involved. It was as if he *had* to talk to her this way, *had* to make things hard for her to keep her from getting the better of him. But he didn't enjoy it.

"Please just bring them up to Southaven and we can hash this all out whenever you want to."

"We could've hashed it out this morning. The kids weren't around. We could have said whatever we needed to. But you bailed out."

"I had to get away, Lloyd. Do you even remember how out of control you were last night? Do you *ever* remember the way you are with me when you get like that?"

"I'm tired of losing my kids every time you go running off to your sister's or your parents."

"It doesn't have to be this way."

Lloyd was wrapping the coiled phone cord around his hand and now he released it with a springy snap. "I'll go to that clinic."

"I would be so happy if you really meant that."

"Just let me keep the kids for the rest of the weekend. I won't drink."

"I don't believe you." Bianca got very quiet. Then she said, "You waved your gun at me last night."

"I waved the gun?"

"Yes."

"Did I say that I wanted to shoot you with it?"

"You don't remember?"

"I can't remember."

"Lloyd. You said that you were going to shoot *yourself*. But then you changed your mind, because you said I didn't deserve to have Shawn and Kimberly all to myself while you were buried six feet under. That kind of talk scares the crap out of me, Lloyd. The kids need to be with me until you can get your head back on. You're sober right now, so you should understand that."

"I'm taking them for pizza. They'll be here later this evening when you get Buzz to drive you down. What did you do with my gun? It needs to be under lock and key when it's in the house."

"It isn't in the house. I disposed of it. I didn't want it around anymore."

Lloyd drove his 1989 Honda Accord coupe up the graveled drive to his neighbor's house a half hour later. Both men were in their late thirties. Jason, like Lloyd, was a weekend farmer. Both men worked weekdays up in Southaven.

"Hey," Lloyd said as Jason answered the door.

"Hey," said Jason. He craned his head to see Shawn and Kimberly sitting in the car, Shawn in the passenger side bucket, Kimberly in the back. "What's up?"

"Did Bianca bring my gun over here this morning?"

Jason's wife Dolly appeared next to her husband. She wore a scarf and there was a smudge of something on her cheek. She'd been cleaning. "We don't have your gun, Lloyd."

"It isn't Bianca's to give away," said Lloyd.

"It *is* if you've been waving it around scaring the daylights out of her."

"Jason, I want my goddamned gun back. I've been using guns *responsibly* since I was fourteen. I'll put it away." Then to Dolly: "I was waving it around for dramatic effect. There weren't any bullets in it."

Jason, over his wife's protests, went to get the gun. He placed it in Lloyd's palm. "And here are the bullets that you said weren't in the gun."

Dolly could hardly speak. "*Why*? *Why*, Jason?"

"Because things aren't going to get better until somebody starts to trust Lloyd again. Don't let me down, Lloyd. Keep the gun away from the kids."

Lloyd nodded. "Thanks, guy."

He didn't say anything to Dolly. Dolly and Bianca were good friends. Bianca told Dolly things.

Lloyd put the gun in the glove compartment of the car. He dropped the bullets into his shirt pocket. "Don't open the glove compartment," he said to Shawn.

Shawn nodded. "Are we going for pizza, Dad?"

"All right."

Lloyd took his son and daughter to a pizzeria close to home. He decided to get the pie and Cokes to go. "We'll drive over to Arkabutla and have a twilight picnic." The sun was going down.

It took almost twenty minutes to get to Arkabutla Lake, where Lloyd knew there would be picnic tables. The three ended up eating in the half dark and swatting at mosquitoes. Lloyd had forgotten to get napkins and Kimberly cried when she couldn't get the tomato sauce off her face and hands.

"This was a mistake," said Lloyd to himself.

"The pizza was good," said Shawn.

"Let's get back to the house. We'll pack your bags and I'll take you up to your Aunt Christine and Uncle Buzz's house like your mother wants."

"Thanks, Dad," said Shawn.

Lloyd drove out of the picnic area. He stopped to let a truck and boat trailer pull up from the concrete boat ramp. The truck turned and drove away. But Lloyd remained parked, his motor idling. Lloyd and his son and daughter were alone now in the dark.

"She's gonna divorce me this time," Lloyd said. "I could spend the next year of my life at that dry-out clinic and it won't matter. She's gonna divorce me and take you kids with her."

Shawn shifted nervously in his seat. "We'll come see you, Dad."

Lloyd stared at the spot where the inky darkness of the lake met the near-darkness of the sky. It was quiet, but he could hear the sound of the water gently lapping the bottom reach of the boat launch.

Shawn fumbled for the dome light in the car and flicked it on. He looked hard at his father's face—a face that he didn't recognize. Lloyd had different faces that he showed his wife and children. This wasn't like any of them: this was the face of a man who seemed to be giving up.

"I don't know. I just don't know anymore." Lloyd turned the steering wheel to the right. He put the Accord at the top of the boat ramp. "Let's see what the bottom of the lake looks like, shall we?"

Lloyd accelerated. The car sped down the ramp, hydroplaned across the water and then settled lambently upon the surface about thirty yards from the shore. "They say most cars can float for a while." Lloyd turned around to address his daughter. "You want to see if Daddy's car can double as a boat?"

Shawn struggled to open the door next to him. He heard the pop of the power locks and looked to his father.

Lloyd's voice was paternal, calm. "If you open that door, son, all the water will rush in and we'll sink like a stone. Why don't we just sit here and float for a while? It's nice, isn't it? The way the car rocks on the water."

Shawn looked at his sister. He couldn't tell if she was enjoying the adventure or not. A moment later, the look of puzzlement on her face turned to fear. Water began to slosh at her feet. Kimberly began to scream.

"We have to get out, Dad," said Shawn. "We have to get out before we sink."

"We have plenty of time."

It was as if Lloyd couldn't hear his daughter wailing. He held his hands at ten o'clock and two o'clock and half smiled to no one in particular. He was in a different place now—Shawn could see that. Still, he tried to reason with his father. The car tipped forward from the weight of the engine. Shawn's tennis shoes were completely under water now. "Roll down the windows, Dad, so we can all get out."

"What if I don't want us to get out, son? What if I happen to think this might be better than giving you over to your bitch of a mother for the rest of your lives?"

Shawn stared at his father.

Kimberly had unfastened her seatbelt. She was trying to climb into the front seat with her brother.

Shawn turned. "Stay back there, Kimmy. I'll get us out. Dad, roll down the window so we can all get out." Shawn looked down at his feet. The water was rushing in faster now. His calves were nearly submerged. The car was tipping even more dramatically forward.

"All right. Don't panic, boy. I'll get us out through the windows. I never liked this Jap car anyway. Arkabutla can have her." Lloyd pushed the power windows button but nothing happened. "The water's probably shorted out the window mechanism. Recline your seat, son. I'm gonna kick out your window." Lloyd unfastened his seatbelt and then positioned himself to kick the glass out of the passenger side front window. After several concerted blows, the glass remained intact. It didn't shatter. It didn't even crack. "I know the windshields are made not to break," he panted, "but I thought it was different with the side windows. Jesus Christ."

"What are we going to do, Dad?"

"Jesus Christ," Lloyd said again, and gave the window another profitless kick.

The water had reached the level of the seats now. Kimberly was hysterical. Shawn was frightened as well. But Shawn was also angry. If his dad wasn't already about to die, Shawn thought that he might kill him. He would put a bullet right through his father's head.

Shawn looked at his father. Then he looked at the window *next* to his father. Ignoring his father's previous order, he opened the glove compartment and pulled out the gun. Without saying a word, he dug his hand into his father's shirt pocket and pulled out a bullet. He loaded the gun, disengaged the safety, and fired at the driver's side window. The gunshot was deafening. Kimberly screamed louder as the window shattered and water began to splash in.

"Kimmy, you first." He pulled his sister with all of his might up into the front seat and passed her to Lloyd, who pushed her through the fully breached window. "Climb up on top of the car and hang on," said Shawn.

Next was Shawn's turn. He crawled jumbly-limbed over his father, making sure to knee him in the groin as he passed. Shawn hung onto his sister on the top of the slippery, bobbing car, not knowing if his father would follow the two of them out or not. And not really caring.

Just as the lake water began to flood through the paneless window, Lloyd emerged from the car. He treaded water next to the car, gasping and half-choking. A fisherman in a rowboat coming in late had watched the car go into the water but had been too far removed to attempt an early rescue on his own. Now he paddled up to the drowning Accord and helped Kimberly and her brother into his boat.

Kimberly cried softly. She didn't look at Lloyd as he lifted himself, heavy with sodden clothing, into the boat from the black water.

Shawn didn't look at him either.

As the fisherman rowed toward the shore Shawn watched the car, still dimly lit inside, sink slowly beneath the surface of the lake and disappear.

Lloyd spent the next several years trying his best to redeem himself in the eyes of his children. Shawn vowed not to have anything to do with him. Kimberly followed her big brother's example. There was, however, one thing that Shawn did for Lloyd, and it was an important thing: he told the sheriff that going into Arkabutla Lake had been an accident. This lie spared his father from spending the rest of his life in prison.

Eventually Lloyd gave up trying to win his children's forgiveness. He moved to another state and was not heard from again.

When, years later, Shawn Toland joined the Mississippi chapter of the NRA, he told a group of fellow gun owners that a gun had protected his sister and him when set upon by a madman. He didn't mention any details, including the most important detail of all: that the madman was a man whom he had once loved with a full filial heart, as every good son is taught to do.

It wasn't any of their business.

1992

GRIEVING IN MINNESOTA

"It just isn't right," said Bonnie. Vicki nodded. The sisters, both in their late thirties, were at their favorite coffeehouse in St. Paul. An acoustic guitar could be heard over the drone of caffeine-fueled customer chatter. The air was infused with the smell of roasting coffee. This was Dunn Brothers' biggest boast: they roasted their own coffee every day right on the premises.

"In fact, it's actually kind of creepy," Bonnie went on. "Having to listen to Dad's voice every time I call home and Mom's not there."

Vicki crunched a biscotto. "Another Vietnamese family moved onto my street. Now we have three."

"I'm talking about Mom."

"What do you want me to do about it?"

"Tell her to record a new greeting for her answering machine. Dad's been dead for six months."

Vicki wet her finger with her tongue and poked at the crumbs of biscotti on her plate. She licked them off her finger.

"Go ahead. Say it."

"Say what?"

"Whatever it is you seem dying to say."

"All right, then. I'll say it. I happen to *like* hearing Dad's voice on Mom's answering machine."

"*Really?*"

Vicki shrugged.

"*Alice and I aren't home right now. Well, I don't know where <u>she</u> is, but I'm currently up in Heaven with Jesus.* That's the vibe it's giving out—you know that, right?"

"Bonnie, do you want me to talk to her? Is that why you're bringing this up?"

"Yes, I want you to talk to her. She listens to you. And make her start giving away some of those clothes to the Goodwill or somebody. It's like he's off on a business trip and she's just waiting for him to get back."

"If that's how she wants to handle this, I think it's her right."

Bonnie stared at her sister. "Pretending he's still alive doesn't help things. Do you remember how hard it was just getting Mom to talk to the man about the life insurance? It was $50,000 and she was dragging her feet."

Vicki looked out the window. She watched the pedestrians walking up and down bustling Grand Avenue. "My whole neighborhood is starting to smell like fried egg rolls."

"You don't want to talk to her."

"Not really."

"All right, then."

"I just think—"

"Let's just drop it."

Vicki turned to the barista wiping down the table next to her. "Can I have another half-cup of the Vienna roast?"

"Six months is a long time for a woman to keep her dead husband's voice on her answering machine, Vicki."

"I thought we weren't discussing it anymore. Are you going to eat the rest of that muffin?"

Alice Schuford had a friend over. Her name was Bettie O'Shield, and she had known Alice since the two had met as twelve-year-olds at Chippewa Ranch Camp in Wisconsin's North Woods. Bettie now lived in Minneapolis. Right after Alice's husband Burl's death, Bettie was with her friend nearly every day. Lately the visits had tapered off, by mutual agreement, to about twice a week.

"So what is the one thing you did *this* week?" asked Bettie. Bettie O'Shield was drinking "French Vanilla Café" in a teacup. Bettie sometimes pretended that she and Alice were the two young women in the General Foods International Coffees commercial, grabbing girl-time together in what looked like the middle of a flower shop. Alice and Bettie were sitting on the sofa in Alice's den. The den had been her husband's domain—everything was either paneled or shagged. There wasn't a bright color, flower, or houseplant in sight.

Alice pointed at her husband's worn Naugahyde recliner. "I almost called St. Vincent de Paul this morning to take this chair away."

"Why didn't you? I had them haul away my old couch last month. They use off-duty firemen. There were two gorgeous off-duty firemen in my house, Alice. I made them stay and have some bundt cake."

"I just can't bring myself to get rid of anything."

"You need to re-record your O.G.M., honey."

"What's my 'O.G.M.'?"

"Your outgoing message. On your answering machine. Don't people call—people who don't know you—don't they call and hear Burl's voice and leave messages for him?"

"Yes, but it doesn't matter because I don't call them back."

"What if *they* call back? What do you say to them?"

"I say he isn't home."

"Then they'll just call back again."

"Sometimes I say he's away on business."

"That's an awfully long business trip your husband's taking."

"Bettie, sometimes what you think is clever is really just rude." Alice stood up. "Can I get you another cup?"

"Only if you want me to go into a diabetic coma. Alice, you need to get rid of all of this furniture. This was *his* room—you need to make it *your* room now. And you need to do something with his clothes. Listen to me, honey. I've been through this before."

"You never lost a husband."

"Not to *death*, but I have certainly lost a husband. Everything Dusty left behind, I burned in the backyard. There were toxic fumes and the fire department showed up. That's the *happy* ending to that story. I gave the firemen apple fritters."

Alice sat back down. "It's hard, Bettie."

"I know, honey. It's one of the hardest things you're ever going to do."

Alice leaned forward. She took her head in her hands and massaged her temples. "I don't even cry anymore," she said, her voice slightly muted. "It's like I don't have any tears left." Alice lifted her head to look directly at her friend. "Why do you and Bonnie and everybody else want me to erase him—to pretend like he was never even here?"

"Bonnie's talked to you about this too?"

Alice nodded. "She came over yesterday."

"None of us want you to erase Burl, honey. You have your memories and your pictures and all your letters. But you're not allowed to pretend like he's still here. Every time you look at that chair, I know a part of you is waiting for him to walk in and sit down. It isn't good for you."

"Why isn't it good? Why can't you hold onto somebody for as long as you want to? There isn't a law."

"What happens when you go to bed? Haven't you got used to him not being in that bed with you?"

Alice shook her head. She took out a handkerchief and blew her nose. "Half the time he'd fall asleep in front of the TV and not come to bed at all."

"Sweetie, I want you to go to that answering machine and erase that O.G.M. and record a new one. I'll be here to help you."

"What do I say?"

"Just say, 'You have reached the Schuford residence. I'm sorry but I can't take your call right now.' They don't have to know if you're out of the house or in the bathtub or whatever. But make it 'I', honey. Not 'we.'"

Alice half-smiled. "I almost thought of taking in several foster children—one of those crazy things that go through your head. I thought about filling my house full of voices because I don't have Burl's voice anymore. Do you know how quiet it is here without Burl going off on first one thing and then another? 'Read my lips: no new taxes,' *my ass!*"

"Burl would have been a Perot man, wouldn't he?"

Alice nodded. After a brief silence, Bettie led her friend to the answering machine. Alice found the owner's manual and together the two figured out what needed to be done to record a new O.G.M.

Vicki was the first to hear it. She called while Alice was out buying groceries at Rainbow Foods. Vicki immediately phoned her sister Bonnie.

Bonnie picked up after three rings. Bonnie was playing her stereo. Vicki could hear someone singing in the background, but she couldn't quite tell who it was.

"Hi, Bonnie. You'll be happy to know that Mom has changed the announcement on her answering machine."

"That's good." Bonnie sniffed.

"Have you been crying?"

"I was thinking about Dad."

"What are you listening to?"

"Natalie Cole. She's singing 'Unforgettable' with her father."

"How can she do that? He's dead."

"It's magic." Vicki could hear Bonnie blowing her nose.

"Is it on the radio or did you put on a record?"

"I put it on. I listen to it every day."

"Do you cry like this every time you hear it?"

"No. Just sometimes." Bonnie cleared her throat. "I'm proud of Mom."

"I am too."

"It hurts so bad sometimes, Vicki."

"I know, baby. I know."

1993

SHELVED IN NEW MEXICO

"Don't Stop (Thinking About Tomorrow)."

It used to be Jocelyn's favorite song. It wasn't anymore. It was one thing for Ernesto to whisper-sing it into Jocelyn's ear. It told her that Ernesto was willing to wait, that he understood her situation, that he understood this culture that valued family above everything else—even personal happiness.

But it was something very different to hear it now. Now that Ernesto had removed himself from Jocelyn's life. The song mocked her. The Clinton campaign had appropriated it for its campaign theme song. The new president had even convinced Fleetwood Mac to reunite—temporarily— so they could perform it at his inaugural ball. This happened only a few weeks after Ernesto and Jocelyn's break-up. It made Jocelyn want to become a Republican.

The break-up took place in two stages; the first came on Christmas Eve in Albuquerque's Old Town, when Jocelyn had gone to help her father close up his jewelry shop. She helped her father in the store whenever she could get away. But there were fewer and fewer chances for her to do this. Her mother required around-the-clock care now. This was also Jocelyn's job—a job for which she didn't get paid.

Christmas Eve was the exception. Jocelyn's brothers and older sister came to the house so that they could shower love and attention on the mother they didn't have to take care of all of the other days and nights of the year. They brought their kids. Luis had even driven up from Las Cruces. Mama could no longer make the Christmas Eve tamales. Luis's wife Marilyn found an old woman in nearby Mesilla who made them. They tasted almost as good as Mama's. *Almost.*

Because of all the people who came to Old Town to see the festive luminarias, Papa kept the shop open late. It was nine o'clock and the streets were crowded with locals and tourists. A mariachi band was playing seasonal music on the plaza just across from San Felipe de Neri Church. The church, constructed of five-foot-thick adobe brick, was being spruced up. It was about to celebrate its bicentennial. San Felipe de Neri reminded Jocelyn of her mother: battered and buffeted by the years, but still standing.

For all of Jocelyn's mother's health problems, she seemed destined to live on and on. Thanks, of course, to Jocelyn's constant care and attention.

Jocelyn and her father, Ruben, had just stepped out of the shop when they saw them coming down the sidewalk: Ernesto and one of the waitresses who worked in the restaurant in Old Town that Ernesto's father owned and Ernesto managed. She was hanging on Ernesto's—on Jocelyn's *boyfriend's* arm, drunkenly nibbling his ear. Ernesto appeared drunk too. He seemed, at first, to be looking right through Jocelyn, but when her presence finally registered, he quickly detached himself from the draping, clinging, nibbling woman who was all flouncy Mexican skirt and ruffled blouse, all lipstick and eyeshadow and everything feminine and desirable that Jocelyn had never allowed herself to be. Jocelyn hadn't time for herself. She was the self-sacrificing caregiver. She was the handsome woman in muted colors who helped the old man in his shop. Jocelyn had to tamp down her vibrant female spirit as she waited for the circumstances of her life to change.

"Hello, Jocelyn. Hello, Ruben," said Ernesto. "This is Rosa."

"I know Rosa," said Jocelyn without smiling.

"Feliz Navidad to you both. Rosa and I are going to a party."

"Tell them the good news, Ernesto," slurred Rosa.

"Oh, yes. My father has decided to retire. He wants me to have Luna's. He's giving me good terms."

"Tell them the other good news, Ernesto."

"Not now, *cariño*."

Ernesto waited until the next day to tell Jocelyn the "good news." It wasn't so good for Jocelyn. As Mama and Papa and Jocelyn's three brothers and one sister and all of her nieces and nephews were sitting themselves down to Christmas dinner, Ernesto came to the door and took Jocelyn out onto the xeriscaped front lawn (though she was needed inside to help serve).

He had to tell Jocelyn something important: he wouldn't be seeing her anymore. He was seeing Rosa now. Soon he would be *marrying* Rosa. He had waited for four years for Jocelyn to come around and he wasn't going to wait anymore.

Jocelyn felt as if the sky had fallen down on top of her. She hated Ernesto for leaving her, for making her stop thinking about tomorrow, but at the same time she was aware of how unfair it had been to leave him on the hook for so long. And yet, was any of it Jocelyn's fault? This was the way it worked: the youngest daughter was required to put her life upon the shelf if this be the mother's wish, to remain in attendance to her mother's later-life needs—to sacrifice a large part of her own life for the woman who bore her.

It had Jocelyn wishing for her mother's death, for which she felt horribly guilty.

Death came during the monsoon rains of the following August. Mama Lucero caught a chill and went to bed with a high fever. The illness taxed her fragile heart. The cause of death was put down as congestive heart failure.

There was a family conference. It was decided that Jocelyn should have the house. It was in her mother's name, and now it would be put in Jocelyn's name. Ruben agreed that this was the right thing to do. The consensus among the four older siblings was that their baby sister could keep working for their father if she liked. Or she could do something entirely different with her life. She had permission now.

Jocelyn nodded and agreed that everything being offered to her was fair and generous. Inside, though, her heart had hardened toward her siblings. She was forty. She had tended to her mother since she was a little girl. In her spare time she had driven to Old Town and worked behind a counter selling Native American jewelry her father had purchased wholesale from the local pueblos. She had made friends with a couple of the neighboring storekeepers, but few others.

Along the way she had fallen in love with an older man named Ernesto, a large man with jet-black hair and bright green eyes, who claimed her virginity at the age of thirty-six in the little apartment he kept over the restaurant. He had asked her to marry him, knowing that her answer could only be "No, not now. Not just yet."

He seemed to understand.

Or was it that he had proposed marriage knowing fully well what the answer would be? Because this was Ernesto's way of keeping *Jocelyn* on the hook: taking her up to his rooms above the restaurant until someone better came along.

Rosa. The whore.

Today was September 14. The rains had tapered off. Fall was in the air. Jocelyn sat in her car. The radio station was playing the song—the song she now despised. She was stopped at the light, waiting to make her left turn onto her street. The house was on Candelaria. It was one of the many streets in Albuquerque's North Valley that still carried vestiges of the neighborhood's farming and ranching past. The street came to a dead end near the Rio Grande, at a place where cottonwood trees grew in the sandy soil of the river's gallery forest.

She didn't want to make the turn. The light had changed to green and the way was clear to go, but she couldn't make herself do it. She didn't even roll forward into the intersection. There was a car behind her. The driver was being polite. He wasn't honking, though she clearly should be turning so that he could then make *his* turn.

The light turned yellow.

Jocelyn Lucero didn't turn.

The light turned red. Jocelyn could see through her rearview mirror the middle-aged man pounding his fist upon his steering wheel in frustration.

She didn't want to make the turn because she didn't want to go home. She had spent forty years of her life in that stucco house, watching each of her three brothers and her sister walk out the door and come back only on his or her own terms. She had stayed home because it was expected of her. And now she was supposed to go home because there was no place else for her to go.

The light turned green. The man behind her tapped his horn lightly.

This time she cooperated. She pulled up. When the way was clear, she made her turn. She drove down Candelaria, a residential street with every house different from the one next to it. The North Valley was home to people who didn't care what the house next to them looked like. Sometimes it wasn't a house at all; it might be an old barn or even a sheep pen.

This was old Albuquerque. This was The Valley.

Jocelyn slowed as she approached the house. The driveway was empty. Her father was staying a little late at the store. She had said she would go home and start dinner for the both of them. Instead, she kept driving. She passed the house and took the street to the place where it came to an end. She parked her car and walked to the river. She had been coming here for years—ever since she was a young girl. Every fall she came to see the majestic cottonwoods put on their leafy coats of brilliant yellow. There were no oranges or reds allowed in this southwestern bosque—only this single, all-pervasive color, like liquid sunshine dripped upon these gnarled, defiant giants of the desert.

She remembered a picnic she once had with Ernesto beneath these trees. He had said he would remain patient, because he loved her. "My love isn't going anywhere, Jocelyn."

Today the trees were green. The wispy cotton they had shed in early summer had been blown away. The path through the bosque was choked by seasonally opportunistic weeds and wild grasses. Jocelyn walked along the river's edge. She looked up at the houses perched upon the western bluff. The forest was too dense for her to see the mountains that towered behind her—the ones given the name *Sandia*, Spanish for "watermelon," because of the watermelon-pinkish color they took on in the waning light of the winter sunsets.

There were Canada geese wading near a sand island in the middle of the river. Jocelyn listened to the sounds of the place where she had grown up: the flutter and cooing of the ubiquitous mourning doves overhead, the distant barking of dogs in this city of canine hegemony, the gentle rustle of a horse brushing the crowding thicket along a nearby bridle trail, the gurgle of the river current purling over rocks and errant branches and other river clutter at her feet.

She loved this city for the sense of place and belonging that it gave her, but she hated it for having held on to her for too long—like the cottonwoods, forever stingy about dropping their leaves. They would shed them only reluctantly, when they were dried and brown and crumbling, and only when the winds shook some sense into their branches. Who was to blame? Her mother needed her, and she didn't want to make a stand. She'd known young women who did—who then became ostracized by family members who had won their own family lotteries of gender and age and didn't understand why their little sister didn't accept her fate with equanimity.

She thought of Ernesto and the way he had wanted to make love to her in the stand of flimsy elms as covert as a chain-link fence. Oh how she had protested, but oh how it had stirred her, had made her feel alive, had made her feel independent even as she was submitting to someone else who had his own idea of what it was that she ought to be doing.

She loved him, of course.

Or did she?

Was Ernesto simply someone who had come along at the right time—when she needed to be loved for the woman she so wanted to be?

They were going to run the restaurant together. They were going to open other Luna's Restaurant in the Northeast Heights, in Bernalillo, perhaps even in Santa Fe. Ernesto's father, Silverio, had been content never to dream big.

Jocelyn and Ernesto dreamed big. They aimed high.

"Someday, *cariño*. Someday soon, yes?"

Someday.

Now Jocelyn felt betrayed. She kicked a rock into the river. She walked back to her car.

Her sister Olivia was waiting at the house. "Weren't you supposed to be home at five thirty?"

It was twenty past six.

"What do you want, Olivia?" asked Jocelyn. "Why are you here?"

"I need Mama's recipe for calavacitas. I'm having some people over tomorrow night."

"You've watched Mama make it all your life. You've watched *me* make it. You don't remember what goes in it?"

"What's wrong?"

"What do you mean, 'what's wrong?' I come home a few minutes late to a house that I assumed would be empty only to find you standing here making demands."

Olivia got her pouty face. "I didn't know I'd be putting you out."

"You mean because I probably wouldn't be doing anything important anyway, except throwing something together for Papa and me to eat? We're having Stouffer's lasagna, if it's any of your business—which it isn't."

"You're too young to be going through the change. I wish you would tell me what this is about."

Jocelyn sat down on the sofa. "The problem, Olivia, is that you don't know *what* the problem is—not you or Luis or Marco or Vic. *Or* Papa."

Olivia sat down on the sofa next to her younger sister. "I miss Mama too. But we all have to get on with our lives, baby sister."

Jocelyn didn't speak at first. She stared at Olivia with disbelief and contempt. Then she said, "I hated our mother. I wanted her dead so my family indentureship would end. She died too late."

"I don't think you mean that."

"I do."

"And Ernesto wasn't good for you. I was happy when the two of you broke up."

"We didn't break up. He left me. He got tired of waiting. How long did you make Mark wait?"

"Our situations are very different. Are you going to give me the recipe or not?"

"Not. And get out of my house. It's the only thing I've ever gotten from this family, and I'm looking forward to the day that Papa drops dead so I can truly have it all to myself."

"I don't believe that you've become this person. I *won't* believe it."

"Please leave, Olivia. Go."

Olivia left, taking her indignation and Reddi-wipped victim complex with her.

Ruben Lucero came home twenty minutes later. Jocelyn served him Stouffer's meat sauce lasagna. They had a beer. Jocelyn and her father didn't usually talk much during the quiet evenings following Francine Lucero's death. They spoke to each other at the store—about shop business—and that seemed enough for one day.

Tonight was different. There was something Ruben very much wanted to discuss with his daughter. And he had something to give her.

It was a brochure for a Caribbean cruise line. "It's for one of those singles cruises. Your mother and I decided after Ernesto—well, we decided that you needed to get away, that you needed to meet some men who weren't anything like that sly little weasel."

"This was Mama's idea too?"

"Yes. In the end. I did have to do a little persuading, but she came around. Then she had all that trouble in the spring, and the woman we were going to get to come in to help her out in the summer—well, it didn't work out. And then, of course, she died, God rest her soul. So go on the cruise. Have a wonderful time. Start your life, *Corazon*."

"You haven't called me that in years."

"It's time I picked it up again."

Jocelyn got up from the table. She reached down and gave him a hug. She picked up the travel brochure. "This is the name of the ship? It's a odd name for a ship."

Ruben agreed.

Deus ex Machina. It was indeed a very odd name for a ship.

* * *

"All right. Comments? Impressions? Yes, Derrick?"

"I understand that we're supposed to make these comments as positive and constructive as possible, but to be honest, I thought the ending sucked."

"That isn't helpful."

"No, that's okay. Tell me, Derrick. Tell me why my ending sucked."

"It was too clever by half. It felt author-intrusive."

"What do you mean by 'author-intrusive'? Your hand is up, Sheila. What do you think Derrick means by 'author-intrusive'?"

"The author calling attention to herself through a transparent manipulation of the story elements. It also sounds like she wrote herself into a corner and had to call upon the proverbial gods for deliverance."

"Derrick's right. I did write myself into a corner. Because I knew that in reality, Jocelyn was destined to spend the rest of her life working for her father—both in the Old Town shop and at home—and then after he died, living alone. Pretty dreary stuff."

"Cynthia, you're being very quiet back there. Perhaps you might like to contribute something here?"

"Not really. It sounds like Campbell knows what's wrong with her story. It doesn't have a realistic ending."

"But taking the story overall, do you think that she did a good job of fleshing out her characters—creating a plausible narrative up to a point?"

"Yes."

Cynthia didn't elaborate. She didn't know Campbell. She knew that Campbell had no window into her own life, yet it was uncanny how closely her own life story resembled that of Jocelyn Lucero's. Cynthia even lived in the Albuquerque's North Valley not that far from Candelaria.

It gave her pause. It gave her chills, actually. She was the youngest. She was left behind to take care of her mother—a mother who was constantly ill but never too ill not to keep plodding on, with the help of Cynthia's filial love and attendance. It was a wonder that Cynthia was able to get away for the creative writing class she took two nights a week at UNM.

Cynthia liked the idea of a cruise. It served her escape fantasy.

Five days later that fantasy became a reality when Cynthia Baca bought a ticket for a Caribbean singles cruise and disappeared for a month. Her two brothers and two sisters were horrified, her mother devastated to be abandoned by her baby—someone who up until that point had been so dependable, so lovingly self-sacrificing.

Cynthia sent Campbell a postcard from the Bahamas in care of the school, thanking her for providing the impetus for her liberation, thanking Campbell for the chance to meet Paul in Freeport and then Kent in Nassau and then Danny in the midnight buffet line aboard ship. Because Cynthia had been transformed by this act of self-empowerment. At the age of thirty-eight she'd finally come into her own.

In Cynthia's enthusiastic opinion, continuing education classes had the potential to be life-altering experiences.

* * *

"That ending is simply horrible, Anita. You can't be serious about entering that story into the writing competition."

"Dead serious, Sis. And I intend to win that all-expenses-paid trip to New York City, and Mama will just have to fend for herself. On second thought, you can drive down from Santa Fe and stay with her yourself. For once."

"What's gotten into you?"

"It's a long story."

"And this is where it ends?"

"Yes."

1994

CROONING AND SWOONING
IN SOUTH DAKOTA

Just as she said she would, Mrs. Richman ("Oh, please, call me Natalia!") arrived at 5:30.

"Is there anybody in America besides bakers and dairy farmers who gets up before 5:30?" Jeremy had groggily inquired as he pulled the coffee pot from the coffee maker.

"Mrs. Richman can hear you," Erin said from the dining room.

"Oh, please, call me Natalia!"

Natalia looked around the room. It was everything Erin and her brother Jeremy had said it would be: a hoarder's trove of Roy Rogers memorabilia. "Your grandfather had quite an extensive collection. I've never seen anything like it, and I've been doing estate sales for over twenty years."

Natalia's hand fell upon a framed, autographed portrait of all the members of the singing group, Sons of the Pioneers, which Roy had formed in the early thirties, back when he was still Leonard Slye of Cincinnati, Ohio. "How long did it take your grandfather to assemble this collection?"

"Almost fifty years," said Erin.

"And where is he now—is he already in the nursing home?"

"As of a couple of weeks ago," offered Jeremy, coming in from the kitchen, a cup of coffee in each hand.

"Thank you, Jeremy," said Erin to her brother, taking a cup. "So Mrs.—I mean, Natalia, how do you think we'll do?"

"Well, I've kept my fee down to twenty percent. That helps. But the fact that the sale will appeal mostly to collectors of Roy Rogers memorabilia—"

"*Serious* collectors."

"True. It is limiting. On the other hand—and I'm definitely an 'other hand' sort of person—I've advertised all over this end of the state. And I'll bet you there will be some Roy Rogers and Dale Evans fans who'll get wind of it from as far away as Nebraska and Minnesota, so we'll just cross our fingers for a good turnout. May I ask: is the collection complete?"

"Complete in what way?" asked Jeremy, who was now sipping from his own cup of coffee.

"Roy Rogers was famous for putting his name on everything. Nobody branded more merchandise in his heyday except Disney. Still, there are a finite variety of items that Rogers collectors are able to get their hands on. Did your grandfather tell you if he'd acquired them all?"

Erin shrugged.

Jeremy picked up a cowboy hat with Roy Rogers' name stitched across the hatband and put it on. "I wouldn't be surprised."

"Is that the only hat?" asked Natalia, pulling out her list.

"Hell no," replied Jeremy.

Erin added, "There are at least a dozen more in the den."

"Oh, goodness," said Natalia Richman, with a slightly avaricious simper.

By sunup there was an orderly line of early-bird customers stretched down the front walk. Cars were continuing to pull onto the street. Mitchell, South Dakota, wasn't a very big town. These people came from other places. Word was out; this had the makings of a good sale.

Natalia Richman understood people. She understood their totemic relationship to things. She also understood how much people of a certain age loved Roy Rogers and his wife, Dale Evans, and Roy's horse, Trigger, and his German Shepherd, Bullet. And yet their popularity didn't last forever. When ABC decided to give Roy and Dale their own comedy-western-variety show in the fall of 1962 (called, naturally, T*he Roy Rogers and Dale Evans Show*), they got clobbered in the ratings by Jackie Gleason and were promptly cancelled—probably because all of Roy's kid-followers had grown up and were busy raising kids of their own, kids who didn't *get* Roy Rogers. Roy and Dale weren't necessarily has-beens. There was still enormous affection for them throughout the country. But for a long while nobody was buying Roy Rogers–approved neckties and frontier shirts and kerchiefs and board games and trick lassos anymore.

It was different now. Now Roy Rogers and Dale Evans, both still living on their ranch in Apple Valley, California, were *nostalgic*. Nostalgia was a good thing for someone like Natalia Richman. A Long Island native in her late forties, Natalia had moved to Sioux Falls with her husband ten years earlier, and, now divorced, was still plying her trade running estate sales and an antique store in Yankton, and actually making a decent living at it.

"Shall we admit the hordes?" she asked Erin and Jeremy.

Both siblings nodded.

"And may I say," said Natalia, going to unlock the front door, "how much I admire the two of you for taking care of your grandfather's estate for him. I should be so lucky to have grandkids like you."

"Thanks," said Jeremy. "But we're a little mercenary. He's giving us a percentage."

Natalia's hand rested on the doorknob but she didn't open the door just yet. "How did he feel, if you don't mind me asking, about getting rid of his collection? I find that people as acquisitive as your grandfather are sometimes reluctant to let go of even a few items, much less their entire collection."

Jeremy looked at his sister, who answered for the both of them: "His mind was going—to put it bluntly. We let him take a few things with him to the rest home. As far as he knows, he's got everything right there with him."

Natalia squinted at the two, perplexed. "But you just said he was giving you a percentage."

"Oh. Well—" Jeremy turned to his sister.

"That was during one of his more lucid moments," explained Erin. "You know how it is with people our grandfather's age: perfectly rational and coherent one moment and totally out of it the next." Erin swallowed. "Don't you think you should let all those people in? It's past time."

Natalia opened the door. There were at least twenty men and women and a couple of children, who now rushed into the room. Their eager entrance was suggestive of a big department store sale, but obviously played out on a slightly smaller scale.

"Please be careful," Natalia had to say to one man right off the bat. He was shaking a Roy Rogers boot bank, apparently trying to discover if there were any coins still left inside.

The memorabilia had been distributed throughout three different rooms. Natalia, Erin, and Jeremy each took a different room so they could keep a close eye on the customers and answer any questions.

"Are these their real autographs?" an overweight, middle-aged woman asked Natalia. The woman was holding an inscribed color photograph of Roy and Dale posed behind a rustic fence railing, each gazing lovingly into the eyes of the other. Both wore excessively fringed Western shirts and colorful kerchiefs around their necks.

"Since they've personalized their sentiments to someone named Patrick, I'd say these are their original signatures." Natalia remembered that the old man's first name was Tyler. Perhaps he bought the picture from someone named Patrick.

"I was only asking," said the woman, clutching the framed photo, "because, as you can see, Roy Rogers' name is on everything in this house. It's hard to tell what's a real signature and what isn't."

The man standing next to the woman, who did not seem to know her, volunteered an opinion: "Whether it's a real signature or a printed one, it doesn't much matter. Roy and Dale are notorious for signing anything you shove in their face. They're real autographing sluts that way."

"That was rude," said the woman to the man.

"I'm just saying, don't let this woman charge you too much for something just because it's been autographed." Then the man turned to Natalia and held up a Roy Rogers rodeo lamp—the kind you'd put next to a kid's bed. "How much for the lamp?"

With a straight face, Natalia replied, "Ten thousand dollars."

At eight o'clock, Erin's friend Betsy came to help out. Betsy was blond and very pretty and lit up the room with her smile, like Mary Tyler Moore.

With Betsy now helping out, Natalia was able to turn the living room over to Erin and let Betsy have the den, and then Natalia moved to the kitchen, where she set herself up at the table with the cash box and the receipt book. This was easier than trying to transact business in a more roving fashion. So far, business had been much better than she expected. Usually the die-hards would come early. After that there would be a lull. The rest of the day would bring a trickle of dilettante collectors and curious locals and those hoping to find something for sale that didn't necessarily have to do with the overriding theme of the collection. Not today. Today there was a good, steady stream of *serious* customers.

Natalia totaled up a large purchase from a man who had been in the house since she first opened the door. He was pulling a Roy Rogers "chuck wagon," which was a little red wagon fitted up to look like a miniature

Conestoga. The man had filled it with Roy Rogers authorized apparel: boots and "bootsters," socks, spurs and cuffs, a rodeo suit and frontier shirt, all imprinted with the same familiar Roy Rogers signature, and one of several different images of Roy mounted on Trigger. The man was also set to purchase a Roy Rogers children's paint set in mint condition, a Roy Rogers harmonica, and Roy Rogers authorized binoculars. He mostly accepted the prices Natalia had scribbled on the tags, but now and then would haggle a little, and Natalia would haggle a little in return until the two had reached an amicable agreement.

Once the man had emptied his wallet and departed, Natalia found herself alone. She took a sip from either her third or fourth cup of coffee of the morning (she'd lost count) and took a bite of her crumbly blueberry muffin. It was a little after ten. There were fewer buyers in the house now, but she could still hear the sound of people commenting to each other on all the remaining merchandise. She could hear something else as well—an odd noise coming from somewhere behind her. The only thing behind her was a door that she assumed opened onto a kitchen pantry.

It was a scratching sound with a little thumping mixed in. A mouse? Do mice "thump"? she wondered. Natalia was frightened to death of mice and had no desire whatsoever to investigate. She tried to distract herself by looking over the contract that Erin and Jeremy had signed. At the top of the page were the words "Estate Sale on Behalf of Tyler Enger. Authorized agents: Jeremy Enger, Erin Enger." This reminded her of the autographed picture that had been personalized to someone named Patrick. It was a little thing, really, but most collectors didn't like to buy items with personalized autographs unless the recipient was somebody famous.

And still there was the scratching and the thumping. This was no mouse. This was something much bigger. A chill shot through Natalia. She got up from her chair to go and ask Erin about it. Then there came from behind the door a different sound altogether: a moan. A *human* moan.

Something was going on—something disturbing that she would have to look into, whether she wanted to or not. Natalia recalled that Erin and her brother had struggled a little with answers to a couple of her questions about their grandfather. And earlier the brother and sister had contradicted their own statement about the arrangement the old man had made in terms of dividing the proceeds from the sale. It had seemed suspicious. Everything seemed suspicious to her now. Where were their parents? Why was it only the old man's grandchildren who had been assigned the task of unloading his extensive Roy Rogers memorabilia collection?

Natalia went to the door. Not knowing what or *who* she might find, but hoping against hope that it had absolutely nothing to do with the old man, she slowly opened the door. It wasn't a pantry that lay on the other side; it was a basement—or rather, stairs leading down to a basement. And it wasn't Tyler Enger whom she found on the stairs. In spite of the disturbing picture in front of her, she almost sighed with relief. Erin and Jeremy *hadn't* imprisoned their grandfather in the basement so they could sell his Roy Rogers collection. They'd imprisoned someone else—a much younger man. The young man was gagged and bound, but had apparently, over some period of time, managed to get himself two-thirds of the way up the stairs. He was looking up at her, pleading with his eyes for assistance.

Natalia found the light switch and flicked on the naked bulb that dangled over the stairs. She descended a couple of the steps and then closed the door behind her. Hopefully, this would buy her a minute or two. If Erin or Jeremy or Erin's friend Betsy came into the kitchen, they would, perhaps, conclude that she had momentarily ducked into the bathroom.

Natalia took the three additional steps necessary to put herself next to the hog-tied young man. She fumbled with the knot that held the gag tightly in place and was able to undo it so that the man could speak.

"Praise Jesus," he said. "Can you untie me?"

"I'll try. Who are you?"

"I'm Patrick. Erin and Jeremy's brother."

"What's going on?"

"Isn't it obvious? My brother and sister tied me up and left me in the cellar so I wouldn't interfere with their plans. We have to hurry or they'll have everything sold right out from under me."

"From under *you*? I thought all of this stuff belonged to your grandfather."

"We don't have a grandfather."

"Everything upstairs—it all belongs to *you*?"

"That's what I'm saying. You're really going to have to work to loosen the rope around my wrists. It's pretty tight."

"Why are they doing this?"

"Why do you think?"

"Because they want to sell all your stuff and run away with the profit?"

"Now *that* would be interesting—a good storyline for one of Roy's Western adventures. No, it's not nearly as thrilling as that. They're doing this for 'my own good.' Because they think I've turned loony after all these years of collecting Roy Rogers memorabilia and living alone and really not getting out very much except to go to my night job at the electrical power plant. This is an intervention. Problem is, they're liquidating my huge investment here, and they aren't even going about it the right way. You don't sell a quality collection like this in a garage sale. You go to dealers who specialize in Royandalabilia. Who are you, anyway?"

"I'm the woman they hired to sell said quality collection."

"Oh. Well, what do *you* know about Roy Rogers?"

"I know that there are some serious collectors out there. I was hoping we'd end the day with a nice chunk of change."

The rope was off Patrick's wrists now. He rubbed them where they were reddened and chafed. "I can't believe that it actually came to this. That's okay. I can do the ankles myself."

"Should I call the police?"

"Yes. And tell them to bring a couple of straitjackets. Talk about loony: my brother and sister should have been put into a padded cell a long time ago. Jeremy tried to burn down the Corn Palace a few years ago. Granted, he was high on patio sealant at the time, but that's no excuse."

"What do I do about the other girl who's been helping them?"

"What other girl?"

"I think her name is Betsy."

"Betsy's here?" Suddenly Patrick's expression changed. It softened. Natalia nodded. "Do you know her?"

"Yeah. Kind of. Isn't that a pip? Betsy's here."

Natalia started up the stairs. "I'll call the police. They can sort everything out when they get here."

"No! Wait!" Patrick grabbed Natalia's leg. It startled her and she almost screamed.

"I don't want *Betsy* arrested."

"Why?"

"Because I'm madly in love with her, that's why. I always thought she considered me a hopeless freak. But now you say she's here. Now you say that she's upstairs helping Erin and Jeremy rid me of this, this, this *sickness*—"

"Patrick. I'm very perplexed."

"Our parents died when we were young—Erin and Jeremy and me. That's not to say we probably wouldn't have been messed up anyway. It's in the genes. Anyway, Erin and Jeremy—*they* decided to engage the world. On *their* terms, obviously, but I have to hand it to them—at times they appear almost normal."

"I thought they *were* normal."

"Whereas I *dis*engaged. I retreated into my—"

"Royandalabilia?"

"That's right. I took the happy trail. You know the song that Dale wrote—their theme song—'Happy Trails'? I've spent my life looking for good role models, you know, being an orphan and all. But you know who it is I need more than anyone else right now?"

"Betsy?"

Patrick nodded. "See? This means she loves me. This means she has hopes that I can turn my life around, begin to get out in the world. If I were to have her thrown in jail, I'm not sure she'd ever forgive me. No, don't call the police, okay?"

"Should I at least stop the sale?"

Patrick didn't reply. He stared off into the middle distance. "In their own way, I do think they mean well."

"*Mean well*? How long have you been tied up in this basement?"

"You're right. I know you're right. I don't know what to do!" Patrick began to claw at his thick mop of hair with restless fingers. "Yes, I do. You better leave me down here. Pretend like you and me—like we never ever saw each other. First bring me a Pop Tart or something. I'm really hungry."

"You're sure about this?"

"No. Not really. But until I get some telepathic advice from the King of the Cowboys, I should probably just stay put. He's all the way down in Southern California, you know, so there's bound to be a delay in the transmission."

"Okay."

"You know I'm kidding, right?"

"I'm not so sure about anything right now." Natalia shook her head slowly in deep befuddlement, then climbed the stairs, opened the door, and went out into the kitchen. There was a woman standing at the table holding a couple of record albums. Natalia quickly shut the door behind her.

"*There* you are!" the woman chirped. "I found two that I didn't have already: 'My Chickashay Gal' and 'I'm Gonna Gallop Gallop to Gallup, New Mexico.'"

"I'm very happy for you," Natalia said.

"I love Roy Rogers. I named my boy Roy and my girl Dale. We have a coon hound named Ghost, just like Roy's champion coon hound."

"Five dollars for each record. That'll be ten all together."

The woman paid and walked out of the kitchen singing "Happy Trails."

A moment later Betsy entered with money from a quick sale she'd made in the den. Natalia couldn't help herself. "Everything's going to be all right," she confided with a comforting smile.

Betsy gave Natalia a quizzical look. "You *know*, don't you?"

Natalia nodded.

"It's probably one of the oddest estate sales you've ever run, right?"

"A little twisted, you know, but I'm trying to adjust to it."

"Twisted? How is that?"

"Well, I mean the fact that Patrick's—"

"Not here? But don't you think it's better this way? And besides, Erin says he's always wanted to go to Mount Rushmore. Last she heard, he was having a wonderful time."

"Oh dear."

"Are you all right, Ms. Richman? You don't look too well."

"I think I'll have a Pop Tart. Let's all have a Pop Tart. Things are about to get very interesting."

Scratch, scratch, thump, thump.

"And please, call me Natalia."

1995

VARIOUSLY BEREFT IN MINNESOTA, CALIFORNIA, OKLAHOMA, AND MONTANA

Melanie Minero lives in Minnesota. She hasn't always lived in Minnesota. The earliest years of her life were spent in the company of four older siblings in Lincoln, Nebraska. Like her three brothers and one sister, Mellie left her hometown as a young adult, and after the death of her remaining parent—her mother—never had much reason to go back.

This story isn't about Lincoln, Nebraska.

It isn't about any one particular place, really. It's about two sisters and two brothers who live in four different states, and about a third brother who's just died in a different state.

A couple of days ago.

May 16.

These five siblings have never been all that close, although they have made a few begrudging attempts to keep themselves loosely inserted into each other's lives. In terms of their feelings for one another, the five Ramseys (including the two female *nee* Ramseys) aren't really all that different from any of the other millions of dissimilar brothers and sisters who make up the majority of modern extended American families: brothers and sisters who share a few of the same genes and a handful of mutual memories of a connected past—brothers and sisters who by convenience of circumstance grew up together in the same house and now live in other houses in other places.

It has been said that death will either bring a family together or pull a family apart. Because death has the tendency to play havoc with relationships and sensibilities as it reshuffles the deck of the card game of life, it rarely makes only a glancing impression upon a family member. However, with the death of Shelby Ramsey, his surviving siblings displayed every point upon the spectrum of familial response, including the one that rests squarely in the middle: marginal interest bordering upon indifference.

Let us begin our examination of these varied responses with Carla Guinter, wife of Captain Virgil Guinter of the United States Navy, and, within the timeframe of our story, a resident of the Mission Hills neighborhood of San Diego. Carla, first in the family birth order, has just received a phone call from her sister Mellie about the death of said brother Shelby (fourth oldest), who for the last twenty years has gone by the name of Sawyer. He chose Sawyer when he began to include in his juggling act three active-duty two-stroke-engine-powered chainsaws. Sawyer used to juggle rubber balls. Then he moved up to dessert plates. He finished his life juggling chainsaws. It was, in fact, one of the chainsaws that prematurely (and violently) brought the curtain down on Shelby/Sawyer's neo-Vaudevillian life.

Mellie is calling from Burnsville, a suburb of Minneapolis. Mellie and her husband Artie are both high school teachers.

"How did he die?" asks Carla, who tries very hard to be attentive to news of her brother's death—the brother she has not seen except on an occasional television variety show for the last dozen years.

"He was performing at Circus Circus Tunica, one of those new Mississippi River casinos, and he lost his concentration, and one of the chainsaws sliced the jugular vein in his neck."

This statement of gruesome fact is followed on the other end of the telephone line by silence.

"I'm sorry, Carla. I didn't know how else to say it. Hello? Carla?"

"I'm back. I dropped the phone. I didn't hear what you just—There is a man on a rampage on channel ten. He's stolen a tank and he's flattening cars and trucks like he was Godzilla's own feet."

"What on earth are you talking about?"

"On the television. They're showing it right now. He's destroying a whole street in Clairemont. It's hard to even watch. He just tried to knock over a house. Now he's backing up. He's running over a fire hy—Jesus God, Mellie. The man has just unleashed a geyser of water three stories high."

"Our brother is dead. He was nearly decapitated."

"Who did it?"

"What do you mean 'who did it?' He did it to himself. It isn't just a severed finger from a misthrown Ginsu knife this time, Carla. It's his neck."

"That's awful. Oh Jesus God, Mellie—the tank maniac just ran over some kind of recreational vehicle. Opened it right up like a loosely wrapped Christmas present."

"Would you turn off the television?" There is the sound of undisguised impatience to Mellie's voice.

"Just a minute. I'm turning the sound down. I'll turn away for a moment, but I have to know what happens I have friends who live in Clairemont. I fear for their safety."

"Buck is handling the arrangements. He's flying down to Memphis tonight. He wants to know if we're okay with cremation."

"I don't have a problem with cre—oooooh!"

"You turned back around, didn't you?"

"I can't help it, Mellie. There's all manner of mayhem being broadcast on my television right now."

"You're disrespecting our brother."

"I hardly knew him"

"That was cold, Carla."

"That didn't come out the way I meant it. I just mean that Shelby and I had so very little to do with each other. He really was a stranger to me. Just as, no doubt, I've always been a stranger to him. I'm a navy wife. Whereas he juggled things for a living. Can you think of any other two people less alike?"

"So you're fine with Buck having him cremated?"

"Yes, of course. Is there going to be a funeral?"

"His friends—his juggling friends—they want to do something special for him at the casino."

"Something like what?"

"They want to put his ashes in little hollow balls and juggle them in tribute."

"Well, that certainly sounds in keeping with the crazy kind of life our brother led. Who am I to object?"

"That's what I needed to know. Buck doesn't like the idea. He thinks it's kitschy. I'll talk to him. What is the tank doing?"

"I can look now?"

"Have they been able to stop it?"

"How do you stop a tank?"

"With an anti-ballistic missile?"

The two women hang up.

Mellie gets her youngest brother Troy on the phone. Troy lives in Oklahoma City.

"Hello, Troy. Has Buck called you?"

"Yeah. Did you know there's a tank on the rampage in San Diego? Is Carla okay?"

"It isn't in her neighborhood."

"I think the whole world has gone batty. We have a little girl who lives next to us. She won't come out of her closet."

"Is it because of the bombing?"

"That's what her mother says. The girl is friends with another little girl whose baby sister was in the Murrah Building when it blew up last month. You can't keep the kids from watching all the coverage on TV. You can't protect your kids from all the shit that's out there these days. Nowhere is safe. Not even the heartland of America. I'm glad Taffy's grown. I still worry about her, though. She's in New York. There could be a sarin gas attack in the subway. She could be downtown when they try to blow up the World Trade Center again. Who's driving that tank? Is it O.J. Simpson?"

"I don't think they know who it is. Maybe it's the Unabomber. That would make sense. Buck wants to have Shelby cremated. He doesn't want all those jugglers juggling Shelby's ashes around, though."

"Yeah, he told me."

"Do you have an opinion one way or another?"

"I think it would be disrespectful to juggle his ashes. Even though this is how he made his living. Mom would have disapproved. But Mom is dead. I don't think Shelby would have minded, but Buck's the one doing all the heavy lifting here. So I vote to let Buck have the final say. And that's what I told him."

"How is it there in Oklahoma City?"

"There's still a pall over the city. You see it in all the faces. And such anger. Before they found out that it was a homegrown lunatic who did it, this East Indian who runs the convenience store in my neighborhood— somebody shot at him with a BB gun. They thought he was Muslim, like the guys who tried to pull down the Twin Towers. He isn't Muslim. He's a

Sikh. They wear turbans too. I hate this country. Full of idiots and crazies."

"I should call Buck."

"Sorry."

"About what?"

"Going off on my rant. And Clinton's no improvement on Bush."

"I'll talk to you later."

"Love you, Sis."

"Love you too."

Mellie phones her oldest brother Buck. Buck owns a ranch on the eastern slopes of the Pryor Mountains, south of Billings, Montana. He breeds champion Friesian stallions.

"He was a crazy sonofabitch, but he always made me laugh."

"Are you flying down tomorrow?"

"Yep."

"Did he have money? Do you need Artie and me to pitch in for the funeral expenses?"

"I talked to his girlfriend. Dawn. She's helping me with the arrangements. She said he was set up okay. Shelby never lived beyond his means. Those chainsaws were probably his biggest expense. How are *you* doing—you and Artie?"

"I'm in shock. You're never prepared for something like this. Although he did live dangerously."

"Everybody seems to be living dangerously these days. How are you doing otherwise? I don't think we've talked since somebody tried to burn your high school down."

"They didn't just try it. They actually succeeded."

"Some literal-minded teenaged hoodlum."

"You mean because the school's in Burnsville? Because the name of our varsity team is the Blaze?"

"No. Because your mascot's called 'Sparky.'"

"This isn't the time to make me laugh, Buck."

"What else can you do? Troy says the whole country's gone off the rails."

"If you live in Oklahoma City right now, you have every right to see things that way."

"This kind of stuff goes in cycles. We're presently in a bad cycle."

"I hate it. Oh, and Carla's bonkers."

"I've known that for quite a while."

"And one of our brothers sawed his head half off."

"The tabloids are having a field day. Some of their reporters have been calling. I guess Dawn gave them my number. But what could I tell them? I hardly knew Shelby. Dawn said he was good soul, though."

A silence.

"Are you still there, Mel?"

"I was looking for a Kleenex. I've never been to your ranch."

"It's nothing special."

"I'd like to see your horses."

"Come on up."

"I will."

"And I wouldn't put it off. You know that we're in the End Times, right?"

Mellie blows her nose. "I feel sometimes like the Rapture's already happened and we *all* got left behind."

Buck laughs.

Mellie says, "I was reading something in a magazine about Christopher Reeve. He's doing equestrian events now. When he's not acting. Take a guess at the name of his horse."

"I know the name of his horse. I pay attention to these things, Mel. It's Buck."

"The world can't just be all doom and gloom, right, Buck? Especially now that we've got Superman riding around on a big, beautiful steed, ready to make things right again."

Nine days later...oh, must I say it?

1996

COPROPHOBIC IN MISSISSIPPI

The Realtor's name was Maggie Kessler. Bill Hollon, the newly married husband of Heather Hollon, sat in the front seat of Maggie's 1995 Buick Century, Heather in the back.

Maggie had jowls. She wore thick mascara that made her eyes pop. She kept her hair short and feathered like Angela Lansbury when she was playing Jessica Fletcher, the mystery-writing sleuthess.

"As you can see, this subdivision is relatively new. In fact, there are several lots still for sale. But I want you to see a finished house which I feel would be just perfect for you."

"Trees are tall," said Bill Hollon, looking at the great leafy oaks that crowded the main entrance to the subdivision.

"You rarely see stands of old growth trees so nicely preserved in this part of Mississippi. Most of the forests that used to cover Desoto County were chopped down and converted to farmland years ago. Not that the developers didn't have to do their own share of bulldozing and leveling off to put these houses in here. It's always a trade-off."

Heather hadn't heard a word Maggie said. She was fascinated by the ducks.

"Look at the duck pond, honey," said Heather, touching her new husband on the shoulder.

"Oh yeah," said Bill. "Nice duck pond."

Maggie the Realtor handed Bill a brochure from her bag on the floor. "There are ten different models in this subdivision, but the builder has been very generous with customizing allowances. I don't work for him, though. I just thought you'd like to—do you like *that* one? It's Number Seven. The Tuscany. Anyway, the one I want to show you is a resale. That's why they're letting an outside broker like me come in here."

"How long did the previous owners live there?"

Bill asked the question; Heather nodded with equal curiosity.

"Not a single day. The house has been empty ever since it was finished last November. Nothing sadder than an empty house. I was here early this morning checking the keys and making sure the power company hadn't turned off the—here we are. Isn't it lovely?"

The house sat on a little hill. It had a steeply pitched roof suggesting a very high living room ceiling. The architectural style was nothing recognizable: an exaggerated Mediterranean arch over the front door, mansard eaves shading the front bedroom windows, a mishmash of different elements that maintained a sense of unity through color and texture, even if a cohesive architectural vision was lacking.

"I like the decorative glass," remarked Heather after the threesome had landed on the porch. She ran her hand along the narrow etched-glass panel next to the front door and went, "Um."

"Yeah. Real nice."

Maggie unlocked the door and opened it upon a large vestibule that led to the expansive living room. "It's 2,200 square feet overall, but the vaulted ceiling makes it feel even bigger—palatial almost. In the summer, all that hot air goes right up to the top. Then in winter the ceiling fan pulls it all right back down."

The Hollons nodded. This was only the third house they'd looked at. Everything about the process of buying a home was new to them. There was a definite mystery to it. Maggie the Realtor was revealing great truths and they were imbibing them, absorbing them into their unformed, protean consciousnesses. They trusted Maggie, welcomed her as their house-buying sherpa, because she had been doing this for over twenty years, and because she was a member of the same Hernando, Mississippi, garden club as Heather's mother.

There were two porthole windows near the ceiling of the living room. Maggie pointed to the one on the right. "When I got here early this morning the sun had just come up, and there was the most beautiful cascade of light coming down. It was dappled by the branches of the tall trees in the backyard. Quite magical. I felt like I was standing in the nave of some great cathedral."

Heather had tuned Maggie out again. She was staring at an electrical outlet on the wall. The top screw had fallen out of the plate and it hung slightly askew. It was a minor thing, really, but her eye was drawn to it.

Bill and Heather followed Maggie into the kitchen. All of the appliances were matching black. There was an island beneath an impressive pot rack. The cabinets in the kitchen were either cherry wood or cherry stained—Maggie wasn't sure which—but Heather thought they were pretty either way. She ran a couple of fingers through her Jennifer Aniston shag and nodded her appreciation.

The two smaller bedrooms shared a Jack-and-Jill bathroom. They seemed perfect for the family that Bill and Heather Hollon planned to start as soon as Bill got his promotion at the bank and Heather had put away some money from her job as a receptionist for a garden seed company. Heather looked out the back bedroom window and noted the large backyard. "A lot of room for a garden," she said to Bill.

"Or for a couple of Golden Retrievers to romp around." Bill winked. He drew Heather to his side and gave her a little squeeze about the hips.

The master bedroom was spacious. There was crown molding around the room and a large walk-in closet nearly the size of a fourth bedroom.

Maggie led her clients into the master bathroom. It was roomy as well. There was a large soaking tub in one corner and a separate shower. The toilet was sequestered in a closet. Bill stepped over to the closet. The door was open. The lid to the toilet was down, but in keeping with his inquisitive nature, he leaned over and lifted it. There, floating in the water, was a large umber-colored turd. It was solid, yet discernibly segmented. There was nothing else in the bowl. No toilet paper. Just the floating turd.

Bill closed the lid, but not fast enough for Heather and Maggie to miss seeing the turd.

Had he been alone in his discovery, Bill would simply have dropped the lid and walked away. But the fact that there were other witnesses to his find required that he do the thing this situation customarily required: he flushed the toilet.

For a long moment no one spoke. Bill could not keep himself from looking at Maggie. Maggie looked at the wall. Heather, for her part, could not avert her eyes from the toilet as hard as she tried. The toilet took its time emptying its tank and then refilling itself with fresh water. The sound of lavatory hydraulics echoed throughout the cavernous bathroom.

Eventually, Maggie led the couple out. A minute or so later, the Hollons and their real estate agent were standing in the backyard, looking at a few of the beautiful oak trees that had given their names to the subdivision: "Towering Oaks."

Maggie, who had previously been sunny and quite chatty in her description of the many winning features of the house, now spoke in dull monosyllables. "Well-kept lawn. Um. Nice deck here."

Heather cast an uneasy glance over her shoulder at the part of the house where the master bathroom was. Where the toilet closet was. Where they had all seen the big, brown, floating fecal log.

Not much was said in the car. Nor did conversation pick up in the fourth house that Maggie showed the Hollons. Bill avoided looking at either of the two toilets in this house, although Heather found herself staring at the closed lid of one of them, her face rigid with worry over dangerous possibilities.

That evening, after Bill and Heather had finished their slices of pizza and Bill had downed almost all of his second beer, the new husband said to the new wife, "So which house did you like the best?"

"The third one," said Heather.

"The one with the shit log?"

Heather nodded. Then she said, "Bill, was that *her* shit log?"

"We'll never know, honey. But probably."

"Why would she leave it there?"

"Maybe it didn't go down when she flushed. Try not to think about it."

"I love that house, Bill, but it had a turd in it."

"I know, angel." Bill put his arm around his new wife consolingly. After a moment, he drew back. "As embarrassing as it was for us, it must have been doubly hard for Maggie."

"I can only imagine," sighed Heather.

"Do you want this last piece of sausage?"

"No," said Heather. "I could not possibly eat it."

Later that night, Bill awoke to the sound of Heather's soft sniffles.

"Are you okay?" he asked with whispered tenderness.

"No, Bill. I'm not okay."

Bill rolled over and enfolded his wife's convulsing body. The tears flowed freely now, great moans of sadness emanating from deep within her throat.

"Oh God, how I loved that house!" she keened, her voice crepitating with pain.

"I know you did, angel. Go ahead and let it out. Let it all out."

1997

COMBUSTIBLE IN OHIO

Randi Bryce didn't like the interrogation room. The overhead light was harsh and the dark concrete walls made her feel as if she were sitting in a prison cell. It was a sobering reminder of her potential fate.

None of it made sense. It was as if she had entered her own *Twilight Zone* episode or one of those stories by Kafka in which one is doomed by circumstances both menacing and illogical. Randi Bryce had stood at the kitchen window and watched her husband burst into flames. She had rushed out with an afghan snatched from the daybed in the adjoining sunroom. Josh was rolling upon the ground, howling in a primal voice she had never heard before. She threw the afghan upon him to put out the fire that still consumed him. Her hands were singed.

She looked down at those hands now, bandaged and lying still upon her lap—hands tremulous beneath the gauze.

Randi was being accused, indirectly, of setting her husband on fire. The police officers who brought her in after the ambulance had taken Josh away wanted to know how such a thing could happen. She hadn't been formally arrested, but she could tell that they were getting close to making it all official. She could tell that they suspected she had used a match and the five-gallon can of gasoline they found sitting accusingly upon the awning-covered patio behind the house. Yet there was no smell of gasoline on her husband, or in the yard. There was no dribbled trail upon the patio's pebbled surface. Moreover, the lawnmower parked next to the can made the container's presence appear even less incriminating.

Maybe this is why they have yet to slap the handcuffs on me, Randi thought.

Josh's burns had been severe, but thankfully, given swift actions on the part of both husband and wife, they weren't life-threatening, barring complications. Randi wanted to see Josh, but being a person of interest in what was now being considered a possible attempted homicide, she could not.

There were injuries to go around. Things had been said by husband and wife the night before during an argument that was unfortunately witnessed by Josh's mother Agnes after Randi and Josh's ten-year-old daughter Brie had been sent up to bed. Randi and Josh had had it out in front of Agnes, and the next morning, a couple of hours after the "incident," Agnes related the vitriolic exchange to the two investigating officers, Lieutenants Selvera and Leggio—willingly, even eagerly, and in great detail.

Now it was Randi's turn to give her side, to try to convince the two detectives that in spite of the obvious motive, she could not possibly have done this terrible thing. Her mother-in-law's allegation was outrageous. She could hardly speak to it. But she calmed herself. A glass of juice had been set before her. She took a drink from the straw.

Randi was well aware that she didn't have to say anything if she didn't want to. But she *wanted* to talk. Randi knew that once she was charged, she could have an attorney at her side advising her as to what she should say and what she shouldn't so that she wouldn't dig herself a deeper hole than the one she was already in, but she didn't care. There was a small chance that by simply telling the truth about what happened, here at this early stage, she might be thoroughly exonerated in the minds of the suspicious officers. In the meantime, the cause of her husband's combustion was still being investigated. Circumstantially, she was the culpable agent. But there was still this: a total absence of any evidence showing how the fire had been ignited.

The pretty female officer sitting across the table from her, Lieutenant Selvera, was patient. Her voice had a slow, soothing cadence. "Take your time," she said. "Tell us everything that happened last night and everything that happened this morning leading up to the incident."

The shovel-nosed young male detective leaning against the dingy cinderblock wall nearest the door agreed with a nod.

"Why do I have to talk about what happened last night? Haven't you heard it all from Agnes? She was right there when the fireworks went off."

"Fireworks?" Lieutenant Leggio raised an eyebrow.

"I don't mean that literally." Randi glanced at the male officer. His face registered nothing. This wasn't going to be good cop and bad cop, Randi thought. It was going to be good cop and rudely indifferent cop.

"Josh and I—I don't think we've ever had a good marriage," Randi began. "It was okay in the beginning, but over time we just found ourselves going through the motions. He never asked me for a divorce and I never sought one from *him*. I don't think either of us had the stomach for it, and there was Brie to consider. We both felt like this would tear her apart—she's a very delicate child." Randi felt weariness creeping in, even though the interview had hardly begun. "We went to the marriage counselor and tried a few things, but we could never make the marriage what we wanted it to be. So we just kept plodding along."

"What do you and your husband do for a living?" asked Lieutenant Leggio.

"I worked for a small investment company until I got sick and haven't gone back."

"Sick?" asked Lieutenant Selvera.

"Yes. I got cancer a couple of years ago. Cervical cancer. Josh and I didn't want to have any more kids, so I opted for a radical hysterectomy and post-op radiation."

"How are you doing?"

"Good for now. Time will tell." Randi stopped her story to take another suck of juice. She couldn't use her hands, so she bent forward like the little toy drinking bird in the top hat.

"Go on," said the female lieutenant, after Randi had swallowed.

"Josh works for a construction supply company."

"What happened last night?" asked Leggio. "What was the fight about?"

"He flipped out. He does this. Something gets to him and he goes postal. Last night it was news from his mother. She was having dinner with us, as she's no doubt already told you. Josh's brother, Stephen, had really started to rake it in with this World Wide Web–based company that he'd gotten in on the ground floor with, and here Josh was, working for the same old walls-and-windows company that hadn't given him a raise in over two years. It started to be about that, and then it morphed into how lousy his life was overall and how even his marriage was just one big fat joke. And he had only stayed with me because of the cancer, but he was miserable. All this in front of his mother."

"What did *she* do? The mother," said Selvera.

"What she always does. She jumped right to his defense. He's so overworked and this and that, and of course he should get a handle on his temper, but he has every right to want his life to go in a different direction. Textbook mother-in-law malarkey. I felt that I was being ganged up on—as usual—and so I fought back."

"How did you fight back?"

"I said that I should have married this guy I dated in college. And Josh said that he should have married some girl he'd known since high school, and this is when things entered uncharted territory. He confessed that he'd been seeing her off and on all through our marriage. Until she died. She also had cancer—the same cancer as me. He wondered why the cancer had taken Teri but didn't take me, as if this were evidence of some cosmic cruelty directed only at him. I was paralyzed. Not only by the fact that my husband wished death upon me, but by his need to mention this longtime affair he'd had with Teri just to hurt me. So I sought a way to hurt *him*. I told him something that just came to me in that moment: that cervical cancer is caused by the human papillomavirus. That I'd never slept with anyone but Josh. That only *he* could have given me that virus—the virus that he had apparently gotten from his old girlfriend. Now I knew why I had gotten cancer and who had given it to me. I knew that if I had died, he would have been responsible for my death. Did Agnes mention this? You should have seen her face when I said it."

Randi took another sip. "This juice is too sweet. Can I just have some water?"

Lieutenant Leggio glanced over at the two-way mirror and nodded. A moment passed and then another officer entered the interrogation room carrying an open plastic water bottle with a straw bobbing inside. He set it down in front of Randi and left.

"Tell me about this morning," said Lieutenant Selvera, after Randi had taken a long drink of water.

"He was still angry. I was downstairs when he got up, getting Brie ready for my next-door neighbor Adelle. She takes Brie, along with her own three kids, to a summer day camp in Shaker Heights that her sister runs. Adelle came and got Brie, and then a few minutes later I could hear him upstairs banging around. Then he comes downstairs and goes into the den and all of the sudden there he is standing in the doorway between the dining room and the kitchen. He's giving me this look—like the way he looks at the cat when she goes on the rug. He's holding the three remote controls that go to each of our three television sets in his hand. He yells at me: 'How can *all three* of our TV remotes be broken at the same time? The law of averages says that's an impossibility.'

"'It's probably the batteries,' I say. I tell him I'll go to Radio Shack and buy replacements.

"He sits down at the kitchen table and starts to take out the batteries, telling me I should take them with me or I'll get the wrong ones. The sliding part doesn't come up very easily on one of them and this ticks him off. And then he says he can't trust me to do it right—this is just plain meanness on his part—and he stuffs them in his pants pocket and says he'll stop by Radio Shack on the way home from work. I tell him I'm sorry about what I said the night before and he says he still wonders if we're going to be able to stay together until Brie goes off to college. I notice that he's cut his neck shaving.

"'I was watching that goddamned Bigham mutt taking a shit in our backyard. We should have fenced in that goddamned yard the day we bought this house, but we didn't, and now all the neighborhood dogs come over at their goddamned leisure to use it for a toilet. I guess my hand slipped. I'm going to shoot me a dog one of these mornings.'

"I got him calmed down. I got his oatmeal and coffee. He ate. Things seemed to be getting back to normal—or at least what *we* call normal. There was so much that we needed to address from the night before, but I was just happy that we weren't at each other's throats anymore. We didn't have to love each other, I thought, but there had to be some way we could learn to tolerate each other while we were still stuck together."

Randi got quiet for a moment. She was replaying the conversation in her head. She had said all the right things and Josh had stopped being hateful, had looked a little contrite even, as the two sat staring at one another in silence across the table. Suddenly, the silence was shattered by the sound of a dog barking in the backyard.

"He flew out of his seat and threw open the back door and went after the dog—I don't know whose dog it was. But he literally chased that dog out of the yard and halfway down the block. He was panting and winded when he got back. I was standing on the patio watching him. I was about to ask whose dog it was this time, when suddenly he burst into flames."

"Spontaneous combustion?" asked Lieutenant Leggio, shaking his head skeptically.

"Yes."

"You know, Ms. Bryce, that we don't believe you."

"But that's what happened. I saw it."

What was to be done? Randi had watched this terrible thing happen to her husband, she had been snatched up before she could see him at the hospital, before she could tell him that she would stand by his side just as he had stood by her side through the cancer. It is the thing that spouses do. Even those who no longer love each other. Randi worried about her daughter, who was, no doubt, worried sick about her mother and father while in the temporary custody of her grandmother. It was a horrible situation made even worse by the alarming accusation leveled against Randi—that she had somehow set her husband on fire.

How had she done it? It baffled the two police detectives. When the Cuyahoga River burst into flames in 1969, some said that it was spontaneous combustion. But it didn't take long to discern the real reason, the one based upon scientific fact: the river was covered with oil slicks, and oil was combustible. One match, dropped in just the right spot, would have done it. Where was Randi's match—both figuratively and literally?

What had happened to Josh Bryce continued to baffle the two detectives as they made their way to the precinct captain's office. It baffled, as well, the medical examiner who had been brought in to answer questions about how a person could set another person on fire and leave no evidentiary trace behind. It was the medical examiner, a thoughtful, deliberate man nearing retirement, who decided, instead, to shine a different sort of light on the incident by asking a question that had not yet been asked: "Why did Ms. Bryce attempt to put out the fire if her purpose had been to see her husband fully consumed by it?"

"A change of heart maybe?" asked Lieutenant Leggio as he and his companions settled into chairs around the police captain's desk, leaving Randi Bryce in temporary limbo in the interrogation room.

"Perhaps. But let us consider the following," said Dr. Graybeal, the M.E., scratching the bristles of his once old-fashioned but now suddenly trendy goatee. "Seemingly spontaneous combustion does on occasion happen. It's a rare, but documented, occurrence."

"*Seemingly*?" asked Captain Samuels.

"Combustion for which a cause can never be determined."

"Uh-uh, Graybeal. Not really buying it." The captain's best detectives weren't buying it either. Leggio all but suggested with his look of amused incredulity that it was time for the good doctor to take his forty-year gold watch and go hit the rocker.

Graybeal had dealt with disrespectful cops before. "What was the victim wearing?" he pursued.

"Well, we're certain it wasn't anything flame retardant," answered Leggio, his mordant humor going unappreciated by the others in the room.

"What was in his pockets?" asked the doctor.

"You're not giving up on this, are you, Henry?" asked Lieutenant Selvera. "Nothing unusual. Keys. A wallet. He was getting ready to leave for work."

"Anything else?"

"There were three lithium batteries. The fire pretty much melted them."

"Oh."

Now the medical examiner smiled. For a brief moment Josh Bryce became not some poor victim of backyard immolation, but a riddle completely soluble. "The batteries weren't melted *by* the fire, officers. They were the *reason* for it. The keys and the batteries jostling together in his pocket. The morning was hot. There must have been some friction. Had he been moving around the yard?"

Lieutenant Selvera nodded. "He'd chased after a dog."

Graybeal nodded. "The friction of the keys rubbing against the batteries short-circuited one or more of them and ignited the fire in his pocket. It happens, and not that infrequently. Have the crime lab run some tests. I'm sure the findings will bear this out."

"The woman was telling the truth?" asked Leggio, after a long, arced whistle of astonishment.

"Lo and behold, she must have been," said his partner. "Okay to get her over to the hospital to be with her husband, captain?"

"Of course. Take one of the patrol cars."

Randi Bryce reached the hospital at six. Josh was awake, but just barely. Their eyes held on one another for a long moment as Randi gently touched her husband's one bandage-free hand with one of her unbandaged fingers. "I told you I'd go to Radio Shack," she said.

"I know," he responded groggily, the intravenous painkillers sucking him back into somnolence. "I know." And then he was asleep.

Randi did not leave her husband's side all night. It is the thing that spouses do.

1998

DENTIGEROUSLY FORTUITIOUS
IN FLORIDA

There are three things that probably shouldn't be said to the victim of a brutal, late-night assault in a dark parking lot.

The first is "How are you holding up, hon?" This from the victim's mother.

The victim—Abby Alpert—didn't know how to answer. She was still having nightmares, although the panic attacks had subsided and she'd even been able to go to the movies with her girlfriends the previous Friday night (something light, a romantic comedy).

The second is "Aren't you glad he didn't rape you?" This from Abby's best girlfriend, Tish.

Abby's reply: "Yes, I'm very glad he didn't rape me. But allow me, please, to still feel violated, nonetheless, by the attack."

The third is "So when do you think you'll be able to come back to work?" This from Abby's sensitivity-challenged employer, Thom Jensen, DDS. Abby had been out for two weeks and Thom the dentist and his office manager Ms. Purdy were getting tired of beating the bushes of Port St. Lucie for part-time hygienists to fill in for all of Abby's appointments, this being August, and so many of Florida's dental hygienists having temporarily fled the state for cooler climes "off-peninsula."

"I'll be back on Monday, Thom."

"You're ready to come back?"

"I'm ready to come back. And even if I'm not, I *need* to come back. I need to get back into my routine."

"Excellent," said Thom. "I'll see you on Monday."

Monday came. Abby rose early. She had an eight-thirty. She showered and dressed, nuked a frozen scone in the microwave, and then steeled herself to spend the day doing what she was very good at: cleaning teeth, making *other* people feel comfortable and relaxed during a sometimes intimidating trip to the dentist's office. Abby was a popular hygienist. Some of her patients had switched dentists just to have Abby clean their teeth. It was a good job, a job she really loved. She hoped that she would be able to concentrate, that her hand wouldn't shake, that memories of the attack wouldn't intrude on her thoughts at inopportune moments.

Her eight-thirty went well. Mrs. Johnstone. One of Abby's oldest patients (among a goodly number of senior-citizen transplants), Mrs. Johnstone was solemnly mindful of what Abby had been through and asked no questions. Her nine-thirty, Ginger Lopez, a bartender in her mid-thirties, was too used to drunken customers spilling their guts. Abby had to make it clear that she didn't feel like doing any spilling that morning.

Her ten-thirty, Mr. Spinella, cancelled at the last minute. He was a real estate attorney and the time of a closing got moved up and he was very sorry—his secretary said—and, of course, he would pay, in full, for the missed appointment.

Abby's eleven-thirty was a new patient—just moved to Port St. Lucie, he told Ms. Purdy on the phone. Abby didn't want any new patients that first week back. She only wanted to clean the teeth of people she knew. She had neglected to tell Ms. Purdy this. It was her own fault.

The man came on time. Abby poked her head out into the waiting room and called his name: Davin Romey. He was a fairly young man, perhaps in his late twenties, with a short and stocky wrestler's build. The first thing that Abby noticed about him was the wide breadth of his chest. He was wearing a fitted ecru-colored t-shirt under a loose blue summer jacket. He got up and took off the jacket. Abby noticed now that he had muscular arms, both biceps and forearms. Abby always thought of Popeye when she met men with overly developed forearms. Normal protocol, especially for a first-time patient, was to greet the patient and shake his hand. But Abby didn't want to shake this man's hand. He obviously wouldn't know her story and might even think her rude, but she didn't care; she didn't want to shake the man's hand. Entering the man's open mouth with all of her dental instruments was intimate enough for her.

As Abby was leading Mr. Romey down the corridor to her room, she asked him how he had come to pick Dr. Jensen's practice. "Did someone recommend us to you?"

The man shrugged. "Phone book. Yellow pages. A dentist is a dentist, right?"

Wrong. But Abby didn't want to engage him. There was something about his voice that didn't sit well with her.

Abby pulled the long arm of the dental unit out of the way so that the man could slide easily into the chair. She took a look at the questionnaire for new patients he'd filled out in the waiting room. "You've had some gum problems?"

The man nodded. "I chewed tobacco for a few years. I think it did a number on my teeth and gums."

I know that voice.

"When was the last time you visited a dentist?"

"Two, maybe three years ago."

Once Romey had settled in, Abby said, "I'm going to take some X-rays." Romey nodded. Abby covered his chest with the lead shield and placed the thyroid collar around his neck. "Open, please," she said, after she had put the unexposed film on the X-ray mount. She inserted the bitewing into the man's mouth. "Bite down, please."

There was a smell about him. Cologne.

When she had finished with the X-rays, she said, "I'll be right back." She took the film down to the room where the X-rays were developed. Suddenly, she felt queasy. Was it the two cups of coffee she'd had with her thawed-out scone? Sometimes coffee gave her a sour stomach.

He's wearing the man's cologne. The man who assaulted me. He's wearing the same brand of cologne as the man who grabbed me and pulled me behind the Dumpster. He pulled me with forceful arms. Strong, muscular arms.

And there were two other smells, along with the cologne. What were those other smells?

Abby had to sit down. Jensen's assistant Loretta—a young woman whom Abby really liked (she didn't ask stupid questions)—appeared in the doorway.

"Are you okay?" This was a legitimate question.

Abby felt weak. Loretta noticed that she was slightly pale.

"I'm okay," said Abby.

"Do you want to go home?"

"I'm in the middle of an appointment."

"Screw that. Go home if you need to."

Abby shook her head. Then she shook her head again, along with her shoulders and arms, in the same way that actors shake themselves to limber up before a performance.

Get a grip. You're being idiotic. You're grasping at coincidences. This is a man named Mr. Romey. He has come in to get his teeth cleaned. The form said that he's employed as a locksmith. This is what he does, Abby. He makes keys. He doesn't terrorize women in late night parking lots. Stop it. Pull yourself together.

Abby pulled herself together. She returned to her patient. She liked it that he wasn't overly friendly, that he only spoke when she asked him a question. Abby liked people as a rule. She liked talking to her patients and having them talk back, but she also liked that other aspect to her job—the option, when she *didn't* feel like listening to people, to put things into their mouths to keep them quiet.

Abby sat down on her wheeled saddle-stool. She depressed the foot pedal to recline the patient chair. She rolled over to the tray of instruments and plucked up her explorer and mirror. She pulled down the lamp and concentrated its beam on Romey's open mouth. She used the explorer and the mirror to look for cavities. Nothing obvious there, but the mouth still showed evidence of some abuse. The chewing tobacco, she imagined. She traded the explorer for the probe so she could look for pockets. There had been a pronounced receding of the gums.

Chewing tobacco. That was one of the other smells. The man smelled of chewing tobacco and cologne. Too much cologne, just like the generous amount that Mr. Romey is wearing now. And there was some smell on his hands. He put his hand up to my mouth to keep me quiet. What was that smell on his palm? Try to remember, Abby.

Abby's hands began to tremble. She withdrew the probe and mirror from Romey's mouth.

His mouth now empty, he was freed up to speak. "Are you okay?"

"I've been ill," was all that Abby could think to say. After all, she *had* been ill. Everything had shut down after the attack. She had lain in bed, not eating, shivering in a warm room. She couldn't sleep, and when she did, her dreams were disjointed, unsettling. They were displaced dreams—not about the attack itself but filled with everything else dark and menacing that her subconscious mind could conjure up.

Such things do not happen. A woman does not get knocked around behind a Dumpster, does not have her handbag ripped from her shoulder with such force that she is left with an ugly strap-width contusion. A woman does not have a strange man's hands on her ass, looking for a way to get inside, and only by the grace of God—(What was it? Did he see someone approaching? Did he lose his nerve? What made him stop?)—a woman does not go through all of this and then find the man who did it to her seated in her dental chair two weeks later. Such things simply do not happen.

"I'm sorry to hear that," said the man. The voice had a slight Brooklyn cadence. Abby knew Brooklyn accents. She had lived in Brooklyn when she went to school there to study dental hygiene. The man who'd attacked her had the same accent.

"It's okay. I'm better now," said Abby. Her hands had stopped shaking. She placed a gloved hand back into the man's mouth to check for bumps and lumps on the floor of his mouth and inside his cheeks. "Stick out your tongue, please." Abby took out a cotton 2 x 2 to look under the tongue. She gave the tongue a careful inspection. The man had said that he used to be a tobacco chewer.

Used to be. Abby's assailant hadn't given it up. In fact, it smelled as if he had been chewing a plug right before the attack. A thousand thoughts had raced through her head as she lay crumpled upon the pavement that night behind the Dumpster. One was this: that she hoped the man would get oral cancer. What a strange thing to think at such a moment. Yet only a minute or two after the attack, Abby was already thinking of how her assailant should be punished for what he did to her. He hadn't raped her—not literally, but she had been raped in every other sense of that word. Men like that should have to pay for what they did.

"I'm sorry to hear that." This was how he had responded. He had asked me, as he held me, as he had pushed himself against my back, as he had breathed his fetid tobacco-breath upon my neck, he had asked me if I had a husband or a boyfriend. I didn't know how to answer. Should I have lied and said yes? How would he have reacted? Would he have shown my made-up husband or boyfriend that he didn't own sole title to me? That I belonged to my assailant as well? Is this the sort of thing that psychotic men do to women in the dark? Assault both the women and the men they love?

So I told the truth. That I didn't have a husband. Nor a boyfriend at the moment. "I'm sorry to hear that," he had said, almost sympathetically—just as Romey had said it. Exactly *as Romey had said it.* "*You're much too pretty not to have a boyfriend.*"

Abby closed her eyes.

Brass.

Abby opened her eyes.

The third smell—the smell on his dirty hands: brass. What is made of brass? Keys are made of brass. Locksmiths smell of brass.

It was clear to Abby now: the man in the chair was the same man who had assaulted her in the corner of the sandy parking lot. He had never asked what she did for a living. He would not have known that she was a dental hygienist. He had said that she was pretty, yet he had never gotten a good look at her face. He had come upon her from behind. He had done his dirty business in the dark. If he had fully seen her, something of this recognition would have registered on his face in the waiting room, wouldn't it? Or there would have been a slow process of recollection there in the chair. Yet there was not.

In this respect, Abby had him at a disadvantage.

Abby rolled over to her ultra-sonic and took the water-blaster into her right hand. With her left hand she took up the suction—her "Mr. Thirsty." She hooked it to one corner of Romey's open mouth. With the foot pedal she turned on the ultra-sonic and began to clean her new patient's teeth as her thoughts ran wild. Every moment of the assault came back to her. Every smell, every sound, the painful grip of her assailant's muscular paws. It all came blasting back into her brain as the ultra-sonic—the sound of its shrill whirring—assailed the silence of the room.

Abby would have to find a way to detain him so that someone could call the police. It shouldn't be that hard to do. He'd have to wait as she went back to retrieve the X-rays. Yes, this was when she would grab Loretta and have her make the call. The police would come quickly. Then it would all be over. He would be put behind bars for what he had done to her.

But I want him dead.

It could not happen that way. He had not killed her. He would be put away. Justice would be served.

But I want him dead.

Abby tried to shake the thought from her head. Her head shook with more violence than she expected. This drew Romey's attention. He pushed her arm away—the arm with the hand that was blasting away at his fetid mouth.

"What is it? What's wrong?" he asked.

She removed her foot from the pedal. The room grew quiet again.

"I'm not feeling well," she said, the words shaped by fear.

"Maybe I should go."

Don't go. You can't go.

"No, it's okay," she said, almost pleading. "Just give me a moment."

Now he was looking at her. Now he was staring at her, studying her. He had not seen her face on the night of the attack. Or *had* he seen her face? In the club. Where Abby had gone for drinks with her friends. Had he been watching her from across the room? Did he follow her out to the parking lot? Is this why he was there, why he was almost on top of her before she had even reached her car? The club had been dark and smoky. Perhaps this is why it took him some time to remember her.

But now he is remembering me. Now he knows it's me.

"You're going to keep your mouth shut. I'm going to walk out of this place and you're going to keep your mouth shut."

"Okay." This is what she had said that night. When he had said that he wasn't going to hurt her, even as he had fumbled with the belt to her jeans. Now she was saying it again. The same way.

This is how he knows.

He sat up quickly. He hit his head against the lamp.

"I haven't finished the cleaning," said Abby with forced placidity. "I haven't polished. We have to look at your X-rays."

"Shut up," he said, rubbing his head. He grabbed her by the wrist to command her complete attention. The tight vise on her wrist was painfully familiar. "Get this bib off of me," he said.

He released her wrist. She put her hand upon the bib. She moved her hand to the bib chain. She turned the bib around so that the chain was touching the front of his neck.

I'm going to strangle him with this chain. That is what I am going to do. I am going to choke him until he dies.

And yet her hands, her own grip would not be strong enough. Abby had "hygienist hands"—often aching, nearly arthritic from the meticulous work they did—the professional downside to being a dental hygienist.

I can't do it.

Yet there was something that she *could* do. Behind her was the drawer with the syringes. Not the innocuous air/water syringes of her trade. The kind that gave injections. Injections of Lidocaine. She threw open the drawer and grabbed the syringe. As Romey was tearing at the bib and flailing at the lamp that was still blocking his escape, she plunged the hypodermic into his chest and injected the air that was inside the syringe. Right where she knew his heart to be. He seized up and fell back into the chair. She grabbed a second syringe, just to be sure, and stabbed him again.

You can't have too many embolisms.

The man was dead within seconds. Abby knew that poor dental hygiene can sometimes lead to heart disease and coronary-related death. But who knew that dental hygienists were capable of achieving that same end all on their own?

Loretta came. And Dr. Jensen. Ms. Purdy phoned the police. Abby was on the floor now. She sat on the floor looking up at the dentist and his assistant. At the man she had just killed, his body slumped in the chair, his limbs flopped out like those of a rag doll. Abby felt weak. But she no longer felt powerless.

To Dr. Jensen she said, in a soft, almost cheerful voice, "The patient is a good candidate for some reparative periodontal work. But at this point, I'd say he probably shouldn't bother."

The dentist gave no reply.

1999

CONSTRUCTIVE IN BOTSWANA

The locals called them the "White Campers," though they didn't do any actual camping until week three of their visit. They were in Botswana under the auspices of Habitat for Humanity's Global Village initiative. The "R and R" component of the trip came only after two weeks of building cement-block houses for residents of the village of Serowe. The fourteen crew members, largely from the Northeastern U.S., finished four houses under the supervision of crew leader Jack Darrigan, a New York City building contractor, and started work on three others.

Each day they hauled blocks (called "bricks" by local builders), mixed mortar, raised wood and tin roofs, sang, prayed (Habitat for Humanity being a Christian organization), and then piled into their chartered mini-bus (called a "combi" by the natives), and headed back to the lodge, where they feasted on samp and beans, mabele, goat seswaa, and braised oxtail, and where they drank too much beer (Habitat for Humanity being a fairly *liberal* Christian organization).

The first two weeks of the trip had been physically grueling but invigorating. The White Campers had definitely earned their R and R: a visit to Moremi Game Reserve in the Okavango Delta in northwest Botswana. There they would take part in a four-day/three-night budget photo-safari with campfire grub and army-issue tents. Offsetting the bare-bones amenities were twice-daily trips through the savanna and wetlands; within the two-thousand-mile reserve, the Habitat crew members had the opportunity to view some of the most diverse and abundant natural habitat wildlife to be found anywhere on the continent. Zebras and greater kudus, cape buffalo, crocodiles, elephants, vervet monkeys, wildebeest, ostriches, giraffes...Ericka Prager tried to keep a list, but she eventually had to stop. The profusion of animal residents of the Okavango defied itemization.

Ericka was from Greenwich, Connecticut. She was a high school biology teacher. Her friend Soumeya Powell, a fellow teacher at the school, had asked her to come. It didn't take much coaxing; Ericka was already familiar with Habitat from having worked on a couple of houses in Stamford. She was young. And she was adventurous.

Ericka was also single.

David Venetti lived in White Plains, New York. He was a computer programmer. David had never given much thought to taking a trip to Africa, but once he *had* started thinking about it—especially the chance to use his weekend carpentry skills for some purpose other than helping his father build a backyard deck—the idea began to appeal to him.

David was also single.

Through the two weeks of home-building, Ericka and David had worked happily side by side. A growing friendship soon moved cautiously into the realm of romance. At twilight on their last day in the village of Serowe, as the two stood on the porch of the cabin David shared with two other single young men on the crew, as David and Ericka stood listening to the herdsmen calling their cows in for the night, as they watched the obedient cattle, their cowbells jangling, lumber through the dusktide shadows to their night pens, David reached over and kissed Ericka.

She was receptive. And she now believed that there was a very good chance that she was in love.

In the bush plane that took the two (along with two other Habitat crew-members) over the salt pans to the Okavango, Ericka and David sat in the back seat. (Roy, who had won the seat lottery for this particular flight, was next to the pilot, and Leonard—poor sad-sack Leonard who could never catch a break—huddled in the far back with all the luggage). It was hard to speak over the drone of the plane's engine. But Ericka tried, nonetheless. She wanted to find out more about David, who hadn't been all that forthcoming with details from his personal life. This, obviously, wasn't the time or place to draw him out, but she definitely needed to know more about him if this relationship was to move forward.

Or *would* it move forward? She just didn't know. But for now, all Ericka said was, "It has a stark beauty, doesn't it? The landscape."

"That's some desert," said David, who had very little of the poet in him.

*

There were a few attempts at singalongs over the campfire that first night, but mostly the group chattered away like the little monkeys who lived in the nearby trees, discussing all that they had seen during their first mini road safari. There was wildlife around every corner, and the lions were especially accommodating, the regal males allowing their human visitors to rumble right up to their open dens and impose upon their privacy without even a half-growl of protest.

Asked Soumeya of her vehicle's driver, a congenial young Motswana named Jacob, "Are they tame? Why don't they get upset when we drive up to them like this?"

Jacob smiled. "They don't see you as prey. They also know that they'll have the chance to come visit *you* tonight."

"What do you mean?" asked Leonard, suddenly troubled by the thought of lions invading the campsite later that evening. With his luck, Leonard was sure that he'd be the first camper to get eaten.

"It's a good idea not to leave your tents once you go in for the night."

That night, David left the tent that he was sharing with Roy. He came over to Ericka and Soumeya's tent. "I've got Amarula, if you girls wanna come out and join me for a nightcap."

Amarula had become the official cream liqueur of the Serowe Habitat build of August, 1999. It was made with the fruit of the African Marula tree, a tree which, as legend had it, was favored by elephants, who enjoyed guttling the fermented yellow fruit and getting drunk. Considering the low alcohol content of the liqueur and the prodigious body weight of your average African elephant, nobody believed there to be much truth to the legend.

A potential visit by the lions of Moremi—now that, of course, was good reason to stay in for the night.

"Count me out," said Soumeya emphatically.

Ericka thought over the invitation. "Maybe for a minute. It's still early. When do you think the lions usually show up?"

"Around one thirty," jested David. "The embers are still warm. Come sit with me." David reached into the small tent to help Ericka out. She was still wearing her safari clothes. She and Soumeya had been sitting up, playing cards.

The night air was filled with the sounds of nocturnal animals broadcasting their moods, summoning their mates, commenting upon their pursuit by other more predatory creatures. Is he pursuing me? asked Ericka of herself, as David led her to the dying campfire.

The two sat for a moment without speaking. David reached out and took Ericka's hand. She sighed. She felt like some lovestruck middle-schooler. In Africa everything you usually think about yourself gets pushed to the margins. Those more primitive, more sublimated parts of you rise impudently to the surface. Sometimes the elemental manifests itself in child-reversion: the need for food, for human comfort and companionship, the need to have one's many fears put to rest. Most children learn in time how to combat their fears, just as a visitor to Africa learns to make similar adjustments to better appreciate the wonders and riches of the continent.

"Can you believe that we're here?" she finally asked her fireside companion. "And not on some fancy linen-tablecloth safari. We've become a part of this place, haven't we?"

"I guess you can say that." David poured Ericka a cup of Amarula. It was better layered above crème de Menthe in a drink that the British expats called a "Springbok." But Amarula straight up would have to suffice this night.

"David, I don't know anything about you." Ericka was looking up into the cloudless sky at Southern Hemisphere constellations that were unfamiliar to her.

David took a swig from the bottle, scanning the black firmament overhead. "What would you like to know?"

"What do you do with computers? My brother-in-law works for Citibank on Y2K."

David chuckled. "It's interesting you should say that. I work for a group that's doing something similar."

"What is it?"

"The techno think tank that employs me—we're addressing the Y10K problem."

There was a roar. It didn't sound leonine.

"Hippopotamus, I think," he said. "One of the guides told me that nighttime is when they generally make the most racket."

"What's the 'Y10K problem'?"

"It's all the potential software bugs and glitches that might emerge when the calendar year moves to five digits. Everything's set up for four digits, you know."

"You're being serious? That's eight thousand years away."

"There isn't a lot of urgency to my job. Sometimes I sleep in."

"I have to ask you something, David. I don't know any way around it. We've got two more nights of safari and then those last two nights in Vic Falls, and then the trip's over. Am I going to see you—I mean, ever again?"

David set the Amarula bottle down and drew his legs up to his chest. "That was really to the point."

"When you're a schoolteacher, you learn not to obfuscate."

"I don't know what that means."

"It means that I have to be very clear. I'm sorry, but don't you think we're starting to feel something for each other?"

"Yeah. Sure. Although I haven't even gotten into your pants yet."

"That was crass."

"Was there some other way you wanted me to say it?"

"Just forget it. I'm sorry I brought it up. It just seemed like it was time to talk about where we go from here. Do you want to see me again?"

"Of course I do. But what I want these days doesn't seem to matter very much. I'm in a kinda strange place in my life right now. Just kinda, you know, *drifting*."

Ericka touched David's shoulder.

"We're *all* drifting. Things are so unsettled these days. In four months we'll be entering a new millennium. I can't even get my brain around that."

"Call me in the year 10,000 and I'll give you something to try to get your brain around."

"I'll bet we're more alike than you think. We're both looking for something. Maybe we're looking for the same thing."

"Could be," said David. He reached over and pulled Ericka's face toward his, and then gave her a long kiss. "I really want to get into your—I really want to make love to you, Ericka. I wish there was someplace we could go."

Ericka thought for a moment. "We could go over to the showers. Do you have your flashlight? I could go into my tent and get mine, but Soumeya will try to talk me out of going."

David got up. "I'll get *mine*."

"We'll have to do it standing up. Those floors are icky."

"Standing up is fine with me."

"Of course, you know we're not supposed to leave the campsite. We're not even supposed to leave our tents once the fire dies down."

"Would you rather we not? I'm okay with that."

"I want you."

"I want you too."

The darkness around them was thick, almost palpable. Although David shone the beam of his flashlight on the ground in front of them, Ericka still took special care in where she put her feet. One of the female crewmembers had met up with a large snake of unknown hazard when she went to take her shower earlier that afternoon.

The two reached the dark cinderblock building that housed the sinks and showers. Within seconds David was pushing Ericka up against the wall and kissing her with unusual force. Ericka welcomed the sloppy animalism in his advance. She writhed and clawed in response. She groaned with matched volume. They ripped their clothes off and tossed them into one of the nearby sinks. David was inside her half a minute later.

"Whatever our differences," said Ericka in that next bliss-filled post-coital moment, "I love you too much to let you go."

Earlier, in the midst of fucking, David had said, "I love you, baby. Oh God, I love you, baby." But now, spent and sleepy, he said, "Uh huh. Oh yeah."

It wasn't a lion that visited Ericka and David in the showers that tenebrous African night. It was a pack of hungry and prowling spotted hyenas.

Ericka was quite familiar with spotted hyenas. One of her students had delivered a paper on them when she had made the assignment in May (a rather self-serving assignment, to be sure) that each of her advanced biology students should take an African mammal (preferably one of the southern African mammals their teacher was likely to see on her late summer safari) and write a paper on it.

The gregarious spotted hyenas have long been regarded as maneaters. Some paleontologists have conjectured that predatory attacks by cave hyenas in Siberia delayed the migration of humans across the Bering Strait into what is now Alaska, perhaps for hundreds of years. Some of these facts flashed through Ericka's head as David began shouting at the hyenas gathering in the doorway, chatter-laughing and bearing their canines.

Ericka picked up the flashlight set upon the side of the sink and began waving it. David grabbed up his pants and started flapping them at the animals, who continued to laugh—as was their hyenine wont—at the negligible defensive actions of the naked humans.

"Where is a lion when you need him?" David tossed to Ericka.

Ericka registered his display of manly pluck, even as terror continued to grip her. The two worked through loud shouts and the air-flaying of their disrobed clothing to push the three or four hyenas (in the darkness there seemed to be even more) out of the shower house. There was no door to shut, so the danger would not be averted altogether until the doglike creatures gave up on human prey for the night and trotted off to find their supper elsewhere.

Or unless David and Ericka were rescued. The latter occurred a couple of minutes later. Jack Darrigan and two of the guides, having heard the commotion, showed up and successfully chased the four-legged predators away. There wasn't time for Ericka and David to dress before the three men stepped into the shower house.

"The same thing happened with a couple of last month's White Campers," said Jacob. "I forgot to tell of the spotted hyenas."

Jacob was staring at Ericka's pubic jungle. In his defense, it was impossible not to.

Over breakfast that morning there was only one topic under discussion. Ericka and David laughed off their encounter with death and both accepted without complaint the good-natured ribbing of those who knew exactly why the two had found themselves in such a predicament. Ruth, the oldest of the group and the most devout, was the least judgmental: "The Lord protects those who love so deeply."

Did Ericka and David love each other so deeply? Was their love, like their naked rendezvous with the man-eating spotted hyenas, something that could jolt them from the doldrums of their fairly vacuous, monotonous lives? Africa, in all its glory, had shown Ericka that there was life—wild, unpredictable, impetuous life—outside of the Greenwich high school where she taught, outside the narrow confines of her stultifying daily routine, outside the small circle of somnolent, adventure-deprived family and friends who kept her dully circumscribed.

Was Africa just a temporary flash of light—an isolated, fugitive moment of emancipating sensuality? Or was it a foretaste of all that could be?

Ericka and David dated long-distance for four months after returning to the States—long enough to greet the new millennium (as the consensus of opinion on century beginnings and endings at the time dictated) together, David pistoning on top and Ericka thrashing below, her eyes pinned to the digits of her clock radio, hoping for perfect millennial-coital synchronicity.

They were off by two and four minutes, respectively.

The next week they parted.

The break-up was amicable. David was a good lover, a most generous lover, but he was not any of those other things that Ericka had sought in a mate. But it came down to one thing more important than anything else: Ericka wanted to return to Africa. She wanted to join another Habitat build, either in Botswana or in some other country. And she wanted David to come with her.

But he had done Africa, and that was that.

She couldn't help thinking, couldn't help imagining whom she might meet on that next trip. Would he take her as David had? And then would they stay together, grow old together? Ericka Prager desperately wanted someone to grow old with.

She had built houses in Africa. Now she wanted to put mortar between the cement blocks—the "bricks"—of her own life.

2000

CONVERGENT IN CONNECTICUT

"I don't know what happened to little Catherine Gallagher. I have always nurtured the wish that she should have a very long and happy life."

Catherine Uhlmyer Gallagher Connelly had been about the business of living a very long (although not uniformly happy) life when Ericka Prager first visited her at her Wilton, Connecticut, nursing home in early January. By Catherine's 107th birthday two months later, the two had become friends. In fact, by early April, Ericka had made friends with several of the other nursing home residents, including a woman named Eunice Ludden—mother of the famed Ludden Sisters singing group— who confessed to Ericka that she wasn't an *official* resident of the facility but was working undercover to investigate patient abuse; and Karen Bailey Kelly, the daughter of famed Boston novelist Dennis Bailey. (Karen had her own connection to sororal singing groups, having written a biography of the Brox Sisters in 1953.)

It had been Ericka's friend and fellow high school teacher Shannon Humphries' idea for Ericka to accompany Shannon and her advanced history students as they each chose a long-lived occupant of the facility and wrote down his or her oral history. The students had a large group of colorful and interesting senior citizens from which to choose; as testament to the migratory nature of Americans over the last one hundred years, the residents hailed from forty-one different states, including Alaska and Hawaii. There was Mr. Grimm, retired administrator of a Presbyterian boarding school in central Utah; and Mrs. Daltry, the wife of a retired U.S. Air Force colonel who had assisted in the investigation of the accidental dropping of a bomb on a rural South Carolina community in 1958; and

Frieda Chapman, whose husband, a U.S. Navy captain, was severely injured during the attack on Pearl Harbor.

Even after the project was completed, Ericka and Shannon continued to visit the nursing home every weekend, each looking forward to attending May 27's "Celebration of Tri-century Centenarians." The special ceremony (with punch and cake and a visit by Senator Joe Lieberman, who was believed to be on Al Gore's short list for vice-presidential running mate that year) would honor fifteen of the home's residents, who, having been born in the "Gay '90s" and having been blessed by the "long genes," were now in the unique position of having lived in three different centuries (if one is to stipulate, of course, to the debatable claim that the twenty-first century owns title to the year 2000).

New Englander Ericka and Mississippi-born Shannon had met at the University of Vermont. Both had been education majors and both had eventually roomed together in a rental house with three other coeds: Tian Gilliam, the adopted daughter of Montana ranchers; Claudia Wilmer, heiress to the Wilmer-HearMore Hearing Aids fortune; and Lindsey Royce from Gainesville, Florida, who was later called "One of America's Thousand Points of Light" by President George H.W. Bush after she rescued an older woman, Josephine Charles, visiting from Derry, New Hampshire, from her car when it accidentally went into the Winooski River. In an amazing and somewhat disturbing coincidence, Shannon's own nephew and niece were in the car with their father when it went into Arkabutla Lake in Mississippi that very same year (all three rescued themselves successfully; Shannon's sister Bianca, alienated from her husband at the time, wasn't present.) The five University of Vermont education majors, each hoping for a career teaching at the high school level, lived, coincidentally, next door to a retired high school principal named Cornell Rodgers (whom they called, with private mischief, "Mr. Rodgers").

Shannon's other sister, Heather, who resided in Hernando, just south of Memphis, suffered a nervous breakdown of unknown origin in 1996 and maintained only tentative ties to her sisters in the years that followed. Shannon and Heather's parents, Piddy and Billy Humphries, lived for many years in their native Yazoo City, Mississippi, before moving up to Memphis, where Billy got a job as manager of a movie theatre in Whitehaven.

Ericka's 107-year-old friend Catherine, who was nearly blind with cataracts and very hard of hearing, wasn't as close to Ericka as was the old woman's roommate, who had just joined the Centenarian Club in March. Gail Hoyt Hopper Rabbitt, who could not say that her one-hundred-plus years were nearly so tragic as those of her fellow centenarian, Mrs. Connelly (for whom the *General Slocum* steamboat fire of 1904 cast a cloud of dark remembrance that scarcely subsided during all the many years of her later life), had, nonetheless, enjoyed a far from trouble-free life herself. In early 1926, Gail's first husband, Tillman Hopper, and his two brothers took all of the money that comprised their large family inheritance and put it into an invention of Tillman's brother Hezekiah's ingenuity and design: a life preserver with attached battery-powered propellers, called the "Poseidon-Peller." The business the three brothers formed was doing well until the Stock Market Crash of 1929, when they lost their shirts, and Tillman, in despair, took a swan dive from his and his wife's twentieth-story apartment on the Upper West Side of Manhattan. As might be guessed, he didn't survive.

At least two of Gail's fellow nursing-home residents were intimately familiar with the incident. Tillman's plummeting body had barely missed landing on top of a friend of Pearl Patz's. Pearl was Gail's dining room companion. Leonora Touliatos was on her honeymoon in New York on that fateful day in late 1930 when the body struck the sidewalk only a few feet away from her. Not wishing to upset his blind wife, Leonora's husband James waited several years before telling her the truth of what had occurred that day, perpetuating, instead, the fiction that the thud she heard next to her was a dead horse keeling over from heat exhaustion.

Also familiar with the incident was another member of the Centenarian Club, a woman from Hartford by the name of Frances Hellman. Frances and her husband Hank had come down from Connecticut for a weekend of sightseeing, dining, and dancing with their friends, the Petersons. When the body smacked the concrete, Frances reacted by slapping her cheeks in hard shock, and for hours thereafter looked as if she had over-applied her rouge that morning.

Though one of the occupants of the room next door to Catherine and Gail, Rory Hillard, had no special connection to the suicide, he nonetheless took an interest in Gail's brother-in-law's ill-fated invention. "It would have come in mighty handy for my buddy Torkleson and me when the *Indianapolis* went down and all the neighborhood sharks became ill-mannered." A retired butcher (previously in the employ of Piggly Wiggly), Rory had moved to Fairfield County, Connecticut, from

Houston after the death of his second wife to be closer to his daughter Regina and his five granddaughters.

The other thing casting a shadow over the life of Gail Hoyt (otherwise known as "The Rock-a-bye Girl" of 1900 Galveston hurricane association) was her rocky marriage to a philandering aviator by the name of Leslie Rabbitt (whom Gail decided had only married her because of their mutual love of flying and because he would be giving his wife the comical extended surname of Hopper Rabbitt).

Leslie, who was himself less rabbit and more pig (and once attended a masquerade party dressed as pig—snout and all—after reading about a World War I soldier who wore a pig nose in battle), descended from two fairly tainted bloodlines. In the late teens and early-to-mid-twenties (up until his arrest in 1926), Leslie's father had performed hundreds of illegal abortions in the town of Winchester, Kentucky, which had resulted in no small number of client deaths. Leslie's mother, Jettie Livergood Rabbitt, served a year in prison for filing a mischievous false police report in 1906 accusing the Livergood Family Association of Warwick, Rhode Island, of running a clandestine white slavery ring. The charge and the subsequent raid on the association's 1906 reunion left the organization in a shambles from which it never recovered.

Leslie's offenses, though comparatively more venial, were ruinous to the marriage: an ongoing affair with a wealthy middle-aged Fall River, Massachusetts lush by the name of Alice Rose Carteret, and an on-again-off-again long-distance relationship with a woman named Patsy Pullen, whom Leslie had met in the lobby of the Blackstone Hotel in Chicago during the city's 1933-34 World's Fair. Leslie continued to pilot airplanes after his messy divorce from Gail, and perished, arguably by his own hand, when in a drunken stunt in late 1944, he painted his personal plane in the colors of the Japanese Zero long-range fighter aircraft and ventured too close to Los Alamos, New Mexico, where he was promptly shot out of the sky. The incident was covered up until 1987, when it was brought to light by a radio documentary producer in Madison, Wisconsin, named Byron Reeves, who was doing a piece on the 1947 Roswell UFO incident at the time, based on a book by two young authors with the Tweedledum-and-dee names of Kirk and Dirk.

Dirk Heinze grew up in Anchorage and wrote a best-selling book about the 1964 Alaskan earthquake, which he had experienced as a young boy, before turning to the true crime genre and penning *An*

Encyclopedia of American Criminality, with entries on everyone from Leopold and Loeb to Russell Edeale, an aeronautical engineer who spent his free time putting guns to people's heads and making them beg for their lives. Shared interest in the criminal mind was the reason that Kirk and Dirk came to their present partnership. Kirk, who was from Vineland, New Jersey, was inspired by Truman Capote's non-fiction novel, *In Cold Blood*, to write a book very much in the same vein: *Double Take*, about Charlie Towers and Bob Fletcher, brothers who murdered each other's wives. The consultant on Kirk's book was Towers' and Fletcher's triplet brother Henry Kierbaum, who had just recently retired from GHH (Grady-Hawthorne-Hay) Enterprises, where he headed up the Genitalia Accessories division.

Gail and Ericka sat sipping tea. On the television across the room (its volume turned down and its closed captioning on), *Inside Edition* was running a story about a dental hygienist in Florida who two years earlier had stabbed one of her clients to death with an air-filled syringe.

"We'll have to suspend our teatime shortly, Ericka," said Gail, setting her teacup down. "They're going to wheel all of us centenarians into the cafeteria and take our picture for the paper tomorrow."

"Are you looking forward to the celebration?" asked Ericka.

"What's that, dear?" Gail was momentarily distracted by a passing fellow resident waving at her from the hallway. Lois Gregory, another centenarian, was smiling smugly in the company of three doting men of various ages: her son Les, her grandson, Ari, and Ari's life-partner, Wayne. Ari, formerly a bookstore owner in Wilmington, Delaware, and Wayne, a building contractor for Holman-Crampo Homes in Dallas, Texas, both of whom had had boyhood crushes on Roy Rogers, had met at a Royandalabilia estate sale six years earlier in Mitchell, South Dakota.

"I was just asking about the celebration tomorrow. Will all of your fellow centenarians be able to attend?"

"Well, dear, we lost Dr. Kleerekoper—the eminent mathematician. He's been moved to hospice care. But the others are doing quite well for their advanced years. Take Penny Rutland, our resident Mainer; she writes for an outrageously funny newsletter about people who can't abide flowers. Can you imagine such a thing? I love her spunk and spice, though. She's the bees' knees."

Ericka smiled at the aged flapper. "What about Adelaide—the woman on your floor from Tarrytown?"

"Adelaide's had a bad cold, but she's much better now. We're always holding our breaths around here, since the Grim Reaper often comes with a hacking pneumonic cough. Adelaide's teacher friend, Carla—I think they met when they did some volunteer work together for the NEA— she's flying all the way from Pocatello, Idaho, just to be in attendance tomorrow."

There was a knock on the room's open door. A pretty woman in her thirties stood in the doorway. "We're going to take you and Mrs. Connelly down to the cafeteria now for the shoot."

Gail winked at Ericka and whispered, "She's new here or she wouldn't have put it that way. When you get to be Catherine's and my age, we generally don't like to hear that we're about to be shot. It sounds a little like 'thinning the herd,' don't you think?"

Ericka grinned and wagged her finger at her playful friend.

"I don't need this wheelchair," said Gail, pointing to her "ride," "but it seems to make them happy to roll us all around in them. Doesn't it, Catherine? Oh, she can't hear me."

Catherine wouldn't have heard Gail even if she could hear. At present she was squinting at and quite engrossed in a television program on the History Channel about Typhoid Mary. Catherine winced to see the house where Mary Mallon was quarantined on Brother's Island, so close to where they had laid out the bodies of Catherine's mother; her nine-year-old brother, Walter; and her baby sister, Agnes.

As Gail and Ericka were waiting for the assembling of all of the centenarians (in company with their respective retinues), Gail turned to her companion and whispered, "Lucinda—that girl there who wants to have us all 'shot'—she was telling me the other day about being nearly kidnapped by a pervert in a mall in Waukegan, when she was no more than five. I have come to the conclusion, Ericka, that life is a perilous journey no matter *who* you are. There are some, like myself, who walk the tightrope and do aerial loop-the-loops to impress the crowds—those who add a layer of additional risk to their lives—*we* constitute a special category and sometimes we get lucky. My good Lord, I'm one hundred years old. I've looked death in the face more times than I can remember, yet here I am!

"But for everyone else, luck plays its part as well. Catherine was lucky to survive what *she* went through; so many who boarded that boat with

her did not. Dorothy, who lives down the hall, survived the sinking of the *Lusitania* when *she* was just a little girl. And Angeline—poor Angeline's face was slashed by her demented father at nearly the same age, but her marriage to her beloved Jake has lasted sixty years. Although, there are so many others I know who have been dealt equally unfortunate hands who did *not* survive, did *not* prevail.

"Do you see Alma there? Doesn't she look exotic in that blueberry-colored gypsy peasant dress her granddaughter Connie got her from the vintage clothing store? Connie's a dear. She's taking over the kitchen and making us linguine tonight—she uses lots of oregano. Alma's brother was shot by his lieutenant for not going 'over the top' in the first World War. Shot pointblank right there in the trenches. Lily Lanham—see her there in the pretty red hat?—Lily's nephew Todd was accidentally pushed off a balcony in a Chicago movie theatre when an usher tried to get him to go home; the young man seemed determined to watch every single screening of *The Harvey Girls*. You know, the one with the song about the Atchison, Topeka, and the Santa Fe? And Amelia Bream's sister Vanessa—Amelia's the handsome woman sitting next to Joanna in the big wool sweater—Vanessa broke her neck in a jitterbug competition back in '39, when she slipped from her partner's arms in an over-the-head throw and had to spend the rest of her life paralyzed from the neck down."

"I was almost devoured by hyenas on my trip to Africa last year," contributed Ericka, almost proudly.

"Yes, I remember you telling me that they invaded your camp one night and tried to get into your tent."

Ericka cleared her throat. "That's right."

Ericka was asked by the photographer to step back. His name was Dack and he wore a deerstalker cap he'd inherited from a favorite great uncle—a Michigan man. Dack was from Wisconsin but had spent most of the last thirty years living in Greenwich in a house he'd bought from an ad man, a Bataan survivor, who'd had the Neocolonial custom-built a few years after the war. The Gold Coast remained very popular with New York "Mad Men." One of Dack's neighbors was a Young and Rubicam account executive named Stewart Selman, who made headlines for himself and his agency in 1970 by putting together a midi-skirt ad campaign for New York clothier Bonwit Teller that depicted iconic Americans of the twentieth century (all men!) wearing midi-skirts: Louis Armstrong, the Wright Brothers, Harold Lloyd (hanging from that detaching skyscraper clock

wearing a paisley print mid-length), and even Louis B. Mayer, bedecked in a chartreuse calf-length and flanked by a conveniently delighted Mickey and Judy. Several years later, Selman won a Clio for a parody ad in which the gunslinger Shane is persuaded to return to the homesteading Starrett family (in the midst of his ride into the proverbial western sunset) for a bowl of "crispy, crunchy" Golden Grahams breakfast cereal.

After the photo shoot, as most of the centenarians were being returned to their rooms, Gail and Ericka went into one of the home's intimate sitting rooms to speak in private. Gail said that she had something important she wanted to talk to Ericka about. There was a travel magazine on the sofa. Ericka moved it to the coffee table before sitting down. On its cover was a picture of the Golden Gate Bridge. Someone had prankishly penned in a little stick man taking a dive from it. Ericka set it down on top of another magazine—this one for senior citizens. The cover article was titled "Fifteen Reasons to Visit Flagstaff, Arizona." Ericka wondered if one of the reasons was souvenirs; her great-aunt had bought her a Grand Canyon pennant at a gift shop in Flagstaff called Gertie's. Ericka had added it to her growing collection of colorful place-pennants, most of them purchased by friends and relatives at Stuckey's roadside stores.

Ericka liked the cozy little room. On the wall across from her was a print of Maxfield Parrish's fantastical *Daybreak*; on the wall behind her a print of van Gogh's reticent "Vase with Poppies." The radio in the room was tuned to a classical station. In honor of Memorial Day weekend, the station was playing works by American composers—at the moment, the first movement of Edward MacDowell's Second Piano Concerto.

"Dear, there is something I'd like you to do for me. While the longevity of my roommate Catherine is something I might wish to aim for, I don't believe for a minute that I'll ever reach the age of 107. When I do die, be it this year or the next, I'd like you to take my cremains—is that the word?—take them down to New York and go to the top of whichever of the World Trade Center towers has the observation deck. I haven't been there since right after they were built. And I want you to cast my ashes to the wind. You must make certain, dear, that the wind is blowing *away* from the building. What I'm asking you to do may very well be illegal, but then again, illegality hasn't stopped *me* from doing a host of things in my life that I thought had value. I very nearly stowed away on the Akron when I was a much younger woman—in protest over the fact that women weren't allowed to serve in any capacity on Uncle Sam's rigid airships. How I envy

you, Ericka—all the wonderful opportunities being afforded to women of your generation."

"I'll do that for you, Gail. I will."

"Of course, my preference has always been to have my ashes taken to the top of Mount Everest, but that's an impossibility, isn't it? You don't happen to know anyone who climbs that mountain on a regular basis, do you?"

"I'm afraid I don't."

"I never had children—wasn't able to. I've met a lot of women over the years who weren't able to bear children but were successful in making of their friendships something very much like family. My trouble is that all of my friends are dead. Except for *you*, Ericka. This is one of the drawbacks to living to be so old. Now, I take that back. I do have a couple of other younger friends besides you of whom I'm relatively fond. My friend Audrey in Austin, for example. And Nona in Marietta, Georgia. Nona's a preschool teacher. And back in the twenties, so many, many years ago, I was good friends with a couple of Bohemian gals in Greenwich Village, Jenny and M.K., and there were the Cadwaladers—Wilberforce and Rosalinda—an older couple I knew in the thirties. She was a crosspatch but he was a dream. The cat's meow, as we used to say. Of course, now I'm talking about people who are dead. I suppose I just made my earlier point, didn't I?"

"Would you like me to take you back to your room now?"

"I *am* a little sleepy. I'm liable to nod off any minute now. Ginger, who lives across the hall from me, does that sometime. She's from Iowa. Red Oak. Lost two brothers in the war. Poor unlucky woman, poor unlucky *town*. And Camilla doesn't so much fall asleep as go into a kind of temporary catatonia. I think she's reliving the death of her teenaged son back in Helena, Montana. He and another boy died in a terrible car crash one night."

Ericka helped Gail to her feet. "Have you traveled much, Gail?"

"Oh good Lord, have I traveled! First Tillman and me, and then me and that cuniculine bastard—we all had the wanderlust, don't you know, and once I was free of Mr. Rabbitt, that wanderlust got even lustier. I flew prop planes all over South America and skydived in Europe and pretty much wore myself out until I was forced to become almost exclusively terrestrial. Even grounded, I've had my share of interesting experiences. I lived with an Indian couple in Old Town Albuquerque, had lunch with

Harry and Bess Truman in Independence, Missouri. I even worked as a counselor at a girl's camp in Wisconsin. I've seen so much that is good about this country, Ericka, honey, and so much that wasn't good at all. I was in Greensboro when they rounded up all those homosexuals in 1957. I was in Nashville, Tennessee, when the women-haters almost killed the Nineteenth Amendment abornin'. And can you believe I was even in Cincinnati the night they arrested that evangelist couple about fifteen years ago—the Swearingens…accounting fraud or tax evasion or some such thing as that. Sometimes I feel like—oh, what was that retarded man's name? Tim Hanks played him in the pictures."

"*Tom Hanks*, I think you mean. Forrest Gump."

"That's right. I feel just like Forrest Gump. Except that I'm allergic to chocolates."

Ericka took Gail by the arm and led her back to her room. Catherine was in bed, taking her afternoon nap. On the television there was a story about the risks to airlines of unsecured lithium batteries in their cargo holds. "Is there anything I can get you before I go?" asked Ericka.

"No, dear, I'm fine. And you've taken such a load off my mind, knowing that you'll dispose of my ashes in the way that I ask. Oh, goodness! That's an awful thought: being 'disposed' of. Will you be coming back tomorrow for the celebration?"

"Of course I will," said Ericka, helping Gail into bed.

"I used to soar. Now I'm earthbound. But at least my ashes will take wing."

Ericka nodded, said goodbye, and stepped from the room. She poked her head into the room of another friend she had made at the home, a spry widow named Jelena from Kansas City, Kansas. Jelena was resting.

On the drive back to her apartment, Ericka gave more serious thought to what Gail had asked her to do. She was touched that she had been asked, but worried over how she would pull it off. It wasn't all that easy to throw things from the World Trade Center. For one thing, the windows were airtight. And what if the wind on the observation deck was uncooperative? It would be terrible to leave Gail's "cremains" scattered about the surface of the building's roof. Ericka wished that Gail wasn't so particular about it having to be the World Trade Center. As skyscrapers went, the Empire State Building was far more useful when it came to putting things into the air from a great height. Ericka learned this when she was a little girl and accidentally sent her Barbie Doll all the way down to Fifth Avenue the fast way. Or how about the Woolworth Building? Wasn't it the tallest building in the world for several years in the early part of the twentieth century?

Ericka switched on her car radio. The station was repeating an audio documentary about the past century that had originally aired in January. There was mention of the "Bonus Army" march on Washington in 1932, the Montgomery bus boycott in 1955, the gas shortage of 1973, and, more recently, the bombing of the Alfred P. Murrah Federal Building in 1995. A middle-aged man, Broderain Tyson III, spoke tearfully of having lost his wife in this act of domestic terrorism.

On May 10, 2001, Gail Hoyt passed away. She was survived, incredibly, by her roommate, Catherine Uhlmyer Gallagher Connelly, who went on to live another year and a half to the chelonian age of 109 (and a half).

Ericka put off doing what she had been charged to do. (The will had given custody of the ashes to Ericka. What she was supposed to do with them was not mentioned.) After all, rationalized Ericka, Gail hadn't said just *when* she wanted her ashen remains sent eternally airborne. This was left to Ericka's discretion.

And then…

On a clear blue morning in September, the opportunity for fulfilling Gail's final request to the letter was lost in the horror and chaos of that epoch of national tragedy. It was an act that clearly belonged to the *new* century, not to the one now past—the century that all of Gail Hoyt's Tri-century Centenarian friends claimed as their own for each of its 36,524 days.

Without the World Trade Center, what was to be done? Ericka could keep the urn with her always and always feel guilty, or she could do the only logical thing that she was sure would appease Gail's hungry, restless, empyreal soul.

Ericka Prager had been to Africa, but she had yet to visit Asia.

She would climb Mount Everest.

AMERICAN DECAMERON
SYNOPSES OF STORIES

1901 ARBOREAL IN TEXAS

A baby girl born on the eve of the Great Galveston Hurricane survives the storm, finds love and then rejection at the orphanage that takes her in, and starts along a life path that parallels the ascension of the much-storied American Century.

1902 VEHICULAR IN NEW YORK

A collision with a tree brings a young man to the door of a wealthy woman and her nubile but querulous daughter. The courteous young man and the discourteous daughter are apparently on more intimate terms than circumstances initially indicate.

1903 DEDUCTIVE IN MICHIGAN

The sudden elopement of their daughter has Mom and Dad scratching their heads, while Younger Brother, sniffing coercion and intrigue, springs into action in the guise of his idol: Sherlock Holmes.

1904 IN MEMORIAM IN PENNSYLVANIA

The wife of the last surviving member of Haverford College's Class of 1904 sees only a man in the final stages of senility, while within the sanctuary of his trapped thoughts, the man revisits his golden college days, when his whole life lay spread out before him.

1905 GENEALOGICAL IN RHODE ISLAND

The unofficial draft of the official record of the 1905 reunion of the Livergood Family Association of Warwick, Rhode Island...with copious commentary.

1906 PUNCH(ING) DRUNK IN PENNSYLVANIA
The painful relationship between two brothers whose lives took wildly different paths reaches a life-threatening climax that neither could have anticipated.

1907 PROBLEMATICALLY BETROTHED IN MASSACHUSETTS
On the eve of their daughter's marriage, a troubling revelation about the groom-to-be causes Mother and Father to consider canceling the wedding, though Daughter doesn't seem bothered in the least.

1908 VOLANT IN NORTH CAROLINA
An expedition to the sandy wilds of the North Carolina coast confirms what most had believed to be a hoax.

1909 MORBIFIC IN NEW YORK
A female reporter scores an interview with a notorious criminal in isolation and comes to sorely regret the trip.

1910 PORCINE IN NORTH CAROLINA
A boy who displayed piggish manners at the table is forced by his aunt to wear a papier mâché pig nose for a week, though his uncle and schoolteacher don't agree that this is the best means of behavioral correction.

1911 EFFLORESCENT IN MAINE
A wealthy grandmother falls short when it comes to guiding her granddaughter easily through the garden of budding adolescence.

1912 TRISKAPHOBIC IN WISCONSIN
A would-be assassin winds up in the history books, but fate, a metal eyeglasses case, and the folded pages of an eighty-minute-long speech keep him from becoming a household name.

1913 CLAIRVOYANT IN NEW YORK
The three grown offspring of a woman being milked of the family fortune by enterprising charlatan-psychics set a trap to drive the scammers out of town.

1914 DEVOTIONAL IN ILLINOIS
An eighteen-year-old woman's diary reveals the details of a life-changing summer upon the grounds of the New Piasa Chautauqua, a spiritual and educational retreat.

1915 HAVING A SINKING FEELING IN THE NORTH ATLANTIC
An accidental reunion provides an opportunity for two couples, survivors of the torpedoing of RMS *Lusitania*, to speak of that which they hadn't been able to talk about before.

1916 INCARCERATED IN OKLAHOMA
A convict reveals to his cellmate the reason for his imprisonment: the murder of his uncle, stopped in the course of trying to drown the convict's mentally challenged brother as directed by the convict's own father.

1917 PRINCIPLED IN MASSACHUSETTS
A short story writer on the staff of a popular magazine must decide whether to serve his country's propaganda machine or be true to his own views about a war he doesn't support.

1918 TREPID IN FRANCE
A World War I doughboy sees fear embodied in a terrified young private, for whom the only thing worse than death is the dread that can often precede it.

1919 VESTAL IN NORTH DAKOTA
A disturbed war veteran finds a tragically counterproductive way to protect womanhood from the depravities of man.

1920 FILIAL IN TENNESSEE
The deciding vote to grant universal suffrage to American women is cast by a young man who has always minded his mother.

1921 COMPOSED (?) IN OREGON
A nationally renown classical composer, commissioned to write a concerto for ukelele and orchestra, finds himself tormented both by the demons of his schizophrenic nature, and by the one from whom he inherited those very demons.

1922 CINEASTIC IN ARKANSAS
A minister learns that his young son has been sneaking off to the wicked picture show. The discovery has an unexpected effect on the relationship between the two.

1923 CONSPIRATORIAL IN NORTH CAROLINA
A jury in Greensboro must decide the fate of a woman who fired a shot at her husband's lover. The case isn't all that it seems, but then again, neither is the jury.

1924 DOUBLE FAULTED IN ILLINOIS AND D.C.
Two teenage boys die within weeks of one another, one the famous son of a sitting U.S. president, the other a soon-to-be famous victim of cold-blooded murder—each death inadvertently brought on by a love of the game of tennis.

1925 ACROPHILIC AND AGORAPHOBIC IN PENNSYLVANIA
1901's high-flying little girl is all grown up now—a daredevil, flag pole-sitting flapper who falls for (and with) the brother of two young men who cannot leave their house until called to the ultimate test: to rescue their fallen brother and his new love.

1926 BETWEEN THE HAMMER AND THE ANVIL IN KENTUCKY
An old woman looks back at the tragic reason behind her parents' divorce.

1927 ASSISIAN IN MASSACHUSETTS
A drunkenly candid supporter of the Fall River Animal Rescue League tells the "true" story of Lizzie Borden and the murderous deed that historical consensus has ascribed to her.

1928 MISDEEMED IN INDIANA
A newlywed wife can't abide her husband's disgustingly peculiar fetish; in an effort to understand it, she solicits the opinion of an ill-equipped door-to-door vacuum cleaner salesman.

1929 TAKING A DIM VIEW IN MICHIGAN
A sexually reticent woman who is losing her eyesight decides to cop a look at a well-formed man in his most natural state before it's too late.

1930 WITHOUT APRON STRINGS IN DELAWARE
A middle-aged man finally tracks down the mother who gave him up for adoption when he was a baby, with unexpected results.

1931 AWED AND WONDERING IN CONNECTICUT
When propositioned by her boss with the admonition that a refusal will result in the loss of her job, a woman gets a response from her unemployed husband that she never expected.

1932 FASCISTIC IN D.C.
A participant in the "Bonus Army" march on Washington gives his account of the last hours of the army's occupancy of the city, with special attention paid to the man whose job it was to clear D.C. of all veteran "vagrants."

1933 LETTING GO IN MISSOURI
While waiting for the midnight legalization of "near" beer, two friends who are also employer and employee at a local ice company discuss the recent crash of the dirigible USS *Akron* and its relevance to a difficult decision the ice company's owner has made.

1934 ADULTEROUS IN ILLINOIS
The husband of one couple and the wife of another decide to confess their affair to their respective spouses at the Chicago World's Fair with disastrous, albeit not unpredictable, results.

1935 PERSEVERINGLY TERPSICHOREAN IN WASHINGTON STATE
Two older women from different sides of the track form a friendship while watching a dance marathon and cheering on their favorite couples—a friendship that is destined to last no longer than the viability of the couples who compete before them.

1936 SHABBY-GENTEEL IN CALIFORNIA
A migrant worker is invited to a proper tea party, but all is not what it seems.

1937 DEPILATED IN OHIO
A teenage girl takes a stand against her adoptive parents' constant displays of hatred for one another; she threatens to cut off all of her luxuriously long

hair, and then promptly follows through with the help of a sympathetic local sheep shearer.

1938 JIVING IN NEBRASKA
A physically disabled, jitterbug-music-crazed young man moves back to Omaha from New York and tries to convince his girlfriend to join him, though she no longer wishes to keep to the sidelines with the whole country jump-jivin' with able-bodied exuberance.

1939 GALACTOPHOROUS IN VIRGINIA
MGM wants to turn a novelist's best-seller into the next *Gone With the Wind*. The problem: the writer has the last word in how the story gets retold for the screen, and pre-emptive censorship on the part of the studio is making it a bad day for all concerned.

1940 AU FAIT IN COLORADO, NEW MEXICO, AND CALIFORNIA
A fifteen-year-old savant on the Santa Fe Super Chief befriends Charlie McCarthy and earns a slot on the *Quiz Kids* radio broadcast, before the tragic truth about the boy's limitations derails his parents' dreams for their child.

1941 UNDER ATTACK IN HAWAII
A Hawaiian third grader writes a personal account of the bombing of Pearl Harbor a few days after the attack.

1942 CERULEAN IN WISCONSIN
A young wife whose husband is serving in World War II suffers debilitating and nearly tragic post-partum depression following the birth of her second child

1943 TELEGRAPHIC IN IOWA
A Western Union messenger boy in a town hard hit by World War II casualties cannot help being regarded by his neighbors as the messenger of death.

1944 SEQUESTERED IN NEW MEXICO
A married couple remembers the Manhattan Project as something both historically monumental and domestically challenging.

1945 HYPERNATREMIC IN THE PACIFIC OCEAN
Two sailors, survivors of the sinking of the USS *Indianapolis*, wait in shark-infested waters for help that doesn't come.

1946 ENNEADIC IN IOWA
A Dutch-American mathematics professor, having lost his family in the Holocaust, finds in his ongoing calculation of pi something that betrays his belief in disbelief.

1947 RACIST IN TENNESSEE
Memphis's censor czar, exercising bigoted and sometimes ridiculously arbitrary control over the movies that will be seen within his jurisdiction, entertains a visiting delegation of movie house managers hoping to convince him to soften his heavy-handed authority.

1948 HAUNTED IN CONNECTICUT
One of the men digging a well for a World War II veteran's new house in Connecticut bears a haunting resemblance to a soldier who saved the man's life during the Bataan death march.

1949 BALL CHANGING IN MISSISSIPPI
A Saturday morning kiddy talent show broadcast takes a few unexpected comical twists and turns before the winners are finally crowned.

1950 POIKILOTHERMAL IN WEST VIRGINIA
Snowbound with his fiancée and her family, a disturbed young man wrestles with sadistic impulses that are ultimately his undoing.

1951 PSITTICINE IN PENNSYLVANIA
A blind woman discovers the troubling truth about her friend's potty-mouthed parrot.

1952 DOUBLY UXORICIDAL IN COLORADO
Separated-from-birth twin brothers discover one another by chance and take advantage of their good fortune by plotting crisscross murders of their respective problem spouses.

1953 PHARISAICAL IN WYOMING

A traveling tent show revivalist preacher becomes self-appointed and unwelcome negotiator on behalf of the hostages in a bank holdup.

1954 FAMISHED IN TEXAS

A self-absorbed suburban wife can't be bothered to help her emotionally fragile, literally starving aunt, even though it means losing her husband and daughter.

1955 AGITATED IN ALABAMA

Riding the bus in Montgomery, two white female friends find little common ground in how they view the city's black bus boycott.

1956 DISCREETLY SILENT IN MONTANA

A doctor and a deputy sheriff must decide what to tell the families of the two closeted teenaged boys whose lives came to a tragic end in a late-night automobile crash.

1957 LOYAL IN UTAH

Faculty and staff of a Presbyterian boarding school are asked to sign a loyalty oath as a condition of their employment.

1958 EXPLOSIVE IN SOUTH CAROLINA

A story told in reverse about the accidental dropping of an atomic bomb (sans nuclear components) on a rural community.

1959 TIGHT IN NEW YORK

It's New Year's Eve in Westchester and the babysitter's balking; she refuses to get in the car with her employer, who's started his potable-partying a little earlier than usual.

1960 SMILING IN CALIFORNIA

A failed writer decides to end his life by jumping off the Golden Gate Bridge. An unlikely heroine makes it her job to stop him.

1961 UNLITERATE IN NEW HAMPSHIRE

A woman buys a first edition of *The Joy of Cooking* at a neighborhood yard sale and discovers an uncashed check inside.

1962 THROWN A CURVE BALL IN NEW YORK
As a boy listens to the very first Mets game alongside his stepfather, to whom he has become closely attached, he learns that his mother and stepfather are divorcing.

1963 ESTIVATING IN NEW JERSEY
An appliance salesman discovers an unexpected link between himself and two children who come in each afternoon to watch cartoons in the store in which he works.

1964 NEARLY INTERRED IN ALASKA
In the aftermath of the great Alaskan Good Friday earthquake, a frightened babysitter is punished for her selfish cowardice by the children in her care, who thoroughly despise her.

1965 MISTRYSTED IN NEW YORK
An Affair to Remember-like rendezvous between two World War II lovers at Grand Central Terminal is impeded by a citywide blackout.

1966 OUTRAGED IN IDAHO
An elementary school concert tribute to the popular musical *The Sound of Music* hits a major snag when the teacher planning the event wants to include a song from the original stage version that few are familiar with—one with a distasteful message.

1967 GOING THE VOLE IN NEVADA
A young man decides to put all the money he and his wife have on one life-changing roll of the roulette wheel.

1968 HIERATIC IN KANSAS
On the night of the Miss America pageant, a wife, husband, and their old friend, a priest, place the feminist movement and the general state of relations between men and women into a decidedly personal context.

1969 PARENTAL IN ARIZONA
Every summer a wealthy couple takes their kids on a joyful "travelcading" adventure through the American West, but this year is different; half-sisters of the father find a fly in the ointment—a fly that they put there themselves.

1970 SKIRTING THE ISSUE IN WEST VIRGINIA
A department store buyer has a personal reason for bemoaning the foisting of the unflattering "midi skirt" on the female American consumer.

1971 BIBLIOPHILIC IN ALABAMA
Members of a family of voracious readers on beach vacation work in concert to use their book smarts to save a drowning fellow vacationer.

1972 PRECIPITATE IN ILLINOIS
A woman at a mall witnesses a child abduction and knows that she is the only person who can save the little girl.

1973 VENGEFUL IN MARYLAND
While waiting in a long gas line, an ex-wife has the opportunity to exact revenge on her former husband.

1974 VICINAL IN TENNESSEE
Twin brothers spend the night of their eighteenth birthday with a neighbor: Elvis Presley.

1975 PHYSICALLY CANDID IN LOUSIANA
Two patio paviors must contend with a provocatively ecdysiastic lady of the house.

1976 THROTTLED IN ARKANSAS AND OKLAHOMA
Feuding sisters drive from Tennessee to Oklahoma to celebrate their mother's birthday in separate cars, though fate refuses to keep them apart.

1977 RECTALLY REMUNERATIVE IN ILLINOIS
Big changes are discussed in the boardroom of a company that has made its reputation manufacturing products best not discussed in mixed company.

1978 TRI-TOASTED IN MISSOURI
Three thirty-something lawyers come together to raise a glass of Johnnie Walker to someone they all have in common and each dearly loved, though the feeling wasn't reciprocal.

1979 GOING THROUGH THE MILL IN TEXAS
The story of a hapless, antisocial Dallas family told through documents filed in a Dallas County Justice Court.

1980 RENOVATIVE IN TEXAS
A boy remembers the summer he spent helping his step-grandfather renovate a house and learns that family isn't always defined by blood.

1981 SELF-ANOINTED ABOVE, LET'S SAY, OKLAHOMA
A woman confronts a famous female televangelist on a plane, accusing her and her husband of keeping the woman's mentally unstable daughter from getting proper medical treatment.

1982 REUNITED IN MISSOURI
Those gathered at a thirty-year high school reunion wonder if the one among them who has just recently been released from prison will make an appearance, and if he does, what will be the consequences?

1983 ETCHED IN STONE IN WASHINGTON, D.C.
A man visits the Vietnam Memorial on his late friend's birthday and finds his friend's kid brother there, ready to topple the man's heart-object from his pedestal.

1984 PATRIARCHAL IN CALIFORNIA
A father of three girls wants to try once more for a boy, and his "son obsession" puts a crimp in the family's enjoyment of the Los Angeles Summer Olympic Games.

1985 SMITTEN IN WISCONSIN AND MINNESOTA
A young man sees a youthful picture of his wife's grandmother and falls in love, inviting consequences that jeopardize his marriage.

1986 LOCKED OUT IN TEXAS
An old man is confronted by the reality of his Alzheimer's as he stands naked before a YMCA locker, having forgotten his lock's combination.

1987 MOTHERLY IN GEORGIA
A middle-aged preschool teacher has a very personal reason for wanting

to teach only three-year-olds—a reason that finally comes out after thirty years.

1988 STOUTHEARTED IN FLORIDA
A teenage girl schemes to make it possible for her grandmother's lesbian partner to see her grandmother when visitation by "non-family" members of ICU patients is disallowed.

1989 MELODIOUS IN OHIO
The four grown members of a teenage singing sister act accidentally learn about a fifth sister they never knew they had.

1990 GERONTOCONCUPISCENT IN VERMONT
An old man—the "guardian angel" of the love between a teenaged boy and girl he befriends—is tempted to exploit the fact that the couple has been sneaking into his house to have sex while he is out.

1991 FILICIDAL IN MISSISSIPPI
A father decides to do the unthinkable: end his own life and the lives of his two children by taking them automotively to the bottom of a lake. His eleven-year-old son is determined not to let him have his way.

1992 GRIEVING IN MINNESOTA
A widow cannot bring herself to remove her husband's voice from the announcement on her home answering machine.

1993 SHELVED IN NEW MEXICO
A young woman must put her life on hold to care for her mother. She isn't alone.

1994 CROONING AND SWOONING IN SOUTH DAKOTA
During a purported estate sale of Will Rogers and Dale Evans memorabilia, the sales coordinator learns the truth behind the sale…from a young man tied up in the basement.

1995 VARIOUSLY BEREFT IN MINNESOTA, CALIFORNIA, OKLAHOMA, AND MONTANA
The death of their brother necessitates various conversations among

the four surviving siblings, during which they assess their tentative relationships with one another and the lunatic state of the country.

1996 COPROPHOBIC IN MISSISSIPPI
A couple looking for a new house find one that could be a good fit if only it weren't for an insurmountable glitch in its presentation.

1997 COMBUSTIBLE IN OHIO
A woman insists to police detectives that she didn't set her husband on fire, even though there is sufficient motive to implicate her.

1998 DENTIGEROUSLY FORTUITOUS IN FLORIDA
A dental hygienist discovers that the man who two weeks earlier tried to rape her in a dark parking lot is sitting in her chair.

1999 CONSTRUCTIVE IN BOTSWANA
A sexual tryst with a fellow Habitat for Humanity crewmember and a life-and-death encounter with a pack of wild hyenas bring a woman to certain enlightening truths about herself.

2000 CONVERGENT IN CONNECTICUT
All of the stories of the century come together in this denouement set in a Wilton nursing home.

ACKNOWLEDGMENTS

There are a lot of people I should thank for help—both direct and indirect—with this book. Inspiration for these stories came from many people and from many different places. I got the idea for "1994: Crooning and Swooning in South Dakota," for example, when my friend Rod Replogle gave me a program from a Roy Rogers traveling variety show he attended as a kid. Likewise, a facsimile of a 1940 Atchison, Topeka, and Santa Fe railroad schedule I received from my friend Steve Marquis was the inspiration for "1940: Au Fait in Colorado, New Mexico, and California." People from all around the country picked up their phones and courteously answered all of my oddball questions about their cities, their churches, their streets, their grocery stores, their Stuckey's roadside gift shops. I rarely got their names, but their assistance is no less appreciated for being undocumented.

Some folks do require a personal thank you:

Thanks to Jack Thayer, admissions director of the Menaul School in Albuquerque, and to the directors and volunteers at the Menaul Historical Library of the Southwest for research assistance pertaining to "1957: Loyal in Utah." Jack was also especially helpful in providing information about his grandfather, a *Titanic* survivor, for a story which, regrettably, I was unable to use (due to a surplus of nautical tales in the book and another story's strong claim to the year 1912).

Thanks to Wayne Taylor for sharing details of the summer he spent with his step-grandfather, many of which ended up in "1980: Renovative in Texas."

Thanks to Laurie Kalet for sharing the particulars of her job as preschool teacher, which I incorporated into "1987: Motherly in Georgia."

Thanks to Jennifer Rodgers for doing the same for her job as dental hygienist, which I used in "1998: Dentigerously Fortuitous in Florida."

Thanks to Scott White for the idea behind "1976: Throttled in Arkansas and Oklahoma," and to Mary Dunn for the idea behind "1961: Unliterate in New Hampshire."

Thanks, as well, to Mets scholar Phil Calbi for making sure that I got the facts right in "1962: Thrown a Curve Ball in New York," and to Los Alamos resident Robert Benjamin for doing the same with "1944: Sequestered in New Mexico."

Thanks to Yazoo City native daughter Cindy Foose for all the help she gave me with "1949: Ball Changing in Mississippi." I appreciate Cindy's willingness to relate so many rich details of her Mississippi youth to me.

Thanks to Jeremy Pena for help with the legal aspects of "1997: Combustible in Ohio."

Thanks, as well, to all the people who put together the Internet Archive digital library and the Wikipedia and Gutenberg websites. As a writer who has spent most of his former research hours sitting in dark, musty libraries for long afternoons, the opportunity to access primary and secondary sources for my historical research with the click of a mouse has made a book about the twentieth century, which previously would have taken me a decade to complete, something I was successful in finishing in less than two years. Each of these websites (along with all the other sites I consulted) was a Godsend for this author of the mother of all cultural research projects. I am also grateful to OTR.net, which offered among its thousands of hours of archived radio programs WJSV's full day of broadcasting from September 21, 1939, which became the inspiration for "1939: Galactophorous in Virginia." How did I know how many songs from *The Wizard of Oz* were sung on CBS radio that day? Because I listened to its entire broadcast day, courtesy of this site—a veritable audio time capsule.

Four very personal thank-yous are in order:

To my literary agent, Amy Rennert, who has stuck by me through thin and thin (her patience in waiting for the "thick" being greatly appreciated).

To my editor, Guy Intoci, not only for his editorial gifts, but for his championing of this very unusual book. It's editors like Guy who, in this era of stultifying caution and conservative retrenchment in the publishing industry, view "different" as actually a positive thing. Without editors like Guy or publishers like Mark Pearce, adventurous writers like me would be woefully under-employed.

To my copy editor, Michelle Dotter, who was Captain Cook-ian in her navigation through a quarter million words of prose, and who went above and beyond her responsibilities—at one point informing me with a heavy heart that I would have to jettison my use of the Alka-Seltzer catchphrase, "I can't believe I ate the whole thing!" because it came out a year later than the story I'd sought to use it in. Michelle's investment in the success of this book, in spite of presumptions tied to her surname, went far beyond dotting "I's" (and crossing "T's").

And thanks, finally, to my wife Mary for all of her editorial input, and for putting up with me and this wildly ambitious fiction project that hijacked nearly three years of our marriage. It's over now, honey. Let's get our lives back.